Great Short Works

of

Leo Tolstoy

Other Books in the Series

Great Short Works of Herman Melville

Great Short Works of Mark Twain

Great Short Works of Fyodor Dostoevsky

Great Short Works of Stephen Crane

Great Short Works of Edgar Allan Poe

Great Short Works

of

Leo Tolstoy

With an Introduction by

John Bayley

In the translations by
Louise and Aylmer Maude

PERENNIAL ▪ CLASSICS

The translations of *The Cossacks, The Death of Ivan Ilych, The Kreutzer Sonata, The Devil, Master and Man, Father Sergius,* and *Hadji Murád* by Louise and Aylmer Maude and the translation of *Family Happiness* by J. D. Duff are reprinted here from the texts of The World's Classics editions by permission of the Oxford University Press, 200 Madison Avenue, New York, New York, 10016.

HarperCollins books may be purchased for educational, business, or sales promotional use. For information please write: Special Markets Department, HarperCollins Publishers Inc., 10 East 53rd Street, New York, NY 10022.

First Perennial Library edition published 1967.

First Perennial Classics edition published 2004.
Perennial Classics are published by Perennial, an imprint of HarperCollins Publishers.

Designed by Darlene Starr Carbone

Library of Congress Cataloging-in-Publication Data is available.

ISBN 0-06-058697-4

04 05 06 07 08 RRD 10 9 8 7 6 5 4 3 2 1

Contents

Introduction by John Bayley   vii

Family Happiness   1
The Cossacks   83
The Death of Ivan Ilych   245
The Devil   303
The Kreutzer Sonata   353
Master and Man   451
Father Sergius   501
Hadji Murád   547
Alyosha the Pot   669

A Chronology   679
A Bibliography   683

Introduction

It is a mistake to regard the writings of Leo Tolstoy too much in the light of a sage's personal utterances rather than as works of art. It is true that the idea of art, with a capital A, the notion of Art as practised by other novelists of his epoch, notably Turgenev, meant little to Tolstoy. When he worked out his own theory about it in *What is Art?*, he had already written his greatest works. After the first three volumes of *War and Peace* had been published, he wrote an article for *The Russian Archive*, from which the following is an extract.

> *War and Peace* is what the author wished, and was able, to express in the form in which it is expressed. Such an announcement of disregard for conventional form in an artistic production might seem presumptuous were it premeditated . . .

"A good work of art," wrote Tolstoy later to his friend Goldenweiser, "can in its entirety be expressed only by itself." It was not Tolstoy's way to compose a work of art in a particular form, as an epic, a chronicle, a *nouvelle*.

Tolstoy's stories are in some sense founded on a paradox. They are carefully and beautifully composed tales by a genius who did not give his whole allegiance to this formal method of composition. It is an exciting paradox, and like many such paradoxes in art it produced with some incidental defects powerful and unforgettable results.

Not the least interesting aspect of these stories by Tolstoy is their use of the same material that is also contained in the bulk of the novels, but altered and in some cases distorted by its deployment in a more rigid and artificial form. In *Family Happiness* (1859) we have the first example of that understanding and analysis of the modes of communication in a marriage that forms such a superb and self-justifying conclusion to *War and Peace*.

Family Happiness was written four years before Tolstoy's
own marriage, which fact shows that he did not necessarily,
as his readers often take for granted, have to experience
what he wrote before he wrote about it. Tolstoy was
imagining what marriage for him might be like. He had
a girl in mind, an acquaintance named Valeria Arseneva,
and he was attempting to forecast how his own relationship with a young girl in marriage might turn out. To
this problem he brought the same kind of honesty and
remorseless self-analysis that he was to show when he came
to write *A Confession* in 1879. He also reveals the amazing insight into a feminine consciousness that he displays
in the presentation of Natasha and of Anna Karenina.
Nonetheless, the theme of *Family Happiness* remains in-
triguingly different because, as I tried to show in my
recent book *Tolstoy and the Novel* (London, 1966; New
York, 1967), it is based on an hypothesis. This *hypo-
thetical* quality is an important aspect of a great many
of his stories.

The account in *War and Peace* of Prince Andrew's last
days and death is strikingly similar to that of the situation
in *The Death of Ivan Ilych*, with the difference, again,
that Tolstoy seems intent on proving something to himself
and to us in the story that is no concern of the novel. It
is the same with Karenin's obsessive and self-destructive
jealousy, emotionally akin to that in *The Devil* and *The
Kreutzer Sonata,* but shown in proportion and against the
perspective of other lives, not pursued to a bitter and
solitary end.

Early stories like *The Wood-felling* and *Sebastopol*
show where Tolstoy acquired his intimate knowledge of
military life. They are frankly reportage of his own experiences in the Caucasus and the Crimea, but reportage
of a singularly vivid and unusual kind. Perhaps the most
striking affinity of all with the longer novels is Tolstoy's
use in *Hadji Murad,* one of his last and finest tales, of
what he called the "peepshow method." This is essentially
the method, on a meticulous and miniature scale, that
makes *War and Peace* a vast scenic panorama. It is as if
Tolstoy had returned at the end of his life to the mood
of his greatest work.

But because they are used on this small clear scale, the
"peepshows" of which *Hadji Murad* is composed make a
very different impression on us. They are pointed, dramatic,

tendentious. For all the majestic clarity and calm with which the story unfolds, it constitutes one of the most ferocious denunciations in all literature of the realities and the necessities of power. It is possible to read *War and Peace* without concerning ourselves, unless we wish, with Tolstoy's views on history in general and on the campaign of 1812 in particular, for the great sweep of the novel holds so much else to engross us. In *Hadji Murad* the *meaning* of the tale presses upon us inescapably and relentlessly, just as do the meanings in Tolstoy's other tales, the meaning of death in *The Death of Ivan Ilych*, of pride in *Father Sergius*, of sexual emotion in *The Devil* and *The Kreutzer Sonata*. We can deny the truth of these meanings if we wish, but we cannot escape the implacable gaze that the author fastens on us, willing us to accept them.

"During the first half of his life," Prince Mirsky notes in his history of Russian literature, "Tolstoy saw the world as an enchanted ball-room. During the second, he saw it as Ivan Ilych's black bag." This may be an oversimplification, but it is a telling one. Certainly the maestro who leads us into the lighted ball-room seems not only a very different kind of man, but a very different kind of writer from the hypnotist whose eyes try to compel us to see the world as he saw it. Like the genius of Shakespeare the genius of Tolstoy can embrace extremes, not only extremes of vision but of technique as well. Yet we feel that the same man is there, experiencing the same continuity of life that we all have to experience.

In his celebrated essay "Goethe and Tolstoy" Thomas Mann takes a subtly patronising line about Tolstoy's moralising earnestness, his search for the meaning of life and the terrible pessimism that he came to feel about the flesh and the life of the body that he had once celebrated. Mann contrasts what seems to him Tolstoy's defeat and collapse with Goethe's development and poise. The contrast is certainly an illuminating one, but few of us feel, I think, that it damages Tolstoy and exalts Goethe quite in the way in which Thomas Mann makes out. All of us are subject to a temporary collapse of our instinct that existence is meaningful and sufficient in itself. Tolstoy, as we know from *A Confession* and elsewhere, experienced such a collapse on an overwhelming scale. His embodiment in his great novels of a kind of universal physical existence would be far less impressive if he had not also been haunted and obsessed by the questions that he asks in the stories, the questions not only of "How should a man live?" but "How should a man die?" A Tolstoy who continued to write novels of the same sort would have been an intolerable phenomenon, for he seems to encompass all physical existence. But what grows with this sense of existence, haunts it and finally dominates it is the admission of its limitations, the confrontation of self with what is not self, of life with death.

The Tolstoy of *A Confession* and of many of the stories is not ill, nor perverse. He plays out in himself and on his huge scale the most universal and inevitable of human dramas. Ultimately, as Thomas Mann comes near to admitting, even so great a humanistic genius as that of Goethe was fundamentally egotistic. Tolstoy was also a gigantic egotist, but an egotist of a very different kind. If Goethe cared for nothing but himself, Tolstoy *was* nothing but himself; and his sense of what awaited him and of what life had come to mean for him is correspondingly more intimate and more moving. He hits us where we live. "Every bosom," as Dr. Johnson observed of the greatest kinds of literature, "returns an echo" to the message of these stories.

As soon as he had finished *Family Happiness*, Tolstoy rejected it with loathing and referred to it as "a foul blot." The reasons for this disgust are interesting. The main one seems to have been because the story was *made up*. All his life Tolstoy detested the idea of invention, the need of the artist to put things together and to work them out in his own head. Of course, he had to do it, in *War and Peace* no less than in *Family Happiness*, but he always maintained that the ultimate test of a writer was whether things happened in his fictions naturally and inevitably or if they seemed inconsistent and artificial. "It is a terrible thing," he wrote to Goldenweiser, "when the characters in a novel do what is not in their nature to do." He maintained that it was Anna Karenina, not he, who decided that she would throw herself under a train. In his long novels we do have a remarkable sense of Tolstoy's waiting on his characters until extended acquaintance told him how they should behave and what their fates should be.

In the stories it is different. The figures in them seem more like Tolstoy's agents and representatives than independent beings. They are aspects of the story's mechanism, and they are to be manipulated to make the story's point, to fulfil its dramatic pattern. In this they resemble significantly the characters of Dostoevsky, for whom *invention* was precisely the point and the privilege of the novelist. *Vdumyvat'*, in Russian, "to think up," was the function on which Dostoevsky prided himself; and, perhaps, this is the reason why we feel in *Crime and Punishment* that the action is taking place in somebody's head rather than in the real world. The events of *The Kreutzer Sonata* might equally be said to take place in the consciousness of the hero Pozdnyshev. His killing of his wife, like Raskolnikov's murder of the old money-lender, is a nightmare about which we are told, rather than an event in which we take part.

This is the note of *hypothesis* that I have mentioned as characteristic of Tolstoy's tales. By inventing a situation they pose a problem. If one married, along what lines might the relation proceed? What would happen if one became murderously jealous or obsessed with desire for another woman? Suppose one were to contract a fatal and painful disease or gave up the world to become a monk or hermit? Even *The Cossacks* shares this element of hypothesis. Its young hero Olenin—who, we should note, is *not* Tolstoy himself—wishes to join in the simple life of the Cossacks and perhaps to marry a Cossack girl. It is the old romantic European dream of "the Noble Savage," of participating in the life of a primitive and unspoiled community; and here we have it in a peculiarly Russian form. Tolstoy's great predecessor Alexander Pushkin had written a long dramatic poem entitled *The Gipsies* which handles a very similar theme. Its hero wishes to abandon civilisation and lead the simple life with a wandering gipsy tribe. He marries a gipsy girl and finds happiness for a time; but when his wife has an affair with a handsome young gipsy, the old standards of civilisation reassert themselves. He kills both his wife and her lover and is cast out by the tribe. At the end of the poem he is left utterly alone. The upshot of *The Gipsies* is starkly tragic; that of *The Cossacks* expansively comic, but in both cases the hero fails to become a different kind of man in a simpler and more heroic world. Both try to change their lives and both fail. The result is a triumph for a certain sort of realism. In Pushkin's case it is highly

economical and poetic; in Tolstoy's, naturalistic and pains-
takingly exact.

The parallel between the poem and the story is empha-
sised by the fact that Tolstoy first had thoughts of treating
his theme in verse, but he wisely abandoned the notion.
Indeed, as far as we know he only once in his life at-
tempted verse, and then only in a letter. His genius was
a more literal one, and in the slow and laborious composition of *The Cossacks*, which extended over a number of
years, he set himself to make the setting and the characters
as real as he knew how. In this he succeeded perfectly.
Olenin's romantic dreams are set against the pungent
physical presence of the Cossack girl Maryanka and old
"Uncle" Eroshka. Maryanka is a superlative creation, for
Tolstoy has deliberately turned the sloe-eyed Circassian
maiden of Russian romance into a real girl, yet a girl
whose physical actuality inspires Olenin as romantically
as the literary heroine of his dreams.

There is a deep and rich comedy in this, and for all its
familiarity with death *The Cossacks* could be called a
comic masterpiece. It is also the only one of Tolstoy's
works that has proved technically influential in the sense
that later writers have found inspiration in its method and
its spirit. We know that Hemingway admired it and can
see how he made use of its unemphatic style, though we
may also feel that he never attains its peculiar depth and
humour of perception. Frederick, the hero of *A Farewell
to Arms*, has something in common with Olenin, but its
heroine is a sad disappointment after Maryanka. The fact
of influence is significant and is surely connected with the
technical originality of Tolstoy's story and its carefully
wrought effects. It has a definite literary progeny in a
sense that *Anna Karenina* and *War and Peace* have never
had and could never have.

* * *

It is not too fanciful to trace a continuity in theme between
The Cossacks and *Father Sergius*, one of Tolstoy's last
and most impressive tales. In *Father Sergius* the moving
power is again Tolstoy's demonstration that men do not
change and that their natures are stronger than their wills.
Father Sergius can no more rid himself of the ground of
pride in his nature than Olenin can rid himself of the
outlook and beliefs of the society in which he has grown

up. As Olenin tries to escape from himself into being a Cossack, Father Sergius tries to escape into the monastic life, and later, in his despair at finding that he is still his old self, into the humble anonymity of a Siberian peasant. But he remains the same, as conscious of what his position demands of him when at the end he is humbly begging alms for his fellow-tramps as when he was on the parade ground in Saint Petersburg, or receiving admirers in his monastic cell.

Though sombre, the end of this story, and particularly the figure of Pashenka, touches us to the heart, as we are touched by a short and simple tale that Tolstoy wrote even later, *Alyosha the Pot*. It is difficult not to feel Tolstoy's own pride and stubborn self-will yearning for the simple goodness of those who have no sense of themselves, the peace that Pashenka and Alyosha possess without knowing, a peace that Father Sergius can never attain. *Father Sergius* is not only an extremely powerful but an agonisingly ambiguous story. It reminds us of Tolstoy's criticism of one of Chekhov's best tales, *The Darling*. *The Darling* presents a woman who has no character or opinions of her own, but adopts them with a simple and comical seriousness from her successive husbands. It is a light-hearted and ironic tale, but in a celebrated essay Tolstoy insisted on its underlying serious charity. He remarks that Chekhov seems to make fun of "the darling," but "by directing the close attention of a poet upon her he has exalted her."

What is interesting about this criticism is that it suggests what we feel in *Father Sergius*, that a great story-teller need not consciously bring off the overt intention of his story, but may involuntarily suggest another and deeper meaning. Whether, as Tolstoy suggests, it is true of Chekhov's story must remain a matter of opinion, but it is significant that Tolstoy should have thought so. For the idea behind his verdict contradicts in some measure his own view of an artist's intention, which should be to infect us, his readers, with the moral that he has in mind. Tolstoy's view of the story, as we can see from *What is Art?*, came to be based on the example of Christ's parables. *Father Sergius* is surely in intention such a parable, a parable on the nature of pride. But the abiding impression it leaves with us, and this was surely not Tolstoy's idea, is that if we are proud we cannot escape pride! We can only try to do so, and in the contrast between the effort and the reality lies the true power and pathos of the tale. In *The Cossacks* Tolstoy shows us deliberately that we cannot escape from what we are and from what our background has made us. In *Father Sergius* he reveals involuntarily, and thus more movingly, the same truth in its starkest form.

"The old man wrote it well," Tolstoy is said to have observed about *Father Sergius*. So indeed he did. But in the greatest art there is always an element of unconscious power that carries it beyond the scope of the author's purpose and preoccupation. We can see this power at work in *Father Sergius* as we see it in *Anna Karenina* and in *War and Peace*. Tolstoy himself admitted it, as we have seen in his perceptive words about *The Darling*. Nonetheless, his own view of art did in some ways contradict his instincts. Speaking of modern authors, he writes in *What is Art?* that one can usually see too clearly what they have in mind. "From the first lines one sees the intention with which the book is written, the details all become superfluous, and one feels dull." There is a strong connection between *artfulness* and the impression that the artist wants to make on us: the two go together. Hence, when Tolstoy himself wants to make a particular impression on us, the story may seem artful as well. The strange thing is that as he came to reject and even to hate the notion of art, he makes more and more use of his own powers of artistry. The reason must be that only by making the most deliberate use of those powers can he persuade us to see what he wants us to see and to feel the impact that he wants us to feel.

Master and Man is a good example of the divided mind of Tolstoy in creation. As he wrote it, he noted in his diary: "It is rather good from the artistic point of view, but the content is still feeble." And then a little later, significantly: "It is no good. No character—neither the one nor the other." Whichever Tolstoy meant here, that neither of the main characters was good or that neither art nor content was, it is clear that he was bothered by the way in which the story was turning out. After making the most elaborate corrections and amendments at proof-stage, he finally wrote: "I have sinned, because I am ashamed to have wasted my time on such stuff." Yet *Master and Man* is a triumph, one of Tolstoy's most superb pieces, and all the more so because we do *not* know how it will turn out. The two characters are not puppets but completely realised, and the motives of Brekhunov remain touchingly ambiguous and absolutely true to his merchant's nature. He sets about saving his servant as if it was a business deal, and he obviously calculates that in keeping Nikita warm he will keep himself warm too. He is wrong: this is the first miscalculation that he has made; yet he comes to realise before he dies that it does not matter.

The heroes of *The Devil* and *The Kreutzer Sonata* have no such independence. Irtenyev in *The Devil* has none at all, and the alternative endings of the tale not only show this, but show that Tolstoy himself realised it. Although much in this piece is strong and vivid—the confrontations between the hero and the servant girl are as terrifyingly potent as those between Maslova and her seducer in *Resurrection*—by Tolstoy's highest standards the story does not come off. The hero is not actualised enough. Is the same true of Pozdnyshev in *The Kreutzer Sonata*? He certainly begins by seeming a mere repository for Tolstoy's more extreme views on sex and marriage, but at the end we realise that he is a human being; and when he says, "Goodbye— Forgive me" (in Russian the two phrases are almost the same word), his case as an individual moves us deeply, though it may be that his theories and denunciations leave us untouched. He has realised that his wife was "another human being," and it is this realisation, coming too late for any recognition between them, that is his tragic and personal experience. That experience is similar to Prince Andrew's in *War and Peace,* who finds that confrontation · with Natasha, about whom he has been consumed with jealousy, leads to a disappearance of all the maddening abstractions that jealousy produces. All his embittered emotions fall away, and he sees only the girl herself. That confrontation was a happy one, even though Andrew was mortally wounded, but Pozdnyshev's is tragic, because his injured wife will not and cannot recognise him as a human being as he has at last recognised her. She only looks at him with "cold animal hatred."

The Kreutzer Sonata caused a sensation, and it was published only after the Countess Tolstoy had persuaded Tsar Alexander III to relax the official censorship on its behalf. It was, of course, the shock effect of the story's views on marriage rather than their artistic presentation that secured its immediate notoriety. But there is some evidence that Tolstoy was well aware in this case of the subtlety with which he had presented the hero, particularly in the final pages. Replying to a criticism of Pozdnyshev as a monstrous being, Tolstoy observed that he "gives himself away not only by abusing himself but by concealing the good sides of his character." That is just it. Pozdnyshev is not unlike one of Dostoevsky's characters, in particular his "Underground Man," in being his own worst advocate. What moves the reader in both cases is the potential for goodness and kindness that has been wasted, distorted by an attitude to life that the conventions and hypocrisies of society have helped to bring about.

Tolstoy worked long on *Hadji Murad* and admitted that it was almost the only one of his later works of which he thought well. In an undisclosed and symbolic way it is one of his most autobiographical works. It is true that Hadji Murad was a real person, a Tartar chieftain who was killed attempting to escape from the Russians after he had gone over to their side; but it is impossible not to be aware of the deep sense of personal identification that Tolstoy feels with him. Tolstoy, too, had cut himself off from his own class and his own life, yet had not been able to find any real peace or solidarity in his new life and among his new disciples. Hadji Murad remembers the tale of the falcon that was caught by men and then pecked to death by its own kind. Tolstoy certainly underwent something of this sort at the hands of his wife during his last days.

And yet *Hadji Murad* is first and foremost a superbly objective tale, a miniature epic or saga, which also shows a penetrating insight into the interplay of power politics, intrigue and colonial conquest. It has something in common, on the one hand, with Shakespeare's plays of power and fate, and on the other, with such a corrosively perceptive study of colonialism as Conrad's *Heart of Darkness*. The episode itself dates from Tolstoy's own early years in the Caucasus, when Shamil, the Moslem religious leader, was trying to unite the Caucasian tribes against Russian annexation. Whether Tolstoy was fair to Nicholas I hardly matters, any more than whether Shakespeare was fair to Octavius Caesar or Richard III. What counts is his masterly indictment not only of the hatefulness of power but the dreadful helplessness of those who exercise it. It becomes necessary to its possessors, who exercise it as unreflectingly as ordinary people run their homes or go to the office. Like almost everything that Tolstoy wrote, the lesson or "moral" involved here is one that we can never forget or afford to ignore. It is significant that Soviet critics have tried to see in the story propaganda for the cause of Russia against Moselm fanaticism and for the new order against the old, but its theme is universal, one that leaders of the West today, no less than those of the Soviet system, would do well to take to heart. As one of Tolstoy's most balanced critics has put it:*

> The story impresses one with the great threat to life and happiness which lies in the contrasting despotisms of Shamil and Nicholas . . . and by its compelling sympathy with the fine wild chieftain, tenacious of life to the last, hanging on like the red wild thistle, the only living thing in the field to survive the passage of the plough—the symbol with which Tolstoy begins his tale, and with which he ends it.

This image of the thistle, which holds the wide range of the story in its emblematic vice, has a curiously similar function to the central symbol in another great Russian tale of power and submission, Pushkin's poem *The Bronze Horseman,* in which the statue of Peter the Great dominates the consciousness of the divided hero and eventually helps to drive him mad.

As usual in Tolstoy's best tales, this final masterpiece contains a great variety of effect. The old general's farewell speech is deliciously funny yet moving. Marya Dimitrievna, the drunken major's mistress, is a fine and unexpectedly sympathetic portrait. When she assails with passionate indignation the officers who are displaying Hadji Murad's severed head, she has something of the grandeur of an Antigone. Death presides over the tale, but not the haunting fear and horror of death in so much of Tolstoy's work. Here death has become the fitting climax to an heroic life and a part of the archaic tranquillity of the narrative form. The vivid pictures of his childhood that fill Hadji Murad's mind during his last moments are like those of Tolstoy

* Theodore Redpath: *Tolstoy* (Studies in Modern European Life and Thought).

himself, and he watches them pass "without evoking any feeling within him—neither pity nor anger nor any kind of desire." When Tolstoy, after his flight from home and his final journey, was lying at the Astapovo railway station, he repeated over and over during the last moments of his life: "I do not understand what it is I have to do." Like Hadji Murad, whom he had imagined so well, he had nothing to do but to die.

John Bayley

New College,
Oxford University.

Family Happiness

[1859]

Part I

I

We were in mourning for my mother, who had died in the autumn, and I spent all that winter alone in the country with Kátya and Sónya.

Kátya was an old friend of the family, our governess who had brought us all up, and I had known and loved her since my earliest recollections. Sónya was my younger sister. It was a dark and sad winter which we spent in our old house of Pokróvskoe. The weather was cold and so windy that the snowdrifts came higher than the windows; the panes were almost always dimmed by frost, and we seldom walked or drove anywhere throughout the winter. Our visitors were few, and those who came brought no addition of cheerfulness or happiness to the household. They all wore sad faces and spoke low, as if they were afraid of waking someone; they never laughed, but sighed and often shed tears as they looked at me and especially at little Sónya in her black frock. The feeling of death clung to the house; the air was still filled with the grief and horror of death. My mother's room was kept locked; and whenever I passed it on my way to bed, I felt a strange uncomfortable impulse to look into that cold empty room.

I was then seventeen; and in the very year of her death my mother was intending to move to Petersburg, in order to take me into society. The loss of my mother was a great grief to me; but I must confess to another feeling behind that grief—a feeling that though I was young and pretty (so everybody told me), I was wasting a second winter in the solitude of the country. Before the winter ended, this sense of dejection, solitude, and simple boredom increased to such an extent that I refused to leave my room or open the piano or take up a book. When Kátya urged me to find some occupation, I said that I did not feel able for

3

it; but in my heart I said, 'What is the good of it? What is the good of doing anything, when the best part of my life is being wasted like this?' And to this question, tears were my only answer.

I was told that I was growing thin and losing my looks; but even this failed to interest me. What did it matter? For whom? I felt that my whole life was bound to go on in the same solitude and helpless dreariness, from which I had myself no strength and even no wish to escape. Towards the end of winter Kátya became anxious about me and determined to make an effort to take me abroad. But money was needed for this, and we hardly knew how our affairs stood after my mother's death. Our guardian, who was to come and clear up our position, was expected every day.

In March he arrived.

'Well, thank God!' Kátya said to me one day, when I was walking up and down the room like a shadow, without occupation, without a thought, and without a wish. 'Sergéy Mikháylych has arrived; he has sent to inquire about us and means to come here for dinner. You must rouse yourself, dear Máshechka,' she added, 'or what will he think of you? He was so fond of you all.'

Sergéy Mikháylych was our near neighbour, and, though a much younger man, had been a friend of my father's. His coming was likely to change our plans and to make it possible to leave the country; and also I had grown up in the habit of love and regard for him; and when Kátya begged me to rouse myself, she guessed rightly that it would give me especial pain to show to disadvantage before him, more than before any other of our friends. Like everyone in the house, from Kátya and his god-daughter Sónya down to the helper in the stables, I loved him from old habit; and also he had a special significance for me, owing to a remark which my mother had once made in my presence. 'I should like you to marry a man like him,' she said. At the time this seemed to me strange and even unpleasant. My ideal husband was quite different: he was to be thin, pale, and sad; and Sergéy Mikháylych was middle-aged, tall, robust, and always, as it seemed to me, in good spirits. But still my mother's words stuck in my head; and even six years before this time, when I was eleven, and he still said 'thou' to me, and played with me, and called me by the pet-name of 'violet'—even then I sometimes asked myself in a fright, 'What *shall* I do, if he suddenly wants to marry me?'

Before our dinner, to which Kátya made an addition of sweets and a dish of spinach, Sergéy Mikháylych arrived. From the window I watched him drive up to the house in a small sleigh; but as soon as it turned the corner, I hastened to the drawing-room, meaning to pretend that his visit was a complete surprise. But when I heard his tramp and loud voice and Kátya's footsteps in the hall, I lost patience and went to meet him myself. He was holding Kátya's hand, talking loud, and smiling. When he saw me, he stopped and looked at me for a time without bowing. I was uncomfortable and felt myself blushing.

'Can this be really you?' he said in his plain decisive way, walking towards me with his arms apart. 'Is so great a change possible? How grown-up you are! I used to call you "violet", but now you are a rose in full bloom!'

He took my hand in his own large hand and pressed it so hard that it almost hurt. Expecting him to kiss my hand, I bent towards him, but he only pressed it again and looked straight into my eyes with the old firmness and cheerfulness in his face.

It was six years since I had seen him last. He was much changed—older and darker in complexion; and he now wore whiskers which did not become him at all; but much remained the same—his simple manner, the large features of his honest open face, his bright intelligent eyes, his friendly, almost boyish, smile.

Five minutes later he had ceased to be a visitor and had become the friend of us all, even of the servants, whose visible eagerness to wait on him proved their pleasure at his arrival.

He behaved quite unlike the neighbours who had visited us after my mother's death. They had thought it necessary to be silent when they sat with us, and to shed tears. He, on the contrary, was cheerful and talkative, and said not a word about my mother, so that this indifference seemed strange to me at first and even improper on the part of so close a friend. But I understood later that what seemed indifference was sincerity, and I felt grateful for it. In the evening Kátya poured out tea, sitting in her old place in the drawing-room, where she used to sit in my mother's lifetime; Sónya and I sat near him; our old butler Grigóri had hunted out one of my father's pipes and brought it to him; and he began to walk up and down the room as he used to do in past days.

'How many terrible changes there are in this house, when one thinks of it all!' he said, stopping in his walk.

'Yes,' said Kátya with a sigh; and then she put the lid on the samovar and looked at him, quite ready to burst out crying.

'I suppose you remember your father?' he said, turning to me.

'Not clearly,' I answered.

'How happy you would have been together now!' he added in a low voice, looking thoughtfully at my face above the eyes. 'I was very fond of him,' he added in a still lower tone, and it seemed to me that his eyes were shining more than usual.

'And now God has taken her too!' said Kátya; and at once she laid her napkin on the teapot, took out her handkerchief, and began to cry.

'Yes, the changes in this house are terrible,' he repeated, turning away. 'Sónya, show me your toys,' he added after a little and went off to the parlour. When he had gone, I looked at Kátya with eyes full of tears.

'What a splendid friend he is!' she said. And, though he was no relation, I did really feel a kind of warmth and comfort in the sympathy of this good man.

I could hear him moving about in the parlour with Sónya, and the sound of her high childish voice. I sent tea to him there; and I heard him sit down at the piano and strike the keys with Sónya's little hands.

Then his voice came—'Márya Alexándrovna, come here and play something.'

I liked his easy behaviour to me and his friendly tone of command; I got up and went to him.

'Play this,' he said, opening a book of Beethoven's music at the *adagio* of the 'Moonlight Sonata.' 'Let me hear how you play,' he added, and went off to a corner of the room, carrying his cup with him.

I somehow felt that with him it was impossible to refuse or to say beforehand that I played badly: I sat down obediently at the piano and began to play as well as I could; yet I was afraid of criticism, because I knew that he understood and enjoyed music. The *adagio* suited the remembrance of past days evoked by our conversation at tea, and I believe that I played it fairly well. But he would not let me play the *scherzo*. 'No,' he said, coming up to me; 'you don't play that right; don't go on; but the first movement was not bad; you seem to be musical.' This moderate praise pleased me so much that I even reddened. I felt it pleasant and strange that a friend of my father's, and his contemporary, should no longer treat me like a child but speak to me seriously. Kátya now went upstairs to put Sónya to bed, and we were left alone in the parlour.

He talked to me about my father, and about the beginning of their friendship and the happy days they had spent together, while I was still busy with lesson-books and toys; and his talk put my father before me in quite a new light, as a man of simple and delightful character. He asked me too about my tastes, what I read and what I intended to do, and gave me advice. The man of mirth and jest who used to tease me and make me toys had disappeared; here was a serious, simple, and affectionate friend, for whom I could not help feeling respect and sympathy. It was easy and pleasant to talk to him; and yet I felt an involuntary strain also. I was anxious about each word I spoke: I wished so much to earn for my own sake the love which had been given me already merely because I was my father's daughter.

After putting Sónya to bed, Kátya joined us and began to complain to him of my·apathy, about which I had said nothing.

'So she never told me the most important thing of all!' he said, smiling and shaking his head reproachfully at me.

'Why tell you?' I said. 'It is very tiresome to talk about, and it will pass off.' (I really felt now, not only that my dejection would pass off, but that it had already passed off, or rather had never existed.)

'It is a bad thing,' he said, 'not to be able to stand solitude. Can it be that you are a young lady?'

'Of course, I am a young lady,' I answered, laughing.

'Well, I can't praise a young lady who is alive only when people are admiring her, but as soon as she is left alone, collapses and finds nothing to her taste—one who is all for show and has no resources in herself.'

'You have a flattering opinion of me!' I said, just for the sake of saying something.

He was silent for a little. Then he said: 'Yes; your likeness to your father means something. There is something in you . . . ,' and his kind attentive look again flattered me and made me feel a pleasant embarrassment.

I noticed now for the first time that his face, which gave one at first the impression of high spirits, had also an expression peculiar to himself—bright at first and then more and more attentive and rather sad.

'You ought not to be bored and you cannot be,' he said; 'you have music, which you appreciate, books, study; your whole life lies before you, and now or never is the time to prepare for it and save yourself future regrets. A year hence it will be too late.'

He spoke to me like a father or an uncle, and I felt that he kept a constant check upon himself, in order to keep on my level. Though I was hurt that he considered me as inferior to himself, I was pleased that for me alone he thought it necessary to try to be different.

For the rest of the evening he talked about business with Kátya.

'Well, good-bye, dear friends,' he said. Then he got up, came towards me, and took my hand.

'When shall we see you again?' asked Kátya.

'In spring,' he answered, still holding my hand. 'I shall go now to Danílovka' (this was another property of ours), 'look into things there and make what arrangements I can; then I go to Moscow on business of my own; and in summer we shall meet again.'

'Must you really be away so long?' I asked, and I felt terribly grieved. I had really hoped to see him every day, and I felt a sudden shock of regret, and a fear that my depression would return. And my face and voice must have made this plain.

'You must find more to do and not get depressed,' he said; and I thought his tone too cool and unconcerned. 'I shall put you through an examination in spring,' he added, letting go my hand and not looking at me.

When we saw him off in the hall, he put on his fur coat in a hurry and still avoided looking at me. 'He is taking a deal of trouble for nothing!' I thought. 'Does he think me so anxious that he should look at me? He is a good man, a very good man; but that's all.'

That evening, however, Kátya and I sat up late, talking, not about him but about our plans for the summer, and where we should spend next winter and what we should do then. I had ceased to ask that terrible question—what is the good of it all? Now it seemed quite plain and simple: the proper object of life was happiness, and I promised myself much happiness ahead. It seemed as if our gloomy old house had suddenly become full of light and life.

II

Meanwhile spring arrived. My old dejection passed away and gave place to the unrest which spring brings with it, full of dreams and vague hopes and desires. Instead of living as I had done at the beginning of winter, I read and played the piano and gave lessons to Sónya; but also I often went into the garden and wandered for long alone through the avenues, or sat on a bench there; and Heaven knows what my thoughts and wishes and hopes were at such times. Sometimes at night, especially if there was a moon, I sat by my bedroom window till dawn; sometimes, when Kátya was not watching, I stole out into the garden wearing only a wrapper and ran through the dew as far as the pond; and once I went all the way to the open fields and walked right round the garden alone at night.

I find it difficult now to recall and understand the dreams which then filled my imagination. Even when I *can* recall them, I find it hard to believe that my dreams were just like that: they were so strange and so remote from life.

Sergéy Mikháylych kept his promise: he returned from his travels at the end of May.

His first visit to us was in the evening and was quite unexpected. We were sitting in the veranda, preparing for tea. By this time the garden was all green, and the nightingales had taken up their quarters for the whole of St. Peter's Fast in the leafy borders. The tops of the round lilac bushes had a sprinkling of white and purple—a sign that their flowers were ready to open. The foliage of the birch avenue was all transparent in the light of the setting sun. In the veranda there was shade and freshness. The evening dew was sure to be heavy in the grass. Out of doors beyond the garden the last sounds of day were audible, and the noise of the sheep and cattle, as they were driven home. Níkon, the half-witted boy, was driving his water-cart along the path outside the veranda, and a cold stream of water from the sprinkler made dark circles on the mould round the stems and supports of the dahlias. In our veranda the polished samovar shone and hissed on the white table-cloth; there were cracknels and biscuits and cream on the table. Kátya was busy washing the cups with her plump hands. I was too hungry after bathing to wait for tea, and was eating bread with thick fresh cream. I was wearing a gingham blouse with loose sleeves, and my hair, still wet, was covered with a kerchief. Kátya saw him first, even before he came in.

'You, Sergéy Mikháylych!' she cried. 'Why, we were just talking about you.'

I got up, meaning to go and change my dress, but he caught me just by the door.

'Why stand on such ceremony in the country?' he said, looking with a smile at the kerchief on my head. 'You don't mind the presence of your butler, and I am really the same to you as Grigóri is.' But I felt just then that he was looking at me in a way quite unlike Grigóri's way, and I was uncomfortable.

'I shall come back at once,' I said, as I left them.

'But what is wrong?' he called out after me; 'it's just the dress of a young peasant woman.'

'How strangely he looked at me!' I said to myself as I was quickly changing upstairs. 'Well, I'm glad he has come; things will be more lively.' After a look in the glass I ran gaily downstairs and into the veranda; I was out of breath and did not disguise my haste. He was sitting at the table, talking to Kátya about our affairs. He glanced at me and smiled; then he went on talking. From what he said it appeared that our affairs were in capital shape: it was now possible for us, after spending the summer in the country, to go either to Petersburg for Sónya's education, or abroad.

'If only you would go abroad with us—' said Kátya; 'without you we shall be quite lost there.'

'Oh, I should like to go round the world with you,' he said, half in jest and half in earnest.

'All right,' I said; 'let us start off and go round the world.'

He smiled and shook his head.

'What about my mother? What about my business?' he said. 'But that's not the question just now: I want to know how you have been spending your time. Not depressed again, I hope?'

When I told him that I had been busy and not bored during his absence, and when Kátya confirmed my report, he praised me as if he had a right to do so, and his words and looks were kind, as they might have been to a child. I felt obliged to tell him, in detail and with perfect frankness, all my good actions, and to confess, as if I were in church, all that he might disapprove of. The evening was so fine that we stayed in the veranda after tea was cleared away; and the conversation interested me so much that I did not notice how we ceased by degrees to hear any sound of the servants indoors. The scent of flowers grew stronger and came from all sides; the grass was drenched with dew; a nightingale struck up in a lilac bush close by and then stopped on hearing our voices; the starry sky seemed to come down lower over our heads.

It was growing dusk, but I did not notice it till a bat suddenly and silently flew in beneath the veranda awning and began to flutter round my white shawl. I shrank back against the wall and nearly cried out; but the bat as silently and swiftly dived out from under the awning and disappeared in the half-darkness of the garden.

'How fond I am of this place of yours!' he said, changing the conversation; 'I wish I could spend all my life here, sitting in this veranda.'

'Well, do then!' said Kátya.

'That's all very well,' he said, 'but life won't sit still.'

'Why don't you marry?' asked Kátya; 'you would make an excellent husband.'

'Because I like sitting still?' and he laughed. 'No, Katerína Kárlovna, too late for you and me to marry. People have long ceased to think of me as a marrying man, and I am even surer of it myself; and I declare I have felt quite comfortable since the matter was settled.'

It seemed to me that he said this in an unnaturally persuasive way.

'Nonsense!' said Kátya; 'a man of thirty-six makes out that he is too old!'

'Too old indeed,' he went on, 'when all one wants is to sit still. For a man who is going to marry that's not enough. Just you ask her,' he added, nodding at me; 'people of her age should marry, and you and I can rejoice in their happiness.'

The sadness and constraint latent in his voice was not

lost upon me. He was silent for a little, and neither Kátya nor I spoke.

'Well, just fancy,' he went on, turning a little on his seat; 'suppose that by some mischance I married a girl of seventeen, Másha, if you like—I mean, Márya Alexándrovna. The instance is good; I am glad it turned up; there could not be a better instance.'

I laughed; but I could not understand why he was glad, or what it was that had turned up.

'Just tell me honestly, with your hand on your heart,' he said, turning as if playfully to me, 'would it not be a misfortune for you to unite your life with that of an old worn-out man who only wants to sit still, whereas Heaven knows what wishes are fermenting in that heart of yours?'

I felt uncomfortable and was silent, not knowing how to answer him.

'I am not making you a proposal, you know,' he said, laughing; 'but am I really the kind of husband you dream of when walking alone in the avenue at twilight? It would be a misfortune, would it not?'

'No, not a misfortune,' I began.

'But a bad thing,' he ended my sentence.

'Perhaps; but I may be mistaken . . .' He interrupted me again.

'There, you see! She is quite right, and I am grateful to her for her frankness, and very glad to have had this conversation. And there is something else to be said'—he added: 'for me too it would be a very great misfortune.'

'How odd you are! You have not changed in the least,' said Kátya, and then left the veranda, to order supper to be served.

When she had gone, we were both silent and all was still around us, but for one exception. A nightingale, which had sung last night by fitful snatches, now flooded the garden with a steady stream of song, and was soon answered by another from the dell below, which had not sung till that evening. The nearer bird stopped and seemed to listen for a moment, and then broke out again still louder than before, pouring out his song in piercing long-drawn cadences. There was a regal calm in the birds' voices, as they floated through the realm of night which belongs to those birds and not to man. The gardener walked past to his sleeping-quarters in the greenhouse, and the noise of his heavy boots grew fainter and fainter along the path. Someone whistled twice sharply at the foot of the hill; and then all was still again. The rustling of leaves could just be heard; the veranda awning flapped; a faint perfume, floating in the air, came down on the veranda and filled it. I felt silence awkward after what had been said, but what to say I did not know. I looked at him. His eyes, bright in the half-darkness, turned towards me.

'How good life is!' he said.

I sighed, I don't know why.

'Well?' he asked.

'Life is good,' I repeated after him.

Again we were silent, and again I felt uncomfortable. I could not help fancying that I had wounded him by agreeing that he was old; and I wished to comfort him but did not know how.

'Well, I must be saying good-bye,' he said, rising; 'my mother expects me for supper; I have hardly seen her all day.'

'I meant to play you the new sonata,' I said.

'That must wait,' he replied; and I thought that he spoke coldly.

'Good-bye.'

I felt still more certain that I had wounded him, and I was sorry. Kátya and I went to the steps to see him off and stood for a while in the open, looking along the road where he had disappeared from view. When we ceased to hear the sound of his horse's hoofs, I walked round the house to the veranda, and again, sat looking into the garden; and all I wished to see and hear, I still saw and heard for a long time in the dewy mist filled with the sounds of night.

He came a second time, and a third; and the awkwardness arising from that strange conversation passed away entirely, never to return. During that whole summer. he came two or three times a week; and I grew so accustomed to his presence, that, when he failed to come for some time, I missed him and felt angry with him, and thought he was behaving badly in deserting me. He treated me like a boy whose company he liked, asked me questions, invited the most cordial frankness on my part, gave me advice and encouragement, or sometimes scolded and checked me. But in spite of his constant effort to keep on my level, I was aware that behind the part of him which I could understand there remained an entire region of mystery, into which he did not consider it necessary to admit me; and this fact did much to preserve my respect for him and his attraction for me. I knew from Kátya and from our neighbours that he had not only to care for his old mother with whom he lived, and to manage his own estate and our affairs, but was also responsible for some public business which was the source of serious worries; but what view he took of all this, what were his convictions, plans, and hopes, I could not in the least find out from him. Whenever I turned the conversation to his affairs, he frowned in a way peculiar to himself and seemed to imply, 'Please stop! That is no business of yours;' and then he changed the subject. This hurt me at first; but I soon grew accustomed to confining our talk to my affairs, and felt this to be quite natural.

There was another thing which displeased me at first and then became pleasant to me. This was his complete indifference and even contempt for my personal appearance. Never by word or look did he imply that I was pretty; on the contrary, he frowned and laughed, whenever the word was applied to me in his presence. He even liked to find fault with my looks and tease me about them. On special days Kátya liked to dress me out in fine clothes and to arrange my hair effectively; but my finery met only with mockery from him, which pained kind-hearted Kátya and at first disconcerted me. She had made up her mind that he admired me; and she could not understand how a man could help wishing a woman whom he admired to appear to the utmost advantage. But I soon understood what he wanted. He wished to make sure that I had not a trace of affectation. And when I understood this I was really quite free from affectation in the clothes I wore, or the arrangement of my hair, or my movements; but a very obvious form of affectation took its place—an affectation of simplicity, at a time when I could not yet be really simple. That he loved me, I knew; but I did not yet ask myself whether he loved me as a child or as a woman. I valued his love; I felt that he thought me better than all other young women in the world, and I could not help wishing him to go on being deceived about me. Without wishing to deceive him, I did deceive him, and I became better myself while deceiving him. I felt it a better and worthier course to show him the good points of my heart and mind than of my body. My hair, hands, face, ways—all these,

whether good or bad, he had appraised at once and knew
so well, that I could add nothing to my external appearance except the wish to deceive him. But my mind and
heart he did not know, because he loved them, and
because they were in the very process of growth and
development; and on this point I could and did deceive
him. And how easy I felt in his company, once I understood this clearly! My causeless bashfulness and awkward
movements completely disappeared. Whether he saw me
from in front, or in profile, sitting or standing, with my
hair up or my hair down, I felt that he knew me from
head to foot, and I fancied, was satisfied with me as I
was. If, contrary to his habit, he had suddenly said to me
as other people did, that I had a pretty face, I believe that
I should not have liked it at all. But, on the other hand,
how light and happy my heart was when, after I had said
something, he looked hard at me and said, hiding emotion
under a mask of raillery:

'Yes, there *is* something in you! you are a fine girl—
that I must tell you.'

And for what did I receive such rewards, which filled
my heart with pride and joy? Merely for saying that I
felt for old Grigóri in his love for his little granddaughter;
or because the reading of some poem or novel moved me
to tears; or because I liked Mozart better than Schulhof.
And I was surprised at my own quickness in guessing what
was good and worthy of love, when I certainly did not
know then what *was* good and worthy to be loved. Most
of my former tastes and habits did not please him; and a
mere look of his, or a twitch of his eyebrow was enough
to show that he did not like what I was trying to say;
and I felt at once that my own standard was changed.
Sometimes, when he was about to give me a piece of
advice, I seemed to know beforehand what he would say.
When he looked in my face and asked me a question, his
very look would draw out of me the answer he wanted.
All my thoughts and feelings of that time were not really
mine: they were his thoughts and feelings, which had
suddenly become mine and passed into my life and lighted
it up. Quite unconsciously I began to look at everything
with different eyes—at Kátya and the servants and Sónya
and myself and my occupations. Books, which I used to
read merely to escape boredom, now became one of the
chief pleasures of my life, merely because he brought me

the books and we read and discussed them together. The lessons I gave to Sónya had been a burdensome obligation which I forced myself to go through from a sense of duty; but, after he was present at a lesson, it became a joy to me to watch Sónya's progress. It used to seem to me an impossibility to learn a whole piece of music by heart; but now, when I knew that he would hear it and might praise it, I would play a single movement forty times over without stopping, till poor Kátya stuffed her ears with cottonwool, while I was still not weary of it. The same old sonatas seemed quite different in their expression, and came out quite changed and much improved. Even Kátya, whom I knew and loved like a second self, became different in my eyes. I now understood for the first time that she was not in the least bound to be the mother, friend, and slave that she was to us. Now I appreciated all the self-sacrifice and devotion of this affectionate creature, and all my obligations to her; and I began to love her even better. It was he too who taught me to take quite a new view of our serfs and servants and maids. It is an absurd confession to make—but I had spent seventeen years among these people and yet knew less about them than about strangers whom I had never seen; it had never once occurred to me that they had their affections and wishes and sorrows, just as I had. Our garden and woods and fields, which I had known so long, became suddenly new and beautiful to me. He was right in saying that the only certain happiness in life is to live for others. At the time his words seemed to me strange, and I did not understand them; but by degrees this became a conviction with me, without thinking about it. He revealed to me a whole new world of joys in the present, without changing anything in my life, without adding anything except himself to each impression in my mind. All that had surrounded me from childhood without saying anything to me, suddenly came to life. The mere sight of him made everything begin to speak and press for admittance to my heart, fiiling it with happiness.

Often during that summer, when I went upstairs to my room and lay down on my bed, the old unhappiness of spring with its desires and hopes for the future gave place to a passionate happiness in the present. Unable to sleep, I often got up and sat on Kátya's bed, and told her how perfectly happy I was, though I now realize that this was quite unnecessary, as she could see it for herself. But she told me that she was quite content and perfectly happy, and kissed me. I believed her—it seemed to me so necessary and just that everyone should be happy. But Kátya could think of sleep too; and sometimes, pretending to be angry, she drove me from her bed and went to sleep, while I turned over and over in my mind all that made me so happy. Sometimes I got up and said my prayers over again, praying in my own words and thanking God for all the happiness he had given me.

All was quiet in the room; there was only the even breathing of Kátya in her sleep, and the ticking of the clock by her bed, while I turned from side to side and whispered words of prayer, or crossed myself and kissed the cross round my neck. The door was shut and the windows shuttered; perhaps a fly or gnat hung buzzing in the air. I felt a wish never to leave that room—a wish that dawn might never come, that my present frame of mind might never change. I felt that my dreams and thoughts and prayers were live things, living there in the dark with me, hovering about my bed, and standing over me. And every thought was his thought, and every feeling his feeling. I did not know yet that this was love; I thought that things might go on so for ever, and that this feeling involved no consequences.

III

One day when the corn was being carried, I went with Kátya and Sónya to our favourite seat in the garden, in the shade of the lime-trees and above the dell, beyond which the fields and woods lay open before us. It was three days since Sergéy Mikháylych had been to see us; we were expecting him, all the more because our bailiff reported that he had promised to visit the harvest-field. At two o'clock we saw him ride on to the rye-field. With a smile and a glance at me, Kátya ordered peaches and cherries, of which he was very fond, to be brought; then she lay down on the bench and began to doze. I tore off a crooked flat lime-tree branch, which made my hand wet with its juicy leaves and juicy bark. Then I fanned Kátya with it and went on with my book, breaking off from time to time, to look at the field-path along which he must come. Sónya was making a dolls' house at the root of an old lime-tree. The day was sultry, windless, and steaming; the clouds were packing and growing blacker; all morning a thunderstorm had been gathering, and I felt restless, as I always did before thunder. But by afternoon the clouds began to part, the sun sailed out into a clear sky, and only in one quarter was there a faint rumbling. A single heavy cloud, louring above the horizon and mingling with the dust from the fields, was rent from time to time by pale zigzags of lightning which ran down to the ground. It was clear that for to-day the storm would pass off, with us at all events. The road beyond the garden was visible in places, and we could see a procession of high creaking carts slowly moving along it with their load of sheaves, while the empty carts rattled at a faster pace to meet them, with swaying legs and shirts fluttering in them. The thick dust neither blew away nor settled down—it stood still beyond the fence, and we could see it through the transparent foliage of the garden trees. A little farther off, in the stackyard, the same voices and the same creaking of wheels were audible; and the same yellow sheaves that had moved slowly past the fence were now flying aloft, and I could see the oval stacks gradually rising higher, and their conspicuous pointed tops, and the labourers swarming upon them. On the dusty field in front more carts were moving and more yellow sheaves were visible; and the noise of the carts, with the sound of talking and singing, came to us from a distance. At one side the bare stubble, with strips of fallow covered with wormwood, came more and more into view. Lower down, to the right, the gay dresses of the women were visible, as they bent down and swung their arms to bind the sheaves. Here the bare stubble looked untidy; but the disorder was cleared by degrees, as the pretty sheaves were ranged at close intervals. It seemed as if summer had suddenly turned to autumn before my eyes. The dust and heat were everywhere, except in our favourite nook in the garden; and everywhere, in this heat and dust and under the burning sun, the labourers carried on their heavy task with talk and noise.

Meanwhile Kátya slept so sweetly on our shady bench, beneath her white cambric handkerchief, the black juicy cherries glistened so temptingly on the plate, our dresses were so clean and fresh, the water in the jug was so bright with rainbow colours in the sun, and I felt so happy! 'How

can I help it?' I thought; 'am I to blame for being happy?
And how can I share my happiness? How and to whom
can I surrender all myself and all my happiness?'

By this time the sun had sunk behind the tops of the
birch avenue, the dust was settling on the fields, the
distance became clearer and brighter in the slanting light.
The clouds had dispersed altogether; I could see through
the trees the thatch of three new corn-stacks. The labourers
came down off the stacks; the carts hurried past, evidently
for the last time, with a loud noise of shouting; the women,
with rakes over their shoulders and straw-bands in their
belts, walked home past us, singing loudly; and still there
was no sign of Sergéy Mikháylych, though I had seen him
ride down the hill long ago. Suddenly he appeared upon
the avenue, coming from a quarter where I was not looking for him. He had walked round by the dell. He came
quickly towards me, with his hat off and radiant with high
spirits. Seeing that Kátya was asleep, he bit his lip, closed
his eyes, and advanced on tiptoe; I saw at once that he
was in that peculiar mood of causeless merriment which
I always delighted to see in him, and which we called
'wild ecstasy'. He was just like a schoolboy playing truant;
his whole figure, from head to foot, breathed content, happiness, and boyish frolic.

'Well, young violet, how are you? All right?' he said in
a whisper, coming up to me and taking my hand. Then,
in answer to my question, 'Oh, I'm splendid to-day, I feel
like a boy of thirteen—I want to play at horses and climb
trees.'

'Is it wild ecstasy?' I asked, looking into his laughing
eyes, and feeling that the 'wild ecstasy' was infecting me.

'Yes,' he answered, winking and checking a smile. 'But
I don't see why you need hit Katerína Kárlovna on the
nose.'

With my eyes on him I had gone on waving the branch,
without noticing that I had knocked the handkerchief off
Kátya's face and was now brushing her with the leaves.
I laughed.

'She will say she was awake all the time,' I whispered,
as if not to awake Kátya; but that was not my real reason
—it was only that I liked to whisper to him.

He moved his lips in imitation of me, pretending that
my voice was too low for him to hear. Catching sight of
the dish of cherries, he pretended to steal it, and carried

it off to Sónya under the lime-tree, where he sat down on
her dolls. Sónya was angry at first, but he soon made his
peace with her by starting a game, to see which of them
could eat cherries faster.

'If you like, I will send for more cherries,' I said; 'or let
us go ourselves.'

He took the dish and set the dolls on it, and we all three
started for the orchard. Sónya ran behind us, laughing and
pulling at his coat, to make him surrender the dolls. He
gave them up and then turned to me, speaking more
seriously.

'You really are a violet,' he said, still speaking low,
though there was no longer any fear of waking anybody;
'when I came to you out of all that dust and heat and toil,
I positively smelt violets at once. But not the sweet violet—
you know, that early dark violet that smells of melting
snow and spring grass.'

'Is harvest going on well?' I asked, in order to hide the
happy agitation which his words produced in me.

'First-rate! Our people are always splendid. The more
you know them, the better you like them.'

'Yes,' I said; 'before you came I was watching them
from the garden, and suddenly I felt ashamed to be so
comfortable myself while they were hard at work, and
so . . .'

He interrupted me, with a kind but grave look: 'Don't
talk like that, my dear; it is too sacred a matter to talk of
lightly. God forbid that you should use fine phrases about
that!'

'But it is only to *you* I say this.'

'All right, I understand. But what about those cherries?'

The orchard was locked, and no gardener to be seen:
he had sent them all off to help with the harvest. Sónya ran
to fetch the key. But he would not wait for her: climbing
up a corner of the wall, he raised the net and jumped
down on the other side.

His voice came over the wall—'If you want some, give
me the dish.'

'No,' I said; 'I want to pick for myself. I shall fetch the
key; Sónya won't find it.'

But suddenly I felt that I must see what he was doing
there and what he looked like—that I must watch his
movements while he supposed that no one saw him. Besides
I was simply unwilling just then to lose sight of him for

a single minute. Running on tiptoe through the nettles to the other side of the orchard where the wall was lower, I mounted on an empty cask, till the top of the wall was on a level with my waist, and then leaned over into the orchard. I looked at the gnarled old trees, with their broad dented leaves and the ripe black cherries hanging straight and heavy among the foliage; then I pushed my head under the net, and from under the knotted bough of an old cherry-tree I caught sight of Sergéy Mikháylych. He evidently thought that I had gone away and that no one was watching him. With his hat off and his eyes shut, he was sitting on the fork of an old tree and carefully rolling into a ball a lump of cherry-tree gum. Suddenly he shrugged his shoulders, opened his eyes, muttered something, and smiled. Both words and smile were so unlike him that I felt ashamed of myself for eavesdropping. It seemed to me that he had said, 'Másha!' 'Impossible,' I thought. 'Darling Másha!' he said again, in a lower and more tender tone. There was no possible doubt about the two words this time. My heart beat hard, and such a passionate joy—illicit joy, as I felt—took hold of me, that I clutched at the wall, fearing to fall and betray myself. Startled by the sound of my movement, he looked round—he dropped his eyes instantly, and his face turned red, even scarlet, like a child's. He tried to speak, but in vain; again and again his face positively flamed up. Still he smiled as he looked at me, and I smiled too. Then his whole face grew radiant with happiness. He had ceased to be the old uncle who spoiled or scolded me; he was a man on my level, who loved and feared me as I loved and feared him. We looked at one another without speaking. But suddenly he frowned; the smile and light in his eyes disappeared, and he resumed his cold paternal tone, just as if we were doing something wrong and he was repenting and calling on me to repent.

'You had better get down, or you will hurt yourself,' he said; 'and do put your hair straight; just think what you look like!'

'What makes him pretend? what makes him want to give me pain?' I thought in my vexation. And the same instant brought an irresistible desire to upset his composure again and test my power over him.

'No,' I said; 'I mean to pick for myself.' I caught hold of the nearest branch and climbed to the top of the wall;

then, before he had time to catch me, I jumped down on the other side.

'What foolish things you do!' he muttered, flushing again and trying to hide his confusion under a pretence of annoyance; 'you might really have hurt yourself. But how do you mean to get out of this?'

He was even more confused than before, but this time his confusion frightened rather than pleased me. It infected me too and made me blush; avoiding his eye and not knowing what to say, I began to pick cherries though I had nothing to put them in. I reproached myself, I repented of what I had done, I was frightened; I felt that I had lost his good opinion for ever by my folly. Both of us were silent and embarrassed. From this difficult situation Sónya rescued us by running back with the key in her hand. For some time we both addressed our conversation to her and said nothing to each other. When we returned to Kátya, who assured us that she had never been asleep and was listening all the time, I calmed down, and he tried to drop into his fatherly patronizing manner again, but I was not taken in by it. A discussion which we had had some days before came back clear before me.

Kátya had been saying that it was easier for a man to be in love and declare his love than for a woman.

'A man may say that he is in love, and a woman can't,' she said.

'I disagree,' said he; 'a man has no business to say, and can't say, that he is in love.'

'Why not?' I asked.

'Because it never can be true. What sort of a revelation is that, that a man is in love? A man seems to think that whenever he says the word, something will go pop!—that some miracle will be worked, signs and wonders, with all the big guns firing at once! In my opinion,' he went on, 'whoever solemnly brings out the words "I love you" is either deceiving himself or, which is even worse, deceiving others.'

'Then how is a woman to know that a man is in love with her, unless he tells her?' asked Kátya.

'That I don't know,' he answered; 'every man has his own way of telling things. If the feeling exists, it will out somehow. But when I read novels, I always fancy the crestfallen look of Lieut. Strélsky or Alfred, when he says, "I love you, Eleanora", and expects something wonderful to happen at once, and no change at all takes place in either of them—their eyes and their noses and their whole selves remain exactly as they were.'

Even then I had felt that this banter covered something serious that had reference to myself. But Kátya resented his disrespectful treatment of the heroes in novels.

'You are never serious,' she said; 'but tell me truthfully, have you never yourself told a woman that you loved her?'

'Never, and never gone down on one knee,' he answered, laughing; 'and never will.'

This conversation I now recalled, and I reflected that there was no need for him to tell me that he loved me. 'I know that he loves me,' I thought, 'and all his endeavours to seem indifferent will not change my opinion.'

He said little to me throughout the evening, but in every word he said to Kátya and Sónya and in every look and movement of his I saw love and felt no doubt of it. I was only vexed and sorry for him, that he thought it necessary still to hide his feelings and pretend coldness, when it was all so clear, and when it would have been so simple and easy to be boundlessly happy. But my jumping down to him in the orchard weighed on me like a crime. I kept feeling that he would cease to respect me and was angry with me.

After tea I went to the piano, and he followed me.

'Play me something—it is long since I heard you,' he said, catching me up in the parlour.

'I was just going to,' I said. Then I looked straight in his face and said quickly, 'Sergéy Mikháylych, you are not angry with me, are you?'

'What for?' he asked.

'For not obeying you this afternoon,' I said, blushing.

He understood me: he shook his head and made a grimace, which implied that I deserved a scolding but that he did not feel able to give it.

'So it's all right, and we are friends again?' I said, sitting down at the piano.

'Of course!' he said.

In the drawing-room, a large lofty room, there were only two lighted candles on the piano, the rest of the room remaining in half-darkness. Outside the open windows the summer night was bright. All was silent, except when the sound of Kátya's footsteps in the unlighted parlour was heard occasionally, or when his horse, which was tied up under the window, snorted or stamped his hoof on the burdocks that grew there. He sat behind me, where I could not see him; but everywhere—in the half-darkness of the room, in every sound, in myself—I felt his presence. Every look, every movement of his, though I could not see them, found an echo in my heart. I played a sonata of Mozart's which he had brought me and which I had learnt in his presence and for him. I was not thinking at all of what I was playing, but I believe that I played it well, and I thought that he was pleased. I was conscious of his pleasure, and conscious too, though I never looked at him, of the gaze fixed on me from behind. Still moving my fingers mechanically, I turned round quite involuntarily and looked at him. The night had grown brighter, and his head stood out on a background of darkness. He was sitting with his head propped on his hands, and his eyes shone as they gazed at me. Catching his look, I smiled and stopped playing. He smiled too and shook his head reproachfully at the music, for me to go on. When I stopped, the moon had grown brighter and was riding high in the heavens; and the faint light of the candles was supplemented by a new silvery light which came in through the windows and fell on the floor. Kátya called out that it was really too bad—that I had stopped at the best part of the piece, and that I was playing badly. But he declared that I had never played so well; and then he began to walk about the rooms—through the drawing-room to the unlighted parlour and back again to the drawing-room, and each time he looked at me and smiled. I smiled too; I wanted even to laugh with no reason; I was so happy at something that had happened that very day. Kátya and I were standing by the piano; and each time that he vanished through the drawing-room door, I started kissing her in my favourite place, the soft part of her neck under the chin; and each time he came back, I made a solemn face and refrained with difficulty from laughing.

'What is the matter with her to-day?' Kátya asked him.

He only smiled at me without answering; he knew what was the matter with me.

'Just look what a night it is!' he called out from the parlour, where he had stopped by the open French window looking into the garden.

We joined him; and it really was such a night as I

have never seen since. The full moon shone above the house and behind us, so that we could not see it, and half the shadow, thrown by the roof and pillars of the house and by the veranda awning, lay slanting and foreshortened on the gravel-path and the strip of turf beyond. Everything else was bright and saturated with the silver of the dew and the moonlight. The broad garden-path, on one side of which the shadows of the dahlias and their supports lay aslant, all bright and cold, and shining on the inequalities of the gravel, ran on till it vanished in the mist. Through the trees the roof of the greenhouse shone bright, and a growing mist rose from the dell. The lilac-bushes, already partly leafless, were all bright to the centre. Each flower was distinguishable apart, and all were drenched with dew. In the avenues light and shade were so mingled that they looked, not like paths and trees but like transparent houses, swaying and moving. To our right, in the shadow of the house, everything was black, indistinguishable, and uncanny. But all the brighter for the surrounding darkness was the top of a poplar, with a fantastic crown of leaves, which for some strange reason remained there close to the house, towering into the bright light, instead of flying away into the dim distance, into the retreating dark-blue of the sky.

'Let us go for a walk,' I said.

Kátya agreed, but said I must put on goloshes.

'I don't want them, Kátya,' I said; 'Sergéy Mikháylych will give me his arm.'

As if that would prevent me from wetting my feet! But to us three this seemed perfectly natural at the time. Though he never used to offer me his arm, I now took it of my own accord, and he saw nothing strange in it. We all went down from the veranda together. That whole world, that sky, that garden, that air, were different from those that I knew.

We were walking along an avenue, and it seemed to me, whenever I looked ahead, that we could go no farther in the same direction, that the world of the possible ended there, and that the whole scene must remain fixed for ever in its beauty. But we still moved on, and the magic wall kept parting to let us in; and still we found the familiar garden with trees and paths and withered leaves. And we were really walking along the paths, treading on patches of light and shade; and a withered leaf was really crackling under my foot, and a live twig brushing my face. And that was really he, walking steadily and slowly at my side, and carefully supporting my arm; and that was really Kátya walking beside us with her creaking shoes. And that must be the moon in the sky, shining down on us through the motionless branches.

But at each step the magic wall closed up again behind us and in front, and I ceased to believe in the possibility of advancing farther——I ceased to believe in the reality of it all.

'Oh, there's a frog!' cried Kátya.

'Who said that? and why?' I thought. But then I realized it was Kátya, and that she was afraid of frogs. Then I looked at the ground and saw a little frog which gave a jump and then stood still in front of me, while its tiny shadow was reflected on the shining clay of the path.

'You're not afraid of frogs, are you?' he asked.

I turned and looked at him. Just where we were there was a gap of one tree in the lime-avenue, and I could see his face clearly——it was so handsome and so happy!

Though he had spoken of my fear of frogs, I knew that he meant to say, 'I love you, my dear one!' 'I love you, I love you' was repeated by his look, by his arm; the light, the shadow, and the air all repeated the same words.

We had gone all round the garden. Kátya's short steps had kept up with us, but now she was tired and out of breath. She said it was time to go in; and I felt very sorry for her. 'Poor thing!' I thought; 'why does not she feel as we do? why are we not all young and happy, like this night and like him and me?'

We went in, but it was a long time before he went away, though the cocks had crowed, and everyone in the house was asleep, and his horse, tethered under the window, snorted continually and stamped his hoof on the burdocks. Kátya never reminded us of the hour, and we sat on talking of the merest trifles and not thinking of the time, till it was past two. The cocks were crowing for the third time and the dawn was breaking when he rode away. He said good-bye as usual and made no special allusion; but I knew that from that day he was mine, and that I should never lose him now. As soon as I had confessed to myself that I loved him, I took Kátya into my confidence. She rejoiced in the news and was touched by my telling her; but she was actually able—poor thing!—to go to bed and sleep! For me, I walked for a long, long time about the veranda; then I went down to the garden, where, recalling each word, each movement, I walked along the same avenues through which I had walked with him. I did not sleep at all that night, and saw sunrise and early dawn for the first time in my life. And never again did I see such a night and such a morning. 'Only why does he not tell me plainly that he loves me?' I thought; 'what makes him invent obstacles and call himself old, when all is so simple and so splendid? What makes him waste this golden time which may never return? Let him say "I love you"—say it in plain words; let him take my hand in his and bend over it and say "I love you". Let him blush and look down before me; and then I will tell him all. No! not tell him, but throw my arms round him and press close to him and weep.' But then a thought came to me—'What if I am mistaken and he does not love me?'

I was startled by this fear—God knows where it might have led me. I recalled his embarrassment and mine, when I jumped down to him in the orchard; and my heart grew very heavy. Tears gushed from my eyes, and I began to pray. A strange thought occurred to me, calming me and bringing hope with it. I resolved to begin fasting on that day, to take the Communion on my birthday, and on that same day to be betrothed to him.

How this result would come to pass I had no idea; but from that moment I believed and felt sure it would be so. The dawn had fully come and the labourers were getting up when I went back to my room.

IV

The Fast of the Assumption falling in August, no one in the house was surprised by my intention of fasting.

During the whole of the week he never once came to see us; but, far from being surprised or vexed or made uneasy by his absence, I was glad of it—I did not expect him until my birthday. Each day during the week I got up early. While the horses were being harnessed, I walked in the garden alone, turning over in my mind the sins of the day before, and considering what I must do to-day, so as to be satisfied with my day and not spoil it by a single sin. It seemed so easy to me then to abstain from sin al-

together; only a trifling effort seemed necessary. When the
horses came round, I got into the carriage with Kátya or
one of the maids, and we drove to the church two miles
away. While entering the church, I always recalled the
prayer for those who 'come unto the Temple in the fear
of God', and tried to get just that frame of mind when
mounting the two grass-grown steps up to the building.
At that hour there were not more than a dozen worship-
pers—household servants or peasant women keeping the
Fast. They bowed to me, and I returned their bows with
studied humility. Then, with what seemed to me a great
effort of courage, I went myself and got candles from the
man who kept them, an old soldier and an Elder; and I
placed the candles before the icons. Through the central
door of the altar-screen I could see the altar-cloth which
my mother had worked; on the screen were the two angels
which had seemed so big to me when I was little, and the
dove with a golden halo which had fascinated me long
ago. Behind the choir stood the old battered font, where
I had been christened myself and had stood godmother to
so many of the servants' children. The old priest came
out, wearing a cope made of the pall that had covered my
father's coffin, and began to read in the same voice that
I had heard all my life—at services held in our house, at
Sónya's christening, at memorial services for my father,
and at my mother's funeral. The same old quavering voice
of the deacon rose in the choir; and the same old woman,
whom I could remember at every service in that church,
crouched by the wall, fixing her streaming eyes on an icon
in the choir, pressing her folded fingers against her faded
kerchief, and muttering with her toothless gums. And these
objects were no longer merely curious to me, merely interesting from old recollections—each had become important and sacred in my eyes and seemed charged with
profound meaning. I listened to each word of the prayers
and tried to suit my feeling to it; and if I failed to understand, I prayed silently that God would enlighten me, or
made up a prayer of my own in place of what I had
failed to catch. When the penitential prayers were repeated, I recalled my past life, and that innocent childish
past seemed to me so black when compared to the present brightness of my soul, that I wept and was horrified
at myself; but I felt too that all those sins would be forgiven, and that if my sins had been even greater, my re-

pentance would be all the sweeter. At the end of the service when the priest said, 'The blessing of the Lord be upon you!' I seemed to feel an immediate sensation of physical well-being, of a mysterious light and warmth that instantly filled my heart. The service over, the priest came and asked me whether he should come to our house to say Mass, and what hour would suit me; and I thanked him for the suggestion, intended, as I thought, to please me, but said that I would come to church instead, walking or driving.

'Is that not too much trouble?' he asked. And I was at a loss for an answer, fearing to commit a sin of pride.

After the Mass, if Kátya was not with me, I always sent the carriage home and walked back alone, bowing humbly to all who passed, and trying to find an opportunity of giving help or advice. I was eager to sacrifice myself for someone, to help in lifting a fallen cart, to rock a child's cradle, to give up the path to others by stepping into the mud. One evening I heard the bailiff report to Kátya that Simon, one of our serfs, had come to beg some boards to make a coffin for his daughter, and a rouble to pay the priest for the funeral; the bailiff had given what he asked. 'Are they as poor as that?' I asked. 'Very poor, Miss,' the bailiff answered; 'they have no salt to their food.' My heart ached to hear this, and yet I felt a kind of pleasure too. Pretending to Kátya that I was merely going for a walk, I ran upstairs, got out all my money (it was very little but it was all I had), crossed myself, and started off alone, through the veranda and the garden, on my way to Simon's hut. It stood at the end of the village, and no one saw me as I went up to the window, placed the money on the sill, and tapped on the pane. Someone came out, making the door creak, and hailed me; but I hurried home, cold and shaking with fear like a criminal. Kátya asked where I had been and what was the matter with me; but I did not answer, and did not even understand what she was saying. Everything suddenly seemed to me so petty and insignificant. I locked myself up in my own room, and walked up and down alone for a long time, unable to do anything, unable to think, unable to understand my own feelings. I thought of the joy of the whole family, and of what they would say of their benefactor; and I felt sorry that I had not given them the money myself. I thought too of what Sergéy Mikháylych would say, if he knew what I had done; and I was glad to think that no one would ever find out. I was so happy, and I felt myself and everyone else so bad, and yet was so kindly disposed to myself and to all the world, that the thought of death came to me as a dream of happiness. I smiled and prayed and wept, and felt at that moment a burning passion of love for all the world, myself included. Between services I used to read the Gospel; and the book became more and more intelligible to me, and the story of that divine life simpler and more touching; and the depths of thought and feeling I found in studying it became more awful and impenetrable. On the other hand, how clear and simple everything seemed to me when I rose from the study of this book and looked again on life around me and reflected on it! It was so difficult, I felt, to lead a bad life, and so simple to love everyone and be loved. All were so kind and gentle to me; even Sónya, whose lessons I had not broken off, was quite different—trying to understand and please me and not to vex me. Everyone treated me as I treated them. Thinking over my enemies, of whom I must ask pardon before confession, I could only remember one—one of our neighbours, a girl, whom I had made fun of in company a year ago, and who had ceased to visit us. I wrote to her, confessing my fault and asking her forgiveness. She replied that she forgave me and wished me to forgive her. I cried for joy over her simple words, and saw in them, at the time, a deep and touching feeling. My old nurse cried, when I asked her to forgive me. 'What makes them all so kind to me? what have I done to deserve their love?' I asked myself. Sergéy Mikháylych would come into my mind, and I thought for long about him. I could not help it, and I did not consider these thoughts sinful. But my thoughts of him were quite different from what they had been on the night when I first realized that I loved him: he seemed to me now like a second self, and became a part of every plan for the future. The inferiority which I had always felt in his presence had vanished entirely: I felt myself his equal, and could understand him thoroughly from the moral elevation I had reached. What had seemed strange in him was now quite clear to me. Now I could see what he meant by saying that to live for others was the only true happiness, and I agreed with him perfectly. I believed that our life together would be endlessly happy and untroubled. I looked forward, not to foreign tours or fashionable society or display, but to a quite different scene—a quiet family life in the country, with constant self-sacrifice, constant mutual love, and constant recognition in all things of the kind hand of Providence.

I carried out my plan of taking the Communion on my birthday. When I came back from church that day, my heart was so swelling with happiness that I was afraid of life, afraid of any feeling that might break in on that happiness. We had hardly left the carriage for the steps in front of the house, when there was a sound of wheels on the bridge, and I saw Sergéy Mikháylych drive up in his well-known trap. He congratulated me, and we went together to the parlour. Never since I had known him had I been so much at my ease with him and so self-possessed as on that morning. I felt in myself a whole new world, out of his reach and beyond his comprehension. I was not conscious of the slightest embarrassment in speaking to him. He must have understood the cause of this feeling; for he was tender and gentle beyond his wont and showed a kind of reverent consideration for me. When I made for the piano, he locked it and put the key in his pocket.

'Don't spoil your present mood,' he said, 'you have the sweetest of all music in your soul just now.'

I was grateful for his words, and yet I was not quite pleased at his understanding too easily and clearly what ought to have been an exclusive secret in my heart. At dinner he said that he had come to congratulate me and also to say good-bye; for he must go to Moscow to-morrow. He looked at Kátya as he spoke; but then he stole a glance at me, and I saw that he was afraid he might detect signs of emotion on my face. But I was neither surprised nor agitated; I did not even ask whether he would be long away. I knew he would say this, and I knew that he would not go. How did I know? I cannot explain that to myself now; but on that memorable day it seemed that I knew everything that had been and that would be. It was like a delightful dream, when all that happens seems to have happened already and to be quite familiar, and it will all happen over again, and one knows that it will happen.

He meant to go away immediately after dinner; but, as Kátya was tired after church and went to lie down for a little, he had to wait until she woke up in order to say good-bye to her. The sun shone into the drawing-room, and we went out to the veranda. When we were seated,

I began at once, quite calmly, the conversation that was bound to fix the fate of my heart. I began to speak, no sooner and no later, but at the very moment when we sat down, before our talk had taken any turn or colour that might have hindered me from saying what I meant to say. I cannot tell myself where it came from—my coolness and determination and preciseness of expression. It was as if something independent of my will was speaking through my lips. He sat opposite me with his elbows resting on the rails of the veranda; he pulled a lilac-branch towards him and stripped the leaves off it. When I began to speak, he let go the branch and leaned his head on one hand. His attitude might have shown either perfect calmness or strong emotion.

'Why are you going?' I asked, significantly, deliberately, and looking straight at him.

He did not answer at once.

'Business!' he muttered at last and dropped his eyes.

I realized how difficult he found it to lie to me, and in reply to such a frank question.

'Listen,' I said; 'you know what to-day is to me, how important for many reasons. If I question you, it is not to show an interest in your doings (you know that I have become intimate with you and fond of you)—I ask you this question, because I *must* know the answer. Why are you going?'

'It is very hard for me to tell you the true reason,' he said. 'During this week I have thought much about you and about myself, and have decided that I must go. You understand why; and if you care for me, you will ask no questions.' He put up a hand to rub his forehead and cover his eyes. 'I find it very difficult . . . But you will understand.'

My heart began to beat fast.

'I cannot understand you,' I said; 'I *cannot! you* must tell me; in God's name and for the sake of this day tell me what you please, and I shall hear it with calmness,' I said.

He changed his position, glanced at me, and again drew the lilac-twig towards him.

'Well!' he said, after a short silence in a voice that tried in vain to seem steady, 'it is a foolish business and impossible to put into words, and I feel the difficulty, but I will try to explain it to you,' he added, frowning as if in bodily pain.

'Well?' I said.

'Just imagine the existence of a man—let us call him A—who has left youth far behind, and of a woman whom we may call B, who is young and happy and has seen nothing as yet of life or of the world. Family circumstances of various kinds brought them together, and he grew to love her as a daughter, and had no fear that his love would change its nature.'

He stopped, but I did not interrupt him.

'But he forgot that B was so young, that life was still all a May-game to her,' he went on with a sudden swiftness and determination and without looking at me, 'and that it was easy to fall in love with her in a different way, and that this would amuse her. He made a mistake and was suddenly aware of another feeling, as heavy as remorse, making its way into his heart, and he was afraid. He was afraid that their old friendly relations would be destroyed, and he made up his mind to go away before that happened.' As he said this, he began again to rub his eyes, with a pretence of indifference, and to close them.

'Why was he afraid to love differently?' I asked very low; but I restrained my emotion and spoke in an even voice. He evidently thought that I was not serious; for he answered as if he were hurt.

'You are young, and I am not young. You want amusement, and I want something different. Amuse yourself, if you like, but not with me. If you do, I shall take it seriously; and then I shall be unhappy, and you will repent. That is what A said,' he added; 'however, this is all nonsense; but you understand why I am going. And don't let us continue this conversation. Please not!'

'No! no!' I said, 'we must continue it,' and tears began to tremble in my voice. 'Did he love her, or not?'

He did not answer.

'If he did not love her, why did he treat her as a child and pretend to her?' I asked.

'Yes, A behaved badly,' he interrupted me quickly; 'but it all came to an end and they parted friends.'

'This is horrible! Is there no other ending?' I said with a great effort, and then felt afraid of what I had said.

'Yes, there is,' he said, showing a face full of emotion

and looking straight at me. 'There are two different endings. But, for God's sake, listen to me quietly and don't interrupt. Some say'—here he stood up and smiled with a smile that was heavy with pain—'some say that A went off his head, fell passionately in love with B, and told her so. But she only laughed. To her it was all a jest, but to him a matter of life and death.'

I shuddered and tried to interrupt him—tried to say that he must not dare to speak for me; but he checked me, laying his hand on mine.

'Wait!' he said, and his voice shook. 'The other story is that she took pity on him, and fancied, poor child, from her ignorance of the world, that she really could love him, and so consented to be his wife. And he, in his madness, believed it—believed that his whole life could begin anew; but she saw herself that she had deceived him and that he had deceived her. . . . But let us drop the subject finally,' he ended, clearly unable to say more; and then he began to walk up and down in silence before me.

Though he had asked that the subject should be dropped, I saw that his whole soul was hanging on my answer. I tried to speak, but the pain at my heart kept me dumb. I glanced at him—he was pale and his lower lip trembled. I felt sorry for him. With a sudden effort I broke the bonds of silence which had held me fast, and began to speak in a low inward voice, which I feared would break every moment.

'There is a third ending to the story,' I said, and then paused, but he said nothing; 'the third ending is that he did not love her, but hurt her, hurt her, and thought that he was right; and he left her and was actually proud of himself. You have been pretending, not I; I have loved you since the first day we met, loved you,' I repeated, and at the word 'loved' my low inward voice changed, without intention of mine, to a wild cry which frightened me myself.

He stood pale before me, his lip trembled more and more violently, and two tears came out upon his cheeks.

'It is wrong!' I almost screamed, feeling that I was choking with angry unshed tears. 'Why do you do it?' I cried, and got up to leave him.

But he would not let me go. His head was resting on my knees, his lips were kissing my still trembling hands, and his tears were wetting them. 'My God! if I had only known!' he whispered.

'Why? why?' I kept on repeating, but in my heart there was happiness, happiness which had now come back, after so nearly departing for ever.

Five minutes later Sónya was rushing upstairs to Kátya and proclaiming all over the house that Másha intended to marry Sergéy Mikháylych.

V

There were no reasons for putting off our wedding, and neither he nor I wished for delay. Kátya, it is true, thought we ought to go to Moscow, to buy and order wedding-clothes; and his mother tried to insist that, before the wedding, he must set up a new carriage, buy new furniture, and re-paper the whole house. But we two together carried our point, that all these things, if they were really indispensable, should be done afterwards, and that we should be married within a fortnight after my birthday, quietly, without wedding-clothes, without a party, without best men and supper and champagne, and all the other conventional features of a wedding. He told me how dissatisfied his mother was that there should be no band, no mountain of luggage, no renovation of the whole house—so unlike her own marriage which had cost thirty thousand roubles; and he told of the solemn and secret confabulations which she held in her store-room with her housekeeper, Maryúshka, rummaging the chests and discussing carpets, curtains, and salvers as indispensable conditions of our happiness. At our house Kátya did just the same with my old nurse, Kuzmínichna. It was impossible to treat the matter lightly with Kátya. She was firmly convinced that he and I, when discussing our future, were merely talking the sentimental nonsense natural to people in our position; and that our real future happiness depended on the hemming of table-cloths and napkins and the proper cutting-out and stitching of under-clothing. Several times a day secret information passed between the two houses, to communicate what was going forward in each; and though the external relations between Kátya and his mother were most affectionate, yet a slightly hostile though very subtle diplomacy was already perceptible in their dealings. I now became more intimate with Tatyána Semënovna, the mother of Sergéy Mikháylych, an old-fashioned lady, strict and formal in the management of her household. Her son loved her, and not merely because she was his mother: he thought her the best, cleverest, kindest, and most affectionate woman in the world. She was always kind to us and to me especially, and was glad that her son should be getting married; but when I was with her after our engagement, I always felt that she wished me to understand that, in her opinion, her son might have looked higher, and that it would be as well for me to keep that in mind. I understood her meaning perfectly and thought her quite right.

During that fortnight he and I met every day. He came to dinner regularly and stayed on till midnight. But though he said—and I knew he was speaking the truth—that he had no life apart from me, yet he never spent the whole day with me, and tried to go on with his ordinary occupations. Our outward relations remained unchanged to the very day of our marriage: we went on saying 'you' and not 'thou' to each other; he did not even kiss my hand; he did not seek, but even avoided, opportunities of being alone with me. It was as if he feared to yield to the harmful excess of tenderness he felt. I don't know which of us had changed; but I now felt myself entirely his equal; I no longer found in him the pretence of simplicity which had displeased me earlier; and I often delighted to see in him, not a grown man inspiring respect and awe but a loving and wildly happy child. 'How mistaken I was about him!' I often thought; 'he is just such another human being as myself!' It seemed to me now, that his whole character was before me and that I thoroughly understood it. And how simple was every feature of his character, and how congenial to my own! Even his plans for our future life together were just my plans, only more clearly and better expressed in his words.

The weather was bad just then, and we spent most of our time indoors. The corner between the piano and the window was the scene of our best intimate talks. The candle-light was reflected on the blackness of the window near us; from time to time drops struck the glistening pane and rolled down. The rain pattered on the roof; the water splashed in a puddle under the spout; it felt damp near the window; but our corner seemed all the brighter and warmer and happier for that.

'Do you know, there is something I have long wished to say to you,' he began one night when we were sitting up late in our corner; 'I was thinking of it all the time you were playing.'

'Don't say it, I know all about it,' I replied.

'All right! mum's the word!'

'No! what is it?' I asked.

'Well, it is this. You remember the story I told you about A and B?'

'I should just think I did! What a stupid story! Lucky that it ended as it did!'

'Yes. I was very near destroying my happiness by my own act. You saved me. But the main thing is that I was always telling lies then, and I'm ashamed of it, and I want to have my say out now.'

'Please don't! you really mustn't!'

'Don't be frightened,' he said, smiling. 'I only want to justify myself. When I began then, I meant to argue.'

'It is always a mistake to argue,' I said.

'Yes, I argued wrong. After all my disappointments and mistakes in life, I told myself firmly when I came to the country this year, that love was no more for me, and that all I had to do was to grow old decently. So for a long time, I was unable to clear up my feeling towards you, or to make out where it might lead me. I hoped, and I didn't hope: at one time I thought you were trifling with me; at another I felt sure of you but could not decide what to do. But after that evening, you remember, when we walked in the garden at night, I got alarmed: the present happiness seemed too great to be real. What if I allowed myself to hope and then failed? But of course I was thinking only of myself, for I am disgustingly selfish.'

He stopped and looked at me.

'But it was not all nonsense that I said then. It was possible and right for me to have fears. I take so much from you and can give so little. You are still a child, a bud that has yet to open; you have never been in love before, and I . . .'

'Yes, do tell me the truth . . . ,' I began, and then stopped, afraid of his answer. 'No, never mind,' I added.

'Have I been in love before? is that it?' he said, guessing

my thoughts at once. 'That I can tell you. No, never before
—nothing at all like what I feel now.' But a sudden painful recollection seemed to flash across his mind. 'No,' he
said sadly; 'in this too I need your compassion, in order
to have the right to love you. Well, was I not bound to
think twice before saying that I loved you? What do I
give you? love, no doubt.'

'And is that little?' I asked, looking him in the face.

'Yes, my dear, it is little to give *you*,' he continued;
'you have youth and beauty. I often lie awake at night from
happiness, and all the time I think of our future life together. I have lived through much, and now I think I
have found what is needed for happiness. A quiet secluded
life in the country, with the possibility of being useful
to people to whom it is easy to do good, and who are not
accustomed to have it done to them; then work which one
hopes may be of some use; then rest, nature, books,
music, love for one's neighbour—such is my idea of happiness. And then, on the top of all that, you for a mate, and
children, perhaps—what more can the heart of man desire?'

'It should be enough,' I said.

'Enough for me whose youth is over,' he went on, 'but
not for you. Life is still before you, and you will perhaps
seek happiness, and perhaps find it, in something different.
You think now that this is happiness, because you love me.'

'You are wrong,' I said; 'I have always desired just that
quiet domestic life and prized it. And you only say just
what I have thought.'

He smiled.

'So you think, my dear; but that is not enough for you.
You have youth and beauty,' he repeated thoughtfully.

But I was angry because he disbelieved me and seemed
to cast my youth and beauty in my teeth.

'Why do you love me then?' I asked angrily; 'for my
youth or for myself?'

'I don't know, but I love you,' he answered, looking
at me with his attentive and attractive gaze.

I did not reply and involuntarily looked into his eyes.
Suddenly a strange thing happened to me: first I ceased
to see what was around me; then his face seemed to vanish
till only the eyes were left, shining over against mine; next
the eyes seemed to be in my own head, and then all became confused—I could see nothing and was forced to

shut my eyes, in order to break loose from the feeling of pleasure and fear which his gaze was producing in me . . .

The day before our wedding-day, the weather cleared up towards evening. The rains which had begun in summer gave place to clear weather, and we had our first autumn evening, bright and cold. It was a wet, cold, shining world, and the garden showed for the first time the spaciousness and colour and bareness of autumn. The sky was clear, cold, and pale. I went to bed happy in the thought that to-morrow, our wedding-day, would be fine. I awoke with the sun, and the thought that this very day . . . seemed alarming and surprising. I went out into the garden. The sun had just risen and shone fitfully through the meagre yellow leaves of the lime avenue. The path was strewn with rustling leaves, clusters of mountain-ash berries hung red and wrinkled on the boughs, with a sprinkling of frost-bitten crumpled leaves; the dahlias were black and wrinkled. The first rime lay like silver on the pale green of the grass and on the broken burdock plants round the house. In the clear cold sky there was not, and could not be, a single cloud.

'Can it possibly be to-day?' I asked myself, incredulous of my own happiness. 'Is it possible that I shall wake to-morrow, not here but in that strange house with the pillars? Is it possible that I shall never again wait for his coming and meet him, and sit up late with Kátya to talk about him? Shall I never sit with him beside the piano in our drawing-room? never see him off and feel uneasy about him on dark nights?' But I remembered that he promised yesterday to pay a last visit, and that Kátya had insisted on my trying on my wedding-dress, and had said 'For to-morrow'. I believed for a moment that it was all real, and then doubted again. 'Can it be that after to-day I shall be living there with a mother-in-law, without Nadézha or old Grigóri or Kátya? Shall I go to bed without kissing my old nurse good-night and hearing her say, while she signs me with the cross from old custom, "Good-night, Miss"? Shall I never again teach Sónya and play with her and knock through the wall to her in the morning and hear her hearty laugh? Shall I become from to-day someone that I myself do not know? and is a new world, that will realize my hopes and desires, opening before me? and will that new world last for ever?' Alone with these thoughts I was depressed and impatient for his arrival. He came early, and it required his presence to convince me that I should really be his wife that very day, and the prospect ceased to frighten me.

Before dinner we walked to our church, to attend a memorial service for my father.

'If only he were living now!' I thought as we were returning and I leant silently on the arm of him who had been the dearest friend of the object of my thoughts. During the service, while I pressed my forehead against the cold stone of the chapel floor, I called up my father so vividly; I was so convinced that he understood me and approved my choice, that I felt as if his spirit were still hovering over us and blessing me. And my recollections and hopes, my joy and sadness, made up one solemn and satisfied feeling which was in harmony with the fresh still air, the silence, the bare fields and pale sky, from which the bright but powerless rays, trying in vain to burn my cheek, fell over all the landscape. My companion seemed to understand and share my feeling. He walked slowly and silently; and his face, at which I glanced from time to time, expressed the same serious mood between joy and sorrow which I shared with nature.

Suddenly he turned to me, and I saw that he intended to speak. 'Suppose he starts some other subject than that which is in my mind?' I thought. But he began to speak of my father and did not even name him.

'He once said to me in jest, "you should marry my Másha",' he began.

'He would have been happy now,' I answered, pressing closer the arm which held mine.

'You were a child then,' he went on, looking into my eyes; 'I loved those eyes then and used to kiss them only because they were like his, never thinking they would be so dear to me for their own sake. I used to call you Másha then.'

'I want you to say "thou" to me,' I said.

'I was just going to,' he answered; 'I feel for the first time that *thou art* entirely mine;' and his calm happy gaze that drew me to him rested on me.

We went on along the footpath over the beaten and trampled stubble; our voices and footsteps were the only sounds. On one side the brownish stubble stretched over a hollow to a distant leafless wood; across it at some distance a peasant was noiselessly ploughing a black strip which grew wider and wider. A drove of horses scattered under the hill seemed close to us. On the other side, as far as the garden and our house peeping through the trees, a field of winter corn, thawed by the sun, showed black with occasional patches of green. The winter sun shone over everything, and everything was covered with long gossamer spider's webs, which floated in the air round us, lay on the frost-dried stubble, and got into our eyes and hair and clothes. When we spoke, the sound of our voices hung in the motionless air above us, as if we two were alone in the whole world—alone under that azure vault, in which the beams of the winter sun played and flashed without scorching.

I too wished to say 'thou' to him, but I felt ashamed.

'Why *dost thou* walk so fast?' I said quickly and almost in a whisper; I could not help blushing.

He slackened his pace, and the gaze he turned on me was even more affectionate, gay, and happy.

At home we found that his mother and the inevitable guests had arrived already, and I was never alone with him again till we came out of church to drive to Nikólskoe.

The church was nearly empty: I just caught a glimpse of his mother standing up straight on a mat by the choir and of Kátya wearing a cap with purple ribbons and with tears on her cheeks, and of two or three of our servants looking curiously at me. I did not look at him, but felt his presence there beside me. I attended to the words of the prayers and repeated them, but they found no echo in my heart. Unable to pray, I looked listlessly at the icons, the candles, the embroidered cross on the priest's cope, the screen, and the window, and took nothing in. I only felt that something strange was being done to me. At last the priest turned to us with the cross in his hand, congratulated us, and said, 'I christened you and by God's mercy have lived to marry you.' Kátya and his mother kissed us, and Grigóri's voice was heard, calling up the carriage. But I was only frightened and disappointed: all was over, but nothing extraordinary, nothing worthy of the Sacrament I had just received, had taken place in myself. He and I exchanged kisses, but the kiss seemed strange and not expressive of our feeling. 'Is this all?' I thought. We went out of church, the sound of wheels reverberated under the vaulted roof, the fresh air blew on my face, he put on his hat and handed me into the carriage. Through the window I could see a frosty moon with a halo round it. He sat down beside me and shut the door after him. I felt a sudden pang. The assurance of his proceedings seemed to me insulting. Kátya called out that I should put something on my head; the wheels rumbled on the stone and then moved along the soft road, and we were off. Huddling in a corner, I looked out at the distant fields and the road flying past in the cold glitter of the moon. Without looking at him, I felt his presence beside me. 'Is this all I have got from the moment, of which I expected so much?' I thought; and still it seemed humiliating and insulting to be sitting alone with him, and so close. I turned to him, intending to speak; but the words would not come, as if my love had vanished, giving place to a feeling of mortification and alarm.

'Till this moment I did not believe it was possible,' he said in a low voice in answer to my look.

'But I am afraid somehow,' I said.

'Afraid of me, my dear?' he said, taking my hand and bending over it.

My hand lay lifeless in his, and the cold at my heart was painful.

'Yes,' I whispered.

But at that moment my heart began to beat faster, my hand trembled and pressed his, I grew hot, my eyes sought his in the half-darkness, and all at once I felt that I did not fear him, that this fear was love—a new love still more tender and stronger than the old. I felt that I was wholly his, and that I was happy in his power over me.

Part II

I

Days, weeks, two whole months of seclusion in the country slipped by unnoticed, as we thought then; and yet those two months comprised feelings, emotions, and happiness, sufficient for a lifetime. Our plans for the regulation of our life in the country were not carried out at all in the way that we expected; but the reality was not inferior to our ideal. There was none of that hard work, performance of duty, self-sacrifice, and life for others, which I had pictured to myself before our marriage; there was, on the contrary, merely a selfish feeling of love for one another, a wish to be loved, a constant causeless gaiety and entire oblivion of all the world. It is true that my husband sometimes went to his study to work, or drove to town on business, or walked about attending to the management of the estate; but I saw what it cost him to tear himself away from me. He confessed later that every occupation, in my absence, seemed to him mere nonsense in which it was impossible to take any interest. It was just the same with me. If I read, or played the piano, or passed my time with his mother, or taught in the school, I did so only because each of these occupations was connected with him and won his approval; but whenever the thought of him was not associated with any duty, my hands fell by my sides and it seemed to me absurd to think that anything existed apart from him. Perhaps it was a wrong and selfish feeling, but it gave me happiness and lifted me high above all the world. He alone existed on earth for me, and I considered him the best and most faultless man in the world; so that I could not live for anything else than for him, and my one object was to realize his conception of me. And in his eyes I was the first and most excellent woman in the world, the possessor of all possible virtues; and I strove to be that woman in the opinion of the first and best of men.

He came to my room one day while I was praying. I looked round at him and went on with my prayers. Not wishing to interrupt me, he sat down at a table and opened a book. But I thought he was looking at me and looked round myself. He smiled, I laughed, and had to stop my prayers.

'Have you prayed already?' I asked.

'Yes. But you go on; I'll go away.'

'You do say your prayers, I hope?'

He made no answer and was about to leave the room when I stopped him.

'Darling, for my sake, please repeat the prayers with me!' He stood up beside me, dropped his arms awkwardly, and began, with a serious face and some hesitation. Occasionally he turned towards me, seeking signs of approval and aid in my face.

When he came to an end, I laughed and embraced him.

'I feel just as if I were ten! And you do it all!' he said, blushing and kissing my hands.

Our house was one of those old-fashioned country houses in which several generations have passed their lives together under one roof, respecting and loving one another. It was all redolent of good sound family traditions, which as soon as I entered it seemed to become mine too. The management of the household was carried on by Tatyána Semënovna, my mother-in-law, on old-fashioned lines. Of grace and beauty there was not much; but, from the servants down to the furniture and food, there was abundance of everything, and a general cleanliness, solidity, and order, which inspired respect. The drawing-room furniture was arranged symmetrically; there were portraits on the walls, and the floor was covered with home-made carpets and mats. In the morning-room there was an old piano, with chiffoniers of two different patterns, sofas, and little carved tables with bronze ornaments. My sitting-room, specially arranged by Tatyána Semënovna, contained the best furniture in the house, of many styles and periods, including an old pierglass, which I was frightened to look into at first, but came to value as an old friend. Though Tatyána Semënovna's voice was never heard, the whole household went like a clock. The number of servants was far too large (they all wore soft boots with no heels, because Tatyána Semënovna had an intense dislike for stamping heels and creaking soles); but they all seemed proud of their calling, trembled before their old mistress, treated my husband and me with an affectionate air of patronage, and performed their duties, to all appearance, with extreme satisfaction. Every Saturday the floors were scoured and the carpets beaten without fail; on the first of every month there was a religious service in the house and holy water was sprinkled; on Tatyána Semënovna's name-day and on her son's (and on mine too, beginning from that autumn) an entertainment was regularly provided for the whole neighbourhood. And all this had gone on without a break ever since the beginning of Tatyána Semënovna's life.

My husband took no part in the household management, he attended only to the farm-work and the labourers, and gave much time to this. Even in winter he got up so early that I often woke to find him gone. He generally came back for early tea, which we drank alone together; and at that time, when the worries and vexations of the farm were over, he was almost always in that state of high spirits which we called 'wild ecstasy'. I often made him tell me what he had been doing in the morning, and he gave such absurd accounts that we both laughed till we cried. Sometimes I insisted on a serious account, and he gave it, restraining a smile. I watched his eyes and moving lips and took nothing in: the sight of him and the sound of his voice was pleasure enough.

'Well, what have I been saying? repeat it,' he would sometimes say. But I could repeat nothing. It seemed so absurd that *he* should talk to *me* of any other subject than ourselves. As if it mattered in the least what went on in the world outside! It was at a much later time that I began to some extent to understand and take an interest in his occupations. Tatyána Semënovna never appeared before dinner: she breakfasted alone and said good-morning to us by deputy. In our exclusive little world of frantic happiness a voice from the staid orderly region in which she dwelt was quite startling: I often lost self-control and could only laugh without speaking, when the maid stood before me with folded hands and made her formal report: 'The mistress bade me inquire how you slept after your walk yesterday evening; and about her I was to report that she had pain in her side all night, and a stupid dog barked in the village and kept her awake: and also I was to ask how you liked the bread this morning, and to tell you that it was not Tarás who baked to-day, but Nikoláshka who was trying his hand for the first time; and she says his baking is not at all bad, especially the cracknels: but the tea-rusks were over-baked.' Before dinner we saw little of each other: he wrote or went out again while I played the piano or read; but at four o'clock we all met in the drawing-room before dinner. Tatyána Semënovna sailed out of her own room, and certain poor and pious maiden ladies, of whom there were always two or three living in the house, made their appearance also. Every day without fail my husband by old habit offered his arm to his mother, to take her in to dinner; but she insisted that I should take the other, so that every day, without fail, we stuck in the doors and got in each other's way. She also presided at dinner, where the conversation, if rather solemn, was polite and sensible. The commonplace talk between my husband and me was a pleasant interruption to the formality of those entertainments. Sometimes there were squabbles between mother and son and they bantered one another; and I especially enjoyed those scenes, because they were the best proof of the strong and tender love which united the two. After dinner Tatyána Semënovna went to the parlour, where she sat in an armchair and ground her snuff or cut the leaves of new books, while we read aloud or went off to the piano in the morning-room. We read much together at this time, but music was our favourite and best enjoyment, always evoking fresh chords in our hearts and as it were revealing each afresh to the other. While I played his favourite pieces, he sat on a distant sofa where I could hardly see him. He was ashamed to betray the impression produced on him by the music; but often, when he was not expecting it, I rose from the piano, went up to him, and tried to detect on his face signs of emotion—the unnatural brightness and moistness of the eyes, which he tried in vain to conceal. Tatyána Semënovna, though she often wanted to take a look at us there, was also anxious to put no constraint upon us. So she always passed through the room with an air of indifference and a pretence of being busy; but I knew that she had no real reason for going to her room and returning so soon. In the evening I poured out tea in the large drawing-room, and all the household met again. This solemn ceremony of distributing cups and glasses before the solemnly shining samovar made me nervous for a long time. I felt myself still unworthy of such a distinction, too young and frivolous to turn the tap of such a big samovar, to put glasses on Nikíta's salver, saying 'For Peter Ivánovich', 'For Márya Mínichna', to ask 'Is it sweet enough?' and to leave out lumps of sugar for Nurse and other deserving persons. 'Capital! capital! Just like a grown-up person!' was a frequent comment from my husband, which only increased my confusion.

After tea Tatyána Semënovna played patience or listened to Márya Mínichna telling fortunes by the cards. Then she kissed us both and signed us with the cross, and we went off to our own rooms. But we generally sat up together till midnight, and that was our best and pleasantest time. He told me stories of his past life; we made plans and sometimes even talked philosophy; but we tried always to speak low, for fear we should be heard upstairs and reported to Tatyána Semënovna, who insisted on our going to bed early. Sometimes we grew hungry; and then we stole off to the pantry, secured a cold supper by the good offices of Nikíta, and ate it in my sitting-room by the light of one candle. He and I lived like strangers in that big old house, where the uncompromising spirit of the past and of Tatyána Semënovna ruled supreme. Not she only, but the servants, the old ladies, the furniture, even the pictures, inspired me with respect and a little alarm, and made me feel that he and I were a little out of place in that house and must always be very careful and cautious in our doings. Thinking it over now, I see that many things—the pressure of that unvarying routine, and that crowd of idle and inquisitive servants—were uncomfortable and oppressive; but at the time that very constraint made our love for one another still keener. Not I only, but he also, never grumbled openly at anything; on the contrary he shut his eyes to what was amiss. Dmítri Sídorov, one of the footmen, was a great smoker; and regularly every day, when we two were in the morning-room after dinner, he went to my husband's study to take tobacco from the jar; and it was a sight to see Sergéy Mikháylych creeping on tiptoe to me with a face between delight and terror, and a wink and a warning forefinger, while he pointed at Dmítri Sídorov, who was quite unconscious of being watched. Then, when Dmítri Sídorov had gone away without having seen us, in his joy that all had passed off successfully, he declared (as he did on every other occasion) that I was a darling, and kissed me. At times his calm connivance and apparent indifference to everything annoyed me, and I took it for weakness, never noticing that I acted in the same way myself. 'It's like a child who dares not show his will,' I thought.

'My dear! my dear!' he said once when I told him that his weakness surprised me; 'how can a man, as happy as I am, be dissatisfied with anything? Better to give way myself than to put compulsion on others; of that I have long been convinced. There is no condition in which one cannot be happy; but our life is such bliss! I simply cannot be angry; to me now nothing seems bad, but only pitiful and amusing. Above all—*le mieux est l'ennemi du bien*. Will you believe it, when I hear a ring at the bell, or receive a letter, or even wake up in the morning, I'm frightened. Life must go on, something may change; and nothing can be better than the present.'

I believed him but did not understand him. I was happy; but I took that as a matter of course, the invariable experience of people in our position, and believed that there was somewhere, I knew not where, a different happiness, not greater but different.

So two months went by and winter came with its cold and snow; and, in spite of his company, I began to feel lonely, that life was repeating itself, that there was nothing new either in him or in myself, and that we were merely going back to what had been before. He began to give more time to business which kept him away from me, and my old feeling returned, that there was a special department of his mind into which he was unwilling to admit me. His unbroken calmness provoked me. I loved him as much as ever and was as happy as ever in his love; but my love, instead of increasing, stood still; and another new and disquieting sensation began to creep into my heart. To love him was not enough for me after the happiness I had felt in falling in love. I wanted movement and not a calm course of existence. I wanted excitement and danger and the chance to sacrifice myself for my love. I felt in myself a superabundance of energy which found no outlet in our quiet life. I had fits of depression which I was ashamed of and tried to conceal from him, and fits of excessive tenderness and high spirits which alarmed him. He realized my state of mind before I did, and proposed a visit to Petersburg; but I begged him to give this up and not to change our manner of life or spoil our happiness. Happy indeed I was; but I was tormented by the thought that this happiness cost me no effort and no sacrifice, though I was even painfully conscious of my power to face both. I loved him and saw that I was all in all to him; but I wanted everyone to see our love; I wanted to love him in spite of obstacles. My mind, and even my senses, were fully occupied; but there was another feeling of youth and craving for movement, which found no satisfaction in our quiet life. What made him say that, whenever I liked, we could go to town? Had he not said so I might have realized that my uncomfortable feelings were my own fault and dangerous nonsense, and that the sacrifice I desired was there before me, in the task of overcoming these feelings. I was haunted by the thought that I could escape from depression by a mere change from the country; and at the same time I felt ashamed and sorry to tear him away, out of selfish motives, from all he cared for. So time went on, the snow grew deeper, and there we remained together, all alone and just the same as before, while outside I knew there was noise and glitter and excitement, and hosts of people suffering or rejoicing without one thought of us and our remote existence. I suffered most from the feeling that custom was daily petrifying our lives into one fixed shape, that our minds were losing their freedom and becoming enslaved to the steady passionless course of time. The morning always found us cheerful; we were polite at dinner, and affectionate in the evening. 'It is all right,' I thought, 'to do good to others and lead upright lives, as he says; but there is time for that later; and there are other things, for which the time is now or never.' I wanted, not what I had got, but a life of struggle; I wanted feeling to be the guide of life, and not life to guide feeling. If only I could go with him to the edge of a precipice and say, 'One step, and I shall fall over—one movement, and I shall be lost!' then, pale with fear, he would catch me in his strong arms and hold me over the edge till my blood froze, and then carry me off whither he pleased.

This state of feeling even affected my health, and I began to suffer from nerves. One morning I was worse than usual. He had come back from the estate-office out of sorts, which was a rare thing with him. I noticed it at once and asked what was the matter. He would not tell me and said it was of no importance. I found out afterwards that the police-inspector, out of spite against my husband, was summoning our peasants, making illegal demands on them, and using threats to them. My husband could not swallow this at once; he could not feel it merely 'pitiful and amusing'. He was provoked, and therefore unwilling to speak of it to me. But it seemed to me that he did not wish to speak to me about it because he considered me a mere child, incapable of understanding his concerns. I turned from him and said no more. I then told the servant to ask Márya Mínichna, who was staying in the house, to join us at breakfast. I ate my breakfast very fast and took her to the morning-room, where I began to talk loudly to her about some trifle which did not interest me in the least. He walked about the room, glancing at us from time to time. This made me more and more inclined to talk and even to laugh; all that I said myself, and all that Márya Mínichna said, seemed to me laughable. Without a word to me he went off to his study and shut the door behind him. When I ceased to hear him, all my high spirits vanished at once: indeed Márya Mínichna was surprised and asked what was the matter. I sat down on a sofa without answering, and felt ready to cry. 'What has he got on his mind?' I wondered; 'some trifle which he thinks important; but, if he tried to tell it me, I should soon show him it was mere nonsense. But he must needs think that I won't understand, must humiliate me by his majestic composure, and always be in the right as against me. But I too am in the right when I find things tiresome and trivial,' I reflected; 'and I do well to want an active life rather than to stagnate in one spot and feel life flowing past me. I want to move forward, to have some new experience every day and every hour, whereas he wants to stand still and to keep me standing beside him. And how easy it would be for him to gratify me! He need not take me to town; he need only be like me and not put compulsion on himself and regulate his feelings, but live simply. That is the advice he gives me, but he is not simple himself. That is what is the matter.'

I felt the tears rising and knew that I was irritated with him. My irritation frightened me, and I went to his study. He was sitting at the table, writing. Hearing my step, he looked up for a moment and then went on writing; he seemed calm and unconcerned. His look vexed me: instead of going up to him, I stood beside his writing-table, opened a book, and began to look at it. He broke off his writing again and looked at me.

'Másha, are you out of sorts?' he asked.

I replied with a cold look, as much as to say, 'You are very polite, but what is the use of asking?' He shook his head and smiled with a tender timid air; but his smile, for the first time, drew no answering smile from me.

'What happened to you to-day?' I asked; 'why did you not tell me?'

'Nothing much—a trifling nuisance,' he said. 'But I might tell you now. Two of our serfs went off to the town . . .'

But I would not let him go on.

'Why would you not tell me, when I asked you at breakfast?'

'I was angry then and should have said something foolish.'

'I wished to know then.'

'Why?'

'Why do you suppose that I can never help you in anything?'

'Not help me!' he said, dropping his pen. 'Why, I believe that without you I could not live. You not only help me in everything I do, but you do it yourself. You are very wide of the mark,' he said, and laughed. 'My life depends on you. I am pleased with things, only because you are there, because I need you . . .'

'Yes, I know; I am a delightful child who must be humoured and kept quiet,' I said in a voice that astonished him, so that he looked up as if this was a new experience; 'but I don't want to be quiet and calm; that is more in your line, and too much in your line,' I added.

'Well,' he began quickly, interrupting me and evidently afraid to let me continue, 'when I tell you the facts, I should like to know your opinion.'

'I don't want to hear them now,' I answered. I did want to hear the story, but I found it so pleasant to break down his composure. 'I don't want to play at life,' I said, 'but to live, as you do yourself.'

His face, which reflected every feeling so quickly and so vividly, now expressed pain and intense attention.

'I want to share your life, to . . . ,' but I could not go on—his face showed such deep distress. He was silent for a moment.

'But what part of my life do you not share?' he asked; 'is it because I, and not you, have to bother with the inspector and with tipsy labourers?'

'That's not the only thing,' I said.

'For God's sake try to understand me, my dear!' he cried. 'I know that excitement is always painful; I have learnt that from the experience of life. I love you, and I can't but wish to save you from excitement. My life consists of my love for you; so you should not make life impossible for me.'

'You are always in the right,' I said without looking at him.

I was vexed again by his calmness and coolness while I was conscious of annoyance and some feeling akin to penitence.

'Másha, what is the matter?' he asked. 'The question is not, which of us is in the right—not at all; but rather, what grievance have you against me? Take time before you answer, and tell me all that is in your mind. You are dissatisfied with me: and you are, no doubt, right; but let me understand what I have done wrong.'

But how could I put my feeling into words? That he understood me at once, that I again stood before him like a child, that I could do nothing without his understanding and foreseeing it—all this only increased my agitation.

'I have no complaint to make of you,' I said; 'I am merely bored and want not to be bored. But you say that it can't be helped, and, as always, you are right.'

I looked at him as I spoke. I had gained my object: his calmness had disappeared, and I read fear and pain in his face.

'Másha,' he began in a low troubled voice, 'this is no mere trifle: the happiness of our lives is at stake. Please hear me out without answering. Why do you wish to torment me?'

But I interrupted him.

'Oh, I know you will turn out to be right. Words are useless; of course you are right.' I spoke coldly, as if some evil spirit were speaking with my voice.

'If you only knew what you are doing!' he said, and his voice shook.

I burst out crying and felt relieved. He sat down beside me and said nothing. I felt sorry for him, ashamed of myself, and annoyed at what I had done. I avoided looking at him. I felt that any look from him at that moment must express severity or perplexity. At last I looked up and saw his eyes: they were fixed on me with a tender gentle expression that seemed to ask for pardon. I caught his hand and said,

'Forgive me! I don't know myself what I have been saying.'

'But I do; and you spoke the truth.'

'What do you mean?' I asked.

'That we must go to Petersburg,' he said; 'there is nothing for us to do here just now.'

'As you please,' I said.

He took me in his arms and kissed me.

'You must forgive me,' he said; 'for I am to blame.'

That evening I played to him for a long time, while he walked about the room. He had a habit of muttering to himself; and when I asked him what he was muttering, he always thought for a moment and then told me exactly what it was. It was generally verse, and sometimes mere nonsense, but I could always judge of his mood by it. When I asked him now, he stood still, thought an instant, and then repeated two lines from Lérmontov:

> *He in his madness prays for storms,*
> *And dreams that storms will bring him peace.*

'He is really more than human,' I thought; 'he knows everything. How can one help loving him?'

I got up, took his arm, and began to walk up and down with him, trying to keep step.

'Well?' he asked, smiling and looking at me.

'All right,' I whispered. And then a sudden fit of merriment came over us both: our eyes laughed, we took longer and longer steps, and rose higher and higher on tiptoe. Prancing in this manner, to the profound dissatisfaction of the butler and astonishment of my mother-in-law, who was playing patience in the parlour, we proceeded through the house till we reached the dining-room; there we stopped, looked at one another, and burst out laughing.

A fortnight later, before Christmas, we were in Petersburg.

II

The journey to Petersburg, a week in Moscow, visits to my own relations and my husband's, settling down in our new quarters, travel, new towns and new faces—all this passed before me like a dream. It was all so new, various, and delightful, so warmly and brightly lighted up by his presence and his love, that our quiet life in the country seemed to me something very remote and unimportant. I had expected to find people in society proud and cold; but to my great surprise, I was received everywhere with unfeigned cordiality and pleasure, not only by relations, but also by strangers. I seemed to be the one object of their thoughts, and my arrival the one thing they wanted, to complete their happiness. I was surprised too to discover in what seemed to me the very best society a number of people acquainted with my husband, though he had never spoken of them to me; and I often felt it odd and disagreeable to hear him now speak disapprovingly of some of these people who seemed to me so kind. I could not understand his coolness towards them or his endeavours to avoid many acquaintances that seemed to me flattering. Surely, the more kind people one knows, the better; and here every-one was kind.

'This is how we must manage, you see,' he said to me before we left the country; 'here we are little Croesuses, but in town we shall not be at all rich. So we must not stay after Easter, or go into society, or we shall get into difficulties. For your sake too I should not wish it.'

'Why should we go into society?' I asked; 'we shall have a look at the theatres, see our relations, go to the opera, hear some good music, and be ready to come home before Easter.'

But these plans were forgotten the moment we got to Petersburg. I found myself at once in such a new and de-lightful world, surrounded by so many pleasures and con-fronted by such novel interests, that I instantly, though un-consciously, turned my back on my past life and its plans. 'All that was preparatory, a mere playing at life; but here is the real thing! And there is the future too!' Such were my thoughts. The restlessness and symptoms of de-pression which had troubled me at home vanished at once and entirely, as if by magic. My love for my husband grew calmer, and I ceased to wonder whether he loved me less. Indeed I could not doubt his love: every thought of mine was understood at once, every feeling shared, and every wish gratified by him. His composure, if it still existed, no longer provoked me. I also began to realize that he not only loved me but was proud of me. If we paid a call, or made some new acquaintance, or gave an evening party at which I, trembling inwardly from fear of disgracing myself, acted as hostess, he often said when it was over: 'Bravo, young woman! capital! you needn't be frightened; a real success!' And his praise gave me great pleasure. Soon after our arrival he wrote to his mother and asked me to add a postscript, but refused to let me see his letter; of course I insisted on reading it; and he had said: 'You would not know Másha again, I don't myself. Where does she get that charming graceful self-confidence and ease, such social gifts with such simplicity and charm and kindliness? Everybody is delighted with her. I can't admire her enough myself, and should be more in love with her than ever, if that were possible.'

'Now I know what I am like,' I thought. In my joy and pride I felt that I loved him more than before. My success with all our new acquaintances was a complete surprise to me. I heard on all sides, how this uncle had taken a special fancy for me, and that aunt was raving about me; I was told by one admirer that I had no rival among the Petersburg ladies, and assured by another, a lady, that I might, if I cared, lead the fashion in society. A cousin of my husband's, in particular, a Princess D., middle-aged and very much at home in society, fell in love with me at first sight and paid me compliments which turned my head. The first time that she invited me to a ball and spoke to my husband about it, he turned to me and asked if I wished to go; I could just detect a sly smile on his face. I nodded assent and felt that I was blushing.

'She looks like a criminal when confessing what she wishes,' he said with a good-natured laugh.

'But you said that we must not go into society, and you don't care for it yourself,' I answered, smiling and looking imploringly at him.

'Let us go, if you want to very much,' he said.

'Really, we had better not.'

'Do you want to? very badly?' he asked again.

I said nothing.

'Society in itself is no great harm,' he went on; 'but unsatisfied social aspirations are a bad and ugly business. We must certainly accept, and we will.'

'To tell you the truth,' I said, "I never in my life longed for anything as much as I do for this ball.'

So we went, and my delight exceeded all my expectations. It seemed to me, more than ever, that I was the centre round which everything revolved, that for my sake alone this great room was lighted up and the band played, and that this crowd of people had assembled to admire me. From the hairdresser and the lady's maid to my partners and the old gentlemen promenading the ball-room, all alike seemed to make it plain that they were in love with me. The general verdict formed at the ball about me and reported by my cousin, came to this: I was quite unlike the other women and had a rural simplicity and charm of my own. I was so flattered by my success that I frankly told my husband I should like to attend two or three more balls during the season, and 'so get thoroughly sick of them', I added; but I did not mean what I said.

He agreed readily; and he went with me at first with

obvious satisfaction. He took pleasure in my success, and seemed to have quite forgotten his former warning or to have changed his opinion.

But a time came when he was evidently bored and wearied by the life we were leading. I was too busy, however, to think about that. Even if I sometimes noticed his eyes fixed questioningly on me with a serious attentive gaze, I did not realize its meaning. I was utterly blinded by this sudden affection which I seemed to evoke in all our new acquaintances, and confused by the unfamiliar atmosphere of luxury, refinement, and novelty. It pleased me so much to find myself in these surroundings not merely his equal but his superior, and yet to love him better and more independently than before, that I could not understand what he could object to for me in society life. I had a new sense of pride and self-satisfaction when my entry at a ball attracted all eyes, while he, as if ashamed to confess his ownership of me in public, made haste to leave my side and efface himself in the crowd of black coats. 'Wait a little!' I often said in my heart, when I identified his obscure and sometimes woebegone figure at the end of the room—'Wait till we get home! Then you will see and understand for whose sake I try to be beautiful and brilliant, and what it is I love in all that surrounds me this evening!' I really believed that my success pleased me only because it enabled me to give it up for his sake. One danger I recognized as possible—that I might be carried away by a fancy for some new acquaintance, and that my husband might grow jealous. But he trusted me so absolutely, and seemed so undisturbed and indifferent, and all the young men were so inferior to him, that I was not alarmed by this one danger. Yet the attention of so many people in society gave me satisfaction, flattered my vanity, and made me think that there was some merit in my love for my husband. Thus I became more offhand and self-confident in my behaviour to him.

'Oh, I saw you this evening carrying on a most animated conversation with Mme N.,' I said one night on returning from a ball, shaking my finger at him. He had really been talking to this lady, who was a well-known figure in Petersburg society. He was more silent and depressed than usual, and I said this to rouse him up.

'What is the good of talking like that, for *you* especially, Másha?' he said with half-closed teeth and frowning as if in pain. 'Leave that to others; it does not suit you and me. Pretence of that sort may spoil the true relation between us, which I still hope may come back.'

I was ashamed and said nothing.

'Will it ever come back, Másha, do you think?' he asked.

'It never was spoilt and never will be,' I said; and I really believed this then.

'God grant that you are right!' he said; 'if not, we ought to be going home.'

But he only spoke like this once—in general he seemed as satisfied as I was, and I was so gay and so happy! I comforted myself too by thinking, 'If he is bored sometimes, I endured the same thing for his sake in the country. If the relation between us has become a little different, everything will be the same again in summer, when we shall be alone in our house at Nikólskoe with Tatyána Semёnovna.'

So the winter slipped by, and we stayed on, in spite of our plans, over Easter in Petersburg. A week later we were preparing to start; our packing was all done; my husband, who had bought things—plants for the garden and presents for people at Nikólskoe, was in a specially cheerful and affectionate mood. Just then Princess D. came and begged us to stay till the Saturday, in order to be present at a reception to be given by Countess R. The Countess was very anxious to secure me, because a foreign prince, who was visiting Petersburg and had seen me already at a ball, wished to make my acquaintance; indeed this was his motive for attending the reception, and he declared that I was the most beautiful woman in Russia. All the world was to be there; and, in a word, it would really be too bad, if I did not go too.

My husband was talking to someone at the other end of the drawing-room.

'So you will go, won't you, Mary?' said the Princess.

'We meant to start for the country the day after tomorrow,' I answered undecidedly, glancing at my husband. Our eyes met, and he turned away at once.

'I must persuade him to stay,' she said, 'and then we can go on Saturday and turn all heads. All right?'

'It would upset our plans; and we have packed,' I answered, beginning to give way.

'She had better go this evening and make her curtsey to the Prince,' my husband called out from the other end of the room; and he spoke in a tone of suppressed irritation which I had never heard from him before.

'I declare he's jealous, for the first time in his life,' said the lady, laughing. 'But it's not for the sake of the Prince I urge it, Sergéy Mikháylych, but for all our sakes. The Countess was so anxious to have her.'

'It rests with her entirely,' my husband said coldly, and then left the room.

I saw that he was much disturbed, and this pained me. I gave no positive promise. As soon as our visitor left, I went to my husband. He was walking up and down his room, thinking, and neither saw nor heard me when I came in on tiptoe.

Looking at him I said to myself: 'He is dreaming already of his dear Nikólskoe, our morning coffee in the bright drawing-room, the land and the labourers, our evenings in the music-room, and our secret midnight suppers.' Then I decided in my own heart: 'Not for all the balls and all the flattering princes in the world will I give up his glad confusion and tender cares.' I was just about to say that I did not wish to go to the ball and would refuse, when he looked round, saw me, and frowned. His face, which had been gentle and thoughtful, changed at once to its old expression of sagacity, penetration, and patronizing composure. He would not show himself to me as a mere man, but had to be a demigod on a pedestal.

'Well, my dear?' he asked, turning towards me with an unconcerned air.

I said nothing. I was provoked, because he was hiding his real self from me, and would not continue to be the man I loved.

'Do you want to go to this reception on Saturday?' he asked.

'I did, but you disapprove. Besides, our things are all packed,' I said.

Never before had I heard such coldness in his tone to me, and never before seen such coldness in his eye.

'I shall order the things to be unpacked,' he said, 'and I shall stay till Tuesday. So you can go to the party, if you like. I hope you will; but I shall not go.'

Without looking at me, he began to walk about the room jerkily, as his habit was when perturbed.

'I simply can't understand you,' I said, following him with my eyes from where I stood. 'You say that you never lose self-control' (he had never really said so); 'then why do you talk to me so strangely? I am ready on your account to sacrifice this pleasure, and then you, in a sarcastic tone which is new from you to me, insist that I should go.'

'So you make a *sacrifice!*' he threw special emphasis on the last word. 'Well, so do I. What could be better? We compete in generosity—what an example of family happiness!'

Such harsh and contemptuous language I had never heard from his lips before. I was not abashed, but mortified by his contempt; and his harshness did not frighten me but made me harsh too. How could *he* speak thus, he who was always so frank and simple and dreaded insincerity in our speech to one another? And what had I done that he should speak so? I really intended to sacrifice for his sake a pleasure in which I could see no harm; and a moment ago I loved him and understood his feelings as well as ever. We had changed parts: now he avoided direct and plain words, and I desired them.

'You are much changed,' I said, with a sigh. 'How am I guilty before you? It is not this party—you have something else, some old count against me. Why this insincerity? You used to be so afraid of it yourself. Tell me plainly what you complain of.' 'What will he say?' thought I, and reflected with some complacency that I had done nothing all winter which he could find fault with.

I went into the middle of the room, so that he had to pass close to me, and looked at him. I thought, 'He will come and clasp me in his arms, and there will be an end of it.' I was even sorry that I should not have the chance of proving him wrong. But he stopped at the far end of the room and looked at me.

'Do you not understand yet?' he asked.

'No, I don't.'

'Then I must explain. What I feel, and cannot help feeling, positively sickens me for the first time in my life.' He stopped, evidently startled by the harsh sound of his own voice.

'What do you mean?' I asked, with tears of indignation in my eyes.

'It sickens me that the Prince admired you, and you therefore run to meet him, forgetting your husband and yourself and womanly dignity; and you wilfully misunderstand what your want of self-respect makes your husband feel for you: you actually come to your husband and speak of the "sacrifice" you are making, by which you mean—"To show myself to His Highness is a great pleasure to me, but I 'sacrifice' it." '

The longer he spoke, the more he was excited by the sound of his own voice, which was hard and rough and cruel. I had never seen him, had never thought of seeing him, like that. The blood rushed to my heart and I was frightened; but I felt that I had nothing to be ashamed of, and the excitement of wounded vanity made me eager to punish him.

'I have long been expecting this,' I said. 'Go on. Go on!'

'What you expected, I don't know,' he went on; 'but I might well expect the worst, when I saw you day after day sharing the dirtiness and idleness and luxury of this foolish society, and it has come at last. Never have I felt such shame and pain as now—pain for myself, when your friend thrusts her unclean fingers into my heart and speaks of my jealousy!—jealousy of a man whom neither you nor I know; and you refuse to understand me and offer to make a sacrifice for me—and what sacrifice? I am ashamed for you, for your degradation! . . . Sacrifice!' he repeated again.

'Ah, so this is a husband's power,' thought I: 'to insult and humiliate a perfectly innocent woman. Such may be a husband's rights, but I will not submit to them.' I felt the blood leave my face and a strange distension of my nostrils, as I said, 'No! I make no sacrifice on your account. I shall go to the party on Saturday without fail.'

'And I hope you may enjoy it. But all is over between us two!' he cried out in a fit of unrestrained fury. 'But you shall not torture me any longer! I was a fool, when I . . .', but his lips quivered, and he refrained with a visible effort from ending the sentence.

I feared and hated him at that moment. I wished to say a great deal to him and punish him for all his insults; but if I had opened my mouth, I should have lost my dignity by bursting into tears. I said nothing and left the room. But as soon as I ceased to hear his footsteps, I was horrified at what we had done. I feared that the tie which had made all my happiness might really be snapped for ever; and I thought of going back. But then I wondered: 'Is he calm enough now to understand me, if I mutely stretch out my hand and look at him? Will he realize my generosity? What if he calls my grief a mere pretence? Or he may feel sure that he is right and accept my repentance and forgive me with unruffled pride. And why, oh why, did he whom I loved so well insult me so cruelly?'

I went not to him but to my own room, where I sat for a long time and cried. I recalled with horror each word of our conversation, and substituted different words, kind words, for those that we had spoken, and added others; and then again I remembered the reality with horror and a feeling of injury. In the evening I went down for tea and met my husband in the presence of a friend who was staying with us; and it seemed to me that a wide gulf had opened between us from that day. Our friend asked me when we were to start; and before I could speak, my husband answered:

'On Tuesday,' he said; 'we have to stay for Countess R.'s reception.' He turned to me: 'I believe you intend to go?' he asked.

His matter-of-fact tone frightened me, and I looked at him timidly. His eyes were directed straight at me with an unkind and scornful expression; his voice was cold and even.

'Yes,' I answered.

When we were alone that evening, he came up to me and held out his hand.

'Please forget what I said to you to-day,' he began.

As I took his hand, a smile quivered on my lips and the tears were ready to flow; but he took his hand away and sat down on an armchair at some distance, as if fearing a sentimental scene. 'Is it possible that he still thinks himself in the right?' I wondered; and, though I was quite ready to explain and to beg that we might not go to the party, the words died on my lips.

'I must write to my mother that we have put off our departure,' he said; 'otherwise she will be uneasy.'

'When do you think of going?' I asked.

'On Tuesday, after the reception,' he replied.

'I hope it is not on my account,' I said, looking into his eyes; but those eyes merely looked—they said nothing, and a veil seemed to cover them from me. His face seemed to me to have grown suddenly old and disagreeable.

We went to the reception, and good friendly relations

between us seemed to have been restored, but these relations were quite different from what they had been.

At the party I was sitting with other ladies when the Prince came up to me, so that I had to stand up in order to speak to him. As I rose, my eyes involuntarily sought my husband. He was looking at me from the other end of the room, and now turned away. I was seized by a sudden sense of shame and pain; in my confusion I blushed all over my face and neck under the Prince's eye. But I was forced to stand and listen, while he spoke, eyeing me from his superior height. Our conversation was soon over: there was no room for him beside me, and he, no doubt, felt that I was uncomfortable with him. We talked of the last ball, of where I should spend the summer, and so on. As he left me, he expressed a wish to make the acquaintance of my husband, and I saw them meet and begin a conversation at the far end of the room. The Prince evidently said something about me; for he smiled in the middle of their talk and looked in my direction.

My husband suddenly flushed up. He made a low bow and turned away from the Prince without being dismissed. I blushed too: I was ashamed of the impression which I and, still more, my husband must have made on the Prince. Everyone, I thought, must have noticed my awkward shyness when I was presented, and my husband's eccentric behaviour. 'Heaven knows how they will interpret such conduct? Perhaps they know already about my scene with my husband!'

Princess D. drove me home, and on the way I spoke to her about my husband. My patience was at an end, and I told her the whole story of what had taken place between us owing to this unlucky party. To calm me, she said that such differences were very common and quite unimportant, and that our quarrel would leave no trace behind. She explained to me her view of my husband's character—that he had become very stiff and unsociable. I agreed, and believed that I had learned to judge him myself more calmly and more truly.

But when I was alone with my husband later, the thought that I had sat in judgement upon him weighed like a crime upon my conscience; and I felt that the gulf which divided us had grown still greater.

III

From that day there was a complete change in our life and our relations to each other. We were no longer as happy when we were alone together as before. To certain subjects we gave a wide berth, and conversation flowed more easily in the presence of a third person. When the talk turned on life in the country, or on a ball, we were uneasy and shrank from looking at one another. Both of us knew where the gulf between us lay, and seemed afraid to approach it. I was convinced that he was proud and irascible, and that I must be careful not to touch him on his weak point. He was equally sure that I disliked the country and was dying for social distraction, and that he must put up with this unfortunate taste of mine. We both avoided frank conversation on these topics, and each misjudged the other. We had long ceased to think each other the most perfect people in the world; each now judged the other in secret, and measured the offender by the standard of other people. I fell ill before we left Petersburg, and we went from there to a house near town, from which my husband went on alone, to join his mother at Nikólskoe. By that time I was well enough to have gone with him, but he urged me to stay on the pretext of my health. I knew, however, that he was really afraid we should be uncomfortable together in the country; so I did not insist much, and he went off alone. I felt it dull and solitary in his absence; but when he came back, I saw that he did not add to my life what he had added formerly. In the old days every thought and experience weighed on me like a crime till I had imparted it to him; every action and word of his seemed to me a model of perfection; we often laughed for joy at the mere sight of each other. But these relations had changed, so imperceptibly that we had not even noticed their disappearance. Separate interests and cares, which we no longer tried to share, made their appearance, and even the fact of our estrangement ceased to trouble us. The idea became familiar, and, before a year had passed, each could look at the other without confusion. His fits of boyish merriment with me had quite vanished; his mood of calm indulgence to all that passed, which used to provoke me, had disappeared; there was an end of those penetrat-

ing looks which used to confuse and delight me, an end
of the ecstasies and prayers which we once shared in common. We did not even meet often: he was continually absent, with no fears or regrets for leaving me alone; and I
was constantly in society, where I did not need him.

There were no further scenes or quarrels between us. I
tried to satisfy him, he carried out all my wishes, and we
seemed to love each other.

When we were by ourselves, which we seldom were, I
felt neither joy nor excitement nor embarrassment in his
company: it seemed like being alone. I realized that he
was my husband and no mere stranger, a good man, and
as familiar to me as my own self. I was convinced that I
knew just what he would say and do, and how he would
look; and if anything he did surprised me, I concluded that
he had made a mistake. I expected nothing from him. In
a word, he was my husband—and that was all. It seemed
to me that things must be so, as a matter of course, and
that no other relations between us had ever existed. When
he left home, especially at first, I was lonely and frightened and felt keenly my need of support; when he came
back, I ran to his arms with joy, though two hours later
my joy was quite forgotten, and I found nothing to say to
him. Only at moments which sometimes occurred between
us of quiet undemonstrative affection, I felt something
wrong and some pain at my heart, and I seemed to read
the same story in his eyes. I was conscious of a limit to
tenderness, which he seemingly would not, and I could not,
overstep. This saddened me sometimes; but I had no leisure
to reflect on anything, and my regret for a change which I
vaguely realized I tried to drown in the distractions which
were always within my reach. Fashionable life, which had
dazzled me at first by its glitter and flattery of my self-love,
now took entire command of my nature, became a habit,
laid its fetters upon me, and monopolized my capacity
for feeling. I could not bear solitude, and was afraid to
reflect on my position. My whole day, from late in the
morning till late at night, was taken up by the claims of
society; even if I stayed at home, my time was not my
own. This no longer seemed to me either gay or dull, but it
seemed that so, and not otherwise, it always had to be.

So three years passed, during which our relations to
one another remained unchanged and seemed to have
taken a fixed shape which could not become either better

or worse. Though two events of importance in our family life took place during that time, neither of them changed my own life. These were the birth of my first child and the death of Tatyána Semënovna. At first the feeling of motherhood did take hold of me with such power, and produce in me such a passion of unanticipated joy, that I believed this would prove the beginning of a new life for me. But, in the course of two months, when I began to go out again, my feeling grew weaker and weaker, till it passed into mere habit and the lifeless performance of a duty. My husband, on the contrary, from the birth of our first boy, became his old self again—gentle, composed, and home-loving, and transferred to the child his old tenderness and gaiety. Many a night when I went, dressed for a ball, to the nursery, to sign the child with the cross before he slept, I found my husband there and felt his eyes fixed on me with something of reproof in their serious gaze. Then I was ashamed and even shocked by my own callousness, and asked myself if I was worse than other women. 'But it can't be helped,' I said to myself; 'I love my child, but to sit beside him all day long would bore me; and nothing will make me pretend what I do not really feel.'

His mother's death was a great sorrow to my husband; he said that he found it painful to go on living at Nikólskoe. For myself, although I mourned for her and sympathized with my husband's sorrow, yet I found life in that house easier and pleasanter after her death. Most of those three years we spent in town: I went only once to Nikólskoe for two months; and the third year we went abroad and spent the summer at Baden.

I was then twenty-one; our financial position was, I believed, satisfactory; my domestic life gave me all that I asked of it; everyone I knew, it seemed to me, loved me; my health was good; I was the best-dressed woman in Baden; I knew that I was good-looking; the weather was fine; I enjoyed the atmosphere of beauty and refinement; and, in short, I was in excellent spirits. They had once been even higher at Nikólskoe, when my happiness was in myself and came from the feeling that I deserved to be happy, and from the anticipation of still greater happiness to come. That was a different state of things; but I did very well this summer also. I had no special wishes or hopes or fears; it seemed to me that my life was full and my conscience easy. Among all the visitors at Baden that season there was no one man whom I preferred to the rest, or even to our old ambassador, Prince K., who was assiduous in his attentions to me. One was young, and another old; one was English and fair, another French and wore a beard—to me they were all alike, but all indispensable. Indistinguishable as they were, they together made up the atmosphere which I found so pleasant. But there was one, an Italian marquis, who stood out from the rest by reason of the boldness with which he expressed his admiration. He seized every opportunity of being with me—danced with me, rode with me, and met me at the casino; and everywhere he spoke to me of my charms. Several times I saw him from my windows loitering round our hotel, and the fixed gaze of his bright eyes often troubled me, and made me blush and turn away. He was young, handsome, and well-mannered; and, above all, by his smile and the expression of his brow, he resembled my husband, though much handsomer than he. He struck me by this likeness, though in general, in his lips, eyes, and long chin, there was something coarse and animal which contrasted with my husband's charming expression of kindness and noble serenity. I supposed him to be passionately in love with me, and thought of him sometimes with proud commiseration. When I tried at times to soothe him and change his tone to one of easy, half-friendly confidence, he resented the suggestion with vehemence, and continued to disquiet me by a smouldering passion which was ready at any moment to burst forth. Though I would not own it even to myself, I feared him and often thought of him against my will. My husband knew him, and treated him—even more than other acquaintances of ours who regarded him only as my husband—with coldness and disdain.

Towards the end of the season I fell ill and stayed indoors for a fortnight. The first evening that I went out again to hear the band, I learnt that Lady S., an Englishwoman famous for her beauty, who had long been expected, had arrived in my absence. My return was welcomed, and a group gathered round me; but a more distinguished group attended the beautiful stranger. She and her beauty were the one subject of conversation around me. When I saw her, she was really beautiful, but her self-satisfied expression struck me as disagreeable, and I said so. That day everything that had formerly seemed amusing, seemed dull. Lady S. arranged an expedition to the ruined castle for the next day; but I declined to be of the party. Almost everyone else went; and my opinion of Baden underwent a complete change. Everything and everybody seemed to me stupid and tiresome; I wanted to cry, to break off my cure, to return to Russia. There was some evil feeling in my soul, but I did not yet acknowledge it to myself. Pretending that I was not strong, I ceased to appear at crowded parties; if I went out, it was only in the morning by myself, to drink the waters; and my only companion was Mme M., a Russian lady, with whom I sometimes took drives in the surrounding country. My husband was absent: he had gone to Heidelberg for a time, intending to return to Russia when my cure was over, and only paid me occasional visits at Baden.

One day when Lady S. had carried off all the company on a hunting-expedition, Mme M. and I drove in the afternoon to the castle. While our carriage moved slowly along the winding road, bordered by ancient chestnut-trees and commanding a vista of the pretty and pleasant country round Baden, with the setting sun lighting it up, our conversation took a more serious turn than had ever happened to us before. I had known my companion for a long time; but she appeared to me now in a new light, as a well-principled and intelligent woman, to whom it was possible to speak without reserve, and whose friendship was worth having. We spoke of our private concerns, of our children, of the emptiness of life at Baden, till we felt a longing for Russia and the Russian countryside. When we entered the castle we were still under the impression of this serious feeling. Within the walls there was shade and coolness; the sunlight played from above upon the ruins. Steps and voices were audible. The landscape, charming enough but cold to a Russian eye, lay before us in the frame made by a doorway. We sat down to rest and watched the sunset in silence. The voices now sounded louder, and I thought I heard my own name. I listened and could not help overhearing every word. I recognized the voices: the speakers were the Italian marquis and a French friend of his whom I knew also. They were talking of me and of Lady S., and the Frenchman was comparing us as rival beauties. Though he said nothing insulting, his words made my pulse quicken. He explained in detail the good points of us both. I was already a mother, while Lady S. was only nineteen; though I had the advantage in hair, my rival had a better figure. 'Besides,' he added, 'Lady S. is a real *grande dame*, and the other is nothing in particular, only one of those obscure Russian princesses who turn up here nowadays in such numbers.' He ended by saying that I was wise in not attempting to compete with Lady S., and that I was completely buried as far as Baden was concerned.

'I am sorry for her—unless indeed she takes a fancy to console herself with you,' he added with a hard ringing laugh.

'If she goes away, I follow her'—the words were blurted out in an Italian accent.

'Happy man! he is still capable of a passion!' laughed the Frenchman.

'Passion!' said the other voice and then was still for a moment. 'It is a necessity to me: I cannot live without it. To make life a romance is the one thing worth doing. And with me romance never breaks off in the middle, and this affair I shall carry through to the end.'

'*Bonne chance, mon ami!*' said the Frenchman.

They now turned a corner, and the voices stopped. Then we heard them coming down the steps, and a few minutes later they came out upon us by a side-door. They were much surprised to see us. I blushed when the marquis approached me, and felt afraid when we left the castle and he offered me his arm. I could not refuse, and we set off for the carriage, walking behind Mme M. and his friend. I was mortified by what the Frenchman had said of me, though I secretly admitted that he had only put in words what I felt myself; but the plain speaking of the Italian had surprised and upset me by its coarseness. I was tormented by the thought that, though I had overheard him, he showed no fear of me. It was hateful to have him so close to me; and I walked fast after the other couple, not looking at him or answering him and trying to hold his arm in such a way as not to hear him. He spoke of the fine view, of the unexpected pleasure of our meeting, and so on; but I was not listening. My thoughts were with my husband, my child, my country; I felt ashamed, distressed, anxious; I was in a hurry to get back to my solitary room in the Hôtel de Bade, there to think at leisure of the storm of feeling that had just risen in my heart. But Mme M. walked slowly, it was still a long way to the carriage, and my escort seemed to loiter on purpose as if he wished to detain me. 'None of that!' I thought, and resolutely quickened my pace. But it soon became unmistakable that he was detaining me and even pressing my arm. Mme M. turned a corner, and we were quite alone. I was afraid.

'Excuse me,' I said coldly and tried to free my arm; but the lace of my sleeve caught on a button of his coat. Bending towards me, he began to unfasten it, and his ungloved fingers touched my arm. A feeling new to me, half horror and half pleasure, sent an icy shiver down my back. I looked at him, intending by my coldness to convey all the contempt I felt for him; but my look expressed nothing but fear and excitement. His liquid blazing eyes, right up against my face, stared strangely at me, at my neck and breast; both his hands fingered my arm above the wrist; his parted lips were saying that he loved me, and that I was all the world to him; and those lips were coming nearer and nearer, and those hands were squeezing mine harder and harder and burning me. A fever ran through my veins, my sight grew dim, I trembled, and the words intended to check him died in my throat. Suddenly I felt a kiss on my cheek. Trembling all over and turning cold, I stood still and stared at him. Unable to speak or move, I stood there, horrified, expectant, even desirous. It was over in a moment, but the moment was horrible! In that short time I saw him exactly as he was—the low straight forehead (that forehead so like my husband's!) under the straw hat; the handsome regular nose and dilated nostrils; the long waxed moustache and short beard; the close-shaved cheeks and sunburnt neck. I hated and feared him; he was utterly repugnant and alien to me. And yet the excitement and passion of this hateful strange man raised a powerful echo in my own heart; I felt an irresistible longing to surrender myself to the kisses of that coarse handsome mouth, and to the pressure of those white hands with their delicate veins and jewelled fingers; I was tempted to throw myself headlong into the abyss of forbidden delights that had suddenly opened up before me.

'I am so unhappy already,' I thought; 'let more and more storms of unhappiness burst over my head!'

He put one arm round me and bent towards my face. 'Better so!' I thought: 'let sin and shame cover me ever deeper and deeper!'

'*Je vous aime!*' he whispered in the voice which was so like my husband's. At once I thought of my husband and child, as creatures once precious to me who had now passed altogether out of my life. At that moment I heard Mme M.'s voice; she called to me from round the corner. I came to myself, tore my hand away without looking at him, and almost ran after her: I only looked at him after she and I were already seated in the carriage. Then I saw him raise his hat and ask some commonplace question with a smile. He little knew the inexpressible aversion I felt for him at that moment.

My life seemed so wretched, the future so hopeless, the past so black! When Mme M. spoke, her words meant nothing to me. I thought that she talked only out of pity, and to hide the contempt I aroused in her. In every word and every look I seemed to detect this contempt and insulting pity. The shame of that kiss burnt my cheek, and the thought of my husband and child was more than I could bear. When I was alone in my own room, I tried to think over my position; but I was afraid to be alone. Without drinking the tea which was brought me, and uncertain of my own motives, I got ready with feverish haste to catch the evening train and join my husband at Heidelberg.

I found seats for myself and my maid in an empty carriage. When the train started and the fresh air blew through the window on my face, I grew more composed and pictured my past and future to myself more clearly. The course of our married life from the time of our first visit to Petersburg now presented itself to me in a new light, and lay like a reproach on my conscience. For the first time I clearly recalled our start at Nikólskoe and our plans for the future; and for the first time I asked myself what happiness had my husband had since then. I felt that I had behaved badly to him. 'But why', I asked myself, 'did he not stop me? Why did he make pretences? Why did he always avoid explanations? Why did he insult me? Why did he not use the power of his love to influence me? Or did he not love me?' But whether he was to blame or not, I still felt the kiss of that strange man upon my cheek. The nearer we got to Heidelberg, the clearer grew my picture of my husband, and the more I dreaded our meeting. 'I shall tell him all,' I thought, 'and wipe out everything with tears of repentance; and he will forgive me.' But I did not know myself what I meant by 'everything'; and I did not believe in my heart that he would forgive me.

As soon as I entered my husband's room and saw his

calm though surprised expression, I felt at once that I had nothing to tell him, no confession to make, and nothing to ask forgiveness for. I had to suppress my unspoken grief and penitence.

'What put this into your head?' he asked. 'I meant to go to Baden to-morrow.' Then he looked more closely at me and seemed to take alarm. 'What's the matter with you? What has happened?' he said.

'Nothing at all,' I replied, almost breaking down. 'I am not going back. Let us go home, to-morrow if you like, to Russia.'

For some time he said nothing but looked at me attentively. Then he said, 'But do tell me what has happened to you.'

I blushed involuntarily and looked down. There came into his eyes a flash of anger and displeasure. Afraid of what he might imagine, I said with a power of pretence that surprised myself:

'Nothing at all has happened. It was merely that I grew weary and sad by myself; and I have been thinking a great deal of our way of life and of you. I have long been to blame towards you. Why do you take me abroad, when you can't bear it yourself? I have long been to blame. Let us go back to Nikólskoe and settle there for ever.'

'Spare us these sentimental scenes, my dear,' he said coldly. 'To go back to Nikólskoe is a good idea, for our money is running short; but the notion of stopping there "for ever" is fanciful. I know you would not settle down. Have some tea, and you will feel better,' and he rose to ring for the waiter.

I imagined all he might be thinking about me; and I was offended by the horrible thoughts which I ascribed to him when I encountered the dubious and shame-faced look he directed at me. 'He will not and cannot understand me.' I said I would go and look at the child, and I left the room. I wished to be alone, and to cry and cry and cry . . .

IV

The house at Nikólskoe, so long unheated and uninhabited, came to life again; but much of the past was dead beyond recall. Tatyána Seménovna was no more, and we were now alone together. But far from desiring such close companionship, we even found it irksome. To me that winter was the more trying because I was in bad health, from which I only recovered after the birth of my second son. My husband and I were still on the same terms as during our life in Petersburg: we were coldly friendly to each other, but in the country each room and wall and sofa recalled what he had once been to me, and what I had lost. It was as if some unforgiven grievance held us apart, as if he were punishing me and pretending not to be aware of it. But there was nothing to ask pardon for, no penalty to deprecate; my punishment was merely this, that he did not give his whole heart and mind to me as he used to do; but he did not give it to anyone or to anything; as though he had no longer a heart to give. Sometimes it occurred to me that he was only pretending to be like that, in order to hurt me, and that the old feeling was still alive in his breast; and I tried to call it forth. But I always failed: he always seemed to avoid frankness, evidently suspecting me of insincerity, and dreading the folly of any emotional display. I could read in his face and the tone of his voice, 'What is the good of talking? I know all the facts already, and I know what is on the tip of your tongue, and I know that you will say one thing and do another.' At first I was mortified by his dread of frankness, but I came later to think that it was rather the absence, on his part, of any need of frankness. It would never have occurred to me now, to tell him of a sudden that I loved him, or to ask him to repeat the prayers with me or listen while I played the piano. Our intercourse came to be regulated by a fixed code of good manners. We lived our separate lives: he had his own occupations in which I was not needed, and which I no longer wished to share, while I continued my idle life which no longer vexed or grieved him. The children were still too young to form a bond between us.

But spring came round and brought Kátya and Sónya to spend the summer with us in the country. As the house at Nikólskoe was under repair, we went to live at my old home at Pokróvskoe. The old house was unchanged— the veranda, the folding table and the piano in the sunny drawing-room, and my old bedroom with its white curtains and the dreams of my girlhood which I seemed to have left behind me there. In that room there were two beds: one had been mine, and in it now my plump little

Kokósha lay sprawling, when I went at night to sign him with the cross; the other was a crib, in which the little face of my baby, Ványa, peeped out from his swaddling-clothes. Often, when I had made the sign over them and remained standing in the middle of the quiet room, suddenly there rose up from all the corners, from the walls and curtains, old forgotten visions of youth. Old voices began to sing the songs of my girlhood. Where were those visions now? where were those dear old sweet songs? All that I had hardly dared to hope for had come to pass. My vague confused dreams had become a reality, and the reality had become an oppressive, difficult, and joyless life. All remained the same—the garden visible through the window, the grass, the path, the very same bench over there above the dell, the same song of the nightingale by the pond, the same lilacs in full bloom, the same moon shining above the house; and yet, in everything such a terrible inconceivable change! Such coldness in all that might have been near and dear! Just as in old times, Kátya and I sit quietly alone together in the parlour and talk, and talk of him. But Kátya has grown wrinkled and pale; and her eyes no longer shine with joy and hope, but express only sympathy, sorrow, and regret. We do not go into raptures as we used to, we judge him coolly; we do not wonder what we have done to deserve such happiness, or long to proclaim our thoughts to all the world. No! we whisper together like conspirators and ask each other for the hundredth time why all has changed so sadly. Yet he was still the same man, save for the deeper furrow between his eyebrows and the whiter hair on his temples; but his serious attentive look was constantly veiled from me by a cloud. And I am the same woman, but without love or desire for love, with no longing for work and no content with myself. My religious ecstasies, my love for my husband, the fullness of my former life—all these now seem utterly remote and visionary. Once it seemed so plain and right that to live for others was happiness; but now it has become unintelligible. Why live for others, when life had no attraction even for oneself?

I had given up my music altogether since the time of our first visit to Petersburg; but now the old piano and the old music tempted me to begin again.

One day I was not well and stayed indoors alone. My husband had taken Kátya and Sónya to see the new buildings at Nikólskoe. Tea was laid; I went downstairs and while waiting for them sat down at the piano. I opened the 'Moonlight Sonata' and began to play. There was no one within sight or sound, the windows were open over the garden, and the familiar sounds floated through the room with a solemn sadness. At the end of the first movement I looked round instinctively to the corner where he used once to sit and listen to my playing. He was not there; his chair, long unmoved, was still in its place; through the window I could see a lilac-bush against the light of the setting sun; the freshness of evening streamed in through the open windows. I rested my elbows on the piano and covered my face with both hands; and so I sat for a long time, thinking. I recalled with pain the irrevocable past, and timidly imagined the future. But for me there seemed to be no future, no desires at all and no hopes. 'Can life be over for me?' I thought with horror; then I looked up, and, trying to forget and not to think, I began playing the same movement over again. 'O God!' I prayed, 'forgive me if I have sinned, or restore to me all that once blossomed in my heart, or teach me what to do and how to live now.' There was a sound of wheels on the grass and before the steps of the house; then I heard cautious and familiar footsteps pass along the veranda and cease; but my heart no longer replied to the sound. When I stopped playing the footsteps were behind me and a hand was laid on my shoulder.

'How clever of you to think of playing that!' he said.

I said nothing.

'Have you had tea?' he asked.

I shook my head without looking at him—I was unwilling to let him see the signs of emotion on my face.

'They'll be here immediately,' he said; 'the horse gave trouble, and they got out on the high road to walk home.'

'Let us wait for them,' I said, and went out to the veranda, hoping that he would follow; but he asked about the children and went upstairs to see them. Once more his presence and simple kindly voice made me doubt if I had really lost anything. What more could I wish? 'He is kind and gentle, a good husband, a good father; I don't know myself what more I want.' I sat down under the veranda awning on the very bench on which I had sat when we became engaged. The sun had set, it was growing dark, and a little spring rain-cloud hung over the house and garden, and only behind the trees the horizon was clear, with the fading glow of twilight, in which one star had just begun to twinkle. The landscape, covered by the shadow of the cloud, seemed waiting for the light spring shower. There was not a breath of wind; not a single leaf or blade of grass stirred; the scent of lilac and bird-cherry was so strong in the garden and veranda that it seemed as if all the air was in flower; it came in wafts, now stronger and now weaker, till one longed to shut both eyes and ears and drink in that fragrance only. The dahlias and rose-bushes, not yet in flower, stood motionless on the black mould of the border, looking as if they were growing slowly upwards on their white-shaved props; beyond the dell, the frogs were making the most of their time before the rain drove them to the pond, croaking busily and loudly. Only the high continuous note of water falling at some distance rose above their croaking. From time to time the nightingales called to one another, and I could hear them flitting restlessly from bush to bush. Again this spring a nightingale had tried to build in a bush under the window, and I heard her fly off across the avenue when I went into the veranda. From there she whistled once and then stopped; she, too, was expecting the rain.

I tried in vain to calm my feelings: I had a sense of anticipation and regret.

He came downstairs again and sat down beside me.

'I am afraid they will get wet,' he said.

'Yes,' I answered; and we sat for long without speaking.

The cloud came down lower and lower with no wind. The air grew stiller and more fragrant. Suddenly a drop fell on the canvas awning and seemed to rebound from it; then another broke on the gravel path; soon there was a splash on the burdock leaves, and a fresh shower of big drops came down faster and faster. Nightingales and frogs were both dumb; only the high note of the falling water, though the rain made it seem more distant, still went on; and a bird, which must have sheltered among the dry leaves near the veranda, steadily repeated its two unvarying notes. My husband got up to go in.

'Where are you going?' I asked, trying to keep him; 'it is so pleasant here.'

'We must send them an umbrella and goloshes,' he replied.

'Don't trouble—it will soon be over.'

He thought I was right, and we remained together in the veranda. I rested one hand upon the wet slippery rail and put my head out. The fresh rain wetted my hair and neck in places. The cloud, growing lighter and thinner, was passing overhead; the steady patter of the rain gave place to occasional drops that fell from the sky or dripped from the trees. The frogs began to croak again in the dell; the nightingales woke up and began to call from the dripping bushes from one side and then from another. The whole prospect before us grew clear.

'How delightful!' he said, seating himself on the veranda rail and passing a hand over my wet hair.

This simple caress had on me the effect of a reproach: I felt inclined to cry.

'What more can a man need?' he said; 'I am so content now that I want nothing; I am perfectly happy!'

He told me a different story once, I thought. He had said that, however great his happiness might be, he always wanted more and more. Now he is calm and contented; while my heart is full of unspoken repentance and unshed tears.

'I think it delightful too,' I said; 'but I am sad just because of the beauty of it all. All is so fair and lovely outside me, while my own heart is confused and baffled and full of vague unsatisfied longing. Is it possible that there is no element of pain, no yearning for the past, in your enjoyment of nature?'

He took his hand off my head and was silent for a little.

'I used to feel that too,' he said, as though recalling it, 'especially in spring. I used to sit up all night too, with my hopes and fears for company, and good company they were! But life was all before me then. Now it is all behind me, and I am content with what I have. I find life capital,' he added with such careless confidence, that I believed, whatever pain it gave me to hear it, that it was the truth.

'But is there nothing you wish for?' I asked.

'I don't ask for impossibilities,' he said, guessing my thoughts. 'You go and get your head wet,' he added, stroking my head like a child's and again passing his hand over the wet hair; 'you envy the leaves and the grass their wetting from the rain, and you would like yourself to be the grass and the leaves and the rain. But I am content to enjoy them and everything else that is good and young and happy.'

'And do you regret nothing of the past?' I asked, while my heart grew heavier and heavier.

Again he thought for a time before replying. I saw that he wished to reply with perfect frankness.

'Nothing,' he said shortly.

'Not true! not true!' I said, turning towards him and looking into his eyes. 'Do you really not regret the past?'

'No!' he repeated; 'I am grateful for it, but I don't regret it.'

'But would you not like to have it back?' I asked.

He turned away and looked out over the garden.

'No; I might as well wish to have wings. It is impossible.'

'And would you not alter the past? do you not reproach yourself or me?'

'No, never! It was all for the best.'

'Listen to me!' I said touching his arm to make him look round. 'Why did you never tell me that you wished me to live as you really wished me to? Why did you give me a freedom for which I was unfit? Why did you stop teaching me? If you had wished it, if you had guided me differently, none of all this would have happened!' said I in a voice that increasingly expressed cold displeasure and reproach in place of the love of former days.

'What would not have happened?' he asked, turning to me in surprise. 'As it is, there is nothing wrong. Things are all right, quite all right,' he added with a smile.

'Does he really not understand?' I thought; 'or still worse, does he not wish to understand?'

Then I suddenly broke out. 'Had you acted differently, I should not now be punished, for no fault at all, by your indifference and even contempt, and you would not have taken from me unjustly all that I valued in life!'

'What do you mean, my dear one?' he asked—he seemed not to understand me.

'No! don't interrupt me! You have taken from me your confidence, your love, even your respect; for I cannot believe, when I think of the past, that you still love me. No! don't speak! I must once for all say out what has long been torturing me. Is it my fault that I knew nothing of life, and that you left me to learn experience for myself? Is it my fault that now, when I have gained the knowledge and have been struggling for nearly a year to come back to you, you push me away and pretend not to understand what I want? And you always do it so that it is impossible to reproach you, while I am guilty and unhappy. Yes, you wish to drive me out again to that life which might rob us both of happiness.'

'How did I show that?' he asked in evident alarm and surprise.

'No later than yesterday you said, and you constantly say, that I can never settle down here, and that we must spend this winter too at Petersburg; and I hate Petersburg!' I went on. 'Instead of supporting me, you avoid all plain speaking, you never say a single frank affectionate word to me. And then, when I fall utterly, you will reproach me and rejoice in my fall.'

'Stop!' he said with cold severity. 'You have no right to say that. It only proves that you are ill-disposed towards me, that you don't . . .'

'That I don't love you? Don't hesitate to say it!' I cried, and the tears began to flow. I sat down on the bench and covered my face with my handkerchief.

'So that is how he understood me!' I thought, trying to restrain the sobs which choked me. 'Gone, gone is our former love!' said a voice at my heart. He did not come close or try to comfort me. He was hurt by what I had said. When he spoke, his tone was cool and dry.

'I don't know what you reproach me with,' he began. 'If you mean that I don't love you as I once did . . .'

'Did love!' I said, with my face buried in the handkerchief, while the bitter tears fell still more abundantly.

'If so, time is to blame for that, and we ourselves. Each time of life has its own kind of love.' He was silent for a moment. 'Shall I tell you the whole truth, if you really wish for frankness? In that summer when I first knew you, I used to lie awake all night, thinking about you, and I made that love myself, and it grew and grew in my heart. So again, in Petersburg and abroad, in the course of horrible sleepless nights, I strove to shatter and destroy that love, which had come to torture me. I did not destroy it, but I destroyed that part of it which gave me pain. Then I grew calm; and I feel love still, but it is a different kind of love.'

'You call it love, but I call it torture!' I said. 'Why did you allow me to go into society, if you thought so badly of it that you ceased to love me on that account?'

'No, it was not society, my dear,' he said.

'Why did you not exercise your authority?' I went on:

'why did you not lock me up or kill me? That would have been better than the loss of all that formed my happiness. I should have been happy, instead of being ashamed.'

I began to sob again and hid my face.

Just then Kátya and Sónya, wet and cheerful, came out to the veranda, laughing and talking loudly. They were silent as soon as they saw us, and went in again immediately.

We remained silent for a long time. I had had my cry out and felt relieved. I glanced at him. He was sitting with his head resting on his hand; he intended to make some reply to my glance, but only sighed deeply and resumed his former position.

I went up to him and removed his hand. His eyes turned thoughtfully to my face.

'Yes,' he began, as if continuing his thoughts aloud, 'all of us, and especially you women, must have personal experience of all the nonsense of life, in order to get back to life itself; the evidence of other people is no good. At that time you had not got near the end of that charming nonsense which I admired in you. So I let you go through it alone, feeling that I had no right to put pressure on you, though my own time for that sort of thing was long past.'

'If you loved me,' I said, 'how could you stand beside me and suffer me to go through it?'

'Because it was impossible for you to take my word for it, though you would have tried to. Personal experience was necessary, and now you have had it.'

'There was much calculation in all that,' I said, 'but little love.'

Again we were silent.

'What you said just now is severe, but it is true,' he began, rising suddenly and beginning to walk about the veranda. 'Yes, it is true. I was to blame,' he added, stopping opposite me; 'I ought either to have kept myself from loving you at all, or to have loved you in a simpler way.'

'Let us forget it all,' I said timidly.

'No,' he said; 'the past can never come back, never;' and his voice softened as he spoke.

'It is restored already,' I said, laying a hand on his shoulder.

He took my hand away and pressed it.

'I was wrong when I said that I did not regret the past. I do regret it; I weep for that past love which can never return. Who is to blame, I do not know. Love remains, but not the old love; its place remains, but it is all wasted away and has lost all strength and substance; recollections are still left, and gratitude; but . . .'

'Do not say that!' I broke in. 'Let all be as it was before! Surely that is possible?' I asked, looking into his eyes; but their gaze was clear and calm, and did not look deeply into mine.

Even while I spoke, I knew that my wishes and my petition were impossible. He smiled calmly and gently; and I thought it the smile of an old man.

'How young you are still!' he said, 'and I am so old. What you seek in me is no longer there. Why deceive ourselves?' he added, still smiling.

I stood silent opposite to him, and my heart grew calmer.

'Don't let us try to repeat life,' he went on. 'Don't let us make pretences to ourselves. Let us be thankful that there is an end of the old emotions and excitements. The excitement of searching is over for us; our quest is done, and happiness enough has fallen to our lot. Now we must stand aside and make room—for him, if you like,' he said, pointing to the nurse who was carrying Ványa out and had stopped at the veranda door. 'That's the truth, my dear one,' he said, drawing down my head and kissing it, not a lover any longer but an old friend.

The fragrant freshness of the night rose ever stronger and sweeter from the garden; the sounds and the silence grew more solemn; star after star began to twinkle overhead. I looked at him, and suddenly my heart grew light; it seemed that the cause of my suffering had been removed like an aching nerve. Suddenly I realized clearly and calmly that the past feeling, like the past time itself, was gone beyond recall, and that it would be not only impossible but painful and uncomfortable to bring it back. And after all, was that time so good which seemed to me so happy? And it was all so long, long ago!

'Time for tea!' he said, and we went together to the parlour. At the door we met the nurse with the baby. I took him in my arms, covered his bare little red legs, pressed him to me, and kissed him with the lightest touch of my lips. Half asleep, he moved the parted fingers of one creased little hand and opened dim little eyes, as if he was looking for something or recalling something. All at once his eyes rested on me, a spark of consciousness shone in them, the little pouting lips, parted before, now met and opened in a smile. 'Mine, mine, mine!' I thought, pressing him to my breast with such an impulse of joy in every limb that I found it hard to restrain myself from hurting him. I fell to kissing the cold little feet, his stomach and hand and head with its thin covering of down. My husband came up to me, and I quickly covered the child's face and uncovered it again.

'Iván Sergéich!' said my husband, tickling him under the chin. But I made haste to cover Iván Sergéich up again. None but I had any business to look long at him. I glanced at my husband. His eyes smiled as he looked at me; and I looked into them with an ease and happiness which I had not felt for a long time.

That day ended the romance of our marriage; the old feeling became a precious irrecoverable remembrance; but a new feeling of love for my children and the father of my children laid the foundation of a new life and a quite different happiness; and that life and happiness have lasted to the present time.

The Cossacks

A Tale of 1852

[1852–1862]

I

All is quiet in Moscow. The squeak of wheels is seldom heard in the snow-covered street. There are no lights left in the windows and the street lamps have been extinguished. Only the sound of bells, borne over the city from the church towers, suggests the approach of morning. The streets are deserted. At rare intervals a night-cabman's sledge kneads up the snow and sand in the street as the driver makes his way to another corner where he falls asleep while waiting for a fare. An old woman passes by on her way to church, where a few wax candles burn with a red light reflected on the gilt mountings of the icons. Workmen are already getting up after the long winter night and going to their work—but for the gentlefolk it is still evening.

From a window in Chevalier's Restaurant a light—illegal at that hour—is still to be seen through a chink in the shutter. At the entrance a carriage, a sledge, and a cabman's sledge, stand close together with their backs to the curbstone. A three-horse sledge from the post-station is there also. A yard-porter muffled up and pinched with cold is sheltering behind the corner of the house.

'And what's the good of all this jawing?' thinks the footman who sits in the hall weary and haggard. 'This always happens when I'm on duty.' From the adjoining room are heard the voices of three young men, sitting there at a table on which are wine and the remains of supper. One, a rather plain, thin, neat little man, sits looking with tired kindly eyes at his friend, who is about to start on a journey. Another, a tall man, lies on a sofa beside a table on which are empty bottles, and plays with his watch-key. A third, wearing a short, fur-lined coat, is pacing up and down the room stopping now and then to crack an almond between his strong, rather thick, but well-tended fingers. He keeps smiling at something and his

85

face and eyes are all aglow. He speaks warmly and ges-
ticulates, but evidently does not find the words he wants
and those that occur to him seem to him inadequate to
express what has risen to his heart.

'Now I can speak out fully,' said the traveller. 'I don't
want to defend myself, but I should like you at least to
understand me as I understand myself, and not look at the
matter superficially. You say I have treated her badly,' he
continued, addressing the man with the kindly eyes who
was watching him.

'Yes, you are to blame,' said the latter, and his look
seemed to express still more kindliness and weariness.

'I know why you say that,' rejoined the one who was
leaving. 'To be loved is in your opinion as great a happiness
as to love, and if a man obtains it, it is enough for his
whole life.'

'Yes, quite enough, my dear fellow, more than enough!'
confirmed the plain little man, opening and shutting his
eyes.

'But why shouldn't the man love too?' said the traveller
thoughtfully, looking at his friend with something like
pity. 'Why shouldn't one love? Because love doesn't
come. . . . No, to be beloved is a misfortune. It is a
misfortune to feel guilty because you do not give something you cannot give. O my God!' he added, with a gesture of his arm. 'If it all happened reasonably, and not all
topsy-turvy—not in our way but in a way of its own! Why,
it's as if I had stolen that love! You think so too, don't
deny it. You must think so. But will you believe it, of all
the horrid and stupid things I have found time to do in
my life—and there are many—this is one I do not and
cannot repent of. Neither at the beginning nor afterwards
did I lie to myself or to her. It seemed to me that I had
at last fallen in love, but then I saw that it was an involuntary falsehood, and that that was not the way to love, and
I could not go on, but she did. Am I to blame that I
couldn't? What was I to do?'

'Well, it's ended now!' said his friend, lighting a cigar
to master his sleepiness. 'The fact is that you have not yet
loved and do not know what love is.'

The man in the fur-lined coat was going to speak again,
and put his hands to his head, but could not express what
he wanted to say.

'Never loved! . . . Yes, quite true, I never have! But
after all, I have within me a desire to love, and nothing
could be stronger than that desire! But then, again, does
such love exist? There always remains something incomplete. Ah well! What's the use of talking? I've made an
awful mess of life! But anyhow it's all over now; you are
quite right. And I feel that I am beginning a new life.'

'Which you will again make a mess of,' said the man
who lay on the sofa playing with his watch-key. But the
traveller did not listen to him.

'I am sad and yet glad to go,' he continued. 'Why I am
sad I don't know.'

And the traveller went on talking about himself, without
noticing that this did not interest the others as much as it
did him. A man is never such an egotist as at moments of
spiritual ecstasy. At such times it seems to him that there
is nothing on earth more splendid and interesting than
himself.

'Dmítri Andréich! The coachman won't wait any longer!'
said a young serf, entering the room in a sheepskin coat,
with a scarf tied round his head. 'The horses have been
standing since twelve, and it's now four o'clock!'

Dmítri Andréich looked at his serf, Vanyúsha. The scarf
round Vanyúsha's head, his felt boots and sleepy face,
seemed to be calling his master to a new life of labour,
hardship, and activity.

'True enough! Good-bye!' said he, feeling for the unfastened hook and eye on his coat.

In spite of advice to mollify the coachman by another
tip, he put on his cap and stood in the middle of the room.
The friends kissed once, then again, and after a pause, a
third time. The man in the fur-lined coat approached
the table and emptied a champagne glass, then took the
plain little man's hand and blushed.

'Ah well, I will speak out all the same. . . . I must and
will be frank with you because I am fond of you. . . . Of
course you love her—I always thought so—don't you?'

'Yes,' answered his friend, smiling still more gently.

'And perhaps . . .'

'Please sir, I have orders to put out the candles,' said
the sleepy attendant, who had been listening to the last
part of the conversation and wondering why gentlefolk
always talk about one and the same thing. 'To whom shall

I make out the bill? To you, sir?' he added, knowing whom to address and turning to the tall man.

'To me,' replied the tall man. 'How much?'

'Twenty-six rubles.'

The tall man considered for a moment, but said nothing and put the bill in his pocket.

The other two continued their talk.

'Good-bye, you are a capital fellow!' said the short plain man with the mild eyes.

Tears filled the eyes of both. They stepped into the porch.

'Oh, by the by,' said the traveller, turning with a blush to the tall man, 'will you settle Chevalier's bill and write and let me know?'

'All right, all right!' said the tall man, pulling on his gloves. 'How I envy you!' he added quite unexpectedly when they were out in the porch.

The traveller got into his sledge, wrapped his coat about him, and said: 'Well then, come along!' He even moved a little to make room in the sledge for the man who said he envied him—his voice trembled.

'Good-bye, Mítya! I hope that with God's help you . . .' said the tall one. But his wish was that the other would go away quickly, and so he could not finish the sentence.

They were silent a moment. Then someone again said, 'Good-bye,' and a voice cried, 'Ready,' and the coachman touched up the horses.

'Hy, Elisár!' One of the friends called out, and the other coachman and the sledge-drivers began moving, clicking their tongues and pulling at the reins. Then the stiffened carriage-wheels rolled squeaking over the frozen snow.

'A fine fellow, that Olénin!' said one of the friends. 'But what an idea to go to the Caucasus—as a cadet, too! I wouldn't do it for anything. . . . Are you dining at the club to-morrow?'

'Yes.'

They separated.

The traveller felt warm, his fur coat seemed too hot. He sat on the bottom of the sledge and unfastened his coat, and the three shaggy post-horses dragged themselves out of one dark street into another, past houses he had never before seen. It seemed to Olénin that only travellers starting on a long journey went through those streets. All was

dark and silent and dull around him, but his soul was full
of memories, love, regrets, and a pleasant tearful feeling.

II

'I'm fond of them, very fond! . . . First-rate fellows!
. . . Fine!' he kept repeating, and felt ready to cry. But
why he wanted to cry, who were the first-rate fellows he
was so fond of—was more than he quite knew. Now and
then he looked round at some house and wondered why
it was so curiously built; sometimes he began wondering
why the post-boy and Vanyúsha, who were so different
from himself, sat so near, and together with him were
being jerked about and swayed by the tugs the side-horses
gave at the frozen traces, and again he repeated: 'First
rate . . . very fond!' and once he even said: 'And how it
seizes one . . . excellent!' and wondered what made him
say it. 'Dear me, am I drunk?' he asked himself. He had
had a couple of bottles of wine, but it was not the wine
alone that was having this effect on Olénin. He remembered all the words of friendship heartily, bashfully, spon-
taneously (as he believed) addressed to him on his departure. He remembered the clasp of hands, glances, the
moments of silence, and the sound of a voice saying,
'*Good-bye, Mítya!*' when he was already in the sledge. He
remembered his own deliberate frankness. And all this
had a touching significance for him. Not only friends and
relatives, not only people who had been indifferent to him,
but even those who did not like him, seemed to have agreed
to become fonder of him, or to forgive him, before his
departure, as people do before confession or death. 'Perhaps I shall not return from the Caucasus,' he thought.
And he felt that he loved his friends and some one besides.
He was sorry for himself. But it was not love for his
friends that so stirred and uplifted his heart that he could
not repress the meaningless words that seemed to rise of
themselves to his lips; nor was it love for a woman (he
had never yet been in love) that had brought on this mood.
Love for himself, love full of hope—warm young love for
all that was good in his own soul (and at that moment it
seemed to him that there was nothing but good in it)—
compelled him to weep and to mutter incoherent words.

Olénin was a youth who had never completed his university course, never served anywhere (having only a

nominal post in some government office or other), who had squandered half his fortune and had reached the age of twenty-four without having done anything or even chosen a career. He was what in Moscow society is termed *un jeune homme*.

At the age of eighteen he was free—as only rich young Russians in the 'forties who had lost their parents at an early age could be. Neither physical nor moral fetters of any kind existed for him; he could do as he liked, lacking nothing and bound by nothing. Neither relatives, nor fatherland, nor religion, nor wants, existed for him. He believed in nothing and admitted nothing. But although he believed in nothing he was not a morose or blasé young man, nor self-opinionated, but on the contrary continually let himself be carried away. He had come to the conclusion that there is no such thing as love, yet his heart always overflowed in the presence of any young and attractive woman. He had long been aware that honours and position were nonsense, yet involuntarily he felt pleased when at a ball Prince Sergius came up and spoke to him affably. But he yielded to his impulses only in so far as they did not limit his freedom. As soon as he had yielded to any influence and became conscious of its leading on to labour and struggle, he instinctively hastened to free himself from the feeling or activity into which he was being drawn and to regain his freedom. In this way he experimented with society-life, the civil service, farming, music—to which at one time he intended to devote his life—and even with the love of women in which he did not believe. He meditated on the use to which he should devote that power of youth which is granted to man only once in a lifetime: that force which gives a man the power of making himself, or even— as it seemed to him—of making the universe, into anything he wishes: should it be to art, to science, to love of woman, or to practical activities? It is true that some people are devoid of this impulse, and on entering life at once place their necks under the first yoke that offers itself and honestly labour under it for the rest of their lives. But Olénin was too strongly conscious of the pres- ence of that all-powerful God of Youth—of that capacity to be entirely transformed into an aspiration or idea—the capacity to wish and to do—to throw oneself headlong into a bottomless abyss without knowing why or wherefore. He bore this consciousness within himself, was proud of it and, without knowing it, was happy in that consciousness. Up to that time he had loved only himself, and could not help loving himself, for he expected nothing but good of himself and had not yet had time to be disillusioned. On leaving Moscow he was in that happy state of mind in which a young man, conscious of past mistakes, suddenly says to himself, 'That was not the real thing.' All that had gone before was accidental and unimportant. Till then he had not really tried to live, but now with his departure from Moscow a new life was beginning—a life in which there would be no mistakes, no remorse, and certainly nothing but happiness.

It is always the case on a long journey that till the first two or three stages have been passed imagination continues to dwell on the place left behind, but with the first morning on the road it leaps to the end of the journey and there begins building castles in the air. So it happened to Olénin.

After leaving the town behind, he gazed at the snowy fields and felt glad to be alone in their midst. Wrapping himself in his fur coat, he lay at the bottom of the sledge, became tranquil, and fell into a doze. The parting with his friends had touched him deeply, and memories of that last winter spent in Moscow and images of the past, mingled with vague thoughts and regrets, rose unbidden in his imagination.

He remembered the friend who had seen him off and his relations with the girl they had talked about. The girl was rich. 'How could he love her knowing that she loved me?' thought he, and evil suspicions crossed his mind. 'There is much dishonesty in men when one comes to reflect.' Then he was confronted by the question: 'But really, how is it I have never been in love? Every one tells me that I never have. Can it be that I am a moral monstrosity?' And he began to recall all his infatuations. He recalled his entry into society, and a friend's sister with whom he spent several evenings at a table with a lamp on it which lit up her slender fingers busy with needlework, and the lower part of her pretty delicate face. He recalled their conversations that dragged on like the game in which one passes on a stick which one keeps alight as long as possible, and the general awkwardness and restraint and his continual feeling of rebellion at all that conventionality. Some voice had always whispered: 'That's not it, that's not it,' and so it had proved. Then he remembered a ball and the mazurka he danced with the beautiful D——. 'How much in love I was that night and how happy! And how hurt and vexed I was next morning when I woke and felt myself still free! Why does not love come and bind me hand and foot?' thought he. 'No, there is no such thing as love! That neighbour who used to tell me, as she told Dubróvin and the Marshal, that she loved the stars, was not *it* either.' And now his farming and work in the country recurred to his mind, and in those recollections also there was nothing to dwell on with pleasure. 'Will they talk long of my departure?' came into his head; but who 'they' were he did not quite know. Next came a thought that made him wince and mutter incoherently. It was the recollection of M. Cappele the tailor, and the six hundred and seventy-eight rubles he still owed him, and he recalled the words in which he had begged him to wait another year, and the look of perplexity and resignation which had appeared on the tailor's face. 'Oh, my God, my God!' he repeated, wincing and trying to drive away the intolerable thought. 'All the same and in spite of everything she loved me,' thought he of the girl they had talked about at the farewell supper. 'Yes, had I married her I should not now be owing anything, and as it is I am in debt to Vasílyev.' Then he remembered the last night he had played with Vasílyev at the club (just after leaving her), and he recalled his humiliating requests for another game and the other's cold refusal. 'A year's economizing and they will all be paid, and the devil take them!' . . . But despite this assurance he again began calculating his outstanding debts, their dates, and when he could hope to pay them off. 'And I owe something to Morell as well as to Chevalier,' thought he, recalling the night when he had run up so large a debt. It was at a carousal at the gipsies arranged by some fellows from Petersburg: Sáshka B——, an aide-de-camp to the Tsar, Prince D——, and that pompous old ——. 'How is it those gentlemen are so self-satisfied?' thought he, 'and by what right do they form a clique to which they think others must be highly flattered to be admitted? Can it be because they are on the Emperor's staff? Why, it's awful what fools and scoundrels they consider other people to be! But I showed them that I at any rate, on the contrary, do not at all want their intimacy. All the same, I fancy Andrew, the steward, would be amazed to know that I am on familiar terms with

a man like Sáshka B——, a colonel and an aide-de-camp
to the Tsar! Yes, and no one drank more than I did that
evening, and I taught the gipsies a new song and everyone listened to it. Though I have done many foolish
things, all the same I am a very good fellow,' thought he.

Morning found him at the third post-stage. He drank
tea, and himself helped Vanyúsha to move his bundles and
trunks and sat down among them, sensible, erect, and
precise, knowing where all his belongings were, how
much money he had and where it was, where he had put
his passport and the post-horse requisition and toll-gate
papers, and it all seemed to him so well arranged that he
grew quite cheerful and the long journey before him
seemed an extended pleasure-trip.

All that morning and noon he was deep in calculations
of how many versts he had travelled, how many remained
to the next stage, how many to the next town, to the
place where he would dine, to the place where he would
drink tea, and to Stavrópol, and what fraction of the whole
journey was already accomplished. He also calculated how
much money he had with him, how much would be left
over, how much would pay off all his debts, and what proportion of his income he would spend each month. Towards
evening, after tea, he calculated that to Stavrópol there
still remained seven-elevenths of the whole journey, that
his debts would require seven months' economy and one-
eighth of his whole fortune; and then, tranquillized, he
wrapped himself up, lay down in the sledge, and again
dozed off. His imagination was now turned to the future:
to the Caucasus. All his dreams of the future were mingled
with pictures of Amalat-Beks, Circassian women, mountains, precipices, terrible torrents, and perils. All these
things were vague and dim, but the love of fame and the
danger of death furnished the interest of that future. Now,
with unprecedented courage and a strength that amazed
everyone, he slew and subdued an innumerable host of
hillsmen; now he was himself a hillsman and with them
was maintaining their independence against the Russians.
As soon as he pictured anything definite, familiar Moscow
figures always appeared on the scene. Sáshka B—— fights
with the Russians or the hillsmen against him. Even the
tailor Cappele in some strange way takes part in the conqueror's triumph. Amid all this he remembered his former
humiliations, weaknesses, and mistakes, and the recollec-

tion was not disagreeable. It was clear that there among the mountains, waterfalls, fair Circassians, and dangers, such mistakes could not recur. Having once made full confession to himself there was an end of it all. One other vision, the sweetest of them all, mingled with the young man's every thought of the future—the vision of a woman. And there, among the mountains, she appeared to his imagination as a Circassian slave, a fine figure with a long plait of hair and deep submissive eyes. He pictured a lonely hut in the mountains, and on the threshold *she* stands awaiting him when, tired and covered with dust, blood, and fame, he returns to her. He is conscious of her kisses, her shoulders, her sweet voice, and her submissiveness. She is enchanting, but uneducated, wild, and rough. In the long winter evenings he begins her education. She is clever and gifted and quickly acquires all the knowledge essential. Why not? She can quite easily learn foreign languages, read the French masterpieces and understand them: *Notre Dame de Paris,* for instance, is sure to please her. She can also speak French. In a drawing-room she can show more innate dignity than a lady of the highest society. She can sing, simply, powerfully, and passionately. . . . 'Oh, what nonsense!' said he to himself. But here they reached a post-station and he had to change into another sledge and give some tips. But his fancy again began searching for the 'nonsense' he had relinquished, and again fair Circassians, glory, and his return to Russia with an appointment as aide-de-camp and a lovely wife rose before his imagination. 'But there's no such thing as love,' said he to himself. 'Fame is all rubbish. But the six hundred and seventy-eight rubles? . . . And the conquered land that will bring me more wealth than I need for a lifetime? It will not be right though to keep all that wealth for myself. I shall have to distribute it. But to whom? Well, six hundred and seventy-eight rubles to Cappele and then we'll see.' . . . Quite vague visions now cloud his mind, and only Vanyúsha's voice and the interrupted motion of the sledge break his healthy youthful slumber. Scarcely conscious, he changes into another sledge at the next stage and continues his journey.

Next morning everything goes on just the same: the same kind of post-stations and tea-drinking, the same moving horses' cruppers, the same short talks with Vanyú-

sha, the same vague dreams and drowsiness, and the same
tired, healthy, youthful sleep at night.

III

The farther Olénin travelled from Central Russia the
farther he left his memories behind, and the nearer he
drew to the Caucasus the lighter his heart became. 'I'll stay
away for good and never return to show myself in society,'
was a thought that sometimes occurred to him. 'These people whom I see here are *not* people. None of them know
me and none of them can ever enter the Moscow society
I was in or find out about my past. And no one in that
society will ever know what I am doing, living among these
people.' And quite a new feeling of freedom from his
whole past came over him among the rough beings he met
on the road whom he did not consider to be *people* in the
sense that his Moscow acquaintances were. The rougher
the people and the fewer the signs of civilization the freer
he felt. Stavrópol, through which he had to pass, irked
him. The signboards, some of them even in French, ladies
in carriages, cabs in the market-place, and a gentleman
wearing a fur cloak and tall hat who was walking along
the boulevard and staring at the passers-by, quite upset
him. 'Perhaps these people know some of my acquaintances,' he thought; and the club, his tailor, cards, society
. . . came back to his mind. But after Stavrópol everything was satisfactory—wild and also beautiful and warlike, and Olénin felt happier and happier. All the Cossacks,
post-boys, and post-station masters seemed to him simple
folk with whom he could jest and converse simply, without having to consider to what class they belonged. They
all belonged to the human race which, without his thinking
about it, all appeared dear to Olénin, and they all treated
him in a friendly way.

Already in the province of the Don Cossacks his sledge
had been exchanged for a cart, and beyond Stavrópol it
became so warm that Olénin travelled without wearing
his fur coat. It was already spring—an unexpected joyous
spring for Olénin. At night he was no longer allowed to
leave the Cossack villages, and they said it was dangerous
to travel in the evening. Vanyúsha began to be uneasy,
and they carried a loaded gun in the cart. Olénin became

still happier. At one of the post-stations the post-master told of a terrible murder that had been committed recently on the high road. They began to meet armed men. 'So this is where it begins!' thought Olénin, and kept expecting to see the snowy mountains of which mention was so often made. Once, towards evening, the Nogáy driver pointed with his whip to the mountains shrouded in clouds. Olénin looked eagerly, but it was dull and the mountains were almost hidden by the clouds. Olénin made out something grey and white and fleecy, but try as he would he could find nothing beautiful in the mountains of which he had so often read and heard. The mountains and the clouds appeared to him quite alike, and he thought the special beauty of the snow peaks, of which he had so often been told, was as much an invention as Bach's music and the love of women, in which he did not believe. So he gave up looking forward to seeing the mountains. But early next morning, being awakened in his cart by the freshness of the air, he glanced carelessly to the right. The morning was perfectly clear. Suddenly he saw, about twenty paces away as it seemed to him at first glance, pure white gigantic masses with delicate contours, the distinct fantastic outlines of their summits showing sharply against the far-off sky. When he had realized the distance between himself and them and the sky and the whole immensity of the mountains, and felt the infinitude of all that beauty, he became afraid that it was but a phantasm or a dream. He gave himself a shake to rouse himself, but the mountains were still the same.

'What's that! What is it?' he said to the driver.

'Why, the mountains,' answered the Nogáy driver with indifference.

'And I too have been looking at them for a long while,' said Vanyúsha. 'Aren't they fine? They won't believe it at home.'

The quick progress of the three-horsed cart along the smooth road caused the mountains to appear to be running along the horizon, while their rosy crests glittered in the light of the rising sun. At first Olénin was only astonished at the sight, then gladdened by it; but later on, gazing more and more intently at that snow-peaked chain that seemed to rise not from among other black mountains, but straight out of the plain, and to glide away into the distance, he began by slow degrees to be penetrated by their beauty and at length to *feel* the mountains. From that moment all he saw, all he thought, and all he felt, acquired for him a new character, sternly majestic like the mountains! All his Moscow reminiscences, shame, and repentance, and his trivial dreams about the Caucasus, vanished and did not return. 'Now it has begun,' a solemn voice seemed to say to him. The road and the Térek, just becoming visible in the distance, and the Cossack villages and the people, all no longer appeared to him as a joke. He looked at himself or Vanyúsha, and again thought of the mountains. . . . Two Cossacks ride by, their guns in their cases swinging rhythmically behind their backs, the white and bay legs of their horses mingling confusedly . . . and the mountains! Beyond the Térek rises the smoke from a Tartar village . . . and the mountains! The sun has risen and glitters on the Térek, now visible beyond the reeds . . . and the mountains! From the village comes a Tartar wagon, and women, beautiful young women, pass by . . . and the mountains! '*Abreks* canter about the plain, and here am I driving along and do not fear them! I have a gun, and strength, and youth . . . and the mountains!'

IV

That whole part of the Térek line (about fifty miles) along which lie the villages of the Grebénsk Cossacks is uniform in character both as to country and inhabitants. The Térek, which separates the Cossacks from the mountaineers, still flows turbid and rapid though already broad and smooth, always depositing greyish sand on its low reedy right bank and washing away the steep, though not high, left bank, with its roots of century-old oaks, its rotting plane trees, and young brushwood. On the right bank lie the villages of pro-Russian, though still somewhat restless, Tartars. Along the left bank, back half a mile from the river and standing five or six miles apart from one another, are Cossack villages. In olden times most of these villages were situated on the banks of the river; but the Térek, shifting northward from the mountains year by year, washed away those banks, and now there remain only the ruins of the old villages and of the gardens of pear and plum trees and poplars, all overgrown with blackberry bushes and wild vines. No one lives there now, and one only sees the tracks of the deer, the wolves, the hares, and the pheasants, who have learned to love these places. From village to village runs a road cut through the forest as a cannon-shot might fly. Along the roads are cordons of Cossacks and watch-towers with sentinels in them. Only a narrow strip about seven hundred yards wide of fertile wooded soil belongs to the Cossacks. To the north of it begin the sand-drifts of the Nogáy or Mozdók steppes, which fetch far to the north and run, Heaven knows where, into the Trukhmén, Astrakhán, and Kirghíz-Kaisátsk steppes. To the south, beyond the Térek, are the Great Chéchnya river, the Kochkálov range, the Black Mountains, yet another range, and at last the snowy mountains, which can just be seen but have never yet been scaled. In this fertile wooded strip, rich in vegetation, has dwelt as far back as memory runs the fine warlike and prosperous Russian tribe belonging to the sect of Old Believers, and called the Grebénsk Cossacks.

Long long ago their Old Believer ancestors fled from Russia and settled beyond the Térek among the Chéchens on the Grében, the first range of wooded mountains of Chéchnya. Living among the Chéchens the Cossacks intermarried with them and adopted the manners and customs of the hill tribes, though they still retained the Russian language in all its purity, as well as their Old Faith. A tradition, still fresh among them, declares that Tsar Iván the Terrible came to the Térek, sent for their Elders, and gave them the land on this side of the river, exhorting them to remain friendly to Russia and promising not to enforce his rule upon them nor oblige them to change their faith. Even now the Cossack families claim relationship with the Chéchens, and the love of freedom, of leisure, of plunder and of war, still form their chief characteristics. Only the harmful side of Russian influence shows itself—by interference at elections, by confiscation of church bells, and by the troops who are quartered in the country or march through it. A Cossack is inclined to hate less the *dzhigit* hillsman who maybe has killed his brother, than the soldier quartered on him to defend his village, but who has defiled his hut with tobacco-smoke. He respects his enemy the hillsman and despises the soldier, who is in his eyes an alien and an oppressor. In reality, from a Cossack's point of view a Russian peasant is a foreign, savage, despicable creature, of whom he sees a sample in the hawkers who come to the country and in the Ukraínian immigrants whom the Cossack contemptuously calls 'wool-beaters'. For him, to be smartly dressed means to be dressed like a Circassian. The best weapons are obtained from the hillsmen and the best horses are bought, or stolen, from them. A dashing young Cossack likes to show off his knowledge of Tartar, and when carousing talks Tartar even to his fellow Cossack. In spite of all these things this small Christian clan stranded in a tiny corner of the earth, surrounded by half-savage Mohammedan tribes and by soldiers, considers itself highly advanced, acknowledges none but Cossacks as human beings, and despises everybody else. The Cossack spends most of his time in the cordon, in action, or in hunting and fishing. He hardly ever works at home. When he stays in the village it is an exception to the general rule and then he is holiday-making. All Cossacks make their own wine, and drunkenness is not so much a general tendency as a rite, the non-fulfilment of which would be considered apostasy. The Cossack looks upon a woman as an instrument for his welfare; only the unmarried girls are allowed to amuse themselves. A married woman has to work for her husband from youth to very old age: his demands on her are the Oriental ones of submission and labour. In consequence of this outlook women are strongly developed both physically and mentally, and though they are—as everywhere in the East—nominally in subjection, they possess far greater influence and importance in family-life than Western women. Their exclusion from public life and inurement to heavy male labour give the women all the more power and importance in the household. A Cossack, who before strangers considers it improper to speak affectionately or needlessly to his wife, when alone with her is involuntarily conscious of her superiority. His house and all his property, in fact the entire homestead, has been acquired and is kept together solely by her labour and care. Though firmly convinced that labour is degrading to a Cossack and is only proper for a Nogáy labourer or a woman, he is vaguely aware of the fact that all he makes use of and calls his own is the result of that toil, and that it is in the power of the woman (his mother or his wife) whom he considers his slave, to deprive him of all he possesses. Besides, the continuous performance of man's heavy work and the responsibilities entrusted to her

have endowed the Grebénsk women with a peculiarly independent masculine character and have remarkably developed their physical powers, common sense, resolution,
and stability. The women are in most cases stronger, more
intelligent, more developed, and handsomer than the men.
A striking feature of a Grebénsk woman's beauty is the
combination of the purest Circassian type of face with the
broad and powerful build of Northern women. Cossack
women wear the Circassian dress—a Tartar smock,
beshmet, and soft slippers—but they tie their kerchiefs
round their heads in the Russian fashion. Smartness, cleanliness and elegance in dress and in the arrangement of
their huts, are with them a custom and a necessity. In their
relations with men the women, and especially the unmarried girls, enjoy perfect freedom.

Novomlínsk village was considered the very heart of
Grebénsk Cossackdom. In it more than elsewhere the
customs of the old Grebénsk population have been preserved, and its women have from time immemorial been
renowned all over the Caucasus for their beauty. A Cossack's livelihood is derived from vineyards, fruit-gardens,
water melon and pumpkin plantations, from fishing, hunting, maize and millet growing, and from war plunder.
Novomlínsk village lies about two and a half miles away
from the Térek, from which it is separated by a dense
forest. On one side of the road which runs through the
village is the river; on the other, green vineyards and
orchards, beyond which are seen the driftsands of the
Nogáy Steppe. The village is surrounded by earth-banks
and prickly bramble hedges, and is entered by tall gates
hung between posts and covered with little reed-thatched
roofs. Beside them on a wooden gun-carriage stands an
unwieldy cannon captured by the Cossacks at some time
or other, and which has not been fired for a hundred years.
A uniformed Cossack sentinel with dagger and gun sometimes stands, and sometimes does not stand, on guard
beside the gates, and sometimes presents arms to a passing
officer and sometimes does not. Below the roof of the
gateway is written in black letters on a white board:
'Houses 266: male inhabitants 897: female 1012.' The
Cossacks' houses are all raised on pillars two and a half
feet from the ground. They are carefully thatched with
reeds and have large carved gables. If not new they are at
least all straight and clean, with high porches of different

shapes; and they are not built close together but have ample space around them, and are all picturesquely placed along broad streets and lanes. In front of the large bright windows of many of the houses, beyond the kitchen gardens, dark green poplars and acacias with their delicate pale verdure and scented v'hite blossoms overtop the houses, and beside them grow flaunting yellow sunflowers, creepers, and grape vines. In the broad open square are three shops where drapery, sunflower and pumpkin seeds, locust beans and gingerbreads are sold; and surrounded by a tall fence, loftier and larger than the other houses, stands the Regimental Commander's dwelling with its casement windows, behind a row of tall poplars. Few people are to be seen in the streets of the village on week-days, especially in summer. The young men are on duty in the cordons or on military expeditions; the old ones are fishing or helping the women in the orchards and gardens. Only the very old, the sick, and the children, remain at home.

V

It was one of those wonderful evenings that occur only in the Caucasus. The sun had sunk behind the mountains but it was still light. The evening glow had spread over a third of the sky, and against its brilliancy the dull white immensity of the mountains was sharply defined. The air was rarefied, motionless, and full of sound. The shadow of the mountains reached for several miles over the steppe. The steppe, the opposite side of the river, and the roads, were all deserted. If very occasionally mounted men appeared, the Cossacks in the cordon and the Chéchens in their *aouls* (villages) watched them with surprised curiosity and tried to guess who those questionable men could be. At nightfall people from fear of one another flock to their dwellings, and only birds and beasts fearless of man prowl in those deserted spaces. Talking merrily, the women who have been tying up the vines hurry away from the gardens before sunset. The vineyards, like all the surrounding district, are deserted, but the villages become very animated at that time of the evening. From all sides, walking, riding, or driving in their creaking carts, people move towards the village. Girls with their smocks tucked up and twigs in their hands run chatting merrily to the village gates to meet the cattle that are crowding together in a cloud of dust and mosquitoes which they bring with them from the steppe. The well-fed cows and buffaloes disperse at a run all over the streets and Cossack women in coloured *beshmets* go to and fro among them. You can hear their merry laughter and shrieks mingling with the lowing of the cattle. There an armed and mounted Cossack, on leave from the cordon, rides up to a hut and, leaning towards the window, knocks. In answer to the knock the handsome head of a young woman appears at the window and you can hear caressing, laughing voices. There a tattered Nogáy labourer, with prominent cheekbones, brings a load of reeds from the steppes, turns his creaking cart into the Cossack captain's broad and clean courtyard, and lifts the yoke off the oxen that stand tossing their heads while he and his master shout to one another in Tartar. Past a puddle that reaches nearly across the street, a barefooted Cossack woman with a bundle of firewood on her back makes her laborious way by clinging to the fences, holding her smock high and exposing her white legs. A Cossack returning from shooting calls out in jest: 'Lift it higher, shameless thing!' and points his gun at her. The woman lets down her smock and drops the wood. An old Cossack, returning home from fishing with his trousers tucked up and his hairy grey chest uncovered, has a net across his shoulder containing silvery fish that are still struggling; and to take a short cut climbs over his neighbour's broken fence and gives a tug to his coat which has caught on the fence. There a woman is dragging a dry branch along and from round the corner comes the sound of an axe. Cossack children, spinning their tops wherever there is a smooth place in the street, are shrieking; women are climbing over fences to avoid going round. From every chimney rises the odorous *kisyak* smoke. From every homestead comes the sound of increased bustle, percursor to the stillness of night.

Granny Ulítka, the wife of the Cossack cornet who is also teacher in the regimental school, goes out to the gates of her yard like the other women, and waits for the cattle which her daughter Maryánka is driving along the street. Before she has had time fully to open the wattle gate in the fence, an enormous buffalo cow surrounded by mosquitoes rushes up bellowing and squeezes in. Several well-fed cows slowly follow her, their large eyes gazing with recognition at their mistress as they swish their sides with their tails. The beautiful and shapely Maryánka enters at the gate and throwing away her switch quickly slams the gate to and rushes with all the speed of her nimble feet to separate and drive the cattle into their sheds. 'Take off your slippers, you devil's wench!' shouts her mother, 'you've worn them into holes!' Maryánka is not at all offended at being called a 'devil's wench', but accepting it as a term of endearment cheerfully goes on with her task. Her face is covered with a kerchief tied round her head. She is wearing a pink smock and a green *beshmet*. She disappears inside the lean-to shed in the yard, following the big fat cattle; and from the shed comes her voice as she speaks gently and persuasively to the buffalo: 'Won't she stand still? What a creature! Come now, come old dear!' Soon the girl and the old woman pass from the shed to the dairy carrying two large pots of milk, the day's yield. From the dairy chimney rises a thin cloud of *kisyak* smoke: the milk is being used to make into clotted cream. The girl makes up the fire while her mother goes to the gate. Twilight has fallen on the village. The air is full of the smell of vegetables, cattle, and scented *kisyak* smoke. From the gates and along the streets Cossack women come running, carrying lighted rags. From the yards one hears the snorting and quiet chewing of the cattle eased of their milk, while in the street only the voices of women and children sound as they call to one another. It is rare on a week-day to hear the drunken voice of a man.

One of the Cossack wives, a tall, masculine old woman, approaches Granny Ulítka from the homestead opposite and asks her for a light. In her hand she holds a rag.

'Have you cleared up, Granny?'

'The girl is lighting the fire. Is it fire you want?' says Granny Ulítka, proud of being able to oblige her neighbour.

Both women enter the hut, and coarse hands unused to dealing with small articles tremblingly lift the lid of a match-box, which is a rarity in the Caucasus. The masculine-looking new-comer sits down on the doorstep with the evident intention of having a chat.

'And is your man at the school, Mother?' she asked.

'He's always teaching the youngsters, Mother. But he writes that he'll come home for the holidays,' said the cornet's wife.

'Yes, he's a clever man, one sees; it all comes useful.'

'Of course it does.'

'And my Lukáshka is at the cordon; they won't let
him come home,' said the visitor, though the cornet's
wife had known all this long ago. She wanted to talk about
her Lukáshka whom she had lately fitted out for service
in the Cossack regiment, and whom she wished to marry to
the cornet's daughter, Maryánka.

'So he's at the cordon?'

'He is, Mother. He's not been home since last holidays.
The other day I sent him some shirts by Fómushkin. He
says he's all right, and that his superiors are satisfied. He
says they are looking out for *abreks* again. Lukáshka is
quite happy, he says.'

'Ah well, thank God,' said the cornet's wife. ' "Snatcher"
is certainly the only word for him.' Lukáshka was surnamed
'the Snatcher' because of his bravery in snatching a boy
from a watery grave, and the cornet's wife alluded to
this, wishing in her turn to say something agreeable to
Lukáshka's mother.

'I thank God, Mother, that he's a good son! He's a fine
fellow, everyone praises him,' says Lukáshka's mother.
'All I wish is to get him married; then I could die in peace.'

'Well, aren't there plenty of young women in the village?'
answered the cornet's wife slyly as she carefully replaced
the lid of the match-box with her horny hands.

'Plenty, Mother, plenty,' remarked Lukáshka's mother,
shaking her head. 'There's your girl now, your Maryánka
—that's the sort of girl! You'd have to search through the
whole place to find such another!'

The cornet's wife knows what Lukáshka's mother is
after, but though she believes him to be a good Cossack
she hangs back: first because she is a cornet's wife and
rich, while Lukáshka is the son of a simple Cossack and
fatherless, secondly because she does not want to part with
her daughter yet, but chiefly because propriety demands it.

'Well, when Maryánka grows up she'll be marriageable
too,' she answers soberly and modestly.

'I'll send the matchmakers to you—I'll send them! Only
let me get the vineyard done and then we'll come and make
our bows to you,' says Lukáshka's mother. 'And we'll
make our bows to Elias Vasílich too.'

'Elias, indeed!' says the cornet's wife proudly. 'It's to me
you must speak! All in its own good time.'

Lukáshka's mother sees by the stern face of the cornet's wife that it is not the time to say anything more just now, so she lights her rag with the match and says, rising: 'Don't refuse us, think of my words. I'll go, it is time to light the fire.'

As she crosses the road swinging the burning rag, she meets Maryánka, who bows.

'Ah, she's a regular queen, a splendid worker, that girl!' she thinks, looking at the beautiful maiden. 'What need for her to grow any more? It's time she was married and to a good home; married to Lukáshka!'

But Granny Ulítka had her own cares and she remained sitting on the threshold thinking hard about something, till the girl called her.

VI

The male population of the village spend their time on military expeditions and in the cordon—or 'at their posts', as the Cossacks say. Towards evening, that same Lukáshka the Snatcher, about whom the old women had been talking, was standing on a watch-tower of the Nízhni-Protótsk post situated on the very banks of the Térek. Leaning on the railing of the tower and screwing up his eyes, he looked now far into the distance beyond the Térek, now down at his fellow Cossacks, and occasionally he addressed the latter. The sun was already approaching the snowy range that gleamed white above the fleecy clouds. The clouds undulating at the base of the mountains grew darker and darker. The clearness of evening was noticeable in the air. A sense of freshness came from the woods, though round the post it was still hot. The voices of the talking Cossacks vibrated more sonorously than before. The moving mass of the Térek's rapid brown waters contrasted more vividly with its motionless banks. The waters were beginning to subside and here and there the wet sands gleamed drab on the banks and in the shallows. The other side of the river, just opposite the cordon, was deserted; only an immense waste of low-growing reeds stretched far away to the very foot of the mountains. On the low bank, a little to one side, could be seen the flat-roofed clay houses and the funnel-shaped chimneys of a Chéchen village. The sharp eyes of the Cossack who stood on the watch-tower followed, through the evening smoke of the pro-Russian village, the tiny moving figures of the Chéchen women visible in the distance in their red and blue garments.

Although the Cossacks expected *abreks* to cross over and attack them from the Tartar side at any moment, especially as it was May when the woods by the Térek are so dense that it is difficult to pass through them on foot and the river is shallow enough in places for a horseman to ford it, and despite the fact that a couple of days before a Cossack had arrived with a circular from the commander of the regiment announcing that spies had reported the intention of a party of some eight men to cross the Térek, and ordering special vigilance—no special vigilance was being observed in the cordon. The Cossacks, unarmed and with their horses unsaddled just as if they were at home, spent their time some in fishing, some in drinking, and some in hunting. Only the horse of the man on duty was saddled, and with its feet hobbled was moving about by the brambles near the wood, and only the sentinel had his Circassian coat on and carried a gun and sword. The corporal, a tall thin Cossack with an exceptionally long back and small hands and feet, was sitting on the earth-bank of a hut with his *beshmet* unbuttoned. On his face was the lazy, bored expression of a superior, and having shut his eyes he dropped his head upon the palm first of one hand and then of the other. An elderly Cossack with a broad greyish-black beard was lying in his shirt, girdled with a black strap, close to the river and gazing lazily at the waves of the Térek as they monotonously foamed and swirled. Others, also overcome by the heat and half naked, were rinsing clothes in the Térek, plaiting a fishing line, or humming tunes as they lay on the hot sand of the river bank. One Cossack, with a thin face much burnt by the sun, lay near the hut evidently dead drunk, by a wall which though it had been in shadow some two hours previously was now exposed to the sun's fierce slanting rays.

Lukáshka, who stood on the watch-tower, was a tall handsome lad about twenty years old and very like his mother. His face and whole build, in spite of the angularity of youth, indicated great strength, both physical and moral. Though he had only lately joined the Cossacks at the front, it was evident from the expression of his face and

the calm assurance of his attitude that he had already acquired the somewhat proud and warlike bearing peculiar
to Cossacks and to men generally who continually carry
arms, and that he felt he was a Cossack and fully knew
his own value. His ample Circassian coat was torn in some
places, his cap was on the back of his head Chéchen
fashion, and his leggings had slipped below his knees.
His clothing was not rich, but he wore it with that
peculiar Cossack foppishness which consists in imitating
the Chéchen brave. Everything on a real brave is ample,
ragged, and neglected, only his weapons are costly. But
these ragged clothes and these weapons are belted and
worn with a certain air and matched in a certain manner,
neither of which can be acquired by everybody and which
at once strike the eye of a Cossack or a hillsman. Lukáshka
had this resemblance to a brave. With his hands folded
under his sword, and his eyes nearly closed, he kept looking at the distant Tartar village. Taken separately his
features were not beautiful, but anyone who saw his stately
carriage and his dark-browed intelligent face would involuntarily say, 'What a fine fellow!'

'Look at the women, what a lot of them are walking
about in the village,' said he in a sharp voice, languidly
showing his brilliant white teeth and not addressing anyone in particular.

Nazárka who was lying below immediately lifted his
head and remarked:

'They must be going for water.'

'Supposing one scared them with a gun?' said Lukáshka,
laughing, 'Wouldn't they be frightened?'

'It wouldn't reach.'

'What! Mine would carry beyond. Just wait a bit, and
when their feast comes round I'll go and visit Giréy Khan
and drink *buza* there,' said Lukáshka, angrily swishing
away the mosquitoes which attached themselves to him.

A rustling in the thicket drew the Cossack's attention.
A pied mongrel half-setter, searching for a scent and violently wagging its scantily furred tail, came running to the
cordon. Lukáshka recognized the dog as one belonging to
his neighbour, Uncle Eróshka, a hunter, and saw, following
it through the thicket, the approaching figure of the hunter
himself.

Uncle Eróshka was a gigantic Cossack with a broad,

snow-white beard and such broad shoulders and chest that in the wood, where there was no one to compare him with, he did not look particularly tall, so well proportioned were his powerful limbs. He wore a tattered coat and, over the bands with which his legs were swathed, sandals made of undressed deer's hide tied on with strings; while on his head he had a rough little white cap. He carried over one shoulder a screen to hide behind when shooting pheasants, and a bag containing a hen for luring hawks, and a small falcon; over the other shoulder, attached by a strap, was a wild cat he had killed; and stuck in his belt behind were some little bags containing bullets, gunpowder, and bread, a horse's tail to swish away the mosquitoes, a large dagger in a torn scabbard smeared with old bloodstains, and two dead pheasants. Having glanced at the cordon he stopped.

'Hi, Lyam!' he called to the dog in such a ringing bass that it awoke an echo far away in the wood; and throwing over his shoulder his big gun, of the kind the Cossacks call a 'flint', he raised his cap.

'Had a good day, good people, eh?' he said, addressing the Cossacks in the same strong and cheerful voice, quite without effort, but as loudly as if he were shouting to someone on the other bank of the river.

'Yes, yes, Uncle!' answered from all sides the voices of the young Cossacks.

'What have you seen? Tell us!' shouted Uncle Eróshka, wiping the sweat from his broad red face with the sleeve of his coat.

'Ah, there's a vulture living in the plane tree here, Uncle. As soon as night comes he begins hovering round,' said Nazárka, winking and jerking his shoulder and leg.

'Come, come!' said the old man incredulously.

'Really, Uncle! You must keep watch,' replied Nazárka with a laugh.

The other Cossacks began laughing.

The wag had not seen any vulture at all, but it had long been the custom of the young Cossacks in the cordon to tease and mislead Uncle Eróshka every time he came to them.

'Eh, you fool, always lying!' exclaimed Lukáshka from the tower to Nazárka.

Nazárka was immediately silenced.

'It must be watched. I'll watch,' answered the old man

to the great delight of all the Cossacks. 'But have you seen any boars?'

'Watching for boars, are you?' said the corporal, bending forward and scratching his back with both hands, very pleased at the chance of some distraction. 'It's *abreks* one has to hunt here and not boars! You've not heard anything, Uncle, have you?' he added, needlessly screwing up his eyes and showing his close-set white teeth.

'*Abreks*,' said the old man. 'No, I haven't. I say, have you any *chikhir*? Let me have a drink, there's a good man. I'm really quite done up. When the time comes I'll bring you some fresh meat, I really will. Give me a drink!' he added.

'Well, and are you going to watch?' inquired the corporal, as though he had not heard what the other said.

'I did mean to watch to-night,' replied Uncle Eróshka. 'Maybe, with God's help, I shall kill something for the holiday. Then you shall have a share, you shall indeed!'

'Uncle! Hallo, Uncle!' called out Lukáshka sharply from above, attracting everybody's attention. All the Cossacks looked up at him. 'Just go to the upper water-course, there's a fine herd of boars there. I'm not inventing, really! The other day one of our Cossacks shot one there. I'm telling you the truth,' added he, readjusting the musket at his back and in a tone that showed he was not joking.

'Ah! Lukáshka the Snatcher is here!' said the old man, looking up. 'Where has he been shooting?'

'Haven't you seen? I suppose you're too young!' said Lukáshka. 'Close by the ditch,' he went on seriously with a shake of the head. 'We were just going along the ditch when all at once we heard something crackling, but my gun was in its case. Elias fired suddenly. . . . But I'll show you the place, it's not far. You just wait a bit. I know every one of their footpaths. . . . Daddy Mósev,' said he, turning resolutely and almost commandingly to the corporal, 'it's time to relieve guard!' and holding aloft his gun he began to descend from the watch-tower without waiting for the order.

'Come down!' said the corporal, after Lukáshka had started, and glanced round. 'Is it your turn, Gúrka? Then go. . . . True enough your Lukáshka has become very skilful,' he went on, addressing the old man. 'He keeps going about just like you, he doesn't stay at home. The other day he killed a boar.'

VII

The sun had already set and the shades of night were rapidly spreading from the edge of the wood. The Cossacks finished their task round the cordon and gathered in the hut for supper. Only the old man still stayed under the plane tree watching for the vulture and pulling the string tied to the falcon's leg, but though a vulture was really perching on the plane tree it declined to swoop down on the lure. Lukáshka, singing one song after another, was leisurely placing nets among the very thickest brambles to trap pheasants. In spite of his tall stature and big hands every kind of work, both rough and delicate, prospered under Lukáshka's fingers.

'Hallo, Luke!' came Nazárka's shrill, sharp voice calling him from the thicket close by. 'The Cossacks have gone in to supper.'

Nazárka, with a live pheasant under his arm, forced his way through the brambles and emerged on the foot-path.

'Oh!' said Lukáshka, breaking off in his song, 'where did you get that cock pheasant? I suppose it was in my trap?'

Nazárka was of the same age as Lukáshka and had also only been at the front since the previous spring.

He was plain, thin and puny, with a shrill voice that rang in one's ears. They were neighbours and comrades. Lukáshka was sitting on the grass crosslegged like a Tartar, adjusting his nets.

'I don't know whose it was—yours, I expect.'

'Was it beyond the pit by the plane tree? Then it is mine! I set the nets last night.'

Lukáshka rose and examined the captured pheasant. After stroking the dark burnished head of the bird, which rolled its eyes and stretched out its neck in terror, Lukáshka took the pheasant in his hands.

'We'll have it in a pilau to-night. You go and kill and pluck it.'

'And shall we eat it ourselves or give it to the corporal?'

'He has plenty!'

'I don't like killing them,' said Nazárka.

'Give it here!'

Lukáshka drew a little knife from under his dagger and gave it a swift jerk. The bird fluttered, but before it could spread its wings the bleeding head bent and quivered.

'That's how one should do it!' said Lukáshka, throwing down the pheasant. 'It will make a fat pilau.'

Nazárka shuddered as he looked at the bird.

'I say, Lukáshka, that fiend will be sending us to the ambush again to-night,' he said, taking up the bird. (He was alluding to the corporal.) 'He has sent Fómushkin to get wine, and it ought to be his turn. He always puts it on us.'

Lukáshka went whistling along the cordon.

'Take the string with you,' he shouted.

Nazárka obeyed.

'I'll give him a bit of my mind to-day, I really will,' continued Nazárka. 'Let's say we won't go; we're tired out and there's an end of it! No, really, you tell him, he'll listen to you. It's too bad!'

'Get along with you! What a thing to make a fuss about!' said Lukáshka, evidently thinking of something else. 'What bosh! If he made us turn out of the village at night now, that would be annoying: there one can have some fun, but here what is there? It's all one whether we're in the cordon or in ambush. What a fellow you are!'

'And are you going to the village?'

'I'll go for the holidays.'

'Gúrka says your Dunáyka is carrying on with Fómushkin,' said Nazárka suddenly.

'Well, let her go to the devil,' said Lukáshka, showing his regular white teeth, though he did not laugh. 'As if I couldn't find another!'

'Gúrka says he went to her house. Her husband was out and there was Fómushkin sitting and eating pie. Gúrka stopped awhile and then went away, and passing by the window he heard her say, "He's gone, the fiend. . . . Why don't you eat your pie, my own? You needn't go home for the night," she says. And Gúrka under the window says to himself, "That's fine!" '

'You're making it up.'

'No, quite true, by Heaven!'

'Well, if she's found another let her go to the devil,' said Lukáshka, after a pause. 'There's no lack of girls and I was sick of her anyway.'

'Well, see what a devil you are!' said Nazárka. 'You should make up to the cornet's girl, Maryánka. Why doesn't she walk out with any one?'

Lukáshka frowned. 'What of Maryánka? They're all alike,' said he.

'Well, you just try . . .'

'What do you think? Are girls so scarce in the village?' And Lukáshka recommenced whistling, and went along the cordon pulling leaves and branches from the bushes as he went. Suddenly, catching sight of a smooth sapling, he drew the knife from the handle of his dagger and cut it down. 'What a ramrod it will make,' he said, swinging the sapling till it whistled through the air.

The Cossacks were sitting round a low Tartar table on the earthen floor of the clay-plastered outer room of the hut, when the question of whose turn it was to lie in ambush was raised. 'Who is to go to-night?' shouted one of the Cossacks through the open door to the corporal in the next room.

'Who is to go?' the corporal shouted back. 'Uncle Burlák has been and Fómushkin too,' said he, not quite confidently. 'You two had better go, you and Nazárka,' he went on, addressing Lukáshka. 'And Ergushóv must go too; surely he has slept it off?'

'You don't sleep it off yourself so why should he?' said Nazárka in a subdued voice.

The Cossacks laughed.

Ergushóv was the Cossack who had been lying drunk and asleep near the hut. He had only that moment staggered into the room rubbing his eyes.

Lukáshka had already risen and was getting his gun ready.

'Be quick and go! Finish your supper and go!' said the corporal; and without waiting for an expression of consent he shut the door, evidently not expecting the Cossack to obey. 'Of course,' thought he, 'if I hadn't been ordered to I wouldn't send anyone, but an officer might turn up at any moment. As it is, they say eight *abreks* have crossed over.'

'Well, I suppose I must go,' remarked Ergushóv, 'it's the regulation. Can't be helped! The times are such. I say, we must go.'

Meanwhile Lukáshka, holding a big piece of pheasant

to his mouth with both hands and glancing now at Nazárka
now at Ergushóv, seemed quite indifferent to what passed
and only laughed at them both. Before the Cossacks were
ready to go into ambush, Uncle Eróshka, who had been
vainly waiting under the plane tree till night fell, entered
the dark outer room.

'Well, lads,' his loud bass resounded through the low-
roofed room drowning all the other voices, 'I'm going with
you. You'll watch for Chéchens and I for boars!'

VIII

It was quite dark when Uncle Eróshka and the three
Cossacks, in their cloaks and shouldering their guns, left
the cordon and went towards the place on the Térek where
they were to lie in ambush. Nazárka did not want to go at
all, but Lukáshka shouted at him and they soon started.
After they had gone a few steps in silence the Cossacks
turned aside from the ditch and went along a path almost hidden by reeds till they reached the river. On its
bank lay a thick black log cast up by the water. The reeds
around it had been recently beaten down.

'Shall we lie here?' asked Nazárka.

'Why not?' answered Lukáshka. 'Sit down here and I'll
be back in a minute. I'll only show Daddy where to go.'

'This is the best place; here we can see and not be
seen,' said Ergushóv, 'so it's here we'll lie. It's a first-rate
place!'

Nazárka and Ergushóv spread out their cloaks and
settled down behind the log, while Lukáshka went on with
Uncle Eróshka.

'It's not far from here, Daddy,' said Lukáshka, stepping
softly in front of the old man; 'I'll show you where they've
been—I'm the only one that knows, Daddy.'

'Show me! You're a fine fellow, a regular Snatcher!'
replied the old man, also whispering.

Having gone a few steps Lukáshka stopped, stooped
down over a puddle, and whistled. 'That's where they come
to drink, d'you see?' He spoke in a scarcely audible voice,
pointing to fresh hoof-prints.

'Christ bless you,' answered the old man. 'The boar
will be in the hollow beyond the ditch,' he added. 'I'll
watch, and you can go.'

Lukáshka pulled his cloak up higher and walked back

alone, throwing swift glances now to the left at the wall of reeds, now to the Térek rushing by below the bank. 'I daresay he's watching or creeping along somewhere,' thought he of a possible Chéchen hillsman. Suddenly a loud rustling and a splash in the water made him start and seize his musket. From under the bank a boar leapt up —his dark outline showing for a moment against the glassy surface of the water and then disappearing among the reeds. Lukáshka pulled out his gun and aimed, but before he could fire the boar had disappeared in the thicket. Lukáshka spat with vexation and went on. On approaching the ambuscade he halted again and whistled softly. His whistle was answered and he stepped up to his comrades.

Nazárka, all curled up, was already asleep. Ergushóv sat with his legs crossed and moved slightly to make room for Lukáshka.

'How jolly it is to sit here! It's really a good place,' said he. 'Did you take him there?'

'Showed him where,' answered Lukáshka, spreading out his cloak. 'But what a big boar I roused just now close to the water! I expect it was the very one! You must have heard the crash?'

'I did hear a beast crashing through. I knew at once it was a beast. I thought to myself: "Lukáshka has roused a beast," ' Ergushóv said, wrapping himself up in his cloak. 'Now I'll go to sleep,' he added. 'Wake me when the cocks crow. We must have discipline. I'll lie down and have a nap, and then you will have a nap and I'll watch—that's the way.'

'Luckily I don't want to sleep,' answered Lukáshka.

The night was dark, warm, and still. Only on one side of the sky the stars were shining, the other and greater part was overcast by one huge cloud stretching from the mountain-tops. The black cloud, blending in the absence of any wind with the mountains, moved slowly onwards, its curved edges sharply defined against the deep starry sky. Only in front of him could the Cossack discern the Térek and the distance beyond. Behind and on both sides he was surrounded by a wall of reeds. Occasionally the reeds would sway and rustle against one another apparently without cause. Seen from down below, against the clear part of the sky, their waving tufts looked like the feathery branches of trees. Close in front at his very feet was the bank, and at its base the rushing torrent. A little farther on was the moving mass of glassy brown water which eddied rhythmically along the bank and round the shallows. Farther still, water, banks, and cloud all merged together in impenetrable gloom. Along the surface of the water floated black shadows, in which the experienced eyes of the Cossack detected trees carried down by the current. Only very rarely sheet-lightning, mirrored in the water as in a black glass, disclosed the sloping bank opposite. The rhythmic sounds of night—the rustling of the reeds, the snoring of the Cossacks, the hum of mosquitoes, and the rushing water, were every now and then broken by a shot fired in the distance, or by the gurgling of water when a piece of bank slipped down, the splash of a big fish, or the crashing of an animal breaking through the thick undergrowth in the wood. Once an owl flew past along the Térek, flapping one wing against the other rhythmically at every second beat. Just above the Cossack's head it turned towards the wood and then, striking its wings no longer after every other flap but at every flap, it flew to an old plane tree where it rustled about for a long time before settling down among the branches. At every one of these unexpected sounds the watching Cossack listened intently, straining his hearing, and screwing up his eyes while he deliberately felt for his musket.

The greater part of the night was past. The black cloud that had moved westward revealed the clear starry sky from under its torn edge, and the golden upturned crescent of the moon shone above the mountains with a reddish light. The cold began to be penetrating. Nazárka awoke, spoke a little, and fell asleep again. Lukáshka feeling bored got up, drew the knife from his dagger-handle and began to fashion his stick into a ramrod. His head was full of the Chéchens who lived over there in the mountains, and of how their brave lads came across and were not afraid of the Cossacks, and might even now be crossing the river at some other spot. He thrust himself out of his hiding-place and looked along the river but could see nothing. And as he continued looking out at intervals upon the river and at the opposite bank, now dimly distinguishable from the water in the faint moonlight, he no longer thought about the Chéchens but only of when it would be time to wake his comrades, and of going home to the village. In the village he imagined Dunáyka, his 'little soul', as the Cossacks call a man's mistress, and thought of her with vexation. Silvery mists, a sign of coming morning, glittered white above the water, and not far from him young eagles were whistling and flapping their wings. At last the crowing of a cock reached him from the distant village, followed by the long-sustained note of another, which was again answered by yet other voices.

'Time to wake them,' thought Lukáshka, who had finished his ramrod and felt his eyes growing heavy. Turning to his comrades he managed to make out which pair of legs belonged to whom, when it suddenly seemed to him that he heard something splash on the other side of the Térek. He turned again towards the horizon beyond the hills, where day was breaking under the upturned crescent, glanced at the outline of the opposite bank, at the Térek, and at the now distinctly visible driftwood upon it. For one instant it seemed to him that he was moving and that the Térek with the drifting wood remained stationary. Again he peered out. One large black log with a branch particularly attracted his attention. The tree was floating in a strange way right down the middle of the stream, neither rocking nor whirling. It even appeared not to be floating altogether with the current, but to be crossing it in the direction of the shallows. Lukáshka stretching out his neck watched it intently. The tree floated to the shallows, stopped, and shifted in a peculiar manner. Lukáshka thought he saw an arm stretched out from beneath the tree. 'Supposing I killed an *abrek* all by myself!' he thought, and seized his gun with a swift, unhurried movement, putting up his gun-rest, placing the gun upon it, and holding it noiselessly in position. Cocking the trigger, with bated breath he took aim, still peering out intently. 'I won't wake them,' he thought. But his heart began beating so fast that he remained motionless, listening. Suddenly the trunk gave a plunge and again began to float across the stream towards our bank. 'Only not to miss . . .' thought he, and now by the faint light of the moon he caught a glimpse of a Tartar's head in front of the floating wood. He aimed straight at the head which appeared to be quite near—just at the end of his rifle's barrel. He glanced across. 'Right enough it is an *abrek*!' he thought joyfully, and suddenly rising to his knees he again took aim. Having found the sight, barely visible at the end of the long gun, he said: 'In the name of the Father and of the Son', in the Cossack way learnt in his childhood, and pulled the trigger. A flash of lightning lit up for an instant the reeds and the water, and the sharp, abrupt report of the shot was carried across the river, changing into a prolonged roll somewhere in the far distance. The piece of driftwood now floated not across, but with the current, rocking and whirling.

'Stop, I say!' exclaimed Ergushóv, seizing his musket and raising himself behind the log near which he was lying.

'Shut up, you devil!' whispered Lukáshka, grinding his teeth. '*Abreks!*'

'Whom have you shot?' asked Nazárka. 'Who was it, Lukáshka?'

Lukáshka did not answer. He was reloading his gun and watching the floating wood. A little way off it stopped on a sand-bank, and from behind it something large that rocked in the water came into view.

'What did you shoot? Why don't you speak?' insisted the Cossacks.

'*Abreks*, I tell you!' said Lukáshka.

'Don't humbug! Did the gun go off? . . .'

'I've killed an *abrek*, that's what I fired at,' muttered Lukáshka in a voice choked by emotion, as he jumped to his feet. 'A man was swimming . . .' he said, pointing to the sand-bank. 'I killed him. Just look there.'

'Have done with your humbugging!' said Ergushóv again, rubbing his eyes.

'Have done with what? Look there,' said Lukáshka, seizing him by the shoulders and pulling him with such force that Ergushóv groaned.

He looked in the direction in which Lukáshka pointed, and discerning a body immediately changed his tone.

'O Lord! But I say, more will come! I tell you the truth,' said he softly, and began examining his musket. 'That was a scout swimming across: either the others are here already or are not far off on the other side—I tell you for sure!'

Lukáshka was unfastening his belt and taking off his Circassian coat.

'What are you up to, you idiot?' exclaimed Ergushóv. 'Only show yourself and you've lost all for nothing, I tell you true! If you've killed him he won't escape. Let me have a little powder for my musket-pan—you have some? Nazárka, you go back to the cordon and look alive; but don't go along the bank or you'll be killed—I tell you true.'

'Catch me going alone! Go yourself!' said Nazárka angrily.

Having taken off his coat, Lukáshka went down to the bank.

'Don't go in, I tell you!' said Ergushóv, putting some powder on the pan. 'Look, he's not moving. I can see. It's nearly morning; wait till they come from the cordon. You go, Nazárka. You're afraid! Don't be afraid, I tell you.'

'Luke, I say, Lukáshka! Tell us how you did it!' said Nazárka.

Lukáshka changed his mind about going into the water just then. 'Go quick to the cordon and I will watch. Tell the Cossacks to send out the patrol. If the *abreks* are on this side they must be caught,' said he.

'That's what I say. They'll get off,' said Ergushóv, rising. 'True, they must be caught!'

Ergushóv and Nazárka rose and, crossing themselves, started off for the cordon—not along the riverbank but breaking their way through the brambles to reach a path in the wood.

'Now mind, Lukáshka—they may cut you down here, so you'd best keep a sharp look-out, I tell you!'

'Go along; I know,' muttered Lukáshka; and having examined his gun again he sat down behind the log.

He remained alone and sat gazing at the shallows and listening for the Cossacks; but it was some distance to the cordon and he was tormented by impatience. He kept thinking that the other *abreks* who were with the one he had killed would escape. He was vexed with the *abreks* who were going to escape just as he had been with the boar that had escaped the evening before. He glanced round and at the opposite bank, expecting every moment to see a man, and having arranged his gun-rest he was ready to fire. The idea that he might himself be killed never entered his head.

IX

It was growing light. The Chéchen's body which was gently rocking in the shallow water was now clearly visible. Suddenly the reeds rustled not far from Luke and he heard steps and saw the feathery tops of the reeds moving. He set his gun at full cock and muttered: 'In the name of the Father and of the Son,' but when the cock clicked the sound of steps ceased.

'Hullo, Cossacks! Don't kill your Daddy!' said a deep bass voice calmly; and moving the reeds apart Daddy Eróshka came up close to Luke.

'I very nearly killed you, by God I did!' said Lukáshka.

'What have you shot?' asked the old man.

His sonorous voice resounded through the wood and downward along the river, suddenly dispelling the mysterious quiet of night around the Cossack. It was as if everything had suddenly become lighter and more distinct.

'There now, Uncle, you have not seen anything, but I've killed a beast,' said Lukáshka, uncocking his gun and getting up with unnatural calmness.

The old man was staring intently at the white back, now clearly visible, against which the Térek rippled.

'He was swimming with a log on his back. I spied him out! . . . Look there. There! He's got blue trousers, and a gun I think. . . . Do you see?' inquired Luke.

'How can one help seeing?' said the old man angrily, and a serious and stern expression appeared on his face. 'You've killed a brave,' he said, apparently with regret.

'Well, I sat here and suddenly saw something dark on the other side. I spied him when he was still over there. It was as if a man had come there and fallen in. Strange! And a piece of driftwood, a good-sized piece, comes floating, not with the stream but across it; and what do I see but a head appearing from under it! Strange! I stretched out of the reeds but could see nothing; then I rose and he must have heard, the beast, and crept out into the shallow and looked about. "No, you don't!" I said, as soon as he landed and looked round, "you won't get away!" Oh, there was something choking me! I got my gun ready but did not stir, and looked out. He waited a little and then swam out again; and when he came into the moonlight I could see his whole back. "In the name of the Father and of the Son and of the Holy Ghost" . . . and through the smoke I see him struggling. He moaned, or so it seemed to me. "Ah," I thought, "the Lord be thanked, I've killed him!" And when he drifted on to the sand-bank I could see him distinctly: he tried to get up but couldn't. He struggled a bit and then lay down. Everything could be seen. Look, he does not move—he must be dead! The Cossacks have gone back to the cordon in case there should be any more of them.'

'And so you got him!' said the old man. 'He is far away now, my lad! . . .' And again he shook his head sadly.

Just then the sound reached them of breaking bushes and the loud voices of Cossacks approaching along the bank on horseback and on foot. 'Are you bringing the skiff?' shouted Lukáshka.

'You're a trump, Luke! Lug it to the bank!' shouted one of the Cossacks.

Without waiting for the skiff Lukáshka began to undress, keeping an eye all the while on his prey.

'Wait a bit, Nazárka is bringing the skiff,' shouted the corporal.

'You fool! Maybe he is alive and only pretending! Take your dagger with you!' shouted another Cossack.

'Get along,' cried Luke, pulling off his trousers. He quickly undressed and, crossing himself, jumped, plunging with a splash into the river. Then with long strokes of his white arms, lifting his back high out of the water and breathing deeply, he swam across the current of the Térek towards the shallows. A crowd of Cossacks stood on the bank talking loudly. Three horsemen rode off to patrol. The skiff appeared round a bend. Lukáshka stood up on the sand-bank, leaned over the body, and gave it a couple of shakes. 'Quite dead!' he shouted in a shrill voice.

The Chéchen had been shot in the head. He had on a pair of blue trousers, a shirt, and a Circassian coat, and a gun and dagger were tied to his back. Above all these a large branch was tied, and it was this which at first had misled Lukáshka.

'What a carp you've landed!' cried one of the Cossacks who had assembled in a circle, as the body, lifted out of the skiff, was laid on the bank, pressing down the grass.

'How yellow he is!' said another.

'Where have our fellows gone to search? I expect the rest of them are on the other bank. If this one had not been a scout he would not have swum that way. Why else should he swim alone?' said a third.

'Must have been a smart one to offer himself before the others; a regular brave!' said Lukáshka mockingly, shivering as he wrung out his clothes that had got wet on the bank.

'His beard is dyed and cropped.'

'And he has tied a bag with a coat in it to his back.'

'That would make it easier for him to swim,' said some one.

'I say, Lukáshka,' said the corporal, who was holding the dagger and gun taken from the dead man. 'Keep the dagger for yourself and the coat too; but I'll give you three rubles for the gun. You see it has a hole in it,' said he, blowing into the muzzle. 'I want it just for a souvenir.'

Lukáshka did not answer. Evidently this sort of begging vexed him but he knew it could not be avoided.

'See, what a devil!' said he, frowning and throwing down the Chéchen's coat. 'If at least it were a good coat, but it's a mere rag.'

'It'll do to fetch firewood in,' said one of the Cossacks.

'Mósev, I'll go home,' said Lukáshka, evidently forgetting his vexation and wishing to get some advantage out of having to give a present to his superior.

'All right, you may go!'

'Take the body beyond the cordon, lads,' said the corporal, still examining the gun, 'and put a shelter over him from the sun. Perhaps they'll send from the mountains to ransom it.'

'It isn't hot yet,' said someone.

'And supposing a jackal tears him? Would that be well?' remarked another Cossack.

'We'll set a watch; if they should come to ransom him it won't do for him to have been torn.'

'Well, Lukáshka, whatever you do you must stand a pail of vodka for the lads,' said the corporal gaily.

'Of course! That's the custom,' chimed in the Cossacks. 'See what luck God has sent you! Without ever having seen anything of the kind before, you've killed a brave!'

'Buy the dagger and coat and don't be stingy, and I'll let you have the trousers too,' said Lukáshka. 'They're too tight for me; he was a thin devil.'

One Cossack bought the coat for a ruble and another gave the price of two pails of vodka for the dagger.

'Drink, lads! I'll stand you a pail!' said Luke. 'I'll bring it myself from the village.'

'And cut up the trousers into kerchiefs for the girls!' said Nazárka.

The Cossacks burst out laughing.

'Have done laughing!' said the corporal. 'And take the body away. Why have you put the nasty thing by the hut?'

'What are you standing there for? Haul him along, lads!' shouted Lukáshka in a commanding voice to the Cossacks, who reluctantly took hold of the body, obeying him as though he were their chief. After dragging the body along for a few steps the Cossacks let fall the legs, which dropped with a lifeless jerk, and stepping apart they then stood silent for a few moments. Nazárka came up and straightened the head, which was turned to one side so that the round wound above the temple and the whole of the dead man's face were visible. 'See what a mark he has made right in the brain,' he said. 'He won't get lost. His owners will always know him!' No one answered, and again the Angel of Silence flew over the Cossacks.

The sun had risen high and its diverging beams were lighting up the dewy grass. Near by, the Térek murmured in the awakened wood and, greeting the morning, the pheasants called to one another. The Cossacks stood still and silent around the dead man, gazing at him. The brown body, with nothing on but the wet blue trousers held by a girdle over the sunken stomach, was well shaped and handsome. The muscular arms lay stretched straight out by his sides; the blue, freshly shaven, round head with the clotted wound on one side of it was thrown back. The smooth tanned forehead contrasted sharply with the shaven part of the head. The open glassy eyes with lowered pupils stared upwards, seeming to gaze past everything. Under the red trimmed moustache the fine lips, drawn at the corners, seemed stiffened into a smile of good-natured subtle raillery. The fingers of the small hands covered with red hairs were bent inward, and the nails were dyed red.

Lukáshka had not yet dressed. He was wet. His neck was redder and his eyes brighter than usual, his broad jaws twitched, and from his healthy body a hardly perceptible steam rose in the fresh morning air.

'He too was a man!' he muttered, evidently admiring the corpse.

'Yes, if you had fallen into his hands you would have had short shrift,' said one of the Cossacks.

The Angel of Silence had taken wing. The Cossacks began bustling about and talking. Two of them went to cut brushwood for a shelter, others strolled towards the cordon. Luke and Nazárka ran to get ready to go to the village.

Half an hour later they were both on their way homewards, talking incessantly and almost running through the dense woods which separated the Térek from the village.

'Mind, don't tell her I sent you, but just go and find out if her husband is at home,' Luke was saying in his shrill voice.

'And I'll go round to Yámka too,' said the devoted Nazárka. 'We'll have a spree, shall we?'

'When should we have one if not to-day?' replied Luke.

When they reached the village the two Cossacks drank, and lay down to sleep till evening.

X

On the third day after the events above described, two companies of a Caucasian infantry regiment arrived at the Cossack village of Novomlínsk. The horses had been unharnessed and the companies' wagons were standing in the square. The cooks had dug a pit, and with logs gathered from various yards (where they had not been sufficiently securely stored) were now cooking the food; the pay-sergeants were settling accounts with the soldiers. The Service Corps men were driving piles in the ground to which to tie the horses, and the quartermasters were going about the streets just as if they were at home, showing officers and men to their quarters. Here were green ammunition boxes in a line, the company's carts, horses, and cauldrons in which buckwheat porridge was being cooked. Here were the captain and the lieutenant and the sergeant-major, Onísim Mikháylovich, and all this was in the Cossack village where it was reported that the companies were ordered to take up their quarters: therefore they were at home here. But why they were stationed there, who the Cossacks were, and whether they wanted the troops to be there, and whether they were Old Believers or not—was all quite immaterial. Having received their pay and been dismissed, tired out and covered with dust, the soldiers noisily and in disorder, like a swarm of bees about to settle, spread over the squares and streets; quite regardless of the Cossacks' ill will, chattering merrily and with their muskets clinking, by twos and threes they entered the huts and hung up their accoutrements, unpacked their bags, and bantered the women. At their favourite spot, round the porridge-cauldrons, a large group of soldiers assembled and with little pipes between their teeth they gazed, now at the smoke which rose into the hot sky, becoming visible when it thickened into white clouds as it rose, and now at the camp fires which were quivering in the pure air like molten glass, and bantered and made fun of the Cossack men and women because they do not live at all like Russians. In all the yards one could see soldiers and hear their laughter and the exasperated and shrill cries of Cossack women defending their houses and refusing to give the soldiers water or cooking utensils. Little boys and girls, clinging to their mothers and to each other, followed all the movements of the troopers (never before seen by them) with frightened curiosity, or ran after them at a respectful distance. The old Cossacks came out silently and dismally and sat on the earthen embankments of their huts, and watched the soldiers' activity with an air of leaving it all to the will of God without understanding what would come of it.

Olénin, who had joined the Caucasian Army as a cadet three months before, was quartered in one of the best houses in the village, the house of the cornet, Elias Vasílich —that is to say at Granny Ulítka's.

'Goodness knows what it will be like, Dmítri Andréich,' said the panting Vanyúsha to Olénin, who, dressed in a Circassian coat and mounted on a Kabardá horse which he had bought in Gróznoe, was after a five-hours' march gaily entering the yard of the quarters assigned to him.

'Why, what's the matter?' he asked, caressing his horse and looking merrily at the perspiring, dishevelled, and worried Vanyúsha, who had arrived with the baggage wagons and was unpacking.

Olénin looked quite a different man. In place of his clean-shaven lips and chin he had a youthful moustache and a small beard. Instead of a sallow complexion, the result of nights turned into day, his cheeks, his forehead, and the skin behind his ears were now red with healthy sunburn. In place of a clean new black suit he wore a dirty white Circassian coat with a deeply pleated skirt, and he bore arms. Instead of a freshly starched collar, his neck was tightly clasped by the red band of his silk *beshmet*. He wore Circassian dress but did not wear it well, and anyone would have known him for a Russian and not a Tartar brave. It was the thing—but not the real thing. But for all that, his whole person breathed health, joy, and satisfaction.

'Yes, it seems funny to you,' said Vanyúsha, 'but just try to talk to these people yourself: they set themselves against one and there's an end of it. You can't get as much as a word out of them.' Vanyúsha angrily threw down a pail on the threshold. 'Somehow they don't seem like Russians.'

'You should speak to the Chief of the Village!'

'But I don't know where he lives,' said Vanyúsha in an offended tone.

'Who has upset you so?' asked Olénin, looking round.

'The devil only knows. Faugh! There is no real master here. They say he has gone to some kind of *kriga,* and the old woman is a real devil. God preserve us!' answered Vanyúsha, putting his hands to his head. 'How we shall live here I don't know. They are worse than Tartars, I do declare—though they consider themselves Christians! A Tartar is bad enough, but all the same he is more noble. Gone to the *kriga* indeed! What this *kriga* they have invented is, I don't know!' concluded Vanyúsha, and turned aside.

'It's not as it is in the serfs' quarters at home, eh?' chaffed Olénin without dismounting.

'Please sir, may I have your horse?' said Vanyúsha, evidently perplexed by this new order of things but resigning himself to his fate.

'So a Tartar is more noble, eh, Vanyúsha?' repeated Olénin, dismounting and slapping the saddle.

'Yes, you're laughing! You think it funny,' muttered Vanyúsha angrily.

'Come, don't be angry, Vanyúsha,' replied Olénin, still smiling. 'Wait a minute, I'll go and speak to the people of the house; you'll see I shall arrange everything. You don't know what a jolly life we shall have here. Only don't get upset.'

Vanyúsha did not answer. Screwing up his eyes he looked contemptuously after his master, and shook his head. Vanyúsha regarded Olénin as only his master, and Olénin regarded Vanyúsha as only his servant; and they would both have been much surprised if anyone had told them that they were friends, as they really were without knowing it themselves. Vanyúsha had been taken into his proprietor's house when he was only eleven and when Olénin was the same age. When Olénin was fifteen he gave Vanyúsha lessons for a time and taught him to read

French, of which the latter was inordinately proud; and when in specially good spirits he still let off French words, always laughing stupidly when he did so.

Olénin ran up the steps of the porch and pushed open the door of the hut. Maryánka, wearing nothing but a pink smock, as all Cossack women do in the house, jumped away from the door, frightened, and pressing herself against the wall covered the lower part of her face with the broad sleeve of her Tartar smock. Having opened the door wider, Olénin in the semi-darkness of the passage saw the whole tall, shapely figure of the young Cossack girl. With the quick and eager curiosity of youth he involuntarily noticed the firm maidenly form revealed by the fine print smock, and the beautiful black eyes fixed on him with childlike terror and wild curiosity. 'This is *she*,' thought Olénin. 'But there will be many others like her' came at once into his head, and he opened the inner door. Old Granny Ulítka, also dressed only in a smock, was stooping with her back turned to him, sweeping the floor.

'Good-day to you, Mother! I've come about my lodgings,' he began.

The Cossack woman, without unbending, turned her severe but still handsome face towards him.

'What have you come here for? Want to mock at us, eh? I'll teach you to mock; may the black plague seize you!' she shouted, looking askance from under her frowning brow at the new-comer.

Olénin had at first imagined that the way-worn, gallant Caucasian Army (of which he was a member) would be everywhere received joyfully, and especially by the Cossacks, our comrades in the war; and he therefore felt perplexed by this reception. Without losing presence of mind however he tried to explain that he meant to pay for his lodgings, but the old woman would not give him a hearing.

'What have you come for? Who wants a pest like you, with your scraped face? You just wait a bit; when the master returns he'll show you your place. I don't want your dirty money! A likely thing—just as if we had never seen any! You'll stink the house out with your beastly tobacco and want to put it right with money! Think we've never seen a pest! May you be shot in your bowels and your heart!' shrieked the old woman in a piercing voice, interrupting Olénin.

'It seems Vanyúsha was right!' thought Olénin. '"A Tartar would be nobler",' and followed by Granny Ulítka's abuse he went out of the hut. As he was leaving, Maryánka, still wearing only her pink smock, but with her forehead covered down to her eyes by a white kerchief, suddenly slipped out from the passage past him. Pattering rapidly down the steps with her bare feet she ran from the porch, stopped, and looking round hastily with laughing eyes at the young man, vanished round the corner of the hut.

Her firm youthful step, the untamed look of the eyes glistening from under the white kerchief, and the firm stately build of the young beauty, struck Olénin even more powerfully than before. 'Yes, it must be *she*,' he thought, and troubling his head still less about the lodgings, he kept looking round at Maryánka as he approached Vanyúsha.

'There you see, the girl too is quite savage, just like a wild filly!' said Vanyúsha, who though still busy with the luggage wagon had now cheered up a bit. '*La fame!*' he added in a loud triumphant voice and burst out laughing.

XI

Towards evening the master of the house returned from his fishing, and having learnt that the cadet would pay for the lodging, pacified the old woman and satisfied Vanyúsha's demands.

Everything was arranged in the new quarters. Their hosts moved into the winter hut and let their summer hut to the cadet for three rubles a month. Olénin had something to eat and went to sleep. Towards evening he woke up, washed and made himself tidy, dined, and having lit a cigarette sat down by the window that looked onto the street. It was cooler. The slanting shadow of the hut with its ornamental gables fell across the dusty road and even bent upwards at the base of the wall of the house opposite. The steep reed-thatched roof of that house shone in the rays of the setting sun. The air grew fresher. Everything was peaceful in the village. The soldiers had settled down and become quiet. The herds had not yet been driven home and the people had not returned from their work.

Olénin's lodging was situated almost at the end of the village. At rare intervals, from somewhere far beyond the Térek in those parts whence Olénin had just come (the

Chéchen or the Kumýtsk plain), came muffled sounds of firing. Olénin was feeling very well contented after three months of bivouac life. His newly washed face was fresh and his powerful body clean (an unaccustomed sensation after the campaign) and in all his rested limbs he was conscious of a feeling of tranquillity and strength. His mind, too, felt fresh and clear. He thought of the campaign and of past dangers. He remembered that he had faced them no worse than other men, and that he was accepted as a comrade among valiant Caucasians. His Moscow recollections were left behind Heaven knows how far! The old life was wiped out and a quite new life had begun in which there were as yet no mistakes. Here as a new man among new men he could gain a new and good reputation. He was conscious of a youthful and unreasoning joy of life. Looking now out of the window at the boys spinning their tops in the shadow of the house, now round his neat new lodging, he thought how pleasantly he would settle down to this new Cossack village life. Now and then he glanced at the mountains and the blue sky, and an appreciation of the solemn grandeur of nature mingled with his reminiscences and dreams. His new life had begun, not as he imagined it would when he left Moscow, but unexpectedly well. 'The mountains, the mountains, the mountains!' they permeated all his thoughts and feelings.

'He's kissed his dog and licked the jug! . . . Daddy Eróshka has kissed his dog!' suddenly the little Cossacks who had been spinning their tops under the window shouted, looking towards the side street. 'He's drunk his bitch, and his dagger!' shouted the boys, crowding together and stepping backwards.

These shouts were addressed to Daddy Eróshka, who with his gun on his shoulder and some pheasants hanging at his girdle was returning from his shooting expedition.

'I have done wrong, lads, I have!' he said, vigorously swinging his arms and looking up at the windows on both sides of the street. 'I have drunk the bitch; it was wrong,' he repeated, evidently vexed but pretending not to care.

Olénin was surprised by the boys' behavior towards the old hunter, but was still more struck by the expressive, intelligent face and the powerful build of the man whom they called Daddy Eróshka.

'Here Daddy, here Cossack!' he called. 'Come here!' The old man looked into the window and stopped.

'Good evening, good man,' he said, lifting his little cap off his cropped head.

'Good evening, good man,' replied Olénin. 'What is it the youngsters are shouting at you?'

Daddy Eróshka came up to the window. 'Why, they're teasing the old man. No matter, I like it. Let them joke about their old daddy,' he said with those firm musical intonations with which old and venerable people speak. 'Are you an army commander?' he added.

'No, I am a cadet. But where did you kill those pheasants?' asked Olénin.

'I dispatched these three hens in the forest,' answered the old man, turning his broad back towards the window to show the hen pheasants which were hanging with their heads tucked into his belt and staining his coat with blood. 'Haven't you seen any?' he asked. 'Take a brace if you like! Here you are,' and he handed two of the pheasants in at the window. 'Are you a sportsman yourself?' he asked.

'I am. During the campaign I killed four myself.'

'Four? What a lot!' said the old man sarcastically. 'And are you a drinker? Do you drink *chikhir?*'

'Why not? I like a drink.'

'Ah, I see you are a trump! We shall be *kunaks*, you and I,' said Daddy Eróshka.

'Step in,' said Olénin. 'We'll have a drop of *chikhir.*'

'I might as well,' said the old man, 'but take the pheasants.' The old man's face showed that he liked the cadet. He had seen at once that he could get free drinks from him, and that therefore it would be all right to give him a brace of pheasants.

Soon Daddy Eróshka's figure appeared in the doorway of the hut, and it was only then that Olénin became fully conscious of the enormous size and sturdy build of this man, whose red-brown face with its perfectly white broad beard was all furrowed by deep lines produced by age and toil. For an old man, the muscles of his legs, arms, and shoulders were quite exceptionally large and prominent. There were deep scars on his head under the short-cropped hair. His thick sinewy neck was covered with deep intersecting folds like a bull's. His horny hands were bruised and scratched. He stepped lightly and easily over the threshold, unslung his gun and placed it in a corner, and casting a rapid glance round the room noted the value of the goods and chattels deposited in the hut, and with out-turned toes stepped softly, in his sandals of raw hide, into the middle of the room. He brought with him a penetrating but not unpleasant smell of *chikhir* wine, vodka, gunpowder, and congealed blood.

Daddy Eróshka bowed down before the icons, smoothed his beard, and approaching Olénin held out his thick brown hand. '*Koshkildy*,' said he; 'That is Tartar for "Good-day"—"Peace be unto you," it means in their tongue.'

'*Koshkildy*, I know,' answered Olénin, shaking hands.

'Eh, but you don't, you won't know the right order! Fool!' said Daddy Eróshka, shaking his head reproachfully. 'If anyone says "*Koshkildy*" to you, you must say "*Allah rasi bo sun*," that is, "God save you." That's the way, my dear fellow, and not "*Koshkildy*." But I'll teach you all about it. We had a fellow here, Elias Mosévich, one of your Russians, he and I were *kunaks*. He was a trump, a drunkard, a thief, a sportsman—and what a sportsman! I taught him everything.'

'And what will you teach me?' asked Olénin, who was becoming more and more interested in the old man.

'I'll take you hunting and teach you to fish. I'll show you Chéchens and find a girl for you, if you like—even that! That's the sort I am! I'm a wag!'—and the old man laughed. 'I'll sit down. I'm tired. *Karga?*' he added inquiringly.

'And what does "*Karga*" mean?' asked Olénin.

'Why, that means "All right" in Georgian. But I say it just so. It is a way I have, it's my favourite word. *Karga, Karga.* I say it just so; in fun I mean. Well, lad, won't you order the *chikhir*? You've got an orderly, haven't you? Hey, Iván!' shouted the old man. 'All your soldiers are Iváns. Is yours Iván?'

'True enough, his name is Iván—Vanyúsha. Here Vanyúsha! Please get some *chikhir* from our landlady and bring it here.'

'Iván or Vanyúsha, that's all one. Why are all your soldiers Iváns? Iván, old fellow,' said the old man, 'you tell them to give you some from the barrel they have begun. They have the best *chikhir* in the village. But don't give more than thirty kopeks for the quart, mind, because that witch would be only too glad. . . . Our people are anathema people; stupid people,' Daddy Eróshka con-

tinued in a confidential tone after Vanyúsha had gone out.
'They do not look upon you as on men, you are worse than
a Tartar in their eyes. "Worldly Russians" they say. But
as for me, though you are a soldier you are still a man,
and have a soul in you. Isn't that right? Elias Mosévich
was a soldier, yet what a treasure of a man he was! Isn't
that so, my dear fellow? That's why our people don't like
me; but I don't care! I'm a merry fellow, and I like everybody. I'm Eróshka; yes, my dear fellow.'

And the old Cossack patted the young man affectionately
on the shoulder.

XII

Vanyúsha, who meanwhile had finished his housekeep-
ing arrangements and had even been shaved by the company's barber and had pulled his trousers out of his high
boots as a sign that the company was stationed in comfortable quarters, was in excellent spirits. He looked attentively but not benevolently at Eróshka, as at a wild
beast he had never seen before, shook his head at the
floor which the old man had dirtied and, having taken two
bottles from under a bench, went to the landlady.

'Good evening, kind people,' he said, having made up
his mind to be very gentle. 'My master has sent me to get
some *chikhir*. Will you draw some for me, good folk?'

The old woman gave no answer. The girl, who was arranging the kerchief on her head before a little Tartar
mirror, looked round at Vanyúsha in silence.

'I'll pay money for it, honoured people,' said Vanyúsha,
jingling the coppers in his pocket. 'Be kind to us and we
too will be kind to you,' he added.

'How much?' asked the old woman abruptly.

'A quart.'

'Go, my own, draw some for them,' said Granny Ulítka
to her daughter. 'Take it from the cask that's begun, my
precious.'

The girl took the keys and a decanter and went out
of the hut with Vanyúsha.

'Tell me, who is that young woman?' asked Olénin,
pointing to Maryánka, who was passing the window. The
old man winked and nudged the young man with his elbow.

'Wait a bit,' said he and reached out of the window.
'Khm,' he coughed, and bellowed, 'Maryánka dear. Hallo,
Maryánka, my girlie, won't you love me, darling? I'm a

wag,' he added in a whisper to Olénin. The girl, not turning her head and swinging her arms regularly and vigorously, passed the window with the peculiarly smart and
bold gait of a Cossack woman and only turned her dark
shaded eyes slowly towards the old man.

'Love me and you'll be happy,' shouted Eróshka, winking, and he looked questioningly at the cadet.

'I'm a fine fellow, I'm a wag!' he added. 'She's a regular
queen, that girl. Eh?'

'She is lovely,' said Olénin. 'Call her here!'

'No, no,' said the old man. 'For that one a match is being arranged with Lukáshka, Luke, a fine Cossack, a brave,
who killed an *abrek* the other day. I'll find you a better
one. I'll find you one that will be all dressed up in silk and
silver. Once I've said it I'll do it. I'll get you a regular
beauty!'

'You, an old man—and say such things,' replied Olénin.
'Why, it's a sin!'

'A sin? Where's the sin?' said the old man emphatically.
'A sin to look at a nice girl? A sin to have some fun with
her? Or is it a sin to love her? Is that so in your parts?
. . . No, my dear fellow, it's not a sin, it's salvation! God
made you and God made the girl too. He made it all; so
it is no sin to look at a nice girl. That's what she was made
for; to be loved and to give joy. That's how I judge it, my
good fellow.'

Having crossed the yard and entered a cool dark store-
room filled with barrels, Maryánka went up to one of them
and repeating the usual prayer plunged a dipper into it.
Vanyúsha standing in the doorway smiled as he looked at
her. He thought it very funny that she had only a smock
on, close-fitting behind and tucked up in front, and still
funnier that she wore a necklace of silver coins. He thought
this quite un-Russian and that they would all laugh in the
serfs' quarters at home if they saw a girl like that. '*La fille
comme c'est tres bien*, for a change,' he thought. 'I'll tell
that to my master.'

'What are you standing in the light for, you devil!' the
girl suddenly shouted. 'Why don't you pass me the decanter!'

Having filled the decanter with cool red wine, Maryánka
handed it to Vanyúsha.

'Give the money to Mother,' she said, pushing away the
hand in which he held the money.

Vanyúsha laughed.

'Why are you so cross, little dear?' he said good-naturedly, irresolutely shuffling with his feet while the girl was covering the barrel.

She began to laugh.

'And you! Are you kind?'

'We, my master and I, are very kind,' Vanyúsha answered decidedly. 'We are so kind that wherever we have stayed our hosts were always very grateful. It's because he's generous.'

The girl stood listening.

'And is your master married?' she asked.

'No. The master is young and unmarried, because noble gentlemen can never marry young,' said Vanyúsha didactically.

'A likely thing! See what a fed-up buffalo he is—and too young to marry! Is he the chief of you all?' she asked.

'My master is a cadet; that means he's not yet an officer, but he's more important than a general—he's an important man! Because not only our colonel, but the Tsar himself, knows him,' proudly explained Vanyúsha. 'We are not like those other beggars in the line regiment, and our papa himself was a Senator. He had more than a thousand serfs, all his own, and they send us a thousand rubles at a time. That's why everyone likes us. Another may be a captain but have no money. What's the use of that?'

'Go away. I'll lock up,' said the girl, interrupting him.

Vanyúsha brought Olénin the wine and announced that *'La fille c'est tres joulie,'* and, laughing stupidly, at once went out.

XIII

Meanwhile the tattoo had sounded in the village square. The people had returned from their work. The herd lowed as in clouds of golden dust it crowded at the village gate. The girls and the women hurried through the streets and yards, turning in their cattle. The sun had quite hidden itself behind the distant snowy peaks. One pale bluish shadow spread over land and sky. Above the darkened gardens stars just discernible were kindling, and the sounds were gradually hushed in the village. The cattle having been attended to and left for the night, the women came out and gathered at the corners of the streets and, cracking sunflower seeds with their teeth, settled down on the earthen embankments of the houses. Later on Maryánka, having finished milking the buffalo and the other two cows, also joined one of these groups.

The group consisted of several women and girls and one old Cossack man.

They were talking about the *abrek* who had been killed. The Cossack was narrating and the women questioning him.

'I expect he'll get a handsome reward,' said one of the women.

'Of course. It's said that they'll send him a cross.'

'Mósev did try to wrong him. Took the gun away from him, but the authorities at Kizlyár heard of it.'

'A mean creature that Mósev is!'

'They say Lukáshka has come home,' remarked one of the girls.

'He and Nazárka are merry-making at Yámka's.' (Yámka was an unmarried, disreputable Cossack woman who kept an illicit pot-house.) 'I heard say they had drunk half a pailful.'

'What luck that Snatcher has,' somebody remarked. 'A real snatcher. But there's no denying he's a fine lad, smart enough for anything, a right-minded lad! His father was just such another, Daddy Kiryák was: he takes after his father. When he was killed the whole village howled. Look, there they are,' added the speaker, pointing to the Cossacks who were coming down the street towards them. 'And Ergushóv has managed to come along with them too! The drunkard!'

Lukáshka, Nazárka, and Ergushóv, having emptied half a pail of vodka, were coming towards the girls. The faces of all three, but especially that of the old Cossack, were redder than usual. Ergushóv was reeling and kept laughing and nudging Nazárka in the ribs.

'Why are you not singing?' he shouted to the girls. 'Sing to our merry-making, I tell you!'

They were welcomed with the words, 'Had a good day? Had a good day?'

'Why sing? It's not a holiday,' said one of the women. 'You're tight, so you go and sing.'

Ergushóv roared with laughter and nudged Nazárka.

'You'd better sing. And I'll begin too. I'm clever, I tell you.'

'Are you asleep, fair ones?' said Nazárka. 'We've come from the cordon to drink your health. We've already drunk Lukáshka's health.'

Lukáshka, when he reached the group, slowly raised his cap and stopped in front of the girls. His broad cheek-bones and neck were red. He stood and spoke softly and sedately, but in his tranquillity and sedateness there was more of animation and strength than in all Nazárka's loquacity and bustle. He reminded one of a playful colt that with a snort and a flourish of its tail suddenly stops short and stands as though nailed to the ground with all four feet. Lukáshka stood quietly in front of the girls, his eyes laughed, and he spoke but little as he glanced now at his drunken companions and now at the girls. When Maryánka joined the group he raised his cap with a firm deliberate movement, moved out of her way and then stepped in front of her with one foot a little forward and with his thumbs in his belt, fingering his dagger. Maryánka answered his greeting with a leisurely bow of her head, settled down on the earth-bank, and took some seeds out of the bosom of her smock. Lukáshka, keeping his eyes fixed on Maryánka, slowly cracked seeds and spat out the shells. All were quiet when Maryánka joined the group.

'Have you come for long?' asked a woman, breaking the silence.

'Till to-morrow morning,' quietly replied Lukáshka.

'Well, God grant you get something good,' said the Cossack; 'I'm glad of it, as I've just been saying.'

'And I say so too,' put in the tipsy Ergushóv, laughing. 'What a lot of visitors have come,' he added, pointing to a soldier who was passing by. 'The soldiers' vodka is good —I like it.'

'They've sent three of the devils to us,' said one of the women. 'Grandad went to the village Elders, but they say nothing can be done.'

'Ah, ha! Have you met with trouble?' said Ergushóv.

'I expect they have smoked you out with their tobacco?' asked another woman. 'Smoke as much as you like in the yard, I say, but we won't allow it inside the hut. Not if the Elder himself comes, I won't allow it. Besides, they may rob you. He's not quartered any of them on himself, no fear, that devil's son of an Elder.'

'You don't like it?' Ergushóv began again.

'And I've also heard say that the girls will have to make the soldiers' beds and offer them *chikhir* and honey,' said Nazárka, putting one foot forward and tilting his cap like Lukáshka.

Ergushóv burst into a roar of laughter, and seizing the girl nearest to him, he embraced her. 'I tell you true.'

'Now then, you black pitch!' squealed the girl, 'I'll tell your old woman.'

'Tell her,' shouted he. 'That's quite right what Nazárka says; a circular has been sent round. He can read, you know. Quite true!' And he began embracing the next girl.

'What are you up to, you beast?' squealed the rosy, round-faced Ústenka, laughing and lifting her arm to hit him.

The Cossack stepped aside and nearly fell.

'There, they say girls have no strength, and you nearly killed me.'

'Get away, you black pitch, what devil has brought you from the cordon?' said Ústenka, and turning away from him she again burst out laughing. 'You were asleep and missed the *abrek*, didn't you? Suppose he had done for you it would have been all the better.'

'You'd have howled, I expect,' said Nazárka, laughing.

'Howled! A likely thing.'

'Just look, she doesn't care. She'd howl, Nazárka, eh? Would she?' said Ergushóv.

Lukáshka all this time had stood silently looking at Maryánka. His gaze evidently confused the girl.

'Well, Maryánka! I hear they've quartered one of the chiefs on you?' he said, drawing nearer.

Maryánka, as was her wont, waited before she replied, and slowly raising her eyes looked at the Cossack. Lukáshka's eyes were laughing as if something special, apart from what was said, was taking place between himself and the girl.

'Yes, it's all right for them as they have two huts,' replied an old woman on Maryánka's behalf, 'but at Fómushkin's now they also have one of the chiefs quartered on them and they say one whole corner is packed full with his things, and the family have no room left. Was such a thing ever heard of as that they should turn a whole horde loose in the village?' she said. 'And what the plague are they going to do here?'

'I've heard say they'll build a bridge across the Térek,' said one of the girls.

'And I've been told that they will dig a pit to put the girls in because they don't love the lads,' said Nazárka, approaching Ústenka; and he again made a whimsical gesture which set everybody laughing, and Ergushóv, passing by Maryánka, who was next in turn, began to embrace an old woman.

'Why don't you hug Maryánka? You should do it to each in turn,' said Nazárka.

'No, my old one is sweeter,' shouted the Cossack, kissing the struggling old woman.

'You'll throttle me,' she screamed, laughing.

The tramp of regular footsteps at the other end of the street interrupted their laughter. Three soldiers in their cloaks, with their muskets on their shoulders, were marching in step to relieve guard by the ammunition wagon.

The corporal, an old cavalry man, looked angrily at the Cossacks and led his men straight along the road where Lukáshka and Nazárka were standing, so that they should have to get out of the way. Nazárka moved, but Lukáshka only screwed up his eyes and turned his broad back without moving from his place.

'People are standing here, so you go round,' he muttered, half turning his head and tossing it contemptuously in the direction of the soldiers.

The soldiers passed by in silence, keeping step regularly along the dusty road.

Maryánka began laughing and all the other girls chimed in.

'What swells!' said Nazárka, 'Just like long-skirted choristers,' and he walked a few steps down the road imitating the soldiers.

Again everyone broke into peals of laughter.

Lukáshka came slowly up to Maryánka.

'And where have you put up the chief?' he asked.

Maryánka thought for a moment.

'We've let him have the new hut,' she said.

'And is he old or young,' asked Lukáshka, sitting down beside her.

'Do you think I've asked?' answered the girl. 'I went to get him some *chikhir* and saw him sitting at the window with Daddy Eróshka. Red-headed he seemed. They've brought a whole cartload of things.'

And she dropped her eyes.

'Oh, how glad I am that I got leave from the cordon!' said Lukáshka, moving closer to the girl and looking straight in her eyes all the time.

'And have you come for long?' asked Maryánka, smiling slightly.

'Till the morning. Give me some sunflower seeds,' he said, holding out his hand.

Maryánka now smiled outright and unfastened the neckband of her smock.

'Don't take them all,' she said.

'Really I felt so dull all the time without you, I swear I did,' he said in a calm, restrained whisper, helping himself to some seeds out of the bosom of the girl's smock, and stooping still closer over her he continued with laughing eyes to talk to her in low tones.

'I won't come, I tell you,' Maryánka suddenly said aloud, leaning away from him.

'No really . . . what I wanted to say to you, . . .' whispered Lukáshka. 'By the Heavens! Do come!'

Maryánka shook her head, but did so with a smile.

'Nursey Maryánka! Hallo Nursey! Mammy is calling! Supper time!' shouted Maryánka's little brother, running towards the group.

'I'm coming,' replied the girl. 'Go, my dear, go alone—I'll come in a minute.'

Lukáshka rose and raised his cap.

'I expect I had better go home too, that will be best,' he said, trying to appear unconcerned but hardly able to repress a smile, and he disappeared behind the corner of the house.

Meanwhile night had entirely enveloped the village. Bright stars were scattered over the dark sky. The streets became dark and empty. Nazárka remained with the women on the earth-bank and their laughter was still heard, but Lukáshka, having slowly moved away from the girls, crouched down like a cat and then suddenly started running lightly, holding his dagger to steady it: not homeward, however, but towards the cornet's house. Having passed two streets he turned into a lane and lifting the skirt of his coat sat down on the ground in the shadow of a fence. 'A regular cornet's daughter!' he thought about Maryánka. 'Won't even have a lark—the devil! But just wait a bit.'

The approaching footsteps of a woman attracted his attention. He began listening, and laughed all by himself. Maryánka with bowed head, striking the pales of the fences with a switch, was walking with rapid regular strides straight towards him. Lukáshka rose. Maryánka started and stopped.

'What an accursed devil! You frightened me! So you have not gone home?' she said, and laughed aloud.

Lukáshka put one arm round her and with the other hand raised her face. 'What I wanted to tell you, by Heaven!' his voice trembled and broke.

'What are you talking of, at night time!' answered Maryánka. 'Mother is waiting for me, and you'd better go to your sweetheart.'

And freeing herself from his arms she ran away a few steps. When she had reached the wattle fence of her home she stopped and turned to the Cossack who was running beside her and still trying to persuade her to stay a while with him.

'Well, what do you want to say, midnight-gadabout?' and she again began laughing.

'Don't laugh at me, Maryánka! By the Heaven! Well, what if I have a sweetheart? May the devil take her! Only say the word and now I'll love *you*—I'll do anything you wish. Here they are!' and he jingled the money in his pocket. 'Now we can live splendidly. Others have pleasures, and I? I get no pleasure from you, Maryánka dear!'

The girl did not answer. She stood before him breaking her switch into little bits with a rapid movement of her fingers.

Lukáshka suddenly clenched his teeth and fists.

'And why keep waiting and waiting? Don't I love you, darling? You can do what you like with me,' said he suddenly, frowning angrily and seizing both her hands.

The calm expression of Maryánka's face and voice did not change.

'Don't bluster, Lukáshka, but listen to me,' she answered, not pulling away her hands but holding the Cossack at arm's length. 'It's true I am a girl, but you listen to me! It does not depend on me, but if you love me I'll tell you this. Let go my hands, I'll tell you without.——I'll marry you, but you'll never get any nonsense from me,' said Maryánka without turning her face.

'What, you'll marry me? Marriage does not depend on

us. Love me yourself, Maryánka dear,' said Lukáshka,
from sullen and furious becoming again gentle, submissive,
and tender, and smiling as he looked closely into her eyes.

Maryánka clung to him and kissed him firmly on the
lips.

'Brother dear!' she whispered, pressing him convulsively
to her. Then, suddenly tearing herself away, she ran into
the gate of her house without looking round.

In spite of the Cossack's entreaties to wait another minute to hear what he had to say, Maryánka did not stop.

'Go,' she cried, 'you'll be seen! I do believe that devil,
our lodger, is walking about the yard.'

'Cornet's daughter,' thought Lukáshka. 'She will marry
me. Marriage is all very well, but you just love me!'

He found Nazárka at Yámka's house, and after having a
spree with him went to Dunáyka's house, where, in spite
of her not being faithful to him, he spent the night.

XIV

It was quite true that Olénin had been walking about
the yard when Maryánka entered the gate, and had heard
her say, 'That devil, our lodger, is walking about.' He had
spent that evening with Daddy Eróshka in the porch of
his new lodging. He had had a table, a samovar, wine, and
a candle brought out, and over a cup of tea and a cigar he
listened to the tales the old man told seated on the threshold at his feet. Though the air was still, the candle
dripped and flickered: now lighting up the post of the
porch, now the table and crockery, now the cropped white
head of the old man. Moths circled round the flame and,
shedding the dust of their wings, fluttered on the table and
in the glasses, flew into the candle flame, and disappeared
in the black space beyond. Olénin and Eróshka had emptied five bottles of *chikhir*. Eróshka filled the glasses every
time, offering one to Olénin, drinking his health, and talking untiringly. He told of Cossack life in the old days: of
his father, 'The Broad', who alone had carried on his back
a boar's carcass weighing three hundredweight, and drank
two pails of *chikhir* at one sitting. He told of his own days
and his chum Gírchik, with whom during the plague he
used to smuggle felt cloaks across the Térek. He told how
one morning he had killed two deer, and about his 'little
soul' who used to run to him at the cordon at night. He

told all this so eloquently and picturesquely that Olénin did not notice how time passed. 'Ah yes, my dear fellow, you did not know me in my golden days; then I'd have shown you things. To-day it's "Eróshka licks the jug", but then Eróshka was famous in the whole regiment. Whose was the finest horse? Who had a Gurda sword? To whom should one go to get a drink? With whom go on the spree? Who should be sent to the mountains to kill Ahmet Khan? Why, always Eróshka! Whom did the girls love? Always Eróshka had to answer for it. Because I was a real brave: a drinker, a thief (I used to seize herds of horses in the mountains), a singer; I was a master of every art! There are no Cossacks like that nowadays. It's disgusting to look at them. When they're that high (Eróshka held his hand three feet from the ground) they put on idiotic boots and keep looking at them—that's all the pleasure they know. Or they'll drink themselves foolish, not like men but all wrong. And who was I? I was Eróshka, the thief; they knew me not only in this village but up in the mountains. Tartar princes, my *kunaks*, used to come to see me! I used to be everybody's *kunak*. If he was a Tartar—with a Tartar; an Armenian—with an Armenian; a soldier—with a soldier; an officer—with an officer! I didn't care as long as he was a drinker. He says you should cleanse yourself from intercourse with the world, not drink with soldiers, not eat with a Tartar.'

'Who says all that?' asked Olénin.

'Why, our teacher! But listen to a Mullah or a Tartar Cadi. He says, "You unbelieving Giaours, why do you eat pig?" That shows that everyone has his own law. But I think it's all one. God has made everything for the joy of man. There is no sin in any of it. Take example from an animal. It lives in the Tartar's reeds or in ours. Wherever it happens to go, there is its home! Whatever God gives it, that it eats! But our people say we have to lick red-hot plates in hell for that. And I think it's all a fraud,' he added after a pause.

'What is a fraud?' asked Olénin.

'Why, what the preachers say. We had an army captain in Chervlëna who was my *kunak*: a fine fellow just like me. He was killed in Chéchnya. Well, he used to say that the preachers invent all that out of their own heads. "When you die the grass will grow on your grave and that's all!" ' The old man laughed. 'He was a desperate fellow.'

'And how old are you?' asked Olénin.

'The Lord only knows! I must be about seventy. When a Tsaritsa reigned in Russia I was no longer very small. So you can reckon it out. I must be seventy.'

'Yes you must, but you are still a fine fellow.'

'Well, thank Heaven I am healthy, quite healthy, except that a woman, a witch, has harmed me. . . .'

'How?'

'Oh, just harmed me.'

'And so when you die the grass will grow?' repeated Olénin.

Eróshka evidently did not wish to express his thought clearly. He was silent for a while.

'And what did you think? Drink!' he shouted suddenly, smiling and handing Olénin some wine.

XV

'Well, what was I saying?' he continued, trying to remember. 'Yes, that's the sort of man I am. I am a hunter. There is no hunter to equal me in the whole army. I will find and show you any animal and any bird, and what and where. I know it all! I have dogs, and two guns, and nets, and a screen and a hawk. I have everything, thank the Lord! If you are not bragging but are a real sportsman, I'll show you everything. Do you know what a man I am? When I have found a track—I know the animal. I know where he will lie down and where he'll drink or wallow. I make myself a perch and sit there all night watching. What's the good of staying at home? One only gets into mischief, gets drunk. And here women come and chatter, and boys shout at me—enough to drive one mad. It's a different matter when you go out at nightfall, choose yourself a place, press down the reeds and sit there and stay waiting, like a jolly fellow. One knows everything that goes on in the woods. One looks up at the sky: the stars move, you look at them and find out from them how the time goes. One looks round—the wood is rustling; one goes on waiting, now there comes a crackling—a boar comes to rub himself; one listens to hear the young eaglets screech and then the cocks give voice in the village, or the geese. When you hear the geese you know it is not yet midnight. And I know all about it! Or when a gun is fired somewhere far away, thoughts come to me. One thinks, who is that firing? Is it another Cossack like myself who has been watching for some animal? And has he killed it? Or only wounded it so that now the poor thing goes through the reeds smearing them with its blood all for nothing? I don't like that! Oh, how I dislike it! Why injure a beast? You fool, you fool! Or one thinks, "Maybe an *abrek* has killed some silly little Cossack." All this passes through one's mind. And once as I sat watching by the river I saw a cradle floating down. It was sound except for one corner which was broken off. Thoughts did come that time! I thought some of your soldiers, the devils, must have got into a Tartar village and seized the Chéchen women, and one of the devils has killed the little one: taken it by its legs, and hit its head against a wall. Don't they do such things? Sh! Men have no souls! And thoughts came to me that filled me with pity. I thought: they've thrown away the cradle and driven the wife out, and her brave has taken his gun and come across to our side to rob us. One watches and thinks. And when one hears a litter breaking through the thicket, something begins to knock inside one. Dear one, come this way! "They'll scent me," one thinks; and one sits and does not stir while one's heart goes dun! dun! dun! and simply lifts you. Once this spring a fine litter came near me, I saw something black. "In the name of the Father and of the Son," and I was just about to fire when she grunts to her pigs: "Danger, children," she says, "there's a man here," and off they all ran, breaking through the bushes. And she had been so close I could almost have bitten her.'

'How could a sow tell her brood that a man was there?' asked Olénin.

'What do you think? You think the beast's a fool? No, he is wiser than a man though you do call him a pig! He knows everything. Take this for instance. A man will pass along your track and not notice it; but a pig as soon as it gets onto your track turns and runs at once: that shows there is wisdom in him, since he scents your smell and you don't. And there is this to be said too: you wish to kill it and it wishes to go about the woods alive. You have one law and it has another. It is a pig, but it is no worse than you—it too is God's creature. Ah, dear! Man is foolish, foolish, foolish!' The old man repeated this several times and then, letting his head drop, he sat thinking.

Olénin also became thoughtful, and descending from the porch with his hands behind his back began pacing up and down the yard.

Eróshka, rousing himself, raised his head and began gazing intently at the moths circling round the flickering flame of the candle and burning themselves in it.

'Fool, fool!' he said. 'Where are you flying to? Fool, fool!' He rose and with his thick fingers began to drive away the moths.

'You'll burn, little fool! Fly this way, there's plenty of room.' He spoke tenderly, trying to catch them delicately by their wings with his thick fingers and then letting them fly again. 'You are killing yourself and I am sorry for you!'

He sat a long time chattering and sipping out of the bottle. Olénin paced up and down the yard. Suddenly he was struck by the sound of whispering outside the gate. Involuntarily holding his breath, he heard a woman's laughter, a man's voice, and the sound of a kiss. Intentionally rustling the grass under his feet he crossed to the opposite side of the yard, but after a while the wattle fence creaked. A Cossack in a dark Circassian coat and a white sheepskin cap passed along the other side of the fence (it was Luke), and a tall woman with a white kerchief on her head went past Olénin. 'You and I have nothing to do with one another' was what Maryánka's firm step gave him to understand. He followed her with his eyes to the porch of the hut, and he even saw her through the window take off her kerchief and sit down. And suddenly a feeling of lonely depression and some vague longings and hopes, and envy of someone or other, overcame the young man's soul.

The last lights had been put out in the huts. The last sounds had died away in the village. The wattle fences and the cattle gleaming white in the yards, the roofs of the houses and the stately poplars, all seemed to be sleeping the labourers' healthy peaceful sleep. Only the incessant ringing voices of frogs from the damp distance reached the young man. In the east the stars were growing fewer and fewer and seemed to be melting in the increasing light, but overhead they were denser and deeper than before. The old man was dozing with his head on his hand. A cock crowed in the yard opposite, but Olénin still paced up and down thinking of something. The sound of a song sung by several voices reached him and he stepped up to the fence and listened. The voices of several young Cossacks carolled a merry song, and one voice was distinguishable among them all by its firm strength.

'Do you know who is singing there?' said the old man, rousing himself. 'It is the Brave, Lukáshka. He has killed a Chéchen and now he rejoices. And what is there to rejoice at? . . . The fool, the fool!'

'And have you ever killed people?' asked Olénin.

'You devil!' shouted the old man. 'What are you asking? One must not talk so. It is a serious thing to destroy a human being. . . . Ah, a very serious thing! Good-bye, my dear fellow. I've eaten my fill and am drunk,' he said rising. 'Shall I come to-morrow to go shooting?'

'Yes, come!'

'Mind, get up early; if you oversleep you will be fined!'

'Never fear, I'll be up before you,' answered Olénin.

The old man left. The song ceased, but one could hear footsteps and merry talk. A little later the singing broke out again but farther away, and Eróshka's loud voice chimed in with the other. 'What people, what a life!' thought Olénin with a sigh as he returned alone to his hut.

XVI

Daddy Eróshka was a superannuated and solitary Cossack: twenty years ago his wife had gone over to the Orthodox Church and run away from him and married a Russian sergeant-major, and he had no children. He was not bragging when he spoke of himself as having been the boldest dare-devil in the village when he was young. Everybody in the regiment knew of his old-time prowess. The death of more than one Russian, as well as Chéchen, lay on his conscience. He used to go plundering in the mountains, and robbed the Russians too; and he had twice been in prison. The greater part of his life was spent in the forests, hunting. There he lived for days on a crust of bread and drank nothing but water. But on the other hand, when he was in the village he made merry from morning to night. After leaving Olénin he slept for a couple of hours and awoke before it was light. He lay on his bed thinking of the man he had become acquainted with the evening before. Olénin's 'simplicity' (simplicity in the sense of not grudging him a drink) pleased him very much, and so did Olénin himself. He wondered why the Russians were all 'simple' and so rich, and why they were educated, and yet knew nothing. He pondered on these questions and also considered what he might get out of Olénin.

Daddy Eróshka's hut was of a good size and not old, but the absence of a woman was very noticeable in it. Contrary to the usual cleanliness of the Cossacks, the whole of this hut was filthy and exceedingly untidy. A blood-stained coat had been thrown on the table, half a dough-cake lay beside a plucked and mangled crow with which to feed the hawk. Sandals of raw hide, a gun, a dagger, a little bag, wet clothes, and sundry rags lay scattered on the benches. In a corner stood a tub with stinking water, in which another pair of sandals were being steeped, and near by was a gun and a hunting-screen. On the floor a net had been thrown down and several dead pheasants lay there, while a hen tied by its leg was walking about near the table pecking among the dirt. In the unheated oven stood a broken pot with some kind of milky liquid. On the top of the oven a falcon was screeching and trying to break the cord by which it was tied, and a moulting hawk sat quietly on the edge of the oven, looking askance at the hen and occasionally bowing its head to right and left. Daddy Eróshka himself, in his shirt, lay on his back on a short bed rigged up between the wall and the oven, with his strong legs raised and his feet on the oven. He was picking with his thick fingers at the scratches left on his hands by the hawk, which he was accustomed to carry without wearing gloves. The whole room, especially near the old man, was filled with that strong but not unpleasant mixture of smells that he always carried about with him.

'*Uyde-ma*, Daddy?' (Is Daddy in?) came through the window in a sharp voice, which he at once recognized as Lukáshka's.

'*Uyde, Uyde, Uyde.* I am in!' shouted the old man. 'Come in, neighbour Mark, Luke Mark. Come to see Daddy? On your way to the cordon?'

At the sound of his master's shout the hawk flapped his wings and pulled at his cord.

The old man was fond of Lukáshka, who was the only man he excepted from his general contempt for the younger generation of Cossacks. Besides that, Lukáshka and his mother, as near neighbours, often gave the old man wine, clotted cream, and other home produce which Eróshka did not possess. Daddy Eróshka, who all his life had allowed himself to get carried away, always explained his infatuations from a practical point of view. 'Well, why not?' he used to say to himself. 'I'll give them some fresh meat, or a bird, and they won't forget Daddy: they'll sometimes bring a cake or a piece of pie.'

'Good morning, Mark! I am glad to see you,' shouted the old man cheerfully, and quickly putting down his bare feet he jumped off his bed and walked a step or two along the creaking floor, looked down at his out-turned toes, and suddenly, amused by the appearance of his feet, smiled, stamped with his bare heel on the ground, stamped again, and then performed a funny dance-step. 'That's clever, eh?' he asked, his small eyes glistening. Lukáshka smiled faintly. 'Going back to the cordon?' asked the old man.

'I have brought the *chikhir* I promised you when we were at the cordon.'

'May Christ save you!' said the old man, and he took up the extremely wide trousers that were lying on the floor, and his *beshmet*, put them on, fastened a strap round his waist, poured some water from an earthenware pot over his hands, wiped them on the old trousers, smoothed his beard with a bit of comb, and stopped in front of Lukáshka. 'Ready,' he said.

Lukáshka fetched a cup, wiped it and filled it with wine, and then handed it to the old man.

'Your health! To the Father and the Son!' said the old man, accepting the wine with solemnity. 'May you have what you desire, may you always be a hero, and obtain a cross.'

Lukáshka also drank a little after repeating a prayer, and then put the wine on the table. The old man rose and brought out some dried fish which he laid on the threshold, where he beat it with a stick to make it tender; then, having put it with his horny hands on a blue plate (his only one), he placed it on the table.

'I have all I want. I have victuals, thank God!' he said proudly. 'Well, and what of Mósev?' he added.

Lukáshka, evidently wishing to know the old man's opinion, told him how the officer had taken the gun from him.

'Never mind the gun,' said the old man. 'If you don't
give the gun you will get no reward.'

'But they say, Daddy, it's little reward a fellow gets
when he is not yet a mounted Cossack; and the gun is a
fine one, a Crimean, worth eighty rubles.'

'Eh, let it go! I had a dispute like that with an officer,
he wanted my horse. "Give it me and you'll be made a
cornet," says he. I wouldn't, and I got nothing!'

'Yes, Daddy, but you see I have to buy a horse; and
they say you can't get one the other side of the river under
fifty rubles, and mother has not yet sold our wine.'

'Eh, we didn't bother,' said the old man; 'when Daddy
Eróshka was your age he already stole herds of horses
from the Nogáy folk and drove them across the Térek.
Sometimes we'd give a fine horse for a quart of vodka or a
cloak.'

'Why so cheap?' asked Lukáshka.

'You're a fool, a fool, Mark,' said the old man contemptuously. 'Why, that's what one steals for, so as not to
be stingy! As for you, I suppose you haven't so much as
seen how one drives off a herd of horses? Why don't you
speak?'

'What's one to say, Daddy?' replied Lukáshka. 'It seems
we are not the same sort of men as you were.'

'You're a fool, Mark, a fool! "Not the same sort of
men!"' retorted the old man, mimicking the Cossack lad.
'I was not that sort of Cossack at your age.'

'How's that?' asked Lukáshka.

The old man shook his head contemptuously.

'Daddy Eróshka was *simple;* he did not grudge anything! That's why I was *kunak* with all Chéchnya. A *kunak*
would come to visit me and I'd make him drunk with
vodka and make him happy and put him to sleep with me,
and when I went to see him I'd take him a present—a
dagger! That's the way it is done, and not as you do
nowadays: the only amusement lads have now is to crack
seeds and spit out the shells!' the old man finished contemptuously, imitating the present-day Cossacks cracking
seeds and spitting out the shells.

'Yes, I know,' said Lukáshka; 'that's so!'

'If you wish to be a fellow of the right sort, be a brave
and not a peasant! Because even a peasant can buy a
horse—pay the money and take the horse.'

They were silent for a while.

'Well, of course it's dull both in the village and the cordon, Daddy: but there's nowhere one can go for a bit of sport. All our fellows are so timid. Take Nazárka. The other day when we went to the Tartar village, Giréy Khan asked us to come to Nogáy to take some horses, but no one went, and how was I to go alone?'

'And what of Daddy? Do you think I am quite dried up? . . . No, I'm not dried up. Let me have a horse and I'll be off to Nogáy at once.'

'What's the good of talking nonsense!' said Luke. 'You'd better tell me what to do about Giréy Khan. He says, "Only bring horses to the Térek, and then even if you bring a whole stud I'll find a place for them." You see he's also a shaven-headed Tartar—how's one to believe him?'

'You may trust Giréy Khan, all his kin were good people. His father too was a faithful *kunak*. But listen to Daddy and I won't teach you wrong: make him take an oath, then it will be all right. And if you go with him, have your pistol ready all the same, especially when it comes to dividing up the horses. I was nearly killed that way once by a Chéchen. I wanted ten rubles from him for a horse. Trusting is all right, but don't go to sleep without a gun.'

Lukáshka listened attentively to the old man.

'I say, Daddy, have you any stone-break grass?' he asked after a pause.

'No, I haven't any, but I'll teach you how to get it. You're a good lad and won't forget the old man. . . . Shall I tell you?'

'Tell me, Daddy.'

'You know a tortoise? She's a devil, the tortoise is!'

'Of course I know!'

'Find her nest and fence it round so that she can't get in. Well, she'll come, go round it, and then will go off to find the stone-break grass and will bring some along and destroy the fence. Anyhow next morning come in good time, and where the fence is broken there you'll find the stone-break grass lying. Take it wherever you like. No lock and no bar will be able to stop you.'

'Have you tried it yourself, Daddy?'

'As for trying, I have not tried it, but I was told of it by good people. I used only one charm: that was to repeat the Pilgrim rhyme when mounting my horse; and no one ever killed me!'

'What is the Pilgrim rhyme, Daddy?'

'What, don't you know it? Oh, what people! You're right to ask Daddy. Well, listen, and repeat after me:

> 'Hail! Ye, living in Sion,
> This is your King,
> Our steeds we shall sit on,
> Sophonius is weeping.
> Zacharias is speaking,
> Father Pilgrim,
> Mankind ever loving.

'Kind ever loving,' the old man repeated. 'Do you know it now? Try it.'

Lukáshka laughed.

'Come, Daddy, was it that that hindered their killing you? Maybe it just happened so!'

'You've grown too clever! You learn it all, and say it. It will do you no harm. Well, suppose you have sung "Pilgrim," it's all right,' and the old man himself began laughing. 'But just one thing, Luke, don't you go to Nogáy!'

'Why?'

'Times have changed. You are not the same men. You've become rubbishy Cossacks! And see how many Russians have come down on us! You'd get to prison. Really, give it up! Just as if you could! Now Gírchik and I, we used . . .'

And the old man was about to begin one of his endless tales, but Lukáshka glanced at the window and interrupted him.

'It is quite light, Daddy. It's time to be off. Look us up some day.'

'May Christ save you! I'll go to the officer; I promised to take him out shooting. He seems a good fellow.'

XVII

From Eróshka's hut Lukáshka went home. As he returned, the dewy mists were rising from the ground and enveloped the village. In various places the cattle, though out of sight, could be heard beginning to stir. The cocks called to one another with increasing frequency and insistence. The air was becoming more transparent, and the villagers were getting up. Not till he was close to it could Lukáshka discern the fence of his yard, all wet with dew, the porch of the hut, and the open shed. From the misty yard he heard the sound of an axe chopping wood. Lukáshka entered the hut. His mother was up, and stood at the oven throwing wood into it. His little sister was still lying in bed asleep.

'Well, Lukáshka, had enough holiday-making?' asked his mother softly. 'Where did you spend the night?'

'I was in the village,' replied her son reluctantly, reaching for his musket, which he drew from its cover and examined carefully.

His mother swayed her head.

Lukáshka poured a little gunpowder onto the pan, took out a little bag from which he drew some empty cartridge cases which he began filling, carefully plugging each one with a ball wrapped in a rag. Then, having tested the loaded cartridges with his teeth and examined them, he put down the bag.

'I say, Mother, I told you the bags wanted mending; have they been done?' he asked.

'Oh yes, our dumb girl was mending something last night. Why, is it time for you to be going back to the cordon? I haven't seen anything of you!'

'Yes, as soon as I have got ready I shall have to go,' answered Lukáshka, tying up the gunpowder. 'And where is our dumb one? Outside?'

'Chopping wood, I expect. She kept fretting for you. "I shall not see him at all!" she said. She puts her hand to her face like this, and clicks her tongue and presses her hands to her heart as much as to say—"sorry." Shall I call her in? She understood all about the *abrek*.'

'Call her,' said Lukáshka. 'And I had some tallow there; bring it: I must grease my sword.'

The old woman went out, and a few minutes later Lukáshka's dumb sister came up the creaking steps and entered the hut. She was six years older than her brother and would have been extremely like him had it not been for the dull and coarsely changeable expression (common to all deaf and dumb people) of her face. She wore a coarse smock all patched; her feet were bare and muddy, and on her head she had an old blue kerchief. Her neck,

arms, and face were sinewy like a peasant's. Her clothing and her whole appearance indicated that she always
did the hard work of a man. She brought in a heap of
logs which she threw down by the oven. Then she went up
to her brother, and with a joyful smile which made her
whole face pucker up, touched him on the shoulder and
began making rapid signs to him with her hands, her face,
and whole body.

'That's right, that's right, Stëpka is a trump!' answered
the brother, nodding. 'She's fetched everything and mended
everything, she's a trump! Here, take this for it!' He
brought out two pieces of gingerbread from his pocket and
gave them to her.

The dumb woman's face flushed with pleasure, and she
began making a weird noise for joy. Having seized the
gingerbread she began to gesticulate still more rapidly,
frequently pointing in one direction and passing her thick
finger over her eyebrows and her face. Lukáshka understood her and kept nodding, while he smiled slightly. She
was telling him to give the girls dainties, and that the girls
liked him, and that one girl, Maryánka—the best of them
all—loved him. She indicated Maryánka by rapidly pointing in the direction of Maryánka's home and to her own
eyebrows and face, and by smacking her lips and swaying
her head. 'Loves' she expressed by pressing her hands to
her breast, kissing her hand, and pretending to embrace
someone. Their mother returned to the hut, and seeing
what her dumb daughter was saying, smiled and shook her
head. Her daughter showed her the gingerbread and again
made the noise which expressed joy.

'I told Ulítka the other day that I'd send a matchmaker
to them,' said the mother. 'She took my words well.'

Lukáshka looked silently at his mother.

'But how about selling the wine, mother? I need a horse.'

'I'll cart it when I have time. I must get the barrels
ready,' said the mother, evidently not wishing her son to
meddle in domestic matters. 'When you go out you'll find
a bag in the passage. I borrowed from the neighbours and
got something for you to take back to the cordon; or shall
I put it in your saddle-bag?'

'All right,' answered Lukáshka. 'And if Giréy Khan
should come across the river send him to me at the cordon, for I shan't get leave again for a long time now; I
have some business with him.'

He began to get ready to start.

'I will send him on,' said the old women. 'It seems you have been spreeing at Yámka's all the time. I went out in the night to see the cattle, and I think it was your voice I heard singing songs.'

Lukáshka did not reply, but went out into the passage, threw the bags over his shoulder, tucked up the skirts of his coat, took his musket, and then stopped for a moment on the threshold.

'Good-bye, mother!' he said as he closed the gate behind him. 'Send me a small barrel with Nazárka. I promised it to the lads, and he'll call for it.'

'May Christ keep you, Lukáshka. God be with you! I'll send you some, some from the new barrel,' said the old woman, going to the fence: 'But listen,' she added, leaning over the fence.

The Cossack stopped.

'You've been making merry here; well, that's all right. Why should not a young man amuse himself? God has sent you luck and that's good. But now look out and mind, my son. Don't you go and get into mischief. Above all, satisfy your superiors: one has to! And I will sell the wine and find money for a horse and will arrange a match with the girl for you.'

'All right, all right!' answered her son, frowning.

His deaf sister shouted to attract his attention. She pointed to her head and the palm of her hand, to indicate the shaved head of a Chéchen. Then she frowned, and pretending to aim with a gun, she shrieked and began rapidly humming and shaking her head. This meant that Lukáshka should kill another Chéchen.

Lukáshka understood. He smiled, and shifting the gun at his back under his cloak stepped lightly and rapidly, and soon disappeared in the thick mist.

The old woman, having stood a little while at the gate, returned silently to the hut and immediately began working.

XVIII

Lukáshka returned to the cordon and at the same time Daddy Eróshka whistled to his dogs and, climbing over his wattle fence, went to Olénin's lodging, passing by the

back of the houses (he disliked meeting women before
going out hunting or shooting). He found Olénin still
asleep, and even Vanyúsha, though awake, was still in bed
and looking round the room considering whether it was
not time to get up, when Daddy Eróshka, gun on shoulder
and in full hunter's trappings, opened the door.

'A cudgel!' he shouted in his deep voice. 'An alarm! The
Chéchens are upon us! Iván! get the samovar ready for
your master, and get up yourself—quick,' cried the old
man. 'That's our way, my good man! Why even the girls
are already up! Look out of the window. See, she's going
for water and you're still sleeping!'

Olénin awoke and jumped up, feeling fresh and light-
hearted at the sight of the old man and at the sound of
his voice.

'Quick, Vanyúsha, quick!' he cried.

'Is that the way you go hunting?' said the old man.
'Others are having their breakfast and you are asleep!
Lyam! Here!' he called to his dog. 'Is your gun ready?' he
shouted, as loud as if a whole crowd were in the hut.

'Well, it's true I'm guilty, but it can't be helped! The
powder, Vanyúsha, and the wads!' said Olénin.

'A fine!' shouted the old man.

'*Du tay voulay vou?*' asked Vanyúsha, grinning.

'You're not one of us—your gabble is not like our
speech, you devil!' the old man shouted at Vanyúsha,
showing the stumps of his teeth.

'A first offence must be forgiven,' said Olénin playfully, drawing on his high boots.

'The first offence shall be forgiven,' answered Eróshka,
'but if you oversleep another time you'll be fined a pail of
chikhir. When it gets warmer you won't find the deer.'

'And even if we do find him he is wiser than we are,'
said Olénin, repeating the words spoken by the old man
the evening before, 'and you can't deceive him!'

'Yes, laugh away! You kill one first, and then you may
talk. Now then, hurry up! Look, there's the master himself
coming to see you,' added Eróshka, looking out of the
window. 'Just see how he's got himself up. He's put on a
new coat so that you should see that he's an officer. Ah,
these people, these people!'

Sure enough Vanyúsha came in and announced that the
master of the house wished to see Olénin.

'L'arjan!' he remarked profoundly, to forewarn his master of the meaning of this visitation. Following him, the master of the house in a new Circassian coat with an officer's stripes on the shoulders and with polished boots (quite exceptional among Cossacks) entered the room, swaying from side to side, and congratulated his lodger on his safe arrival.

The cornet, Elias Vasílich, was an *educated* Cossack. He had been to Russia proper, was a regimental school-teacher, and above all he was noble. He wished to appear noble, but one could not help feeling beneath his grotesque pretence of polish, his affectation, his self-confidence, and his absurd way of speaking, he was just the same as Daddy Eróshka. This could also be clearly seen by his sunburnt face and his hands and his red nose. Olénin asked him to sit down.

'Good morning, Father Elias Vasílich,' said Eróshka, rising with (or so it seemed to Olénin) an ironically low bow.

'Good morning, Daddy. So you're here already,' said the cornet, with a careless nod.

The cornet was a man of about forty, with a grey pointed beard, skinny and lean, but handsome and very fresh-looking for his age. Having come to see Olénin he was evidently afraid of being taken for an ordinary Cossack, and wanted to let Olénin feel his importance from the first.

'That's our Egyptian Nimrod,' he remarked, addressing Olénin and pointing to the old man with a self-satisfied smile. 'A mighty hunter before the Lord! He's our foremost man on every hand. You've already been pleased to get acquainted with him.'

Daddy Eróshka gazed at his feet in their shoes of wet raw hide and shook his head thoughtfully at the cornet's ability and learning, and muttered to himself: 'Gyptian Nimvrod! What things he invents!'

'Yes, you see we mean to go hunting,' answered Olénin.

'Yes, sir, exactly,' said the cornet, 'but I have a small business with you.'

'What do you want?'

'Seeing that you are a gentleman,' began the cornet, 'and as I may understand myself to be in the rank of an officer too, and therefore we may always progressively negotiate,

as gentlemen do.' (He stopped and looked with a smile at
Olénin and at the old man.) 'But if you have the desire
with my consent, then, as my wife is a foolish woman of
our class, she could not quite comprehend your words of
yesterday's date. Therefore my quarters might be let for
six rubles to the Regimental Adjutant, without the stables;
but I can always avert that from myself free of charge.
But, as you desire, therefore I, being myself of an officer's
rank, can come to an agreement with you in everything
personally, as an inhabitant of this district, not according
to our customs, but can maintain the conditions in every
way. . . .'

'Speaks clearly!' muttered the old man.

The cornet continued in the same strain for a long time.
At last, not without difficulty, Olénin gathered that the
cornet wished to let his rooms to him, Olénin, for six
rubles a month. The latter gladly agreed to this, and
offered his visitor a glass of tea. The cornet declined it.

'According to our silly custom we consider it a sort of
sin to drink out of a "worldly" tumbler,' he said. 'Though,
of course, with my education I may understand, but my
wife from her human weakness . . .'

'Well then, will you have some tea?'

'If you will permit me, I will bring my own particular
glass,' answered the cornet, and stepped out into the porch.
'Bring me my glass!' he cried.

In a few minutes the door opened and a young sunburnt arm in a print sleeve thrust itself in, holding a tumbler in the hand. The cornet went up, took it, and whispered something to his daughter. Olénin poured tea for
the cornet into the latter's own 'particular' glass, and for
Eróshka into a 'worldly' glass.

'However, I do not desire to detain you,' said the cornet,
scalding his lips and emptying his tumbler. 'I too have a
great liking for fishing, and I am here, so to say, only on
leave of absence for recreation from my duties. I too have
the desire to tempt fortune and see whether some *Gifts
of the Térek* may not fall to my share. I hope you too
will come and see us and have a drink of our wine, according to the custom of our village,' he added.

The cornet bowed, shook hands with Olénin, and went
out. While Olénin was getting ready, he heard the cornet
giving orders to his family in an authoritative and sensible
tone, and a few minutes later he saw him pass by the

window in a tattered coat with his trousers rolled up to his knees and a fishing net over his shoulder.

'A rascal!' said Daddy Eróshka, emptying his 'worldly' tumbler. 'And will you really pay him six rubles? Was such a thing ever heard of? They would let you the best hut in the village for two rubles. What a beast! Why, I'd let you have mine for three!'

'No, I'll remain here,' said Olénin.

'Six rubles! . . . Clearly it's a fool's money. Eh, eh, eh!" answered the old man. 'Let's have some *chikhir,* Iván!'

Having had a snack and a drink of vodka to prepare themselves for the road, Olénin and the old man went out together before eight o'clock.

At the gate they came up against a wagon to which a pair of oxen were harnessed. With a white kerchief tied round her head down to her eyes, a coat over her smock, and wearing high boots, Maryánka with a long switch in her hand was dragging the oxen by a cord tied to their horns.

'Mammy,' said the old man, pretending that he was going to seize her.

Maryánka flourished her switch at him and glanced merrily at them both with her beautiful eyes.

Olénin felt still more light-hearted.

'Now then, come on, come on,' he said, throwing his gun on his shoulder and conscious of the girl's eyes upon him.

'Gee up!' sounded Maryánka's voice behind them, followed by the creak of the moving wagon.

As long as their road lay through the pastures at the back of the village Eróshka went on talking. He could not forget the cornet and kept on abusing him.

'Why are you so angry with him?' asked Olénin.

'He's stingy. I don't like it,' answered the old man. 'He'll leave it all behind when he dies! Then who's he saving up for? He's built two houses, and he's got a second garden from his brother by a law-suit. And in the matter of papers what a dog he is! They come to him from other villages to fill up documents. As he writes it out, exactly so it happens. He gets it quite exact. But who is he saving for? He's only got one boy and the girl; when she's married who'll be left?'

'Well then, he's saving up for her dowry,' said Olénin.

'What dowry? The girl is sought after, she's a fine girl. But he's such a devil that he must yet marry her to a rich fellow. He wants to get a big price for her. There's Luke, a Cossack, a neighbour and a nephew of mine, a fine lad. It's he who killed the Chéchen—he has been wooing her for a long time, but he hasn't let him have her. He's given one excuse, and another, and a third. "The girl's too young," he says. But I know what he is thinking. He wants to keep them bowing to him. He's been acting shamefully about that girl. Still, they will get her for Lukáshka, because he is the best Cossack in the village, a brave, who has killed an *abrek* and will be rewarded with a cross.'

'But how about this? When I was walking up and down the yard last night, I saw my landlord's daughter and some Cossack kissing,' said Olénin.

'You're pretending!' cried the old man, stopping.

'On my word,' said Olénin.

'Women are the devil,' said Eróshka pondering. 'But what Cossack was it?'

'I couldn't see.'

'Well, what sort of a cap had he, a white one?'

'Yes.'

'And a red coat? About your height?'

'No, a bit taller.'

'It's he!' and Eróshka burst out laughing. 'It's himself, it's Mark. He is Luke, but I call him Mark for a joke. His very self! I love him. I was just such a one myself. What's the good of minding them? My sweetheart used to sleep with her mother and her sister-in-law, but I managed to get in. She used to sleep upstairs; that witch her mother was a regular demon; it's awful how she hated me. Well, I used to come with a chum, Gírchik his name was. We'd come under her window and I'd climb on his shoulders, push up the window and begin groping about. She used to sleep just there on a bench. Once I woke her up and she nearly called out. She hadn't recognized me. "Who is there?" she said, and I could not answer. Her mother was even beginning to stir, but I took off my cap and shoved it over her mouth; and she at once knew it by a seam in it, and ran out to me. I used not to want anything then. She'd bring along clotted cream and grapes and everything,' added Eróshka (who always explained things practically), 'and she wasn't the only one. It was a life!'

'And what now?'

'Now we'll follow the dog, get a pheasant to settle on a tree, and then you may fire.'

'Would you have made up to Maryánka?'

'Attend to the dogs. I'll tell you to-night,' said the old man, pointing to his favourite dog, Lyam.

After a pause they continued talking, while they went about a hundred paces. Then the old man stopped again and pointed to a twig that lay across the path.

'What do you think of that?' he said. 'You think it's nothing? It's bad that this stick is lying so.'

'Why is it bad?'

He smiled.

'Ah, you don't know anything. Just listen to me. When a stick lies like that don't you step across it, but go round it or throw it off the path this way, and say "Father and Son and Holy Ghost," and then go on with God's blessing. Nothing will happen to you. That's what the old men used to teach me.'

'Come, what rubbish!' said Olénin. 'You'd better tell me more about Maryánka. Does she carry on with Lukáshka?'

'Hush, . . . be quiet now!' the old man again interrupted in a whisper: 'just listen, we'll go round through the forest.'

And the old man, stepping quietly in his soft shoes, led the way by a narrow path leading into the dense, wild, overgrown forest. Now and again with a frown he turned to look at Olénin, who rustled and clattered with his heavy boots and, carrying his gun carelessly, several times caught the twigs of trees that grew across the path.

'Don't make a noise. Step softly, soldier!' the old man whispered angrily.

There was a feeling in the air that the sun had risen. The mist was dissolving but it still enveloped the tops of the trees. The forest looked terribly high. At every step the aspect changed: what had appeared like a tree proved to be a bush, and a reed looked like a tree.

XIX

The mist had partly lifted, showing the wet reed thatches, and was now turning into dew that moistened the road and the grass beside the fence. Smoke rose everywhere in clouds from the chimneys. The people were going out of the village, some to their work, some to the river, and some to the cordon. The hunters walked together along the damp, grass-grown path. The dogs, wagging their tails and looking at their masters, ran on both sides of them. Myriads of gnats hovered in the air and pursued the hunters, covering their backs, eyes, and hands. The air was fragrant with the grass and with the dampness of the forest. Olénin continually looked round at the ox-cart in which Maryánka sat urging on the oxen with a long switch.

It was calm. The sounds from the village, audible at first, now no longer reached the sportsmen. Only the brambles cracked as the dogs ran under them, and now and then birds called to one another. Olénin knew that danger lurked in the forest, that *abreks* always hid in such places. But he knew too that in the forest, for a man on foot, a gun is a great protection. Not that he was afraid, but he felt that another in his place might be; and looking into the damp misty forest and listening to the rare and faint sounds with strained attention, he changed his hold on his gun and experienced a pleasant feeling that was new to him. Daddy Eróshka went in front, stopping and carefully scanning every puddle where an animal had left a double track, and pointing it out to Olénin. He hardly spoke at all and only occasionally made remarks in a whisper. The track they were following had once been made by wagons, but the grass had long overgrown it. The elm and plane-tree forest on both sides of them was so dense and overgrown with creepers that it was impossible to see anything through it. Nearly every tree was enveloped from top to bottom with wild grape vines, and dark bramble bushes covered the ground thickly. Every little glade was overgrown with blackberry bushes and grey feathery reeds. In places, large hoof-prints and small funnel-shaped pheasant-trails led from the path into the thicket. The vigour of the growth of this forest, untrampled by cattle, struck Olénin at every turn, for he had never seen anything like it. This forest, the danger, the old man and his mysterious whispering, Maryánka with her virile upright bearing, and the mountains—all this seemed to him like a dream.

'A pheasant has settled,' whispered the old man, looking round and pulling his cap over his face—'Cover your

mug! A pheasant!' he waved his arm angrily at Olénin and
pushed forward almost on all fours. 'He don't like a man's
mug.'

Olénin was still behind him when the old man stopped
and began examining a tree. A cock-pheasant on the tree
clucked at the dog that was barking at it, and Olénin saw
the pheasant; but at that moment a report, as of a cannon,
came from Eróshka's enormous gun, the bird fluttered up
and, losing some feathers, fell to the ground. Coming up
to the old man Olénin disturbed another, and raising his
gun he aimed and fired. The pheasant flew swiftly up and
then, catching at the branches as he fell, dropped like a
stone to the ground.

'Good man!' the old man (who could not hit a flying
bird) shouted, laughing.

Having picked up the pheasants they went on. Olénin,
excited by the exercise and the praise, kept addressing remarks to the old man.

'Stop! Come this way,' the old man interrupted. 'I noticed the track of deer here yesterday.'

After they had turned into the thicket and gone some
three hundred paces they scrambled through into a glade
overgrown with reeds and partly under water. Olénin failed
to keep up with the old huntsman and presently Daddy
Eróshka, some twenty paces in front, stooped down, nodding and beckoning with his arm. On coming up with him
Olénin saw a man's footprint to which the old man was
pointing.

'D'you see?'

'Yes, well?' said Olénin, trying to speak as calmly as he
could. 'A man's footstep!'

Involuntarily a thought of Cooper's *Pathfinder* and of
abreks flashed through Olénin's mind, but noticing the
mysterious manner with which the old man moved on, he
hesitated to question him and remained in doubt whether
this mysteriousness was caused by fear of danger or by
the sport.

'No, it's my own footprint,' the old man said quietly,
and pointed to some grass under which the track of an
animal was just perceptible.

The old man went on, and Olénin kept up with him.
Descending to lower ground some twenty paces farther

on they came upon a spreading pear-tree, under which, on the black earth, lay the fresh dung of some animal.

The spot, all covered over with wild vines, was like a cosy arbour, dark and cool.

'He's been here this morning,' said the old man with a sigh; 'the lair is still damp, quite fresh.'

Suddenly they heard a terrible crash in the forest some ten paces from where they stood. They both started and seized their guns, but they could see nothing and only heard the branches breaking. The rhythmical rapid thud of galloping was heard for a moment and then changed into a hollow rumble which resounded farther and farther off, re-echoing in wider and wider circles through the forest. Olénin felt as though something had snapped in his heart. He peered carefully but vainly into the green thicket and then turned to the old man. Daddy Eróshka with his gun pressed to his breast stood motionless; his cap was thrust backwards, his eyes gleamed with an unwonted glow, and his open mouth, with its worn yellow teeth, seemed to have stiffened in that position.

'A horned stag!' he muttered, and throwing down his gun in despair he began pulling at his grey beard, 'Here it stood. We should have come round by the path. . . . Fool! fool!' and he gave his beard an angry tug. 'Fool! Pig!' he repeated, pulling painfully at his own beard. Through the forest something seemed to fly away in the mist, and ever farther and farther off was heard the sound of the flight of the stag.

It was already dusk when, hungry, tired, but full of vigour, Olénin returned with the old man. Dinner was ready. He ate and drank with the old man till he felt warm and merry. Olénin then went out into the porch. Again, to the west, the mountains rose before his eyes. Again the old man told his endless stories of hunting, of *abreks*, of sweethearts, and of all that free and reckless life. Again the fair Maryánka went in and out and across the yard, her beautiful powerful form outlined by her smock.

XX

The next day Olénin went alone to the spot where he and the old man startled the stag. Instead of passing round through the gate he climbed over the prickly hedge, as

everybody else did, and before he had had time to pull out
the thorns that had caught in his coat, his dog, which had
run on in front, started two pheasants. He had hardly
stepped among the briers when the pheasants began to
rise at every step (the old man had not shown him that
place the day before as he meant to keep it for shooting
from behind the screen). Olénin fired twelve times and
killed five pheasants, but clambering after them through
the briers he got so fatigued that he was drenched with
perspiration. He called off his dog, uncocked his gun, put
in a bullet above the small shot, and brushing away the
mosquitoes with the wide sleeve of his Circassian coat he
went slowly to the spot where they had been the day
before. It was however impossible to keep back the dog,
who found trails on the very path, and Olénin killed two
more pheasants, so that after being detained by this it was
getting towards noon before he began to find the place he
was looking for.

The day was perfectly clear, calm, and hot. The morning moisture had dried up even in the forest, and myriads
of mosquitoes literally covered his face, his back, and his
arms. His dog had turned from black to grey, its back
being covered with mosquitoes, and so had Olénin's coat
through which the insects thrust their stings. Olénin was
ready to run away from them and it seemed to him that
it was impossible to live in this country in the summer.
He was about to go home, but remembering that other
people managed to endure such pain he resolved to bear it
and gave himself up to be devoured. And strange to say,
by noontime the feeling became actually pleasant. He even
felt that without this mosquito-filled atmosphere around
him, and that mosquito-paste mingled with perspiration
which his hand smeared over his face, and that unceasing
irritation all over his body, the forest would lose for him
some of its character and charm. These myriads of insects
were so well suited to that monstrously lavish wild vegetation, these multitudes of birds and beasts which filled the
forest, this dark foliage, this hot scented air, these runlets
filled with turbid water which everywhere soaked through
from the Térek and gurgled here and there under the
overhanging leaves, that the very thing which had at first
seemed to him dreadful and intolerable now seemed pleasant. After going round the place where yesterday they had

found the animal and not finding anything, he felt inclined
to rest. The sun stood right above the forest and poured its
perpendicular rays down on his back and head whenever
he came out into a glade or onto the road. The seven
heavy pheasants dragged painfully at his waist. Having
found the traces of yesterday's stag he crept under a bush
into the thicket just where the stag had lain, and lay down
in its lair. He examined the dark foliage around him, the
place marked by the stag's perspiration and yesterday's
dung, the imprint of the stag's knees, the bit of black earth
it had kicked up, and his own footprints of the day before.
He felt cool and comfortable and did not think of or wish
for anything. And suddenly he was overcome by such a
strange feeling of causeless joy and of love for everything,
that from an old habit of his childhood he began crossing
himself and thanking someone. Suddenly, with extraordinary clearness, he thought: 'Here am I, Dmítri Olénin,
a being quite distinct from every other being, now lying all
alone Heaven only knows where—where a stag used to
live—an old stag, a beautiful stag who perhaps had never
seen a man, and in a place where no human being has
ever sat or thought these thoughts. Here I sit, and around
me stand old and young trees, one of them festooned with
wild grape vines, and pheasants are fluttering, driving one
another about and perhaps scenting their murdered brothers.' He felt his pheasants, examined them, and wiped
the warm blood off his hand onto his coat. 'Perhaps the
jackals scent them and with dissatisfied faces go off in
another direction: above me, flying in among the leaves
which to them seem enormous islands, mosquitoes hang
in the air and buzz: one, two, three, four, a hundred, a
thousand, a million mosquitoes, and all of them buzz
something or other and each one of them is separate from
all else and is just such a separate Dmítri Olénin as I am
myself.' He vividly imagined what the mosquitoes buzzed:
'This way, this way, lads! Here's some one we can eat!'
They buzzed and stuck to him. And it was clear to him
that he was not a Russian nobleman, a member of Moscow
society, the friend and relation of so-and-so and so-and-so,
but just such a mosquito, or pheasant, or deer, as those
that were now living all around him. 'Just as they, just as
Daddy Eróshka, I shall live awhile and die, and as he
says truly: "grass will grow and nothing more".'
'But what though the grass does grow?' he continued

thinking. 'Still I must live and be happy, because happiness is all I desire. Never mind what I am—an animal like all the rest, above whom the grass will grow and nothing more; or a frame in which a bit of the one God has been set,—still I must live in the very best way. How then must I live to be happy, and why was I not happy before?' And he began to recall his former life and he felt disgusted with himself. He appeared to himself to have been terribly exacting and selfish, though he now saw that all the while he really needed nothing for himself. And he looked round at the foliage with the light shining through it, at the setting sun and the clear sky, and he felt just as happy as before. 'Why am I happy, and what used I to live for?' thought he. 'How much I exacted for myself; how I schemed and did not manage to gain anything but shame and sorrow! and, there now, I require nothing to be happy;' and suddenly a new light seemed to reveal itself to him. 'Happiness is this!' he said to himself. 'Happiness lies in living for others. That is evident. The desire for happiness is innate in every man; therefore it is legitimate. When trying to satisfy it selfishly—that is, by seeking for oneself riches, fame, comforts, or love—it may happen that circumstances arise which make it impossible to satisfy these desires. It follows that it is these desires that are illegitimate, but not the need for happiness. But what desires can always be satisfied despite external circumstances? What are they? Love, self-sacrifice.' He was so glad and excited when he had discovered this, as it seemed to him, new truth, that he jumped up and began impatiently seeking some one to sacrifice himself for, to do good to and to love. 'Since one wants nothing for oneself,' he kept thinking, 'why not live for others?' He took up his gun with the intention of returning home quickly to think this out and to find an opportunity of doing good. He made his way out of the thicket. When he had come out into the glade he looked around him; the sun was no longer visible above the tree-tops. It had grown cooler and the place seemed to him quite strange and not like the country round the village. Everything seemed changed—the weather and the character of the forest; the sky was wrapped in clouds, the wind was rustling in the tree-tops, and all around nothing was visible but reeds and dying broken-down trees. He called to his dog who had run away to follow some animal, and his voice came back as in a desert. And suddenly he was seized with a terrible sense of weirdness. He grew frightened. He remembered the *abreks* and the murders he had been told about, and he expected every moment that an *abrek* would spring from behind every bush and he would have to defend his life and die, or be a coward. He thought of God and of the future life as for long he had not thought about them. And all around was that same gloomy stern wild nature. 'And is it worth while living for oneself,' thought he, 'when at any moment you may die, and die without having done any good, and so that no one will know of it?' He went in the direction where he fancied the village lay. Of his shooting he had no further thought; but he felt tired to death and peered round at every bush and tree with particular attention and almost with terror, expecting every moment to be called to account for his life. After having wandered about for a considerable time he came upon a ditch down which was flowing cold sandy water from the Térek, and, not to go astray any longer, he decided to follow it. He went on without knowing where the ditch would lead him. Suddenly the reeds behind him crackled. He shuddered and seized his gun, and then felt ashamed of himself: the over-excited dog, panting hard, had thrown itself into the cold water of the ditch and was lapping it!

He too had a drink, and then followed the dog in the direction it wished to go, thinking it would lead him to the village. But despite the dog's company everything around him seemed still more dreary. The forest grew darker and the wind grew stronger and stronger in the tops of the broken old trees. Some large birds circled screeching round their nests in those trees. The vegetation grew poorer and he came oftener and oftener upon rustling reeds and bare sandy spaces covered with animal footprints. To the howling of the wind was added another kind of cheerless monotonous roar. Altogether his spirits became gloomy. Putting his hand behind him he felt his pheasants, and found one missing. It had broken off and was lost, and only the bleeding head and beak remained sticking in his belt. He felt more frightened than he had ever done before. He began to pray to God, and feared above all that he might die without having done anything good or kind; and he so wanted to live, and to live so as to perform a feat of self-sacrifice.

XXI

Suddenly it was as though the sun had shone into his soul. He heard Russian being spoken, and also heard the rapid smooth flow of the Térek, and a few steps farther in front of him saw the brown moving surface of the river, with the dim-coloured wet sand of its banks and shallows, the distant steppe, the cordon watch-tower outlined above the water, a saddled and hobbled horse among the brambles, and then the mountains opening out before him. The red sun appeared for an instant from under a cloud and its last rays glittered brightly along the river over the reeds, on the watch-tower, and on a group of Cossacks, among whom Lukáshka's vigorous figure attracted Olénin's involuntary attention.

Olénin felt that he was again, without any apparent cause, perfectly happy. He had come upon the Nízhni-Protótsk post on the Térek, opposite a pro-Russian Tartar village on the other side of the river. He accosted the Cossacks, but not finding as yet any excuse for doing anyone a kindness, he entered the hut; nor in the hut did he find any such opportunity. The Cossacks received him coldly. On entering the mud hut he lit a cigarette. The Cossacks paid little attention to him, first because he was smoking a cigarette, and secondly because they had something else to divert them that evening. Some hostile Chéchens, relatives of the *abrek* who had been killed, had come from the hills with a scout to ransom the body; and the Cossacks were waiting for their Commanding Officer's arrival from the village. The dead man's brother, tall and well shaped with a short cropped beard which was dyed red, despite his very tattered coat and cap was calm and majestic as a king. His face was very like that of the dead *abrek*. He did not deign to look at anyone and never once glanced at the dead body, but sitting on his heels in the shade he spat as he smoked his short pipe, and occasionally uttered some few guttural sounds of command, which were respectfully listened to by his companion. He was evidently a brave who had met Russians more than once before in quite other circumstances, and nothing about them could astonish or even interest him. Olénin was about to approach the dead body and had begun to look at it when the brother, looking up at him from under his brows with

calm contempt, said something sharply and angrily. The
scout hastened to cover the dead man's face with his coat.
Olénin was struck by the dignified and stern expression
of the brave's face. He began to speak to him, asking from
what village he came, but the Chéchen, scarcely giving
him a glance, spat contemptuously and turned away.
Olénin was so surprised at the Chéchen not being interested in him that he could only put it down to the
man's stupidity or ignorance of Russian; so he turned to
the scout, who also acted as interpreter. The scout was as
ragged as the other, but instead of being red-haired he
was black-haired, restless, with extremely white gleaming
teeth and sparkling black eyes. The scout willingly entered
into conversation and asked for a cigarette.   .

'There were five brothers,' began the scout in his broken
Russian. 'This is the third brother the Russians have killed,
only two are left. He is a brave, a great brave!' he said,
pointing to the Chéchen. 'When they killed Ahmet Khan
(the dead brave) this one was sitting on the opposite bank
among the reeds. He saw it all. Saw him laid in the skiff
and brought to the bank. He sat there till the night and
wished to kill the old man, but the others would not let
him.'

Lukáshka went up to the speaker, and sat down.

'Of what village?' asked he.

'From there in the hills,' replied the scout, pointing to
the misty bluish gorge beyond the Térek. 'Do you know
Suuk-su? It is about eight miles beyond that.'

'Do you know Giréy Khan in Suuk-su?' asked Lukáshka, evidently proud of the acquaintance. 'He is my
kunak.'

'He is my neighbour,' answered the scout.

'He's a trump!' and Lukáshka, evidently much interested, began talking to the scout in Tartar.

Presently a Cossack captain, with the head of the village,
arrived on horseback with a suite of two Cossacks. The
captain—one of the new type of Cossack officers—wished
the Cossacks 'Good health,' but no one shouted in reply,
'Hail! Good health to your honour,' as is customary in the
Russian Army, and only a few replied with a bow. Some,
and among them Lukáshka, rose and stood erect. The
corporal replied that all was well at the outposts. All this
seemed ridiculous: it was as if these Cossacks were playing at being soldiers. But these formalities soon gave place

to ordinary ways of behaviour, and the captain, who was a smart Cossack just like the others, began speaking fluently in Tartar to the interpreter. They filled in some document, gave it to the scout, and received from him some money. Then they approached the body.

'Which of you is Luke Gavrílov?' asked the captain.

Lukáshka took off his cap and came forward.

'I have reported your exploit to the Commander. I don't know what will come of it. I have recommended you for a cross; you're too young to be made a sergeant. Can you read?'

'I can't.'

'But what a fine fellow to look at!' said the captain, again playing the commander. 'Put on your cap. Which of the Gavrílovs does he come of? . . . the Broad, eh?'

'His nephew,' replied the corporal.

'I know, I know. Well, lend a hand, help them,' he said, turning to the Cossacks.

Lukáshka's face shone with joy and seemed handsomer than usual. He moved away from the corporal, and having put on his cap sat down beside Olénin.

When the body had been carried to the skiff the brother Chéchen descended to the bank. The Cossacks involuntarily stepped aside to let him pass. He jumped into the boat and pushed off from the bank with his powerful leg, and now, as Olénin noticed, for the first time threw a rapid glance at all the Cossacks and then abruptly asked his companion a question. The latter answered something and pointed to Lukáshka. The Chéchen looked at him and, turning slowly away, gazed at the opposite bank. That look expressed not hatred but cold contempt. He again made some remark.

'What is he saying?' Olénin asked of the fidgety scout.

'Yours kill ours, ours slay yours. It's always the same,' replied the scout, evidently inventing, and he smiled, showing his white teeth, as he jumped into the skiff.

The dead man's brother sat motionless, gazing at the opposite bank. He was so full of hatred and contempt that there was nothing on this side of the river that moved his curiosity. The scout, standing up at one end of the skiff and dipping his paddle now on one side now on the other, steered skilfully while talking incessantly. The skiff became smaller and smaller as it moved obliquely across the stream, the voices became scarcely audible, and at last,

still within sight, they landed on the opposite bank where
their horses stood waiting. There they lifted out the corpse
and (though the horse shied) laid it across one of the
saddles, mounted, and rode at a foot-pace along the road
past a Tartar village from which a crowd came out to
look at them. The Cossacks on the Russian side of the
river were highly satisfied and jovial. Laughter and jokes
were heard on all sides. The captain and the head of the
village entered the mud hut to regale themselves. Lukáshka, vainly striving to impart a sedate expression to
his merry face, sat down with his elbows on his knees
beside Olénin and whittled away at a stick.

'Why do you smoke?' he said with assumed curiosity.
'Is it good?'

He evidently spoke because he noticed Olénin felt ill
at ease and isolated among the Cossacks.

'It's just a habit,' answered Olénin. 'Why?'

'H'm, if one of us were to smoke there would be a
row! Look there now, the mountains are not far off,' continued Lukáshka, 'yet you can't get there! How will you
get back alone? It's getting dark. I'll take you, if you like.
You ask the corporal to give me leave.'

'What a fine fellow!' thought Olénin, looking at the
Cossack's bright face. He remembered Maryánka and the
kiss he had heard by the gate, and he was sorry for Lukáshka and his want of culture. 'What confusion it is,'
he thought. 'A man kills another and is happy and satisfied
with himself as if he had done something excellent. Can
it be that nothing tells him that it is not a reason for any
rejoicing, and that happiness lies not in killing, but in
sacrificing oneself?'

'Well, you had better not meet him again now, mate!'
said one of the Cossacks who had seen the skiff off, addressing Lukáshka. 'Did you hear him asking about you?'

Lukáshka raised his head.

'My godson?' said Lukáshka, meaning by that word the
dead Chéchen.

'Your godson won't rise, but the red one is the godson's
brother!'

'Let him thank God that he got off whole himself,'
replied Lukáshka.

'What are you glad about?' asked Olénin. 'Supposing
your brother had been killed; would you be glad?'

The Cossack looked at Olénin with laughing eyes. He

seemed to have understood all that Olénin wished to say to him, but to be above such considerations.

'Well, that happens too! Don't our fellows get killed sometimes?'

XXII

The captain and the head of the village rode away, and Olénin, to please Lukáshka as well as to avoid going back alone through the dark forest, asked the corporal to give Lukáshka leave, and the corporal did so. Olénin thought that Lukáshka wanted to see Maryánka and he was also glad of the companionship of such a pleasant-looking and sociable Cossack. Lukáshka and Maryánka he involuntarily united in his mind, and he found pleasure in thinking about them. 'He loves Maryánka,' thought Olénin, 'and I could love her,' and a new and powerful emotion of tenderness overcame him as they walked homewards together through the dark forest. Lukáshka too felt happy; something akin to love made itself felt between these two very different young men. Every time they glanced at one another they wanted to laugh.

'By which gate do you enter?' asked Olénin.

'By the middle one. But I'll see you as far as the marsh. After that you have nothing to fear.'

Olénin laughed.

'Do you think I am afraid? Go back, and thank you. I can get on alone.'

'It's all right! What have I to do? And how can you help being afraid? Even we are afraid,' said Lukáshka to set Olénin's self-esteem at rest, and he laughed too.

'Then come in with me. We'll have a talk and a drink and in the morning you can go back.'

'Couldn't I find a place to spend the night?' laughed Lukáshka. 'But the corporal asked me to go back.'

'I heard you singing last night, and also saw you.'

'Every one . . .' and Luke swayed his head.

'Is it true you are getting married?' asked Olénin.

'Mother wants me to marry. But I have not got a horse yet.'

'Aren't you in the regular service?'

'Oh dear no! I've only just joined, and have not got a horse yet, and don't know how to get one. That's why the marriage does not come off.'

'And what would a horse cost?'

'We were bargaining for one beyond the river the other day and they would not take sixty rubles for it, though it is a Nogáy horse.'

'Will you come and be my drabánt?' (A drabánt was a kind of orderly attached to an officer when campaigning.) 'I'll get it arranged and will give you a horse,' said Olénin suddenly. 'Really now, I have two and I don't want both.'

'How—don't want it?' Lukáshka said, laughing. 'Why should you make me a present? We'll get on by ourselves by God's help.'

'No, really! Or don't you want to be a drabánt?' said Olénin, glad that it had entered his head to give a horse to Lukáshka, though, without knowing why, he felt uncomfortable and confused and did not know what to say when he tried to speak.

Lukáshka was the first to break the silence.

'Have you a house of your own in Russia?' he asked.

Olénin could not refrain from replying that he had not only one, but several houses.

'A good house? Bigger than ours?' asked Lukáshka good-naturedly.

'Much bigger; ten times as big and three stories high,' replied Olénin.

'And have you horses such as ours?'

'I have a hundred horses, worth three or four hundred rubles each, but they are not like yours. They are trotters, you know. . . . But still, I like the horses here best.'

'Well, and did you come here of your own free will, or were you sent?' said Lukáshka, laughing at him. 'Look! that's where you lost your way,' he added, 'you should have turned to the right.'

'I came by my own wish,' replied Olénin. 'I wanted to see your parts and to join some expeditions.'

'I would go on an expedition any day,' said Lukáshka. 'D'you hear the jackals howling?' he added, listening.

'I say, don't you feel any horror at having killed a man?' asked Olénin.

'What's there to be frightened about? But I should like to join an expedition,' Lukáshka repeated. 'How I want to! How I want to!'

'Perhaps we may be going together. Our company is going before the holidays, and your "hundred" too.'

'And what did you want to come here for? You've a house and horses and serfs. In your place I'd do nothing but make merry! And what is your rank?'

'I am a cadet, but have been recommended for a commission.'

'Well, if you're not bragging about your home, if I were you I'd never have left it! Yes, I'd never have gone away anywhere. Do you find it pleasant living among us?'

'Yes, very pleasant,' answered Olénin.

It had grown quite dark before, talking in this way, they approached the village. They were still surrounded by the deep gloom of the forest. The wind howled through the tree-tops. The jackals suddenly seemed to be crying close beside them, howling, chuckling, and sobbing; but ahead of them in the village the sounds of women's voices and the barking of dogs could already be heard; the outlines of the huts were clearly to be seen; lights gleamed and the air was filled with the peculiar smell of *kisyak* smoke. Olénin felt keenly, that night especially, that here in this village was his home, his family, all his happiness, and that he never had and never would live so happily anywhere as he did in this Cossack village. He was so fond of everybody and especially of Lukáshka that night. On reaching home, to Lukáshka's great surprise, Olénin with his own hands led out of the shed a horse he had bought in Gróznoe—it was not the one he usually rode but another—not a bad horse though no longer young, and gave it to Lukáshka.

'Why should you give me a present?' said Lukáshka, 'I have not yet done anything for you.'

'Really it is nothing,' answered Olénin. 'Take it, and you will give me a present, and we'll go on an expedition against the enemy together.'

Lukáshka became confused.

'But what d'you mean by it? As if a horse were of little value,' he said without looking at the horse.

'Take it, take it! If you don't you will offend me. Vanyúsha! Take the grey horse to his house.'

Lukáshka took hold of the halter.

'Well then, thank you! This is something unexpected, undreamt of.'

Olénin was as happy as a boy of twelve.

'Tie it up here. It's a good horse. I bought it in Gróznoe;

it gallops splendidly! Vanyúsha, bring us some *chikhir*. Come into the hut.'

The wine was brought. Lukáshka sat down and took the wine-bowl.

'God willing I'll find a way to repay you,' he said, finishing his wine. 'How are you called?'

'Dmítri Andréich.'

'Well, 'Mítry Andréich, God bless you. We will be *kunaks*. Now you must come to see us. Though we are not rich people still we can treat a *kunak*, and I will tell mother in case you need anything—clotted cream or grapes—and if you come to the cordon I'm your servant to go hunting or to go across the river, anywhere you like! There now, only the other day, what a boar I killed, and I divided it among the Cossacks, but if I had only known, I'd have given it to you.'

'That's all right, thank you! But don't harness the horse, it has never been in harness.'

'Why harness the horse? And there is something else I'll tell you if you like,' said Lukáshka, bending his head. 'I have a *kunak*, Giréy Khan. He asked me to lie in ambush by the road where they come down from the mountains. Shall we go together? I'll not betray you. I'll be your *murid*.'

'Yes, we'll go; we'll go some day.'

Lukáshka seemed quite to have quieted down and to have understood Olénin's attitude towards him. His calmness and the ease of his behaviour surprised Olénin, and he did not even quite like it. They talked long, and it was late when Lukáshka, not tipsy (he never was tipsy) but having drunk a good deal, left Olénin after shaking hands.

Olénin looked out of the window to see what he would do. Lukáshka went out, hanging his head. Then, having led the horse out of the gate, he suddenly shook his head, threw the reins of the halter over its head, sprang onto its back like a cat, gave a wild shout, and galloped down the street. Olénin expected that Lukáshka would go to share his joy with Maryánka, but though he did not do so Olénin still felt his soul more at ease than ever before in his life. He was as delighted as a boy, and could not refrain from telling Vanyúsha not only that he had given Lukáshka the horse, but also why he had done it, as well as his new theory of happiness. Vanyúsha did not approve of his theory, and announced that *'l'argent il n'y a pas!'* and that therefore it was all nonsense.

Lukáshka rode home, jumped off the horse, and handed it over to his mother, telling her to let it out with the communal Cossack herd. He himself had to return to the cordon that same night. His deaf sister undertook to take the horse, and explained by signs that when she saw the man who had given the horse, she would bow down at his feet. The old woman only shook her head at her son's story, and decided in her own mind that he had stolen it. She therefore told the deaf girl to take it to the herd before daybreak.

Lukáshka went back alone to the cordon pondering over Olénin's action. Though he did not consider the horse a good one, yet it was worth at least forty rubles and Lukáshka was very glad to have the present. But why it had been given him he could not at all understand, and therefore he did not experience the least feeling of gratitude. On the contrary, vague suspicions that the cadet had some evil intentions filled his mind. What those intentions were he could not decide, but neither could he admit the idea that a stranger would give him a horse worth forty rubles for nothing, just out of kindness; it seemed impossible. Had he been drunk one might understand it! He might have wished to show off. But the cadet had been sober, and therefore must have wished to bribe him to do something wrong. 'Eh, humbug!' thought Lukáshka. 'Haven't I got the horse and we'll see later on. I'm not a fool myself and we shall see who'll get the better of the other,' he thought, feeling the necessity of being on his guard, and therefore arousing in himself unfriendly feelings towards Olénin. He told no one how he had got the horse. To some he said he had bought it, to others he replied evasively. However, the truth soon got about in the village, and Lukáshka's mother and Maryánka, as well as Elias Vasílich and other Cossacks, when they heard of Olénin's unnecessary gift, were perplexed, and began to be on their guard against the cadet. But despite their fears his action aroused in them a great respect for his simplicity and wealth.

'Have you heard,' said one, 'that the cadet quartered on Elias Vasílich has thrown a fifty-ruble horse at Lukáshka? He's rich! . . .'

'Yes, I heard of it,' replied another profoundly, 'he

must have done him some great service. We shall see what
will come of this cadet. Eh! what luck that Snatcher has!'

'Those cadets are crafty, awfully crafty,' said a third.
'See if he don't go setting fire to a building, or doing
something!'

XXIII

Olénin's life went on with monotonous regularity. He
had little intercourse with the commanding officers or with
his equals. The position of a rich cadet in the Caucasus was
peculiarly advantageous in this respect. He was not sent
out to work, or for training. As a reward for going on
an expedition he was recommended for a commission, and
meanwhile he was left in peace. The officers regarded him
as an aristocrat and behaved towards him with dignity.
Card-playing and the officers' carousals accompanied by
the soldier-singers, of which he had had experience when
he was with the detachment, did not seem to him attractive,
and he also avoided the society and life of the officers in
the village. The life of officers stationed in a Cossack
village has long had its own definite form. Just as every
cadet or officer when in a fort regularly drinks porter,
plays cards, and discusses the rewards given for taking
part in the expeditions, so in the Cossack villages he regularly drinks *chikhir* with his hosts, treats the girls to sweetmeats and honey, dangles after the Cossack women, and
falls in love, and occasionally marries there. Olénin always
took his own path and had an unconscious objection to
the beaten tracks. And here, too, he did not follow the
ruts of a Caucasian officer's life.

It came quite naturally to him to wake up at daybreak.
After drinking tea and admiring from his porch the mountains, the morning, and Maryánka, he would put on a tattered ox-hide coat, sandals of soaked raw hide, buckle on a
dagger, take a gun, put cigarettes and some lunch in a little
bag, call his dog, and soon after five o'clock would start for
the forest beyond the village. Towards seven in the evening
he would return tired and hungry with five or six pheasants
hanging from his belt (sometimes with some other animal)
and with his bag of food and cigarettes untouched. If the
thoughts in his head had lain like the lunch and cigarettes
in the bag, one might have seen that during all those fourteen hours not a single thought had moved in it. He re-

turned morally fresh, strong, and perfectly happy, and he could not tell what he had been thinking about all the time. Were they ideas, memories, or dreams that had been flitting through his mind? They were frequently all three. He would rouse himself and ask what he had been thinking about; and would see himself as a Cossack working in a vineyard with his Cossack wife, or an *abrek* in the mountains, or a boar running away from himself. And all the time he kept peering and watching for a pheasant, a boar, or a deer.

In the evening Daddy Eróshka would be sure to be sitting with him. Vanyúsha would bring a jug of *chikhir*, and they would converse quietly, drink, and separate to go quite contentedly to bed. The next day he would again go shooting, again be healthily weary, again they would sit conversing and drink their fill, and again be happy. Sometimes on a holiday or day of rest Olénin spent the whole day at home. Then his chief occupation was watching Maryánka, whose every movement, without realizing it himself, he followed greedily from his window or his porch. He regarded Maryánka and loved her (so he thought) just as he loved the beauty of the mountains and the sky, and he had no thought of entering into any relations with her. It seemed to him that between him and her such relations as there were between her and the Cossack Lukáshka could not exist, and still less such as often existed between rich officers and other Cossack girls. It seemed to him that if he tried to do as his fellow officers did, he would exchange his complete enjoyment of contemplation for an abyss of suffering, disillusionment, and remorse. Besides, he had already achieved a triumph of self-sacrifice in connexion with her which had given him great pleasure, and above all he was in a way afraid of Maryánka and would not for anything have ventured to utter a word of love to her lightly.

Once during the summer, when Olénin had not gone out shooting but was sitting at home, quite unexpectedly a Moscow acquaintance, a very young man whom he had met in society, came in.

'Ah, *mon cher*, my dear fellow, how glad I was when I heard that you were here!' he began in his Moscow French, and he went on intermingling French words in his remarks. 'They said, "Olénin". What Olénin? and I was so pleased. . . . Fancy fate bringing us together here! Well, and how are you? How? Why?' and Prince Belétski told his whole story: how he had temporarily entered the regiment, how the Commander-in-Chief had offered to take him as an adjutant, and how he would take up the post after this campaign although personally he felt quite indifferent about it.

'Living here in this hole one must at least make a career—get a cross—or a rank—be transferred to the Guards. That is quite indispensable, not for myself but for the sake of my relations and friends. The prince received me very well; he is a very decent fellow,' said Belétski, and went on unceasingly. 'I have been recommended for the St. Anna Cross for the expedition. Now I shall stay here a bit until we start on the campaign. It's capital here. What women! Well, and how are you getting on? I was told by our captain, Stártsev you know, a kind-hearted stupid creature. . . . Well, he said you were living like an awful savage, seeing no one! I quite understand you don't want to be mixed up with the set of officers we have here. I am so glad now you and I will be able to see something of one another. I have put up at the Cossack corporal's house. There is such a girl there. Ústenka! I tell you she's just charming.'

And more and more French and Russian words came pouring forth from that world which Olénin thought he had left for ever. The general opinion about Belétski was that he was a nice, good-natured fellow. Perhaps he really was; but in spite of his pretty, good-natured face, Olénin thought him extremely unpleasant. He seemed just to exhale that filthiness which Olénin had forsworn. What vexed him most was that he could not—had not the strength—abruptly to repulse this man who came from that world: as if that old world he used to belong to had an irresistible claim on him. Olénin felt angry with Belétski and with himself, yet against his wish he introduced French phrases into his own conversation, was interested in the Commander-in-Chief and in their Moscow acquaintances, and because in this Cossack village he and Belétski both spoke French, he spoke contemptuously of their fellow officers and of the Cossacks, and was friendly with Belétski, promising to visit him and inviting him to drop in to see him. Olénin however did not himself go to see Belétski.

Vanyúsha for his part approved of Belétski, remarking that he was a real gentleman.

Belétski at once adopted the customary life of a rich officer in a Cossack village. Before Olénin's eyes, in one month he came to be like an old resident of the village; he made the old men drunk, arranged evening parties, and himself went to parties arranged by the girls—bragged of his conquests, and even got so far that, for some unknown reason, the women and girls began calling him grandad, and the Cossacks, to whom a man who loved wine and women was clearly understandable, got used to him and even liked him better than they did Olénin, who was a puzzle to them.

XXIV

It was five in the morning. Vanyúsha was in the porch heating the samovar, and using the leg of a long boot instead of bellows. Olénin had already ridden off to bathe in the Térek. (He had recently invented a new amusement: to swim his horse in the river.) His landlady was in her outhouse, and the dense smoke of the kindling fire rose from the chimney. The girl was milking the buffalo-cow in the shed. 'Can't keep quiet, the damned thing!' came her impatient voice, followed by the rhythmical sound of milking.

From the street in front of the house horses' hoofs were heard clattering briskly, and Olénin, riding bareback on a handsome dark-grey horse which was still wet and shining, rode up to the gate. Maryánka's handsome head, tied round with a red kerchief, appeared from the shed and again disappeared. Olénin was wearing a red silk shirt, a white Circassian coat girdled with a strap which carried a dagger, and a tall cap. He sat his well-fed wet horse with a slightly conscious elegance and, holding his gun at his back, stooped to open the gate. His hair was still wet, and his face shone with youth and health. He thought himself handsome, agile, and like a brave; but he was mistaken. To any experienced Caucasian he was still only a soldier. When he noticed that the girl had put out her head he stooped with particular smartness, threw open the gate and, tightening the reins, swished his whip and entered the yard. 'Is tea ready, Vanyúsha?' he cried gaily, not looking at the door of the shed. He felt with pleasure how his fine horse, pressing down its flanks, pulling at the bridle and with every muscle quivering and with each foot ready to leap over the fence, pranced on the hard clay of the yard. *'C'est prêt,'* answered Vanyúsha. Olénin felt as if Maryánka's beautiful head was still looking out of the shed but he did not turn to look at her. As he jumped down from his horse he made an awkward movement and caught his gun against the porch, and turned a frightened look towards the shed, where there was no one to be seen and whence the sound of milking could still be heard.

Soon after he had entered the hut he came out again and sat down with his pipe and a book on the side of the porch which was not yet exposed to the rays of the sun. He meant not to go anywhere before dinner that day, and to write some long-postponed letters; but somehow he felt disinclined to leave his place in the porch, and he was as reluctant to go back into the hut as if it had been a prison. The housewife had heated her oven, and the girl, having driven the cattle, had come back and was collecting *kisyak* and heaping it up along the fence. Olénin went on reading, but did not understand a word of what was written in the book that lay open before him. He kept lifting his eyes from it and looking at the powerful young woman who was moving about. Whether she stepped into the moist morning shadow thrown by the house, or went out into the middle of the yard lit up by the joyous young light, so that the whole of her stately figure in its bright coloured garment gleamed in the sunshine and cast a black shadow—he always feared to lose any one of her movements. It delighted him to see how freely and gracefully her figure bent: into what folds her only garment, a pink smock, draped itself on her bosom and along her shapely legs; how she drew herself up and her tight-drawn smock showed the outline of her heaving bosom, how the soles of her narrow feet in her worn red slippers rested on the ground without altering their shape; how her strong arms with the sleeves rolled up, exerting the muscles, used the spade almost as if in anger, and how her deep dark eyes sometimes glanced at him. Though the delicate brows frowned, yet her eyes expressed pleasure and a knowledge of her own beauty.

'I say, Olénin, have you been up long?' said Belétski as he entered the yard dressed in the coat of a Caucasian officer.

'Ah, Belétski,' replied Olénin, holding out his hand. 'How is it you are out so early?'

'I had to. I was driven out; we are having a ball to-night. Maryánka, of course you'll come to Ústenka's?' he added, turning to the girl.

Olénin felt surprised that Belétski could address this woman so easily. But Maryánka, as though she had not heard him, bent her head, and throwing the spade across her shoulder went with her firm masculine tread towards the outhouse.

'She's shy, the wench is shy,' Belétski called after her. 'Shy of you,' he added as, smiling gaily, he ran up the steps of the porch.

'How is it you are having a ball and have been driven out?'

'It's at Ústenka's, at my landlady's, that the ball is, and you two are invited. A ball consists of a pie and a gathering of girls.'

'What should we do there?'

Belétski smiled knowingly and winked, jerking his head in the direction of the outhouse into which Maryánka had disappeared.

Olénin shrugged his shoulders and blushed.

'Well, really you are a strange fellow!' said he.

'Come now, don't pretend!'

Olénin frowned, and Belétski noticing this smiled insinuatingly. 'Oh, come, what do you mean?' he said, 'living in the same house—and such a fine girl, a splendid girl, a perfect beauty——'

'Wonderfully beautiful! I never saw such a woman before,' replied Olénin.

'Well then?' said Belétski, quite unable to understand the situation.

'It may be strange,' replied Olénin, "but why should I not say what is true? Since I have lived here women don't seem to exist for me. And it is so good, really! Now what can there be in common between us and women like these? Eróshka—that's a different matter! He and I have a passion in common—sport.'

'There now! In common! And what have I in common with Amália Ivánovna? It's the same thing! You may say they're not very clean—that's another matter . . . *À la guerre, comme à la guerre!* . . .'

'But I have never known any Amália Ivánovnas, and have never known how to behave with women of that sort,' replied Olénin. 'One cannot respect them, but these I do respect.'

'Well go on respecting them! Who wants to prevent you?'

Olénin did not reply. He evidently wanted to complete what he had begun to say. It was very near his heart.

'I know I am an exception . . .' He was visibly confused. 'But my life has so shaped itself that I not only see no necessity to renounce my rules, but I could not live here, let alone live as happily as I am doing, were I to live as you do. Therefore I look for something quite different from what you look for.'

Belétski raised his eyebrows incredulously. 'Anyhow, come to me this evening; Maryánka will be there and I will make you acquainted. Do come, please! If you feel dull you can go away. Will you come?'

'I would come, but to speak frankly I am afraid of being seriously carried away.'

'Oh, oh, oh!' shouted Belétski. 'Only come, and I'll see that you aren't. Will you? On your word?'

'I would come, but really I don't understand what we shall do; what part we shall play!'

'Please, I beg of you. You will come?'

'Yes, perhaps I'll come,' said Olénin.

'Really now! Charming women such as one sees nowhere else, and to live like a monk! What an idea! Why spoil your life and not make use of what is at hand? Have you heard that our company is ordered to Vozdvízhensk?'

'Hardly. I was told the 8th Company would be sent there,' said Olénin.

'No. I have had a letter from the adjutant there. He writes that the Prince himself will take part in the campaign. I am very glad I shall see something of him. I'm beginning to get tired of this place.'

'I hear we shall start on a raid soon.'

'I have not heard of it; but I have heard that Krinovítsin has received the Order of St. Anna for a raid. He expected a lieutenancy,' said Belétski laughing. 'He was let in! He has set off for headquarters.'

It was growing dusk and Olénin began thinking about the party. The invitation he had received worried him. He felt inclined to go, but what might take place there seemed strange, absurd, and even rather alarming. He knew that neither Cossack men nor older women, nor anyone besides the girls, were to be there. What was going to happen? How was he to behave? What would they talk about? What connexion was there between him and those wild Cossack girls? Belétski had told him of such curious, cynical, and yet rigid relations. It seemed strange to think that he would be there in the same hut with Maryánka and perhaps might have to talk to her. It seemed to him impossible when he remembered her majestic bearing. But Belétski spoke of it as if it were all perfectly simple. 'Is it possible that Belétski will treat Maryánka in the same way? That is interesting,' thought he. 'No, better not go. It's all so horrid, so vulgar, and above all—it leads to nothing!' But again he was worried by the question of what would take place; and besides he felt as if bound by a promise. He went out without having made up his mind one way or the other, but he walked as far as Belétski's, and went in there.

The hut in which Belétski lived was like Olénin's. It was raised nearly five feet from the ground on wooden piles, and had two rooms. In the first (which Olénin entered by the steep flight of steps) feather beds, rugs, blankets, and cushions were tastefully and handsomely arranged, Cossack fashion, along the main wall. On the side wall hung brass basins and weapons, while on the floor, under a bench, lay water-melons and pumpkins. In the second room there was a big brick oven, a table, and sectarian icons. It was here that Belétski was quartered, with his camp-bed and his pack and trunks. His weapons hung on the wall with a little rug behind them, and on the table were his toilet appliances and some portraits. A silk dressing-gown had been thrown on the bench. Belétski himself, clean and good looking, lay on the bed in his underclothing, reading *Les Trois Mousquetaires*.

He jumped up.

'There, you see how I have arranged things. Fine! Well, it's good that you have come. They are working furiously. Do you know what the pie is made of? Dough with a stuffing of pork and grapes. But that's not the point. You just look at the commotion out there!'

And really, on looking out of the window they saw an unusual bustle going on in the hut. Girls ran in and out, now for one thing and now for another.

'Will it soon be ready?' cried Belétski.

'Very soon! Why? Is Grandad hungry?' and from the hut came the sound of ringing laughter.

Ústenka, plump, small, rosy, and pretty, with her sleeves turned up, ran into Belétski's hut to fetch some plates.

'Get away or I shall smash the plates!' she squeaked, escaping from Belétski. 'You'd better come and help,' she shouted to Olénin, laughing. 'And don't forget to get some refreshments for the girls.' ('Refreshments' meaning spice-bread and sweets.)

'And has Maryánka come?'

'Of course! She brought some dough.'

'Do you know,' said Belétski, 'if one were to dress Ústenka up and clean and polish her up a bit, she'd be better than all our beauties. Have you ever seen that Cossack woman who married a colonel; she was charming! Bórsheva? What dignity! Where do they get it . . .'

'I have not seen Bórsheva, but I think nothing could be better than the costume they wear here.'

'Ah, I'm first-rate at fitting into any kind of life,' said Belétski with a sigh of pleasure. 'I'll go and see what they are up to.'

He threw his dressing-gown over his shoulders and ran out, shouting, 'And you look after the "refreshments".'

Olénin sent Belétski's orderly to buy spice-bread and honey; but it suddenly seemed to him so disgusting to give money (as if he were bribing someone) that he gave no definite reply to the orderly's question: 'How much spice-bread with peppermint, and how much with honey?'

'Just as you please.'

'Shall I spend all the money,' asked the old soldier impressively. 'The peppermint is dearer. It's sixteen kopeks.'

'Yes, yes, spend it all,' answered Olénin and sat down by the window, surprised that his heart was thumping as if he were preparing himself for something serious and wicked.

He heard screaming and shrieking in the girls' hut when Belétski went there, and a few moments later saw how he jumped out and ran down the steps, accompanied by shrieks, bustle, and laughter.

'Turned out,' he said.

A little later Ústenka entered and solemnly invited her visitors to come in: announcing that all was ready.

When they came into the room they saw that everything

was really ready. Ústenka was rearranging the cushions along the wall. On the table, which was covered by a disproportionately small cloth, was a decanter of *chikhir* and some dried fish. The room smelt of dough and grapes. Some half dozen girls in smart tunics, with their heads not covered as usual with kerchiefs, were huddled together in a corner behind the oven, whispering, giggling, and spluttering with laughter.

'I humbly beg you to do honour to my patron saint,' said Ústenka, inviting her guests to the table.

Olénin noticed Maryánka among the group of girls, who without exception were all handsome, and he felt vexed and hurt that he met her in such vulgar and awkward circumstances. He felt stupid and awkward, and made up his mind to do what Belétski did. Belétski stepped to the table somewhat solemnly yet with confidence and ease, drank a glass of wine to Ústenka's health, and invited the others to do the same. Ústenka announced that girls don't drink.

'We might with a little honey,' exclaimed a voice from among the group of girls.

The orderly, who had just returned with the honey and spice-cakes, was called in. He looked askance (whether with envy or with contempt) at the gentlemen, who in his opinion were on the spree; and carefully and conscientiously handed over to them a piece of honeycomb and the cakes wrapped up in a piece of greyish paper, and began explaining circumstantially all about the price and the change, but Belétski sent him away.

Having mixed honey with wine in the glasses, and having lavishly scattered the three pounds of spice-cakes on the table, Belétski dragged the girls from their corners by force, made them sit down at the table, and began distributing the cakes among them. Olénin involuntarily noticed how Maryánka's sunburnt but small hand closed on two round peppermint nuts and one brown one, and that she did not know what to do with them. The conversation was halting and constrained, in spite of Ústenka's and Belétski's free and easy manner and their wish to enliven the company. Olénin faltered, and tried to think of something to say, feeling that he was exciting curiosity and perhaps provoking ridicule and infecting the others with his shyness. He blushed, and it seemed to him that Maryánka in particular was feeling uncomfortable. 'Most likely they are expecting us to give them some money,' thought he. 'How are we to do it? And how can we manage quickest to give it and get away?'

XXV

'How is it you don't know your own lodger?' said Belétski, addressing Maryánka.

'How is one to know him if he never comes to see us?' answered Maryánka, with a look at Olénin.

Olénin felt frightened, he did not know of what. He flushed and, hardly knowing what he was saying, remarked; 'I'm afraid of your mother. She gave me such a scolding the first time I went in.'

Maryánka burst out laughing.

'And so you were frightened?' she said, and glanced at him and turned away.

It was the first time Olénin had seen the whole of her beautiful face. Till then he had seen her with her kerchief covering her to the eyes. It was not for nothing that she was reckoned the beauty of the village. Ústenka was a pretty girl, small, plump, rosy, with merry brown eyes, and red lips which were perpetually smiling and chattering. Maryánka on the contrary was certainly not pretty but beautiful. Her features might have been considered too masculine and almost harsh had it not been for her tall stately figure, her powerful chest and shoulders, and especially the severe yet tender expression of her long dark eyes which were darkly shadowed beneath their black brows, and for the gentle expression of her mouth and smile. She rarely smiled, but her smile was always striking. She seemed to radiate virginal strength and health. All the girls were good-looking, but they themselves and Belétski, and the orderly when he brought in the spice-cakes, all involuntarily gazed at Maryánka, and anyone addressing the girls was sure to address her. She seemed a proud and happy queen among them.

Belétski, trying to keep up the spirit of the party, chattered incessantly, made the girls hand round *chikhir,* fooled about with them, and kept making improper remarks in French about Maryánka's beauty to Olénin, calling her 'yours' (*la vôtre*), and advising him to behave as he did himself. Olénin felt more and more uncomfortable. He was devising an excuse to get out and run away when

Belétski announced that Ústenka, whose saint's day it was, must offer *chikhir* to everybody with a kiss. She consented on condition that they should put money on her plate, as is the custom at weddings. 'What fiend brought me to this disgusting feast?' thought Olénin, rising to go away.

'Where are you off to?'

'I'll fetch some tobacco,' he said, meaning to escape, but Belétski seized his hand.

'I have some money,' he said to him in French.

'One can't go away, one has to pay here,' thought Olénin bitterly, vexed at his own awkwardness. 'Can't I really behave like Belétski? I ought not to have come, but once I am here I must not spoil their fun. I must drink like a Cossack,' and taking the wooden bowl (holding about eight tumblers) he almost filled it with *chikhir* and drank it almost all. The girls looked at him, surprised and almost frightened, as he drank. It seemed to them strange and not right. Ústenka brought them another glass each, and kissed them both. 'There girls, now we'll have some fun,' she said, clinking on the plate the four rubles the men had put there.

Olénin no longer felt awkward, but became talkative.

'Now, Maryánka, it's your turn to offer us wine and a kiss,' said Belétski, seizing her hand.

'Yes, I'll give you such a kiss!' she said playfully, preparing to strike at him.

'One can kiss Grandad without payment,' said another girl.

'There's a sensible girl,' said Belétski, kissing the struggling girl. 'No, you must offer it,' he insisted, addressing Maryánka. 'Offer a glass to your lodger.'

And taking her by the hand he led her to the bench and sat her down beside Olénin.

'What a beauty,' he said, turning her head to see it in profile.

Maryánka did not resist but proudly smiling turned her long eyes towards Olénin.

'A beautiful girl,' repeated Belétski.

'Yes, see what a beauty I am,' Maryánka's look seemed to endorse. Without considering what he was doing Olénin embraced Maryánka and was going to kiss her, but she suddenly extricated herself, upsetting Belétski and pushing the top off the table, and sprang away towards the oven. There was much shouting and laughter. Then Belétski whispered something to the girls and suddenly they all ran out into the passage and locked the door behind them.

'Why did you kiss Belétski and won't kiss me?' asked Olénin.

'Oh, just so. I don't want to, that's all!' she answered, pouting and frowning. 'He's Grandad,' she added with a smile. She went to the door and began to bang at it. 'Why have you locked the door, you devils?'

'Well, let them be there and us here,' said Olénin, drawing closer to her.

She frowned, and sternly pushed him away with her hand. And again she appeared so majestically handsome to Olénin that he came to his senses and felt ashamed of what he was doing. He went to the door and began pulling at it himself.

'Belétski! Open the door! What a stupid joke!'

Maryánka again gave a bright happy laugh. 'Ah, you're afraid of me?' she said.

'Yes, you know you're as cross as your mother.'

'Spend more of your time with Eróshka; that will make the girls love you!' And she smiled, looking straight and close into his eyes.

He did not know what to reply. 'And if I were to come to see you——' he let fall.

'That would be a different matter,' she replied, tossing her head.

At that moment Belétski pushed the door open, and Maryánka sprang away from Olénin and in doing so her thigh struck his leg.

'It's all nonsense what I have been thinking about—love and self-sacrifice and Lukáshka. Happiness is the one thing. He who is happy is right,' flashed through Olénin's mind, and with a strength unexpected to himself he seized and kissed the beautiful Maryánka on her temple and her cheek. Maryánka was not angry, but only burst into a loud laugh and ran out to the other girls.

That was the end of the party. Ústenka's mother, returned from her work, gave all the girls a scolding, and turned them all out.

XXVI

'Yes,' thought Olénin, as he walked home. 'I need only slacken the reins a bit and I might fall desperately in love with this Cossack girl.' He went to bed with these thoughts, but expected it all to blow over and that he would continue to live as before.

But the old life did not return. His relations to Maryánka were changed. The wall that had separated them was broken down. Olénin now greeted her every time they met.

The master of the house having returned to collect the rent, on hearing of Olénin's wealth and generosity invited him to his hut. The old woman received him kindly, and from the day of the party onwards Olénin often went in of an evening and sat with them till late at night. He seemed to be living in the village just as he used to, but within him everything had changed. He spent his days in the forest, and towards eight o'clock, when it began to grow dusk, he would go to see his hosts, alone or with Daddy Eróshka. They grew so used to him that they were surprised when he stayed away. He paid well for his wine and was a quiet fellow. Vanyúsha would bring him his tea and he would sit down in a corner near the oven. The old woman did not mind him but went on with her work, and over their tea or their *chikhir* they talked about Cossack affairs, about the neighbours, or about Russia: Olénin relating and the others inquiring. Sometimes he brought a book and read to himself. Maryánka crouched like a wild goat with her feet drawn up under her, sometimes on the top of the oven, sometimes in a dark corner. She did not take part in the conversations, but Olénin saw her eyes and face and heard her moving or cracking sunflower seeds, and he felt that she listened with her whole being when he spoke, and was aware of his presence while he silently read to himself. Sometimes he thought her eyes were fixed on him, and meeting their radiance he involuntarily became silent and gazed at her. Then she would instantly hide her face and he would pretend to be deep in conversation with the old woman, while he listened all the time to her breathing and to her every movement and waited for her to look at him again. In the presence of others she was generally bright and friendly with him, but when they were alone together she was shy and rough. Sometimes he came in before Maryánka had returned home. Suddenly he would hear her firm footsteps and catch- a glimmer of her blue cotton smock at the open door. Then she would step into the middle of the hut, catch sight of him, and her eyes would give a scarcely perceptible kindly smile, and he would feel happy and frightened.

He neither sought for nor wished for anything from her, but every day her presence became more and more necessary to him.

Olénin had entered into the life of the Cossack village so fully that his past seemed quite foreign to him. As to the future, especially a future outside the world in which he was now living, it did not interest him at all. When he received letters from home, from relatives and friends, he was offended by the evident distress with which they regarded him as a lost man, while he in his village considered those as lost who did not live as he was living. He felt sure he would never repent of having broken away from his former surroundings and of having settled down in this village to such a solitary and original life. When out on expeditions, and when quartered at one of the forts, he felt happy too; but it was here, from under Daddy Eróshka's wing, from the forest and from his hut at the end of the village, and especially when he thought of Maryánka and Lukáshka, that he seemed to see the falseness of his former life. That falseness used to rouse his indignation even before, but now it seemed inexpressibly vile and ridiculous. Here he felt freer and freer every day and more and more of a man. The Caucasus now appeared entirely different to what his imagination had painted it. He had found nothing at all like his dreams, nor like the descriptions of the Caucasus he had heard and read. 'There are none of all those chestnut steeds, precipices, Amalet Beks, heroes or villains,' thought he. 'The people live as nature lives: they die, are born, unite, and more are born—they fight, eat and drink, rejoice and die, without any restrictions but those that nature imposes on sun and grass, on animal and tree. They have no other laws.' Therefore these people, compared to himself, appeared to him beautiful, strong, and free, and the sight of them made him feel ashamed and sorry for himself. Often it seriously occurred to him to throw up everything, to get registered as a Cossack, to buy a hut and cattle and marry a Cossack woman (only

not Maryánka, whom he conceded to Lukáshka), and to
live with Daddy Eróshka and go shooting and fishing with
him, and go with the Cossacks on their expeditions. 'Why
ever don't I do it? What am I waiting for?' he asked himself, and he egged himself on and shamed himself. 'Am I
afraid of doing what I hold to be reasonable and right? Is
the wish to be a simple Cossack, to live close to nature, not
to injure anyone but even to do good to others, more stupid
than my former dreams, such as those of becoming a
minister of state or a colonel?' but a voice seemed to say
that he should wait, and not take any decision. He was held
back by a dim consciousness that he could not live altogether like Eróshka and Lukáshka because he had a different idea of happiness—he was held back by the thought
that happiness lies in self-sacrifice. What he had done for
Lukáshka continued to give him joy. He kept looking for
occasions to sacrifice himself for others, but did not meet
with them. Sometimes he forgot this newly discovered
recipe for happiness and considered himself capable of
identifying his life with Daddy Eróshka's, but then he
quickly bethought himself and promptly clutched at the idea
of conscious self-sacrifice, and from that basis looked
calmly and proudly at all men and at their happiness.

XXVII

Just before the vintage Lukáshka came on horseback to
see Olénin. He looked more dashing than ever.

'Well? Are you getting married?' asked Olénin, greeting
him merrily.

Lukáshka gave no direct reply.

'There, I've exchanged your horse across the river. This
is a horse! A Kabardá horse from the Lov stud. I know
horses.'

They examined the new horse and made him caracole
about the yard. The horse really was an exceptionally fine
one, a broad and long gelding, with glossy coat, thick silky
tail, and the soft fine mane and crest of a thoroughbred. He
was so well fed that 'you might go to sleep on his back' as
Lukáshka expressed it. His hoofs, eyes, teeth, were ex-
quisitely shaped and sharply outlined, as one only finds
them in very pure-bred horses. Olénin could not help admiring the horse, he had not yet met with such a beauty in
the Caucasus.

'And how it goes!' said Lukáshka, patting its neck.
'What a step! And so clever—he simply runs after his
master.'

'Did you have to add much to make the exchange?'
asked Olénin.

'I did not count it,' answered Lukáshka with a smile. 'I
got him from a *kunak*.'

'A wonderfully beautiful horse! What would you take
for it?' asked Olénin.

'I have been offered a hundred and fifty rubles for it, but
I'll give it you for nothing,' said Lukáshka, merrily. 'Only
say the word and it's yours. I'll unsaddle it and you may
take it. Only give me some sort of a horse for my duties.'

'No, on no account.'

'Well then, here is a dagger I've brought you,' said
Lukáshka, unfastening his girdle and taking out one of the
two daggers which hung from it. 'I got it from across the
river.'

'Oh, thank you!'

'And mother has promised to bring you some grapes
herself.'

'That's quite unnecessary. We'll balance up some day.
You see I don't offer you any money for the dagger!'

'How could you? We are *kunaks*. It's just the same as
when Giréy Khan across the river took me into his home
and said, "Choose what you like!" So I took this sword. It's
our custom.'

They went into the hut and had a drink.

'Are you staying here awhile?' asked Olénin.

'No, I have come to say good-bye. They are sending me
from the cordon to a company beyond the Térek. I am
going to-night with my comrade Nazárka.'

'And when is the wedding to be?'

'I shall be coming back for the betrothal, and then I
shall return to the company again,' Lukáshka replied reluctantly.

'What, and see nothing of your betrothed?'

'Just so—what is the good of looking at her? When
you go on campaign ask in our company for Lukáshka
the Broad. But what a lot of boars there are in our parts!
I've killed two. I'll take you.'

'Well, good-bye! Christ save you.'

Lukáshka mounted his horse, and without calling on

Maryánka, rode caracoling down the street, where Nazárka was already awaiting him.

'I say, shan't we call round?' asked Nazárka, winking in the direction of Yámka's house.

'That's a good one!' said Lukáshka. 'Here, take my horse to her and if I don't come soon give him some hay. I shall reach the company by the morning any way.'

'Hasn't the cadet given you anything more?'

'I am thankful to have paid him back with a dagger—he was going to ask for the horse,' said Lukáshka, dismounting and handing over the horse to Nazárka.

He darted into the yard past Olénin's very window, and came up to the window of the cornet's hut. It was already quite dark. Maryánka, wearing only her smock, was combing her hair preparing for bed.

'It's I——' whispered the Cossack.

Maryánka's look was severely indifferent, but her face suddenly brightened up when she heard her name. She opened the window and leant out, frightened and joyous.

'What—what do you want?' she said.

'Open!' uttered Lukáshka. 'Let me in for a minute. I am so sick of waiting! It's awful!'

He took hold of her head through the window and kissed her.

'Really, do open!'

'Why do you talk nonsense? I've told you I won't! Have you come for long?'

He did not answer but went on kissing her, and she did not ask again.

'There, through the window one can't even hug you properly,' said Lukáshka.

'Maryánka dear!' came the voice of her mother, 'who is that with you?'

Lukáshka took off his cap, which might have been seen, and crouched down by the window.

'Go, be quick!' whispered Maryánka.

'Lukáshka called round,' she answered; 'he was asking for Daddy.'

'Well then send him here!'

'He's gone; said he was in a hurry.'

In fact, Lukáshka, stooping, as with big strides he passed under the windows, ran out through the yard and towards Yámka's house unseen by anyone but Olénin. After drinking two bowls of *chikhir* he and Nazárka rode away to the outpost. The night was warm, dark, and calm. They rode in silence, only the footfall of their horses˙was heard. Lukáshka started a song about the Cossack, Mingál, but stopped before he had finished the first verse, and after a pause, turning to Nazárka, said:

'I say, she wouldn't let me in!'

'Oh?' rejoined Nazárka. 'I knew she wouldn't. D'you know what Yámka told me? The cadet has begun going to their house. Daddy Eróshka brags that he got a gun from the cadet for getting him Maryánka.'

'He lies, the old devil!' said Lukáshka, angrily. 'She's not such a girl. If he does not look out I'll wallop that old devil's sides,' and he began his favourite song:

'From the village of Izmáylov,
   From the master's favourite garden,
   Once escaped a keen-eyed falcon.
Soon after him a huntsman came a-riding,
   And he beckoned to the falcon that had strayed,
   But the bright-eyed bird thus answered:
"In gold cage you could not keep me,
On your hand you could not hold me,
   So now I fly to blue seas far away.
There a white swan I will kill,
Of sweet swan-flesh have my fill." '

XXVIII

The betrothal was taking place in the cornet's hut. Lukáshka had returned to the village, but had not been to see Olénin, and Olénin had not gone to the betrothal though he had been invited. He was sad as he had never been since he settled in this Cossack village. He had seen Lukáshka earlier in the evening and was worried by the question why Lukáshka was so cold towards him. Olénin shut himself up in his hut and began writing in his diary as follows:

'Many things have I pondered over lately and much have I changed,' wrote he, 'and I have come back to the copybook maxim: The one way to be happy is to love, to love self-denyingly, to love everybody and everything; to spread a web of love on all sides and to take all who come into it. In this way I caught Vanyúsha, Daddy Eróshka, Lukáshka, and Maryánka.'

As Olénin was finishing this sentence Daddy Eróshka entered the room.

Eróshka was in the happiest frame of mind. A few evenings before this, Olénin had gone to see him and had found him with a proud and happy face deftly skinning the carcass of a boar with a small knife in the yard. The dogs (Lyam his pet among them) were lying close by watching what he was doing and gently wagging their tails. The little boys were respectfully looking at him through the fence and not even teasing him as was their wont. His women neighbours, who were as a rule not too gracious towards him, greeted him and brought him, one a jug of *chikhir*, another some clotted cream, and a third a little flour. The next day Eróshka sat in his store-room all covered with blood, and distributed pounds of boar-flesh, taking in payment money from some and wine from others. His face clearly expressed, 'God has sent me luck. I have killed a boar, so now I am wanted.' Consequently, he naturally began to drink, and had gone on for four days never leaving the village. Besides which he had had something to drink at the betrothal.

He came to Olénin quite drunk: his face red, his beard tangled, but wearing a new *beshmet* trimmed with gold braid; and he brought with him a *balaláyka* which he had obtained beyond the river. He had long promised Olénin this treat, and felt in the mood for it, so that he was sorry to find Olénin writing.

'Write on, write on, my lad,' he whispered, as if he thought that a spirit sat between him and the paper and must not be frightened away, and he softly and silently sat down on the floor. When Daddy Eróshka was drunk his favourite position was on the floor. Olénin looked round, ordered some wine to be brought, and continued to write. Eróshka found it dull to drink by himself and he wished to talk.

'I've been to the betrothal at the cornet's. But there! They're shwine!—Don't want them!—Have come to you.'

'And where did you get your *balaláyka?*' asked Olénin, still writing.

'I've been beyond the river and got it there, brother mine,' he answered, also very quietly. 'I'm a master at it. Tartar or Cossack, squire or soldiers' songs, any kind you please.'

Olénin looked at him again, smiled, and went on writing.

That smile emboldened the old man.

'Come, leave off, my lad, leave off!' he said with sudden firmness.

'Well, perhaps I will.'

'Come, people have injured you but leave them alone, spit at them! Come, what's the use of writing and writing, what's the good?'

And he tried to mimic Olénin by tapping the floor with his thick fingers, and then twisted his big face to express contempt.

'What's the good of writing quibbles. Better have a spree and show you're a man!'

No other conception of writing found place in his head except that of legal chicanery.

Olénin burst out laughing and so did Eróshka. Then, jumping up from the floor, the latter began to show off his skill on the *balaláyka* and to sing Tartar songs.

'Why write, my good fellow! You'd better listen to what I'll sing to you. When you're dead you won't hear any more songs. Make merry now!'

First he sang a song of his own composing accompanied by a dance:

> 'Ah, dee, dee, dee, dee, dee, dim,
> Say where did they last see him?
> In a booth, at the fair,
> He was selling pins, there.'

Then he sang a song he had learnt from his former sergeant-major:

> 'Deep I fell in love on Monday,
> Tuesday nothing did but sigh,
> Wednesday I popped the question,
> Thursday waited her reply.
> Friday, late, it came at last,
> Then all hope for me was past!
> Saturday my life to take
> I determined like a man,
> But for my salvation's sake
> Sunday morning changed my plan!'

Then he sang again:

> 'Oh dee, dee, dee, dee, dee, dim,
> Say where did they last see him?'

And after that, winking, twitching his shoulders, and footing it to the tune, he sang:

> 'I will kiss you and embrace,
> Ribbons red twine round you;
> And I'll call you little Grace.
> Oh, you little Grace now do
> Tell me, do you love me true?'

And he became so excited that with a sudden dashing movement he started dancing around the room accompanying himself the while.

Songs like 'Dee, dee, dee'—'gentlemen's songs'—he sang for Olénin's benefit, but after drinking three more tumblers of *chikhir* he remembered old times and began singing real Cossack and Tartar songs. In the midst of one of his favourite songs his voice suddenly trembled and he ceased singing, and only continued strumming on the *balaláyka*.

'Oh, my dear friend!' he said.

The peculiar sound of his voice made Olénin look round. The old man was weeping. Tears stood in his eyes and one tear was running down his cheek.

'You are gone, my young days, and will never come back!' he said, blubbering and halting. 'Drink, why don't you drink!' he suddenly shouted with a deafening roar, without wiping away his tears.

There was one Tartar song that specially moved him. It had few words, but its charm lay in the sad refrain. 'Ay day, dalalay!' Eróshka translated the words of the song: 'A youth drove his sheep from the *aoul* to the mountains: the Russians came and burnt the *aoul*, they killed all the men and took all the women into bondage. The youth returned from the mountains. Where the *aoul* had stood was an empty space; his mother not there, nor his brothers, nor his house; one tree alone was left standing. The youth sat beneath the tree and wept. "Alone like thee, alone am I left," ' and Eróshka began singing: 'Ay day, dalalay!' and the old man repeated several times this wailing, heart-rending refrain.

When he had finished the refrain Eróshka suddenly seized a gun that hung on the wall, rushed hurriedly out into the yard and fired off both barrels into the air. Then again he began, more dolefully, his 'Ay day, dalalay—ah, ah,' and ceased.

Olénin followed him into the porch and looked up into the starry sky in the direction where the shots had flashed. In the cornet's house there were lights and the sound of voices. In the yard girls were crowding round the porch and the windows, and running backwards and forwards between the hut and the outhouse. Some Cossacks rushed out of the hut and could not refrain from shouting, re-echoing the refrain of Daddy Eróshka's song and his shots.

'Why are you not at the betrothal?' asked Olénin.

'Never mind them! Never mind them!' muttered the old man, who had evidently been offended by something there. 'Don't like them, I don't. Oh, those people! Come back into the hut! Let them make merry by themselves and we'll make merry by ourselves.'

Olénin went in.

'And Lukáshka, is he happy? Won't he come to see me?' he asked.

'What, Lukáshka? They've lied to him and said I am getting his girl for you,' whispered the old man. 'But what's the girl? She will be ours if we want her. Give enough money—and she's ours. I'll fix it up for you. Really!'

'No, Daddy, money can do nothing if she does not love me. You'd better not talk like that!'

'We are not loved, you and I. We are forlorn,' said Daddy Eróshka suddenly, and again he began to cry.

Listening to the old man's talk Olénin had drunk more than usual. 'So now my Lukáshka is happy,' thought he; yet he felt sad. The old man had drunk so much that evening that he fell down on the floor and Vanyúsha had to call soldiers in to help, and spat as they dragged the old man out. He was so angry with the old man for his bad behaviour that he did not even say a single French word.

XXIX

It was August. For days the sky had been cloudless, the sun scorched unbearably and from early morning the warm wind raised a whirl of hot sand from the sand-drifts and from the road, and bore it in the air through the reeds, the trees, and the village. The grass and the leaves on the trees were covered with dust, the roads and dried-up salt marshes were baked so hard that they rang when trodden on. The water had long since subsided in the Térek and rapidly vanished and dried up in the ditches. The slimy banks of the pond near the village were trodden bare by the cattle and all day long you could hear the splashing of water and the shouting of girls and boys bathing. The sand-drifts and the reeds were already drying up in the steppes, and the cattle, lowing, ran into the fields in the day-time. The boars migrated into the distant reed-beds and to the hills beyond the Térek. Mosquitoes and gnats swarmed in thick clouds over the low lands and villages. The snow-peaks were hidden in grey mist. The air was rarefied and smoky. It was said that *abreks* had crossed the now shallow river and were prowling on this side of it. Every night the sun set in a glowing red blaze. It was the busiest time of the year. The villagers all swarmed in the melon-fields and the vineyards. The vineyards thickly overgrown with twining verdure lay in cool, deep shade. Everywhere between the broad translucent leaves, ripe, heavy, black clusters peeped out. Along the dusty road from the vineyards the creaking carts moved slowly, heaped up with black grapes. Clusters of them, crushed by the wheels, lay in the dirt. Boys and girls in smocks stained with grape-juice, with grapes in their hands and mouths, ran after their mothers. On the road you continually came across tattered labourers with baskets of grapes on their powerful shoulders; Cossack maidens, veiled with kerchiefs to their eyes, drove bullocks harnessed to carts laden high with grapes. Soldiers who happened to meet these carts asked for grapes, and the maidens, clambering up without stopping their carts, would take an armful of grapes and drop them into the skirts of the soldiers' coats. In some homesteads they had already begun pressing the grapes; and the smell of the emptied skins filled the air. One saw the blood-red troughs in the pent-houses in the yards and Nogáy labourers with their trousers rolled up and their legs stained with the juice. Grunting pigs gorged themselves with the empty skins and rolled about in them. The flat roofs of the outhouses were all spread over with the dark amber clusters drying in the sun. Daws and magpies crowded round the roofs, picking the seeds and fluttering from one place to another.

The fruits of the year's labour were being merrily gathered in, and this year the fruit was unusually fine and plentiful.

In the shady green vineyards amid a sea of vines, laughter, songs, merriment, and the voices of women were to be heard on all sides, and glimpses of their bright-coloured garments could be seen.

Just at noon Maryánka was sitting in their vineyard in the shade of a peach-tree, getting out the family dinner from under an unharnessed cart. Opposite her, on a spread-out horse-cloth, sat the cornet (who had returned from the school) washing his hands by pouring water on them from a little jug. Her little brother, who had just come straight out of the pond, stood wiping his face with his wide sleeves, and gazed anxiously at his sister and his mother and breathed deeply, awaiting his dinner. The old mother, with her sleeves rolled up over her strong sunburnt arms, was arranging grapes, dried fish, and clotted cream on a little low, circular Tartar table. The cornet wiped his hands, took off his cap, crossed himself, and moved nearer to the table. The boy seized the jug and eagerly began to drink. The mother and daughter crossed their legs under them and sat down by the table. Even in the shade it was intolerably hot. The air above the vineyard smelt unpleasant: the strong warm wind passing amid the branches brought no coolness, but only monotonously bent the tops of the pear, peach, and mulberry trees with which the vineyard was sprinkled. The cornet, having crossed himself once more, took a little jug of *chikhir* that stood behind him covered with a vine-leaf, and having had a drink from the mouth of the jug passed it to the old woman. He had nothing on over his shirt, which was un-fastened at the neck and showed his shaggy muscular chest. His fine-featured cunning face looked cheerful; neither in his attitude nor in his words was his usual wiliness to be seen; he was cheerful and natural.

'Shall we finish the bit beyond the shed to-night?' he asked, wiping his wet beard.

'We'll manage it,' replied his wife, 'if only the weather does not hinder us. The Dëmkins have not half finished yet,' she added. 'Only Ústenka is at work there, wearing herself out.'

'What can you expect of them?' said the old man proudly.

'Here, have a drink, Maryánka dear!' said the old woman, passing the jug to the girl. 'God willing we'll have enough to pay for the wedding feast,' she added.

'That's not yet awhile,' said the cornet with a slight frown.

The girl hung her head.

'Why shouldn't we mention it?' said the old woman. 'The affair is settled, and the time is drawing near too.'

'Don't make plans beforehand,' said the cornet. 'Now we have the harvest to get in.'

'Have you seen Lukáshka's new horse?' asked the old woman. 'That which Dmítri Andréich Olénin gave him is gone—he's exchanged it.'

'No, I have not; but I spoke with the servant to-day,' said the cornet, 'and he said his master has again received a thousand rubles.'

'Rolling in riches, in short,' said the old woman.

The whole family felt cheerful and contented.

The work was progressing successfully. The grapes were more abundant and finer than they had expected.

After dinner Maryánka threw some grass to the oxen, folded her *beshmet* for a pillow, and lay down under the wagon on the juicy down-trodden grass. She had on only a red kerchief over her head and a faded blue print smock, yet she felt unbearably hot. Her face was burning, and she did not know where to put her feet, her eyes were moist with sleepiness and weariness, her lips parted involuntarily, and her chest heaved heavily and deeply.

The busy time of year had begun a fortnight ago and the continuous heavy labour had filled the girl's life. At dawn she jumped up, washed her face with cold water, wrapped herself in a shawl, and ran out barefoot to see to the cattle. Then she hurriedly put on her shoes and her *beshmet* and, taking a small bundle of bread, she harnessed the bullocks and drove away to the vineyards for the whole day. There she cut the grapes and carried the baskets with only an hour's interval for rest, and in the evening she returned to the village, bright and not tired, dragging the bullocks by a rope or driving them with a long stick. After attending to the cattle, she took some sunflower seeds in the wide sleeve of her smock and went to the corner of the street to crack them and have some fun with the other girls. But as soon as it was dusk she returned home, and after having supper with her parents and her brother in the dark outhouse, she went into the hut, healthy and free from care, and climbed onto the oven, where half drowsing she listened to their lodger's conversation. As soon as he went away she would throw herself down on her bed and sleep soundly and quietly till

morning. And so it went on day after day. She had not
seen Lukáshka since the day of their betrothal, but calmly
awaited the wedding. She had got used to their lodger and
felt his intent looks with pleasure.

XXX

Although there was no escape from the heat and the
mosquitoes swarmed in the cool shadow of the wagons,
and her little brother tossing about beside her kept pushing
her, Maryánka having drawn her kerchief over her head
was just falling asleep, when suddenly their neighbour
Ústenka came running towards her and, diving under the
wagon, lay down beside her.

'Sleep, girls, sleep!' said Ústenka, making herself comfortable under the wagon. 'Wait a bit,' she exclaimed,
'this won't do!'

She jumped up, plucked some green branches, and
stuck them through the wheels on both sides of the wagon
and hung her *beshmet* over them.

'Let me in,' she shouted to the little boy as she again
crept under the wagon. 'Is this the place for a Cossack—
with the girls? Go away!'

When alone under the wagon with her friend, Ústenka
suddenly put both her arms round her, and clinging close
to her began kissing her cheeks and neck.

'Darling, sweetheart,' she kept repeating, between bursts
of shrill, clear laughter.

'Why, you've learnt it from grandad,' said Maryánka,
struggling. 'Stop it!'

And they both broke into such peals of laughter that
Maryánka's mother shouted to them to be quiet.

'Are you jealous?' asked Ústenka in a whisper.

'What humbug! Let me sleep. What have you come for?'

But Ústenka kept on, 'I say! But I wanted to tell you
such a thing.'

Maryánka raised herself on her elbow and arranged
the kerchief which had slipped off.

'Well, what is it?'

'I know something about your lodger!'

'There's nothing to know,' said Maryánka.

'Oh, you rogue of a girl!' said Ústenka, nudging her
with her elbow and laughing. 'Won't tell anything. Does he
come to you?'

'He does. What of that?' said Maryánka with a sudden blush.

'Now I'm a simple lass. I tell everybody. Why should I pretend?' said Ústenka, and her bright rosy face suddenly became pensive. 'Whom do I hurt? I love him, that's all about it.'

'Grandad, do you mean?'

'Well, yes!'

'And the sin?'

'Ah, Maryánka! When is one to have a good time if not while one's still free? When I marry a Cossack I shall bear children and shall have cares. There now, when you get married to Lukáshka not even a thought of joy will enter your head: children will come, and work!'

'Well? Some who are married live happily. It makes no difference!' Maryánka replied quietly.

'Do tell me just this once what has passed between you and Lukáshka?'

'What has passed? A match was proposed. Father put it off for a year, but now it's been settled and they'll marry us in autumn.'

'But what did he say to you?'

Maryánka smiled.

'What should he say? He said he loved me. He kept asking me to come to the vineyards with him.'

'Just see what pitch! But you didn't go, did you? And what a dare-devil he has become: the first among the braves. He makes merry out there in the army too! The other day our Kírka came home; he says: "What a horse Lukáshka's got in exchange!" But all the same I expect he frets after you. And what else did he say?'

'Must you know everything?' said Maryánka laughing. 'One night he came to my window tipsy, and asked me to let him in.'

'And you didn't let him?'

'Let him, indeed! Once I have said a thing I keep to it firm as a rock,' answered Maryánka seriously.

'A fine fellow! If he wanted her, no girl would refuse him.'

'Well, let him go to the others,' replied Maryánka proudly.

'You don't pity him?'

'I do pity him, but I'll have no nonsense. It is wrong.'

Ústenka suddenly dropped her head on her friend's

breast, seized hold of her, and shook with smothered laughter. 'You silly fool!' she exclaimed, quite out of breath. 'You don't want to be happy,' and she began tickling Maryánka.

'Oh, leave off!' said Maryánka, screaming and laughing. 'You've crushed Lazútka.'

'Hark at those young devils! Quite frisky! Not tired yet!' came the old woman's sleepy voice from the wagon.

'Don't want happiness,' repeated Ústenka in a whisper, insistently. 'But you are lucky, that you are! How they love you! You are so crusty, and yet they love you. Ah, if I were in your place I'd soon turn the lodger's head! I noticed him when you were at our house. He was ready to eat you with his eyes. What things grandad has given me! And yours they say is the richest of the Russians. His orderly says they have serfs of their own.'

Maryánka raised herself, and after thinking a moment, smiled.

'Do you know what he once told me: the lodger I mean?' she said, biting a bit of grass. 'He said, "I'd like to be Lukáshka the Cossack, or your brother Lazútka——." What do you think he meant?'

'Oh, just chattering what came into his head,' answered Ústenka. 'What does mine not say! Just as if he was possessed!'

Maryánka dropped her hand on her folded *beshmet*, threw her arm over Ústenka's shoulder, and shut her eyes.

'He wanted to come and work in the vineyard to-day: father invited him,' she said, and after a short silence she fell asleep.

XXXI

The sun had come out from behind the pear-tree that had shaded the wagon, and even through the branches that Ústenka had fixed up it scorched the faces of the sleeping girls. Maryánka woke up and began arranging the kerchief on her head. Looking about her, beyond the pear-tree she noticed their lodger, who with his gun on his shoulder stood talking to her father. She nudged Ústenka and smilingly pointed him out to her.

'I went yesterday and didn't find a single one,' Olénin was saying as he looked about uneasily, not seeing Maryánka through the branches.

'Ah, you should go out there in that direction, go right as by compasses, there in a disused vineyard denominated as the Waste, hares are always to be found,' said the cornet, having at once changed his manner of speech.

'A fine thing to go looking for hares in these busy times! You had better come and help us, and do some work with the girls,' the old woman said merrily. 'Now then, girls, up with you!' she cried.

Maryánka and Ústenka under the cart were whispering and could hardly restrain their laughter.

Since it had become known that Olénin had given a horse worth fifty rubles to Lukáshka, his hosts had become more amiable and the cornet in particular saw with pleasure his daughter's growing intimacy with Olénin.

'But I don't know how to do the work,' replied Olénin, trying not to look through the green branches under the wagon where he had now noticed Maryánka's blue smock and red kerchief.

'Come, I'll give you some peaches,' said the old woman.

'It's only according to the ancient Cossack hospitality. It's her old woman's silliness,' said the cornet, explaining and apparently correcting his wife's words. 'In Russia, I expect, it's not so much peaches as pineapple jam and preserves you have been accustomed to eat at your pleasure.'

'So you say hares are to be found in the disused vineyard?' asked Olénin. 'I will go there,' and throwing a hasty glance through the green branches he raised his cap and disappeared between the regular rows of green vines.

The sun had already sunk behind the fence of the vineyards, and its broken rays glittered through the translucent leaves when Olénin returned to his host's vineyard. The wind was falling and a cool freshness was beginning to spread around. By some instinct Olénin recognized from afar Maryánka's blue smock among the rows of vine, and, picking grapes on his way, he approached her. His highly excited dog also now and then seized a low-hanging cluster of grapes in his slobbering mouth. Maryánka, her face flushed, her sleeves rolled up, and her kerchief down below her chin, was rapidly cutting the heavy clusters and laying them in a basket. Without letting go of the vine she had hold of, she stopped to smile pleasantly at him and resumed her work. Olénin drew near and threw his gun behind his back to have his hands free. 'Where are your people? May God aid you! Are you alone?' he meant to say but did not say, and only raised his cap in silence.

He was ill at ease alone with Maryánka, but as if purposely to torment himself he went up to her.

'You'll be shooting the women with your gun like that,' said Maryánka.

'No, I shan't shoot them.'

They were both silent.

Then after a pause she said: 'You should help me.'

He took out his knife and began silently to cut off the clusters. He reached from under the leaves low down a thick bunch weighing about three pounds, the grapes of which grew so close that they flattened each other for want of space. He showed it to Maryánka.

'Must they all be cut? Isn't this one too green?'

'Give it here.'

Their hands touched. Olénin tóok her hand, and she looked at him smiling.

'Are you going to be married soon?' he asked.

She did not answer, but turned away with a stern look.

'Do you love Lukáshka?'

'What's that to you?'

'I envy him!'

'Very likely!'

'No really. You are so beautiful!'

And he suddenly felt terribly ashamed of having said it, so commonplace did the words seem to him. He flushed, lost control of himself, and seized both her hands.

'Whatever I am, I'm not for you. Why do you make fun of me?' replied Maryánka, but her look showed how certainly she knew he was not making fun.

'Making fun? If you only knew how I——'

The words sounded still more commonplace, they accorded still less with what he felt, but yet he continued, 'I don't know what I would not do for you——'

'Leave me alone, you pitch!'

But her face, her shining eyes, her swelling bosom, her shapely legs, said something quite different. It seemed to him that she understood how petty were all things he had said, but that she was superior to such considerations. It seemed to him she had long known all he wished and was not able to tell her, but wanted to hear how he would say it. 'And how can she help knowing,' he thought, 'since

I only want to tell her all that she herself is? But she does not wish to understand, does not wish to reply.'

'Hullo!' suddenly came Ústenka's high voice from behind the vine at no great distance, followed by her shrill laugh. 'Come and help me, Dmítri Andréich. I am all alone,' she cried, thrusting her round, naïve little face through the vines.

Olénin did not answer nor move from his place.

Maryánka went on cutting and continually looked up at Olénin. He was about to say something, but stopped, shrugged his shoulders and, having jerked up his gun, walked out of the vineyard with rapid strides.

XXXII

He stopped once or twice, listening to the ringing laughter of Maryánka and Ústenka who, having come together, were shouting something. Olénin spent the whole evening hunting in the forest and returned home at dusk without having killed anything. When crossing the road he noticed her open the door of the outhouse, and her blue smock showed through it. He called to Vanyúsha very loud so as to let her know that he was back, and then sat down in the porch in his usual place. His hosts now returned from the vineyard; they came out of the outhouse and into their hut, but did not ask him in. Maryánka went twice out of the gate. Once in the twilight it seemed to him that she was looking at him. He eagerly followed her every movement, but could not make up his mind to approach her. When she disappeared into the hut he left the porch and began pacing up and down the yard, but Maryánka did not come out again. Olénin spent the whole sleepless night out in the yard listening to every sound in his hosts' hut. He heard them talking early in the evening, heard them having their supper and pulling out their cushions, and going to bed; he heard Maryánka laughing at something, and then heard everything growing gradually quiet. The cornet and his wife talked a while in whispers, and someone was breathing. Olénin re-entered his hut. Vanyúsha lay asleep in his clothes. Olénin envied him, and again went out to pace the yard, always expecting something, but no one came, no one moved, and he only heard the regular breathing of three people. He knew Maryánka's breathing and listened to it and to the beating of his own heart. In the village everything was quiet. The waning moon rose late, and the deep-breathing cattle in the yard became more visible as they lay down and slowly rose. Olénin angrily asked himself, 'What is it I want?' but could not tear himself away from the enchantment of the night. Suddenly he thought he distinctly heard the floor creak and the sound of footsteps in his hosts' hut. He rushed to the door, but all was silent again except for the sound of regular breathing, and in the yard the buffalo-cow, after a deep sigh, again moved, rose on her foreknees and then on her feet, swished her tail, and something splashed steadily on the dry clay ground; then she lay down again in the dim moonlight. He asked himself: 'What am I to do?' and definitely decided to go to bed, but again he heard a sound, and in his imagination there arose the image of Maryánka coming out into this moonlit misty night, and again he rushed to her window and again heard the sound of footsteps. Not till just before dawn did he go up to her window and push at the shutter and then run to the door, and this time he really heard Maryánka's deep breathing and her footsteps. He took hold of the latch and knocked. The floor hardly creaked under the bare cautious footsteps which approached the door. The latch clicked, the door creaked, and he noticed a faint smell of marjoram and pumpkin, and Maryánka's whole figure appeared in the doorway. He saw her only for an instant in the moonlight. She slammed the door and, muttering something, ran lightly back again. Olénin began rapping softly but nothing responded. He ran to the window and listened. Suddenly he was startled by a shrill, squeaky man's voice.

'Fine!' exclaimed a rather small young Cossack in a white cap, coming across the yard close to Olénin. 'I saw . . . fine!'

Olénin recognized Nazárka, and was silent, not knowing what to do or say.

'Fine! I'll go and tell them at the office, and I'll tell her father! That's a fine cornet's daughter! One's not enough for her.'

'What do you want of me, what are you after?' uttered Olénin.

'Nothing; only I'll tell them at the office.'

Nazárka spoke very loud, and evidently did so intentionally, adding: 'Just see what a clever cadet!'

Olénin trembled and grew pale.

'Come here, here!' He seized the Cossack firmly by the arm and drew him towards his hut.

'Nothing happened, she did not let me in, and I too mean no harm. She is an honest girl——'

'Eh, discuss——'

'Yes, but all the same I'll give you something now. Wait a bit!'

Nazárka said nothing. Olénin ran into his hut and brought out ten rubles, which he gave to the Cossack.

'Nothing happened, but still I was to blame, so I give this!—— Only for God's sake don't let anyone know, for nothing happened . . .'

'I wish you joy,' said Nazárka laughing, and went away.

Nazárka had come to the village that night at Lukáshka's bidding to find a place to hide a stolen horse, and now, passing by on his way home, had heard the sound of footsteps. When he returned next morning to his company he bragged to his chum, and told him how cleverly he had got ten rubles. Next morning Olénin met his hosts and they knew nothing about the events of the night. He did not speak to Maryánka, and she only laughed a little when she looked at him. Next night he also passed without sleep, vainly wandering about the yard. The day after he purposely spent shooting, and in the evening he went to see Belétski to escape from his own thoughts. He was afraid of himself, and promised himself not to go to his hosts' hut any more.

That night he was roused by the sergeant-major. His company was ordered to start at once on a raid. Olénin was glad this had happened, and thought he would not again return to the village.

The raid lasted four days. The commander, who was a relative of Olénin's, wished to see him and offered to let him remain with the staff, but this Olénin declined. He found that he could not live away from the village, and asked to be allowed to return to it. For having taken part in the raid he received a soldier's cross, which he had formerly greatly desired. Now he was quite indifferent about it, and even more indifferent about his promotion, the order for which had still not arrived. Accompanied by Vanyúsha he rode back to the cordon without any accident several hours in advance of the rest of the company. He spent the whole evening in his porch watching Maryánka, and he again walked about the yard, without aim or thought, all night.

XXXIII

It was late when he awoke the next day. His hosts were no longer in. He did not go shooting, but now took up a book, and now went out into the porch, and now again re-entered the hut and lay down on the bed. Vanyúsha thought he was ill.

Towards evening Olénin got up, resolutely began writing, and wrote on till late at night. He wrote a letter, but did not post it because he felt that no one would have understood what he wanted to say, and besides it was not necessary that anyone but himself should understand it. This is what he wrote:

'I receive letters of condolence from Russia. They are afraid that I shall perish, buried in these wilds. They say about me: "He will become coarse; he will be behind the times in everything; he will take to drink, and who knows but that he may marry a Cossack girl." It was not for nothing, they say, that Ermólov declared: "Anyone serving in the Caucasus for ten years either becomes a confirmed drunkard or marries a loose woman." How terrible! Indeed it won't do for me to ruin myself when I might have the great happiness of even becoming the Countess B——'s husband, or a Court chamberlain, or a *Maréchal de noblesse* of my district. Oh, how repulsive and pitiable you all seem to me! You do not know what happiness is and what life is! One must taste life once in all its natural beauty, must see and understand what I see every day before me—those eternally unapproachable snowy peaks, and a majestic woman in that primitive beauty in which the first woman must have come from her creator's hands—and then it becomes clear who is ruining himself and who is living truly or falsely—you or I. If you only knew how despicable and pitiable you, in your delusions, seem to me! When I picture to myself—in place óf my hut, my forests, and my love—those drawing-rooms, those women with their pomatum-greased hair eked out with false curls, those unnaturally grimacing lips, those hidden, feeble, distorted limbs, and that chatter of obligatory drawing-room conversation which has no right to the name—I feel unendurably revolted. I then see before me those obtuse faces, those rich eligible girls whose looks seem to say: "It's all right, you may come near though I am rich and eligible" —and that arranging and rearranging of seats, that shameless match-making and that eternal tittle-tattle and pretence; those rules—with whom to shake hands, to whom only to nod, with whom to converse (and all this done deliberately with a conviction of its inevitability), that continual ennui in the blood passing on from generation to generation. Try to understand or believe just this one thing: you need only see and comprehend what truth and beauty are, and all that you now say and think and all your wishes for me and for yourselves will fly to atoms! Happiness is being with nature, seeing her, and conversing with her. "He may even (God forbid) marry a common Cossack girl, and be quite lost socially" I can imagine them saying of me with sincere pity! Yet the one thing I desire is to be quite "lost" in your sense of the word. I wish to marry a Cossack girl, and dare not because it would be a height of happiness of which I am unworthy.

'Three months have passed since I first saw the Cossack girl, Maryánka. The views and prejudices of the world I had left were still fresh in me. I did not then believe that I could love that woman. I delighted in her beauty just as I delighted in the beauty of the mountains and the sky, nor could I help delighting in her, for she is as beautiful as they. I found that the sight of her beauty had become a necessity of my life and I began asking myself whether I did not love her. But I could find nothing within myself at all like love as I had imagined it to be. Mine was not the restlessness of loneliness and desire for marriage, nor was it platonic, still less a carnal love such as I have experienced. I needed only to see her, to hear her, to know that she was near—and if I was not happy, I was at peace.

'After an evening gathering at which I met her and touched her, I felt that between that woman and myself there existed an indissoluble though unacknowledged bond against which I could not struggle, yet I did struggle. I asked myself: "Is it possible to love a woman who will never understand the profoundest interests of my life? Is it possible to love a woman simply for her beauty, to love the statue of a woman?" But I was already in love with her, though I did not yet trust to my feelings.

'After that evening when I first spoke to her our relations changed. Before that she had been to me an extraneous but majestic object of external nature: but since then she has become a human being. I began to meet her, to talk to her, and sometimes to go to work for her father and to spend whole evenings with them, and in, this intimate intercourse she remained still in my eyes just as pure, inaccessible, and majestic. She always responded with equal calm, pride, and cheerful equanimity. Sometimes she was friendly, but generally her every look, every word, and every movement expressed equanimity—not contemptuous, but crushing and bewitching. Every day with a feigned smile on my lips I tried to play a part, and with torments of passion and desire in my heart I spoke banteringly to her. She saw that I was dissembling, but looked straight at me cheerfully and simply. This position became unbearable. I wished not to deceive her but to tell her all I thought and felt. I was extremely agitated. We were in the vineyard when I began to tell her of my love, in words I am now ashamed to remember. I am ashamed because I ought not to have dared to speak so to her because she stood far above such words and above the feeling they were meant to express. I said no more, but from that day my position has been intolerable. I did not wish to demean myself by continuing our former flippant relations, and at the same time I felt that I had not yet reached the level of straight and simple relations with her. I asked myself despairingly, "What am I to do?" In foolish dreams I imagined her now as my mistress and now as my wife, but rejected both ideas with disgust. To make her a wanton woman would be dreadful. It would be murder. To turn her into a fine lady, the wife of Dmítri Andréich Olénin, like a Cossack woman here who is married to one of our officers, would be still worse. Now could I turn Cossack like Lukáshka, and steal horses, get drunk on *chikhir,* sing rollicking songs, kill people, and when drunk climb in at her window for the night without a thought of who and what I am, it would be different: then we might understand one another and I might be happy.

'I tried to throw myself into that kind of life but was still more conscious of my own weakness and artificiality. I cannot forget myself and my complex, distorted past, and my future appears to me still more hopeless. Every day I have before me the distant snowy mountains and this majestic, happy woman. But not for me is the only happiness possible in the world; I cannot have this woman!

What is most terrible and yet sweetest in my condition is that I feel that I understand her but that she will never understand me; not because she is inferior: on the contrary she ought not to understand me. She is happy, she is like nature: consistent, calm, and self-contained; and I, a weak distorted being, want her to understand my deformity and my torments! I have not slept at night, but have aimlessly passed under her windows not rendering account to myself of what was happening to me. On the 18th our company started on a raid, and I spent three days away from the village. I was sad and apathetic, the usual songs, cards, drinking-bouts, and talk of rewards in the regiment, were more repulsive to me than usual. Yesterday I returned home and saw her, my hut, Daddy Eróshka, and the snowy mountains, from my porch, and was seized by such a strong, new feeling of joy that I understood it all. I love this woman; I feel real love for the first and only time in my life. I know what has befallen me. I do not fear to be degraded by this feeling, I am not ashamed of my love, I am proud of it. It is not my fault that I love. It has come about against my will. I tried to escape from my love by self-renunciation, and tried to devise a joy in the Cossack Lukáshka's and Maryánka's love, but thereby only stirred up my own love and jealousy. This is not the ideal, the so-called exalted love which I have known before; not that sort of attachment in which you admire your own love and feel that the source of your emotion is within yourself and do everything yourself. I have felt that too. It is still less a desire for enjoyment: it is something different. Perhaps in her I love nature: the personification of all that is beautiful in nature; but yet I am not acting by my own will, but some elemental force loves through me; the whole of God's world, all nature, presses this love into my soul and says, "Love her." I love her not with my mind or my imagination, but with my whole being. Loving her I feel myself to be an integral part of all God's joyous world. I wrote before about the new convictions to which my solitary life had brought me, but no one knows with what labour they shaped themselves within me and with what joy I realized them and saw a new way of life opening out before me; nothing was dearer to me than those convictions . . . Well! . . . love has come and neither they nor any regrets for them remain! It is even difficult for me to believe that I could prize such a one-sided, cold, and abstract state of mind. Beauty came and scattered to the winds all that laborious inward toil, and no regret remains for what has vanished! Self-renunciation is all nonsense and absurdity! That is pride, a refuge from well-merited unhappiness, and salvation from the envy of others' happiness: "Live for others, and do good!"——Why? when in my soul there is only love for myself and the desire to love her and to live her life with her? Not for others, not for Lukáshka, I now desire happiness. I do not now love those others. Formerly I should have told myself that this is wrong. I should have tormented myself with the questions: What will become of her, of me, and of Lukáshka? Now I don't care. I do not live my own life, there is something stronger than me which directs me. I suffer; but formerly I was dead and only now do I live. To-day I will go to their house and tell her everything.'

XXXIV

Late that evening, after writing this letter, Olénin went to his hosts' hut. The old woman was sitting on a bench behind the oven unwinding cocoons. Maryánka with her head uncovered sat sewing by the light of a candle. On seeing Olénin she jumped up, took her kerchief and stepped to the oven.

'Maryánka dear,' said her mother, 'won't you sit here with me a bit?'

'No, I'm bareheaded,' she replied, and sprang up on the oven.

Olénin could only see a knee, and one of her shapely legs hanging down from the oven. He treated the old woman to tea. She treated her guest to clotted cream which she sent Maryánka to fetch. But having put a plateful on the table Maryánka again sprang on the oven from whence Olénin felt her eyes upon him. They talked about household matters. Granny Ulítka became animated and went into raptures of hospitality. She brought Olénin preserved grapes and a grape tart and some of her best wine, and pressed him to eat and drink with the rough yet proud hospitality of country folk, only found among those who produce their bread by the labour of their own hands. The old woman, who had at first struck Olénin so much by her rudeness, now often touched him by her simple tenderness towards her daughter.

'Yes, we need not offend the Lord by grumbling! We have enough of everything, thank God. We have pressed sufficient *chikhir* and have preserved and shall sell three or four barrels of grapes and have enough left to drink. Don't be in a hurry to leave us. We will make merry together at the wedding.'

'And when is the wedding to be?' asked Olénin, feeling his blood suddenly rush to his face while his heart beat irregularly and painfully.

He heard a movement on the oven and the sound of seeds being cracked.

'Well, you know, it ought to be next week. We are quite ready,' replied the old woman, as simply and quietly as though Olénin did not exist. 'I have prepared and have procured everything for Maryánka. We will give her away properly. Only there's one thing not quite right. Our Lukáshka has been running rather wild. He has been too much on the spree! He's up to tricks! The other day a Cossack came here from his company and said he had been to Nogáy.'

'He must mind he does not get caught,' said Olénin.

'Yes, that's what I tell him. "Mind, Lukáshka, don't you get into mischief. Well, of course, a young fellow naturally wants to cut a dash. But there's a time for everything. Well, you've captured or stolen something and killed an *abrek*! Well, you're a fine fellow! But now you should live quietly for a bit, or else there'll be trouble."'

'Yes, I saw him a time or two in the division, he was always merry-making. He has sold another horse,' said Olénin, and glanced towards the oven.

A pair of large, dark, and hostile eyes glittered as they gazed severely at him.

He became ashamed of what he had said. 'What of it? He does no one any harm,' suddenly remarked Maryánka. 'He makes merry with his own money,' and lowering her legs she jumped down from the oven and went out banging the door.

Olénin followed her with his eyes as long as she was in the hut, and then looked at the door and waited, understanding nothing of what Granny Ulítka was telling him.

A few minutes later some visitors arrived: an old man, Granny Ulítka's brother, with Daddy Eróshka, and following them came Maryánka and Ústenka.

'Good evening,' squeaked Ústenka. 'Still on holiday?' she added, turning to Olénin.

'Yes, still on holiday,' he replied, and felt, he did not know why, ashamed and ill at ease.

He wished to go away but could not. It also seemed to him impossible to remain silent. The old man helped him by asking for a drink, and they had a drink. Olénin drank with Eróshka, with the other Cossack, and again with Eróshka, and the more he drank the heavier was his heart. But the two old men grew merry. The girls climbed onto the oven, where they sat whispering and looking at the men, who drank till it was late. Olénin did not talk, but drank more than the others. The Cossacks were shouting. The old woman would not let them have any more *chikhir*, and at last turned them out. The girls laughed at Daddy Eróshka, and it was past ten when they all went out into the porch. The old men invited themselves to finish their merry-making at Olénin's. Ústenka ran off home and Eróshka led the old Cossack to Vanyúsha. The old woman went out to tidy up the shed. Maryánka remained alone in the hut. Olénin felt fresh and joyous, as if he had only just woke up. He noticed everything, and having let the old men pass ahead he turned back to the hut where Maryánka was preparing for bed. He went up to her and wished to say something, but his voice broke. She moved away from him, sat down cross-legged on her bed in the corner, and looked at him silently with wild and frightened eyes. She was evidently afraid of him. Olénin felt this. He felt sorry and ashamed of himself, and at the same time proud and pleased that he aroused even that feeling in her.

'Maryánka!' he said. 'Will you never take pity on me? I can't tell you how I love you.'

She moved still farther away.

'Just hear how the wine is speaking! . . . You'll get nothing from me!'

'No, it is not the wine. Don't marry Lukáshka. I will marry you.' ('What am I saying,' he thought as he uttered these words. 'Shall I be able to say the same to-morrow?' 'Yes, I shall, I am sure I shall, and I will repeat them now,' replied an inner voice.)

'Will you marry me?'

She looked at him seriously and her fear seemed to have passed.

'Maryánka, I shall go out of my mind! I am not myself. I will do whatever you command,' and madly tender words came from his lips of their own accord.

'Now then, what are you drivelling about?' she interrupted, suddenly seizing the arm he was stretching towards her. She did not push his arm away but pressed it firmly with her strong hard fingers. 'Do gentlemen marry Cossack girls? Go away!'

'But will you? Everything . . .'

'And what shall we do with Lukáshka?' said she, laughing.

He snatched away the arm she was holding and firmly embraced her young body, but she sprang away like a fawn and ran barefoot into the porch: Olénin came to his senses and was terrified at himself. He again felt himself inexpressibly vile compared to her, yet not repenting for an instant of what he had said he went home, and without even glancing at the old men who were drinking in his room he lay down and fell asleep more soundly than he had done for a long time.

XXXV

The next day was a holiday. In the evening all the villagers, their holiday clothes shining in the sunset, were out in the street. That season more wine than usual had been produced, and the people were now free from their labours. In a month the Cossacks were to start on a campaign and in many families preparations were being made for weddings.

Most of the people were standing in the square in front of the Cossack Government Office and near the two shops, in one of which cakes and pumpkin seeds were sold, in the other kerchiefs and cotton prints. On the earth-embankment of the office-building sat or stood the old men in sober grey, or black coats without gold trimmings or any kind of ornament. They conversed among themselves quietly in measured tones, about the harvest, about the young folk, about village affairs, and about old times, looking with dignified equanimity at the younger generation. Passing by them, the women and girls stopped and bent their heads. The young Cossacks respectfully slackened their pace and raised their caps, holding them for a while over their heads. The old men then stopped speaking.

Some of them watched the passers-by severely, others kindly, and in their turn slowly took off their caps and put them on again.

The Cossack girls had not yet started dancing their *khorovóds*, but having gathered in groups, in their bright-coloured *beshmets* with white kerchiefs on their heads pulled down to their eyes, they sat either on the ground or on the earth-banks about the huts sheltered from the oblique rays of the sun, and laughed and chattered in their ringing voices. Little boys and girls playing in the square sent their balls high up into the clear sky, and ran about squealing and shouting. The half-grown girls had started dancing their *khorovóds*, and were timidly singing in their thin shrill voices. Clerks, lads not in the service, or home for the holiday, bright-faced and wearing smart white or new red Circassian gold-trimmed coats, went about arm in arm in twos or threes from one group of women or girls to another, and stopped to joke and chat with the Cossack girls. The Armenian shopkeeper, in a gold-trimmed coat of fine blue cloth, stood at the open door through which piles of folded bright-coloured kerchiefs were visible and, conscious of his own importance and with the pride of an oriental tradesman, waited for customers. Two red-bearded, barefooted Chéchens, who had come from beyond the Térek to see the fête, sat on their heels outside the house of a friend, negligently smoking their little pipes and occasionally spitting, watching the villagers and exchanging remarks with one another in their rapid guttural speech. Occasionally a workaday-looking soldier in an old overcoat passed across the square among the bright-clad girls. Here and there the songs of tipsy Cossacks who were merry-making could already be heard. All the huts were closed; the porches had been scrubbed clean the day before. Even the old women were out in the street, which was everywhere sprinkled with pumpkin and melon seed-shells. The air was warm and still, the sky deep and clear. Beyond the roofs the dead-white mountain range, which seemed very near, was turning rosy in the glow of the evening sun. Now and then from the other side of the river came the distant roar of a cannon, but above the village, mingling with one another, floated all sorts of merry holiday sounds.

Olénin had been pacing the yard all that morning hoping

to see Maryánka. But she, having put on holiday clothes, went to Mass at the chapel and afterwards sat with the other girls on an earth-embankment cracking seeds; sometimes again, together with her companions, she ran home, and each time gave the lodger a bright and kindly look. Olénin felt afraid to address her playfully or in the presence of others. He wished to finish telling her what he had begun to say the night before, and to get her to give him a definite answer. He waited for another moment like that of yesterday evening, but the moment did not come, and he felt that he could not remain any longer in this uncertainty. She went out into the street again, and after waiting awhile he too went out and without knowing where he was going he followed her. He passed by the corner where she was sitting in her shining blue satin *beshmet,* and with an aching heart he heard behind him the girls laughing.

Belétski's hut looked out onto the square. As Olénin was passing it he heard Belétski's voice calling to him, 'Come in,' and in he went.

After a short talk they both sat down by the window and were soon joined by Eróshka, who entered dressed in a new *beshmet* and sat down on the floor beside them.

'There, that's the aristocratic party,' said Belétski, pointing with his cigarette to a brightly coloured group at the corner. 'Mine is there too. Do you see her? in red. That's a new *beshmet.* Why don't you start the *khorovód?*' he shouted, leaning out of the window. 'Wait a bit, and then when it grows dark let us go too. Then we will invite them to Ústenka's. We must arrange a ball for them!'

'And I will come to Ústenka's,' said Olénin in a decided tone. 'Will Maryánka be there?'

'Yes, she'll be there. Do come!' said Belétski, without the least surprise. 'But isn't it a pretty picture?' he added, pointing to the motley crowds.

'Yes, very!' Olénin assented, trying to appear indifferent. 'Holidays of this kind,' he added, 'always make me wonder why all these people should suddenly be contented and jolly. To-day for instance, just because it happens to be the fifteenth of the month, everything is festive. Eyes and faces and voices and movements and garments, and the air and the sun, are all in a holiday mood. And we no longer have any holidays!'

'Yes,' said Belétski, who did not like such reflections. 'And why are you not drinking, old fellow?' he said, turning to Eróshka.

Eróshka winked at Olénin, pointing to Belétski. 'Eh, he's a proud one that *kunak* of yours,' he said.

Belétski raised his glass. '*Allah birdy*' he said, emptying it. (*Allah birdy*, 'God has given!'—the usual greeting of Caucasians when drinking together.)

'*Sau bul*' ('Your health'), answered Eróshka smiling, and emptied his glass.

'Speaking of holidays!' he said, turning to Olénin as he rose and looked out of the window, 'What sort of holiday is that! You should have seen them make merry in the old days! The women used to come out in their gold-trimmed *sarafáns*. Two rows of gold coins hanging round their necks and gold-cloth diadems on their heads, and when they passed they made a noise, "flu, flu," with their dresses. Every woman looked like a princess. Sometimes they'd come out, a whole herd of them, and begin singing songs so that the air seemed to rumble, and they went on making merry all night. And the Cossacks would roll out a barrel into the yards and sit down and drink till break of day, or they would go hand-in-hand sweeping the village. Whoever they met they seized and took along with them, and went from house to house. Sometimes they used to make merry for three days on end. Father used to come home—I still remember it—quite red and swollen, without a cap, having lost everything: he'd come and lie down. Mother knew what to do: she would bring him some fresh caviar and a little *chikhir* to sober him up, and would herself run about in the village looking for his cap. Then he'd sleep for two days! That's the sort of fellows they were then! But now what are they?'

'Well, and the girls in the *sarafáns*, did they make merry all by themselves?' asked Belétski.

'Yes, they did! Sometimes Cossacks would come on foot or on horse and say, "Let's break up the *khorovóds*," and they'd go, but the girls would take up cudgels. Carnival week, some young fellow would come galloping up, and they'd cudgel his horse and cudgel him too. But he'd break through, seize the one he loved, and carry her off. And his sweetheart would love him to his heart's content! Yes, the girls in those days, they were regular queens!'

XXXVI

Just then two men rode out of the side street into the square. One of them was Nazárka. The other, Lukáshka, sat slightly sideways on his well-fed bay Kabardá horse which stepped lightly over the hard road jerking its beautiful head with its fine glossy mane. The well-adjusted gun in its cover, the pistol at his back, and the cloak rolled up behind his saddle showed that Lukáshka had not come from a peaceful place or from one near by. The smart way in which he sat a little sideways on his horse, the careless motion with which he touched the horse under its belly with his whip, and especially his half-closed black eyes, glistening as he looked proudly around him, all expressed the conscious strength and self-confidence of youth. 'Ever seen as fine a lad?' his eyes, looking from side to side, seemed to say. The elegant horse with its silver ornaments and trappings, the weapons, and the handsome Cossack himself attracted the attention of everyone in the square. Nazárka, lean and short, was much less well dressed. As he rode past the old men, Lukáshka paused and raised his curly white sheepskin cap above his closely cropped black head.

'Well, have you carried off many Nogáy horses?' asked a lean old man with a frowning, lowering look.

'Have you counted them, Grandad, that you ask?' replied Lukáshka, turning away.

'That's all very well, but you need not take my lad along with you,' the old man muttered with a still darker frown.

'Just see the old devil, he knows everything,' muttered Lukáshka to himself, and a worried expression came over his face; but then, noticing a corner where a number of Cossack girls were standing, he turned his horse towards them.

'Good evening, girls!' he shouted in his powerful, resonant voice, suddenly checking his horse. 'You've grown old without me, you witches!' and he laughed.

'Good evening, Lukáshka! Good evening, laddie!' the merry voices answered. 'Have you brought much money? Buy some sweets for the girls! . . . Have you come for long? True enough, it's long since we saw you. . . .'

'Nazárka and I have just flown across to make a night of it,' replied Lukáshka, raising his whip and riding straight at the girls.

'Why, Maryánka has quite forgotten you,' said Ústenka, nudging Maryánka with her elbow and breaking into a shrill laugh.

Maryánka moved away from the horse and throwing back her head calmly looked at the Cossack with her large sparkling eyes.

'True enough, you have not been home for a long time! Why are you trampling us under your horse?' she remarked dryly, and turned away.

Lukáshka had appeared particularly merry. His face shone with audacity and joy. Obviously staggered by Maryánka's cold reply he suddenly knitted his brow.

'Step up on my stirrup and I'll carry you away to the mountains, Mammy!' he suddenly exclaimed, and as if to disperse his dark thoughts he caracoled among the girls. Stooping down towards Maryánka, he said, 'I'll kiss, oh, how I'll kiss you! . . .'

Maryánka's eyes met his and she suddenly blushed and stepped back.

'Oh, bother you! you'll crush my feet,' she said, and bending her head looked at her well-shaped feet in their tightly fitting light blue stockings with clocks and her new red slippers trimmed with narrow silver braid.

Lukáshka turned towards Ústenka, and Maryánka sat down next to a woman with a baby in her arms. The baby stretched his plump little hands towards the girl and seized a necklace string that hung down onto her blue *beshmet*. Maryánka bent towards the child and glanced at Lukáshka from the corner of her eyes. Lukáshka just then was getting out from under his coat, from the pocket of his black *beshmet*, a bundle of sweetmeats and seeds.

'There, I give them to all of you,' he said, handing the bundle to Ústenka and smiling at Maryánka.

A confused expression again appeared on the girl's face. It was as though a mist gathered over her beautiful eyes. She drew her kerchief down below her lips, and leaning her head over the fair-skinned face of the baby that still held her by her coin necklace she suddenly began to kiss it greedily. The baby pressed his little hands against the girl's high breasts, and opening his toothless mouth screamed loudly.

'You're smothering the boy!' said the little one's mother, taking him away; and she unfastened her *beshmet* to give him the breast. 'You'd better have a chat with the young fellow.'

'I'll only go and put up my horse and then Nazárka and I will come back; we'll make merry all night,' said Lukáshka, touching his horse with his whip and riding away from the girls.

Turning into a side street, he and Nazárka rode up to two huts that stood side by side.

'Here we are all right, old fellow! Be quick and come soon!' called Lukáshka to his comrade, dismounting in front of one of the huts; then he carefully led his horse in at the gate of the wattle fence of his own home.

'How d'you do, Stëpka?' he said to his dumb sister, who, smartly dressed like the others, came in from the street to take his horse; and he made signs to her to take the horse to the hay, but not to unsaddle it.

The dumb girl made her usual humming noise, smacked her lips as she pointed to the horse and kissed it on the nose, as much as to say that she loved it and that it was a fine horse.

'How d'you do, Mother? How is it that you have not gone out yet?' shouted Lukáshka, holding his gun in place as he mounted the steps of the porch.

His old mother opened the door.

'Dear me! I never expected, never thought, you'd come,' said the old woman. 'Why, Kírka said you wouldn't be here.'

'Go and bring some *chikhir*, Mother. Nazárka is coming here and we will celebrate the feast day.'

'Directly, Lukáshka, directly!' answered the old woman. 'Our women are making merry. I expect our dumb one has gone too.'

She took her keys and hurriedly went to the outhouse.

Nazárka, after putting up his horse and taking the gun off his shoulder, returned to Lukáshka's house and went in.

XXXVII

'Your health!' said Lukáshka, taking from his mother's hands a cup filled to the brim with *chikhir* and carefully raising it to his bowed head.

'A bad business!' said Nazárka. 'You heard how Daddy

Burlák said, "Have you stolen many horses?" He seems to know!'

'A regular wizard!' Lukáshka replied shortly. 'But what of it!' he added, tossing his head. 'They are across the river by now. Go and find them!'

'Still it's a bad lookout.'

'What's a bad lookout? Go and take some *chikhir* to him to-morrow and nothing will come of it. Now let's make merry. Drink!' shouted Lukáshka, just in the tone in which old Eróshka uttered the word. 'We'll go out into the street and make merry with the girls. You go and get some honey; or no, I'll send our dumb wench. We'll make merry till morning.'

Nazárka smiled.

'Are we stopping here long?' he asked.

'Till we've had a bit of fun. Run and get some vodka. Here's the money.'

Nazárka ran off obediently to get the vodka from Yámka's.

Daddy Eróshka and Ergushóv, like birds of prey, scenting where the merry-making was going on, tumbled into the hut one after the other, both tipsy.

'Bring us another half-pail,' shouted Lukáshka to his mother, by way of reply to their greeting.

'Now then, tell us where did you steal them, you devil?' shouted Eróshka. 'Fine fellow, I'm fond of you!'

'Fond indeed . . .' answered Lukáshka laughing, 'carrying sweets from cadets to lasses! Eh, you old . . .'

'That's not true, not true! . . . Oh, Mark,' and the old man burst out laughing. 'And how that devil begged me. "Go," he said, "and arrange it." He offered me a gun! But no. I'd have managed it, but I feel for you. Now tell us where have you been?' And the old man began speaking in Tartar.

Lukáshka answered him promptly.

Ergushóv, who did not know much Tartar, only occasionally put in a word in Russian:

'What I say is he's driven away the horses. I know it for a fact,' he chimed in.

'Giréy and I went together.' (His speaking of Giréy Khan as 'Giréy' was, to the Cossack mind, evidence of his boldness.) 'Just beyond the river he kept bragging that he knew the whole of the steppe and would lead the way straight, but we rode on and the night was dark, and my Giréy lost his way and began wandering in a circle without getting anywhere: couldn't find the village, and there we were. We must have gone too much to the right. I believe we wandered about well-nigh till midnight. Then, thank goodness, we heard dogs howling.'

'Fools!' said Daddy Eróshka. 'There now, we too used to lose our way in the steppe. (Who the devil can follow it?) But I used to ride up a hillock and start howling like the wolves, like this!' He placed his hands before his mouth, and howled like a pack of wolves, all on one note. 'The dogs would answer at once. . . . Well, go on—so you found them?'

'We soon led them away! Nazárka was nearly caught by some Nogáy women, he was!'

'Caught indeed,' Nazárka, who had just come back, said in an injured tone.

'We rode off again, and again Giréy lost his way and almost landed us among the sand-drifts. We thought we were just getting to the Térek but we were riding away from it all the time!'

'You should have steered by the stars,' said Daddy Eróshka.

'That's what I say,' interjected Ergushóv.

'Yes, steer when all is black; I tried and tried all about . . . and at last I put the bridle on one of the mares and let my own horse go free—thinking he'll lead us out, and what do you think! he just gave a snort or two with his nose to the ground, galloped ahead, and led us straight to our village. Thank goodness! It was getting quite light. We barely had time to hide them in the forest. Nagím came across the river and took them away.'

Ergushóv shook his head. 'It's just what I said. Smart. Did you get much for them?'

'It's all here,' said Lukáshka, slapping his pocket.

Just then his mother came into the room, and Lukáshka did not finish what he was saying.

'Drink!' he shouted.

'We too, Gírich and I, rode out late one night . . .' began Eróshka.

'Oh bother, we'll never hear the end of you!' said Lukáshka. 'I am going.' And having emptied his cup and tightened the strap of his belt he went out.

XXXVIII

It was already dark when Lukáshka went out into the street. The autumn night was fresh and calm. The full golden moon floated up behind the tall dark poplars that grew on one side of the square. From the chimneys of the outhouses smoke rose and spread above the village, mingling with the mist. Here and there lights shone through the windows, and the air was laden with the smell of *kisyak*, grape-pulp, and mist. The sounds of voices, laughter, songs, and the cracking of seeds mingled just as they had done in the daytime, but were now more distinct. Clusters of white kerchiefs and caps gleamed through the darkness near the houses and by the fences.

In the square, before the shop door which was lit up and open, the black and white figures of Cossack men and maids showed through the darkness, and one heard from afar their loud songs and laughter and talk. The girls, hand in hand, went round and round in a circle stepping lightly in the dusty square. A skinny girl, the plainest of them all, set the tune:

'From beyond the wood, from the forest dark,
From the garden green and the shady park,
There came out one day two young lads so gay.
Young bachelors, hey!' brave and smart were they!
And they walked and walked, then stood still, each man,
And they talked and soon to dispute began!
Then a maid came out; as she came along,
Said, "To one of you I shall soon belong!"
'Twas the fair-faced lad got the maiden fair,
Yes, the fair-faced lad with the golden hair!
Her right hand so white in his own took he,
And he led her round for his mates to see!
And said, "Have you ever in all your life,
Met a lass as fair as my sweet little wife?" '

The old women stood round listening to the songs. The little boys and girls ran about chasing one another in the dark. The men stood by, catching at the girls as the latter moved round, and sometimes breaking the ring and entering it. On the dark side of the doorway stood Belétski and Olénin, in their Circassian coats and sheepskin caps, and talked together in a style of speech unlike that of the Cossacks, in low but distinct tones, conscious that they were attracting attention. Next to one another in the *khorovód* circle moved plump little Ústenka in her red *beshmet* and the stately Maryánka in her new smock and *beshmet*. Olénin and Belétski were discussing how to snatch Ústenka and Maryánka out of the ring. Belétski thought that Olénin wished only to amuse himself, but Olénin was expecting his fate to be decided. He wanted at any cost to see Maryánka alone that very day and to tell her everything, and ask her whether she could and would be his wife. Although that question had long been answered in the negative in his own mind, he hoped he would be able to tell her all he felt, and that she would understand him.

'Why did you not tell me sooner?' said Belétski. 'I would have got Ústenka to arrange it for you. You are such a queer fellow! . . .'

'What's to be done! . . . Some day, very soon, I'll tell you all about it. Only now, for Heaven's sake, arrange so that she should come to Ústenka's.'

'All right, that's easily done! Well, Maryánka, will you belong to the "fair-faced lad," and not to Lukáshka?' said Belétski, speaking to Maryánka first for propriety's sake, but having received no reply he went up to Ústenka and begged her to bring Maryánka home with her. He had hardly time to finish what he was saying before the leader began another song and the girls started pulling each other round in the ring by the hand.

They sang:

'Past the garden, by the garden,
A young man came strolling down,
Up the street and through the town.
And the first time as he passed
He did wave his strong right hand.
As the second time he passed
Waved his hat with silken band.
But the third time as he went
He stood still: before her bent.

"How is it that thou, my dear,
My reproaches dost not fear?
In the park don't come to walk
That we there might have a talk?
Come now, answer me, my dear,
Dost thou hold me in contempt?
Later on, thou knowest, dear,
Thou'lt get sober and repent.

Soon to woo thee I will come,
And when we shall married be
Thou wilt weep because of me!"

"Though I knew what to reply,
Yet I dared not him deny,
No, I dared not him deny!
So into the park went I,
In the park my lad to meet,
There my dear one I did greet."

"Maiden dear, I bow to thee!
Take this handkerchief from me.
In thy white hand take it, see!
Say I am beloved by thee.
I don't know at all, I fear,
What I am to give thee, dear!
To my dear I think I will
Of a shawl a present make—
And five kisses for it take." '

Lukáshka and Nazárka broke into the ring and started
walking about among the girls. Lukáshka joined in the
singing, taking seconds in his clear voice as he walked in
the middle of the ring swinging his arms. "Well, come in,
one of you!' he said. The other girls pushed Maryánka,
but she would not enter the ring. The sound of shrill laughter, slaps, kisses, and whispers mingled with the singing.

As he went past Olénin, Lukáshka gave a friendly nod.

'Dmítri Andréich! Have you too come to have a look?'
he said.

'Yes,' answered Olénin dryly.

Belétski stooped and whispered something into Ústenka's
ear. She had not time to reply till she came round again,
when she said:

'All right, we'll come.'

'And Maryánka too?'

Olénin stooped towards Maryánka. 'You'll come? Please
do, if only for a minute. I must speak to you.'

'If the other girls come, I will.'

'Will you answer my question?' said he, bending towards
her. 'You are in good spirits to-day.'

She had already moved past him. He went after her.

'Will you answer?'

'Answer what?'

'The question I asked you the other day,' said Olénin,
stooping to her ear. 'Will you marry me?'

Maryánka thought for a moment.

'I'll tell you,' said she, 'I'll tell you to-night.'

And through the darkness her eyes gleamed brightly and kindly at the young man.

He still followed her. He enjoyed stooping closer to her.

But Lukáshka, without ceasing to sing, suddenly seized her firmly by the hand and pulled her from her place in the ring of girls into the middle. Olénin had only time to say, 'Come to Ústenka's,' and stepped back to his companion. The song came to an end. Lukáshka wiped his lips, Maryánka did the same, and they kissed. 'No, no, kisses five!' said Lukáshka. Chatter, laughter, and running about, succeeded to the rhythmic movements and sound. Lukáshka, who seemed to have drunk a great deal, began to distribute sweetmeats to the girls.

'I offer them to everyone!' he said with proud, comically pathetic self-admiration. 'But anyone who goes after soldiers goes out of the ring!' he suddenly added, with an angry glance at Olénin.

The girls grabbed his sweetmeats from him, and, laughing, struggled for them among themselves. Belétski and Olénin stepped aside.

Lukáshka, as if ashamed of his generosity, took off his cap and wiping his forehead with his sleeve came up to Maryánka and Ústenka.

'Answer me, my dear, dost thou hold me in contempt?' he said in the words of the song they had just been singing, and turning to Maryánka he angrily repeated the words: 'Dost thou hold me in contempt? When we shall married be thou wilt weep because of me!' he added, embracing Ústenka and Maryánka both together.

Ústenka tore herself away, and swinging her arm gave him such a blow on the back that she hurt her hand.

'Well, are you going to have another turn?' he asked.

'The other girls may if they like,' answered Ústenka, 'but I am going home and Maryánka was coming to our house too.'

With his arm still round her, Lukáshka led Maryánka away from the crowd to the darker corner of a house.

'Don't go, Maryánka,' he said, 'let's have some fun for the last time. Go home and I will come to you!'

'What am I to do at home? Holidays are meant for merry-making. I am going to Ústenka's,' replied Maryánka.

'I'll marry you all the same, you know!'

'All right,' said Maryánka, 'we shall see when the time comes.'.

'So you are going,' said Lukáshka sternly, and, pressing her close, he kissed her on the cheek.

'There, leave off! Don't bother,' and Maryánka, wrenching herself from his arms, moved away.

'Ah my girl, it will turn out badly,' said Lukáshka reproachfully and stood still, shaking his head. 'Thou wilt weep because of me . . .' and turning away from her he shouted to the other girls:

'Now then! Play away!'

What he had said seemed to have frightened and vexed Maryánka. She stopped, 'What will turn out badly?'

'Why, that!'

'That what?'

'Why, that you keep company with a soldier-lodger and no longer care for me!'

'I'll care just as long as I choose. You're not my father, nor my mother. What do you want? I'll care for whom I like!'

'Well, all right . . .' said Lukáshka, 'but remember!' He moved towards the shop. 'Girls!' he shouted, 'why have you stopped? Go on dancing. Nazárka, fetch some more *chikhir.*'

'Well, will they come?' asked Olénin, addressing Belétski.

'They'll come directly,' replied Belétski. 'Come along, we must prepare the ball.'

XXXIX

It was already late in the night when Olénin came out of Belétski's hut following Maryánka and Ústenka. He saw in the dark street before him the gleam of the girl's white kerchief. The golden moon was descending towards the steppe. A silvery mist hung over the village. All was still; there were no lights anywhere and one heard only the receding footsteps of the young women. Olénin's heart beat fast. The fresh moist atmosphere cooled his burning face. He glanced at the sky and turned to look at the hut he had just come out of: the candle was already out. Then he again peered through the darkness at the girls' retreating shadows. The white kerchief disappeared in the mist. He was afraid to remain alone, he was so happy. He jumped down from the porch and ran after the girls.

'Bother you, someone may see . . .' said Ústenka.

'Never mind!'

Olénin ran up to Maryánka and embraced her.

Maryánka did not resist.

'Haven't you kissed enough yet?' said Ústenka. 'Marry and then kiss, but now you'd better wait.'

'Good-night, Maryánka. To-morrow I will come to see your father and tell him. Don't you say anything.'

'Why should I!' answered Maryánka.

Both the girls started running. Olénin went on by himself thinking over all that had happened. He had spent the whole evening alone with her in a corner by the oven. Ústenka had not left the hut for a single moment, but had romped about with the other girls and with Belétski all the time. Olénin had talked in whispers to Maryánka.

'Will you marry me?' he had asked.

'You'd deceive me and not have me,' she replied cheerfully and calmly.

'But do you love me? Tell me for God's sake!'

'Why shouldn't I love you? You don't squint,' answered Maryánka, laughing and with her hard hands squeezing his. . . .

'What whi-ite, whi-i-ite, soft hands you've got—so like clotted cream,' she said.

'I am in earnest. Tell me, will you marry me?'

'Why not, if father gives me to you?'

'Well then remember, I shall go mad if you deceive me. To-morrow I will tell your mother and father. I shall come and propose.'

Maryánka suddenly burst out laughing.

'What's the matter?'

'It seems so funny!'

'It's true! I will buy a vineyard and a house and will enroll myself as a Cossack.'

'Mind you don't go after other women then. I am severe about that.'

Olénin joyfully repeated all these words to himself. The memory of them now gave him pain and now such joy that it took away his breath. The pain was because she had remained as calm as usual while talking to him. She did not seem at all agitated by these new conditions. It was as if she did not trust him and did not think of the future. It seemed to him that she only loved him for the present moment, and that in her mind there was no future with him. He was happy because her words sounded to him true, and she had consented to be his. 'Yes,' thought he to himself, 'we shall only understand one another when she is quite mine. For such love there are no words. It needs life—the whole of life. To-morrow everything will be cleared up. I cannot live like this any longer; to-morrow I will tell everything to her father, to Belétski, and to the whole village.'

Lukáshka, after two sleepless nights, had drunk so much at the fête that for the first time in his life his feet would not carry him, and he slept in Yámka's house.

XL

The next day Olénin awoke earlier than usual, and immediately remembered what lay before him, and he joyfully recalled her kisses, the pressure of her hard hands, and her words, 'What white hands you have!' He jumped up and wished to go at once to his hosts' hut to ask for their consent to his marriage with Maryánka. The sun had not yet risen, but it seemed that there was an unusual bustle in the street and side-street: people were moving about on foot and on horseback, and talking. He threw on his Circassian coat and hastened out into the porch. His hosts were not yet up. Five Cossacks were riding past and talking loudly together. In front rode Lukáshka on his broad-backed Kabardá horse. The Cossacks were all speaking and shouting so that it was impossible to make out exactly what they were saying.

'Ride to the Upper Post,' shouted one.

'Saddle and catch us up, be quick,' said another.

'It's nearer through the other gate!'

'What are you talking about?' cried Lukáshka. 'We must go through the middle gates, of course.'

'So we must, it's nearer that way,' said one of the Cossacks who was covered with dust and rode a perspiring horse. Lukáshka's face was red and swollen after the drinking of the previous night and his cap was pushed to the back of his head. He was calling out with authority as though he were an officer.

'What is the matter? Where are you going?' asked Olénin, with difficulty attracting the Cossacks' attention.

'We are off to catch *abreks*. They're hiding among the sand-drifts. We are just off, but there are not enough of us yet.'

And the Cossacks continued to shout, more and more of them joining as they rode down the street. It occurred to Olénin that it would not look well for him to stay behind; besides he thought he could soon come back. He dressed, loaded his gun with bullets, jumped onto his horse which Vanyúsha had saddled more or less well, and overtook the Cossacks at the village gates. The Cossacks had dismounted, and filling a wooden bowl with *chikhir* from a little cask which they had brought with them, they passed the bowl round to one another and drank to the success of their expedition. Among them was a smartly dressed young cornet, who happened to be in the village and who took command of the group of nine Cossacks who had joined for the expedition. All these Cossacks were privates, and although the cornet assumed the airs of a commanding officer, they only obeyed Lukáshka. Of Olénin they took no notice at all, and when they had all mounted and started, and Olénin rode up to the cornet and began asking him what was taking place, the cornet, who was usually quite friendly, treated him with marked condescension. It was with great difficulty that Olénin managed to find out from him what was happening. Scouts who had been sent out to search for *abreks* had come upon several hillsmen some six miles from the village. These *abreks* had taken shelter in pits and had fired at the scouts, declaring they would not surrender. A corporal who had been scouting with two Cossacks had remained to watch the *abreks*, and had sent one Cossack back to get help.

The sun was just rising. Three miles beyond the village the steppe spread out and nothing was visible except the dry, monotonous, sandy, dismal plain covered with the footmarks of cattle, and here and there with tufts of withered grass, with low reeds in the flats, and rare, little-trodden footpaths, and the camps of the nomad Nogáy tribe just visible far away. The absence of shade and the austere aspect of the place were striking. The sun always rises and sets red in the steppe. When it is windy whole hills of sand are carried by the wind from place to place.

When it is calm, as it was that morning, the silence, uninterrupted by any movement or sound, is peculiarly striking. That morning in the steppe it was quiet and dull, though the sun had already risen. It all seemed specially soft and desolate. The air was hushed, the footfalls and the snorting of the horses were the only sounds to be heard, and even they quickly died away.

The men rode almost silently. A Cossack always carries his weapons so that they neither jingle nor rattle. Jingling weapons are a terrible disgrace to a Cossack. Two other Cossacks from the village caught the party up and exchanged a few words. Lukáshka's horse either stumbled or caught its foot in some grass, and became restive—which is a sign of bad luck among the Cossacks, and at such a time was of special importance. The others exchanged glances and turned away, trying not to notice what had happened. Lukáskha pulled at the reins, frowned sternly, set his teeth, and flourished his whip above his head. His good Kabardá horse, prancing from one foot to another not knowing with which to start, seemed to wish to fly upwards on wings. But Lukáshka hit its well-fed sides with his whip once, then again, and a third time, and the horse, showing its teeth and spreading out its tail, snorted and reared and stepped on its hind legs a few paces away from the others.

'Ah, a good steed that!' said the cornet.

That he said *steed* instead of *horse* indicated special praise.

'A lion of a horse,' assented one of the others, an old Cossack.

The Cossacks rode forward silently, now at a footpace, then at a trot, and these changes were the only incidents that interrupted for a moment the stillness and solemnity of their movements.

Riding through the steppe for about six miles, they passed nothing but one Nogáy tent, placed on a cart and moving slowly along at a distance of about a mile from them. A Nogáy family was moving from one part of the steppe to another. Afterwards they met two tattered Nogáy women with high cheekbones, who with baskets on their backs were gathering dung left by the cattle that wandered over the steppe. The cornet, who did not know their language well, tried to question them, but they did not understand him and, obviously frightened, looked at one another.

Lukáshka rode up to them both, stopped his horse, and promptly uttered the usual greeting. The Nogáy women were evidently relieved, and began speaking to him quite freely as to a brother.

'*Áy-ay, kop abrek!*' they said plaintively, pointing in the direction in which the Cossacks were going. Olénin understood that they were saying, 'Many *abreks.*'

Never having seen an engagement of that kind, and having formed an idea of them only from Daddy Eróshka's tales, Olénin wished not to be left behind by the Cossacks, but wanted to see it all. He admired the Cossacks, and was on the watch, looking and listening and making his own observations. Though he had brought his sword and a loaded gun with him, when he noticed that the Cossacks avoided him he decided to take no part in the action, as in his opinion his courage had already been sufficiently proved when he was with his detachment, and also because he was very happy.

Suddenly a shot was heard in the distance.

The cornet became excited, and began giving orders to the Cossacks as to how they should divide and from which side they should approach. But the Cossacks did not appear to pay any attention to these orders, listening only to what Lukáshka said and looking to him alone. Lukáshka's face and figure were expressive of calm solemnity. He put his horse to a trot with which the others were unable to keep pace, and screwing up his eyes kept looking ahead.

'There's a man on horseback,' he said, reining in his horse and keeping in line with the others.

Olénin looked intently, but could not see anything. The Cossacks soon distinguished two riders and quietly rode straight towards them.

'Are those the *abreks?*' asked Olénin.

The Cossacks did not answer his question, which appeared quite meaningless to them. The *abreks* would have been fools to venture across the river on horseback.

'That's friend Ródka waving to us, I do believe,' said Lukáshka, pointing to the two mounted men who were now clearly visible. 'Look, he's coming to us.'

A few minutes later it became plain that the two horsemen were the Cossack scouts. The corporal rode up to Lukáshka.

XLI

'Are they far?' was all Lukáshka said.

Just then they heard a sharp shot some thirty paces off. The corporal smiled slightly.

'Our Gúrka is having shots at them,' he said, nodding in the direction of the shot.

Having gone a few paces farther they saw Gúrka sitting behind a sand-hillock and loading his gun. To while away the time he was exchanging shots with the *abreks,* who were behind another sand-heap. A bullet came whistling from their side.

The cornet was pale and grew confused. Lukáshka dismounted from his horse, threw the reins to one of the other Cossacks, and went up to Gúrka. Olénin also dismounted and, bending down, followed Lukáshka. They had hardly reached Gúrka when two bullets whistled above them. Lukáshka looked around laughing at Olénin and stooped a little.

'Look out or they will kill you, Dmítri Andréich,' he said. 'You'd better go away—you have no business here.'

But Olénin wanted absolutely to see the *abreks.*

From behind the mound he saw caps and muskets some two hundred paces off. Suddenly a little cloud of smoke appeared from thence, and again a bullet whistled past. The *abreks* were hiding in a marsh at the foot of the hill. Olénin was much impressed by the place in which they sat. In reality it was very much like the rest of the steppe, but because the *abreks* sat there it seemed to detach itself from all the rest and to have become distinguished. Indeed it appeared to Olénin that it was the very spot for *abreks* to occupy. Lukáshka went back to his horse and Olénin followed him.

'We must get a hay-cart,' said Lukáshka, 'or they will be killing some of us. There behind that mound is a Nogáy cart with a load of hay.'

The cornet listened to him and the corporal agreed. The cart of hay was fetched, and the Cossacks, hiding behind it, pushed it forward. Olénin rode up a hillock from whence he could see everything. The hay-cart moved on and the Cossacks crowded together behind it. The Cossacks advanced, but the Chéchens, of whom there were nine, sat with their knees in a row and did not fire.

All was quiet. Suddenly from the Chéchens arose the sound of a mournful song, something like Daddy Eróshka's 'Ay day, dalalay.' The Chéchens knew that they could not escape, and to prevent themselves from being tempted to take to flight they had strapped themselves together, knee to knee, had got their guns ready, and were singing their death-song.

The Cossacks with their hay-cart drew closer and closer, and Olénin expected the firing to begin at any moment, but the silence was only broken by the *abreks'* mournful song. Suddenly the song ceased; there was a sharp report, a bullet struck the front of the cart, and Chéchen curses and yells broke the silence and shot followed on shot and one bullet after another struck the cart. The Cossacks did not fire and were now only five paces distant.

Another moment passed and the Cossacks with a whoop rushed out on both sides from behind the cart—Lukáshka in front of them. Olénin heard only a few shots, then shouting and moans. He thought he saw smoke and blood, and abandoning his horse and quite beside himself he ran towards the Cossacks. Horror seemed to blind him. He could not make out anything, but understood that all was over. Lukáshka, pale as death, was holding a wounded Chéchen by the arms and shouting, 'Don't kill him. I'll take him alive!' The Chéchen was the red-haired man who had fetched his brother's body away after Lukáshka had killed him. Lukáshka was twisting his arms. Suddenly the Chéchen wrenched himself free and fired his pistol. Lukáshka fell, and blood began to flow from his stomach. He jumped up, but fell again, swearing in Russian and in Tartar. More and more blood appeared on his clothes and under him. Some Cossacks approached him and began loosening his girdle. One of them, Nazárka, before beginning to help, fumbled for some time unable to put his sword in its sheath: it would not go the right way. The blade of the sword was blood-stained.

The Chéchens with their red hair and clipped moustaches lay dead and hacked about. Only the one we know of, who had fired at Lukáshka, though wounded in many places was still alive. Like a wounded hawk all covered with blood (blood was flowing from a wound under his right eye), pale and gloomy, he looked about him with wide-open excited eyes and clenched teeth as he crouched, dagger in hand, still prepared to defend himself. The cornet went up to him as if intending to pass by, and with a quick movement shot him in the ear. The Chéchen started up, but it was too late, and he fell.

The Cossacks, quite out of breath, dragged the bodies aside and took the weapons from them. Each of the red-haired Chéchens had been a man, and each one had his own individual expression. Lukáshka was carried to the cart. He continued to swear in Russian and in Tartar.

'No fear, I'll strangle him with my hands. *Anna seni!*' he cried, struggling. But he soon became quiet from weakness.

Olénin rode home. In the evening he was told that Lukáshka was at death's door, but that a Tartar from beyond the river had undertaken to cure him with herbs.

The bodies were brought to the village office. The women and the little boys hastened to look at them.

It was growing dark when Olénin returned, and he could not collect himself after what he had seen. But towards night memories of the evening before came rushing to his mind. He looked out of the window, Maryánka was passing to and fro from the house to the cowshed, putting things straight. Her mother had gone to the vineyard and her father to the office. Olénin could not wait till she had quite finished her work, but went out to meet her. She was in the hut standing with her back towards him. Olénin thought she felt shy.

'Maryánka,' said he, 'I say, Maryánka! May I come in?'

She suddenly turned. There was a scarcely perceptible trace of tears in her eyes and her face was beautiful in its sadness. She looked at him in silent dignity.

Olénin again said:

'Maryánka, I have come——'

'Leave me alone!' she said. Her face did not change but the tears ran down her cheeks.

'What are you crying for? What is it?'

'What?' she repeated in a rough voice. 'Cossacks have been killed, that's what for.'

'Lukáshka?' said Olénin.

'Go away! What do you want?'

'Maryánka!' said Olénin, approaching her.

'You will never get anything from me!'

'Maryánka, don't speak like that,' Olénin entreated.

'Get away. I'm sick of you!' shouted the girl, stamping her foot, and moved threateningly towards him. And her face expressed such abhorrence, such contempt, and such anger that Olénin suddenly understood that there was no hope for him, and that his first impression of this woman's inaccessibility had been perfectly correct.

Olénin said nothing more, but ran out of the hut.

XLII

For two hours after returning home he lay on his bed motionless. Then he went to his company commander and obtained leave to visit the staff. Without taking leave of anyone, and sending Vanyúsha to settle his accounts with his landlord, he prepared to leave for the fort where his regiment was stationed. Daddy Eróshka was the only one to see him off. They had a drink, and then a second, and then yet another. Again as on the night of his departure from Moscow, a three-horsed conveyance stood waiting at the door. But Olénin did not confer with himself as he had done then, and did not say to himself that all he had thought and done here was 'not it'. He did not promise himself a new life. He loved Maryánka more than ever, and knew that he could never be loved by her.

'Well, good-bye, my lad!' said Daddy Eróshka. 'When you go on an expedition, be wise and listen to my words— the words of an old man. When you are out on a raid or the like (you know I'm an old wolf and have seen things), and when they begin firing, don't get into a crowd where there are many men. When you fellows get frightened you always try to get close together with a lot of others. You think it is merrier to be with others, but that's where it is worst of all! They always aim at a crowd. Now I used to keep farther away from the others and went alone, and I've never been wounded. Yet what things haven't I seen in my day?'

'But you've got a bullet in your back,' remarked Vanyúsha, who was clearing up the room.

'That was the Cossacks fooling about,' answered Eróshka.

'Cossacks? How was that?' asked Olénin.

'Oh, just so. We were drinking. Vánka Sítkin, one of the Cossacks, got merry, and puff! he gave me one from his pistol just here.'

'Yes, and did it hurt?' asked Olénin. 'Vanyúsha, will you soon be ready?' he added.

'Ah, where's the hurry! Let me tell you. When he banged into me, the bullet did not break the bone but remained here. And I say: "You've killed me, brother. Eh! What have you done to me? I won't let you off! You'll have to stand me a pailful!" '

'Well, but did it hurt?' Olénin asked again, scarcely listening to the tale.

'Let me finish. He stood a pailful, and we drank it, but the blood went on flowing. The whole room was drenched and covered with blood. Grandad Burlák, he says, "The lad will give up the ghost. Stand a bottle of the sweet sort, or we shall have you taken up!" They bought more drink, and boozed and boozed——'

'Yes, but did it hurt you much?' Olénin asked once more.

'Hurt, indeed! Don't interrupt: I don't like it. Let me finish. We boozed and boozed till morning, and I fell asleep on the top of the oven, drunk. When I woke in the morning I could not unbend myself anyhow——'

'Was it very painful?' repeated Olénin, thinking that now he would at last get an answer to his question.

'Did I tell you it was painful? I did not say it was painful, but I could not bend and could not walk.'

'And then it healed up?' said Olénin, not even laughing, so heavy was his heart.

'It healed up, but the bullet is still there. Just feel it!' And lifting his shirt he showed his powerful back, where just near the bone a bullet could be felt and rolled about.

'Feel how it rolls,' he said, evidently amusing himself with the bullet as with a toy. 'There now, it has rolled to the back.'

'And Lukáshka, will he recover?' asked Olénin.

'Heaven only knows! There's no doctor. They've gone for one.'

'Where will they get one? From Gróznoe?' asked Olénin.

'No, my lad. Were I the Tsar I'd have hung all your Russian doctors long ago. Cutting is all they know! There's our Cossack Bakláshka, no longer a real man now that they've cut off his leg! That shows they're fools. What's Bakláshka good for now? No, my lad, in the mountains there are real doctors. There was my chum, Vórchik, he was on an expedition and was wounded just here in the chest. Well, your doctors gave him up, but one of theirs came from the mountains and cured him! They understand herbs, my lad!'

'Come, stop talking rubbish,' said Olénin. 'I'd better send a doctor from head-quarters.'

'Rubbish!' the old man said mockingly. 'Fool, fool! Rubbish. You'll send a doctor!——If yours cured people, Cossacks and Chéchens would go to you for treatment, but as it is your officers and colonels send to the mountains for doctors. Yours are all humbugs, all humbugs.'

Olénin did not answer. He agreed only too fully that all was humbug in the world in which he had lived and to which he was now returning.

'How is Lukáshka? You've been to see him?' he asked.

'He just lies as if he were dead. He does not eat nor drink. Vodka is the only thing his soul accepts. But as long as he drinks vodka it's well. I'd be sorry to lose the lad. A fine lad—a brave, like me. I too lay dying like that once. The old women were already wailing. My head was burning. They had already laid me out under the holy icons. So I lay there, and above me on the oven little drummers, no bigger than this, beat the tattoo. I shout at them and they drum all the harder.' (The old man laughed.) 'The women brought our church elder. They were getting ready to bury me. They said, "He defiled himself with worldly unbelievers; he made merry with women; he ruined people; he did not fast, and he played the *balaláyka*. Confess," they said. So I began to confess. "I've sinned!" I said. Whatever the priest said, I always answered "I've sinned." He began to ask me about the *balaláyka*. "Where is the accursed thing," he says. "Show it me and smash it." But I say, "I've not got it." I'd hidden it myself in a net in the out-house. I knew they could not find it. So they left me. Yet after all I recovered. When I went for my *balaláyka*—— What was I saying?' he continued. 'Listen to me, and keep farther away from the other men or you'll get killed foolishly. I feel for you, truly: you are a drinker—I love you! And fellows like you like riding up the mounds. There was one who lived here who had come from Russia, he always would ride up the mounds (he called the mounds so funnily, "hillocks"). Whenever he saw a mound, off he'd gallop. Once he galloped off that way and rode to the top quite pleased, but a Chéchen fired at him and killed him! Ah, how well they shoot from their gun-rests, those Chéchens! Some of them shoot even better than I do. I don't like it when a fellow gets killed so foolishly! Sometimes I used to look at your soldiers and wonder at them. There's foolishness for you! They go, the poor fellows, all in a clump, and even sew red collars to their coats! How can they help being hit! One gets killed, they drag him away and another takes his place! What foolishness!' the old man repeated, shaking his head. 'Why not scatter, and go one by one? So you just go like that and they won't notice you. That's what you must do.'

'Well, thank you! Good-bye, Daddy. God willing we may meet again,' said Olénin, getting up and moving towards the passage.

The old man, who was sitting on the floor, did not rise.

'Is that the way one says "Good-bye"? Fool, fool!' he began. 'Oh dear, what has come to people? We've kept company, kept company for well-nigh a year, and now "Good-bye!" and off he goes! Why, I love you, and how I pity you! You are so forlorn, always alone, always alone. You're somehow so unsociable. At times I can't sleep for thinking about you. I am so sorry for you. As the song has it:

> "It is very hard, dear brother,
> In a foreign land to live."

So it is with you.'

'Well, good-bye,' said Olénin again.

The old man rose and held out his hand. Olénin pressed it and turned to go.

'Give us your mug, your mug!'

And the old man took Olénin by the head with both hands and kissed him three times with wet moustaches and lips, and began to cry.

'I love you, good-bye!'

Olénin got into the cart.

'Well, is that how you're going? You might give me something for a remembrance. Give me a gun! What do you want two for?' said the old man, sobbing quite sincerely.

Olénin got out a musket and gave it to him.

'What a lot you've given the old fellow,' murmured Vanyúsha, 'he'll never have enough! A regular old beggar. They are all such irregular people,' he remarked, as he wrapped himself in his overcoat and took his seat on the box.

'Hold your tongue, swine!' exclaimed the old man, laughing. 'What a stingy fellow!'

Maryánka came out of the cowshed, glanced indifferently at the cart, bowed and went towards the hut.

'*La fille!*' said Vanyúsha, with a wink, and burst out into a silly laugh.

'Drive on!' shouted Olénin, angrily.

'Good-bye, my lad! Good-bye. I won't forget you!' shouted Eróshka.

Olénin turned round. Daddy Eróshka was talking to Maryánka, evidently about his own affairs, and neither the old man nor the girl looked at Olénin.

The Death of Iván Ilých

[1886]

I

During an interval in the Melvínski trial in the large building of the Law Courts the members and public prosecutor met in Iván Egórovich Shébek's private room, where the conversation turned on the celebrated Krasóvski case. Fëdor Vasílievich warmly maintained that it was not subject to their jurisdiction, Iván Egórovich maintained the contrary, while Peter Ivánovich, not having entered into the discussion at the start, took no part in it but looked through the *Gazette* which had just been handed in.

'Gentlemen,' he said, 'Iván Ilých has died!'

'You don't say so!'

'Here, read it yourself,' replied Peter Ivánovich, handing Fëdor Vasílievich the paper still damp from the press. Surrounded by a black border were the words: 'Praskóvya Fëdorovna Goloviná, with profound sorrow, informs relatives and friends of the demise of her beloved husband Iván Ilých Golovín, Member of the Court of Justice, which occurred on February the 4th of this year 1882. The funeral will take place on Friday at one o'clock in the afternoon.'

Iván Ilých had been a colleague of the gentlemen present and was liked by them all. He had been ill for some weeks with an illness said to be incurable. His post had been kept open for him, but there had been conjectures that in case of his death Alexéev might receive his appointment, and that either Vínnikov or Shtábel would succeed Alexéev. So on receiving the news of Iván Ilých's death the first thought of each of the gentlemen in that private room was of the changes and promotions it might occasion among themselves or their acquaintances.

'I shall be sure to get Shtábel's place or Vínnikov's,' thought Fëdor Vasílievich. 'I was promised that long ago, and the promotion means an extra eight hundred rubles a year for me besides the allowance.'

247

'Now I must apply for my brother-in-law's transfer from Kalúga,' thought Peter Ivánovich. 'My wife will be very glad, and then she won't be able to say that I never do anything for her relations.'

'I thought he would never leave his bed again,' said Peter Ivánovich aloud. 'It's very sad.'

'But what really was the matter with him?'

'The doctors couldn't say—at least they could, but each of them said something different. When last I saw him I thought he was getting better.'

'And I haven't been to see him since the holidays. I always meant to go.'

'Had he any property?'

'I think his wife had a little—but something quite trifling.'

'We shall have to go to see her, but they live so terribly far away.'

'Far away from you, you mean. Everything's far away from your place.'

'You see, he never can forgive my living on the other side of the river,' said Peter Ivánovich, smiling at Shébek. Then, still talking of the distances between different parts of the city, they returned to the Court.

Besides considerations as to the possible transfers and promotions likely to result from Iván Ilých's death, the mere fact of the death of a near acquaintance aroused, as usual, in all who heard of it the complacent feeling that, 'it is he who is dead and not I.'

Each one thought or felt, 'Well, he's dead but I'm alive!' But the more intimate of Iván Ilých's acquaintances, his so-called friends, could not help thinking also that they would now have to fulfil the very tiresome demands of propriety by attending the funeral service and paying a visit of condolence to the widow.

Fëdor Vasílievich and Peter Ivánovich had been his nearest acquaintances. Peter Ivánovich had studied law with Iván Ilých and had considered himself to be under obligations to him.

Having told his wife at dinner-time of Iván Ilých's death, and of his conjecture that it might be possible to get her brother transferred to their circuit, Peter Ivánovich sacrificed his usual nap, put on his evening clothes and drove to Iván Ilých's house.

At the entrance stood a carriage and two cabs. Leaning

against the wall in the hall downstairs near the cloakstand was a coffin-lid covered with cloth of gold, ornamented with gold cord and tassels, that had been polished up with metal powder. Two ladies in black were taking off their fur cloaks. Peter Ivánovich recognized one of them as Iván Ilých's sister, but the other was a stranger to him. His colleague Schwartz was just coming downstairs, but on seeing Peter Ivánovich enter he stopped and winked at him, as if to say: 'Iván Ilých has made a mess of things—not like you and me.'

Schwartz's face with his Piccadilly whiskers, and his slim figure in evening dress, had as usual an air of elegant solemnity which contrasted with the playfulness of his character and had a special piquancy here, or so it seemed to Peter Ivánovich.

Peter Ivánovich allowed the ladies to precede him and slowly followed them upstairs. Schwartz did not come down but remained where he was, and Peter Ivánovich understood that he wanted to arrange where they should play bridge that evening. The ladies went upstairs to the widow's room, and Schwartz with seriously compressed lips but a playful look in his eyes, indicated by a twist of his eyebrows the room to the right where the body lay.

Peter Ivánovich, like everyone else on such occasions, entered feeling uncertain what he would have to do. All he knew was that at such times it is always safe to cross oneself. But he was not quite sure whether one should make obeisances while doing so. He therefore adopted a middle course. On entering the room he began crossing himself and made a slight movement resembling a bow. At the same time, as far as the motion of his head and arm allowed, he surveyed the room. Two young men—apparently nephews, one of whom was a high-school pupil —were leaving the room, crossing themselves as they did so. An old woman was standing motionless, and a lady with strangely arched eyebrows was saying something to her in a whisper. A vigorous, resolute Church Reader, in a frock-coat, was reading something in a loud voice with an expression that precluded any contradiction. The butler's assistant, Gerásim, stepping lightly in front of Peter Ivánovich, was strewing something on the floor. Noticing this, Peter Ivánovich was immediately aware of a faint odour of a decomposing body.

The last time he had called on Iván Ilých, Peter Ivánovich had seen Gerásim in the study. Iván Ilých had been particularly fond of him and he was performing the duty of a sick nurse.

Peter Ivánovich continued to make the sign of the cross slightly inclining his head in an intermediate direction between the coffin, the Reader, and the icons on the table in a corner of the room. Afterwards, when it seemed to him that this movement of his arm in crossing himself had gone on too long, he stopped and began to look at the corpse.

The dead man lay, as dead men always lie, in a specially heavy way, his rigid limbs sunk in the soft cushions of the coffin, with the head forever bowed on the pillow. His yellow waxen brow with bald patches over his sunken temples was thrust up in the way peculiar to the dead, the protruding nose seeming to press on the upper lip. He was much changed and had grown even thinner since Peter Ivánovich had last seen him, but, as is always the case with the dead, his face was handsomer and above all more dignified than when he was alive. The expression on the face said that what was necessary had been accomplished, and accomplished rightly. Besides this there was in that expression a reproach and a warning to the living. This warning seemed to Peter Ivánovich out of place, or at least not applicable to him. He felt a certain discomfort and so he hurriedly crossed himself once more and turned and went out of the door—too hurriedly and too regardless of propriety, as he himself was aware.

Schwartz was waiting for him in the adjoining room with legs spread wide apart and both hands toying with his top-hat behind his back. The mere sight of that playful, well-groomed, and elegant figure refreshed Peter Ivánovich. He felt that Schwartz was above all these happenings and would not surrender to any depressing influences. His very look said that this incident of a church service for Iván Ilých could not be a sufficient reason for infringing the order of the session—in other words, that it would certainly not prevent his unwrapping a new pack of cards and shuffling them that evening while a footman placed four fresh candles on the table: in fact, that there was no reason for supposing that this incident would hinder their spending the evening agreeably. Indeed he said this in a whisper as Peter Ivánovich passed him, proposing that they should meet for a game at Fëdor Vasílievich's. But apparently Peter Ivánovich was not destined to play bridge that evening. Praskóvya Fëdorovna (a short, fat woman who despite all efforts to the contrary had continued to broaden steadily from her shoulders downwards and who had the same extraordinarily arched eyebrows as the lady who had been standing by the coffin), dressed all in black, her head covered with lace, came out of her own room with some other ladies, conducted them to the room where the dead body lay, and said: 'The service will begin immediately. Please go in.'

Schwartz, making an indefinite bow, stood still, evidently neither accepting nor declining this invitation. Praskóvya Fëdorovna recognizing Peter Ivánovich, sighed, went close up to him, took his hand, and said: 'I know you were a true friend to Iván Ilých . . .' and looked at him awaiting some suitable response. And Peter Ivánovich knew that, just as it had been the right thing to cross himself in that room, so what he had to do here was to press her hand, sigh, and say, 'Believe me . . .' So he did all this and as he did it felt that the desired result had been achieved: that both he and she were touched.

'Come with me. I want to speak to you before it begins,' said the widow. 'Give me your arm.'

Peter Ivánovich gave her his arm and they went to the inner rooms, passing Schwartz who winked at Peter Ivánovich compassionately.

'That does for our bridge! Don't object if we find another player. Perhaps you can cut in when you do escape,' said his playful look.

Peter Ivánovich sighed still more deeply and despondently, and Praskóvya Fëdorovna pressed his arm gratefully. When they reached the drawing-room, upholstered in pink cretonne and lighted by a dim lamp, they sat down at the table—she on a sofa and Peter Ivánovich on a low pouffe, the springs of which yielded spasmodically under his weight. Praskóvya Fëdorovna had been on the point of warning him to take another seat, but felt that such a warning was out of keeping with her present condition and so changed her mind. As he sat down on the pouffe Peter Ivánovich recalled how Iván Ilých had arranged this room and had consulted him regarding this pink cretonne with green leaves. The whole room was full of furniture and knick-knacks, and on her way to the sofa the lace of the widow's black shawl caught on the carved edge of the

table. Peter Ivánovich rose to detach it, and the springs of
the pouffe, relieved of his weight, rose also and gave him
a push. The widow began detaching her shawl herself, and
Peter Ivánovich again sat down, suppressing the rebellious
springs of the pouffe under him. But the widow had not
quite freed herself and Peter Ivánovich got up again, and
again the pouffe rebelled and even creaked. When this
was all over she took out a clean cambric handkerchief
and began to weep. The episode with the shawl and the
struggle with the pouffe had cooled Peter Ivánovich's
emotions and he sat there with a sullen look on his face.
This awkward situation was interrupted by Sokolóv, Iván
Ilých's butler, who came to report that the plot in the
cemetery that Praskóvya Fëdorovna had chosen would
cost two hundred rubles. She stopped weeping and, looking
at Peter Ivánovich with the air of a victim, remarked in
French that it was very hard for her. Peter Ivánovich
made a silent gesture signifying his full conviction that it
must indeed be so.

'Please smoke,' she said in a magnanimous yet crushed
voice, and turned to discuss with Sokolóv the price of the
plot for the grave.

Peter Ivánovich while lighting his cigarette heard her
inquiring very circumstantially into the prices of different
plots in the cemetery and finally decide which she would
take. When that was done she gave instructions about
engaging the choir. Sokolóv then left the room.

'I look after everything myself,' she told Peter Ivánovich,
shifting the albums that lay on the table; and noticing that
the table was endangered by his cigarette-ash, she immediately passed him an ash-tray, saying as she did so: 'I
consider it an affectation to say that my grief prevents
my attending to practical affairs. On the contrary, if anything can—I won't say console me, but—distract me, it
is seeing to everything concerning him.' She again took
out her handkerchief as if preparing to cry, but suddenly,
as if mastering her feeling, she shook herself and began to
speak calmly. 'But there is something I want to talk to you
about.'

Peter Ivánovich bowed, keeping control of the springs of
the pouffe, which immediately began quivering under him.

'He suffered terribly the last few days.'

'Did he?' said Peter Ivánovich.

'Oh, terribly! He screamed unceasingly, not for minutes

but for hours. For the last three days he screamed incessantly. It was unendurable. I cannot understand how I bore it; you could hear him three rooms off. Oh, what I have suffered!'

'Is it possible that he was conscious all that time?' asked Peter Ivánovich.

'Yes,' she whispered. 'To the last moment. He took leave of us a quarter of an hour before he died, and asked us to take Volódya away.'

The thought of the suffering of this man he had known so intimately, first as a merry little boy, then as a schoolmate, and later as a grown-up colleague, suddenly struck Peter Ivánovich with horror, despite an unpleasant consciousness of his own and this woman's dissimulation. He again saw that brow, and that nose pressing down on the lip, and felt afraid for himself.

'Three days of frightful suffering and the death! Why, that might suddenly, at any time, happen to me,' he thought, and for a moment felt terrified. But—he did not himself know how—the customary reflection at once occurred to him that this had happened to Iván Ilých and not to him, and that it should not and could not happen to him, and that to think that it could would be yielding to depression which he ought not to do, as Schwartz's expression plainly showed. After which reflection Peter Ivánovich felt reassured, and began to ask with interest about the details of Iván Ilých's death, as though death was an accident natural to Iván Ilých but certainly not to himself.

After many details of the really dreadful physical sufferings Iván Ilých had endured (which details he learnt only from the effect those sufferings had produced on Praskóvya Fëdorovna's nerves) the widow apparently found it necessary to get to business.

'Oh, Peter Ivánovich, how hard it is! How terribly, terribly hard!' and she again began to weep.

Peter Ivánovich sighed and waited for her to finish blowing her nose. When she had done so he said, 'Believe me . . .' and she again began talking and brought out what was evidently her chief concern with him—namely, to question him as to how she could obtain a grant of money from the government on the occasion of her husband's death. She made it appear that she was asking Peter Ivánovich's advice about her pension, but he soon saw that she already knew about that to the minutest detail, more even than he did himself. She knew how much could be got out of the government in consequence of her husband's death, but wanted to find out whether she could not possibly extract something more. Peter Ivánovich tried to think of some means of doing so, but after reflecting for a while and, out of propriety, condemning the government for its niggardliness, he said he thought that nothing more could be got. Then she sighed and evidently began to devise means of getting rid of her visitor. Noticing this, he put out his cigarette, rose, pressed her hand, and went out into the anteroom.

In the dining-room where the clock stood that Iván Ilých had liked so much and had bought at an antique shop, Peter Ivánovich met a priest and a few acquaintances who had come to attend the service, and he recognized Iván Ilých's daughter, a handsome young woman. She was in black and her slim figure appeared slimmer than ever. She had a gloomy, determined, almost angry expression, and bowed to Peter Ivánovich as though he were in some way to blame. Behind her, with the same offended look, stood a wealthy young man, an examining magistrate, whom Peter Ivánovich also knew and who was her fiancé, as he had heard. He bowed mournfully to them and was about to pass into the death-chamber, when from under the stairs appeared the figure of Iván Ilých's schoolboy son, who was extremely like his father. He seemed a little Iván Ilých, such as Peter Ivánovich remembered when they studied law together. His tear-stained eyes had in them the look that is seen in the eyes of boys of thirteen or fourteen who are not pure-minded. When he saw Peter Ivánovich he scowled morosely and shamefacedly. Peter Ivánovich nodded to him and entered the death-chamber. The service began: candles, groans, incense, tears, and sobs. Peter Ivánovich stood looking gloomily down at his feet. He did not look once at the dead man, did not yield to any depressing influence, and was one of the first to leave the room. There was no one in the anteroom, but Gerásim darted out of the dead man's room, rummaged with his strong hands among the fur coats to find Peter Ivánovich's and helped him on with it.

'Well, friend Gerásim,' said Peter Ivánovich, so as to say something. 'It's a sad affair, isn't it?'

'It's God's will. We shall all come to it some day,' said

Gerásim, displaying his teeth—the even, white teeth of a healthy peasant—and, like a man in the thick of urgent work, he briskly opened the front door, called the coachman, helped Peter Ivánovich into the sledge, and sprang back to the porch as if in readiness for what he had to do next.

Peter Ivánovich found the fresh air particularly pleasant after the smell of incense, the dead body, and carbolic acid.

'Where to, sir?' asked the coachman.

'It's not too late even now. . . . I'll call round on Fëdor Vasílievich.'

He accordingly drove there and found them just finishing the first rubber, so that it was quite convenient for him to cut in.

II

Iván Ilých's life had been most simple and most ordinary and therefore most terrible.

He had been a member of the Court of Justice, and died at the age of forty-five. His father had been an official who after serving in various ministries and departments in Petersburg had made the sort of career which brings men to positions from which by reason of their long service they cannot be dismissed, though they are obviously unfit to hold any responsible position, and for whom therefore posts are specially created, which though fictitious carry salaries of from six to ten thousand rubles that are not fictitious, and in receipt of which they live on to a great age.

Such was the Privy Councillor and superfluous member of various superfluous institutions, Ilyá Epímovich Golovín.

He had three sons, of whom Iván Ilých was the second. The eldest son was following in his father's footsteps only in another department, and was already approaching that stage in the service at which a similar sinecure would be reached. The third son was a failure. He had ruined his prospects in a number of positions and was now serving in the railway department. His father and brothers, and still more their wives, not merely disliked meeting him, but avoided remembering his existence unless compelled to do so. His sister had married Baron Greff, a Petersburg official of her father's type. Iván Ilých was *le phénix de la famille* as people said. He was neither as cold and formal as his elder brother nor as wild as the younger, but was a happy mean between them—an intelligent, polished, lively and agreeable man. He had studied with his younger brother at the School of Law, but the latter had failed to complete the course and was expelled when he was in the fifth class. Iván Ilých finished the course well. Even when he was at the School of Law he was just what he remained for the rest of his life: a capable, cheerful, good-natured, and sociable man, though strict in the fulfilment of what he considered to be his duty: and he considered his duty to be what was so considered by those in authority. Neither as a boy nor as a man was he a toady, but from early youth was by nature attracted to people of high station as a fly is drawn to the light, assimilating their ways and views of life and establishing friendly relations with them. All the enthusiasms of childhood and youth passed without leaving much trace on him; he succumbed to sensuality, to vanity, and latterly among the highest classes to liberalism, but always within limits which his instinct unfailingly indicated to him as correct.

At school he had done things which had formerly seemed to him very horrid and made him feel disgusted with himself when he did them; but when later on he saw that such actions were done by people of good position and that they did not regard them as wrong, he was able not exactly to regard them as right, but to forget about them entirely or not be at all troubled at remembering them.

Having graduated from the School of Law and qualified for the tenth rank of the civil service, and having received money from his father for his equipment, Iván Ilých ordered himself clothes at Scharmer's, the fashionable tailor, hung a medallion inscribed *respice finem* on his watch-chain, took leave of his professor and the prince who was patron of the school, had a farewell dinner with his comrades at Donon's first-class restaurant, and with his new and fashionable portmanteau. linen, clothes, shaving and other toilet appliances, and a travelling rug, all purchased at the best shops, he set off for one of the provinces where through his father's influence, he had been attached to the governor as an official for special service.

In the province Iván Ilých soon arranged as easy and agreeable a position for himself as he had had at the

School of Law. He performed his official task, made his career, and at the same time amused himself pleasantly and decorously. Occasionally he paid official visits to country districts where he behaved with dignity both to his superiors and inferiors, and performed the duties entrusted to him, which related chiefly to the sectarians, with an exactness and incorruptible honesty of which he could not but feel proud.

In official matters, despite his youth and taste for frivolous gaiety, he was exceedingly reserved, punctilious, and even severe; but in society he was often amusing and witty, and always good-natured, correct in his manner, and *bon enfant*, as the governor and his wife—with whom he was like one of the family—used to say of him.

In the province he had an affair with a lady who made advances to the elegant young lawyer, and there was also a milliner; and there were carousals with aides-de-camp who visited the district, and after-supper visits to a certain outlying street of doubtful reputation; and there was too some obsequiousness to his chief and even to his chief's wife, but all this was done with such a tone of good breeding that no hard names could be applied to it. It all came under the heading of the French saying: '*Il faut que jeunesse se passe.*' It was all done with clean hands, in clean linen, with French phrases, and above all among people of the best society and consequently with the approval of people of rank.

So Iván Ilých served for five years and then came a change in his official life. The new and reformed judicial institutions were introduced, and new men were needed. Iván Ilých became such a new man. He was offered the post of examining magistrate, and he accepted it though the post was in another province and obliged him to give up the connexions he had formed and to make new ones. His friends met to give him a send-off; they had a group-photograph taken and presented him with a silver cigarette-case, and he set off to his new post.

As examining magistrate Iván Ilých was just as *comme il faut* and decorous a man, inspiring general respect and capable of separating his official duties from his private life, as he had been when acting as an official on special service. His duties now as examining magistrate were far more interesting and attractive than before. In his former position it had been pleasant to wear an undress uniform made by Scharmer, and to pass through the crowd of petitioners and officials who were timorously awaiting an audience with the governor, and who envied him as with free and easy gait he went straight into his chief's private room to have a cup of tea and a cigarette with him. But not many people had then been directly dependent on him —only police officials and the sectarians when he went on special missions—and he liked to treat them politely, almost as comrades, as if he were letting them feel that he who had the power to crush them was treating them in this simple, friendly way. There were then but few such people. But now, as an examining magistrate, Iván Ilých felt that everyone without exception, even the most important and self-satisfied, was in his power, and that he need only write a few words on a sheet of paper with a certain heading, and this or that important, self-satisfied person would be brought before him in the role of an accused person or a witness, and if he did not choose to allow him to sit down, would have to stand before him and answer his questions. Iván Ilých never abused his power; he tried on the contrary to soften its expression, but the consciousness of it and of the possibility of softening its effect, supplied the chief interest and attraction of his office. In his work itself, especially in his examinations, he very soon acquired a method of eliminating all considerations irrelevant to the legal aspect of the case, and reducing even the most complicated case to a form in which it would be presented on paper only in its externals, completely excluding his personal opinion of the matter, while above all observing every prescribed formality. The work was new and Iván Ilých was one of the first men to apply the new Code of 1864.

On taking up the post of examining magistrate in a new town, he made new acquaintances and connexions, placed himself on a new footing, and assumed a somewhat different tone. He took up an attitude of rather dignified aloofness towards the provincial authorities, but picked out the best circle of legal gentlemen and wealthy gentry living in the town and assumed a tone of slight dissatisfaction with the government, of moderate liberalism, and of enlightened citizenship. At the same time, without at all altering the elegance of his toilet, he ceased shaving his chin and allowed his beard to grow as it pleased.

Iván Ilých settled down very pleasantly in this new

town. The society there, which inclined towards opposition to the governor, was friendly, his salary was larger, and he began to play *vint* [a form of bridge], which he found added not a little to the pleasure of life, for he had a capacity for cards, played good-humouredly, and calculated rapidly and astutely, so that he usually won.

After living there for two years he met his future wife, Praskóvya Fëdorovna Míkhel, who was the most attractive, clever, and brilliant girl of the set in which he moved, and among other amusements and relaxations from his labours as examining magistrate, Iván Ilých established light and playful relations with her.

While he had been an official on special service he had been accustomed to dance, but now as an examining magistrate it was exceptional for him to do so. If he danced now, he did it as if to show that though he served under the reformed order of things, and had reached the fifth official rank, yet when it came to dancing he could do it better than most people. So at the end of an evening he sometimes danced with Praskóvya Fëdorovna, and it was chiefly during these dances that he captivated her. She fell in love with him. Iván Ilých had at first no definite intention of marrying, but when the girl fell in love with him he said to himself: 'Really, why shouldn't I marry?'

Praskóvya Fëdorovna came of a good family, was not bad looking, and had some little property. Iván Ilých might have aspired to a more brilliant match, but even this was good. He had his salary, and she, he hoped, would have an equal income. She was well connected, and was a sweet, pretty, and thoroughly correct young woman. To say that Iván Ilých married because he fell in love with Praskóvya Fëdorovna and found that she sympathized with his views of life would be as incorrect as to say that he married because his social circle approved of the match. He was swayed by both these considerations: the marriage gave him personal satisfaction, and at the same time it was considered the right thing by the most highly placed of his associates.

So Iván Ilých got married.

The preparations for marriage and the beginning of married life, with its conjugal caresses, the new furniture, new crockery, and new linen, were very pleasant until his wife became pregnant—so that Iván Ilých had begun to think that marriage would not impair the easy, agreeable, gay and always decorous character of his life, approved of by society and regarded by himself as natural, but would even improve it. But from the first months of his wife's pregnancy, something new, unpleasant, depressing, and unseemly, and from which there was no way of escape, unexpectedly showed itself.

His wife, without any reason—*de gaieté de cœur* as Iván Ilých expressed it to himself—began to disturb the pleasure and propriety of their life. She began to be jealous without any cause, expected him to devote his whole attention to her, found fault with everything, and made coarse and ill-mannered scenes.

At first Iván Ilých hoped to escape from the unpleasantness of this state of affairs by the same easy and decorous relation to life that had served him heretofore: he tried to ignore his wife's disagreeable moods, continued to live in his usual easy and pleasant way, invited friends to his house for a game of cards, and also tried going out to his club or spending his evenings with friends. But one day his wife began upbraiding him so vigorously, using such coarse words, and continued to abuse him every time he did not fulfil her demands, so resolutely and with such evident determination not to give way till he submitted—that is, till he stayed at home and was bored just as she was—that he became alarmed. He now realized that matrimony—at any rate with Praskóvya Fëdorovna—was not always conducive to the pleasures and amenities of life, but on the contrary often infringed both comfort and propriety, and that he must therefore entrench himself against such infringement. And Iván Ilých began to seek for means of doing so. His official duties were the one thing that imposed upon Praskóvya Fëdorovna, and by means of his official work and the duties attached to it he began struggling with his wife to secure his own independence.

With the birth of their child, the attempts to feed it and the various failures in doing so, and with the real and imaginary illnesses of mother and child, in which Iván Ilých's sympathy was demanded but about which he understood nothing, the need of securing for himself an existence outside his family life became still more imperative.

As his wife grew more irritable and exacting and Iván Ilých transferred the centre of gravity of his life more and more to his official work, so did he grow to like his work better and became more ambitious than before.

Very soon, within a year of his wedding, Iván Ilých had realized that marriage, though it may add some comforts to life, is in fact a very intricate and difficult affair towards which in order to perform one's duty, that is, to lead a decorous life approved of by society, one must adopt a definite attitude just as towards one's official duties.

And Iván Ilých evolved such an attitude towards married life. He only required of it those conveniences—dinner at home, housewife, and bed—which it could give him, and above all that propriety of external forms required by public opinion. For the rest he looked for light-hearted pleasure and propriety, and was very thankful when he found them, but if he met with antagonism and querulousness he at once retired into his separate fenced-off world of official duties, where he found satisfaction.

Iván Ilých was esteemed a good official, and after three years was made Assistant Public Prosecutor. His new duties, their importance, the possibility of indicting and imprisoning anyone he chose, the publicity his speeches received, and the success he had in all these things, made his work still more attractive.

More children came. His wife became more and more querulous and ill-tempered, but the attitude Iván Ilých had adopted towards his home life rendered him almost impervious to her grumbling.

After seven years' service in that town he was transferred to another province as Public Prosecutor. They moved, but were short of money and his wife did not like the place they moved to. Though the salary was higher the cost of living was greater, besides which two of their children died and family life became still more unpleasant for him.

Praskóvya Fëdorovna blamed her husband for every inconvenience they encountered in their new home. Most of the conversations between husband and wife, especially as to the children's education, led to topics which recalled former disputes, and these disputes were apt to flare up again at any moment. There remained only those rare periods of amorousness which still came to them at times but did not last long. These were islets at which they anchored for a while and then again set out upon that ocean of veiled hostility which showed itself in their aloofness from one another. This aloofness might have grieved Iván Ilých had he considered that it ought not to exist, but he now regarded the position as normal, and even made it the goal at which he aimed in family life. His aim was to free himself more and more from those unpleasant-nesses and to give them a semblance of harmlessness and propriety. He attained this by spending less and less time with his family, and when obliged to be at home he tried to safeguard his position by the presence of outsiders. The chief thing however was that he had his official duties. The whole interest of his life now centred in the official world and that interest absorbed him. The consciousness of his power, being able to ruin anybody he wished to ruin, the importance, even the external dignity of his entry into court, or meetings with his subordinates, his success with superiors and inferiors, and above all his masterly han-dling of cases, of which he was conscious—all this gave him pleasure and filled his life, together with chats with his colleagues, dinners, and bridge. So that on the whole Iván Ilých's life continued to flow as he considered it should do—pleasantly and properly.

So things continued for another seven years. His eldest daughter was already sixteen, another child had died, and only one son was left, a schoolboy and a subject of dis-sension. Iván Ilých wanted to put him in the School of Law, but to spite him Praskóvya Fëdorovna entered him at the High School. The daughter had been educated at home and had turned out well: the boy did not learn badly either.

III

So Iván Ilých lived for seventeen years after his mar-riage. He was already a Public Prosecutor of long stand-ing, and had declined several proposed transfers while awaiting a more desirable post, when an unanticipated and unpleasant occurrence quite upset the peaceful course of his life. He was expecting to be offered the post of presid-ing judge in a University town, but Happe somehow came to the front and obtained the appointment instead. Iván Ilých became irritable, reproached Happe, and quarrelled both with him and with his immediate superiors—who became colder to him and again passed him over when other appointments were made.

This was in 1880, the hardest year of Iván Ilých's life. It was then that it became evident on the one hand that

his salary was insufficient for them to live on, and on the
other that he had been forgotten, and not only this, but
that what was for him the greatest and most cruel injustice appeared to others a quite ordinary occurrence.
Even his father did not consider it his duty to help him.
Iván Ilých felt himself abandoned by everyone, and that
they regarded his position with a salary of 3,500 rubles
[about £350] as quite normal and even fortunate. He
alone knew that with the consciousness of the injustices
done him, with his wife's incessant nagging, and with the
debts he had contracted by living beyond his means, his
position was far from normal.

In order to save money that summer he obtained leave
of absence and went with his wife to live in the country
at her brother's place.

In the country, without his work, he experienced *ennui*
for the first time in his life, and not only *ennui* but intolerable depression, and he decided that it was impossible
to go on living like that, and that it was necessary to take
energetic measures.

Having passed a sleepless night pacing up and down
the veranda, he decided to go to Petersburg and bestir
himself, in order to punish those who had failed to appreciate him and to get transferred to another ministry.

Next day, despite many protests from his wife and her
brother, he started for Petersburg with the sole object of
obtaining a post with a salary of five thousand rubles a
year. He was no longer bent on any particular department,
or tendency, or kind of activity. All he now wanted was
an appointment to another post with a salary of five thousand rubles, either in the administration, in the banks, with
the railways in one of the Empress Márya's Institutions, or
even in the customs—but it had to carry with it a salary
of five thousand rubles and be in a ministry other than
that in which they had failed to appreciate him.

And this quest of Iván Ilých's was crowned with remarkable and unexpected success. At Kursk an acquaintance of his, F. I. Ilyín, got into the first-class carriage,
sat down beside Iván Ilých, and told him of a telegram
just received by the governor of Kursk announcing that
a change was about to take place in the ministry: Peter
Ivánovich was to be superseded by Iván Seménovich.

The proposed change, apart from its significance for
Russia, had a special significance for Iván Ilých, because

by bringing forward a new man, Peter Petróvich, and consequently his friend Zachár Ivánovich, it was highly favourable for Iván Ilých, since Zachár Ivánovich was a friend and colleague of his.

In Moscow this news was confirmed, and on reaching Petersburg Iván Ilých found Zachár Ivánovich and received a definite promise of an appointment in his former Department of Justice.

A week later he telegraphed to his wife: 'Zachár in Miller's place. I shall receive appointment on presentation of report.'

Thanks to this change of personnel, Iván Ilých had unexpectedly obtained an appointment in his former ministry which placed him two stages above his former colleagues besides giving him five thousand rubles salary and three thousand five hundred rubles for expenses connected with his removal. All his ill humour towards his former enemies and the whole department vanished, and Iván Ilých was completely happy.

He returned to the country more cheerful and contented than he had been for a long time. Praskóvya Fëdorovna also cheered up and a truce was arranged between them. Iván Ilých told of how he had been fêted by everybody in Petersburg, how all those who had been his enemies were put to shame and now fawned on him, how envious they were of his appointment, and how much everybody in Petersburg had liked him.

Praskóvya Fëdorovna listened to all this and appeared to believe it. She did not contradict anything, but only made plans for their life in the town to which they were going. Iván Ilých saw with delight that these plans were his plans, that he and his wife agreed, and that, after a stumble, his life was regaining its due and natural character of pleasant lightheartedness and decorum.

Iván Ilých had come back for a short time only, for he had to take up his new duties on the 10th of September. Moreover, he needed time to settle into the new place, to move all his belongings from the province, and to buy and order many additional things: in a word, to make such arrangements as he had resolved on, which were almost exactly what Praskóvya Fëdorovna too had decided on.

Now that everything had happened so fortunately, and that he and his wife were at one in their aims and moreover saw so little of one another, they got on together better than they had done since the first years of marriage. Iván Ilých had thought of taking his family away with him at once, but the insistence of his wife's brother and her sister-in-law, who had suddenly become particularly amiable and friendly to him and his family, induced him to depart alone.

So he departed, and the cheerful state of mind induced by his success and by the harmony between his wife and himself, the one intensifying the other, did not leave him. He found a delightful house, just the thing both he and his wife had dreamt of. Spacious, lofty reception rooms in the old style, a convenient and dignified study, rooms for his wife and daughter, a study for his son—it might have been specially built for them. Iván Ilých himself superintended the arrangements, chose the wallpapers, supplemented the furniture (preferably with antiques which he considered particularly *comme il faut*), and supervised the upholstering. Everything progressed and progressed and approached the ideal he had set himself: even when things were only half completed they exceeded his expectations. He saw what a refined and elegant character, free from vulgarity, it would all have when it was ready. On falling asleep he pictured to himself how the reception-room would look. Looking at the yet unfinished drawing-room he could see the fireplace, the screen, the what-not, the little chairs dotted here and there, the dishes and plates on the walls, and the bronzes, as they would be when everything was in place. He was pleased by the thought of how his wife and daughter, who shared his taste in this matter, would be impressed by it. They were certainly not expecting as much. He had been particularly successful in finding, and buying cheaply, antiques which gave a particularly aristocratic character to the whole place. But in his letters he intentionally understated everything in order to be able to surprise them. All this so absorbed him that his new duties—though he liked his official work —interested him less than he had expected. Sometimes he even had moments of absent-mindedness during the court sessions, and would consider whether he should have straight or curved cornices for his curtains. He was so interested in it all that he often did things himself, rearranging the furniture, or rehanging the curtains. Once when mounting a step-ladder to show the upholsterer, who did not understand, how he wanted the hangings draped, he made a false step and slipped, but being a strong and agile man he clung on and only knocked his side against the knob of the window frame. The bruised place was painful but the pain soon passed, and he felt particularly bright and well just then. He wrote: 'I feel fifteen years younger.' He thought he would have everything ready by September, but it dragged on till mid-October. But the result was charming not only in his eyes but to everyone who saw it.

In reality it was just what is usually seen in the houses of people of moderate means who want to appear rich, and therefore succeed only in resembling others like themselves: there were damasks, dark wood, plants, rugs, and dull and polished bronzes—all the things people of a certain class have in order to resemble other people of that class. His house was so like the others that it would never have been noticed, but to him it all seemed to be quite exceptional. He was very happy when he met his family at the station and brought them to the newly furnished house all lit up, where a footman in a white tie opened the door into the hall decorated with plants, and when they went on into the drawing-room and the study uttering exclamations of delight. He conducted them everywhere, drank in their praises eagerly, and beamed with pleasure. At tea that evening, when Praskóvya Fëdorovna among other things asked him about his fall, he laughed, and showed them how he had gone flying and had frightened the upholsterer.

'It's a good thing I'm a bit of an athlete. Another man might have been killed, but I merely knocked myself, just here; it hurts when it's touched, but it's passing off already —it's only a bruise.'

So they began living in their new home—in which, as always happens, when they got thoroughly settled in they found they were just one room short—and with the increased income, which as always was just a little (some five hundred rubles) too little, but it was all very nice.

Things went particularly well at first, before everything was finally arranged and while something had still to be done: this thing bought, that thing ordered, another thing moved, and something else adjusted. Though there were some disputes between husband and wife, they were both so well satisfied and had so much to do that it all passed off without any serious quarrels. When nothing was left to arrange it became rather dull and something seemed to be lacking, but they were then making acquaintances, forming habits, and life was growing fuller.

Iván Ilých spent his mornings at the law court and came home to dinner, and at first he was generally in a good humour, though he occasionally became irritable just on account of his house. (Every spot on the tablecloth or the upholstery, and every broken window-blind string, irritated him. He had devoted so much trouble to arranging it all that every disturbance of it distressed him.) But on the whole his life ran its course as he believed life should do: easily, pleasantly, and decorously.

He got up at nine, drank his coffee, read the paper, and then put on his undress uniform and went to the law courts. There the harness in which he worked had already been stretched to fit him and he donned it without a hitch: petitioners, inquiries at the chancery, the chancery itself, and the sittings public and administrative. In all this the thing was to exclude everything fresh and vital, which always disturbs the regular course of official business, and to admit only official relations with people, and then only on official grounds. A man would come, for instance, wanting some information. Iván Ilých, as one in whose sphere the matter did not lie, would have nothing to do with him: but if the man had some business with him in his official capacity, something that could be expressed on officially stamped paper, he would do everything, positively everything he could within the limits of such relations, and in doing so would maintain the semblance of friendly human relations, that is, would observe the courtesies of life. As soon as the official relations ended, so did everything else. Iván Ilých possessed this capacity to separate his real life from the official side of affairs and not mix the two, in the highest degree, and by long practice and natural aptitude had brought it to such a pitch that sometimes, in the manner of a virtuoso, he would even allow himself to let the human and official relations mingle. He let himself do this just because he felt that he could at any time he chose resume the strictly official attitude again and drop the human relation. And he did it all easily, pleasantly, correctly, and even artistically. In the intervals between the sessions he smoked, drank tea, chatted a little about politics, a little about general topics, a little about cards, but most of all about official appointments. Tired, but

with the feelings of a virtuoso—one of the first violins
who has played his part in an orchestra with precision—
he would return home to find that his wife and daughter
had been out paying calls, or had a visitor, and that his
son had been to school, had done his homework with his
tutor, and was duly learning what is taught at High
Schools. Everything was as it should be. After dinner, if
they had no visitors, Iván Ilých sometimes read a book that
was being much discussed at the time, and in the evening
settled down to work, that is, read official papers, compared the depositions of witnesses, and noted paragraphs
of the Code applying to them. This was neither dull nor
amusing. It was dull when he might have been playing
bridge, but if no bridge was available it was at any rate
better than doing nothing or sitting with his wife. Iván
Ilých's chief pleasure was giving little dinners to which
he invited men and women of good social position, and
just as his drawing-room resembled all other drawing-
rooms so did his enjoyable little parties resemble all other
such parties.

Once they even gave a dance. Iván Ilých enjoyed it and
everything went off well, except that it led to a violent
quarrel with his wife about the cakes and sweets. Praskóvya Fëdorovna had made her own plans, but Iván
Ilých insisted on getting everything from an expensive
confectioner and ordered too many cakes, and the quarrel
occurred because some of those cakes were left over and
the confectioner's bill came to forty-five rubles. It was
a great and disagreeable quarrel. Praskóvya Fëdorovna
called him 'a fool and an imbecile,' and he clutched at his
head and made angry allusions to divorce.

But the dance itself had been enjoyable. The best people
were there, and Iván Ilých had danced with Princess Trú-
fonova, a sister of the distinguished founder of the Society
'Bear My Burden.'

The pleasures connected with his work were pleasures
of ambition; his social pleasures were those of vanity; but
Iván Ilých's greatest pleasure was playing bridge. He
acknowledged that whatever disagreeable incident happened in his life, the pleasure that beamed like a ray of
light above everything else was to sit down to bridge with
good players, not noisy partners, and of course to four-
handed bridge (with five players it was annoying to have
to stand out, though one pretended not to mind), to play

a clever and serious game (when the cards allowed it) and then to have supper and drink a glass of wine. After a game of bridge, especially if he had won a little (to win a large sum was unpleasant), Iván Ilých went to bed in specially good humour.

So they lived. They formed a circle of acquaintances among the best people and were visited by people of importance and by young folk. In their views as to their acquaintances, husband, wife and daughter were entirely agreed, and tacitly and unanimously kept at arm's length and shook off the various shabby friends and relations who, with much show of affection, gushed into the drawing-room with its Japanese plates on the walls. Soon these shabby friends ceased to obtrude themselves and only the best people remained in the Golovíns' set.

Young men made up to Lisa, and Petríshchev, an examining magistrate and Dmítri Ivánovich Petríshchev's son and sole heir, began to be so attentive to her that Iván Ilých had already spoken to Praskóvya Fëdorovna about it, and considered whether they should not arrange a party for them, or get up some private theatricals.

So they lived, and all went well, without change, and life flowed pleasantly.

IV

They were all in good health. It could not be called ill health if Iván Ilých sometimes said that he had a queer taste in his mouth and felt some discomfort in his left side.

But this discomfort increased and, though not exactly painful, grew into a sense of pressure in his side accompanied by ill humour. And his irritability became worse and worse and began to mar the agreeable, easy, and correct life that had established itself in the Golovín family. Quarrels between husband and wife became more and more frequent, and soon the ease and amenity disappeared and even the decorum was barely maintained. Scenes again became frequent, and very few of those islets remained on which husband and wife could meet without an explosion. Praskóvya Fëdorovna now had good reason to say that her husband's temper was trying. With characteristic exaggeration she said he had always had a dreadful temper, and that it had needed all her good nature to put up with it for twenty years. It was true that now the quarrels were started by him. His bursts of temper always came just before dinner, often just as he began to eat his soup. Sometimes he noticed that a plate or dish was chipped, or the food was not right, or his son put his elbow on the table, or his daughter's hair was not done as he liked it, and for all this he blamed Praskóvya Fëdorovna. At first she retorted and said disagreeable things to him, but once or twice he fell into such a rage at the beginning of dinner that she realized it was due to some physical derangement brought on by taking food, and so she restrained herself and did not answer, but only hurried to get the dinner over. She regarded this self-restraint as highly praise-worthy. Having come to the conclusion that her husband had a dreadful temper and made her life miserable, she began to feel sorry for herself, and the more she pitied herself the more she hated her husband. She began to wish he would die; yet she did not want him to die because then his salary would cease. And this irritated her against him still more. She considered herself dreadfully unhappy just because not even his death could save her, and though she concealed her exasperation, that hidden exasperation of hers increased his irritation also.

After one scene in which Iván Ilých had been particularly unfair and after which he had said in explanation that he certainly was irritable but that it was due to his not being well, she said that if he was ill it should be attended to, and insisted on his going to see a celebrated doctor.

He went. Everything took place as he had expected and as it always does. There was the usual waiting and the important air assumed by the doctor, with which he was so familiar (resembling that which he himself assumed in court), and the sounding and listening, and the questions which called for answers that were foregone conclusions and were evidently unnecessary, and the look of importance which implied that 'if only you put yourself in our hands we will arrange everything—we know indubitably how it has to be done, always in the same way for everybody alike.' It was all just as it was in the law courts. The doctor put on just the same air towards him as he himself put on towards an accused person.

The doctor said that so-and-so indicated that there was so-and-so inside the patient, but if the investigation of so-

and-so did not confirm this, then he must assume that and
that. If he assumed that and that, then . . . and so on.
To Iván Ilých only one question was important: was his
case serious or not? But the doctor ignored that inappropriate question. From his point of view it was not the one
under consideration, the real question was to decide between a floating kidney, chronic catarrh, or appendicitis.
It was not a question of Iván Ilých's life or death, but
one between a floating kidney and appendicitis. And that
question the doctor solved brilliantly, as it seemed to Iván
Ilých, in favour of the appendix, with the reservation that
should an examination of the urine give fresh indications
the matter would be reconsidered. All this was just what
Iván Ilých had himself brilliantly accomplished a thousand times in dealing with men on trial. The doctor
summed up just as brilliantly, looking over his spectacles
triumphantly and even gaily at the accused. From the
doctor's summing up Iván Ilých concluded that things were
bad, but that for the doctor, and perhaps for everybody
else, it was a matter of indifference, though for him it
was bad. And this conclusion struck him painfully, arousing in him a great feeling of pity for himself and of bit-
terness towards the doctor's indifference to a matter of
such importance.

He said nothing of this, but rose, placed the doctor's fee
on the table, and remarked with a sigh: 'We sick people
probably often put inappropriate questions. But tell me, in
general, is this complaint dangerous, or not? . . .'

The doctor looked at him sternly over his spectacles
with one eye, as if to say: 'Prisoner, if you will not keep
to the questions put to you, I shall be obliged to have you
removed from the court.'

'I have already told you what I consider necessary and
proper. The analysis may show something more.' And the
doctor bowed.

Iván Ilých went out slowly, seated himself disconsolately
in his sledge, and drove home. All the way home he was
going over what the doctor had said, trying to translate
those complicated, obscure, scientific phrases into plain
language and find in them an answer to the question: 'Is
my condition bad? Is it very bad? Or is there as yet nothing much wrong?' And it seemed to him that the meaning of what the doctor had said was that it was very bad.
Everything in the streets seemed depressing. The cabmen,

the houses, the passers-by, and the shops, were dismal. His ache, this dull gnawing ache that never ceased for a moment, seemed to have acquired a new and more serious significance from the doctor's dubious remarks. Iván Ilých now watched it with a new and oppressive feeling.

He reached home and began to tell his wife about it. She listened, but in the middle of his account his daughter came in with her hat on, ready to go out with her mother. She sat down reluctantly to listen to this tedious story, but could not stand it long, and her mother too did not hear him to the end.

'Well, I am very glad,' she said. 'Mind now to take your medicine regularly. Give me the prescription and I'll send Gerásim to the chemist's.' And she went to get ready to go out.

While she was in the room Iván Ilých had hardly taken time to breathe, but he sighed deeply when she left it.

'Well,' he thought, 'perhaps it isn't so bad after all.'

He began taking his medicine and following the doctor's directions, which had been altered after the examination of the urine. But then it happened that there was a contradiction between the indications drawn from the examination of the urine and the symptoms that showed themselves. It turned out that what was happening differed from what the doctor had told him, and that he had either forgotten, or blundered, or hidden something from him. He could not, however, be blamed for that, and Iván Ilých still obeyed his orders implicitly and at first derived some comfort from doing so.

From the time of his visit to the doctor, Iván Ilých's chief occupation was the exact fulfillment of the doctor's instructions regarding hygiene and the taking of medicine, and the observation of his pain and his excretions. His chief interests came to be people's ailments and people's health. When sickness, deaths, or recoveries were mentioned in his presence, especially when the illness resembled his own, he listened with agitation which he tried to hide, asked questions, and applied what he heard to his own case.

The pain did not grow less, but Iván Ilých made efforts to force himself to think that he was better. And he could do this so long as nothing agitated him. But as soon as he had any unpleasantness with his wife, any lack of success in his official work, or held bad cards at bridge, he was at

once acutely sensible of his disease. He had formerly
borne such mischances, hoping soon to adjust what was
wrong, to master it and attain success, or make a grand
slam. But now every mischance upset him and plunged
him into despair. He would say to himself: 'There now,
just as I was beginning to get better and the medicine had
begun to take effect, comes this accursed misfortune, or
unpleasantness . . .' And he was furious with the mishap,
or with the people who were causing the unpleasantness
and killing him, for he felt that this fury was killing him
but he could not restrain it. One would have thought that it
should have been clear to him that this exasperation with
circumstances and people aggravated his illness, and that
he ought therefore to ignore unpleasant occurrences. But
he drew the very opposite conclusion: he said that he
needed peace, and he watched for everything that might
disturb it and became irritable at the slightest infringement
of it. His condition was rendered worse by the fact that
he read medical books and consulted doctors. The progress
of his disease was so gradual that he could deceive himself when comparing one day with another—the difference
was so slight. But when he consulted the doctors it seemed
to him that he was getting worse, and even very rapidly.
Yet despite this he was continually consulting them.

That month he went to see another celebrity, who told
him almost the same as the first had done but put his
questions rather differently, and the interview with this
celebrity only increased Iván Ilých's doubts and fears.
A friend of a friend of his, a very good doctor, diagnosed
his illness again quite differently from the others, and
though he predicted recovery, his questions and supposi-
tions bewildered Iván Ilých still more and increased his
doubts. A homeopathist diagnosed the disease in yet another way, and prescribed medicine which Iván Ilých took
secretly for a week. But after a week, not feeling any
improvement and having lost confidence both in the former
doctor's treatment and in this one's, he became still more
despondent. One day a lady acquaintance mentioned a
cure effected by a wonder-working icon. Iván Ilých caught
himself listening attentively and beginning to believe that
it had occurred. This incident alarmed him. 'Has my mind
really weakened to such an extent?' he asked himself.
'Nonsense! It's all rubbish. I mustn't give way to nervous
fears but having chosen a doctor must keep strictly to his

treatment. That is what I will do. Now it's all settled. I won't think about it, but will follow the treatment seriously till summer, and then we shall see. From now there must be no more of this wavering!' This was easy to say but impossible to carry out. The pain in his side oppressed him and seemed to grow worse and more incessant, while the taste in his mouth grew stranger and stranger. It seemed to him that his breath had a disgusting smell, and he was conscious of a loss of appetite and strength. There was no deceiving himself: something terrible, new, and more important than anything before in his life, was taking place within him of which he alone was aware. Those about him did not understand or would not understand it, but thought everything in the world was going on as usual. That tormented Iván Ilých more than anything. He saw that his household, especially his wife and daughter who were in a perfect whirl of visiting, did not understand anything of it and were annoyed that he was so depressed and so exacting, as if he were to blame for it. Though they tried to disguise it he saw that he was an obstacle in their path, and that his wife had adopted a definite line in regard to his illness and kept to it regardless of anything he said or did. Her attitude was this: 'You know,' she would say to her friends, 'Iván Ilých can't do as other people do, and keep to the treatment prescribed for him. One day he'll take his drops and keep strictly to his diet and go to bed in good time, but the next day unless I watch him he'll suddenly forget his medicine, eat sturgeon —which is forbidden—and sit up playing cards till one o'clock in the morning.'

'Oh, come, when was that?' Iván Ilých would ask in vexation. 'Only once at Peter Ivánovich's.'

'And yesterday with Shébek.'

'Well, even if I hadn't stayed up, this pain would have kept me awake.'

'Be that as it may you'll never get well like that, but will always make us wretched.'

Praskóvya Fëdorovna's attitude to Iván Ilých's illness, as she expressed it both to others and to him, was that it was his own fault and was another of the annoyances he caused her. Iván Ilých felt that this opinion escaped her involuntarily—but that did not make it easier for him.

At the law courts too, Iván Ilých noticed, or thought he noticed, a strange attitude towards himself. It sometimes seemed to him that people were watching him inquisitively as a man whose place might soon be vacant. Then again, his friends would suddenly begin to chaff him in a friendly way about his low spirits, as if the awful, horrible, and unheard-of thing that was going on within him, incessantly gnawing at him and irresistibly drawing him away, was a very agreeable subject for jests. Schwartz in particular irritated him by his jocularity, vivacity, and *savoir-faire*, which reminded him of what he himself had been ten years ago.

Friends came to make up a set and they sat down to cards. They dealt, bending the new cards to soften them, and he sorted the diamonds in his hand and found he had seven. His partner said 'No trumps' and supported him with two diamonds. What more could be wished for? It ought to be jolly and lively. They would make a grand slam. But suddenly Iván Ilých was conscious of that gnawing pain, that taste in his mouth, and it seemed ridiculous that in such circumstances he should be pleased to make a grand slam.

He looked at his partner Mikháil Mikháylovich, who rapped the table with his strong hand and instead of snatching up the tricks pushed the cards courteously and indulgently towards Iván Ilých that he might have the pleasure of gathering them up without the trouble of stretching out his hand for them. 'Does he think I am too weak to stretch out my arm?' thought Iván Ilých, and forgetting what he was doing he over-trumped his partner, missing the grand slam by three tricks. And what was most awful of all was that he saw how upset Mikháil Mikháylovich was about it but did not himself care. And it was dreadful to realize why he did not care.

They all saw that he was suffering, and said: 'We can stop if you are tired. Take a rest.' Lie down? No, he was not at all tired, and he finished the rubber. All were gloomy and silent. Iván Ilých felt that he had diffused this gloom over them and could not dispel it. They had supper and went away, and Iván Ilých was left alone with the consciousness that his life was poisoned and was poisoning the lives of others, and that this poison did not weaken but penetrated more and more deeply into his whole being.

With this consciousness, and with physical pain besides the terror, he must go to bed, often to lie awake the greater part of the night. Next morning he had to get up again, dress, go to the law courts, speak, and write; or if he did not go out, spend at home those twenty-four hours a day each of which was a torture. And he had to live thus all alone on the brink of an abyss, with no one who understood or pitied him.

V

So one month passed and then another. Just before the New Year his brother-in-law came to town and stayed at their house. Iván Ilých was at the law courts and Praskóvya Fëdorovna had gone shopping. When Iván Ilých came home and entered his study he found his brother-in-law there—a healthy, florid man—unpacking his portmanteau himself. He raised his head on hearing Iván Ilých's footsteps and looked up at him for a moment without a word. That stare told Iván Ilých everything. His brother-in-law opened his mouth to utter an exclamation of surprise but checked himself, and that action confirmed it all.

'I have changed, eh?'

'Yes, there is a change.'

And after that, try as he would to get his brother-in-law to return to the subject of his looks, the latter would say nothing about it. Praskóvya Fëdorovna came home and her brother went out to her. Iván Ilých locked the door and began to examine himself in the glass, first full face, then in profile. He took up a portrait of himself taken with his wife, and compared it with what he saw in the glass. The change in him was immense. Then he bared his arms to the elbow, looked at them, drew the sleeves down again, sat down on an ottoman, and grew blacker than night.

'No, no, this won't do!' he said to himself, and jumped up, went to the table, took up some law papers and began to read them, but could not continue. He unlocked the door and went into the reception-room. The door leading to the drawing-room was shut. He approached it on tiptoe and listened.

'No, you are exaggerating!' Praskóvya Fëdorovna was saying.

'Exaggerating! Don't you see it? Why, he's a dead man! Look at his eyes—there's no light in them. But what is it that is wrong with him?'

'No one knows. Nikoláevich [that was another doctor] said something, but I don't know what. And Leshchetítsky [this was the celebrated . specialist] said quite the contrary . . .'

Iván Ilých walked away, went to his own room, lay down, and began musing: 'The kidney, a floating kidney.' He recalled all the doctors had told him of how it detached itself and swayed about. And by an effort of imagination he tried to catch that kidney and arrest it and support it. So little was needed for this, it seemed to him. 'No, I'll go to see Peter Ivánovich again.' [That was the friend whose friend was a doctor.] He rang, ordered the carriage, and got ready to go.

'Where are you going, Jean?' asked his wife, with a specially sad and exceptionally kind look.

This exceptionally kind look irritated him. He looked morosely at her.

'I must go to see Peter Ivánovich.'

He went to see Peter Ivánovich, and together they went to see his friend, the doctor. He was in, and Iván Ilých had a long talk with him.

Reviewing the anatomical and physiological details of what in the doctor's opinion was going on inside him, he understood it all.

There was something, a small thing, in the vermiform appendix. It might all come right. Only stimulate the energy of one organ and check the activity of another, then absorption would take place and everything would come right. He got home rather late for dinner, ate his dinner, and conversed cheerfully, but could not for a long time bring himself to go back to work in his room. At last, however, he went to his study and did what was necessary, but the consciousness that he had put something aside—an important, intimate matter which he would revert to when his work was done—never left him. When he had finished his work he remembered that this intimate matter was the thought of his vermiform appendix. But he did not give himself up to it, and went to the drawing-room for tea. There were callers there, including the examining magistrate who was a desirable match for his daughter, and they were conversing, playing the piano, and singing. Iván Ilých, as Praskóvya Fёdorovna remarked, spent that evening more cheerfully than usual, but he never for a moment forgot that he had postponed the important

matter of the appendix. At eleven o'clock he said good-
night and went to his bedroom. Since his illness he had
slept alone in a small room next to his study. He undressed
and took up a novel by Zola, but instead of reading it he
fell into thought, and in his imagination that desired improvement in the vermiform appendix occurred. There
was the absorption and evacuation and the re-establish-
ment of normal activity. 'Yes, that's it!' he said to himself.
'One need only assist nature, that's all.' He remembered his
medicine, rose, took it, and lay down on his back watching
for the beneficent action of the medicine and for it to
lessen the pain. 'I need only take it regularly and avoid
all injurious influences. I am already feeling better, much
better.' He began touching his side: it was not painful to
the touch. 'There, I really don't feel it. It's much better
already.' He put out the light and turned on his side . . .
'The appendix is getting better, absorption is occurring.'
Suddenly he felt the old, familiar, dull, gnawing pain,
stubborn and serious. There was the same familiar loathsome taste in his mouth. His heart sank and he felt dazed.
'My God! My God!' he muttered. 'Again, again! And it will
never cease.' And suddenly the matter presented itself in
a quite different aspect. 'Vermiform appendix! Kidney!'
he said to himself. 'It's not a question of appendix or
kidney, but of life and . . . death. Yes, life was there and
now it is going, going and I cannot stop it. Yes. Why
deceive myself? Isn't it obvious to everyone but me that
I'm dying, and that it's only a question of weeks, days
. . . it may happen this moment. There was light and
now there is darkness. I was here and now I'm going there!
Where?' A chill came over him, his breathing ceased, and
he felt only the throbbing of his heart.

'When I am not, what will there be? There will be
nothing. Then where shall I be when I am no more? Can
this be dying? No, I don't want to!' He jumped up and
tried to light the candle, felt for it with trembling hands,
dropped candle and candlestick on the floor, and fell back
on his pillow.

'What's the use? It makes no difference,' he said to himself, staring with wide-open eyes into the darkness. 'Death.
Yes, death. And none of them knows or wishes to know
it, and they have no pity for me. Now they are playing.'
(He heard through the door the distant sound of a song
and its accompaniment.) 'It's all the same to them, but

they will die too! Fools! I first, and they later, but it will be the same for them. And now they are merry . . . the beasts!'

Anger choked him and he was agonizingly, unbearably miserable. 'It is impossible that all men have been doomed to suffer this awful horror!' He raised himself.

'Something must be wrong. I must calm myself—must think it all over from the beginning.' And he again began thinking. 'Yes, the beginning of my illness: I knocked my side, but I was still quite well that day and the next. It hurt a little, then rather more. I saw the doctors, then followed despondency and anguish, more doctors, and I drew nearer to the abyss. My strength grew less and I kept coming nearer and nearer, and now I have wasted away and there is no light in my eyes. I think of the appendix—but this is death! I think of mending the appendix, and all the while here is death! Can it really be death?' Again terror seized him and he gasped for breath. He leant down and began feeling for the matches, pressing with his elbow on the stand beside the bed. It was in his way and hurt him, he grew furious with it, pressed on it still harder, and upset it. Breathless and in despair he fell on his back, expecting death to come immediately.

Meanwhile the visitors were leaving. Praskóvya Fëdorovna was seeing them off. She heard something fall and came in.

'What has happened?'

'Nothing. I knocked it over accidentally.'

She went out and returned with a candle. He lay there panting heavily, like a man who has run a thousand yards, and stared upwards at her with a fixed look.

'What is it, Jean?'

'No . . . o . . . thing. I upset it.' ('Why speak of it? She won't understand,' he thought.)

And in truth she did not understand. She picked up the stand, lit his candle, and hurried away to see another visitor off. When she came back he still lay on his back, looking upwards.

'What is it? Do you feel worse?'

'Yes.'

She shook her head and sat down.

'Do you know, Jean, I think we must ask Leshchetítsky to come and see you here.'

This meant calling in the famous specialist, regardless

of expense. He smiled malignantly and said 'No.' She remained a little longer and then went up to him and kissed his forehead.

While she was kissing him he hated her from the bottom of his soul and with difficulty refrained from pushing her away.

'Good-night. Please God you'll sleep.'

'Yes.'

VI

Iván Ilých saw that he was dying, and he was in continual despair.

In the depth of his heart he knew he was dying, but not only was he not accustomed to the thought, he simply did not and could not grasp it.

The syllogism he had learnt from Kiesewetter's Logic: 'Caius is a man, men are mortal, therefore Caius is mortal,' had always seemed to him correct as applied to Caius, but certainly not as applied to himself. That Caius—man in the abstract—was mortal, was perfectly correct, but he was not Caius, not an abstract man, but a creature quite, quite separate from all others. He had been little Ványa, with a mamma and a papa, with Mítya and Volódya, with the toys, a coachman and a nurse, afterwards with Kátenka and with all the joys, griefs, and delights of childhood, boyhood, and youth. What did Caius know of the smell of that striped leather ball Ványa had been so fond of? Had Caius kissed his mother's hand like that, and did the silk of her dress rustle so for Caius? Had he rioted like that at school when the pastry was bad? Had Caius been in love like that? Could Caius preside at a session as he did? 'Caius really was mortal, and it was right for him to die; but for me, little Ványa, Iván Ilých, with all my thoughts and emotions, it's altogether a different matter. It cannot be that I ought to die. That would be too terrible.'

Such was his feeling.

'If I had to die like Caius I should have known it was so. An inner voice would have told me so, but there was nothing of the sort in me and I and all my friends felt that our case was quite different from that of Caius. And now here it is!' he said to himself. 'It can't be. It's impossible! But here it is. How is this? How is one to understand it?'

He could not understand it, and tried to drive this false, incorrect, morbid thought away and to replace it by other proper and healthy thoughts. But that thought, and not the thought only but the reality itself, seemed to come and confront him.

And to replace that thought he called up a succession of others, hoping to find in them some support. He tried to get back into the former current of thoughts that had once screened the thought of death from him. But strange to say, all that had formerly shut off, hidden, and destroyed his consciousness of death, no longer had that effect. Iván Ilých now spent most of his time in attempting to re-establish that old current. He would say to himself: 'I will take up my duties again—after all I used to live by them.' And banishing all doubts he would go to the law courts, enter into conversation with his colleagues, and sit carelessly as was his wont, scanning the crowd with a thoughtful look and leaning both his emaciated arms on the arms of his oak chair; bending over as usual to a colleague and drawing his papers nearer he would interchange whispers with him, and then suddenly raising his eyes and sitting erect would pronounce certain words and open the proceedings. But suddenly in the midst of those proceedings the pain in his side, regardless of the stage the proceedings had reached, would begin its own gnawing work. Iván Ilých would turn his attention to it and try to drive the thought of it away, but without success. *It* would come and stand before him and look at him, and he would be petrified and the light would die out of his eyes, and he would again begin asking himself whether *It* alone was true. And his colleagues and subordinates would see with surprise and distress that he, the brilliant and subtle judge, was becoming confused and making mistakes. He would shake himself, try to pull himself together, manage somehow to bring the sitting to a close, and return home with the sorrowful consciousness that his judicial labours could not as formerly hide from him what he wanted them to hide, and could not deliver him from *It*. And what was worst of all was that *It* drew his attention to itself not in order to make him take some action but only that he should look at *It*, look it straight in the face: look at it and without doing anything, suffer inexpressibly.

And to save himself from this condition Iván Ilých

looked for consolations—new screens—and new screens were found and for a while seemed to save him, but then they immediately fell to pieces or rather became transparent, as if *It* penetrated them and nothing could veil *It*.

In these latter days he would go into the drawing-room he had arranged—that drawing-room where he had fallen and for the sake of which (how bitterly ridiculous it seemed) he had sacrificed his life—for he knew that his illness originated with that knock. He would enter and see that something had scratched the polished table. He would look for the cause of this and find that it was the bronze ornamentation of an album, that had got bent. He would take up the expensive album which he had lovingly arranged, and feel vexed with his daughter and her friends for their untidiness—for the album was torn here and there and some of the photographs turned upside down. He would put it carefully in order and bend the ornamentation back into position. Then it would occur to him to place all those things in another corner of the room, near the plants. He would call the footman, but his daughter or wife would come to help him. They would not agree, and his wife would contradict him, and he would dispute and grow angry. But that was all right, for then he did not think about *It*. *It* was invisible.

But then, when he was moving something himself, his wife would say: 'Let the servants do it. You will hurt yourself again.' And suddenly *It* would flash through the screen and he would see it. It was just a flash, and he hoped it would disappear, but he would involuntarily pay attention to his side. 'It sits there as before, gnawing just the same!' And he could no longer forget *It*, but could distinctly see it looking at him from behind the flowers. 'What is it all for?'

'It really is so! I lost my life over that curtain as I might have done when storming a fort. Is that possible? How terrible and how stupid. It can't be true! It can't, but it is.'

He would go to his study, lie down, and again be alone with *It*: face to face with *It*. And nothing could be done with *It* except to look at it and shudder.

VII

How it happened it is impossible to say because it came about step by step, unnoticed, but in the third month of Iván Ilých's illness, his wife, his daughter, his son, his acquaintances, the doctors, the servants, and above all he himself, were aware that the whole interest he had for other people was whether he would soon vacate his place, and at last release the living from the discomfort caused by his presence and be himself released from his sufferings.

He slept less and less. He was given opium and hypodermic injections of morphine, but this did not relieve him. The dull depression he experienced in a somnolent condition at first gave him a little relief, but only as something new, afterwards it became as distressing as the pain itself or even more so.

Special foods were prepared for him by the doctors' orders, but all those foods became increasingly distasteful and disgusting to him.

For his excretions also special arrangements had to be made, and this was a torment to him every time—a torment from the uncleanliness, the unseemliness, and the smell, and from knowing that another person had to take part in it.

But just through this most unpleasant matter, Iván Ilých obtained comfort. Gerásim, the butler's young assistant, always came in to carry the things out. Gerásim was a clean, fresh peasant lad, grown stout on town food and always cheerful and bright. At first the sight of him, in his clean Russian peasant costume, engaged on that disgusting task embarrassed Iván Ilých.

Once when he got up from the commode too weak to draw up his trousers, he dropped into a soft armchair and looked with horror at his bare, enfeebled thighs with the muscles so sharply marked on them.

Gerásim with a firm light tread, his heavy boots emitting a pleasant smell of tar and fresh winter air, came in wearing a clean Hessian apron, the sleeves of his print shirt tucked up over his strong bare young arms; and refraining from looking at his sick master out of consideration for his feelings, and restraining the joy of life that beamed from his face, he went up to the commode.

'Gerásim!' said Iván Ilých in a weak voice.

Gerásim started, evidently afraid he might have committed some blunder, and with a rapid movement turned his fresh, kind, simple young face which just showed the first downy signs of a beard.

'Yes, sir?'

'That must be very unpleasant for you. You must forgive me. I am helpless.'

'Oh, why, sir,' and Gerásim's eyes beamed and he showed his glistening white teeth, 'what's a little trouble? It's a case of illness with you, sir.'

And his deft strong hands did their accustomed task, and he went out of the room stepping lightly. Five minutes later he as lightly returned.

Iván Ilých was still sitting in the same position in the armchair.

'Gerásim,' he said when the latter had replaced the freshly-washed utensil. 'Please come here and help me.' Gerásim went up to him. 'Lift me up. It is hard for me to get up, and I have sent Dmítri away.'

Gerásim went up to him, grasped his master with his strong arms deftly but gently, in the same way that he stepped—lifted him, supported him with one hand, and with the other drew up his trousers and would have set him down again, but Iván Ilých asked to be led to the sofa. Gerásim, without an effort and without apparent pressure, led him, almost lifting him, to the sofa and placed him on it.

'Thank you. How easily and well you do it all!'

Gerásim smiled again and turned to leave the room. But Iván Ilých felt his presence such a comfort that he did not want to let him go.

'One thing more, please move up that chair. No, the other one—under my feet. It is easier for me when my feet are raised.'

Gerásim brought the chair, set it down gently in place, and raised Iván Ilých's legs on to it. It seemed to Iván Ilých that he felt better while Gerásim was holding up his legs.

'It's better when my legs are higher,' he said. 'Place that cushion under them.'

Gerásim did so. He again lifted the legs and placed them, and again Iván Ilých felt better while Gerásim held

his legs. When he set them down Iván Ilých fancied he
felt worse.

'Gerásim,' he said. 'Are you busy now?'

'Not at all, sir,' said Gerásim, who had learnt from the
townsfolk how to speak to gentlefolk.

'What have you still to do?'

'What have I to do? I've done everything except chopping the logs for to-morrow.'

'Then hold my legs up a bit higher, can you?'

'Of course I can. Why not?' And Gerásim raised his
master's legs higher and Iván Ilých thought that in that
position he did not feel any pain at all.

'And how about the logs?'

'Don't trouble about that, sir. There's plenty of time.'

Iván Ilých told Gerásim to sit down and hold his legs,
and began to talk to him. And strange to say it seemed
to him that he felt better while Gerásim held his legs up.

After that Iván Ilých would sometimes call Gerásim
and get him to hold his legs on his shoulders, and he liked
talking to him. Gerásim did it all easily, willingly, simply,
and with a good nature that touched Iván Ilých. Health,
strength, and vitality in other people were offensive to him,
but Gerásim's strength and vitality did not mortify but
soothed him.

What tormented Iván Ilých most was the deception, the
lie, which for some reason they all accepted, that he was
not dying but was simply ill, and that he only need keep
quiet and undergo a treatment and then something very
good would result. He however knew that do what they
would nothing would come of it, only still more agonizing
suffering and death. This deception tortured him—their
not wishing to admit what they all knew and what he knew,
but wanting to lie to him concerning his terrible condition,
and wishing and forcing him to participate in that lie. Those
lies—lies enacted over him on the eve of his death and
destined to degrade this awful, solemn act to the level of
their visitings, their curtains, their sturgeon for dinner—
were a terrible agony for Iván Ilých. And strangely enough,
many times when they were going through their antics over
him he had been within a hairbreadth of calling out to
them: 'Stop lying! You know and I know that I am dying.
Then at least stop lying about it!' But he had never had
the spirit to do it. The awful, terrible act of his dying

was, he could see, reduced by those about him to the
level of a casual, unpleasant, and almost indecorous incident (as if someone entered a drawing-room diffusing an
unpleasant odour) and this was done by that very decorum
which he had served all his life long. He saw that no one
felt for him, because no one even wished to grasp his
position. Only Gerásim recognized it and pitied him. And
so Iván Ilých felt at ease only with him. He felt comforted when Gerásim supported his legs (sometimes all
night long) and refused to go to bed, saying: 'Don't you
worry, Iván Ilých. I'll get sleep enough later on,' or when
he suddenly became familiar and exclaimed: 'If you weren't
sick it would be another matter, but as it is, why should
I grudge a little trouble?' Gerásim alone did not lie; everything showed that he alone understood the facts of the
case and did not consider it necessary to disguise them,
but simply felt sorry for his emaciated and enfeebled
master. Once when Iván Ilých was sending him away he
even said straight out: 'We shall all of us die, so why
should I grudge a little trouble?'—expressing the fact that
he did not think his work burdensome, because he was
doing it for a dying man and hoped someone would do
the same for him when his time came.

Apart from this lying, or because of it, what most
tormented Iván Ilých was that no one pitied him as he
wished to be pitied. At certain moments after prolonged
suffering he wished most of all (though he would have
been ashamed to confess it) for someone to pity him as
a sick child is pitied. He longed to be petted and comforted. He knew he was an important functionary, that
he had a beard turning grey, and that therefore what he
longed for was impossible, but still he longed for it. And
in Gerásim's attitude towards him there was something
akin to what he wished for, and so that attitude comforted
him. Iván Ilých wanted to weep, wanted to be petted and
cried over, and then his colleague Shébek would come,
and instead of weeping and being petted, Iván Ilých
would assume a serious, severe, and profound air, and by
force of habit would express his opinion on a decision of
the Court of Cassation and would stubbornly insist on that
view. This falsity around him and within him did more
than anything else to poison his last days.

VIII

It was morning. He knew it was morning because Gerásim had gone, and Peter the footman had come and put out the candles, drawn back one of the curtains, and begun quietly to tidy up. Whether it was morning or evening, Friday or Sunday, made no difference, it was all just the same: the gnawing, unmitigated, agonizing pain, never ceasing for an instant, the consciousness of life inexorably waning but not yet extinguished, the approach of that ever dreaded and hateful Death which was the only reality, and always the same falsity. What were days, weeks, hours, in such a case?

'Will you have some tea, sir?'

'He wants things to be regular, and wishes the gentle-folk to drink tea in the morning,' thought Iván Ilých, and only said 'No.'

'Wouldn't you like to move onto the sofa, sir?'

'He wants to tidy up the room, and I'm in the way. I am uncleanliness and disorder,' he thought, and said only:

'No, leave me alone.'

The man went on bustling about. Iván Ilých stretched out his hand. Peter came up, ready to help.

'What is it, sir?'

'My watch.'

Peter took the watch which was close at hand and gave it to his master.

'Half-past eight. Are they up?'

'No sir, except Vladímir Ivánich' (the son) 'who has gone to school. Praskóvya Fëdorovna ordered me to wake her if you asked for her. Shall I do so?'

'No, there's no need to.' 'Perhaps I'd better have some tea,' he thought, and added aloud: 'Yes, bring me some tea.'

Peter went to the door, but Iván Ilých dreaded being left alone. 'How can I keep him here? Oh yes, my medicine.' 'Peter, give me my medicine.' 'Why not? Perhaps it may still do me some good.' He took a spoonful and swallowed it. 'No, it won't help. It's all tomfoolery, all deception,' he decided as soon as he became aware of the familiar, sickly, hopeless taste. 'No, I can't believe in it any longer. But the pain, why this pain? If it would only cease just for a moment!' And he moaned. Peter turned towards him. 'It's all right. Go and fetch me some tea.'

Peter went out. Left alone Iván Ilých groaned not so much with pain, terrible though that was, as from mental anguish. Always and for ever the same, always these endless days and nights. If only it would come quicker! If only *what* would come quicker? Death, darkness? . . . No, no! Anything rather than death!

When Peter returned with the tea on a tray, Iván Ilých stared at him for a time in perplexity, not realizing who and what he was. Peter was disconcerted by that look and his embarrassment brought Iván Ilých to himself.

'Oh, tea! All right, put it down. Only help me to wash and put on a clean shirt.'

And Iván Ilých began to wash. With pauses for rest, he washed his hands and then his face, cleaned his teeth, brushed his hair, and looked in the glass. He was terrified by what he saw, especially by the limp way in which his hair clung to his pallid forehead.

While his shirt was being changed he knew that he would be still more frightened at the sight of his body, so he avoided looking at it. Finally he was ready. He drew on a dressing-gown, wrapped himself in a plaid, and sat down in the armchair to take his tea. For a moment he felt refreshed, but as soon as he began to drink the tea he was again aware of the same taste, and the pain also returned. He finished it with an effort, and then lay down stretching out his legs, and dismissed Peter.

Always the same. Now a spark of hope flashes up, then a sea of despair rages, and always pain; always pain, always despair, and always the same. When alone he had a dreadful and distressing desire to call someone, but he knew beforehand that with others present it would be still worse. 'Another dose of morphine—to lose consciousness. I will tell him, the doctor, that he must think of something else. It's impossible, impossible, to go on like this.'

An hour and another pass like that. But now there is a ring at the door bell. Perhaps it's the doctor? It is. He comes in fresh, hearty, plump, and cheerful, with that look on his face that seems to say: 'There now, you're in a panic about something, but we'll arrange it all for you directly!' The doctor knows this expression is out of place here, but he has put it on once for all and can't take it off—like a man who has put on a frock-coat in the morning to pay a round of calls.

The doctor rubs his hands vigorously and reassuringly.

'Brr! How cold it is! There's such a sharp frost; just let me warm myself!' he says, as if it were only a matter of waiting till he was warm, and then he would put everything right.

'Well now, how are you?'

Iván Ilých feels that the doctor would like to say: 'Well, how are our affairs?' but that even he feels that this would not do, and says instead: 'What sort of a night have you had?'

Iván Ilých looks at him as much as to say: 'Are you really never ashamed of lying?' But the doctor does not wish to understand this question, and Iván Ilých says: 'Just as terrible as ever. The pain never leaves me and never subsides. If only something . . .'

'Yes, you sick people are always like that. . . . There, now I think I am warm enough. Even Praskóvya Fëdorovna, who is so particular, could find no fault with my temperature. Well, now I can say good-morning,' and the doctor presses his patient's hand.

Then, dropping his former playfulness, he begins with a most serious face to examine the patient, feeling his pulse and taking his temperature, and then begins the sounding and auscultation.

Iván Ilých knows quite well and definitely that all this is nonsense and pure deception, but when the doctor, getting down on his knee, leans over him, putting his ear first higher then lower, and performs various gymnastic movements over him with a significant expression on his face, Iván Ilých submits to it all as he used to submit to the speeches of the lawyers, though he knew very well that they were all lying and why they were lying.

The doctor, kneeling on the sofa, is still sounding him when Praskóvya Fëdorovna's silk dress rustles at the door and she is heard scolding Peter for not having let her know of the doctor's arrival.

She comes in, kisses her husband, and at once proceeds to prove that she has been up a long time already, and only owing to a misunderstanding failed to be there when the doctor arrived.

Iván Ilých looks at her, scans her all over, sets against her the whiteness and plumpness and cleanness of her hands and neck, the gloss of her hair, and the sparkle of her vivacious eyes. He hates her with his whole soul. And the thrill of hatred he feels for her makes him suffer from her touch.

Her attitude towards him and his disease is still the same. Just as the doctor had adopted a certain relation to his patient which he could not abandon, so had she formed one towards him—that he was not doing something he ought to do and was himself to blame, and that she reproached him lovingly for this—and she could not now change that attitude.

'You see he doesn't listen to me and doesn't take his medicine at the proper time. And above all he lies in a position that is no doubt bad for him—with his legs up.'

She described how he made Gerásim hold his legs up.

The doctor smiled with a contemptuous affability that said: 'What's to be done? These sick people do have foolish fancies of that kind, but we must forgive them.'

When the examination was over the doctor looked at his watch, and then Praskóvya Fëdorovna announced to Iván Ilých that it was of course as he pleased, but she had sent to-day for a celebrated specialist who would examine him and have a consultation with Michael Danílovich (their regular doctor).

'Please don't raise any objections. I am doing this for my own sake,' she said ironically, letting it be felt that she was doing it all for his sake and only said this to leave him no right to refuse. He remained silent, knitting his brows. He felt that he was so surrounded and involved in a mesh of falsity that it was hard to unravel anything.

Everything she did for him was entirely for her own sake, and she told him she was doing for herself what she actually was doing for herself, as if that was so incredible that he must understand the opposite.

At half-past eleven the celebrated specialist arrived. Again the sounding began and the significant conversations in his presence and in another room, about the kidneys and the appendix, and the questions and answers, with such an air of importance that again, instead of the real question of life and death which now alone confronted him, the question arose of the kidney and appendix which were not behaving as they ought to and would now be attacked by Michael Danílovich and the specialist and forced to amend their ways.

The celebrated specialist took leave of him with a serious though not hopeless look, and in reply to the timid question Iván Ilých, with eyes glistening with fear and hope, put to him as to whether there was a chance of recovery, said that he could not vouch for it but there was a possibility. The look of hope with which Iván Ilých watched the doctor out was so pathetic that Praskóvya Fëdorovna, seeing it, even wept as she left the room to hand the doctor his fee.

The gleam of hope kindled by the doctor's encouragement did not last long. The same room, the same pictures, curtains, wall-paper, medicine bottles, were all there, and the same aching suffering body, and Iván Ilých began to moan. They gave him a subcutaneous injection and he sank into oblivion.

It was twilight when he came to. They brought him his dinner and he swallowed some beef tea with difficulty, and then everything was the same again and night was coming on.

After dinner, at seven o'clock, Praskóvya Fëdorovna came into the room in evening dress, her full bosom pushed up by her corset, and with traces of powder on her face. She had reminded him in the morning that they were going to the theatre. Sarah Bernhardt was visiting the town and they had a box, which he had insisted on their taking. Now he had forgotten about it and her toilet offended him, but he concealed his vexation when he remembered that he had himself insisted on their securing a box and going because it would be an instructive and aesthetic pleasure for the children.

Praskóvya Fëdorovna came in, self-satisfied but yet with a rather guilty air. She sat down and asked how he was, but, as he saw, only for the sake of asking and not in order to learn about it, knowing that there was nothing to learn—and then went on to what she really wanted to say: that she would not on any account have gone but that the box had been taken and Helen and their daughter were going, as well as Petríshchev (the examining magistrate, their daughter's fiancé) and that it was out of the question to let them go alone; but that she would have much preferred to sit with him for a while; and he must be sure to follow the doctor's orders while she was away.

'Oh, and Fëdor Petróvich' (the fiancé) 'would like to come in. May he? And Lisa?'

'All right.'

Their daughter came in in full evening dress, her fresh young flesh exposed (making a show of that very flesh which in his own case caused so much suffering), strong, healthy, evidently in love, and impatient with illness, suffering, and death, because they interfered with her happiness.

Fëdor Petróvich came in too, in evening dress, his hair curled à la Capoul, a tight stiff collar round his long sinewy neck, an enormous white shirt-front and narrow black trousers tightly stretched over his strong thighs. He had one white glove tightly drawn on, and was holding his opera hat in his hand.

Following him the schoolboy crept in unnoticed, in a new uniform, poor little fellow, and wearing gloves. Terribly dark shadows showed under his eyes, the meaning of which Iván Ilých knew well.

His son had always seemed pathetic to him, and now it was dreadful to see the boy's frightened look of pity. It seemed to Iván Ilých that Vásya was the only one besides Gerásim who understood and pitied him.

They all sat down and again asked how he was. A silence followed. Lisa asked her mother about the opera-glasses, and there was an altercation between mother and daughter as to who had taken them and where they had been put. This occasioned some unpleasantness.

Fëdor Petróvich inquired of Iván Ilých whether he had ever seen Sarah Bernhardt. Iván Ilých did not at first catch the question, but then replied: 'No, have you seen her before?'

'Yes, in *Adrienne Lecouvreur*.'

Praskóvya Fëdorovna mentioned some rôles in which Sarah Bernhardt was particularly good. Her daughter disagreed. Conversation sprang up as to the elegance and realism of her acting—the sort of conversation that is always repeated and is always the same.

In the midst of the conversation Fëdor Petróvich glanced at Iván Ilých and became silent. The others also looked at him and grew silent. Iván Ilých was staring with glittering eyes straight before him, evidently indignant with them. This had to be rectified, but it was impossible to do so. The silence had to be broken, but for a time no one dared to break it and they all became afraid that the conventional deception would suddenly become obvious and the truth become plain to all. Lisa was the first to pluck up courage and break that silence, but by trying to hide what everybody was feeling, she betrayed it.

'Well, if we are going it's time to start,' she said, looking at her watch, a present from her father, and with a faint and significant smile at Fëdor Petróvich relating to something known only to them. She got up with a rustle of her dress.

They all rose, said good-night, and went away.

When they had gone it seemed to Iván Ilých that he felt better; the falsity had gone with them. But the pain remained—that same pain and that same fear that made everything monotonously alike, nothing harder and nothing easier. Everything was worse.

Again minute followed minute and hour followed hour. Everything remained the same and there was no cessation. And the inevitable end of it all became more and more terrible.

'Yes, send Gerásim here,' he replied to a question Peter asked.

IX

His wife returned late at night. She came in on tiptoe, but he heard her, opened his eyes, and made haste to close them again. She wished to send Gerásim away and to sit with him herself, but he opened his eyes and said: 'No, go away.'

'Are you in great pain?'

'Always the same.'

'Take some opium.'

He agreed and took some. She went away.

Till about three in the morning he was in a state of stupefied misery. It seemed to him that he and his pain were being thrust into a narrow, deep black sack, but though they were pushed further and further in they could not be pushed to the bottom. And this, terrible enough in itself, was accompanied by suffering. He was frightened yet wanted to fall through the sack, he struggled but yet co-operated. And suddenly he broke through, fell, and regained consciousness. Gerásim was sitting at the foot of the bed dozing quietly and patiently, while he himself lay with his emaciated stockinged legs resting on Gerásim's shoulders; the same shaded candle was there and the same unceasing pain.

'Go away, Gerásim,' he whispered.

'It's all right, sir. I'll stay a while.'

'No. Go away.'

He removed his legs from Gerásim's shoulders, turned sideways onto his arm, and felt sorry for himself. He only waited till Gerásim had gone into the next room and then restrained himself no longer but wept like a child. He wept on account of his helplessness, his terrible loneliness, the cruelty of man, the cruelty of God, and the absence of God.

'Why hast Thou done all this? Why hast Thou brought me here? Why, why dost Thou torment me so terribly?'

He did not expect an answer and yet wept because there was no answer and could be none. The pain again grew more acute, but he did not stir and did not call. He said to himself: 'Go on! Strike me! But what is it for? What have I done to Thee? What is it for?'

Then he grew quiet and not only ceased weeping but even held his breath and became all attention. It was as though he were listening not to an audible voice but to the voice of his soul, to the current of thoughts arising within him.

'What is it you want?' was the first clear conception capable of expression in words, that he heard.

'What do you want? What do you want?' he repeated to himself.

'What do I want? To live and not to suffer,' he answered.

And again he listened with such concentrated attention that even his pain did not distract him.

'To live? How?' asked his inner voice.

'Why, to live as I used to—well and pleasantly.'

'As you lived before, well and pleasantly?' the voice repeated.

And in imagination he began to recall the best moments of his pleasant life. But strange to say none of those best moments of his pleasant life now seemed at all what they had then seemed—none of them except the first recollections of childhood. There, in childhood, there had been something really pleasant with which it would be possible to live if it could return. But the child who had expe-

rienced that happiness existed no longer, it was like a
reminiscence of somebody else.

As soon as the period began which had produced the
present Iván Ilých, all that had then seemed joys now
melted before his sight and turned into something trivial
and often nasty.

And the further he departed from childhood and the
nearer he came to the present the more worthless and
doubtful were the joys. This began with the School of
Law. A little that was really good was still found there—
there was light-heartedness, friendship, and hope. But in
the upper classes there had already been fewer of such
good moments. Then during the first years of his official
career, when he was in the service of the governor, some
pleasant moments again occurred: they were the memories
of love for a woman. Then all became confused and there
was still less of what was good; later on again there was
still less that was good, and the further he went the less
there was. His marriage, a mere accident, then the disen-
chantment that followed it, his wife's bad breath and the
sensuality and hypocrisy: then that deadly official life
and those preoccupations about money, a year of it, and
two, and ten, and twenty, and always the same thing. And
the longer it lasted the more deadly it became. 'It is as if
I had been going downhill while I imagined I was going
up. And that is really what it was. I was going up in public
opinion, but to the same extent life was ebbing away from
me. And now it is all done and there is only death.

'Then what does it mean? Why? It can't be that life is
so senseless and horrible. But if it really has been so horrible and senseless, why must I die and die in agony?
There is something wrong!

'Maybe I did not live as I ought to have done,' it suddenly occurred to him. 'But how could that be, when I
did everything properly?' he replied, and immediately
dismissed from his mind this, the sole solution of all the
riddles of life and death, as something quite impossible.

'Then what do you want now? To live? Live how? Live
as you lived in the law courts when the usher proclaimed
"The judge is coming!" The judge is coming, the judge!'
he repeated to himself. 'Here he is, the judge. But I am not
guilty!' he exclaimed angrily. 'What is it for?' And he
ceased crying, but turning his face to the wall continued

to ponder on the same question: Why, and for what purpose, is there all this horror? But however much he pondered he found no answer. And whenever the thought occurred to him, as it often did, that it all resulted from his not having lived as he ought to have done, he at once recalled the correctness of his whole life and dismissed so strange an idea.

X

Another fortnight passed. Iván Ilých now no longer left his sofa. He would not lie in bed but lay on the sofa, facing the wall nearly all the time. He suffered ever the same unceasing agonies and in his loneliness pondered always on the same insoluble question: 'What is this? Can it be that it is Death?' And the inner voice answered: 'Yes, it is Death.'

'Why these sufferings?' And the voice answered, 'For no reason—they just are so.' Beyond and besides this there was nothing.

From the very beginning of his illness, ever since he had first been to see the doctor, Iván Ilých's life had been divided between two contrary and alternating moods: now it was despair and the expectation of this uncomprehended and terrible death, and now hope and an intently interested observation of the functioning of his organs. Now before his eyes there was only a kidney or an intestine that temporarily evaded its duty, and now only that incomprehensible and dreadful death from which it was impossible to escape.

These two states of mind had alternated from the very beginning of his illness, but the further it progressed the more doubtful and fantastic became the conception of the kidney, and the more real the sense of impending death.

He had but to call to mind what he had been three months before and what he was now, to call to mind with what regularity he had been going downhill, for every possibility of hope to be shattered.

Latterly during that loneliness in which he found himself as he lay facing the back of the sofa, a loneliness in the midst of a populous town and surrounded by numerous acquaintances and relations but that yet could not have been more complete anywhere—either at the bottom of the sea or under the earth—during that terrible loneliness

Iván Ilých had lived only in memories of the past. Pictures of his past rose before him one after another. They always began with what was nearest in time and then went back to what was most remote—to his childhood—and rested there. If he thought of the stewed prunes that had been offered him that day, his mind went back to the raw shrivelled French plums of his childhood, their peculiar flavour and the flow of saliva when he sucked their stones, and along with the memory of that taste came a whole series of memories of those days: his nurse, his brother, and their toys. 'No, I mustn't think of that. . . . It is too painful,' Iván Ilých said to himself, and brought himself back to the present—to the button on the back of the sofa and the creases in its morocco. 'Morocco is expensive, but it does not wear well: there had been a quarrel about it. It was a different kind of quarrel and a different kind of morocco that time when we tore father's portfolio and were punished, and mamma brought us some tarts. . . .' And again his thoughts dwelt on his childhood, and again it was painful and he tried to banish them and fix his mind on something else.

Then again together with that chain of memories another series passed through his mind—of how his illness had progressed and grown worse. There also the further back he looked the more life there had been. There had been more of what was good in life and more of life itself. The two merged together. 'Just as the pain went on getting worse and worse, so my life grew worse and worse,' he thought. 'There is one bright spot there at the back, at the beginning of life, and afterwards all becomes blacker and blacker and proceeds more and more rapidly—in inverse ratio to the square of the distance from death,' thought Iván Ilých. And the example of a stone falling downwards with increasing velocity entered his mind. Life, a series of increasing sufferings, flies further and further towards its end—the most terrible suffering. 'I am flying. . . .' He shuddered, shifted himself, and tried to resist, but was already aware that resistance was impossible, and again with eyes weary of gazing but unable to cease seeing what was before them, he stared at the back of the sofa and waited—awaiting that dreadful fall and shock and destruction.

'Resistance is impossible!' he said to himself. 'If I could only understand what it is all for! But that too is impossible. An explanation would be possible if it could be said that I have not lived as I ought to. But it is impossible to say that,' and he remembered all the legality, correctitude, and propriety of his life. 'That at any rate can certainly not be admitted,' he thought, and his lips smiled ironically as if someone could see that smile and be taken in by it. 'There is no explanation! Agony, death. . . . What for?'

XI

Another two weeks went by in this way and during that fortnight an event occurred that Iván Ilých and his wife had desired. Petríshchev formally proposed. It happened in the evening. The next day Praskóvya Fëdorovna came into her husband's room considering how best to inform him of it, but that very night there had been a fresh change for the worse in his condition. She found him still lying on the sofa but in a different position. He lay on his back, groaning and staring fixedly straight in front of him.

She began to remind him of his medicines, but he turned his eyes towards her with such a look that she did not finish what she was saying; so great an animosity, to her in particular, did that look express.

'For Christ's sake let me die in peace!' he said.

She would have gone away, but just then their daughter came in and went up to say good morning. He looked at her as he had done at his wife, and in reply to her inquiry about his health said dryly that he would soon free them all of himself. They were both silent and after sitting with him for a while went away.

'Is it our fault?' Lisa said to her mother. 'It's as if we were to blame! I am sorry for papa, but why should we be tortured?'

The doctor came at his usual time. Iván Ilých answered 'Yes' and 'No,' never taking his angry eyes from him, and at last said: 'You know you can do nothing for me, so leave me alone.'

'We can ease your sufferings.'

'You can't even do that. Let me be.'

The doctor went into the drawing-room and told Praskóvya Fëdorovna that the case was very serious and that the only resource left was opium to allay her husband's sufferings, which must be terrible.

It was true, as the doctor said, that Iván Ilých's physical sufferings were terrible, but worse than the physical sufferings were his mental sufferings which were his chief torture.

His mental sufferings were due to the fact that that night, as he looked at Gerásim's sleepy, good-natured face with its prominent cheek-bones, the question suddenly occurred to him: 'What if my whole life has been wrong?'

It occurred to him that what had appeared perfectly impossible before, namely that he had not spent his life as he should have done, might after all be true. It occurred to him that his scarcely perceptible attempts to struggle against what was considered good by the most highly placed people, those scarcely noticeable impulses which he had immediately suppressed, might have been the real thing, and all the rest false. And his professional duties and the whole arrangement of his life and of his family, and all his social and official interests, might all have been false. He tried to defend all those things to himself and suddenly felt the weakness of what he was defending. There was nothing to defend.

'But if that is so,' he said to himself, 'and I am leaving this life with the consciousness that I have lost all that was given me and it is impossible to rectify it—what then?'

He lay on his back and began to pass his life in review in quite a new way. In the morning when he saw first his footman, then his wife, then his daughter, and then the doctor, their every word and movement confirmed to him the awful truth that had been revealed to him during the night. In them he saw himself—all that for which he had lived—and saw clearly that it was not real at all, but a terrible and huge deception which had hidden both life and death. This consciousness intensified his physical suffering tenfold. He groaned and tossed about, and pulled at his clothing which choked and stifled him. And he hated them on that account.

He was given a large dose of opium and became unconscious, but at noon his sufferings began again. He drove everybody away and tossed from side to side.

His wife came to him and said:

'Jean, my dear, do this for me. It can't do any harm and often helps. Healthy people often do it.'

He opened his eyes wide.

'What? Take communion? Why? It's unnecessary! How-ever . . .'

She began to cry.

'Yes, do, my dear. I'll send for our priest. He is such a nice man.'

'All right. Very well,' he muttered.

When the priest came and heard his confession, Iván Ilých was softened and seemed to feel a relief from his doubts and consequently from his sufferings, and for a moment there came a ray of hope. He again began to think of the vermiform appendix and the possibility of correcting it. He received the sacrament with tears in his eyes.

When they laid him down again afterwards he felt a moment's ease, and the hope that he might live awoke in him again. He began to think of the operation that had been suggested to him. 'To live! I want to live!' he said to himself.

His wife came in to congratulate him after his communion, and when uttering the usual conventional words she added:

'You feel better, don't you?'

Without looking at her he said 'Yes.'

Her dress, her figure, the expression of her face, the tone of her voice, all revealed the same thing. 'This is wrong, it is not as it should be. All you have lived for and still live for is falsehood and deception, hiding life and death from you.' And as soon as he admitted that thought, his hatred and his agonizing physical suffering again sprang up, and with that suffering a consciousness of the unavoidable, approaching end. And to this was added a new sensation of grinding shooting pain and a feeling of suffocation.

The expression of his face when he uttered that 'Yes' was dreadful. Having uttered it, he looked her straight in the eyes, turned on his face with a rapidity extraordinary in his weak state and shouted:

'Go away! Go away and leave me alone!'

XII

From that moment the screaming began that continued for three days, and was so terrible that one could not hear it through two closed doors without horror. At the moment he answered his wife he realized that he was lost, that there was no return, that the end had come, the very end, and his doubts were still unsolved and remained doubts.

'Oh! Oh! Oh!' he cried in various intonations. He had begun by screaming 'I won't!' and continued screaming on the letter 'O'.

For three whole days, during which time did not exist for him, he struggled in that black sack into which he was being thrust by an invisible, resistless force. He struggled as a man condemned to death struggles in the hands of the executioner, knowing that he cannot save himself. And every moment he felt that despite all his efforts he was drawing nearer and nearer to what terrified him. He felt that his agony was due to his being thrust into that black hole and still more to his not being able to get right into it. He was hindered from getting into it by his conviction that his life had been a good one. That very justification of his life held him fast and prevented his moving forward, and it caused him most torment of all.

Suddenly some force struck him in the chest and side, making it still harder to breathe, and he fell through the hole and there at the bottom was a light. What had happened to him was like the sensation one sometimes experiences in a railway carriage when one thinks one is going backwards while one is really going forwards and suddenly becomes aware of the real direction.

'Yes, it was all not the right thing,' he said to himself, 'but that's no matter. It can be done. But what *is* the right thing?' he asked himself, and suddenly grew quiet.

This occurred at the end of the third day, two hours before his death. Just then his schoolboy son had crept softly in and gone up to the bedside. The dying man was still screaming desperately and waving his arms. His hand fell on the boy's head, and the boy caught it, pressed it to his lips, and began to cry.

At that very moment Iván Ilých fell through and caught sight of the light, and it was revealed to him that though his life had not been what it should have been, this could still be rectified. He asked himself, 'What *is* the right thing?' and grew still, listening. Then he felt that someone was kissing his hand. He opened his eyes, looked at his son, and felt sorry for him. His wife came up to him and he glanced at her. She was gazing at him open-mouthed, with undried tears on her nose and cheek and a despairing look on her face. He felt sorry for her too.

'Yes, I am making them wretched,' he thought. 'They are sorry, but it will be better for them when I die.' He wished to say this but had not the strength to utter it. 'Besides, why speak? I must act,' he thought. With a look at his wife he indicated his son and said: 'Take him away . . . sorry for him . . . sorry for you too. . . .' He tried to add, 'Forgive me', but said 'Forego' and waved his hand, knowing that He whose understanding mattered would understand.

And suddenly it grew clear to him that what had been oppressing him and would not leave him was all dropping away at once from two sides, from ten sides, and from all sides. He was sorry for them, he must act so as not to hurt them: release them and free himself from these sufferings. 'How good and how simple!' he thought. 'And the pain?' he asked himself. 'What has become of it? Where are you, pain?'

He turned his attention to it.

'Yes, here it is. Well, what of it? Let the pain be.'

'And death . . . where is it?'

He sought his former accustomed fear of death and did not find it. 'Where is it? What death?' There was no fear because there was no death.

In place of death there was light.

'So that's what it is!' he suddenly exclaimed aloud. 'What joy!'

To him all this happened in a single instant, and the meaning of that instant did not change. For those present his agony continued for another two hours. Something rattled in his throat, his emaciated body twitched, then the gasping and rattle became less and less frequent.

'It is finished!' said someone near him.

He heard these words and repeated them in his soul.

'Death is finished,' he said to himself. 'It is no more!'

He drew in a breath, stopped in the midst of a sigh, stretched out, and died.

The Devil

[1889]

But I say unto you, that every one that looketh on a woman to lust after her hath committed adultery with her already in his heart.

And if thy right eye causeth thee to stumble, pluck it out, and cast it from thee: for it is profitable for thee that one of thy members should perish, and not thy whole body be cast into hell.

And if thy right hand causeth thee to stumble, cut it off, and cast it from thee: for it is profitable for thee that one of thy members should perish, and not thy whole body go into hell. Matthew v. 28, 29, 30.

I

A brilliant career lay before Eugène Irténev. He had everything necessary to attain it: an admirable education at home, high honours when he graduated in law at Petersburg University, and connexions in the highest society through his recently deceased father; he had also already begun service in one of the Ministries under the protection of the Minister. Moreover he had a fortune; even a large one, though insecure. His father had lived abroad and in Petersburg, allowing his sons, Eugène and Andrew (who was older than Eugène and in the Horse Guards), six thousand rubles a year each, while he himself and his wife spent a great deal. He only used to visit his estate for a couple of months in summer and did not concern himself with its direction, entrusting it all to an unscrupulous manager who also failed to attend to it, but in whom he had complete confidence.

After the father's death, when the brothers began to divide the property, so many debts were discovered that their lawyer even advised them to refuse the inheritance and retain only an estate left them by their grandmother, which was valued at a hundred thousand rubles. But a neighbouring landed-proprietor who had done business with old Irténev, that is to say, who had promissory notes from him and had come to Petersburg on that account, said that in spite of the debts they could straighten out affairs so as to retain a large fortune (it would only be necessary to sell the forest and some outlying land, retaining the rich Semënov estate with four thousand desyatins of black earth, the sugar factory, and two hundred desyatins of water-meadows) if one devoted oneself to the management of the estate, settled there, and farmed it wisely and economically.

And so, having visited the estate in spring (his father

had died in Lent), Eugène looked into everything, resolved
to retire from the Civil Service, settle in the country with
his mother, and undertake the management with the object of preserving the main estate. He arranged with his
brother, with whom he was very friendly, that he would
pay him either four thousand rubles a year, or a lump sum
of eighty thousand, for which Andrew would hand over to
him his share of the inheritance.

So he arranged matters and, having settled down with
his mother in the big house, began managing the estate
eagerly, yet cautiously.

It is generally supposed that Conservatives are usually
old people, and that those in favour of change are the
young. That is not quite correct. Usually Conservatives are
young people: those who want to live but who do not
think about how to live, and have not time to think, and
therefore take as a model for themselves a way of life that
they have seen.

Thus it was with Eugène. Having settled in the village,
his aim and ideal was to restore the form of life that had
existed, not in his father's time—his father had been a bad
manager—but in his grandfather's. And now he tried to
resurrect the general spirit of his grandfather's life—in the
house, the garden, and in the estate management—of course
with changes suited to the times—everything on a large
scale—good order, method, and everybody satisfied. But
to do this entailed much work. It was necessary to meet
the demands of the creditors and the banks, and for that
purpose to sell some land and arrange renewals of credit.
It was also necessary to get money to carry on (partly by
farming out land, and partly by hiring labour) the immense operations on the Semënov estate, with its four
hundred desyatins of ploughland and its sugar factory, and
to deal with the garden so that it should not seem to be
neglected or in decay.

There was much work to do, but Eugène had plenty of
strength—physical and mental. He was twenty-six, of
medium height, strongly built, with muscles developed by
gymnastics. He was full-blooded and his whole neck was
very red, his teeth and lips were bright, and his hair soft
and curly though not thick. His only physical defect was
short-sightedness, which he had himself developed by using
spectacles, so that he could not now do without a pince-nez,

which had already formed a line on the bridge of his nose.

Such he was physically. For his spiritual portrait it might be said that the better people knew him the better they liked him. His mother had always loved him more than anyone else, and now after her husband's death she concentrated on him not only her whole affection but her whole life. Nor was it only his mother who so loved him. All his comrades at the high school and the university not merely liked him very much, but respected him. He had this effect on all who met him. It was impossible not to believe what he said, impossible to suspect any deception or falseness in one who had such an open, honest face and in particular such eyes.

In general his personality helped him much in his affairs. A creditor who would have refused another trusted him. The clerk, the village Elder, or a peasant, who would have played a dirty trick and cheated someone else, forgot to deceive under the pleasant impression of intercourse with this kindly, agreeable, and above all candid man.

It was the end of May. Eugène had somehow managed in town to get the vacant land freed from the mortgage, so as to sell it to a merchant, and had borrowed money from that same merchant to replenish his stock, that is to say, to procure horses, bulls, and carts, and in particular to begin to build a necessary farm-house. The matter had been arranged. The timber was being carted, the carpenters were already at work, and manure for the estate was being brought on eighty carts, but everything still hung by a thread.

II

Amid these cares something came about which though unimportant tormented Eugène at the time. As a young man he had lived as all healthy young men live, that is, he had had relations with women of various kinds. He was not a libertine but neither, as he himself said, was he a monk. He only turned to this, however, in so far as was necessary for physical health and to have his mind free, as he used to say. This had begun when he was sixteen and had gone on satisfactorily—in the sense that he had never given himself up to debauchery, never once been infatu-

ated, and had never contracted a disease. At first he had
had a seamstress in Petersburg, then she got spoilt and he
made other arrangements, and that side of his affairs was
so well secured that it did not trouble him.

But now he was living in the country for the second
month and did not at all know what he was to do. Com-
pulsory self-restraint was beginning to have a bad effect on
him.

Must he really go to town for that purpose? And where
to? How? That was the only thing that disturbed him; but
as he was convinced that the thing was necessary and that
he needed it, it really became a necessity, and he felt that
he was not free and that his eyes involuntarily followed
every young woman.

He did not approve of having relations with a married
woman or a maid in his own village. He knew by report
that both his father and grandfather had been quite different in this matter from other landowners of that time.
At home they had never had any entanglements with
peasant-women, and he had decided that he would not do
so either; but afterwards, feeling himself ever more and
more under compulsion and imagining with horror what
might happen to him in the neighbouring country town,
and reflecting on the fact that the days of serfdom were
now over, he decided that it might be done on the spot.
Only it must be done so that no one should know of it, and
not for the sake of debauchery but merely for health's sake
—as he said to himself. And when he had decided this he
became still more restless. When talking to the village
Elder, the peasants, or the carpenters, he involuntarily
brought the conversation round to women, and when it
turned to women he kept it on that theme. He noticed the
women more and more.

III

To settle the matter in his own mind was one thing but
to carry it out was another. To approach a woman himself
was impossible. Which one? Where? It must be done
through someone else, but to whom should he speak about
it?

He happened to go into a watchman's hut in the forest
to get a drink of water. The watchman had been his

father's huntsman, and Eugène Ivánich chatted with him, and the man began telling some strange tales of hunting sprees. It occurred to Eugène Ivánich that it would be convenient to arrange matters in this hut, or in the wood, only he did not know how to manage it and whether old Daniel would undertake the arrangement. 'Perhaps he will be horrified at such a proposal and I shall have disgraced myself, but perhaps he will agree to it quite simply.' So he thought while listening to Daniel's stories. Daniel was telling how once when they had been stopping at the hut of the sexton's wife in an outlying field, he had brought a woman for Fëdor Zakhárich Pryánishnikov.

'It will be all right,' thought Eugène.

'Your father, may the kingdom of heaven be his, did not go in for nonsense of that kind.'

'It won't do,' thought Eugène. But to test the matter he said: 'How was it you engaged on such bad things?'

'But what was there bad in it? She was glad, and Fëdor Zakhárich was satisfied, very satisfied. I got a ruble. Why, what was he to do? He too is a lively limb apparently, and drinks wine.'

'Yes, I may speak,' thought Eugène, and at once proceeded to do so.

'And do you know, Daniel, I don't know how to endure it,'—he felt himself going scarlet.

Daniel smiled.

'I am not a monk—I have been accustomed to it.'

He felt that what he was saying was stupid, but was glad to see that Daniel approved.

'Why of course, you should have told me long ago. It can all be arranged,' said he: 'only tell me which one you want.'

'Oh, it is really all the same to me. Of course not an ugly one, and she must be healthy.'

'I understand!' said Daniel briefly. He reflected.

'Ah! There is a tasty morsel,' he began. Again Eugène went red. 'A tasty morsel. See here, she was married last autumn.' Daniel whispered,—'and he hasn't been able to do anything. Think what that is worth to one who wants it!'

Eugène even frowned with shame.

'No, no,' he said. 'I don't want that at all. I want, on the contrary (what could the contrary be?), on the contrary I only want that she should be healthy and that there should be as little fuss as possible—a woman whose husband is away in the army or something of that kind.'

'I know. It's Stepanída I must bring you. Her husband is away in town, just the same as a soldier. And she is a fine woman, and clean. You will be satisfied. As it is I was saying to her the other day—you should go, but she . . .'

'Well then, when is it to be?'

'To-morrow if you like. I shall be going to get some tobacco and I will call in, and at the dinner-hour come here, or to the bath-house behind the kitchen garden. There will be nobody about. Besides after dinner everybody takes a nap.'

'All right then.'

A terrible excitement seized Eugène as he rode home. 'What will happen? What is a peasant woman like? Suppose it turns out that she is hideous, horrible? No, she is handsome,' he told himself, remembering some he had been noticing. 'But what shall I say? What shall I do?'

He was not himself all that day. Next day at noon he went to the forester's hut. Daniel stood at the door and silently and significantly nodded towards the wood. The blood rushed to Eugène's heart, he was conscious of it and went to the kitchen garden. No one was there. He went to the bath-house—there was no one about, he looked in, came out, and suddenly heard the crackling of a breaking twig. He looked round—and she was standing in the thicket beyond the little ravine. He rushed there across the ravine. There were nettles in it which he had not noticed. They stung him and, losing the pince-nez from his nose, he ran up the slope on the farther side. She stood there, in a white embroidered apron, a red-brown skirt, and a bright red kerchief, barefoot, fresh, firm, and handsome, and smiling shyly.

'There is a path leading round—you should have gone round,' she said. 'I came long ago, ever so long.'

He went up to her and, looking her over, touched her.

A quarter of an hour later they separated; he found his pince-nez, called in to see Daniel, and in reply to his question: 'Are you satisfied, master?' gave him a ruble and went home.

He was satisfied. Only at first had he felt ashamed, then it had passed off. And everything had gone well. The best thing was that he now felt at ease, tranquil and vigorous.

As for her, he had not even seen her thoroughly. He remembered that she was clean, fresh, not bad-looking, and simple, without any pretence. 'Whose wife is she?' said he to himself. 'Péchnikov's, Daniel said. What Péchnikov is that? There are two households of that name. Probably she is old Michael's daughter-in-law. Yes, that must be it. His son does live in Moscow. I'll ask Daniel about it some time.'

From then onward that previously important drawback to country life—enforced self-restraint—was eliminated. Eugène's freedom of mind was no longer disturbed and he was able to attend freely to his affairs.

And the matter Eugène had undertaken was far from easy: before he had time to stop up one hole a new one would unexpectedly show itself, and it sometimes seemed to him that he would not be able to go through with it and that it would end in his having to sell the estate after all, which would mean that all his efforts would be wasted and that he had failed to accomplish what he had undertaken. That prospect disturbed him most of all.

All this time more and more debts of his father's unexpectedly came to light. It was evident that towards the end of his life he had borrowed right and left. At the time of the settlement in May, Eugène had thought he at last knew everything, but in the middle of the summer he suddenly received a letter from which it appeared that there was still a debt of twelve thousand rubles to the widow Esípova. There was no promissory note, but only an ordinary receipt which his lawyer told him could be disputed. But it did not enter Eugène's head to refuse to pay a debt of his father's merely because the document could be challenged. He only wanted to know for certain whether there had been such a debt.

'Mamma! Who is Kalériya Vladímirovna Esípova?' he asked his mother when they met as usual for dinner.

'Esípova? She was brought up by your grandfather. Why?'

Eugène told his mother about the letter.

'I wonder she is not ashamed to ask for it. Your father gave her so much!'

'But do we owe her this?'

'Well now, how shall I put it? It is not a debt. Papa, out of his unbounded kindness . . .'

'Yes, but did Papa consider it a debt?'

'I cannot say. I don't know. I only know it is hard enough for you without that.'

Eugène saw that Mary Pávlovna did not know what to say, and was as it were sounding him.

'I see from what you say that it must be paid,' said he. 'I will go to see her to-morrow and have a chat, and see if it cannot be deferred.'

'Ah, how sorry I am for you, but you know that will be best. Tell her she must wait,' said Mary Pávlovna, evidently tranquillized and proud of her son's decision.

Eugène's position was particularly hard because his mother, who was living with him, did not at all realize his position. She had been so accustomed all her life long to live extravagantly that she could not even imagine to herself the position her son was in, that is to say, that to-day or to-morrow matters might shape themselves so that they would have nothing left and he would have to sell everything and live and support his mother on what salary he could earn, which at the very most would be two thousand rubles. She did not understand that they could only save themselves from that position by cutting down expense in everything, and so she could not understand why Eugène was so careful about trifles, in expenditure on gardeners, coachmen, servants—even on food. Also, like most widows, she nourished feelings of devotion to the memory of her departed spouse quite different from those she had felt for him while he lived, and she did not admit the thought that anything the departed had done or arranged could be wrong or could be altered.

Eugène by great efforts managed to keep up the garden and the conservatory with two gardeners, and the stables with two coachmen. And Mary Pávlovna naïvely thought that she was sacrificing herself for her son and doing all a mother could do, by not complaining of the food which the old man-cook prepared, of the fact that the paths in the park were not all swept clean, and that instead of footmen they had only a boy.

So, too, concerning this new debt, in which Eugène saw an almost crushing blow to all his undertakings, Mary Pávlovna only saw an incident displaying Eugène's noble nature. Moreover she did not feel much anxiety about Eugène's position, because she was confident that he would make a brilliant marriage which would put everything right. And he could make a very brilliant marriage: she knew a dozen families who would be glad to give their daughters to him. And she wished to arrange the matter as soon as possible.

IV

Eugène himself dreamt of marriage, but not in the same way as his mother. The idea of using marriage as a means of putting his affairs in order was repulsive to him. He wished to marry honourably, for love. He observed the girls whom he met and those he knew, and compared himself with them, but no decision had yet been taken. Meanwhile, contrary to his expectations, his relations with Stepanída continued, and even acquired the character of a settled affair. Eugène was so far from debauchery, it was so hard for him secretly to do this thing which he felt to be bad, that he could not arrange these meetings himself and even after the first one hoped not to see Stepanída again; but it turned out that after some time the same restlessness (due he believed to that cause) again overcame him. And his restlessness this time was no longer impersonal, but suggested just those same bright, black eyes, and that deep voice, saying, 'ever so long,' that same scent of something fresh and strong, and that same full breast lifting the bib of her apron, and all this in that hazel and maple thicket, bathed in bright sunlight.

Though he felt ashamed he again approached Daniel. And again a rendezvous was fixed for midday in the wood. This time Eugène looked her over more carefully and everything about her seemed attractive. He tried talking to her and asked about her husband. He really was Michael's son and lived as a coachman in Moscow.

'Well, then, how is it you . . .' Eugène wanted to ask how it was she was untrue to him.

'What about "how is it"?' asked she. Evidently she was clever and quick-witted.

'Well, how is it you come to me?'

'There now,' said she merrily. 'I bet he goes on the spree there. Why shouldn't I?'

Evidently she was putting on an air of sauciness and assurance, and this seemed charming to Eugène. But all the same he did not himself fix a rendezvous with her. Even when she proposed that they should meet without the aid of Daniel, to whom she seemed not very well disposed, he did not consent. He hoped that this meeting would be the last. He liked her. He thought such intercourse was necessary for him and that there was nothing bad about it, but in the depth of his soul there was a stricter judge who did not approve of it and hoped that this would be the last time, or if he did not hope that, at any rate did not wish to participate in arrangements to repeat it another time.

So the whole summer passed, during which they met a dozen times and always by Daniel's help. It happened once that she could not be there because her husband had come home, and Daniel proposed another woman, but Eugène refused with disgust. Then the husband went away and the meetings continued as before, at first through Daniel, but afterwards he simply fixed the time and she came with another woman, Prókhorova—as it would not do for a peasant-woman to go about alone.

Once at the very time fixed for the rendezvous a family came to call on Mary Pávlovna, with the very girl she wished Eugène to marry, and it was impossible for Eugène to get away. As soon as he could do so, he went out as though to the thrashing-floor, and round by the path to their meeting-place in the wood. She was not there, but at the accustomed spot everything within reach had been broken—the black alder, the hazel-twigs, and even a young maple the thickness of a stake. She had waited, had become excited and angry, and had skittishly left him a remembrance. He waited and waited, and then went to Daniel to ask him to call her for to-morrow. She came and was just as usual.

So the summer passed. The meetings were always arranged in the wood, and only once, when it grew towards autumn, in the shed that stood in her backyard.

It did not enter Eugène's head that these relations of his had any importance for him. About her he did not even think. He gave her money and nothing more. At first he did not know and did not think that the affair was known and that she was envied throughout the village, or that her relations took money from her and encouraged her, and that her conception of any sin in the matter had been quite obliterated by the influence of the money and her family's approval. It seemed to her that if people envied her, then what she was doing was good.

'It is simply necessary for my health,' thought Eugène. 'I grant it is not right, and though no one says anything, everybody, or many people, know of it. The woman who comes with her knows. And once she knows she is sure to have told others. But what's to be done? I am acting badly,' thought Eugène, 'but what's one to do? Anyhow it is not for long.'

What chiefly disturbed Eugène was the thought of the husband. At first for some reason it seemed to him that the husband must be a poor sort, and this as it were partly justified his conduct. But he saw the husband and was struck by his appearance: he was a fine fellow and smartly dressed, in no way a worse man than himself, but surely better. At their next meeting he told her he had seen her husband and had been surprised to see that he was such a fine fellow.

'There's not another man like him in the village,' said she proudly.

This surprised Eugène, and the thought of the husband tormented him still more after that. He happened to be at Daniel's one day and Daniel, having begun chatting, said to him quite openly:

'And Michael asked me the other day: "Is it true that the master is living with my wife?" I said I did not know. "Anyway," I said, "better with the master than with a peasant." '

'Well, and what did he say?'

'He said: "Wait a bit. I'll get to know and I'll give it her all the same." '

'Yes, if the husband returned to live here I would give her up,' thought Eugène.

But the husband lived in town and for the present their intercourse continued.

'When necessary I will break it off, and there will be nothing left of it,' thought he.

And this seemed to him certain, especially as during the whole summer many different things occupied him very fully: the erection of the new farm-house, and the harvest, and building, and above all meeting the debts and selling the wasteland. All these were affairs that completely absorbed him and on which he spent his thoughts when he lay down and when he got up. All that was real life. His intercourse—he did not even call it connexion—with Stepanída he paid no attention to. It is true that when the wish to see her arose it came with such strength that he could think of nothing else. But this did not last long. A meeting was arranged, and he again forgot her for a week or even for a month.

In autumn Eugène often rode to town, and there became friendly with the Ánnenskis. They had a daughter who had just finished the Institute. And then, to Mary Pávlovna's great grief, it happened that Eugène 'cheapened himself,' as she expressed it, by falling in love with Liza Ánnenskaya and proposing to her.

From that time his relations with Stepanída ceased.

V

It is impossible to explain why Eugène chose Liza Ánnenskaya, as it is always impossible to explain why a man chooses this and not that woman. There were many reasons—positive and negative. One reason was that she was not a very rich heiress such as his mother sought for him, another that she was naïve and to be pitied in her relations with her mother, another that she was not a beauty who attracted general attention to herself, and yet she was not bad-looking. But the chief reason was that his acquaintance with her began at the time when he was ripe for marriage. He fell in love because he knew that he would marry.

Liza Ánnenskaya was at first merely pleasing to Eugène, but when he decided to make her his wife his feelings for her became much stronger. He felt that he was in love.

Liza was tall, slender, and long. Everything about her was long; her face, and her nose (not prominently but downwards), and her fingers, and her feet. The colour of her face was very delicate, creamy white and delicately pink; she had long, soft, and curly, light-brown hair, and beautiful eyes, clear, mild, and confiding. Those eyes especially struck Eugène, and when he thought of Liza he always saw those clear, mild, confiding eyes.

Such was she physically; he knew nothing of her spiritually, but only saw those eyes. And those eyes seemed to tell him all he needed to know. The meaning of their expression was this:

While still in the Institute, when she was fifteen, Liza used continually to fall in love with all the attractive men she met and was animated and happy only when she was in love. After leaving the Institute she continued to fall in love in just the same way with all the young men she met,

and of course fell in love with Eugène as soon as she made
his acquaintance. It was this being in love which gave her
eyes that particular expression which so captivated Eugène.
Already that winter she had been in love with two young
men at one and the same time, and blushed and became
excited not only when they entered the room but whenever their names were mentioned. But afterwards, when
her mother hinted to her that Irténev seemed to have
serious intentions, her love for him increased so that she
became almost indifferent to the two previous attractions,
and when Irténev began to come to their balls and parties
and danced with her more than with others and evidently
only wished to know whether she loved him, her love for
him became painful. She dreamed of him in her sleep and
seemed to see him when she was awake in a dark-room,
and everyone else vanished from her mind. But when he
proposed and they were formally engaged, and when they
had kissed one another and were a betrothed couple, then
she had no thoughts but of him, no desire but to be with
him, to love him, and to be loved by him. She was also
proud of him and felt emotional about him and herself and
her love, and quite melted and felt faint from love of him.

The more he got to know her the more he loved her. He
had not at all expected to find such love, and it strengthened his own feeling still more.

VI

Towards spring he went to his estate at Semënovskoe
to have a look at it and to give directions about the management, and especially about the house which was being
done up for his wedding.

Mary Pávlovna was dissatisfied with her son's choice,
not only because the match was not as brilliant as it
might have been, but also because she did not like Varvára
Alexéevna, his future mother-in-law. Whether she was
good-natured or not she did not know and could not
decide, but that she was not well-bred, not *comme il faut*
—'not a lady' as Mary Pávlovna said to herself—she saw
from their first acquaintance, and this distressed her; distressed her because she was accustomed to value breeding
and knew that Eugène was sensitive to it, and she foresaw
that he would suffer much annoyance on this account. But
she liked the girl. Liked her chiefly because Eugène did.

One could not help loving her, and Mary Pávlovna was quite sincerely ready to do so.

Eugène found his mother contented and in good spirits. She was getting everything straight in the house and preparing to go away herself as soon as he brought his young wife. Eugène persuaded her to stay for the time being, and the future remained undecided.

In the evening after tea Mary Pávlovna played patience as usual. Eugène sat by, helping her. This was the hour of their most intimate talks. Having finished one game and while preparing to begin another, she looked up at him and, with a little hesitation, began thus:

'I wanted to tell you, Jénya—of course I do not know, but in general I wanted to suggest to you—that before your wedding it is absolutely necessary to have finished with all your bachelor affairs so that nothing may disturb either you or your wife. God forbid that it should. You understand me?'

And indeed Eugène at once understood that Mary Pávlovna was hinting at his relations with Stepanída which had ended in the previous autumn, and that she attributed much more importance to those relations than they deserved, as solitary women always do. Eugène blushed, not from shame so much as from vexation that good-natured Mary Pávlovna was bothering—out of affection no doubt, but still was bothering—about matters that were not her business and that she did not and could not understand. He answered that there was nothing that needed concealment, and that he had always conducted himself so that there should be nothing to hinder his marrying.

'Well, dear, that is excellent. Only, Jénya . . . don't be vexed with me,' said Mary Pávlovna, and broke off in confusion.

Eugène saw that she had not finished and had not said what she wanted to. And this was confirmed when a little later she began to tell him how, in his absence, she had been asked to stand godmother at . . . the Péchnikovs.

Eugène flushed again, not with vexation or shame this time, but with some strange consciousness of the importance of what was about to be told him—an involuntary consciousness quite at variance with his conclusions. And what he expected happened. Mary Pávlovna, as if merely by way of conversation, mentioned that this year only boys

were being born—evidently a sign of a coming war. Both
at the Vásins and the Péchnikovs the young wife had a first
child—at each house a boy. Mary Pávlovna wanted to say
this casually, but she herself felt ashamed when she saw
the colour mount to her son's face and saw him nervously
removing, tapping, and replacing his pince-nez and hurriedly lighting a cigarette. She became silent. He too was
silent and could not think how to break that silence. So
they both understood that they had understood one
another.

'Yes, the chief thing is that there should be justice and
no favouritism in the village—as under your grandfather.'

'Mamma,' said Eugène suddenly, 'I know why you are
saying this. You have no need to be disturbed. My future
family-life is so sacred to me that I should not infringe it
in any case. And as to what occurred in my bachelor days,
that is quite ended. I never formed any union and no one
has any claims on me.'

'Well, I am glad,' said his mother. 'I know how noble
your feelings are.'

Eugène accepted his mother's words as a tribute due to
him, and did not reply.

Next day he drove to town thinking of his fiancée and
of anything in the world except of Stepanída. But, as if
purposely to remind him, on approaching the church he
met people walking and driving back from it. He met old
Matvéy with Simon, some lads and girls, and then two
women, one elderly, the other, who seemed familiar,
smartly dressed and wearing a bright-red kerchief. This
woman was walking lightly and boldly, carrying a child in
her arms. He came up to them, and the elder woman
bowed, stopping in the old-fashioned way, but the young
woman with the child only bent her head, and from under
the kerchief gleamed familiar, merry, smiling eyes.

Yes, this was she, but all that was over and it was no
use looking at her: 'and the child may be mine,' flashed
through his mind. No, what nonsense! There was her husband, she used to see him. He did not even consider the
matter further, so settled in his mind was it that it had
been necessary for his health—he had paid her money and
there was no more to be said; there was, there had been,
and there could be, no question of any union between
them. It was not that he stifled the voice of conscience, no

—his conscience simply said nothing to him. And he thought no more about her after the conversation with his mother and this meeting. Nor did he meet her again.

Eugène was married in town the week after Easter, and left at once with his young wife for his country estate. The house had been arranged as usual for a young couple. Mary Pávlovna wished to leave, but Eugène begged her to remain, and Liza still more strongly, and she only moved into a detached wing of the house.

And so a new life began for Eugène.

VII

The first year of his marriage was a hard one for Eugène. It was hard because affairs he had managed to put off during the time of his courtship now, after his marriage, all came upon him at once.

To escape from debts was impossible. An outlying part of the estate was sold and the most pressing obligations met, but others remained, and he had no money. The estate yielded a good revenue, but he had had to send payments to his brother and to spend on his own marriage, so that there was no ready money and the factory could not carry on and would have to be closed down. The only way of escape was to use his wife's money; and Liza, having realized her husband's position, insisted on this herself. Eugène agreed, but only on condition that he should give her a mortgage on half his estate, which he did. Of course this was done not for his wife's sake, who felt offended at it, but to appease his mother-in-law.

These affairs with various fluctuations of success and failure helped to poison Eugène's life that first year. Another thing was his wife's ill-health. That same first year in autumn, seven months after their marriage, a misfortune befell Liza. She was driving out to meet her husband on his return from town, and the quiet horse became rather playful and she was frightened and jumped out. Her jump was comparatively fortunate—she might have been caught by the wheel—but she was pregnant, and that same night the pains began and she had a miscarriage from which she was long in recovering. The loss of the expected child and his wife's illness, together with the disorder in his affairs, and above all the presence of his mother-in-law,

who arrived as soon as Liza fell ill—all this together made
the year still harder for Eugène.

But notwithstanding these difficult circumstances, towards the end of the first year Eugène felt very well. First
of all his cherished hope of restoring his fallen fortune and
renewing his grandfather's way of life in a new form, was
approaching accomplishment, though slowly and with difficulty. There was no longer any question of having to sell
the whole estate to meet the debts. The chief estate, though
transferred to his wife's name, was saved, and if only the
beet crop succeeded and the price kept up, by next year
his position of want and stress might be replaced by one of
complete prosperity. That was one thing.

Another was that however much he had expected from
his wife, he had never expected to find in her what he
actually found. He found not what he had expected, but
something much better. Raptures of love—though he tried
to produce them—did not take place or were very slight,
but he discovered something quite different, namely, that
he was not merely more cheerful and happier but that it
had become easier to live. He did not know why this
should be so, but it was.

And it was so because immediately after marriage his
wife decided that Eugène Irténev was superior to anyone
else in the world: wiser, purer, and nobler than they, and
that therefore it was right for everyone to serve him and
please him; but that as it was impossible to make everyone
do this, she must do it herself to the limit of her strength.
And she did; directing all her strength of mind towards
learning and guessing what he liked, and then doing just
that thing, whatever it was and however difficult it might
be.

She had the gift which furnishes the chief delight of
intercourse with a loving woman: thanks to her love of
her husband she penetrated into his soul. She knew his
every state and his every shade of feeling—better it seemed
to him than he himself—and she behaved correspondingly
and therefore never hurt his feelings, but always lessened
his distresses and strengthened his joys. And she understood not only his feelings but also his joys. Things quite
foreign to her—concerning the farming, the factory, or the
appraisement of others—she immediately understood so
that she could not merely converse with him, but could

often, as he himself said, be a useful and irreplaceable counsellor. She regarded affairs and people and everything in the world only through his eyes. She loved her mother, but having seen that Eugène disliked his mother-in-law's interference in their life she immediately took her husband's side, and did so with such decision that he had to restrain her.

Besides all this she had very good taste, much tact, and above all she had repose. All that she did, she did unnoticed; only the results of what she did were observable, namely, that always and in everything there was cleanliness, order, and elegance. Liza had at once understood in what her husband's ideal of life consisted, and she tried to attain, and in the arrangement and order of the house did attain, what he wanted. Children it is true were lacking, but there was hope of that also. In winter she went to Petersburg to see a specialist and he assured them that she was quite well and could have children.

And this desire was accomplished. By the end of the year she was again pregnant.

The one thing that threatened, not to say poisoned, their happiness was her jealousy—a jealousy she restrained and did not exhibit, but from which she often suffered. Not only might Eugène not love any other woman—because there was not a woman on earth worthy of him (as to whether she herself was worthy or not she never asked herself),—but not a single woman might therefore dare to love him.

VIII

This was how they lived: he rose early, as he always had done, and went to see to the farm or the factory where work was going on, or sometimes to the fields. Towards ten o'clock he would come back for his coffee, which they had on the veranda: Mary Pávlovna, an uncle who lived with them, and Liza. After a conversation which was often very animated while they drank their coffee, they dispersed till dinner-time. At two o'clock they dined and then went for a walk or a drive. In the evening when he returned from his office they drank their evening tea and sometimes he read aloud while she worked, or when there were guests they had music or conversation. When he went away on business he wrote to his wife and received letters

from her every day. Sometimes she accompanied him, and
then they were particularly merry. On his name-day and
on hers guests assembled, and it pleased him to see how
well she managed to arrange things so that everybody
enjoyed coming. He saw and heard that they all admired
her—the young, agreeable hostess—and he loved her still
more for this.

All went excellently. She bore her pregnancy easily and,
though they were afraid, they both began making plans
as to how they would bring the child up. The system of
education and the arrangements were all decided by
Eugène, and her only wish was to carry out his desires
obediently. Eugène on his part read up medical works
and intended to bring the child up according to all the
precepts of science. She of course agreed to everything and
made preparations, making warm and also cool 'envelopes',
and preparing a cradle. Thus the second year of their marriage arrived and the second spring.

IX

It was just before Trinity Sunday. Liza was in her fifth
month, and though careful she was still brisk and active.
Both his mother and hers were living in the house, but
under pretext of watching and safeguarding her only
upset her by their tiffs. Eugène was specially engrossed
with a new experiment for the cultivation of sugar-beet on
a large scale.

Just before Trinity Liza decided that it was necessary
to have a thorough house-cleaning as it had not been
done since Easter, and she hired two women by the day
to help the servants wash the floors and windows, beat
the furniture and the carpets, and put covers on them.
These women came early in the morning, heated the coppers, and set to work. One of the two was Stepanída, who
had just weaned her baby boy and had begged for the
job of washing the floors through the office-clerk—whom
she now carried on with. She wanted to have a good
look at the new mistress. Stepanída was living by herself
as formerly, her husband being away, and she was up to
tricks as she had formerly been first with old Daniel (who
had once caught her taking some logs of firewood), afterwards with the master, and now with the young clerk.
She was not concerning herself any longer about her

master. 'He has a wife now,' she thought. But it would be good to have a look at the lady and at her establishment: folk said it was well arranged.

Eugène had not seen her since he had met her with the child. Having a baby to attend to she had not been going out to work, and he seldom walked through the village. That morning, on the eve of Trinity Sunday, he got up at five o'clock and rode to the fallow land which was to be sprinkled with phosphates, and had left the house before the women were about, and while they were still engaged lighting the copper fires.

He returned to breakfast merry, contented, and hungry; dismounting from his mare at the gate and handing her over to the gardener. Flicking the high grass with his whip and repeating a phrase he had just uttered, as one often does, he walked towards the house. The phrase was: 'phosphates justify'—what or to whom, he neither knew nor reflected.

They were beating a carpet on the grass. The furniture had been brought out.

'There now! What a house-cleaning Liza has undertaken! . . . Phosphates justify. . . . What a manageress she is! A manageress! Yes, a manageress,' said he to himself, vividly imagining her in her white wrapper and with her smiling joyful face, as it nearly always was when he looked at her. 'Yes, I must change my boots, or else "phosphates justify", that is, smell of manure, and the manageress is in such a condition. Why "in such a condition"? Because a new little Irténev is growing there inside her,' he thought. 'Yes, phosphates justify,' and smiling at his thoughts he put his hand to the door of his room.

But he had not time to push the door before it opened of itself and he came face to face with a woman coming towards him carrying a pail, barefoot and with sleeves turned up high. He stepped aside to let her pass and she too stepped aside, adjusting her kerchief with a wet hand.

'Go on, go on, I won't go in, if you . . .' began Eugène and suddenly stopped, recognizing her.

She glanced merrily at him with smiling eyes, and pulling down her skirt went out at the door.

'What nonsense! . . . It is impossible,' said Eugène to himself, frowning and waving his hand as though to get rid of a fly, displeased at having noticed her. He was vexed that he had noticed her and yet he could not take his eyes from her strong body, swayed by her agile strides, from her bare feet, or from her arms and shoulders, and the pleasing folds of her shirt and the handsome skirt tucked up high above her white calves.

'But why am I looking?' said he to himself, lowering his eyes so as not to see her. 'And anyhow I must go in to get some other boots.' And he turned back to go into his own room, but had not gone five steps before he again glanced round to have another look at her without knowing why or wherefore. She was just going round the corner and also glanced at him.

'Ah, what am I doing!' said he to himself. 'She may think . . . It is even certain that she already does think . . .'

He entered his damp room. Another woman, an old and skinny one, was there, and was still washing it. Eugène passed on tiptoe across the floor, wet with dirty water, to the wall where his boots stood, and he was about to leave the room when the woman herself went out.

'This one has gone and the other, Stepanída, will come here alone,' someone within him began to reflect.

'My God, what am I thinking of and what am I doing!' He seized his boots and ran out with them into the hall, put them on there, brushed himself, and went out onto the veranda where both the mammas were already drinking coffee. Liza had evidently been expecting him and came onto the veranda through another door at the same time.

'My God! If she, who considers me so honourable, pure, and innocent—if she only knew!'—thought he.

Liza as usual met him with shining face. But to-day somehow she seemed to him particularly pale, yellow, long, and weak.

X

During coffee, as often happened, a peculiarly feminine kind of conversation went on which had no logical sequence but which evidently was connected in some way for it went on uninterruptedly.

The two old ladies were pin-pricking one another, and Liza was skilfully manœuvring between them.

'I am so vexed that we had not finished washing your room before you got back,' she said to her husband. 'But I do so want to get everything arranged.'

'Well, did you sleep well after I got up?'

'Yes, I slept well and I feel well.'

'How can a woman be well in her condition during this intolerable heat, when her windows face the sun,' said Varvára Alexéevna, her mother. 'And they have no venetian-blinds or awnings. I always had awnings.'

'But you know we are in the shade after ten o'clock,' said Mary Pávlovna.

'That's what causes fever; it comes of dampness,' said Varvára Alexéevna, not noticing that what she was saying did not agree with what she had just said. 'My doctor always says that it is impossible to diagnose an illness unless one knows the patient. And he certainly knows, for he is the leading physician and we pay him a hundred rubles a visit. My late husband did not believe in doctors, but he did not grudge me anything.'

'How can a man grudge anything to a woman when perhaps her life and the child's depend . . .'

'Yes, when she has means a wife need not depend on her husband. A good wife submits to her husband,' said Varvára Alexéevna—'only Liza is too weak after her illness.'

'Oh no, mamma, I feel quite well. But why have they not brought you any boiled cream?'

'I don't want any. I can do with raw cream.'

'I offered some to Varvára Alexéevna, but she declined,' said Mary Pávlovna, as if justifying herself.

'No, I don't want any to-day.' And as if to terminate an unpleasant conversation and yield magnanimously, Varvára Alexéevna turned to Eugène and said: 'Well, and have you sprinkled the phosphates?'

Liza ran to fetch the cream.

'But I don't want it. I don't want it.'

'Liza, Liza, go gently,' said Mary Pávlovna. 'Such rapid movements do her harm.'

'Nothing does harm if one's mind is at peace,' said Varvára Alexéevna as if referring to something, though she knew that there was nothing her words could refer to.

Liza returned with the cream and Eugène drank his coffee and listened morosely. He was accustomed to these conversations, but to-day he was particularly annoyed by its lack of sense. He wanted to think over what had happened to him but this chatter disturbed him. Having finished her coffee Varvára Alexéevna went away in a bad humour. Liza, Eugène, and Mary Pávlovna stayed behind, and their conversation was simple and pleasant. But Liza, being sensitive, at once noticed that something was tormenting Eugène, and she asked him whether anything unpleasant had happened. He was not prepared for this question and hesitated a little before replying that there had been nothing. This reply made Liza think all the more. That something was tormenting him, and greatly tormenting, was as evident to her as that a fly had fallen into the milk, yet he would not speak of it. What could it be?

XI

After breakfast they all dispersed. Eugène as usual went to his study, but instead of beginning to read or write his letters, he sat smoking one cigarette after another and thinking. He was terribly surprised and disturbed by the unexpected recrudescence within him of the bad feeling from which he had thought himself free since his marriage. Since then he had not once experienced that feeling, either for her—the woman he had known—or for any other woman except his wife. He had often felt glad of this emancipation, and now suddenly a chance meeting, seemingly so unimportant, revealed to him the fact that he was not free. What now tormented him was not that he was yielding to that feeling and desired her—he did not dream of so doing—but that the feeling was awake within him and he had to be on his guard against it. He had no doubt but that he would suppress it.

He had a letter to answer and a paper to write, and sat down at his writing-table and began to work. Having finished it and quite forgotten what had disturbed him, he went out to go to the stables. And again as ill-luck would have it, either by unfortunate chance or intentionally, as soon as he stepped from the porch a red skirt and red kerchief appeared from round the corner, and she went past him swinging her arms and swaying her body. She not only went past him, but on passing him ran, as if playfully, to overtake her fellow-servant.

Again the bright midday, the nettles, the back of Daniel's hut, and in the shade of the plane-trees her smiling face biting some leaves, rose in his imagination.

'No, it is impossible to let matters continue so,' he said to himself, and waiting till the women had passed out of sight he went to the office.

It was just the dinner-hour and he hoped to find the steward still there, and so it happened. The steward was just waking up from his after-dinner nap, and stretching himself and yawning was standing in the office, looking at the herdsman who was telling him something.

'Vasíli Nikoláich!' said Eugène to the steward.

'What is your pleasure?'

'I want to speak to you.'

'What is your pleasure?'

'Just finish what you are saying.'

'Aren't you going to bring it in?' said Vasíli Nikoláich to the herdsman.

'It's heavy, Vasíli Nikoláich.'

'What is it?' asked Eugène.

'Why, a cow has calved in the meadow. Well, all right, I'll order them to harness a horse at once. Tell Nicholas Lysúkh to get out the dray cart.'

The herdsman went out.

'Do you know,' began Eugène, flushing and conscious that he was doing so, 'do you know, Vasíli Nikoláich, while I was a bachelor I went off the track a bit. . . . You may have heard . . .'

Vasíli Nikoláich, evidently sorry for his master, said with smiling eyes: 'Is it about Stepanída?'

'Why, yes. Look here. Please, please do not engage her to help in the house. You understand, it is very awkward for me . . .'

'Yes, it must have been Ványa the clerk who arranged it.'

'Yes, please . . . and hadn't the rest of the phosphates better be strewn?' said Eugène, to hide his confusion.

'Yes, I am just going to see to it.'

So the matter ended, and Eugène calmed down, hoping that as he had lived for a year without seeing her, so things would go on now. 'Besides, Vasíli Nikoláich will speak to Iván the clerk; Iván will speak to her, and she will understand that I don't want it,' said Eugène to himself, and he was glad that he had forced himself to speak to Vasíli Nikoláich, hard as it had been to do so.

'Yes, it is better, much better, than that feeling of doubt, that feeling of shame.' He shuddered at the mere remembrance of his sin in thought.

XII

The moral effort he had made to overcome his shame and speak to Vasíli Nikoláich tranquillized Eugène. It seemed to him that the matter was all over now. Liza at once noticed that he was quite calm, and even happier than usual. 'No doubt he was upset by our mothers pin-pricking one another. It really is disagreeable, especially for him who is so sensitive and noble, always to hear such unfriendly and ill-mannered insinuations,' thought she.

The next day was Trinity Sunday. It was a beautiful day, and the peasant-women, on their way into the woods to plait wreaths, came, according to custom, to the land-owner's home and began to sing and dance. Mary Pávlovna and Varvára Alexéevna came out onto the porch in smart clothes, carrying sunshades, and went up to the ring of singers. With them, in a jacket of Chinese silk, came out the uncle, a flabby libertine and drunkard, who was living that summer with Eugène.

As usual there was a bright, many-coloured ring of young women and girls, the centre of everything, and around these from different sides like attendant planets that had detached themselves and were circling round, went girls hand in hand, rustling in their new print gowns; young lads giggling and running backwards and forwards after one another; full-grown lads in dark blue or black coats and caps and with red shirts, who unceasingly spat out sunflower-seed shells; and the domestic servants or other outsiders watching the dance-circle from aside. Both the old ladies went close up to the ring, and Liza accompanied them in a light blue dress, with light blue ribbons on her head, and with wide sleeves under which her long white arms and angular elbows were visible.

Eugène did not wish to come out, but it was ridiculous to hide, and he too came out onto the porch smoking a cigarette, bowed to the men and lads, and talked with one of them. The women meanwhile shouted a dance-song with all their might, snapping their fingers, clapping their hands, and dancing.

'They are calling for the master,' said a youngster com-

ing up to Eugène's wife, who had not noticed the call.
Liza called Eugène to look at the dance and at one of the
women dancers who particularly pleased her. This was
Stepanída. She wore a yellow skirt, a velveteen sleeveless
jacket and a silk kerchief, and was broad, energetic, ruddy,
and merry. No doubt she danced well. He saw nothing.
'Yes, yes,' he said, removing and replacing his pince-nez.
'Yes, yes,' he repeated. 'So it seems I cannot be rid of her,'
he thought.

He did not look at her, fearing her attraction, and just
on that account what his passing glance caught of her
seemed to him especially attractive. Besides this he saw by
her sparkling look that she saw him and saw that he
admired her. He stood there as long as propriety demanded,
and seeing that Varvára Alexéevna had called her 'my
dear' senselessly and insincerely and was talking to her,
he turned aside and went away.

He went into the house in order not to see her, but on
reaching the upper story he approached the window,
without knowing how or why, and as long as the women
remained at the porch he stood there and looked and looked
at her, feasting his eyes on her.

He ran, while there was no one to see him, and then
went with quiet steps onto the veranda, and from there,
smoking a cigarette, he passed through the garden as if
going for a stroll, and followed the direction she had taken.
He had not gone two steps along the alley before he
noticed behind the trees a velveteen sleeveless jacket, with a
pink and yellow skirt and a red kerchief. She was going
somewhere with another woman. 'Where are they going?'
And suddenly a terrible desire scorched him as though
a hand were seizing his heart. As if by someone else's wish
he looked round and went towards her.

'Eugène Ivánich, Eugène Ivánich! I have come to see
your honour,' said a voice behind him, and Eugène, seeing
old Samókhin who was digging a well for him, roused
himself and turning quickly round went to meet Samókhin.
While speaking with him he turned sideways and saw
that she and the woman who was with her went down the
slope, evidently to the well or making an excuse of the
well, and having stopped there a little while ran back
to the dance-circle.

XIII

After talking to Samókhin, Eugène returned to the house as depressed as if he had committed a crime. In the first place she had understood him, believed that he wanted to see her, and desired it herself. Secondly that other woman, Anna Prókhorova, evidently knew of it.

Above all he felt that he was conquered, that he was not master, of his own will but that there was another power moving him, that he had been saved only by good fortune, and that if not to-day then to-morrow or a day later, he would perish all the same.

'Yes, perish,' he did not understand it otherwise: to be unfaithful to his young and loving wife with a peasant-woman in the village, in the sight of everyone—what was it but to perish, perish utterly, so that it would be impossible to live? No, something must be done.

'My God, my God! What am I to do? Can it be that I shall perish like this?' said he to himself. Is it not possible to do anything? Yet something must be done. Do not think about her'—he ordered himself. 'Do not think!' and immediately he began thinking and seeing her before him, and seeing also the shade of the plane-tree.

He remembered having read of a hermit who, to avoid the temptation he felt for a woman on whom he had to lay his hand to heal her, thrust his other hand into a brazier and burnt his fingers. He called that to mind. 'Yes, I am ready to burn my fingers rather than to perish.' He looked round to make sure that there was no one in the room, lit a candle, and put a finger into the flame. 'There, now think about her,' he said to himself ironically. It hurt him and he withdrew his smoke-stained finger, threw away the match, and laughed at himself. What nonsense! That was not what had to be done. But it was necessary to do something, to avoid seeing her—either to go away himself or to send her away. Yes—send her away. Offer her husband money to remove to town or to another village. People would hear of it and would talk about it. Well, what of that? At any rate it was better than this danger. 'Yes, that must be done,' he said to himself, and at that very moment he was looking at her without moving his eyes. 'Where is she going?' he suddenly asked

himself. She, it seemed to him, had seen him at the
window and now, having glanced at him and taken another
woman by the hand, was going towards the garden swinging her arm briskly. Without knowing why or wherefore,
merely in accord with what he had been thinking, he went
to the office.

Vasíli Nikoláich in holiday costume and with oiled hair
was sitting at tea with his wife and a guest who was wearing an oriental kerchief.

'I want a word with you, Vasíli Nikoláich!'

'Please say what you want to. We have finished tea.'

'No. I'd rather you came out with me.'

'Directly; only let me get my cap. Tánya, put out the
samovár,' said Vasíli Nikoláich, stepping outside cheerfully.

It seemed to Eugène that Vasíli had been drinking, but
what was to be done? It might be all the better—he would
sympathize with him in his difficulties the more readily.

'I have come again to speak about that same matter,
Vasíli Nikoláich,' said Eugène—'about that woman.'

'Well, what of her? I told them not to take her again
on any account.'

'No, I have been thinking in general, and this is what
I wanted to take your advice about. Isn't it possible to get
them away, to send the whole family away?'

'Where can they be sent?' said Vasíli, disapprovingly and
ironically as it seemed to Eugène.

'Well, I thought of giving them money, or even some
land in Koltóvski,—so that she should not be here.'

'But how can they be sent away? Where is he to go—
torn up from his roots? And why should you do it? What
harm can she do you?'

'Ah, Vasíli Nikoláich, you must understand that it
would be dreadful for my wife to hear of it.'

'But who will tell her?'

'How can I live with this dread? The whole thing is
very painful for me.'

'But really, why should you distress yourself? Whoever stirs up the past—out with his eye! Who is not a
sinner before God and to blame before the Tsar, as the
saying is?'

'All the same it would be better to get rid of them.
Can't you speak to the husband?'

'But it is no use speaking! Eh, Eugène Ivánich, what is

the matter with you? It is all past and forgotten. All sorts
of things happen. Who is there that would now say anything bad of you? Everybody sees you.'

'But all the same go and have a talk with him.'

'All right, I will speak to him.'

Though he knew that nothing would come of it, this
talk somewhat calmed Eugène. Above all, it made him
feel that through excitement he had been exaggerating the
danger.

Had he gone to meet her by appointment? It was impossible. He had simply gone to stroll in the garden and
she had happened to run out at the same time.

XIV

After dinner that very Trinity Sunday Liza while walking from the garden to the meadow, where her husband
wanted to show her the clover, took a false step and fell
when crossing a little ditch. She fell gently, on her side;
but she gave an exclamation, and her husband saw an expression in her face not only of fear but of pain. He was
about to help her up, but she motioned him away with
her hand.

'No, wait a bit, Eugène,' she said, with a weak smile,
and looked up guiltily as it seemed to him. 'My foot only
gave way under me.'

'There, I always say,' remarked Varvára Alexéevna, 'can
anyone in her condition possibly jump over ditches?'

'But it is all right, mamma. I shall get up directly.' With
her husband's help she did get up, but she immediately
turned pale, and looked frightened.

'Yes, I am not well!' and she whispered something to
her mother.

'Oh, my God, what have you done! I said you ought
not to go there,' cried Varvára Alexéevna. 'Wait—I will
call the servants. She must not walk. She must be carried!'

'Don't be afraid, Liza, I will carry you,' said Eugène,
putting his left arm round her. 'Hold me by the neck.
Like that.' And stooping down he put his right arm under
her knees and lifted her. He could never afterwards
forget the suffering and yet beatific expression of her
face.

'I am too heavy for you, dear,' she said with a smile.

'Mamma is running, tell her!' And she bent towards him and kissed him. She evidently wanted her mother to see how he was carrying her.

Eugène shouted to Varvára Alexéevna not to hurry, and that he would carry Liza home. Varvára Alexéevna stopped and began to shout still louder.

'You will drop her, you'll be sure to drop her. You want to destroy her. You have no conscience!'

'But I am carrying her excellently.'

'I do not want to watch you killing my daughter, and I can't.' And she ran round the bend in the alley.

'Never mind, it will pass,' said Liza, smiling.

'Yes. If only it does not have consequences like last time.'

'No. I am not speaking of that. That is all right. I mean mamma. You are tired. Rest a bit.'

But though he found it heavy, Eugène carried his burden proudly and gladly to the house and did not hand her over to the housemaid and the man-cook whom Varvára Alexéevna had found and sent to meet them. He carried her to the bedroom and put her on the bed.

'Now go away,' she said, and drawing his hand to her she kissed it. 'Ánnushka and I will manage all right.'

Mary Pávlovna also ran in from her rooms in the wing. They undressed Liza and laid her on the bed. Eugène sat in the drawing-room with a book in his hand, waiting. Varvára Alexéevna went past him with such a reproachfully gloomy air that he felt alarmed.

'Well, how is it?' he asked.

'How is it? What's the good of asking? It is probably what you wanted when you made your wife jump over the ditch.'

'Varvára Alexéevna!' he cried. 'This is impossible. If you want to torment people and to poison their life' (he wanted to say, 'then go elsewhere to do it,' but restrained himself). 'How is it that it does not hurt you?'

'It is too late now.' And shaking her cap in a triumphant manner she passed out by the door.

The fall had really been a bad one; Liza's foot had twisted awkwardly and there was danger of her having another miscarriage. Everyone knew that there was nothing to be done but that she must just lie quietly, yet all the same they decided to send for a doctor.

'Dear Nikoláy Seménich,' wrote Eugène to the doctor,

'you have always been so kind to us that I hope you will not refuse to come to my wife's assistance. She . . .' and so on. Having written the letter he went to the stables to arrange about the horses and the carriage. Horses had to be got ready to bring the doctor and others to take him back. When an estate is not run on a large scale, such things cannot be quickly decided but have to be considered. Having arranged it all and dispatched the coachman, it was past nine before he got back to the house. His wife was lying down, and said that she felt perfectly well and had no pain. But Varvára Alexéevna was sitting with a lamp screened from Liza by some sheets of music and knitting a large red coverlet, with a mien that said that after what had happened peace was impossible, but that she at any rate would do her duty no matter what anyone else did.

Eugène noticed this, but, to appear as if he had not done so, tried to assume a cheerful and tranquil air and told how he had chosen the horses and how capitally the mare, Kabúshka, had galloped as left trace-horse in the troyka.

'Yes, of course, it is just the time to exercise the horses when help is needed. Probably the doctor will also be thrown into the ditch,' remarked Varvára Alexéevna, examining her knitting from under her pince-nez and moving it close up to the lamp.

'But you know we had to send one way or other, and I made the best arrangement I could.'

'Yes, I remember very well how your horses galloped with me under the arch of the gateway.' This was a long-standing fancy of hers, and Eugène now was injudicious enough to remark that that was not quite what had happened.

'It is not for nothing that I have always said, and have often remarked to the prince, that it is hardest of all to live with people who are untruthful and insincere. I can endure anything except that.'

'Well, if anyone has to suffer more than another, it is certainly I,' said Eugène. 'But you . . .'

'Yes, it is evident.'

'What?'

'Nothing, I am only counting my stitches.'

Eugène was standing at the time by the bed and Liza was looking at him, and one of her moist hands outside the coverlet caught his hand and pressed it. 'Bear with her for my sake. You know she cannot prevent our loving one another,' was what her look said.

'I won't do so again. It's nothing,' he whispered, and he kissed her damp, long hand and then her affectionate eyes, which closed while he kissed them.

'Can it be the same thing over again?' he asked. 'How are you feeling?'

'I am afraid to say for fear of being mistaken, but I feel that he is alive and will live,' said she, glancing at her stomach.

'Ah, it is dreadful, dreadful to think of.'

Notwithstanding Liza's insistence that he should go away, Eugène spent the night with her, hardly closing an eye and ready to attend on her.

But she passed the night well, and had they not sent for the doctor she would perhaps have got up.

By dinner-time the doctor arrived and of course said that though if the symptoms recurred there might be cause for apprehension, yet actually there were no positive symptoms, but as there were also no contrary indications one might suppose on the one hand that—and on the other hand that . . . And therefore she must lie still, and that 'though I do not like prescribing, yet all the same she should take this mixture and should lie quiet.' Besides this, the doctor gave Varvára Alexéevna a lecture on woman's anatomy, during which Varvára Alexéevna nodded her head significantly. Having received his fee, as usual into the backmost part of his palm, the doctor drove away and the patient was left to lie in bed for a week.

XV

Eugène spent most of his time by his wife's bedside, talking to her, reading to her, and what was hardest of all, enduring without murmur Varvára Alexéevna's attacks, and even contriving to turn these into jokes.

But he could not stay at home all the time. In the first place his wife sent him away, saying that he would fall ill if he always remained with her; and secondly the farming was progressing in a way that demanded his presence at every step. He could not stay at home, but had to be in the fields, in the wood, in the garden, at the thrashing-floor; and everywhere he was pursued not merely by the thought but by the vivid image of Stepanída, and he only occasionally forgot her. But that would not have mattered, he could perhaps have mastered his feeling; what was worst of all was that, whereas he had previously lived for months without seeing her, he now continually came across her. She evidently understood that he wished to renew relations with her and tried to come in his way. Nothing was said either by him or by her, and therefore neither he nor she went directly to a rendezvous, but only sought opportunities of meeting.

The most possible place for them to meet was in the forest, where peasant-women went with sacks to collect grass for their cows. Eugène knew this and therefore went there every day. Every day he told himself that he would not go, and every day it ended by his making his way to the forest and, on hearing the sound of voices, standing behind the bushes with sinking heart looking to see if she was there.

Why he wanted to know whether it was she who was there, he did not know. If it had been she and she had been alone, he would not have gone to her—so he believed —he would have run away; but he wanted to see her.

Once he met her. As he was entering the forest she came out of it with two other women, carrying a heavy sack full of grass on her back. A little earlier he would perhaps have met her in the forest. Now, with the other women there, she could not go back to him. But though he realized this impossibility, he stood for a long time behind a hazelbush, at the risk of attracting the other women's attention. Of course she did not return, but he stayed there a long time. And, great heavens, how delightful his imagination made her appear to him! And this not only once, but five or six times, and each time more intensely. Never had she seemed so attractive, and never had he been so completely in her power.

He felt that he had lost control of himself and had become almost insane. His strictness with himself had not weakened a jot; on the contrary he saw all the abomination of his desire and even of his action, for his going to the wood was an action. He knew that he only need come near her anywhere in the dark, and if possible touch her, and he would yield to his feelings. He knew that it was only shame before people, before her, and no doubt before himself also, that restrained him. And he knew too that he had sought conditions in which that shame would not be apparent—darkness or proximity—in which it would be stifled by animal passion. And therefore he knew that he was a wretched criminal, and despised and hated himself with all his soul. He hated himself because he still had not surrendered: every day he prayed God to strengthen him, to save him from perishing; every day he determined that from to-day onward he would not take a step to see her, and would forget her. Every day he devised means of delivering himself from this enticement, and he made use of those means.

But it was all in vain.

One of the means was continual occupation; another was intense physical work and fasting; a third was imagining clearly to himself the shame that would fall upon him when everybody knew of it—his wife, his mother-in-law, and the folk around. He did all this and it seemed to him that he was conquering, but midday came—the hour of their former meetings and the hour when he had met her carrying the grass—and he went to the forest. Thus five days of torment passed. He only saw her from a distance, and did not once encounter her.

XVI

Liza was gradually recovering, she could move about and was only uneasy at the change that had taken place in her husband, which she did not understand.

Varvára Alexéevna had gone away for a while, and the only visitor was Eugène's uncle. Mary Pávlovna was as usual at home.

Eugène was in his semi-insane condition when there came two days of pouring rain, as often happens after thunder in June. The rain stopped all work. They even ceased carting manure on account of the dampness and dirt. The peasants remained at home. The herdsmen wore themselves out with the cattle, and eventually drove them home. The cows and sheep wandered about in the pasture-land and ran loose in the grounds. The peasant-women, barefoot and wrapped in shawls, splashing through the mud, rushed about to seek the runaway cows. Streams flowed everywhere along the paths, all the leaves and all the grass were saturated with water, and streams flowed unceasingly from the spouts into the bubbling puddles.

Eugène sat at home with his wife, who was particularly wearisome that day. She questioned Eugène several times as to the cause of his discontent, and he replied with vexation that nothing was the matter. She ceased questioning him but was still distressed.

They were sitting after breakfast in the drawing-room. His uncle for the hundredth time was recounting fabrications about his society acquaintances. Liza was knitting a jacket and sighed, complaining of the weather and of a pain in the small of her back. The uncle advised her to lie down, and asked for vodka for himself. It was terribly dull for Eugène in the house. Everything was weak and dull. He read a book and a magazine, but understood nothing of them.

'I must go out and look at the rasping-machine they brought yesterday,' said he, and got up and went out.

'Take an umbrella with you.'

'Oh, no, I have a leather coat. And I am only going as far as the boiling-room.'

He put on his boots and his leather coat and went to the factory; and he had not gone twenty steps before he met her coming towards him, with her skirts tucked up high above her white calves. She was walking, holding down the shawl in which her head and shoulders were wrapped.

'Where are you going?' said he, not recognizing her the first instant. When he recognized her it was already too late. She stopped, smiling, and looked long at him.

'I am looking for a calf. Where are you off to in such weather?' said she, as if she were seeing him every day.

'Come to the shed,' said he suddenly, without knowing how he said it. It was as if someone else had uttered the words.

She bit her shawl, winked, and ran in the direction which led from the garden to the shed, and he continued his path, intending to turn off beyond the lilac-bush and go there too.

'Master,' he heard a voice behind him. 'The mistress is calling you, and wants you to come back for a minute.'

This was Mísha, his man-servant.

'My God! This is the second time you have saved me,' thought Eugène, and immediately turned back. His wife reminded him that he had promised to take some medicine at the dinner-hour to a sick woman, and he had better take it with him.

While they were getting the medicine some five minutes elapsed, and then, going away with the medicine, he hesitated to go direct to the shed lest he should be seen from the house, but as soon as he was out of sight he promptly turned and made his way to it. He already saw her in imagination inside the shed smiling gaily. But she was not there, and there was nothing in the shed to show that she had been there.

He was already thinking that she had not come, had not heard or understood his words—he had muttered them through his nose as if afraid of her hearing them—or perhaps she had not wanted to come. 'And why did I imagine that she would rush to me? She has her own husband; it is only I who am such a wretch as to have a wife, and a good one, and to run after another.' Thus he thought sitting in the shed, the thatch of which had a leak and dripped from its straw. 'But how delightful it would be if she did come—alone here in this rain. If only I could embrace her once again, then let happen what may. But I could tell if she has been here by her footprints,' he reflected. He looked at the trodden ground near the shed and at the path overgrown by grass, and the fresh print of bare feet, and even of one that had slipped, was visible.

'Yes, she has been here. Well, now it is settled. Wherever I may see her I shall go straight to her. I will go to her at night.' He sat for a long time in the shed and left it exhausted and crushed. He delivered the medicine, returned home, and lay down in his room to wait for dinner.

XVII

Before dinner Liza came to him and, still wondering what could be the cause of his discontent, began to say that she was afraid he did not like the idea of her going to Moscow for her confinement, and that she had decided that she would remain at home and on no account go to Moscow. He knew how she feared both her confinement itself and the risk of not having a healthy child, and therefore he could not help being touched at seeing how ready she was to sacrifice everything for his sake. All was so nice, so pleasant, so clean, in the house; and in his soul it was so dirty, despicable, and foul. The whole evening Eugène was tormented by knowing that notwithstanding his sincere repulsion at his own weakness, notwithstanding his firm intention to break off,—the same thing would happen again to-morrow.

'No, this is impossible,' he said to himself, walking up and down in his room. 'There must be some remedy for it. My God! What am I to do?'

Someone knocked at the door as foreigners do. He knew this must be his uncle. 'Come in,' he said.

The uncle had come as a self-appointed ambassador from Liza.

'Do you know, I really do notice that there is a change in you,' he said,—'and Liza—I understand how it troubles her. I understand that it must be hard for you to leave all the business you have so excellently started, but *que veux-tu*? I should advise you to go away. It will be more satisfactory both for you and for her. And do you know, I should advise you to go to the Crimea. The climate is beautiful and there is an excellent *accoucheur* there, and you would be just in time for the best of the grape season.'

'Uncle,' Eugène suddenly exclaimed. 'Can you keep a secret? A secret that is terrible to me, a shameful secret.'

'Oh, come—do you really feel any doubt of me?'

'Uncle, you can help me. Not only help, but save me!' said Eugène. And the thought of disclosing his secret to his uncle whom he did not respect, the thought that he would show himself in the worst light and humiliate himself before him, was pleasant. He felt himself to be despicable and guilty, and wished to punish himself.

'Speak, my dear fellow, you know how fond I am of you,' said the uncle, evidently well content that there was a secret and that it was a shameful one, and that it would be communicated to him, and that he could be of use.

'First of all I must tell you that I am a wretch, a good-for-nothing, a scoundrel—a real scoundrel.'

'Now what are you saying . . .' began his uncle, as if he were offended.

'What! Not a wretch when I—Liza's husband, Liza's! One has only to know her purity, her love—and that I, her husband, want to be untrue to her with a peasant-woman!'

'What is this? Why do you want to—you have not been unfaithful to her?'

'Yes, at least just the same as being untrue, for it did not depend on me. I was ready to do so. I was hindered, or else I should . . . now. I do not know what I should have done . . .'

'But please, explain to me . . .'

'Well, it is like this. When I was a bachelor I was stupid enough to have relations with a woman here in our village. That is to say, I used to have meetings with her in the forest, in the field . . .'

'Was she pretty?' asked his uncle.

Eugène frowned at this question, but he was in such need of external help that he made as if he did not hear it, and continued:

'Well, I thought this was just casual and that I should break it off and have done with it. And I did break it off before my marriage. For nearly a year I did not see her or think about her.' It seemed strange to Eugène himself to hear the description of his own condition. 'Then suddenly, I don't myself know why—really one sometimes believes in witchcraft—I saw her, and a worm crept into my heart; and it gnaws. I reproach myself, I understand the full horror of my action, that is to say, of the act I may commit any moment, and yet I myself turn to it, and if I have not committed it, it is only because God preserved me. Yesterday I was on my way to see her when Liza sent for me.'

'What, in the rain?'

'Yes. I am worn out, Uncle, and have decided to confess to you and to ask your help.'

'Yes, of course, it's a bad thing on your own estate. People will get to know. I understand that Liza is weak and that it is necessary to spare her, but why on your own estate?'

Again Eugène tried not to hear what his uncle was saying, and hurried on to the core of the matter.

'Yes, save me from myself. That is what I ask of you. To-day I was hindered by chance. But to-morrow or next time no one will hinder me. And she knows now. Don't leave me alone.'

'Yes, all right,' said his uncle,—'but are you really so much in love?'

'Oh, it is not that at all. It is not that, it is some kind of power that has seized me and holds me. I do not know what to do. Perhaps I shall gain strength, and then . . .'

'Well, it turns out as I suggested,' said his uncle. 'Let us be off to the Crimea.'

'Yes, yes, let us go, and meanwhile you will be with me and will talk to me.'

XVIII

The fact that Eugène had confided his secret to his uncle, and still more the sufferings of his conscience and the feeling of shame he experienced after that rainy day, sobered him. It was settled that they would start for Yálta in a week's time. During that week Eugène drove to town to get money for the journey, gave instructions from the house and from the office concerning the management of the estate, again became gay and friendly with his wife, and began to awaken morally.

So without having once seen Stepanída after that rainy day he left with his wife for the Crimea. There he spent an excellent two months. He received so many new impressions that it seemed to him that the past was obliterated from his memory. In the Crimea they met former acquaintances and became particularly friendly with them, and they also made new acquaintances. Life in the Crimea was a continual holiday for Eugène, besides being instructive and beneficial. They became friendly there with the former Marshal of the Nobility of their province, a clever and liberal-minded man who became fond of Eugène and coached him, and attracted him to his Party.

At the end of August Liza gave birth to a beautiful, healthy daughter, and her confinement was unexpectedly easy.

In September they returned home, the four of them, including the baby and its wet-nurse, as Liza was unable to nurse it herself. Eugène returned home entirely free from the former horrors and quite a new and happy man. Having gone through all that a husband goes through when his wife bears a child, he loved her more than ever. His feeling for the child when he took it in his arms was a funny, new, very pleasant and, as it were, a tickling feeling. Another new thing in his life now was that, besides his occupation with the estate, thanks to his acquaintance with Dúmchin (the ex-Marshal) a new interest occupied his mind, that of the Zémstvo—partly an ambitious interest, partly a feeling of duty. In October there was to be a special Assembly, at which he was to be elected. After arriving home he drove once to town and another time to Dúmchin.

Of the torments of his temptation and struggle he had forgotten even to think, and could with difficulty recall them to mind. It seemed to him something like an attack of insanity he had undergone.

To such an extent did he now feel free from it that he was not even afraid to make inquiries on the first occasion when he remained alone with the steward. As he had previously spoken to him about the matter he was not ashamed to ask.

'Well, and is Sídor Péchnikov still away from home?' he inquired.

'Yes, he is still in town.'

'And his wife?'

'Oh, she is a worthless woman. She is now carrying on with Zenóvi. She has gone quite on the loose.'

'Well, that is all right,' thought Eugène. 'How wonderfully indifferent to it I am! How I have changed.'

XIX

All that Eugène had wished had been realized. He had obtained the property, the factory was working successfully, the beet-crops were excellent, and he expected a large income; his wife had borne a child satisfactorily, his mother-in-law had left, and he had been unanimously elected to the Zémstvo.

He was returning home from town after the election. He had been congratulated and had had to return thanks. He had had dinner and had drunk some five glasses of champagne. Quite new plans of life now presented themselves to him, and he was thinking about these as he drove home. It was the Indian summer: an excellent road and a hot sun. As he approached his home Eugène was thinking of how, as a result of this election, he would occupy among the people the position he had always dreamed of; that is to say, one in which he would be able to serve them not only by production, which gave employment, but also by direct influence. He imagined what his own and the other peasants would think of him in three years' time. 'For instance this one,' he thought, driving just then through the village and glancing at a peasant who with a peasant-woman was crossing the street in front of him carrying a full water-tub. They stopped to let his carriage pass. The peasant was old Péchnikov, and the woman was Stepanída. Eugène looked at her, recognized her, and was glad to feel that he remained quite tranquil. She was still as good-looking as ever, but this did not touch him at all. He drove home.

'Well, may we congratulate you?' said his uncle.

'Yes, I was elected.'

'Capital! We must drink to it!'

Next day Eugène drove about to see to the farming which he had been neglecting. At the outlying farmstead a new thrashing machine was at work. While watching it Eugène stepped among the women, trying not to take notice of them; but try as he would he once or twice noticed the black eyes and red kerchief of Stepanída, who was carrying away the straw. Once or twice he glanced sideways at her and felt that something was happening, but could not account for it to himself. Only next day, when he again drove to the thrashing-floor and spent two hours there quite unnecessarily, without ceasing to caress with his eyes the familiar, handsome figure of the young woman, did he feel that he was lost, irremediably lost. Again those torments! Again all that horror and fear, and there was no saving himself.

What he expected happened to him. The evening of the next day, without knowing how, he found himself at her back-yard, by her hay-shed, where in autumn they had once had a meeting. As though having a stroll, he stopped there lighting a cigarette. A neighbouring peasant-woman saw him, and as he turned back he heard her say to some-one: 'Go, he is waiting for you—on my dying word he is standing there. Go, you fool!'

He saw how a woman—she—ran to the hay-shed; but as a peasant had met him it was no longer possible for him to turn back, and so he went home.

XX

When he entered the drawing-room everything seemed strange and unnatural to him. He had risen that morning vigorous, determined to fling it all aside, to forget it and not allow himself to think about it. But without noticing

how it occurred he had all the morning not merely not
interested himself in the work, but tried to avoid it. What
had formerly cheered him and been important was now
insignificant. Unconsciously he tried to free himself from
business. It seemed to him that he had to do so in order
to think and to plan. And he freed himself and remained
alone. But as soon as he was alone he began to wander
about in the garden and the forest. And all those spots
were besmirched in his recollection by memories that
gripped him. He felt that he was walking in the garden and
pretending to himself that he was thinking out something,
but that really he was not thinking out anything, but in-
sanely and unreasonably expecting her; expecting that by
some miracle she would be aware that he was expecting
her, and would come here at once and go somewhere
where no one would see them, or would come at night
when there would be no moon, and no one, not even she
herself, would see—on such a night she would come and
he would touch her body. . . .

'There now, talking of breaking off when I wish to,'
said he to himself. 'Yes, and that is having a clean healthy
woman for one's health sake! No, it seems one can't play
with her like that. I thought I had taken her, but it was
she who took me; took me and does not let me go. Why,
I thought I was free, but I was not free and was deceiving
myself when I married. It was all nonsense—fraud. From
the time I had her I experienced a new feeling, the real
feeling of a husband. Yes, I ought to have lived with her.

'One of two lives is possible for me: that which I began
with Liza: service, estate management, the child, and
people's respect. If that is life, it is necessary that she,
Stepanída, should not be there. She must be sent away,
as I said, or destroyed so that she shall not exist. And the
other life—is this: For me to take her away from her husband, pay him money, disregard the shame and disgrace,
and live with her. But in that case it is necessary that Liza
should not exist, nor Mimi (the baby). No, that is not so,
the baby does not matter, but it is necessary that there
should be no Liza—that she should go away—that she
should know, curse me, and go away. That she should
know that I have exchanged her for a peasant-woman,
that I am a deceiver and a scoundrel!—No, that is too terrible! It is impossible. But it might happen,' he went on

thinking,—'it might happen that Liza might fall ill and die. Die, and then everything would be capital.

'Capital! Oh, scoundrel! No, if someone must die it should be Stepanída. If she were to die, how good it would be.

'Yes, that is how men come to poison or kill their wives or lovers. Take a revolver and go and call her, and instead of embracing her, shoot her in the breast and have done with it.

'Really she is—a devil. Simply a devil. She has possessed herself of me against my own will.

'Kill? Yes. There are only two ways out: to kill my wife or her. For it is impossible to live like this.* It is impossible! I must consider the matter and look ahead. If things remain as they are what will happen? I shall again be saying to myself that I do not wish it and that I will throw her off, but it will be merely words; in the evening I shall be at her back-yard, and she will know it and will come out. And if people know of it and tell my wife, or if I tell her myself—for I can't lie—I shall not be able to live so. I cannot! People will know. They will all know —Parásha and the blacksmith. Well, is it possible to live so?

'Impossible! There are only two ways out: to kill my wife, or to kill her. Yes, or else . . . Ah, yes, there is a third way: to kill myself,' said he softly, and suddenly a shudder ran over his skin. 'Yes, kill myself, then I shall not need to kill them.' He became frightened, for he felt that only that way was possible. He had a revolver. 'Shall I really kill myself? It is something I never thought of— how strange it will be . . .'

He returned to his study and at once opened the cupboard where the revolver lay, but before he had taken it out of its case his wife entered the room.

XXI

He threw a newspaper over the revolver.

'Again the same!' said she aghast when she had looked at him.

'What is the same?'

* At this place the alternative ending, printed at the end of the story, begins.—A.M.

'The same terrible expression that you had before and would not explain to me. Jénya, dear one, tell me about it. I see that you are suffering. Tell me and you will feel easier. Whatever it may be, it will be better than for you to suffer so. Don't I know that it is nothing bad?'

'You know? While . . .'

'Tell me, tell me, tell me. I won't let you go.'

He smiled a piteous smile.

'Shall I?—No, it is impossible. And there is nothing to tell.'

Perhaps he might have told her, but at that moment the wet-nurse entered to ask if she should go for a walk. Liza went out to dress the baby.

'Then you will tell me? I will be back directly.'

'Yes, perhaps . . .'

She never could forget the piteous smile with which he said this. She went out.

Hurriedly, stealthily like a robber, he seized the revolver and took it out of its case. It was loaded, yes, but long ago, and one cartridge was missing.

'Well, how will it be?' He put it to his temple and hesitated a little, but as soon as he remembered Stepanída—his decision not to see her, his struggle, temptation, fall, and renewed struggle—he shuddered with horror. 'No, this is better,' and he pulled the trigger . . .

When Liza ran into the room—she had only had time to step down from the balcony—he was lying face downwards on the floor: black, warm blood was gushing from the wound, and his corpse was twitching.

There was an inquest. No one could understand or explain the suicide. It never even entered his uncle's head that its cause could be anything in common with the confession Eugène had made to him two months previously.

Varvára Alexéevna assured them that she had always foreseen it. It had been evident from his way of disputing. Neither Liza nor Mary Pávlovna could at all understand why it had happened, but still they did not believe what the doctors said, namely, that he was mentally deranged—a psychopath. They were quite unable to accept this, for they knew he was saner than hundreds of their acquaintances.

And indeed if Eugène Irténev was mentally deranged

everyone is in the same case; the most mentally deranged people are certainly those who see in others indications of insanity they do not notice in themselves.

Variation of the Conclusion of *The Devil*

'To kill, yes. There are only two ways out: to kill my wife, or to kill her. For it is impossible to live like this,' said he to himself, and going up to the table he took from it a revolver and, having examined it—one cartridge was wanting—he put it in his trouser pocket.

'My God! What am I doing?' he suddenly exclaimed, and folding his hands he began to pray.

'O God, help me and deliver me! Thou knowest that I do not desire evil, but by myself am powerless. Help me,' said he, making the sign of the cross on his breast before the icon.

'Yes, I can control myself. I will go out, walk about and think things over.'

He went to the entrance-hall, put on his overcoat and went out onto the porch. Unconsciously his steps took him past the garden along the field path to the outlying farmstead. There the thrashing machine was still droning and the cries of the driver-lads were heard. He entered the barn. She was there. He saw her at once. She was raking up the corn, and on seeing him she ran briskly and merrily about, with laughing eyes, raking up the scattered corn with agility. Eugène could not help watching her though he did not wish to do so. He only recollected himself when she was no longer in sight. The clerk informed him that they were now finishing thrashing the corn that had been beaten down—that was why it was going slower and the output was less. Eugène went up to the drum, which occasionally gave a knock as sheaves not evenly fed in passed under it, and he asked the clerk if there were many such sheaves of beaten-down corn.

'There will be five cartloads of it.'

'Then look here . . .' began Eugène, but he did not finish the sentence. She had gone close up to the drum and was raking the corn from under it, and she scorched him with her laughing eyes. That look spoke of a merry, careless love between them, of the fact that she knew he wanted her and had come to her shed, and that she as always was ready to live and be merry with him regardless of all conditions or consequences. Eugène felt himself to be in her power but did not wish to yield.

He remembered his prayer and tried to repeat it. He began saying it to himself, but at once felt that it was useless. A single thought now engrossed him entirely: how to arrange a meeting with her so that the others should not notice it.

'If we finish this lot to-day, are we to start on a fresh stack or leave it till to-morrow?' asked the clerk.

'Yes, yes,' replied Eugène, involuntarily following her to the heap to which with the other women she was raking the corn.

'But can I really not master myself?' said he to himself. 'Have I really perished? O God! But there is no God. There is only a devil. And it is she. She has possessed me. But I won't, I won't! A devil, yes, a devil.'

Again he went up to her, drew the revolver from his pocket and shot her, once, twice, thrice, in the back. She ran a few steps and fell on the heap of corn.

'My God, my God! What is that?' cried the women.

'No, it was not an accident. I killed her on purpose,' cried Eugène. 'Send for the police-officer.'

He went home and went to his study and locked himself in, without speaking to his wife.

'Do not come to me,' he cried to her through the door. 'You will know all about it.'

An hour later he rang, and bade the man-servant who answered the bell: 'Go and find out whether Stepanída is alive.'

The servant already knew all about it, and told him she had died an hour ago.

'Well, all right. Now leave me alone. When the police-officer or the magistrate comes, let me know.'

The police-officer and magistrate arrived next morning, and Eugène, having bidden his wife and baby farewell, was taken to prison.

He was tried. It was during the early days of trial by jury, and the verdict was one of temporary insanity, and he was sentenced only to perform church penance.

He had been kept in prison for nine months and was then confined in a monastery for one month.

He had begun to drink while still in prison, continued

to do so in the monastery, and returned home an enfeebled, irresponsible drunkard.

Varvára Alexéevna assured them that she had always predicted this. It was, she said, evident from the way he disputed. Neither Liza nor Mary Pávlovna could understand how the affair had happened, but for all that, they did not believe what the doctors said, namely, that he was mentally deranged—a psychopath. They could not accept that, for they knew that he was saner than hundreds of their acquaintances.

And indeed, if Eugène Irténev was mentally deranged when he committed this crime, then everyone is similarly insane. The most mentally deranged people are certainly those who see in others indications of insanity they do not notice in themselves.

The Kreutzer Sonata

[1889]

*But I say unto you, that every one that looketh
on a woman to lust after her hath committed
adultery with her already in his heart.* Matt. v. 28.
*The disciples say unto him, If the case of the man
is so with his wife, it is not expedient to marry. But
he said unto them, All men cannot receive this saying, but they to whom it is given.* Ibid. xix. 10, 11.

[The superscribed numerals within the text refer to the variant
readings of the lithographed version that was privately cir-
culated in Russia. These variants are reprinted here in an
appendix at the end of the story.]

I

It was early spring, and the second day of our journey. Passengers going short distances entered and left our carriage, but three others, like myself, had come all the way with the train. One was a lady, plain and no longer young, who smoked, had a harassed look, and wore a mannish coat and cap; another was an acquaintance of hers, a talkative man of about forty, whose things looked neat and new; the third was a rather short man[1] who kept himself apart. He was not old, but his curly hair had gone prematurely grey. His movements were abrupt and his unusually glittering eyes moved rapidly from one object to another. He wore an old overcoat, evidently from a first-rate tailor, with an astrakhan collar, and a tall astrakhan cap. When he unbuttoned his overcoat a sleeveless Russian coat and embroidered shirt showed beneath it. A peculiarity of this man was a strange sound he emitted, something like a clearing of his throat, or a laugh begun and sharply broken off.

All the way this man had carefully avoided making acquaintance or making any intercourse with his fellow passengers. When spoken to by those near him he gave short and abrupt answers, and at other times read, looked out of the window, smoked, or drank tea and ate something he took out of an old bag.

It seemed to me that his loneliness depressed him, and I made several attempts to converse with him, but whenever our eyes met, which happened often as he sat nearly opposite me, he turned away and took up his book or looked out of the window.

Towards the second evening, when our train stopped at a large station, this nervous man fetched himself some boiling water and made tea. The man with the neat new things —a lawyer as I found out later—and his neighbour, the smoking lady with the mannish coat, went to the refreshment-room to drink tea.

During their absence several new passengers entered the carriage, among them a tall, shaven, wrinkled old man, evidently a tradesman, in a coat lined with skunk fur, and a cloth cap with an enormous peak. The tradesman sat down opposite the seats of the lady and the lawyer, and immediately started a conversation with a young man who had also entered at that station and, judging by his appearance, was a tradesman's clerk.[2]

I was sitting the other side of the gangway and as the train was standing still I could hear snatches of their conversation when nobody was passing between us. The tradesman began by saying that he was going to his estate which was only one station farther on; then as usual the conversation turned to prices and trade, and they spoke of the state of business in Moscow and then of the Nizhni-Nóvgorod Fair. The clerk began to relate how a wealthy merchant, known to both of them, had gone on the spree at the fair, but the old man interrupted him by telling of the orgies he had been at in former times at Kunávin Fair. He evidently prided himself on the part he had played in them, and [3] recounted with pleasure how he and some acquaintances, together with the merchant they had been speaking of, had once got drunk at Kunávin and played such a trick that he had to tell of it in a whisper. The clerk's roar of laughter filled the whole carriage; the old man laughed also, exposing two yellow teeth.

Not expecting to hear anything interesting, I got up to stroll about the platform till the train should start. At the carriage door I met the lawyer and the lady who were talking with animation as they approached.

'You won't have time,' said the sociable lawyer, 'the second bell will ring in a moment.'

And the bell did ring before I had gone the length of the train. When I returned, the animated conversation between the lady and the lawyer was proceeding. The old tradesman sat silent opposite to them, looking sternly before him, and occasionally mumbled disapprovingly as if chewing something.

'Then she plainly informed her husband,' the lawyer was smilingly saying as I passed him, 'that she was not able, and did not wish, to live with him since . . .'

He went on to say something I could not hear. Several other passengers came in after me. The guard passed, a porter hurried in, and for some time the noise made their voices inaudible. When all was quiet again the conversation had evidently turned from the particular case to general considerations.

The lawyer was saying that public opinion in Europe was occupied with the question of divorce, and that cases of 'that kind' were occurring more and more often in Russia. Noticing that his was the only voice audible, he stopped his discourse and turned to the old man.[4]

'Those things did not happen in the old days, did they?' he said, smiling pleasantly.

The old man was about to reply, but the train moved and he took off his cap, crossed himself, and whispered a prayer. The lawyer turned away his eyes and waited politely. Having finished his prayer and crossed himself three times the old man set his cap straight, pulled it well down over his forehead, changed his position, and began to speak.

'They used to happen even then, sir, but less often,' he said. 'As times are now they can't help happening. People have got too educated.'

The train moved faster and faster and jolted over the joints of the rails, making it difficult to hear, but being interested I moved nearer. The nervous man with the glittering eyes opposite me, evidently also interested, listened without changing his place.

'What is wrong with education?' said the lady, with a scarcely perceptible smile. 'Surely it can't be better to marry as they used to in the old days when the bride and bridegroom did not even see one another before the wedding,' she continued, answering not what her interlocutor had said but what she thought he would say, in the way many ladies have. 'Without knowing whether they loved, or whether they could love, they married just anybody, and were wretched all their lives. And you think that was better?' she said, evidently addressing me and the lawyer chiefly and least of all the old man with whom she was talking.

'They've got so very educated,' the tradesman reiterated, looking contemptuously at the lady and leaving her question unanswered.

'It would be interesting to know how you explain the connexion between education and matrimonial discord,' said the lawyer, with a scarcely perceptible smile.

The tradesman was about to speak, but the lady interrupted him.

'No,' she said, 'those times have passed.' But the lawyer stopped her.

'Yes, but allow the gentleman to express his views.'

'Foolishness comes from education,' the old man said categorically.

'They make people who don't love one another marry, and then wonder that they live in discord,' the lady hastened to say, turning to look at the lawyer, at me, and even at the clerk, who had got up and, leaning on the back of the seat, was smilingly listening to the conversation. 'It's only animals, you know, that can be paired off as their master likes; but human beings have their own inclinations and attachments,' said the lady, with an evident desire to annoy the tradesman.

'You should not talk like that, madam,' said the old man, 'animals are cattle, but human beings have a law given them.'

'Yes, but how is one to live with a man when there is no love?' the lady again hastened to express her argument, which probably seemed very new to her.[5]

'They used not to go into that,' said the old man in an impressive tone. 'It is only now that all this has sprung up. The least thing makes them say: "I will leave you!" The fashion has spread even to the peasants. "Here you are!" she says. "Here, take your shirts and trousers and I will go with Vánka; his head is curlier than yours." What can you say? The first thing that should be required of a woman is fear!'

The clerk glanced at the lawyer, at the lady, and at me, apparently suppressing a smile and prepared to ridicule or to approve of the tradesman's words according to the reception they met with.

'Fear of what?' asked the lady.

'Why this: Let her fear her husband! That fear!'

'Oh, the time for that, sir, has passed,' said the lady with a certain viciousness.

'No, madam, that time cannot pass. As she, Eve, was made from the rib of a man, so it will remain to the end of time,' said the old man, jerking his head with such sternness and such a victorious look that the clerk at once concluded that victory was on his side, and laughed loudly.

'Ah yes, that's the way you men argue,' said the lady unyieldingly, and turned to us. 'You have given yourselves freedom but want to shut women up in a tower. You no doubt permit yourselves everything.'

'⁶ No one is permitting anything, but a man does not bring offspring into the home; while a woman—a wife—is a leaky vessel,' the tradesman continued insistently. His tone was so impressive that it evidently vanquished his hearers, and even the lady felt crushed but still did not give in.

'Yes, but I think you will agree that a woman is a human being and has feelings as a man has. What is she to do then, if she does not love her husband?'

'Does not love!' said the tradesman severely, moving his brows and lips. 'She'll love, no fear!' This unexpected argument particularly pleased the clerk, and he emitted a sound of approval.

'Oh, no, she won't!' the lady began. 'And when there is no love you can't enforce it.'

'Well, and supposing the wife is unfaithful, what then?' asked the lawyer.

'That is not admissible,' said the old man. 'One has to see to that.'

'But if it happens, what then? You know it does occur.'

'It happens among some, but not among us,' said the old man.⁷

All were silent. The clerk moved, came still nearer, and, evidently unwilling to be behindhand, began with a smile.

'Yes, a young fellow of ours had a scandal. It was a difficult case to deal with. It too was a case of a woman who was a bad lot. She began to play the devil, and the young fellow is respectable and cultured. At first it was with one of the office-clerks. The husband tried to persuade her with kindness. She would not stop, but played all sorts of dirty tricks. Then she began to steal his money. He beat her, but she only grew worse. Carried on intrigues, if I may mention it, with an unchristened Jew. What was he to do? He turned her out altogether and lives as a bachelor, while she gads about.'

'Because he is a fool,' said the old man. 'If he'd pulled her up properly from the first and not let her have way, she'd be living with him, no fear! It's giving way at first that counts. Don't trust your horse in the field, or your wife in the house.'

At that moment the guard entered to collect the tickets for the next station. The old man gave up his.

'Yes, the female sex must be curbed in time or else all is lost!'

'Yes, but you yourself just now were speaking about the way married men amuse themselves at the Kunávin Fair,' I could not help saying.[8]

'That's a different matter,' said the old man and relapsed into silence.

When the whistle sounded the tradesman rose, got out his bag from under the seat, buttoned up his coat, and slightly lifting his cap went out of the carriage.

II

As soon as the old man had gone several voices were raised.

'A daddy of the old style!' remarked the clerk.

'A living *Domostróy!*' said the lady. 'What barbarous views of women and marriage!'

'Yes, we are far from the European understanding of marriage,' said the lawyer.

'The chief thing such people do not understand,' continued the lady, 'is that marriage without love is not marriage; that love alone sanctifies marriage, and that real marriage is only such as is sanctified by love.'

The clerk listened smilingly, trying to store up for future use all he could of the clever conversation.

In the midst of the lady's remarks we heard, behind me, a sound like that of a broken laugh or sob; and on turning round we saw my neighbour, the lonely grey-haired man with the glittering eyes, who had approached unnoticed during our conversation, which evidently interested him. He stood with his arms on the back of the seat, evidently much excited; his face was red [9] and a muscle twitched in his cheek.

'What kind of love . . . love . . . is it that sanctifies marriage?' he asked hesitatingly.[10]

Noticing the speaker's agitation, the lady tried to answer him as gently and fully as possible.

'True love . . . When such love exists between a man and a woman, then marriage is possible,' she said.

'Yes, but how is one to understand what is meant by "true love"?' said the gentleman with the glittering eyes timidly and with an awkward smile.

'Everybody knows what love is,' replied the lady, evidently wishing to break off her conversation with him.

'But I don't,' said the man. 'You must define what you understand . . .'

'Why? It's very simple,' she said, but stopped to consider. 'Love? Love is an exclusive preference for one above everybody else,' said the lady.

'Preference for how long? A month, two days, or half an hour?' said the grey-haired man and began to laugh.

'Excuse me, we are evidently not speaking of the same thing.'

'Oh, yes! Exactly the same.'

'She means,' interposed the lawyer, pointing to the lady, 'that in the first place marriage must be the outcome of attachment—or love, if you please—and only where that exists is marriage sacred, so to speak. Secondly, that marriage when not based on natural attachment—love, if you prefer the word—lacks the element that makes it morally binding. Do I understand you rightly?' he added, addressing the lady.

The lady indicated her approval of his explanation by a nod of her head.

'It follows . . .' the lawyer continued—but the nervous man whose eyes now glowed as if aflame and who had evidently restrained himself with difficulty, began without letting the lawyer finish:

'Yes, I mean exactly the same thing, a preference for one person over everybody else, and I am only asking: a preference for how long?'

'For how long? For a long time; for life sometimes,' replied the lady, shrugging her shoulders.

'Oh, but that happens only in novels and never in real life. In real life this preference for one may last for years (that happens very rarely), more often for months, or perhaps for weeks, days, or hours,' he said, evidently aware that he was astonishing everybody by his views and pleased that it was so.

'Oh, what are you saying?' 'But no . . .' 'No, allow

me . . .' we all three began at once. Even the clerk uttered an indefinite sound of disapproval.

'Yes, I know,' the grey-haired man shouted above our voices, 'you are talking about what is supposed to be, but I am speaking of what is. Every man experiences what you call love for every pretty woman.' [11]

'Oh, what you say is awful! But the feeling that is called love does exist among people, and is given not for months or years, but for a lifetime!'

'No, it does not! Even if we should grant that a man might prefer a certain woman all his life, the woman in all probability would prefer someone else;[12] and so it always has been and still is in the world,' he said, and taking out his cigarette-case he began to smoke.

'But the feeling may be reciprocal,' said the lawyer.

'No, sir, it can't!' rejoined the other. 'Just as it cannot be that in a cartload of peas, two marked peas will lie side by side. Besides, it is not merely this impossibility, but the inevitable satiety.[13] To love one person for a whole lifetime is like saying that one candle will burn a whole life,' he said, greedily inhaling the smoke.

'But you are talking all the time about physical love. Don't you acknowledge love based on identity of ideals, on spiritual affinity?' asked the lady.

'Spiritual affinity! Identity of ideals!' he repeated, emitting his peculiar sound. 'But in that case why go to bed together? (Excuse my coarseness!) Or do people go to bed together because of the identity of their ideals?' he said, bursting into a nervous laugh.[14]

'But permit me,' said the lawyer. 'Facts contradict you. We do see that matrimony exists, that all mankind, or the greater part of it, lives in wedlock, and many people honourably live long married lives.'

The grey-haired man again laughed.

'First you say that marriage is based on love, and when I express a doubt as to the existence of a love other than sensual, you prove the existence of love by the fact that marriages exist. But marriages in our days are mere deception!'

'No, allow me!' said the lawyer. 'I only say that marriages have existed and do exist.'

'They do! But why? They have existed and do exist among people who see in marriage something sacramental, a mystery binding them in the sight of God. Among them marriages do exist. Among us, people marry regarding marriage as nothing but copulation, and the result is either deception or coercion.[15] When it is deception it is easier to bear. The husband and wife merely deceive people by pretending to be monogamists, while living polygamously. That is bad, but still bearable. But when, as most frequently happens, the husband and wife have undertaken the external duty of living together all their lives,[16] and begin to hate each other after a month, and wish to part but still continue to live together, it leads to that terrible hell which makes people take to drink, shoot themselves, and kill or poison themselves or one another,' he went on, speaking more and more rapidly, not allowing anyone to put in a word and becoming more and more excited. We all felt embarrassed.

'Yes, undoubtedly there are critical episodes in married life,' said the lawyer, wishing to end this disturbingly heated conversation.

'I see you have found out who I am!' said the grey-haired man softly, and with apparent calm.

'No, I have not that pleasure.'

'It is no great pleasure. I am that Pózdnyshev in whose life that critical episode occurred to which you alluded; the episode when he killed his wife,' he said, rapidly glancing at each of us.

No one knew what to say and all remained silent.

'Well, never mind,' he said with that peculiar sound of his. 'However, pardon me. Ah! . . . I won't intrude on you.'

'Oh, no, if you please . . .' said the lawyer, himself not knowing 'if you please' what.

But Pózdnyshev, without listening to him, rapidly turned away and went back to his seat. The lawyer and the lady whispered together. I sat down beside Pózdnyshev in silence, unable to think of anything to say. It was too dark to read, so I shut my eyes pretending that I wished to go to sleep. So we travelled in silence to the next station.

At that station the lawyer and the lady moved into another car, having some time previously consulted the guard about it. The clerk lay down on the seat and fell asleep. Pózdnyshev kept smoking and drinking tea which he had made at the last station.

When I opened my eyes and looked at him he suddenly addressed me resolutely and irritably:

'Perhaps it is unpleasant for you to sit with me, knowing who I am? In that case I will go away.'

'Oh no, not at all.'

'Well then, won't you have some? Only it's very strong.'

He poured out some tea for me.

'They talk . . . and they always lie . . .' he remarked.

'What are you speaking about?' I asked.

'Always about the same thing. About that love of theirs and what it is! Don't you want to sleep?'

'Not at all.'

'Then would you like me to tell you how that love led to what happened to me?'

'Yes, if it will not be painful for you.'

'No, it is painful for me to be silent. Drink the tea . . . or is it too strong?'

The tea was really like beer, but I drank a glass of it. Just then the guard entered. Pózdnyshev followed him with angry eyes, and only began to speak after he had left.[17]

III

'Well then, I'll tell you.[18] But do you really want to hear it?'

I repeated that I wished it very much. He paused, rubbed his face with his hands, and began:

'If I am to tell it, I must tell everything from the beginning: I must tell how and why I married, and the kind of man I was before my marriage.[19]

'Till my marriage I lived as everybody does, that is, everybody in our class. I am a landowner and a graduate of the university, and was a marshal of the gentry. Before my marriage I lived as everyone does, that is, dissolutely; and while living dissolutely I was convinced, like everybody in our class, that I was living as one has to. I thought I was a charming fellow and quite a moral man.[20] I was not a seducer, had no unnatural tastes, did not make that the chief purpose of my life as many of my associates did, but I practised debauchery in a steady, decent way for health's sake.[21] I avoided women who might tie my hands by having a child or by attachment for me. However, there may have been children and attachments, but I acted as if there were not. And this I not only considered moral, but I was even proud of it.'

He paused and gave vent to his peculiar sound, as he evidently did whenever a new idea occurred to him.

'And you know, that is the chief abomination!' he exclaimed. 'Dissoluteness does not lie in anything physical—no kind of physical misconduct is debauchery; real debauchery lies precisely in freeing oneself from moral relations with a woman with whom you have physical intimacy. And such emancipation I regarded as a merit. I remember how I once worried because I had not had an opportunity to pay a woman who gave herself to me (having probably taken a fancy to me) and how I only became tranquil after having sent her some money—thereby intimating that I did not consider myself in any way morally bound to her . . . Don't nod as if you agreed with me,' he suddenly shouted at me. 'Don't I know these things? We all, and you too unless you are a rare exception, hold those same views, just as I used to. Never mind, I beg your pardon, but the fact is that it's terrible, terrible, terrible!'

'What is terrible?' I asked.

'That abyss of error in which we live[22] regarding women and our relations with them. No, I can't speak calmly about it, not because of that "episode," as he called it, in my life, but because since that "episode" occurred my eyes have been opened and I have seen everything in quite a different light. Everything reversed, everything reversed!'

He lit a cigarette and began to speak, leaning his elbows on his knees.

It was too dark to see his face, but, above the jolting of the train, I could hear his impressive and pleasant voice.

IV

'Yes, only after such torments as I have endured, only by their means, have I understood where the root of the matter lies—understood what ought to be, and therefore seen all the horror of what is.[23]

'So you will see how and when that which led up to my "episode" began. It began when I was not quite sixteen. It happened when I still went to the grammar school and my elder brother was a first-year student at the university. I had not yet known any woman, but, like all the unfortunate children of our class, I was no longer an innocent boy. I had been depraved two years before that by other boys.

Already woman, not some particular woman but woman as something to be desired, woman, every woman, woman's nudity, tormented me. My solitude was not pure. I was tormented, as ninety-nine per cent. of our boys are. I was horrified, I suffered, I prayed, and I fell. I was already depraved in imagination and in fact, but I had not yet taken the last step. I was perishing, but I had not yet laid hands on another human being. But one day a comrade of my brother's, a jolly student, a so-called good fellow, that is, the worst kind of good-for-nothing, who had taught us to drink and to play cards, persuaded us after a carousal to go *there*. We went. My brother was also still innocent, and he fell that same night. And I, a fifteen-year-old boy, defiled myself and took part in defiling a woman, without at all understanding what I was doing. I had never heard from any of my elders that what I was doing was wrong, you know. And indeed no one hears it now. It is true it is in the Commandments but then the Commandments are only needed to answer the priest at Scripture examination, and even then they are not very necessary, not nearly as necessary as the commandment about the use of *ut* in conditional sentences in Latin.

'And so I never heard those older persons whose opinions I respected say that it was an evil. On the contrary, I heard people I respected say it was good. I had heard that my struggles and sufferings would be eased after that. I heard this and read it, and heard my elders say it would be good for my health, while from my comrades I heard that it was rather a fine, spirited thing to do. So in general I expected nothing but good from it. The risk of disease? But that too had been foreseen. A paternal government saw to that. It sees to the correct working of the brothels, and makes profligacy safe for schoolboys. Doctors too deal with it for a consideration. That is proper. They assert that debauchery is good for the health, and they organize proper well-regulated debauchery. I know some mothers who attend to their sons' health in that sense. And science sends them to the brothels.'

'Why do you say "science"?' I asked.

'Why, who are the doctors? The priests of science. Who deprave youths[?] by maintaining that this is necessary for their health? They do.

'Yet if a one-hundredth part of the efforts devoted to the cure of syphilis were devoted to the eradication of debauchery there would long ago not have been a trace of syphilis left. But as it is, efforts are made not to eradicate debauchery but to encourage it and to make debauchery safe. That is not the point however. The point is that with me—and with nine-tenths, if not more, not of our class only but of all classes, even the peasants—this terrible thing happens that happened to me; I fell not because I succumbed to the natural temptation of a particular woman's charm—no, I was not seduced by a woman—but I fell because, in the set around me, what was really a fall was regarded by some as a most legitimate function good for one's health, and by others as a very natural and not only excusable but even innocent amusement for a young man. I did not understand that it was a fall, but simply indulged in that half-pleasure, half-need, which, as was suggested to me, was natural at a certain age. I began to indulge in debauchery as I began to drink and to smoke. Yet in that first fall there was something special and pathetic. I remember that at once, on the spot before I left the room, I felt sad, so sad that I wanted to cry—to cry for the loss of my innocence and for my relationship with women, now sullied for ever. Yes, my natural, simple relationship with women was spoilt for ever. From that time I have not had, and could not have, pure relations with women. I had become what is called a libertine. To be a libertine is a physical condition like that of a morphinist, a drunkard, or a smoker. As a morphinist, a drunkard, or a smoker is no longer normal, so too a man who has known several women for his pleasure is not normal but is a man perverted for ever, a libertine. As a drunkard or a morphinist can be recognized at once by his face and manner, so it is with a libertine. A libertine may restrain himself, may struggle, but he will never have those pure, simple, clear, brotherly relations with a woman. By the way he looks at a young woman and examines her, a libertine can always be recognized. And I had become and I remained a libertine, and it was this that brought me to ruin.

V

'Ah, yes! After that things went from bad to worse, and there were all sorts of deviations. Oh, God! When I recall the abominations I committed in this respect I am seized with horror! And that is true of me, whom my companions, I remember, ridiculed for my so-called innocence. And when one hears of the "gilded youths," of officers, of the Parisians . . . ! And when all these gentlemen, and I— who have on our souls hundreds of the most varied and horrible crimes against women—when we thirty-year-old profligates, very carefully washed, shaved, perfumed, in clean linen and in evening dress or uniform, enter a drawing-room or ball-room, we are emblems of purity, charming!

'Only think of what ought to be, and of what is! When in society such a gentleman comes up to my sister or daughter, I, knowing his life, ought to go up to him, take him aside, and say quietly, "My dear fellow, I know the life you lead, and how and with whom you pass your nights. This is no place for you. There are pure, innocent girls here. Be off!" That is what ought to be; but what happens is that when such a gentleman comes and dances, embracing our sister or daughter, we are jubilant, if he is rich and well-connected. Maybe after Rigulboche he will honour my daughter! Even if traces of disease remain, no matter! They are clever at curing that nowadays. Oh, yes, I know several girls in the best society whom their parents enthusiastically gave in marriage to men suffering from a certain disease. Oh, oh . . . the abomination of it! But a time will come when this abomination and falsehood will be exposed!'

He made his strange noise several times and again drank tea. It was fearfully strong and there was no water with which to dilute it. I felt that I was much excited by the two glasses I had drunk. Probably the tea affected him too, for he became more and more excited. His voice grew increasingly mellow and expressive. He continually changed his position, now taking off his cap and now putting it on again, and his face changed strangely in the semi-darkness in which we were sitting.

'Well, so I lived till I was thirty, not abandoning for a moment the intention of marrying and arranging for myself a most elevated and pure family life. With that purpose I observed the girls suitable for that end,' he continued. 'I weltered in a mire of debauchery and at the same time was on the lookout for a girl pure enough to be worthy of me.

'I rejected many just because they were not pure enough to suit me, but at last I found one whom I considered worthy. She was one of two daughters of a once-wealthy Pénza landowner who had been ruined.

'25One evening after we had been out in a boat and had returned by moonlight, and I was sitting beside her admiring her curls and her shapely figure in a tight-fitting jersey, I suddenly decided that it was she! It seemed to me that evening that she understood all that I felt and thought, and that what I felt and thought was very lofty. In reality it was only that the jersey and the curls were particularly becoming to her and that after a day spent near her I wanted to be still closer.

'It is amazing how complete is the delusion that beauty is goodness. A handsome woman talks nonsense, you listen and hear not nonsense but cleverness. She says and does horrid things, and you see only charm. And if a handsome woman does not say stupid or horrid things, you at once persuade yourself that she is wonderfully clever and moral.

'I returned home in rapture, decided that she was the acme of moral perfection, and that therefore she was worthy to be my wife, and I proposed to her next day.

'26What a muddle it is! Out of a thousand men who marry (not only among us but unfortunately also among the masses) there is hardly one who has not already been married ten, a hundred, or even, like Don Juan, a thousand times, before his wedding.

'It is true as I have heard and have myself observed that there are nowadays some chaste young men who feel and know that this thing is not a joke but an important matter.

'God help them! But in my time there was not one such in ten thousand. And everybody knows this and pretends not to know it. In all the novels they describe in detail the heroes' feelings and the ponds and bushes beside which they walk, but when their great love for some maiden is described, nothing is said about what has happened to these interesting heroes before: not a word about their frequenting certain houses, or about the servant-girls, cooks, and other people's wives! If there are such improper novels they are not put into the hands of those who most need this information—the unmarried girls.

'We first pretend to these girls that the profligacy which fills half the life of our towns, and even of the villages, does not exist at all.

'Then we get so accustomed to this pretence that at last,

like the English, we ourselves really begin to believe that we are all moral people and live in a moral world. The girls, poor things, believe this quite seriously. So too did my unfortunate wife. I remember how, when we were engaged, I showed her my diary, from which she could learn something, if but a little, of my past, especially about my last *liaison*, of which she might hear from others, and about which I therefore felt it necessary to inform her. I remember her horror, despair, and confusion, when she learnt of it and understood it. I saw that she then wanted to give me up. And why did she not do so? . . .' [27]

He again made that sound, swallowed another mouthful of tea, and remained silent for a while.

VI

'No, after all, it is better, better so!' he exclaimed. 'It serves me right! But that's not to the point—I meant to say that it is only the unfortunate girls who are deceived.

'The mothers know it, especially mothers educated by their own husbands—they know it very well. While pretending to believe in the purity of men, they act quite differently. They know with what sort of bait to catch men for themselves and for their daughters.

'You see it is only we men who don't know (because we don't wish to know) what women know very well, that the most exalted poetic love, as we call it, depends not on moral qualities but on physical nearness and on the *coiffure*, and the colour and cut of the dress. Ask an expert coquette who has set herself the task of captivating a man, which she would prefer to risk: to be convicted in his presence of lying, of cruelty, or even of dissoluteness, or to appear before him in an ugly and badly made dress— she will always prefer the first. She knows that we are continually lying about high sentiments, but really only want her body and will therefore forgive any abomination except an ugly tasteless costume that is in bad style.

'A coquette knows that consciously, and every innocent girl knows it unconsciously just as animals do.

'That is why there are those detestable jerseys, bustles, and naked shoulders, arms, almost breasts. A woman, especially if she has passed the male school, knows very well that all the talk about elevated subjects is just talk, but that what a man wants is her body and all that pre-

sents it in the most deceptive but alluring light; and she acts
accordingly.[28] If we only throw aside our familiarity with
this indecency, which has become a second nature to us,
and look at the life of our upper classes as it is, in all its
shamelessness—why, it is simply a brothel . . . You don't
agree? Allow me, I'll prove it,' he said, interrupting me.
'You say that the women of our society have other interests
in life than prostitutes have, but I say no, and will prove it.
If people differ in the aims of their lives, by the inner content of their lives, this difference will necessarily be reflected in externals and their externals will be different.
But look at those unfortunate despised women and at the
highest society ladies: the same costumes, the same fash-
ions, the same perfumes, the exposure of arms, shoulders,
and breasts, the same tight skirts over prominent bustles,
the same passion for little stones, for costly, glittering objects, the same amusements, dances, music, and singing.
As the former employ all means to allure, so do these
others.[29]

VII

'Well, so these jerseys and curls and bustles caught me!
'It was very easy to catch me for I was brought up in
the conditions in which amorous young people are forced
like cucumbers in a hot-bed. You see our stimulating super-
abundance of food, together with complete physical idleness, is nothing but a systematic excitement of desire.[80]
Whether this astonishes you or not, it is so. Why, till quite
recently I did not see anything of this myself, but now I
have seen it. That is why it torments me that nobody knows
this, and people talk such nonsense as that lady did.
'Yes, last spring some peasants were working in our
neighbourhood on a railway embankment. The usual food
of a young peasant is rye-bread, kvas, and onions; he keeps
alive and is vigorous and healthy; his work is light agri-
cultural work. When he goes to railway-work his rations
are buckwheat porridge and a pound of meat a day. But
he works off that pound of meat during his sixteen hours'
work wheeling barrow-loads of half-a-ton weight, so it is
just enough for him. But we who every day consume two
pounds of meat, and game, and fish and all sorts of heating
foods and drinks—where does that go to? Into excesses of
sensuality. And if it goes there and the safety-valve is open,

all is well; but try and close the safety-valve, as I closed it temporarily, and at once a stimulus arises which, passing[31] through the prism of our artificial life, expresses itself in utter infatuation, sometimes even platonic. And I fell in love as they all do.

'Everything was there to hand: raptures, tenderness, and poetry. In reality that love of mine was the result, on the one hand of her mamma's and the dressmakers' activity, and on the other of the super-abundance of food consumed by me while living an idle life. If on the one hand there had been no boating, no dressmaker with her waists and so forth, and had my wife been sitting at home in a shapeless dressing-gown, and had I on the other hand been in circumstances normal to man—consuming just enough food to suffice for the work I did, and had the safety-valve been open—it happened to be closed at the time—I should not have fallen in love and nothing of all this would have happened.

VIII

'Well, and now it so chanced that everything combined —my condition, her becoming dress, and the satisfactory boating. It had failed twenty times but now it succeeded. Just like a trap! I am not joking. You see nowadays marriages are arranged that way—like traps. What is the natural way? The lass is ripe, she must be given in marriage. It seems very simple if the girl is not a fright and there are men wanting to marry. That is how it was done in olden times. The lass was grown up and her parents arranged the marriage.[32] So it was done, and is done, among all mankind—Chinese, Hindus, Mohammedans, and among our own working classes; so it is done among at least ninety-nine per cent. of the human race. Only among one per cent. or less, among us libertines, has it been discovered that that is not right, and something new has been invented. And what is this novelty? It is that the maidens sit around and the men walk about, as at a bazaar, choosing. And the maidens wait and think, but dare not say: "Me, please!" "No me!" "Not her, but me!" "Look what shoulders and other things I have!" And we men stroll around and look,[33] and are very pleased. "Yes, I know! I won't be caught!" They stroll about and look, and are very pleased

that everything is arranged like that for them. And then in
an unguarded moment—snap! He is caught!'

'Then how ought it to be done?' I asked. 'Should the
woman propose?'

'Oh, I don't know how; only if there's to be equality, let
it be equality. If they have discovered that pre-arranged
matches are degrading, why this is a thousand times worse!
Then the rights and chances were equal, but here the
woman is a slave in a bazaar[34] or the bait in a trap. Tell
any mother, or the girl herself, the truth, that she is only
occupied in catching a husband . . . oh dear! what an insult! Yet they all do it and have nothing else to do. What
is so terrible is to see sometimes quite innocent poor young
girls engaged on it. And again, if it were but done openly
—but it is always done deceitfully. "Ah, the origin of
species, how interesting!" "Oh, Lily takes such an interest
in painting! And will you be going to the exhibition? How
instructive!" And the troyka-drives, and shows, and sym-
phonies! "Oh! how remarkable! My Lily is mad on music."
"And why don't you share these convictions?" And boating
. . . But their one thought is: "Take me, take me!" "Take
my Lily!" "Or try—at least!" Oh, what an abomination!
What falsehood!' he concluded, finishing his tea and beginning to put away the tea-things.

IX

'You know,' he began while packing the tea and sugar
into his bag. 'The domination of women from which the
world suffers all arises from this.'

'What "domination of women"?' I asked.[35] 'The rights,
the legal privileges, are on the man's side.'

'Yes, yes! That's just it,' he interrupted me. 'That's just
what I want to say. It explains the extraordinary phenomenon that on the one hand woman is reduced to the
lowest stage of humiliation, while on the other she dominates. Just like the Jews: as they pay us back for their op-
pression by a financial domination, so it is with women.
"Ah, you want us to be traders only—all right, as traders
we will dominate you!" say the Jews. "Ah, you want us to
be merely objects of sensuality—all right, as objects of
sensuality we will enslave you," say the women. Woman's
lack of rights arises not from the fact that she must not

vote or be a judge—to be occupied with such affairs is no privilege—but from the fact that she is not man's equal in sexual intercourse and has not the right to use a man or abstain from him as she likes—is not allowed to choose a man at her pleasure instead of being chosen by him. You say that is monstrous. Very well! Then a man must not have those rights either. As it is at present, a woman is deprived of that right while a man has it. And to make up for that right she acts on man's sensuality, and through his sensuality subdues him so that he only chooses formally, while in reality it is she who chooses. And once she has obtained these means she abuses them and acquires a terrible power over people.'

'But where is this special power?' I inquired.

'Where is it? Why everywhere, in everything! Go round the shops in any big town. There are goods worth millions and you cannot estimate the human labour expended on them, and look whether in nine-tenths of these shops there is anything for the use of men. All the luxuries of life are demanded and maintained by women.

'Count all the factories. An enormous proportion of them produce useless ornaments, carriages, furniture, and trinkets, for women. Millions of people, generations of slaves, perish at hard labour in factories merely to satisfy woman's caprice. Women, like queens, keep nine-tenths of mankind in bondage to heavy labour. And all because they have been abased and deprived of equal rights with men. And they revenge themselves by acting on our sensuality and catch us in their nets. Yes, it all comes of that.

'Women have made of themselves such an instrument for acting upon our sensuality that a man cannot quietly consort with a woman.[36] As soon as a man approaches a woman he succumbs to her stupefying influence and becomes intoxicated and crazy. I used formerly to feel uncomfortable and uneasy when I saw a lady dressed up for a ball, but now I am simply frightened and plainly see her as something dangerous and illicit. I want to call a policeman and ask for protection from the peril, and demand that the dangerous object be removed and put away.

'Ah, you are laughing!' he shouted at me, 'but it is not at all a joke. I am sure a time will come, and perhaps very soon, when people will understand this and will wonder how a society could exist in which actions were permitted which so disturb social tranquillity as those adornments of the body directly evoking sensuality, which we tolerate for women in our society. Why, it's like setting all sorts of traps along the paths and promenades—it is even worse! Why is gambling forbidden while women in costumes which evoke sensuality are not forbidden? They are a thousand times more dangerous!

X

'Well, you see, I was caught that way. I was what is called in love. I not only imagined her to be the height of perfection, but during the time of our engagement I regarded myself also as the height of perfection. You know there is no rascal who cannot, if he tries, find rascals in some respects worse than himself, and who consequently cannot find reasons for pride and self-satisfaction. So it was with me: I was not marrying for money—covetousness had nothing to do with it—unlike the majority of my acquaintances who married for money or connexions—I was rich, she was poor. That was one thing. Another thing I prided myself on was that while others married intending to continue in future the same polygamous life they had lived before marriage, I was firmly resolved to be monogamous after marriage, and there was no limit to my pride on that score. Yes, I was a dreadful pig and imagined myself to be an angel.

'Our engagement did not last long. I cannot now think of that time without shame! What nastiness! Love is supposed to be spiritual and not sensual. Well, if the love is spiritual, a spiritual communion, then that spiritual communion should find expression in words, in conversations, in discourse. There was nothing of the kind. It used to be dreadfully difficult to talk when we were left alone. It was the labour of Sisyphus. As soon as we thought of something to say and said it, we had again to be silent, devising something else. There was nothing to talk about. All that could be said about the life that awaited us, our arrangements and plans, had been said, and what was there more? Now if we had been animals we should have known that speech was unnecessary; but here on the contrary it was necessary to speak, and there was nothing to say, because we were not occupied with what finds vent in speech. And moreover there was that ridiculous custom of giving sweets, of coarse gourmandizing on sweets, and all those abominable preparations for the wedding: remarks about the house, the bedroom, beds, wraps, dressing-gowns, underclothing, costumes. You must remember that if one married according to the injunctions of *Domostróy*, as that old fellow was saying, then the feather-beds, the trousseau, and the bedstead are all but details appropriate to the sacrament. But among us, when of ten who marry there are certainly nine who not only do not believe in the sacrament,[37] but do not even believe that what they are doing entails certain obligations—where scarcely one man out of a hundred has not been married before, and of fifty scarcely one is not preparing in advance to be unfaithful to his wife at every convenient opportunity—when the majority regard the going to church as only a special condition for obtaining possession of a certain woman—think what a dreadful significance all these details acquire. They show that the whole business is only that; they show that it is a kind of sale. An innocent girl is sold to a profligate, and the sale is accompanied by certain formalities.

XI

'That is how everybody marries and that is how I married, and the much vaunted honeymoon began. Why, its very name is vile!' he hissed viciously. 'In Paris I once went to see the sights, and noticing a bearded woman and a water-dog on a sign-board, I entered the show. It turned out to be nothing but a man in a woman's low-necked dress, and a dog done up in walrus skin and swimming in a bath. It was very far from being interesting; but as I was leaving, the showman politely saw me out and, addressing the public at the entrance, pointed to me and said, "Ask the gentleman whether it is not worth seeing! Come in, come in, one franc apiece!" I felt ashamed to say it was not worth seeing, and the showman had probably counted on that. It must be the same with those who have experienced the abomination of a honeymoon and who do not disillusion others. Neither did I disillusion anyone, but I do not now see why I should not tell the truth. Indeed, I think it needful to tell the truth about it. One felt awkward, ashamed, repelled, sorry, and above all dull, intolerably dull! It was something like what I felt when I learnt to smoke—when I felt sick and the saliva gathered in my mouth and I swallowed it and pretended that it was very pleasant. Pleasure from smoking, just as from that, if it comes at all, comes later. The husband must cultivate that vice in his wife in order to derive pleasure from it.'

'Why vice?' I said. 'You are speaking of the most natural human functions.'

'Natural?' he said. 'Natural? No, I may tell you that I have come to the conclusion that it is, on the contrary, *un*-natural. Yes, quite *un*natural. Ask a child, ask an unperverted girl.[38]

'Natural, you say!

'It is natural to eat. And to eat is, from the very beginning, enjoyable, easy, pleasant, and not shameful; but this is horrid, shameful, and painful. No, it is unnatural! And an unspoilt girl, as I have convinced myself, always hates it.' [39]

'But how,' I asked, 'would the human race continue?'

'Yes, would not the human race perish?' he said, irritably and ironically, as if he had expected this familiar and insincere objection. 'Teach abstention from child-bearing so that English lords may always gorge themselves—that is all right. Preach it for the sake of greater pleasure—that is all right; but just hint at abstention from child-bearing in the name of morality—and, my goodness, what a rumpus . . . ! Isn't there a danger that the human race may die out because they want to cease to be swine? But forgive me! This light is unpleasant, may I shade it?' he said, pointing to the lamp. I said I did not mind; and with the haste with which he did everything, he got up on the seat and drew the woollen shade over the lamp.

'All the same,' I said, 'if everyone thought this the right thing to do, the human race would cease to exist.'

He did not reply at once.

'You ask how the human race will continue to exist,' he said, having again sat down in front of me, and spreading his legs far apart he leant his elbows on his knees. 'Why should it continue?'

'Why? If not, we should not exist.'

'And why should we exist?'

'Why? In order to live, of course.'

'But why live? [40] If life has no aim, if life is given us for life's sake, there is no reason for living. And if it is so, then the Schopenhauers, the Hartmanns, and all the Buddhists as well, are quite right. But if life has an aim, it is clear that it ought to come to an end when that aim is reached.

And so it turns out,' he said with noticeable agitation, evidently prizing his thought very highly. 'So it turns out. Just think: if the aim of humanity is goodness, righteousness, love—call it what you will—if it is what the prophets have said, that all mankind should be united together in love, that the spears should be beaten into pruning-hooks and so forth, what is it that hinders the attainment of this aim? The passions hinder it. Of all the passions the strongest, cruellest, and most stubborn is the sex-passion, physical love; and therefore if the passions are destroyed, including the strongest of them—physical love—the prophecies will be fulfilled, mankind will be brought into a unity, the aim of human existence will be attained, and there will be nothing further to live for. As long as mankind exists the ideal is before it, and of course not the rabbits' and pigs' ideal of breeding as fast as possible, nor that of monkeys or Parisians—to enjoy sex-passion in the most refined manner, but the ideal of goodness attained by continence and purity. Towards that people have always striven and still strive. You see what follows.

'It follows that physical love is a safety-valve. If the present generation has not attained its aim, it has not done so because of its passions, of which the sex-passion is the strongest. And if the sex-passion endures there will be a new generation and consequently the possibility of attaining the aim in the next generation. If the next one does not attain it, then the next after that may, and so on, till the aim is attained, the prophecies fulfilled, and mankind attains unity. If not, what would result? If one admits that God created men for the attainment of a certain aim, and created them mortal but sexless, or created them immortal, what would be the result? Why, if they were mortal but without the sex-passion, and died without attaining the aim, God would have had to create new people to attain his aim. If they were immortal, let us grant that (though it would be more difficult for the same people to correct their mistakes and approach perfection than for those of another generation) they might attain that aim after many thousands of years, but then what use would they be afterwards? What could be done with them? It is best as it is. . . . But perhaps you don't like that way of putting it? Perhaps you are an evolutionist? It comes to the same thing. The highest race of animals, the human race, in order to maintain itself in the struggle with other animals

ought to unite into one whole like a swarm of bees, and
not breed continually; it should bring up sexless members
as the bees do; that is, again, it should strive towards continence and not towards inflaming desire—to which the
whole system of our life is now directed.' He paused. 'The
human race will cease? But can anyone doubt it, whatever
his outlook on life may be? Why, it is as certain as death.
According to all the teaching of the Church the end of the
world will come, and according to all the teaching of science the same result is inevitable.

XII [41]

'In our world it is just the reverse: even if a man does
think of continence while he is a bachelor, once married
he is sure to think continence no longer necessary. You
know those wedding tours—the seclusion into which, with
their parents' consent, the young couple go—are nothing
but licensed debauchery. But a moral law avenges itself
when it is violated. Hard as I tried to make a success of my
honeymoon, nothing came of it. It was horrid, shameful,
and dull, the whole time. And very soon I began also to
experience a painful, oppressive feeling. That began very
quickly. I think it was on the third or fourth day that I
found my wife depressed. I began asking her the reason
and embracing her, which in my view was all she could
want, but she removed my arm and began to cry. What
about? She could not say. But she felt sad and distressed.
Probably her exhausted nerves suggested to her the truth
as to the vileness of our relation but she did not know how
to express it. I began to question her, and she said something about feeling sad without her mother. It seemed to
me that this was untrue, and I began comforting her without alluding to her mother. I did not understand that she
was simply depressed and her mother was merely an excuse. But she immediately took offence because I had not
mentioned her mother, as though I did not believe her.
She told me she saw that I did not love her. I reproached
her with being capricious, and suddenly her face changed
entirely and instead of sadness it expressed irritation, and
with the most venomous words she began accusing me of
selfishness and cruelty. I gazed at her. Her whole face
showed complete coldness and hostility, almost hatred. I
remember how horror-struck I was when I saw this. "How?

What?" I thought. "Love is a union of souls—and instead of that there is this! Impossible, this is not she!" I tried to soften her, but encountered such an insuperable wall of cold virulent hostility that before I had time to turn round I too was seized with irritation and we said a great many unpleasant things to one another. The impression of that first quarrel was dreadful. I call it a quarrel, but it was not a quarrel but only the disclosure of the abyss that really existed between us. Amorousness was exhausted by the satisfaction of sensuality and we were left confronting one another in our true relation: that is, as two egotists quite alien to each other who wished to get as much pleasure as possible each from the other. I call what took place between us a quarrel, but it was not a quarrel, only the consequence of the cessation of sensuality—revealing our real relations to one another. I did not understand that this cold and hostile relation was our normal state, I did not understand it because at first this hostile attitude was very soon concealed from us by a renewal of redistilled sensuality, that is by love-making.

'I thought we had quarrelled and made it up again, and that it would not recur. But during that same first month of honeymoon a period of satiety soon returned, we again ceased to need one another, and another quarrel supervened. This second quarrel struck me even more painfully than the first. "So the first one was not an accident but was bound to happen and will happen again," I thought. I was all the more staggered by that second quarrel because it arose from such an impossible pretext. It had something to do with money, which I never grudged and could certainly not have grudged to my wife. I only remember that she gave the matter such a twist that some remark of mine appeared to be an expression of a desire on my part to dominate over her by means of money, to which I was supposed to assert an exclusive right—it was something impossibly stupid, mean, and not natural either to me or to her. I became exasperated, and upbraided her with lack of consideration for me. She accused me of the same thing, and it all began again. In her words and in the expression of her face and eyes I again noticed the cruel cold hostility that had so staggered me before. I had formerly quarrelled with my brother, my friends, and my father, but there had never, I remember, been the special venomous malice which there was here. But after a while this mutual hatred was screened by amorousness, that is sensuality, and I still consoled myself with the thought that these two quarrels had been mistakes and could be remedied. But then a third and a fourth quarrel followed and I realized that it was not accidental, but that it was bound to happen and would happen so, and I was horrified at the prospect before me. At the same time I was tormented by the terrible thought that I alone lived on such bad terms with my wife, so unlike what I had expected, whereas this did not happen between other married couples. I did not know then that it is our common fate, but that everybody imagines, just as I did, that it is their peculiar misfortune, and everyone conceals this exceptional and shameful misfortune not only from others but even from himself and does not acknowledge it to himself.

'It began during the first days and continued all the time, ever increasing and growing more obdurate. In the depths of my soul I felt from the first weeks that I was lost, that things had not turned out as I expected, that marriage was not only no happiness but a very heavy burden; but like everybody else I did not wish to acknowledge this to myself (I should not have acknowledged it even now but for the end that followed) and I concealed it not only from others but from myself too. Now I am astonished that I failed to see my real position. It might have been seen from the fact that the quarrels began on pretexts it was impossible to remember when they were over. Our reason was not quick enough to *devise* sufficient excuses for the animosity that always existed between us.[42] But more striking still was the insufficiency of the excuses for our reconciliations. Sometimes there were words, explanations, even tears, but sometimes . . . oh! it is disgusting even now to think of it—after the most cruel words to one another, came sudden silent glances, smiles, kisses, embraces. . . . Faugh, how horrid! How is it I did not then see all the vileness of it?'

XIII

Two fresh passengers entered and settled down on the farthest seats. He was silent while they were seating themselves but as soon as they had settled down continued, evidently not for a moment losing the thread of his idea.

[43] 'You know, what is vilest about it,' he began, 'is that

in theory love is something ideal and exalted, but in practice it is something abominable, swinish, which it is horrid and shameful to mention or remember. It is not for nothing that nature has made it disgusting and shameful. And if it is disgusting and shameful one must understand that it is so. But here, on the contrary, people pretend that what is disgusting and shameful is beautiful and lofty. What were the first symptoms of my love? Why that I gave way to animal excesses, not only without shame but being somehow even proud of the possibility of these physical excesses, and without in the least considering either her spiritual or even her physical life. I wondered what embittered us against one another, yet it was perfectly simple: that animosity was nothing but the protest of our human nature against the animal nature that overpowered it.

'I was surprised at our enmity to one another; yet it could not have been otherwise. That hatred was nothing but the mutual hatred of accomplices in a crime—both for the incitement to the crime and for the part taken in it. What was it but a crime when she, poor thing, became pregnant in the first month and our *swinish* connexion continued? You think I am straying from my subject? Not at all! I am telling you *how* I killed my wife. They asked me at the trial with what and how I killed her. Fools! They thought I killed her with a knife, on the 5th of October. It was not then I killed her, but much earlier. Just as they are all now killing, all, all. . . .'

'But with what?' I asked.

'That is just what is so surprising, that nobody wants to see what is so clear and evident, what doctors ought to know and preach, but are silent about. Yet the matter is very simple. Men and women are created like the animals so that physical love is followed by pregnancy and then by suckling—conditions under which physical love is bad for the woman and for her child. There are an equal number of men and women. What follows from this? It seems clear, and no great wisdom is needed to draw the conclusion that animals do, namely, the need of continence. But no. Science has been able to discover some kind of leucocytes that run about in the blood, and all sorts of useless nonsense, but cannot understand that. At least one does not hear of science teaching it!

'And so a woman has only two ways out: one is to make a monster of herself, to destroy and go on destroying

within herself to such degree as may be necessary the
capacity of being a woman, that is, a mother, in order that
a man may quietly and continuously get his enjoyment;
the other way out—and it is not even a way out but a
simple, coarse, and direct violation of the laws of nature—
practised in all so-called decent families—is that, contrary
to her nature, the woman must be her husband's mistress
even while she is pregnant or nursing—must be what not
even an animal descends to, and for which her strength is
insufficient. That is what causes nerve troubles and hysteria
in our class, and among the peasants causes what they call
being "possessed by the devil"—epilepsy. You will notice
that no pure maidens are ever "possessed," but only married women living with their husbands. That is so here,
and it is just the same in Europe. All the hospitals for
hysterical women are full of those who have violated nature's law. The epileptics and Charcot's patients are complete wrecks, you know, but the world is full of half-crip-
pled women. Just think of it, what a great work goes on
within a woman when she conceives or when she is nursing
an infant. That is growing which will continue us and replace us. And this sacred work is violated—by what? It is
terrible to think of it! And they prate about the freedom
and the rights of women! It is as if cannibals fattened their
captives to be eaten, and at the same time declared that
they were concerned about their prisoners' rights and
freedom.'

All this was new to me and startled me.

'What is one to do? If that is so,' I said, 'it means that
one may love one's wife once in two years, yet men . . .'

'Men must!' he interrupted me. 'It is again those precious
priests of science who have persuaded everybody of that.[44]
Imbue a man with the idea that he requires vodka, tobacco, or opium, and all these things will be indispensable
to him. It seems that God did not understand what was
necessary and therefore, omitting to consult those wizards,
arranged things badly. You see matters do not tally. They
have decided that it is essential for a man to satisfy his desires, and the bearing and nursing of children comes and
interferes with it and hinders the satisfaction of that need.
What is one to do then? Consult the wizards! They will arrange it. And they have devised something. Oh! when will
those wizards with their deceptions be dethroned? It is
high time! It has come to such a point that people go mad

and shoot themselves and all because of this. How could it be otherwise? The animals seem to know that their progeny continue their race, and they keep to a certain law in this matter. Man alone neither knows it nor wishes to know, but is concerned only to get all the pleasure he can. And who is doing that? The lord of nature—man! Animals, you see, only come together at times when they are capable of producing progeny, but the filthy lord of nature is at it any time if only it pleases him! And as if that were not sufficient, he exalts this apish occupation into the most precious pearl of creation, into love. In the name of this love, that is, this filth, he destroys—what? Why, half the human race! All the women who might help the progress of mankind towards truth and goodness he converts, for the sake of his pleasure, into enemies instead of helpmates. See what it is that everywhere impedes the forward movement of mankind. Women! And why are they what they are? Only because of that. Yes, yes . . .' he repeated several times, and began to move about, and to get out his cigarettes and to smoke, evidently trying to calm himself.

XIV

'I too lived like a pig of that sort,' he continued in his former tone. 'The worst thing about it was that while living that horrid life I imagined that, because I did not go after other women, I was living an honest family life, that I was a moral man and in no way blameworthy, and if quarrels occurred it was her fault and resulted from her character.

'Of course the fault was not hers. She was like everybody else—like the majority of women. She had been brought up as the position of women in our society requires, and as therefore all women of the leisured classes without exception are brought up and cannot help being brought up. People talk about some new kind of education for women. It is all empty words: their education is exactly what it has to be in view of our unfeigned, real, general opinion about women.[45]

'The education of women will always correspond to men's opinion about them. Don't we know how men regard women:[46] *Wein, Weib, und Gesang,* and what the poets say in their verses? Take all poetry, all pictures and sculpture, beginning with love poems[47] and the nude

Venuses and Phrynes, and you will see that woman is an instrument of enjoyment; she is so on the Trubá and the Grachévka, and also at the Court balls. And note the devil's cunning: if they are here for enjoyment and pleasure, let it be known that it is pleasure and that woman is a sweet morsel. But no, first the knights-errant declare that they worship women (worship her, and yet regard her as an instrument of enjoyment), and now people assure us that they respect women. Some give up their places to her, pick up her handkerchief; others acknowledge her right to occupy all positions and to take part in the government, and so on. They do all that, but their outlook on her remains the same. She is a means of enjoyment. Her body is a means of enjoyment. And she knows this. It is just as it is with slavery. Slavery, you know, is nothing else than the exploitation by some of the unwilling labour of many. Therefore to get rid of slavery it is necessary that people should not wish to profit by the forced labour of others and should consider it a sin and a shame. But they go and abolish the external form of slavery and arrange so that one can no longer buy and sell slaves, and they imagine and assure themselves that slavery no longer exists, and do not see or wish to see that it does, because people still want and consider it good and right to exploit the labour of others. And as long as they consider that good, there will always be people stronger or more cunning than others who will succeed in doing it. So it is with the emancipation of woman: the enslavement of woman lies simply in the fact that people desire, and think it good, to avail themselves of her as a tool of enjoyment. Well, and they liberate woman, give her all sorts of rights equal to man, but continue to regard her as an instrument of enjoyment, and so educate her in childhood and afterwards by public opinion. And there she is, still the same humiliated and depraved slave, and the man still a depraved slave-owner.

48 'They emancipate women in universities and in law courts, but continue to regard her as an object of enjoyment. Teach her, as she is taught among us, to regard herself as such, and she will always remain an inferior being. Either with the help of those scoundrels the doctors she will prevent the conception of offspring—that is, will be a complete prostitute, lowering herself not to the level of an animal but to the level of a thing—or she will be what the majority of women are, mentally diseased, hysterical,

unhappy, and lacking capacity for spiritual development. High schools and universities cannot alter that. It can only be changed by a change in men's outlook on women and women's way of regarding themselves. It will change only when woman regards virginity as the highest state, and does not, as at present, consider the highest state of a human being a shame and a disgrace. While that is not so, the ideal of every girl, whatever her education may be, will continue to be to attract as many men as possible, as many males as possible, so as to have the possibility of choosing.

'But the fact that one of them knows more mathematics, and another can play the harp, makes no difference. A woman is happy and attains all she can desire when she has bewitched a man. Therefore the chief aim of a woman is to be able to bewitch him. So it has been and will be. So it is in her maiden life in our society, and so it continues to be in her married life. For a maiden this is necessary in order to have a choice, for the married woman in order to have power over her husband.

'The one thing that stops this or at any rate suppresses it for a time, is children, and then only if the mother is not a monster, that is, if she nurses them herself. But here the doctors again come in.

'My wife, who wanted to nurse, and did nurse the four later children herself, happened to be unwell after the birth of her first child. And those doctors, who cynically undressed her and felt her all over—for which I had to thank them and pay them money—those dear doctors considered that she must not nurse the child; and that first time she was deprived of the only means which might have kept her from coquetry. We engaged a wet nurse, that is, we took advantage of the poverty, the need, and the ignorance of a woman, tempted her away from her own baby to ours, and in return gave her a fine head-dress with gold lace. But that is not the point. The point is that during that time when my wife was free from pregnancy and from suckling, the feminine coquetry which had lain dormant within her manifested itself with particular force. And coinciding with this the torments of jealousy rose up in me with a special force. They tortured me all my married life, as they cannot but torture all husbands who live with their wives as I did with mine, that is, immorally.

XV [49]

'During the whole of my married life I never ceased to be tormented by jealousy, but there were periods when I specially suffered from it. One of these periods was when, after the birth of our first child, the doctors forbade my wife to nurse it. I was particularly jealous at that time, in the first place because my wife was experiencing that unrest natural to a mother which is sure to be aroused when the natural course of life is needlessly violated; and secondly, because seeing how easily she abandoned her moral obligations as a mother, I rightly though unconsciously concluded that it would be equally easy for her to disregard her duty as a wife, especially as she was quite well and in spite of the precious doctors' prohibition was able to nurse her later children admirably.'

'I see you don't like doctors,' I said, noticing a peculiarly malevolent tone in his voice whenever he alluded to them.

'It is not a case of liking or disliking. They have ruined my life as they have ruined and are ruining the lives of thousands and hundreds of thousands of human beings, and I cannot help connecting the effect with the cause. I understand that they want to earn money like lawyers and others, and I would willingly give them half my income, and all who realize what they are doing would willingly give them half of their possessions, if only they would not interfere with our family life and would never come near us. I have not collected evidence, but I know dozens of cases (there are any number of them!) where they have killed a child in its mother's womb asserting that she could not give it birth, though she has had children quite safely later on; or they have killed the mother on the pretext of performing some operation. No one reckons these murders any more than they reckoned the murders of the Inquisition, because it is supposed that it is done for the good of mankind. It is impossible to number all the crimes they commit. But, all those crimes are as nothing compared to the moral corruption of materialism they introduce into the world, especially through women.

'I don't lay stress on the fact that if one is to follow their instructions, then on account of the infection which exists everywhere and in everything, people would not progress towards greater unity but towards separation; for according to their teaching we ought all to sit apart and not remove the carbolic atomizer from our mouths (though now they have discovered that even that is of no avail). But that does not matter either. The principal poison lies in the demoralization of the world, especially of women.

'To-day one can no longer say: "You are not living rightly, live better." One can't say that, either to oneself or to anyone else. If you live a bad life it is caused by the abnormal functioning of your nerves, &c. So you must go to them, and they will prescribe eight penn'orth of medicine from a chemist, which you must take!

'You get still worse: then more medicine and the doctor again. An excellent trick!

'That however is not the point. All I wish to say is that she nursed her babies perfectly well and that only her pregnancy and the nursing of her babies saved me from the torments of jealousy. Had it not been for that it would all have happened sooner. The children saved me and her. In eight years she had five children and nursed all except the first herself.'

'And where are your children now?' I asked.

'The children?' he repeated in a frightened voice.

'Forgive me, perhaps it is painful for you to be reminded of them.'

'No, it does not matter. My wife's sister and brother have taken them. They would not let me have them. I gave them my estate, but they did not give them up to me. You know I am a sort of lunatic. I have left them now and am going away. I have seen them, but they won't let me have them because I might bring them up so that they would not be like their parents, and they have to be just like them. Oh well, what is to be done? Of course they won't let me have them and won't trust me. Besides, I do not know whether I should be able to bring them up. I think not. I am a ruin, a cripple. Still I have one thing in me. I know! Yes, that is true, I know what others are far from knowing.

'Yes, my children are living and growing up just such savages as everybody around them. I saw them, saw them three times. I can do nothing for them, nothing. I am now going to my place in the south. I have a little house and a small garden there.

'Yes, it will be a long time before people learn what I know. How much of iron and other metal there is in the sun and the stars is easy to find out, but anything that exposes our swinishness is difficult, terribly difficult!

'You at least listen to me, and I am grateful for that.

XVI

'You mentioned my children. There again, what terrible lies are told about children! Children a blessing from God, a joy! That is all a lie. It was so once upon a time, but now it is not so at all. Children are a torment and nothing else. Most mothers feel this quite plainly, and sometimes inadvertently say so. Ask most mothers of our propertied classes and they will tell you that they do not want to have children for fear of their falling ill and dying.[50] They don't want to nurse them if they do have them, for fear of becoming too much attached to them and having to suffer. The pleasure a baby gives them by its loveliness, its little hands and feet, and its whole body, is not as great as the suffering caused by the very fear of its possibly falling ill and dying, not to speak of its actual illness or death. After weighing the advantages and disadvantages it seems disadvantageous, and therefore undesirable, to have children. They say this quite frankly and boldly, imagining that these feelings of theirs arise from their love of children, a good and laudable feeling of which they are proud. They do not notice that by this reflection they plainly repudiate love, and only affirm their own selfishness. They get less pleasure from a baby's loveliness than suffering from fear on its account, and therefore the baby they would love is not wanted. They do not sacrifice themselves for a beloved being, but sacrifice a being whom they might love, for their own sakes.

'It is clear that this is not love but selfishness. But one has not the heart to blame them—the mothers in well-to-do families—for that selfishness, when one remembers how dreadfully they suffer on account of their children's health, again thanks to the influence of those same doctors among our well-to-do classes. Even now, when I do but remember my wife's life and the condition she was in during the first years when we had three or four children and she was absorbed in them, I am seized with horror! We led no life at all, but were in a state of constant danger, of escape from it, recurring danger, again followed by a desperate struggle and another escape—always as if we were on a sinking ship. Sometimes it seemed to me that this was done on purpose and that she pretended to be anxious about the children in order to subdue me. It solved all questions in her favour with such tempting simplicity. It sometimes seemed as if all she did and said on these occasions was pretence. But no! She herself suffered terribly, and continually tormented herself about the children and their health and illnesses. It was torture for her and for me too;[51] and it was impossible for her not to suffer. After all, the attachment to her children, the animal need of feeding, caressing, and protecting them, was there as with most women, but there was not the lack of imagination and reason that there is in animals. A hen is not afraid of what may happen to her chick, does not know all the diseases that may befall it, and does not know all those remedies with which people imagine that they can save from illness and death. And for a hen her young are not a source of torment. She does for them what it is natural and pleasurable for her to do; her young ones are a pleasure to her. When a chick falls ill her duties are quite definite: she warms and feeds it. And doing this she knows that she is doing all that is necessary. If her chick dies she does not ask herself why it died, or where it has gone to; she cackles for a while, and then leaves off and goes on living as before. But for our unfortunate women, my wife among them, it was not so. Not to mention illnesses and how to cure them, she was always hearing and reading from all sides endless rules for the rearing and educating of children, which were continually being superseded by others. This is the way to feed a child: feed it in this way, on such a thing; no, not on such a thing, but in this way; clothes, drinks, baths, putting to bed, walking, fresh air,—for all these things we, especially she, heard of new rules every week, just as if children had only begun to be born into the world since yesterday. And if a child that had not been fed or bathed in the right way or at the right time fell ill, it appeared that we were to blame for not having done what we ought.

'That was so while they were well. It was a torment even then. But if one of them happened to fall ill, it was all up: a regular hell! It is supposed that illness can be cured and that there is a science about it, and people—doctors—who know about it. Ah, but not all of them know—only the very best. When a child is ill one must get hold of the very best one, the one who saves, and then the child is saved; but if you don't get that doctor, or if you don't live in the place where that doctor lives, the child is lost. This was not a creed peculiar to her, it is the creed of all the women of our class, and she heard nothing else from all sides. Catherine Semënovna lost two children because Iván Zakhárych was not called in in time, but Iván Zakhárych saved Mary Ivánovna's eldest girl, and the Petróvs moved in time to various hotels by the doctor's advice, and the children remained alive; but if they had not been segregated the children would have died.[52] Another who had a delicate child moved south by the doctor's advice and saved the child. How can she help being tortured and agitated all the time, when the lives of the children for whom she has an animal attachment depend on her finding out in time what Iván Zakhárych will say! But what Iván Zakhárych will say nobody knows, and he himself least of all, for he is well aware that he knows nothing and therefore cannot be of any use, but just shuffles about at random so that people should not cease to believe that he knows something or other. You see, had she been wholly an animal she would not have suffered so, and if she had been quite a human being she would have had faith in God and would have said and thought, as a believer does: "The Lord gave and the Lord hath taken away. One can't escape from God."

'Our whole life with the children, for my wife and consequently for me, was not a joy but a torment. How could she help torturing herself? She tortured herself incessantly. Sometimes when we had just made peace after some scene of jealousy, or simply after a quarrel, and thought we should be able to live, to read, and to think a little, we had no sooner settled down to some occupation than the news came that Vásya was being sick, or Másha showed symptoms of dysentery, or Andrúsha had a rash, and there was an end to peace, it was not life any more. Where was one to drive to? For what doctor? How isolate the child? And then it's a case of enemas, temperatures, medicines, and doctors. Hardly is that over before something else begins. We had no regular settled family life but only, as I have already said, continual escapes from imaginary and real dangers. It is like that in most families nowadays, you know, but in my family it was especially acute. My wife was a child-loving and a credulous woman.

'So the presence of children not only failed to improve our life but poisoned it. Besides, the children were a new cause of dissension. As soon as we had children they became the means and the object of our discord, and more often the older they grew. They were not only the object of discord but the weapons of our strife. We used our children, as it were, to fight one another with. Each of us had a favourite weapon among them for our strife. I used to fight her chiefly through Vásya, the eldest boy, and she me through Lisa. Besides that, as they grew older and their characters became defined, it came about that they grew into allies whom each of us tried to draw to his or her side. They, poor things, suffered terribly from this, but we, with our incessant warfare, had no time to think of that. The girl was my ally, and the eldest boy, who resembled his mother and was her favourite, was often hateful to me.

XVII

'Well, and so we lived.[53] Our relations to one another grew more and more hostile and at last reached a stage where it was not disagreement that caused hostility but hostility that caused disagreement. Whatever she might say I disagreed with beforehand, and it was just the same with her.

'In the fourth year we both, it seemed, came to the conclusion that we could not understand one another. We no longer tried to bring any dispute to a conclusion. We invariably kept to our own opinions even about the most trivial questions,[54] but especially about the children. As I now recall them the views I maintained were not at all so dear to me that I could not have given them up; but she was of the opposite opinion and to yield meant yielding to her, and that I could not do. It was the same with her. She probably considered herself quite in the right towards me, and as for me I always thought myself a saint towards her. When we were alone together we were doomed almost to silence, or to conversations such as I am convinced animals can carry on with one another: "What is the time? Time to go to bed. What is to-day's dinner? Where shall we go? What is there in the papers? Send for the doctor; Másha has a sore throat." We only needed to go a hairbreadth beyond this impossibly limited circle of conversation for irritation to flare up.[55] We had collisions and acrimonious words about the coffee, a tablecloth, a trap, a lead at bridge, all of them things that could not be of any importance to either of us. In me at any rate there often raged a terrible hatred of her. Sometimes I watched her pouring out tea, swinging her leg, lifting a spoon to her mouth, smacking her lips and drawing in some liquid, and I hated her for these things as though they were the worst possible actions. I did not then notice that the periods of anger corresponded quite regularly and exactly to the periods of what we called love. A period of love—then a period of animosity; an energetic period of love, then a long period of animosity; a weaker manifestation of love, and a shorter period of animosity. We did not then understand that this love and animosity were one and the same animal feeling only at opposite poles. To live like that would have been awful had we understood our position; but we neither understood nor saw it. Both salvation and punishment for man lie in the fact that if he lives wrongly he can befog himself so as not to see the misery of his position. And this we did. She tried to forget herself in intense and always hurried occupation with household affairs, busying herself with the arrangements of the house, her own and the children's clothes, their lessons, and their health;[56] while I had my own occupations: wine, my office duties, shooting, and cards. We were both continually occupied, and we both felt that the busier we were the nastier we might be to each other. "It's all very well for you to grimace," I thought, "but you have harassed me all night with your scenes, and I have a meeting on." "It's all very well for you," she not only thought but said, "but I have been awake all night with the baby." Those new theories of hypnotism, psychic diseases, and hysterics are not a simple folly, but a dangerous and repulsive one. Charcot would certainly have said that my wife was hysterical, and that I was abnormal, and he would no doubt have tried to cure me. But there was nothing to cure.[57]

'Thus we lived in a perpetual fog, not seeing the condition we were in. And if what did happen had not happened, I should have gone on living so to old age and should have thought, when dying, that I had led a good life. I should not have realized the abyss of misery and the horrible falsehood in which I wallowed.

'We were like two convicts hating each other and

chained together, poisoning óne another's lives and trying not to see it. I did not then know that ninety-nine per cent. of married people live in a similar hell to the one I was in and that it cannot be otherwise. I did not then know this either about others or about myself.

'It is strange what coincidences there are in regular, or even in irregular, lives! Just when the parents find life together unendurable, it becomes necessary to move to town for the children's education.'

He stopped, and once or twice gave vent to his strange sounds, which were now quite like suppressed sobs. We were approaching a station.

'What is the time?' he asked.

I looked at my watch. It was two o'clock.

'You are not tired?' he asked.

'No, but you are?'

'I am suffocating. Excuse me, I will walk up and down and drink some water.'

He went unsteadily through the carriage. I remained alone thinking over what he had said, and I was so engrossed in thought that I did not notice when he re-entered by the door at the other end of the carriage.

XVIII

'Yes, I keep diverging,' he began. 'I have thought much over it. I now see many things differently and I want to express it.

'Well, so we lived in town.[58] In town a man can live for a hundred years without noticing that he has long been dead and has rotted away. He has no time to take account of himself, he is always occupied. Business affairs, social intercourse, health, art, the children's health and their education. Now one has to receive so-and-so and so-and-so, go to see so-and-so and so-and-so; now one has to go and look at this, and hear this man or that woman. In town, you know, there are at any given moment one or two, or even three, celebrities whom one must on no account miss seeing. Then one has to undergo a treatment oneself or get some-one else attended to, then there are teachers, tutors, and governesses, but one's own life is quite empty. Well, so we lived and felt less the painfulness of living together. Besides at first we had splendid occupations, arranging things in a new place, in new quarters; and we were also occupied in going from the town to the country and back to town again.

'We lived so through one winter, and the next there occurred, unnoticed by anyone, an apparently unimportant thing, but the cause of all that happened later.

'She was not well and the doctors told her not to have children, and taught her how to avoid it. To me it was disgusting. I struggled against it, but she with frivolous obstinacy insisted on having her own way and I submitted. The last excuse for our swinish life—children—was then taken away, and life became viler than ever.

'To a peasant, a labouring man, children are necessary; though it is hard for him to feed them, still he needs them, and therefore his marital relations have a justification. But to us who have children, more children are unnecessary; they are an additional care and expense, a further division of property, and a burden. So our swinish life has no justification. We either artificially deprive ourselves of children or regard them as a misfortune, the consequences of carelessness, and that is still worse.

'We have no justification. But we have fallen morally so low that we do not even feel the need of any justification.

'The majority of the present educated world devote themselves to this kind of debauchery without the least qualm of conscience.

'There is indeed nothing that can feel qualms, for conscience in our society is non-existent, unless one can call public opinion and the criminal law a "conscience." In this case neither the one nor the other is infringed: there is no reason to be ashamed of public opinion for everybody acts in the same way—Mary Pávlovna, Iván Zakhárych, and the rest. Why breed paupers or deprive oneself of the possibility of social life? There is no need to fear or be ashamed in face of the criminal law either. Those shameless hussies, or soldiers' wives, throw their babies into ponds or wells, and they of course must be put into prison, but we do it all at the proper time and in a clean way.

'We lived like that for another two years. The means employed by those scoundrel-doctors evidently began to bear fruit; she became physically stouter and handsomer, like the late beauty of summer's end. She felt this and paid attention to her appearance. She developed a provocative kind of beauty which made people restless. She was in the full vigour of a well-fed and excited woman of thirty who is not bearing children. Her appearance disturbed people. When she passed men she attracted their notice. She was like a fresh, well-fed, harnessed horse, whose bridle has been removed. There was no bridle, as is the case with ninety-nine hundredths of our women. And I felt this— and was frightened.'

XIX

He suddenly rose and sat down close to the window.

'Pardon me,' he muttered and, with his eyes fixed on the window, he remained silent for about three minutes. Then he sighed deeply and moved back to the seat opposite mine. His face was quite changed, his eyes looked pathetic, and his lips puckered strangely, almost as if he were smiling. 'I am rather tired but I will go on with it. We have still plenty of time, it is not dawn yet. Ah, yes,' he began after lighting a cigarette, 'she grew plumper after she stopped having babies, and her malady—that everlasting worry about the children—began to pass . . . at least not actually to pass, but she as it were woke up from an intoxication, came to herself, and saw that there was a whole divine world with its joys which she had forgotten, but a divine world she did not know how to live in and did not at all understand. "I must not miss it! Time is passing and won't come back!" So, I imagine, she thought, or rather felt, nor could she have thought or felt differently: she had been brought up in the belief that there was only one thing in the world worthy of attention—love. She had married and received something of that love, but not nearly what had been promised and was expected. Even that had been accompanied by many disappointments and sufferings, and then this unexpected torment: so many children! The torments exhausted her. And then, thanks to the obliging doctors, she learnt that it is possible to avoid having children. She was very glad, tried it, and became alive again for the one thing she knew—for love. But love with a husband, befouled by jealousy and all kinds of anger, was no longer the thing she wanted. She had visions of some other, clean, new love; at least I thought she had. And she began to look about her as if expecting something. I saw this and could not help feeling

anxious. It happened again and again that while talking to
me, as usual through other people—that is, telling a third
person what she meant for me—she boldly, without remembering that she had expressed the opposite opinion
an hour before, declared, though half-jokingly, that a
mother's cares are a fraud, and that it is not worth while
to devote one's life to children when one is young and can
enjoy life. She gave less attention to the children, and less
frenziedly than before, but gave more and more attention
to herself, to her appearance (though she tried to conceal
this), and to her pleasures, even to her accomplishments.
She again enthusiastically took to the piano which she had
quite abandoned, and it all began from that.'

He turned his weary eyes to the window again but,
evidently making an effort, immediately continued once
more.

'Yes, that man made his appearance . . .' he became
confused and once or twice made that peculiar sound with
his nose.

I could see that it was painful for him to name that man,
to recall him, or speak about him. But he made an effort
and, as if he had broken the obstacle that hindered him,
continued resolutely.

'He was a worthless man in my opinion and according
to my estimate. And not because of the significance he
acquired in my life but because he really was so. However,
the fact that he was a poor sort of fellow only served to
show how irresponsible she was. If it had not been he then
it would have been another. It had to be!'

Again he paused. 'Yes, he was a musician, a violinist;
not a professional, but a semi-professional semi-society
man.

'His father, a landowner, was a neighbour of my
father's. He had been ruined, and his children—there were
three boys—had obtained settled positions; only this one,
the youngest, had been handed over to his godmother in
Paris. There he was sent to the *Conservatoire* because he
had a talent for music, and he came out as a violinist and
played at concerts. He was a man . . .' Having evidently
intended to say something bad about him, Pózdnyshev restrained himself and rapidly said: 'Well, I don't really
know how he lived, I only know that he returned to Russia
that year and appeared in my house.

'With moist almond-shaped eyes, red smiling lips, a

small waxed moustache, hair done in the latest fashion, and an insipidly pretty face, he was what women call "not bad looking." His figure was weak though not misshapen, and he had a specially developed posterior, like a woman's, or such as Hottentots are said to have. They too are reported to be musical. Pushing himself as far as possible into familiarity, but sensitive and always ready to yield at the slightest resistance, he maintained his dignity in externals, wore buttoned boots of a special Parisian fashion, bright-coloured ties, and other things foreigners acquire in Paris, which by their noticeable novelty always attract women. There was an affected external gaiety in his manner. That manner, you know, of speaking about everything in allusions and unfinished sentences, as if you knew it all, remembered it, and could complete it yourself.

'It was he with his music who was the cause of it all. You know at the trial the case was put as if it was all caused by jealousy. No such thing; that is, I don't mean "no such thing," it was and yet it was not. At the trial it was decided that I was a wronged husband and that I had killed her while defending my outraged honour (that is the phrase they employ, you know). That is why I was acquitted. I tried to explain matters at the trial but they took it that I was trying to rehabilitate my wife's honour.

'What my wife's relations with that musician may have been has no meaning for me, or for her either. What has a meaning is what I have told you about—my swinishness. The whole thing was an outcome of the terrible abyss between us of which I have told you—that dreadful tension of mutual hatred which made the first excuse sufficient to produce a crisis. The quarrels between us had for some time past become frightful, and were all the more startling because they alternated with similarly intense animal passion.

'If he had not appeared there would have been someone else. If the occasion had not been jealousy it would have been something else. I maintain that all husbands who live as I did, must either live dissolutely, separate, or kill themselves or their wives as I have done. If there is anybody who has not done so, he is a rare exception. Before I ended as I did, I had several times been on the verge of suicide, and she too had repeatedly tried to poison herself.

XX

'Well, that is how things were going not long before it happened. We seemed to be living in a state of truce and had no reason to infringe it. Then we chanced to speak about a dog which I said had been awarded a medal at an exhibition. She remarked, "Not a medal, but an honourable mention." A dispute ensues. We jump from one subject to another, reproach one another, "Oh, that's nothing new, it's always been like that." "You said . . ." "No, I didn't say so." "Then I am telling lies! . . ." You feel that at any moment that dreadful quarrelling which makes you wish to kill yourself or her will begin. You know it will begin immediately, and fear it like fire and therefore wish to restrain yourself, but your whole being is seized with fury. She being in the same or even a worse condition purposely misinterprets every word you say, giving it a wrong meaning. Her every word is venomous; where she alone knows that I am most sensitive, she stabs. It gets worse and worse. I shout: "Be quiet!" or something of that kind.

'She rushes out of the room and into the nursery. I try to hold her back in order to finish what I was saying, to prove my point, and I seize her by the arm. She pretends that I have hurt her and screams: "Children, your father is striking me!" I shout: "Don't lie!" "But it's not the first time!" she screams, or something like that. The children rush to her. She calms them down. I say, "Don't sham!" She says, "Everything is sham in your eyes, you would kill any one and say they were shamming. Now I have understood you. That's just what you want!" "Oh, I wish you were dead as a dog!" I shout. I remember how those dreadful words horrified me. I never thought I could utter such dreadful, coarse words, and am surprised that they escaped me. I shout them and rush away into my study and sit down and smoke. I hear her go out into the hall preparing to go away. I ask, "Where are you going to?" She does not reply. "Well, devil take her," I say to myself, and go back to my study and lie down and smoke. A thousand different plans of how to revenge myself on her and get rid of her, and how to improve matters and go on as if nothing had happened, come into my head. I think all that and go on smoking and smoking. I think of

running away from her, hiding myself, going to America.
I get as far as dreaming of how I shall get rid of her, how
splendid that will be, and how I shall unite with another,
an admirable woman—quite different. I shall get rid of
her either by her dying or by a divorce, and I plan how
it is to be done. I notice that I am getting confused and
not thinking of what is necessary, and to prevent myself
from perceiving that my thoughts are not to the point I
go on smoking.

'Life in the house goes on. The governess comes in and
asks: "Where is madame? When will she be back?" The
footman asks whether he is to serve tea. I go to the dining-
room. The children, especially Lisa who already understands, gaze inquiringly and disapprovingly at me. We
drink tea in silence. She has still not come back. The
evening passes, she has not returned, and two different
feelings alternate within me. Anger because she torments
me and all the children by her absence which will end
by her returning; and fear that she will not return but
will do something to herself. I would go to fetch her, but
where am I to look for her? At her sister's? But it would
be so stupid to go and ask. And it's all the better: if she
is bent on tormenting someone, let her torment herself.
Besides, that is what she is waiting for; and next time it
would be worse still. But suppose she is not with her
sister but is doing something to herself, or has already done
it! It's past ten, past eleven! I don't go to the bedroom—it
would be stupid to lie there alone waiting—but I'll not lie
down here either. I wish to occupy my mind, to write a
letter or to read, but I can't do anything. I sit alone in my
study, tortured, angry, and listening. It's three o'clock,
four o'clock, and she is not back. Towards morning I fall
asleep. I wake up, she has still not come!

'Everything in the house goes on in the usual way, but
all are perplexed and look at me inquiringly and reproachfully, considering me to be the cause of it all. And in me
the same struggle still continues: anger that she is torturing
me, and anxiety for her.

'At about eleven in the morning her sister arrives as her
envoy. And the usual talk begins. "She is in a terrible state.
What does it all mean?" "After all, nothing has happened."
I speak of her impossible character and say that I have not
done anything.

' "But, you know, it can't go on like this," says her sister.

' "It's all her doing and not mine," I say. "I won't take the first step.[59] If it means separation, let it be separation."

'My sister-in-law goes away having achieved nothing. I had boldly said that I would not take the first step; but after her departure, when I came out of my study and saw the children piteous and frightened, I was prepared to take the first step. I should be glad to do it, but[60] I don't know how. Again I pace up and down and smoke; at lunch I drink vodka and wine and attain what I unconsciously desire—I no longer see the stupidity and humiliation of my position.

'At about three she comes. When she meets me she does not speak. I imagine that she has submitted, and begin to say that I had been provoked by her reproaches. She, with the same stern expression on her terribly harassed face, says that she has not come for explanations but to fetch the children, because we cannot live together. I begin telling her that the fault is not mine and that she provoked me beyond endurance. She looks severely and solemnly at me and says: "Do not say any more, you will repent it." I tell her that I cannot stand comedies. Then she cries out something I don't catch, and rushes into her room. The key clicks behind her—she has locked herself in. I try the door, but getting no answer, go away angrily. Half-an-hour later Lisa runs in crying. "What is it? Has anything happened?" "We can't hear mama." We go. I pull at the double doors with all my might. The bolt had not been firmly secured, and the two halves both open. I approach the bed, on which she is lying awkwardly in her petticoats and with a pair of high boots on. An empty opium bottle is on the table. She is brought to herself. Tears follow, and a reconciliation. No, not a reconciliation: in the heart of each there is still the old animosity, with the additional irritation produced by the pain of this quarrel which each attributes to the other. But one must of course finish it all somehow, and life goes on in the old way. And so the same kind of quarrel, and even worse ones, occurred continually: once a week, once a month, or at times every day. It was always the same. Once I had already procured a passport to go abroad—the quarrel had continued for two days. But there was again a partial explanation, a partial reconciliation, and I did not go.

XXI

'So those were our relations when that man appeared.
He arrived in Moscow—his name is Trukhachévski—and
came to my house. It was in the morning. I received him.
We had once been on familiar terms and he tried to
maintain a familiar tone by using non-committal expressions, but I definitely adopted a conventional tone and he
at once submitted to it. I disliked him from the first
glance.[61] But curiously enough a strange and fatal force
led me not to repulse him, not to keep him away, but
on the contrary to invite him to the house. After all, what
could have been simpler than to converse with him coldly,
and say good-bye without introducing him to my wife?
But no, as if purposely, I began talking about his playing,
and said I had been told he had given up the violin. He
replied that, on the contrary, he now played more than
ever. He referred to the fact that there had been a time
when I myself played. I said I had given it up but that
my wife played well. It is an astonishing thing[62] that
from the first day, from the first hour of my meeting him,
my relations with him were such as they might have been
only after all that subsequently happened.[63] There was
something strained in them: I noticed every word, every
expression he or I used, and attributed importance to them.

'I introduced him to my wife. The conversation immediately turned to music, and he offered to be of use
to her by playing with her. My wife was, as usual of late,
very elegant, attractive, and disquietingly beautiful. He
evidently pleased her at first sight. Besides she was glad
that she would have someone to accompany her on a violin,
which she was so fond of that she used to engage a violinist
from the theatre for the purpose; and her face reflected
her pleasure. But catching sight of me she at once understood my feeling and changed her expression, and a game
of mutual deception began. I smiled pleasantly to appear
as if I liked it. He, looking at my wife as all immoral men
look at pretty women, pretended that he was only interested in the subject of the conversation—which no longer
interested him at all; while she tried to seem indifferent,
though my false smile of jealousy with which she was
familiar, and his lustful gaze, evidently excited her. I
saw that from their first encounter her eyes were particu-

larly bright and, probably as a result of my jealousy, it seemed as if an electric current had been established between them, evoking as it were an identity of expressions, looks, and smiles. She blushed and he blushed. She smiled and he smiled. We spoke about music, Paris, and all sorts of trifles. Then he rose to go, and stood smilingly, holding his hat against his twitching thigh and looking now at her and now at me, as if in expectation of what we would do. I remember that instant just because at that moment I might not have invited him, and then nothing would have happened. But I glanced at him and at her and said silently to myself, "Don't suppose that I am jealous," "or that I am afraid of you," I added mentally addressing him, and I invited him to come some evening and bring his violin to play with my wife. She glanced at me with surprise, flushed, and as if frightened began to decline, saying that she did not play well enough. This refusal irritated me still more, and I insisted the more on his coming. I remember the curious feeling with which I looked at the back of his head, with the black hair parted in the middle contrasting with the white nape of his neck, as he went out with his peculiar springing gait suggestive of some kind of a bird. I could not conceal from myself that that man's presence tormented me. "It depends on me," I reflected, "to act so as to see nothing more of him. But that would be to admit that I am afraid of him. No, I am not afraid of him; it would be too humiliating," I said to myself. And there in the ante-room, knowing that my wife heard me, I insisted that he should come that evening with his violin. He promised to do so, and left.

'In the evening he brought his violin and they played. But it took a long time to arrange matters—they had not the music they wanted, and my wife could not without preparation play what they had. I was very fond of music and sympathized with their playing, arranging a music-stand for him and turning over the pages. They played a few things, some songs without words, and a little sonata by Mozart. They played splendidly,[64] and he had an exceptionally fine tone. Besides that, he had a refined and elevated taste not at all in correspondence with his character.

'He was of course a much better player than my wife, and he helped her, while at the same time politely praising her playing. He behaved himself very well. My wife seemed interested only in music and was very simple and

natural.[65] But though I pretended to be interested in the
music I was tormented by jealousy all the evening.

'From the first moment his eyes met my wife's I saw
that the animal in each of them, regardless of all conditions of their position and of society, asked, "May I?"
and answered, "Oh, yes, certainly." I saw that he had not
at all expected to find my wife, a Moscow lady, so attractive, and that he was very pleased. For he had no doubt
whatever that she was *willing*. The only crux was whether
that unendurable husband could hinder them. Had I been
pure I should not have understood this, but, like the
majority of men, I had myself regarded women in that
way before I married and therefore could read his mind like
a manuscript. I was particularly tormented because I saw
without doubt that she had no other feeling towards me
than a continual irritation only occasionally interrupted
by the habitual sensuality; but that this man—by his
external refinement and novelty and still more by his
undoubtedly great talent for music, by the nearness that
comes of playing together, and by the influence music,
especially the violin, exercises on impressionable natures—
was sure not only to please but certainly and without the
least hesitation to conquer, crush, bind her, twist her
round his little finger and do whatever he liked with her.
I could not help seeing this and I suffered terribly. But
for all that, or perhaps on account of it, some force obliged
me against my will to be not merely polite but amiable to
him. Whether I did it for my wife or for him, to show
that I was not afraid of him, or whether I did it to deceive
myself—I don't know, but I know that from the first I
could not behave naturally with him. In order not to yield
to my wish to kill him there and then, I had to make
much of him. I gave him expensive wines at supper, went
into raptures over his playing, spoke to him with a particularly amiable smile, and invited him to dine and play
with my wife again the next Sunday. I told him I would
ask a few friends who were fond of music to hear him.
And so it ended.'

Greatly agitated, Pózdnyshev changed his position and
emitted his peculiar sound.

'It is strange how the presence of that man acted on me,'
he began again, with an evident effort to keep calm. 'I
come home from the Exhibition a day or two later, enter

the ante-room, and suddenly feel something heavy, as if a stone had fallen on my heart, and I cannot understand what it is. It was that passing through the ante-room I noticed something which reminded me of him. I realized what it was only in my study, and went back to the ante-room to make sure. Yes, I was not mistaken, there was his overcoat. A fashionable coat, you know. (Though I did not realize it, I observed everything connected with him with extraordinary attention.) I inquire: sure enough he is there. I pass on to the dancing-room, not through the drawing-room but through the schoolroom. My daughter, Lisa, sits reading a book and the nurse sits with the youngest boy at the table, making a lid of some kind spin round. The door to the dancing-room is shut but I hear the sound of a rhythmic arpeggio and his[66] and her voices. I listen, but cannot make out anything.

'Evidently the sound of the piano is purposely made to drown the sound of their voices, their kisses . . . perhaps. My God! What was aroused in me! Even to think of the beast that then lived in me fills me with horror! My heart suddenly contracted, stopped, and then began to beat like a hammer. My chief feeling, as usual whenever I was enraged, was one of self-pity. "In the presence of the children! of their nurse!" [67] thought I. Probably I looked awful, for Lisa gazed at me with strange eyes. "What am I to do?" I asked myself. "Go in? I can't: heaven only knows what I should do. But neither can I go away." The nurse looked at me as if she understood my position.[68] "But it is impossible not to go in," I said to myself, and I quickly opened the door. He was sitting at the piano playing those arpeggios with his large white upturned fingers. She was standing in the curve of the piano, bending over some open music. She was the first to see or hear, and glanced at me. Whether she was frightened and pretended not to be, or whether she was really not frightened, anyway she did not start or move but only blushed, and that not at once.

' "How glad I am that you have come: we have not decided what to play on Sunday," she said in a tone she would not have used to me had we been alone. This and her using the word "we" of herself and him, filled me with indignation. I greeted him silently.

He pressed my hand, and at once, with a smile which

I thought distinctly ironic, began to explain that he had brought some music to practise for Sunday, but that they disagreed about what to play: a classical but more difficult piece, namely Beethoven's sonata for the violin, or a few little pieces. It was all so simple and natural that there was nothing one could cavil at, yet I felt certain that it was all untrue and that they had agreed how to deceive me.

'One of the most distressing conditions of life for a jealous man (and everyone is jealous in our world) are certain society conventions which allow a man and woman the greatest and most dangerous proximity. You would become a laughing-stock to others if you tried to prevent such nearness at balls, or the nearness of doctors to their women-patients, or of people occupied with art, sculpture, and especially music. A couple are occupied with the noblest of arts, music; this demands a certain nearness, and there is nothing reprehensible in that and only a stupid jealous husband can see anything undesirable in it.[69] Yet everybody knows that it is by means of those very pursuits, especially of music, that the greater part of the adulteries in our society occur. I evidently confused them by the confusion I betrayed: for a long time I could not speak. I was like a bottle held upside down from which the water does not flow because it is too full. I wanted to abuse him and to turn him out, but again felt that I must treat him courteously and amiably. And I did so. I acted as though I approved of it all, and again because of the strange feeling which made me behave to him the more amiably the more his presence distressed me, I told him that I trusted his taste and advised her to do the same. He stayed as long as was necessary to efface the unpleasant impression caused by my sudden entrance— looking frightened and remaining silent—and then left, pretending that it was now decided what to play next day. I was however fully convinced that compared to what interested them the question of what to play was quite indifferent.

'I saw him out to the ante-room with special politeness. (How could one do less than accompany a man who had come to disturb the peace and destroy the happiness of a whole family?) And I pressed his soft white hand with particular warmth.

XXII

'I did not speak to her all that day—I could not. Nearness to her aroused in me such hatred of her that I was afraid of myself. At dinner in the presence of the children she asked me when I was going away. I had to go next week to the District Meetings of the Zémstvo. I told her the date. She asked whether I did not want anything for the journey. I did not answer but sat silent at table and then went in silence to my study. Latterly she used never to come to my room, especially not at that time of day. I lay in my study filled with anger. Suddenly I heard her familiar step, and the terrible, monstrous idea entered my head that she, like Uriah's wife, wished to conceal the sin she had already committed and that that was why she was coming to me at such an unusual time. "Can she be coming to me?" thought I, listening to her approaching footsteps. "If she is coming here, then I am right," and an inexpressible hatred of her took possession of me. Nearer and nearer came the steps. Is it possible that she won't pass on to the dancing-room? No, the door creaks and in the doorway appears her tall [70] handsome figure, on her face and in her eyes a timid ingratiating look which she tries to hide, but which I see and the meaning of which I know. I almost choked, so long did I hold my breath, and still looking at her I grasped my cigarette-case and began to smoke.

'"Now how can you? One comes to sit with you for a bit, and you begin smoking"—and she sat down close to me on the sofa, leaning against me. I moved away so as not to touch her.

'"I see you are dissatisfied at my wanting to play on Sunday," she said.

'"I am not at all dissatisfied," I said.

'"As if I don't see!"

'"Well, I congratulate you on seeing. But I only see that you behave like a coquette. . . . You always find pleasure in all kinds of vileness, but to me it is terrible!"

'"Oh, well, if you are going to scold like a cabman I'll go away."

'"Do, but remember that if you don't value the family honour, I value not you (devil take you) but the honour of the family!"

' "But what is the matter? What?"

' "Go away, for God's sake be off!"

'Whether she pretended not to understand what it was about or really did not understand, at any rate she took offence, grew angry, and did not go away but stood in the middle of the room.

' "You have really become impossible," she began.[71] "You have a character that even an angel could not put up with." And as usual trying to sting me as painfully as possible, she reminded me of my conduct to my sister (an incident when, being exasperated, I said rude things to my sister); she knew I was distressed about it and she stung me just on that spot. "After that, nothing from you will surprise me," she said.

' "Yes! Insult me, humiliate me, disgrace me, and then put the blame on me," I said to myself, and suddenly I was seized by such terrible rage as I had never before experienced.

'For the first time I wished to give physical expression to that rage. I jumped up and went towards her; but just as I jumped up I remembered becoming conscious of my rage and asking myself: "Is it right to give way to this feeling?" and at once I answered that it was right, that it would frighten her, and instead of restraining my fury I immediately began inflaming it still further, and was glad it burnt yet more fiercely within me.

' "Be off, or I'll kill you!" I shouted,[72] going up to her and seizing her by the arm. I consciously intensified the anger in my voice as I said this. And I suppose I was terrible, for she was so frightened that she had not even the strength to go away, but only said: "Vásya, what is it? What is the matter with you?"

' "Go!" I roared louder still.[73] "No one but you can drive me to fury. I do not answer for myself!"

'Having given reins to my rage, I revelled in it and wished to do something still more unusual to show the extreme degree of my anger. I felt a terrible desire to beat her, to kill her, but knew that this would not do, and so[74] to give vent to my fury I seized a paper-weight from my table, again shouting "Go!" and hurled it to the floor near her. I aimed it very exactly past her. Then she left the room, but stopped at the doorway, and immediately, while she still saw it (I did it so that she might see), I began snatching things from the table—candlesticks and ink-stand—and hurling them on the floor still shouting "Go! Get out! I don't answer for myself!" She went away—and I immediately stopped.

'An hour later the nurse came to tell me that my wife was in hysterics. I went to her; she sobbed, laughed, could not speak, and her whole body was convulsed. She was not pretending, but was really ill.[75]

'Towards morning she grew quiet, and we made peace under the influence of the feeling we called love.

'In the morning when, after our reconciliation, I confessed to her that I was jealous of Trukhachévski, she was not at all confused, but laughed most naturally; so strange did the very possibility of an infatuation for such a man seem to her, she said.

' "Could a decent woman have any other feeling for such a man than the pleasure of his music? Why, if you like I am ready never to see him again . . . not even on Sunday, though everybody has been invited. Write and tell him that I am ill, and there's an end of it! Only it is unpleasant that anyone, especially he himself, should imagine that he is dangerous. I am too proud to allow anyone to think that of me!"

'And you know, she was not lying, she believed what she was saying; she hoped by those words to evoke in herself contempt for him and so to defend herself from him, but she did not succeed in doing so. Everything was against her, especially that accursed music. So it all ended, and on the Sunday the guests assembled and they again played together.

XXIII

'I suppose it is hardly necessary to say that I was very vain: if one is not vain there is nothing to live for in our usual way of life. So on that Sunday I arranged the dinner and the musical evening with much care. I bought the provisions myself and invited the guests.

'Towards six the visitors assembled. He came in evening dress with diamond studs that showed bad taste. He behaved in a free and easy manner, answered everything hurriedly with a smile of agreement and understanding, you know, with that peculiar expression which seems to say that all you may do or say is just what he expected. Everything that was not in good taste about him I noticed with particular pleasure, because it ought all to have had the effect of tranquillizing me and showing that he was so far beneath my wife that, as she had said, she could not lower herself to his level. I did not now allow myself to be jealous.[76] In the first place I had worried through that torment and needed rest, and secondly I wanted to believe my wife's assurances and did believe them. But though I was not jealous I was nevertheless not natural with either of them, and at dinner and during the first half of the evening before the music began I still followed their movements and looks.

'The dinner was, as dinners are, dull and pretentious. The music began pretty early.[77] Oh, how I remember every detail of that evening! I remember how he brought in his violin, unlocked the case, took off the cover a lady had embroidered for him, drew out the violin, and began tuning it. I remember how my wife sat down at the piano with pretended unconcern, under which I saw that she was trying to conceal great timidity—chiefly as to her own ability—and then the usual A on the piano began, the pizzicato of the violin, and the arrangement of the music. Then I remember how they glanced at one another, turned to look at the audience who were seating themselves, said something to one another, and began. He took the first chords. His face grew serious, stern, and sympathetic, and listening to the sounds he produced, he touched the strings with careful fingers. The piano answered him. The music began. . . .'

Pózdnyshev paused and produced his strange sound several times in succession. He tried to speak, but sniffed, and stopped.

'They played Beethoven's Kreutzer Sonata,' he continued. 'Do you know the first presto? You do?' he cried.[78] 'Ugh! Ugh! It is a terrible thing, that sonata. And especially that part. And in general music is a dreadful thing! What is it? I don't understand it. What is music? What does it do? And why does it do what it does? They say music exalts the soul. Nonsense, it is not true! It has an effect, an awful effect—I am speaking of myself—but not of an exalting kind. It has neither an exalting nor a debasing effect but it produces agitation. How can I put it? Music makes me forget myself, my real position; it transports me to some other position not my own. Under the influence of music it seems to me that I feel what I do not really feel, that I understand what I do not understand, that I can do what I cannot do. I explain it by the fact that music acts like yawning, like laughter: I am not sleepy, but I yawn when I see someone yawning; there is nothing for me to laugh at, but I laugh when I hear people laughing.

'Music carries me immediately and directly into the mental condition in which the man was who composed it. My soul merges with his and together with him I pass from one condition into another, but why this happens I don't know. You see, he who wrote, let us say, the Kreutzer Sonata—Beethoven—knew of course why he was in that condition; that condition caused him to do certain actions and therefore that condition had a meaning for him, but for me—none at all. That is why music only agitates and doesn't lead to a conclusion. Well, when a military march is played the soldiers march to the music and the music has achieved its object. A dance is played, I dance and the music has achieved its object. Mass has been sung, I receive Communion, and that music too has reached a conclusion. Otherwise it is only agitating, and what ought to be done in that agitation is lacking. That is why music sometimes acts so dreadfully, so terribly. In China, music is a State affair. And that is as it should be. How can one allow anyone who pleases to hypnotize another, or many others, and do what he likes with them? And especially that this hypnotist should be the first immoral man who turns up?

'It is a terrible instrument in the hands of any chance user! Take that Kreutzer Sonata, for instance, how can that first presto be played in a drawing-room among ladies in low-necked dresses? To hear that played, to clap a little, and then to eat ices and talk of the latest scandal? Such things should only be played on certain important significant occasions, and then only when certain actions answering to such music are wanted; play it then and do what the music has moved you to. Otherwise an awakening of energy and feeling unsuited both to the time and the place, to which no outlet is given, cannot but act harmfully. At any rate that piece had a terrible effect on me; it was as if quite new feelings, new possibilities, of which I had till then been unaware, had been revealed to me. "That's how it is: not at all as I used to think and live, but that way," something seemed to say within me.

What this new thing was that had been revealed to me I could not explain to myself, but the consciousness of this new condition was very joyous.[79] All those same people, including my wife and him, appeared in a new light.[80]

'After that allegro they played the beautiful, but common and unoriginal, andante with trite variations, and the very weak finale. Then, at the request of the visitors, they played Ernst's Elegy and a few small pieces. They were all good, but they did not produce on me a one-hundredth part of the impression the first piece had. The effect of the first piece formed the background for them all.

'I felt light-hearted and cheerful the whole evening. I had never seen my wife as she was that evening. Those shining eyes, that severe, significant expression while she played, and her melting languor and feeble, pathetic, and blissful smile after they had finished. I saw all that but did not attribute any meaning to it except that she was feeling what I felt, and that to her as to me new feelings, never before experienced, were revealed or, as it were, recalled.[81] The evening ended satisfactorily and the visitors departed.

'Knowing that I had to go away to attend the Zémstvo Meetings two days later, Trukhachévski on leaving said he hoped to repeat the pleasure of that evening when he next came to Moscow. From this I concluded that he did not consider it possible to come to my house during my absence, and this pleased me.

'It turned out that as I should not be back before he left town, we should not see one another again.

'For the first time I pressed his hand with real pleasure, and thanked him for the enjoyment he had given us. In the same way he bade a final farewell to my wife. Their leave-taking seemed to be most natural and proper. Everything was splendid. My wife and I were both very well satisfied with our evening party.[82]

XXIV

'Two days later I left for the Meetings, parting from my wife in the best and most tranquil of moods.

'In the district there was always an enormous amount to do and a quite special life, a special little world of its own. I spent two ten-hour days at the Council. A letter from my wife was brought me on the second day and I read it there and then.

'She wrote about the children, about uncle, about the nurse, about shopping, and among other things she mentioned, as a most natural occurrence, that Trukhachévski had called, brought some music he had promised, and had offered to play again, but that she had refused.

'I did not remember his having promised any music, but thought he had taken leave for good, and I was therefore unpleasantly struck by this. I was however so busy that I had no time to think of it, and it was only in the evening when I had returned to my lodgings that I re-read her letter.

'Besides the fact that Trukhachévski had called at my house during my absence, the whole tone of the letter seemed to me unnatural. The mad beast of jealousy began to growl in its kennel and wanted to leap out, but I was afraid of that beast and quickly fastened him in. "What an abominable feeling this jealousy is!" I said to myself. "What could be more natural than what she writes?"

'I went to bed and began thinking about the affairs awaiting me next day. During those Meetings, sleeping in a new place, I usually slept badly, but now I fell asleep very quickly. And as sometimes happens, you know, you feel a kind of electric shock and wake up. So I awoke thinking of her, of my physical love for her, and of Trukhachévski, and of everything being accomplished between them. Horror and rage compressed my heart. But I began to reason with myself. "What nonsense!" said I to myself. "There are no grounds to go on, there is nothing and there has been nothing. How can I so degrade her and myself as to imagine such horrors? He is a sort of hired violinist, known as a worthless fellow, and suddenly an honourable woman, the respected mother of a family, *my* wife. . . . What absurdity!" So it seemed to me on the one hand. "How could it help being so?" it seemed on the other. "How could that simplest and most intelligible thing help happening—that for the sake of which I married her, for the sake of which I have been living with her, what alone I wanted of her, and which others including this musician must therefore also want? He is an unmarried man, healthy (I remember how he crunched the gristle of a cutlet and how greedily his red lips clung to the glass of wine), well-fed, plump, and not merely unprincipled but evidently making it a principle to accept the pleasures that present themselves. And they have music, that most exquisite voluptuousness of the senses, as a link between them. What then could make him refrain? She? But who is she? She was, and still is, a mystery. I don't know her. I only know her as an animal. And nothing can or should restrain an animal."

'Only then did I remember their faces that evening when, after the Kreutzer Sonata, they played some impassioned little piece, I don't remember by whom, impassioned to the point of obscenity. "How dared I go away?" I asked myself, remembering their faces. Was it not clear that everything had happened between them that evening? Was it not evident already then that there was not only no barrier between them, but that they both, and she chiefly, felt a certain measure of shame after what had happened? I remember her weak, piteous, and beatific smile as she wiped the perspiration from her flushed face when I came up to the piano. Already then they avoided looking at one another, and only at supper when he was pouring out some water for her, they glanced at each other with the vestige of a smile. I now recalled with horror the glance and scarcely perceptible smile I had then caught. "Yes, it is all over," said one voice, and immediately the other voice said something entirely different. "Something has come over you, it can't be that it is so," said that other voice. It felt uncanny lying in the dark and I struck a light, and felt a kind of terror in that little room with its yellow wall-paper. I lit a cigarette and, as always happens when one's thoughts go round and round in a circle of insoluble contradictions, I smoked, taking one cigarette after another in order to befog myself so as not to see those contradictions.

'I did not sleep all night, and at five in the morning,[83] having decided that I could not continue in such a state of tension, I rose, woke the caretaker who attended me and sent him to get horses. I sent a note to the Council saying that I had been recalled to Moscow on urgent business and asking that one of the members should take my place. At eight o'clock I got into my trap and started.'

XXV

The conductor entered and seeing that our candle had burnt down put it out, without supplying a fresh one. The day was dawning. Pózdnyshev was silent, but sighed deeply all the time the conductor was in the carriage. He continued his story only after the conductor had gone out, and in the semi-darkness of the carriage only the rattle of the windows of the moving carriage and the rhythmic snoring of the clerk could be heard. In the half-light of dawn I could not see Pózdnyshev's face at all, but only heard his voice becoming ever more and more excited and full of suffering.

'I had to travel twenty-four miles by road and eight hours by rail. It was splendid driving. It was frosty autumn weather, bright and sunny. The roads were in that condition when the tyres leave their dark imprint on them, you know. They were smooth, the light brilliant, and the air invigorating. It was pleasant driving in the tarantas. When it grew lighter and I had started I felt easier. Looking at the houses, the fields, and the passers-by, I forgot where I was going. Sometimes I felt that I was simply taking a drive,[84] and that nothing of what was calling me back had taken place. This oblivion was peculiarly enjoyable. When I remembered where I was going to, I said to myself, "We shall see when the time comes; I must not think about it." When we were halfway an incident occurred which detained me and still further distracted my thoughts. The tarantas[85] broke down and had to be repaired. That break-down had a very important effect, for it caused me to arrive in Moscow at midnight, instead of at seven o'clock as I had expected, and to reach home between twelve and one, as I missed the express and had to travel by an ordinary train. Going to fetch a cart, having the tarantas mended, settling up, tea at the inn, a talk with the innkeeper—all this still further diverted my attention. It was twilight before all was ready and I started again. By night it was even pleasanter driving than during the day. There was a new moon, a slight frost, still good roads, good horses, and a jolly driver, and as I went on I enjoyed it, hardly thinking at all of what lay before me; or perhaps I enjoyed it just because I knew what awaited me and was saying good-bye to the joys of life. But that tranquil mood, that ability to suppress my feelings, ended with my drive. As soon as I entered the train something entirely different began. That eight-hour journey in a railway carriage was something dreadful, which I shall never forget all my life. Whether it was that having taken my seat in the carriage I vividly imagined myself as having already arrived, or that railway travelling has such an exciting effect on people, at any rate from the moment I sat down in the train I could no longer control my imagination, and with extraordinary vividness which inflamed my jealousy it painted incessantly, one after another, pictures[86] of what had gone on in my absence, of how she had been false to me. I burnt with indignation, anger, and a peculiar feeling of intoxication with my own humiliation, as I gazed at those pictures, and I could not tear myself away from them; I could not help looking at them, could not efface them, and could not help evoking them.

'That was not all. The more I gazed at those imaginary pictures the stronger grew my belief in their reality.[87] The vividness with which they presented themselves to me seemed to serve as proof that what I imagined was real. It was as if some devil against my will invented and suggested to me the most terrible reflections. An old conversation I had had with Trukhachévski's brother came to my mind, and in a kind of ecstasy I rent my heart with that conversation, making it refer to Trukhachévski and my wife.

'That had occurred long before, but I recalled it. Trukhachévski's brother, I remember, in reply to a question whether he frequented houses of ill-fame, had said that a decent man would not go to places where there was danger of infection and it was dirty and nasty, since he could always find a decent woman. And now his brother had found my wife! "True, she is not in her first youth, has lost a side-tooth, and there is a slight puffiness about her; but it can't be helped, one has to take advantage of what one can get," I imagined him to be thinking. "Yes, it is condescending of him to take her for his mistress!" I said to myself. "And she is safe. . . ." "No, it is impossible!" I thought horror-struck. "There is nothing of the kind, nothing! There are not even any grounds for suspecting such things. Didn't she tell me that the very thought that I could be jealous of him was degrading to her? Yes, but she is lying, she is always lying!" [88] I exclaimed, and everything began anew. . . . There were only two other people in the carriage; an old woman and her husband, both very taciturn, and even they got out at one of the stations and I was quite alone. I was like a caged animal: now I jumped up and went to the window, now I began to walk up and down trying to speed the carriage up; but the carriage with all its seats and windows went jolting on in the same way, just as ours does. . . .'

Pózdnyshev jumped up, took a few steps, and sat down again.

'Oh, I am afraid, afraid of railway carriages, I am seized with horror. Yes, it is awful!' he continued. 'I said to myself, "I will think of something else. Suppose I think of the innkeeper where I had tea," and there in my mind's eye appears the innkeeper with his long beard and his grandson, a boy of the age of my Vásya! He will see how the musician kisses his mother. What will happen in his poor soul? But what does she care? She loves . . ." [89] and again the same thing rose up in me. "No, no . . . I will think about the inspection of the District Hospital. Oh, yes, about the patient who complained of the doctor yesterday. The doctor has a moustache like Trukhachévski's. And how impudent he is . . . they both deceived me when he said he was leaving Moscow," and it began afresh. Everything I thought of had some connexion with them. I suffered dreadfully. The chief cause of the suffering was my ignorance, my doubt, and the contradictions within me: my not knowing whether I ought to love or hate her. My suffering was of a strange kind. I felt a hateful consciousness of my humiliation and of his victory, but a terrible hatred for her. "It will not do to put an end to myself and leave her; she must at least suffer to some extent, and at least understand that I have suffered," I said to myself. I got out at every station to divert my mind. At one station I saw some people drinking, and I immediately drank some vodka. Beside me stood a Jew who was also drinking. He began to talk, and to avoid being alone in my carriage I went with him into his dirty third-class carriage reeking with smoke and bespattered with shells of sunflower seeds. There I sat down beside him and he chattered a great deal and told anecdotes. I listened to him, but could not take in what he was saying because I continued to think about my own affairs. He noticed this and demanded my attention. Then I rose and went back to my carriage. "I must think it over," I said to myself. "Is what I suspect true, and is there any reason for me to suffer?" I sat down, wishing to think it over calmly, but immediately, instead of calm reflection, the same thing began again: instead of reflection, pictures and fancies. "How often I have suffered like this," I said to myself (recalling former similar attacks of jealousy), "and afterwards it all ended in nothing. So it will be now perhaps, yes certainly it will. I shall find her calmly asleep, she will wake up, be pleased to see me, and by her words and looks I shall know that there has been nothing and that this is all nonsense. Oh, how good that would be! But no, that has happened too often and won't happen again now," some voice seemed to say; and it began again. Yes, that was where the punishment lay! I wouldn't take a young man to a lock-hospital to knock the hankering after women out of him, but into my soul, to see the devils that were rending it! What was terrible, you know, was that I considered myself to have a complete right to her body as if it were my own, and yet at the same time I felt I could not control that body, that it was not mine and she could dispose of it as she pleased, and that she wanted to dispose of it not as I wished her to. And I could do nothing either to her or to him. He, like Vánka the Steward, could sing a song before the gallows of how he kissed the sugared lips and so forth. And he would triumph. If she has not yet done it but wishes to—and I know that she does wish to—it is still worse; it would be better if she had done it and I knew it, so that there would be an end to this uncertainty. I could not have said what it was I wanted. I wanted her not to desire that which she was bound to desire. It was utter insanity.

XXVI

'At the last station but one, when the conductor had been to collect the tickets, I gathered my things together and went out onto the brake-platform, and the consciousness that the crisis was at hand still further increased my agitation. I felt cold, and my jaw trembled so that my teeth chattered. I automatically left the terminus with the crowd, took a cab, got in, and drove off. I rode looking at the few passers-by, the night-watchmen,[90] and the shadows of my trap thrown by the street lamps, now in front and now behind me, and did not think of anything. When we had gone about half a mile my feet felt cold, and I remembered that I had taken off my woollen stockings in the train and put them in my satchel. "Where is the satchel? Is it here? Yes." And my wicker trunk? I remembered that I had entirely forgotten about my luggage, but finding that I had the luggage-ticket I decided that it was not worth while going back for it, and so continued my way.

[91] 'Try now as I will, I cannot recall my state of mind at the time. What did I think? What did I want? I don't know at all. All I remember is a consciousness that something dreadful and very important in my life was imminent. Whether that important event occurred because I thought it would, or whether I had a presentiment of what was to happen, I don't know. It may even be that after what has happened all the foregoing moments have acquired a certain gloom in my mind. I drove up to the front porch. It was past midnight. Some cabmen were waiting in front of the porch expecting, from the fact that there were lights in the windows, to get fares. (The lights were in our flat, in the dancing-room and drawing-room.) Without considering why it was still light in our windows so late, I went upstairs in the same state of expectation of something dreadful, and rang. Egór, a kind, willing, but very stupid footman, opened the door. The first thing my eyes fell on in the hall was a man's cloak hanging on the stand with other outdoor coats. I ought to have been surprised but was not, for I had expected it. "That's it!" I said to myself. When I asked Egór who the visitor was and he named Trukhachévski, I inquired whether there was anyone else. He replied, "Nobody, sir." I remember that he replied in a tone as if he wanted to cheer me and dissipate my doubts of there being anybody else there. "So it is, so it is," I seemed to be saying to myself. "And the children?" "All well, heaven be praised. In bed, long ago."

'I could not breathe, and could not check the trembling of my jaw. "Yes, so it is not as I thought: I used to expect a misfortune but things used to turn out all right and in the usual way. Now it is not as usual, but is all as I pictured to myself. I thought it was only fancy, but here it is, all real. Here it all is . . . !"

'I almost began to sob, but the devil immediately suggested to me: "Cry, be sentimental, and they will get away quietly. You will have no proof and will continue to suffer and doubt all your life." And my self-pity immediately vanished, and [92] a strange sense of joy arose in me, that my torture would now be over, that now I could punish her, could get rid of her, and could vent my anger. And I gave vent to it—I became a beast, a cruel and cunning beast.

' "Don't!" I said to Egór, who was about to go to the
drawing-room. "Here is my luggage-ticket, take a cab as
quick as you can and go and get my luggage. Go!" He
went down the passage to fetch his overcoat. Afraid that
he might alarm them, I went as far as his little room and
waited while he put on his overcoat. From the drawing-
room, beyond another room, one could hear voices and the
clatter of knives and plates. They were eating and had not
heard the bell. "If only they don't come out now," thought
I. Egór put on his overcoat, which had an astrakhan collar,
and went out. I locked the door after him and felt creepy
when I knew I was alone and must act at once. How, I
did not yet know. I only knew that all was now over,
that there could be no doubt as to her guilt, and that I
should punish her immediately and end my relations with
her.

'Previously I had doubted and had thought: "Perhaps
after all it's not true, perhaps I am mistaken." But now it
was so no longer. It was all irrevocably decided. "Without
my knowledge she is alone with him at night! That is a
complete disregard of everything! Or worse still: it is
intentional boldness and impudence in crime, that the
boldness may serve as a sign of innocence. All is clear.
There is no doubt." I only feared one thing—their parting
hastily, inventing some fresh lie, and thus depriving me of
clear evidence[93] and of the possibility of proving the fact.
So as to catch them more quickly I went on tiptoe to the
dancing-room where they were, not through the drawing-
room but through the passage and nurseries.

'In the first nursery slept the boys. In the second nursery
the nurse moved and was about to wake, and I imagined
to myself what she would think when she knew all; and
such pity for myself seized me at that thought that I
could not restrain my tears, and not to wake the children
I ran on tiptoe into the passage and on into my study,
where I fell sobbing on the sofa.

' "I, an honest man, I, the son of my parents, I, who
have all my life dreamt of the happiness of married
life; I, a man who was never unfaithful to her. . . . And
now! Five children, and she is embracing a musician because he has red lips!

' "No, she is not a human being. She is a bitch, an
abominable bitch! In the next room to her children whom
she has all her life pretended to love. And writing to me

as she did! Throwing herself so barefacedly on his neck! But what do I know? Perhaps she long ago carried on with the footmen, and so got the children who are considered mine!

' "To-morrow I should have come back and she would have met me with her fine coiffure, with her elegant waist and her indolent, graceful movements" (I saw all her attractive, hateful face), "and that beast of jealousy would for ever have sat in my heart lacerating it. What will the nurse think? . . . And Egór? And poor little Lisa! She already understands something. Ah, that impudence, those lies! And that animal sensuality which I know so well," I said to myself.

'I tried to get up but could not. My heart was beating so that I could not stand on my feet. "Yes, I shall die of a stroke. She will kill me. That is just what she wants. What is killing to her? But no, that would be too advantageous for her and I will not give her that pleasure. Yes, here I sit while they eat and laugh and . . . Yes, though she was no longer in her first freshness he did not disdain her. For in spite of that she is not bad looking, and above all she is at any rate not dangerous to his precious health. And why did I not throttle her then?" I said to myself, recalling the moment when, the week before, I drove her out of my study and hurled things about. I vividly recalled the state I had then been in; I not only recalled it, but again felt the need to strike and destroy that I had felt then. I remember how I wished to act, and how all considerations except those necessary for action went out of my head. I entered into that condition when an animal or a man, under the influence of physical excitement at a time of danger, acts with precision and deliberation but without losing a moment and always with a single definite aim in view.

'The first thing I did was to take off my boots and, in my socks, approach the sofa, on the wall above which guns and daggers were hung. I took down a curved Damascus dagger that had never been used and was very sharp. I drew it out of its scabbard. I remember the scabbard fell behind the sofa, and I remember thinking "I must find it afterwards or it will get lost." Then I took off my overcoat which I was still wearing, and stepping softly in my socks I went there.[94]

XXVII

'Having crept up stealthily to the door, I suddenly opened it.[95] I remember the expression of their faces. I remember that expression because it gave me a painful pleasure—it was an expression of terror. That was just what I wanted. I shall never forget the look of desperate terror that appeared on both their faces the first instant they saw me. He I think was sitting at the table, but on seeing or hearing me he jumped to his feet and stood with his back to the cupboard. His face expressed nothing but quite unmistakable terror. Her face too expressed terror but there was something else besides. If it had expressed only terror, perhaps what happened might not have happened; but on her face there was, or at any rate so it seemed to me at the first moment, also an expression of regret and annoyance that love's raptures and her happiness with him had been disturbed. It was as if she wanted nothing but that her present happiness should not be interfered with. These expressions remained on their faces but an instant. The look of terror on his changed immediately to one of inquiry: might he, or might he not, begin lying? If he might, he must begin at once; if not, something else would happen. But what? . . . He looked inquiringly at her face. On her face the look of vexation and regret changed as she looked at him (so it seemed to me) to one of solicitude for him.

'For an instant I stood in the doorway holding the dagger behind my back.

'At that moment he smiled, and in a ridiculously indifferent tone remarked: "And we have been having some music."

' "What a surprise!" she began, falling into his tone. But neither of them finished; the same fury I had experienced the week before overcame me. Again I felt that need of destruction, violence, and a transport of rage, and yielded to it. Neither finished what they were saying. That something else began which he had feared and which immediately destroyed all they were saying. I rushed towards her, still hiding the dagger that he might not prevent my striking her in the side under her breast. I selected that spot from the first. Just as I rushed at her he saw it, and—a thing I never expected of him—seized me by the arm and shouted: "Think what you are doing! . . . Help, some-one! . . ."

'I snatched my arm away and rushed at him in silence. His eyes met mine and he suddenly grew as pale as a sheet to his very lips. His eyes flashed in a peculiar way, and—what again I had not expected—he darted under the piano and out at the door. I was going to rush after him, but a weight hung on my left arm. It was she. I tried to free myself, but she hung on yet more heavily and would not let me go. This unexpected hindrance, the weight, and her touch which was loathsome to me, inflamed me still more. I felt that I was quite mad and that I must look frightful, and this delighted me. I swung my left arm with all my might, and my elbow hit her straight in the face. She cried out and let go my arm. I wanted to run after him, but remembered that it is ridiculous to run after one's wife's lover in one's socks; and I did not wish to be ridiculous but terrible. In spite of the fearful frenzy I was in, I was all the time aware of the impression I might produce on others, and was even partly guided by that impression. I turned towards her. She fell on the couch, and holding her hand to her bruised eyes, looked at me. Her face showed fear and hatred of me, the enemy, as a rat's does when one lifts the trap in which it has been caught. At any rate I saw nothing in her expression but this fear and hatred of me. It was just the fear and hatred of me which would be evoked by love for another. But still I might perhaps have restrained myself and not done what I did had she remained silent. But she suddenly began to speak and to catch hold of the hand in which I held the dagger.

' "Come to yourself! What are you doing? What is the matter? There has been nothing, nothing, nothing. . . . 'I swear it!"

'I might still have hesitated, but those last words of hers, from which I concluded just the opposite—that everything had happened—called forth a reply. And the reply had to correspond to the temper to which I had brought myself, which continued to increase and had to go on increasing. Fury, too, has its laws.

' "Don't lie, you wretch!" I howled, and seized her arm with my left hand, but she wrenched herself away. Then, still without letting go of the dagger, I seized her by the throat with my left hand, threw her backwards, and began

throttling her. What a firm neck it was . . . ! She seized
my hand with both hers trying to pull it away from her
throat, and as if I had only waited for that, I struck her
with all my might with the dagger in the side below the
ribs.

'When people say they don't remember what they do in
a fit of fury, it is rubbish, falsehood. I remembered everything and did not for a moment lose consciousness of what
I was doing. The more frenzied I became the more brightly
the light of consciousness burnt in me, so that I could not
help knowing everything I did. I knew what I was doing
every second. I cannot say that I knew beforehand what I
was going to do; but I knew what I was doing when I did
it, and even I think a little before, as if to make repentance
possible and to be able to tell myself that I could stop. I
knew I was hitting below the ribs and that the dagger
would enter. At the moment I did it I knew I was doing
an awful thing such as I had never done before, which
would have terrible consequences. But that consciousness
passed like a flash of lightning and the deed immediately
followed the consciousness. I realized the action with extraordinary clearness. I felt, and remember, the momentary resistance of her corset and of something else, and
then the plunging of the dagger into something soft. She
seized the dagger with her hands, and cut them, but
could not hold it back.

'For a long time afterwards, in prison when the moral
change had taken place in me, I thought of that moment,
recalled what I could of it, and considered it. I remembered that for an instant, only an instant, before the action
I had a terrible consciousness that I was killing, had killed,
a defenceless woman, my wife! I remember the horror
of that consciousness and conclude from that, and even
dimly remember, that having plunged the dagger in I
pulled it out immediately, trying to remedy what had been
done and to stop it. I stood for a second motionless waiting
to see what would happen, and whether it could be
remedied.

'She jumped to her feet and screamed: "Nurse! He has
killed me."

'Having heard the noise the nurse was standing by the
door. I continued to stand waiting, and not believing the
truth. But the blood rushed from under her corset.[96] Only
then did I understand that it could not be remedied, and

I immediately decided that it was not necessary it should be, that I had done what I wanted and had to do. I waited till she fell down, and the nurse, crying "Good God!" ran to her, and only then did I throw away the dagger and leave the room.

' "I must not be excited; I must know what I am doing," I said to myself without looking at her and at the nurse. The nurse was screaming—calling for the maid. I went down the passage, sent the maid, and went into my study. "What am I to do now?" I asked myself, and immediately realized what it must be. On entering the study I went straight to the wall, took down a revolver and examined it—it was loaded—I put it on the table. Then I picked up the scabbard from behind the sofa and sat down there.

'I sat thus for a long time. I did not think of anything or call anything to mind. I heard the sounds of bustling outside. I heard someone drive up, then someone else. Then I heard and saw Egór bring into the room my wicker trunk he had fetched. As if anyone wanted that!

' "Have you heard what has happened?" I asked. "Tell the yard-porter to inform the police." He did not reply, and went away. I rose, locked the door, got out my cigarettes and matches and began to smoke. I had not finished the cigarette before sleep overpowered me. I must have slept for a couple of hours. I remember dreaming that she and I were friendly together, that we had quarrelled but were making it up, there was something rather in the way, but we were friends. I was awakened by someone knocking at the door. "That is the police!" I thought, waking up. "I have committed murder, I think. But perhaps it is *she*, and nothing has happened." There was again a knock at the door. I did not answer, but was trying to solve the question whether it had happened or not. Yet, it had! I remembered the resistance of the corset and the plunging in of the dagger, and a cold shiver ran down my back. "Yes, it has. Yes, and now I must do away with myself too," I thought. But I thought this knowing that I should *not* kill myself. Still I got up and took the revolver in my hand. But it is strange: I remember how I had many times been near suicide, how even that day on the railway it had seemed easy, easy just because I thought how it would stagger her—now I was not only unable to kill myself but even to think of it. "Why should I do it?" I asked myself, and there was no reply. There was more knocking at the door. "First I must find out who is knocking. There will still be time for this." I put down the revolver and covered it with a newspaper. I went to the door and unlatched it. It was my wife's sister, a kindly, stupid widow. "Vásya, what is this?" and her ever ready tears began to flow.

' "What do you want?" I asked rudely. I knew I ought not to be rude to her and had no reason to be, but I could think of no other tone to adopt.

' "Vásya, she is dying! Iván Zakhárych says so." Iván Zakhárych was her doctor and adviser.

' "Is he here?" I asked, and all my animosity against her surged up again. "Well, what of it?"

' "Vásya, go to her. Oh, how terrible it is!" said she.

' "Shall I go to her?" I asked myself, and immediately decided that I must go to her. Probably it is always done, when a husband has killed his wife, as I had—he must certainly go to her. "If that is what is done, then I must go," I said to myself. "If necessary I shall always have time," I reflected, referring to the shooting of myself, and I went to her. "Now we shall have phrases, grimaces, but I will not yield to them," I thought. "Wait," I said to her sister, "it is silly without boots, let me at least put on slippers."

XXVIII

'Wonderful to say, when I left my study and went through the familiar rooms, the hope that nothing had happened again awoke in me; but the smell of that doctor's nastiness—iodoform and carbolic—took me aback. "No, it had happened." Going down the passage past the nursery I saw little Lisa. She looked at me with frightened eyes. It even seemed to me that all the five children were there and all looked at me. I approached the door, and the maid opened it from inside for me and passed out. The first thing that caught my eye was her light-grey dress thrown on a chair and all stained black with blood. She was lying on one of the twin beds (on mine because it was easier to get at), with her knees raised. She lay in a very sloping position supported by pillows, with her dressing jacket unfastened. Something had been put on the wound. There was a heavy smell of iodoform in the room. What struck me first and most of all was her swollen and bruised face, blue on part of the nose and under the eyes. This was the result of the blow with my elbow when she had tried to hold me back. There was nothing beautiful about her, but something repulsive as it seemed to me. I stopped on the threshold. "Go up to her, do," said her sister. "Yes, no doubt she wants to confess," I thought. "Shall I forgive her? Yes, she is dying and may be forgiven," I thought, trying to be magnanimous. I went up close to her. She raised her eyes to me with difficulty, one of them was black, and with an effort said falteringly:

' "You've got your way, killed . . ." and through the look of suffering and even the nearness of death her face had the old expression of cold animal hatred that I knew so well. "I shan't . . . let you have . . . the children, all the same. . . . She (her sister) will take . . ."

'Of what to me was the most important matter, her guilt, her faithlessness, she seemed to consider it beneath her to speak.

' "Yes, look and admire what you have done," she said looking towards the door, and she sobbed. In the doorway stood her sister with the children. "Yes, see what you have done."

'I looked at the children and at her bruised disfigured face, and for the first time I forgot myself, my rights, my pride, and for the first time saw a human being in her.[97] And so insignificant did all that had offended me, all my jealousy, appear, and so important what I had done, that I wished to fall with my face to her hand, and say: "Forgive me," but dared not do so.

'She lay silent with her eyes closed, evidently too weak to say more. Then her disfigured face trembled and puckered. She pushed me feebly away.

' "Why did it all happen? Why?"

' "Forgive me," I said.

[98] ' "Forgive! That's all rubbish! . . . Only not to die! . . ." she cried, raising herself, and her glittering eyes were bent on me. "Yes, you have had your way! . . . I hate you! Ah! Ah!" she cried, evidently already in delirium and frightened at something. "Shoot! I'm not afraid! . . . Only kill everyone . . . ! He has gone . . . ! Gone . . . !"

'After that the delirium continued all the time. She did not recognize[99] anyone. She died towards noon that same day. Before that they had taken me to the police-station and from there to prison. There, during the eleven months I remained awaiting trial, I examined myself and my past, and understood it. I began to understand it on the third day: on the third day they took me *there* . . .'

He was going on but, unable to repress his sobs, he stopped. When he recovered himself he continued:

'I only began to understand when I saw her in her coffin . . .'

He gave a sob, but immediately continued hurriedly:

'Only when I saw her dead face did I understand all that I had done. I realized that I, I, had killed her; that it was my doing that she, living, moving, warm, had now become motionless, waxen, and cold, and that this could never, anywhere, or by any means, be remedied. He who has not lived through it cannot understand. . . . Ugh! Ugh! Ugh! . . .' he cried several times and then was silent.

We sat in silence a long while. He kept sobbing and trembling as he sat opposite me without speaking. His face had grown narrow and elongated and his mouth seemed to stretch right across it.

'Yes,' he suddenly said. 'Had I then known what I know now, everything would have been different. Nothing would have induced me to marry her. . . . I should not have married at all.'

Again we remained silent for a long time.

100 'Well, forgive me. . . .' He turned away from me and lay down on the seat, covering himself up with his plaid. At the station where I had to get out (it was at eight o'clock in the morning) I went up to him to say good-bye. Whether he was asleep or only pretended to be, at any rate he did not move. I touched him with my hand. He uncovered his face, and I could see he had not been asleep.

'Good-bye,' I said, holding out my hand. He gave me his and smiled slightly, but so piteously that I felt ready to weep.

'Yes, forgive me . . .' he said, repeating the same words with which he had concluded his story.

Appendix

The following are the readings of the lithograph:

[1] *Add:* with remarkable glittering eyes of an indefinite colour, which attracted attention. *Some of the description that follows is omitted.*

[2] *Read:* At first the clerk said that the place opposite was engaged; to which the old man replied that he was only going as far as the next station.

[3] *Read:* considering probably that this did not at all infringe the dignity his figure and manner denoted, . . .

[4] *For the above paragraph read:* 'And then come discord, financial troubles, mutual recrimination, and the married couple separate,' said the lawyer.

[5] *In place of the two preceding lines, read:* said the lady, evidently encouraged by the general attention and approval.

[6] *The old man here replies*: 'Men are a different matter.' *And the lady says*: 'Then to a man, in your opinion, everything is permitted.'

[7] *Add*: 'Or if some stupid man cannot control his wife —it serves him right. But all the same one must not create a scandal about it. Love or don't love, but don't break up the home. Every husband can keep his wife in order, he has the right to do it. Only a fool can't manage it.'

[8] *In place of this paragraph read*: 'But you yourself may go on the spree with the girls at Kunávin,' said the lawyer with a smile.

[9] *Add*: a vein on his forehead stood out,

[10] *The lithograph here reads differently, and the words that follow are*: 'How do you mean "what kind of love"?' said the lady. 'The ordinary love of married couples.'

'But how can ordinary love sanctify marriage?' continued the nervous gentleman. He was as agitated as though he were angry and wished to speak unpleasantly to the lady. She felt this and was also agitated.

'How? Very simply,' said she. The nervous gentleman at once seized on the word.

'No, not simply!'

[11] *Add*: and least of all for his wife. That is what the

proverb says, and it is a true one. "Another's wife is a swan, but one's own is bitter wormwood." '

[12] *Read*: Even if one admits that Menelaus might prefer Helen for his whole lifetime, Helen would prefer Paris.

[13] *Add*: . . . of Helen with Menelaus or vice versa. The only difference is that with one it comes sooner and with another later. It is only written in stupid novels that they loved one another all their lives, and only children can believe that.

[14] *Add*: 'This identity of ideals does not occur among old people, but always between handsome and young ones. And I assert that love, real love, does not sanctify marriage as we are accustomed to suppose for one's whole life, but on the contrary destroys it.'

[15] *Add:* 'And we feel this, and to avoid it we preach "love." In reality the preaching of free love is only a call to return to the mingling of the sexes—excuse me,' said he, turning to the lady, 'to fornication. The old basis has worn out, and we must find a new one, but not preach depravity!' He had become so excited that we all remained silent and looked at him.

'And at present the transition stage is terrible. People feel that it will not do to allow adultery, and that sexual relations must in some way be defined; but bases for this are lacking, except the old ones in which no one any longer believes. And the people go on getting married in the old way without believing in what they are doing, and the result is either deception or coercion.

[16] *Add*: and do not themselves know why or what for,

[17] *Add*: In the course of his story he did not once stop after that, and not even the entry of fresh passengers interrupted him. During his narration his face completely changed several times so that nothing resembling the former face remained: his eyes, his mouth, his moustache and even his beard were all different—it was a beautiful, touching, new face. These changes occurred suddenly in the dim light, and for some five minutes there was one face and it was impossible to see the former face, and then, one did not know how, another face appeared and again it was impossible to see it otherwise.

[18] *Add:* . . . my life and all my terrible story. Terrible, really terrible. The whole story is more terrible than the end.

[19] *Add*: In the first place let me tell you who I am. I

am the son of a rich landowner in the steppes, and I took a degree in law at the university. I married when I was rather over thirty, but before telling of my marriage I must say how I lived previously and how I regarded family life.

²⁰ *Add*: This—the fact that I considered myself moral —came about because in our family there was not any of that particular specialized vice which was so common in our landowning class, and therefore, being brought up in a family where neither my father nor my mother was unfaithful, I nursed the dream of a most elevated and poetic family life from my early years. My wife had to be the height of perfection. Our mutual love had to be most elevated. The purity of our family life was to be dove-like. So I thought, and I praised myself all the time for having such elevated thoughts. And at the same time, for ten years, I lived as an adult, in no haste to get married, and led what I called a respectable, reasonable, bachelor life.

²¹ *Add*: and I was naïvely confident that I was quite a moral man. The women I was intimate with were not mine, and I had nothing to do with them except for the pleasure they afforded me. And I saw nothing disgraceful in this.

²² *Add*: . . . in regard to the real woman-question . . .'

'That is to say . . . what do you understand to be the real woman-question?'

'The question of what this organic creature that is distinct from man is, and how she herself and men also should regard her.

²³ *For this paragraph read*: 'Yes, for ten years I lived in most disgraceful debauchery, dreaming of a pure, elevated love—and even in the name of that love. Yes, I want to tell of how I killed my wife, and to tell that I must tell how I became depraved.

'I killed her before I met her; I killed a woman the first time I knew one without loving her, and it was already then that I killed my wife.

²⁴ *Read*: Who deprave youths? They do! Who deprave women by devising means for them and teaching them not to bear children? Who treat syphilis with enthusiasm? They.'

'But why not treat syphilis?'

'Because to cure syphilis is the same as to safeguard

vice; it is the same as the Foundlings Hospital for discarded babies.

'No, not the same . . . *Then omit to end of paragraph.*

[25] *Insert here*: To tell the truth without false shame, I was trapped and caught. Her mamma—her papa was dead—arranged all sorts of traps and one of them—namely boating—succeeded.

[26] *Insert*: No, say what you will, we live up to our ears in such a swamp of lies that unless we have our heads bumped, as I did, we cannot come to our senses.

[27] *Add*: How fortunate that would have been for us!

[28] *Add:* If we only reject the conventional explanations of why and for what reason these things are done, if we . . .'

[29] *Add*: There is no difference. Strictly defining the matter, one must say that prostitutes for short terms are usually despised, while prostitutes for long terms are respected.

[30] *Add*: The men of our circle are kept and fed like breeding stallions. It is only necessary, you know, to close the safety-valve—that is, for a vicious young man to live a continent life for a little while—and immediately a terrible restlessness and excitement is caused, which passing through the prism of the artificial conditions of our social life shows itself in the guise of falling in love. Our love affairs and marriages, for the most part, are conditioned by our food. You are surprised: one ought to be surprised that we have not noticed it sooner.

[31] *Read*: through the prism of novels, stories, verses, music—through the idle, luxurious setting of our life—and there will be amorousness of the purest water.

[32] *Read*: . . . her parents, knowing more of life and not distracted by a momentary infatuation, but yet loving her not less than they loved themselves—arranged the marriage.

[33] *Instead of the following lines, read*: And we talk of woman's rights, of "freedom" which is somehow obtainable at university lectures.'

[34] *Add*: and as she cannot consent to be a slave and cannot herself propose, there begins that other abominable lie which is sometimes called "coming out into society," and sometimes "amusing themselves," and which is nothing but husband-hunting.

⁸⁵ *Add*: 'They all complain that they are deprived of rights and are oppressed.

⁸⁶ *Add*: Look at the people's fêtes, and at our balls and parties. Woman knows how she acts, you can see that by her triumphant smile.

⁸⁷ *Add*: whether they believe in that or not—is unimportant.

⁸⁸ *Add:* My sister, when very young, married a man twice her age and a debauchee. I remember how astonished we were the night of the wedding, when she ran out of her bedroom in tears and, shaking all over, said that she could on no account even tell us what he had wanted to do to her.

⁸⁹ *Add*: A pure girl only wants children. Children,—yes, but not a husband.'

'How then,' I said with astonishment, 'how is the human race to be continued?'

'And why should it be continued?' was his unexpected rejoinder.

⁴⁰ *Add*: You know that Schopenhauer, Hartmann, and all the Buddhists too, declare that it is a blessing not to live. And they are so far right that welfare for humanity coincides with self-annihilation, only they have not expressed themselves rightly: they say that the human race should destroy itself to escape from suffering—that its aim should be self-destruction. That is wrong. The aim of humanity cannot be to escape from suffering by self-destruction, because sufferings are the result of activity, and the aim of an activity cannot be to destroy its consequences. The aim both of men and of humanity is blessedness. For the attainment of blessedness a law has been given to humanity which it should fulfil. The law is that of the union of mankind.

⁴¹ *In the lithographed version there are a number of small differences in the last paragraphs of Chapter XI, and Chapter XII commences with the words:* 'It is a strange story,' said I.

'What is there strange about it? According to all Church teaching the end of the world is coming, and according to all that science teaches the same thing is inevitable. So what is there strange in the fact that moral teaching reaches the same result? "He that is able to receive it, let him receive it," said Christ. And I understand that just as he said it. For morality to exist between people in sexual relations it is necessary that the aim they set themselves should be complete chastity. In striving towards chastity, man falls; he falls, and the result is a moral marriage; but if, as in our society, man aims directly at physical love, then though it may clothe itself in the pseudo-moral form of marriage, that will merely be permitted debauchery with one woman—and will none the less be an immoral life, such as that in which I perished and destroyed her, and such as among us is called moral family life. Note what a perverse conception exists among us, when the happiest position for a man—that of freedom, celibacy—is considered pitiable and ridiculous. And the highest ideal, the best position, for a woman—that of being pure, a vestal, a virgin—is a thing to be afraid of and a subject for ridicule in our society. How many and many young girls have offered up their purity to that Moloch of opinion by marrying good-for-nothing fellows, merely to avoid remaining virgin, which is the highest state. For fear that she may remain in that highest state she ruins herself! But I did not then understand that the words in the Gospel—that he who looks upon a woman with desire has already committed adultery with her in his heart—refer not to other wives only, but specially and chiefly to one's own. I did not understand that, and thought that this honeymoon and my behavior on this honeymoon were most excellent, and that to satisfy desire with my own wife was a perfectly right thing. *Then follow in the lithographed version the words*: You know those wedding tours, &c.

[42] *Read*: As happens with mirthful young people who, unable to devise funny things to laugh at quickly enough, laugh at their own laughter, so we had not time to devise excuses for our hatred.

[43] *Read*: 'We all—men and women—are brought up to a kind of veneration for that feeling which we are accustomed to call love. From childhood I prepared to fall in love, and I fell in love; all my youth I was in love and was glad to be so. It was instilled into me that there was no nobler and more exalted business in the world than to be in love. Well at last the expected feeling comes, and a man devotes himself to it. But that is where the deception appears. In theory love is something ideal . . .

[44] *Add*: I would order them—those wizards—to per-

form the office of those women who, in their opinion, are necessary to men—and then let them talk!

[45] *Add*: According to the view existing in our society a woman's vocation is to afford pleasure to man, and the education given her corresponds with this view. From childhood she learns only how to be more attractive. Girls are all taught to think entirely of that. As serfs were brought up to satisfy their masters and it could not be otherwise, so also all our women are educated to attract men and this too cannot be otherwise. But you will perhaps say that this is true only of badly brought-up girls— those who among us are contemptuously called "young ladies"—you will say there is another, a serious education, supplied in high-schools—even classical ones—in mid-wifery, and in medical and university courses. That is not true. All female education of whatever kind has in view only the capture of men. Some girls captivate men by music and curls; others by learning and by political services. But the aim is always the same and cannot be other, because there is no other than that of charming a man so as to capture him. Can you imagine courses for women, and scholarship for women, without men: that is to say, that they should be educated but that men should not know about it? I cannot! No bringing up, no education, can alter this as long as woman's highest ideal remains marriage, and not virginity and freedom from sensuality. Till then she will be a slave. You know one need only think—forgetting how customary they are—of the conditions in which our young ladies are brought up, and we shall be surprised not at the vice which rules among the women of our propertied classes, but on the contrary that there is so little vice. Only think of the finery from early childhood, the adorning of herself, the cleanliness, the grace, the music, the reading of verses and novels, the songs and theatres and concerts for external and internal application, that is those they hear and those in which they perform. And with it all their complete physical idleness and the food they eat, with so much sweetness and so much fat in it. You see, it is only because it is all wrapped up and concealed that we do not know what those unfortunate girls suffer from the excitation of their sensuality: nine out of ten suffer and are unendurably tormented at the period of adolescence and later, if they do not get married by twenty. You know it

is only that we do not want to see it, but anyone who has eyes sees that the majority of these unfortunates are so excited by this concealed sensuality (it is well if it is concealed) that they can do nothing, they only begin to live in the presence of a man. Their whole life is passed in preparations for coquetry and in coquetting. In the presence of men they overflow with life and become animated with sensual energy, but as soon as the man goes away their energy all droops and they cease to live. And this is not with some particular man but with any man, if only he is not quite repulsive. You will say, that is exceptional. No, this is the rule. Only it shows itself more strongly in some girls and less in others; none of them however lives a full life of her own, but only in dependence on man. When he is absent they are all alike and cannot help being alike, because for them all to attract to themselves as many men as possible is the highest ideal both of their girlhood and of their married life. And from this arises a feeling stronger than that one which I will not call their feminine vanity—the animal need of every female animal to attract to herself as many males as possible in order to have a chance of choosing. So it is in their girlhood and so it continues to be after marriage.

⁴⁶ *Insert:* You must understand that in our world an opinion exists, shared by everyone, that woman is there to afford man enjoyment (and vice versa probably, but I don't know about that, I know my own part).

⁴⁷ *Add:* from Pushkin's lines about "little feet."

⁴⁸ *Read:* 'The emancipation of woman lies not in universities and law-courts but in the bedroom. Yes, and the struggle against prostitution lies not in the brothels but in the families.'

The arrangement of this chapter differs in the two versions, and the following passage occurs in the lithographed but is omitted in the printed version:

'But why so?' I asked.

'That is what is surprising—that no one wishes to know what is so clear and evident, and what the doctors ought to know and to preach, but about which they are silent. Man desires the law of nature—children; but the coming of children presents an obstacle to continuous enjoyment, and people who only desire continuous enjoyment have to devise means to evade that obstacle. And they have devised three such means. One is, by the receipt the rascals give, to cripple the woman by making her barren—which has always been, and must be, a misfortune for a woman —then man can quietly and constantly enjoy himself; the second way is polygamy, not honourable polygamy as among the Mohammedans but our base European polygamy, replete with falsehood and hypocrisy; and there is the third evasion—which is not even an evasion, but a simple, coarse, direct infringement of the laws of nature, and which is committed by all the husbands among the peasants and by most husbands in our so-called honourable families. I too lived in that way. We have not even reached the level of Europe, of Paris, of the *Zwei Kinder System*, or of the Mohammedans, and we have devised nothing of our own because we have not thought at all about the matter. We feel that there is something nasty in the one plan and in the other, and we wish to have families, but our barbarous view of woman remains the same and the result is yet worse. A woman with us must at one and the same time be pregnant and be her husband's mistress—must be a nursing mother and his mistress. But her strength cannot stand it.'

⁴⁹ *The lithographed version of Chapter XV begins with a long section on jealousy, omitted in the printed version:*

'Yes, jealousy is one of the secrets of marriage that are known to all and hidden from everybody. Besides the general reason for married couples' hatred of one another—which is their co-operation in defiling a human being—mutual jealousy is continually gnawing at them. But by mutual agreement it is generally decided to conceal this from everyone, and it is so concealed. Knowing that this is so, each assumes that it is an unhappy peculiarity of his own and not the common lot. So it was with me. So it must be. Jealousy must exist between married couples who live immorally with one another. If they are both unable to sacrifice their own pleasure for the welfare of their child, each rightly concludes that the other will certainly not sacrifice pleasure—I will not say for welfare or tranquillity (for one may sin so as not to be found out), but—merely for conscience' sake. Each knows that no strong moral obstacle to unfaithfulness exists in the other. They know this because they infringe the demands of morality with one another, and therefore they distrust and watch each other. Oh, what an awful feeling jealousy is! I am not speaking of that real jealousy which at any rate has some basis. That real jealousy is tormenting but it has, and promises, a result; but I am speaking of the unconscious jealousy which inevitably accompanies every immoral marriage, and which, having no definite cause, has also no end. The other is an abscess on a tooth, but this is a tooth aching with its bone—unchanging pain day and night, and again day and night, and unendingly. This jealousy is dreadful, really dreadful! It is like this: a young man is pleasantly talking to my wife and looking at her, as it seems to me, examining her body. How dare he think about her, or dream of a romance with her! But she not merely tolerates it, she is apparently quite pleased. I even see that she is behaving in the same way to him as he is doing to her. And in my soul there arises such a hatred of her that every word of hers and every gesture becomes repulsive. She notices this, and does not know what she is to do, and she puts on an air of animated indifference. "Ah! I suffer and she finds it amusing, she is well satisfied!" And the hatred increases tenfold but I dare not give it vent, for in the depth of my soul I know that there is no real ground for it. And I sit, pretending to be indifferent, and put on an air of special regard and politeness towards him. Then I become angry with myself and wish to get out of the room and leave them alone, and I really go out. But as soon as I am out I am seized with horror at what is going on in my absence. I go back—inventing some excuse for doing so; or sometimes I do not re-enter the room but stop at the door and listen. How can she humiliate herself and me, putting me—me—in such a mean position of suspicion and eaves-dropping! What meanness! Oh, the nasty beast! And he, he! What about him? He is what all men are, what I was when a bachelor. For him it is a pleasure. He even smiles when he looks at me as though saying: "What can you say about it? It is my turn now!" Oh, that feeling is terrible! The sting of that feeling is terrible: I had only to let loose that feeling on anyone if but once—it was enough if once I suspected a man of having designs on my wife—and that man was for ever spoilt for me, as if vitriol had been poured over him. It was enough for me to be jealous of a man once and I could never afterwards renew simple human relations with him. For ever after that, our eyes flashed when we looked at one another. As for my wife, whom I deluged with quantities of this vitriol of jealous hatred, I entirely disfigured her. During this period of unfounded hatred, I quite dethroned and shamed her in my imagination. I imagined the most impossible tricks on her part. I suspected her, I am ashamed to say, of behaving like the queen in the *Arabian Nights*: being unfaithful to me with a slave almost before my very eyes, and then laughing at me. So that with each fresh access of jealousy (I am still speaking of groundless jealousy) I fell into an already prepared rut of filthy suspicions about her and I made the rut deeper and deeper. She did the same. If I had reasons for jealousy, she, knowing my past, had a thousand times more. And she was even more jealous of me. And the sufferings I experienced from her jealousy were quite different and were also very severe. They occurred like this: we are living more or less quietly; I am even merry and tranquil, when we happen to begin a most ordinary conversation and all at once she does not agree with things she had always agreed with. More than that, I notice that she is becoming irritable without a cause. I think she is upset or that what we are saying is really unpleasant to her. But we turn to something else and the same thing happens, she again attacks me and is again irritable. I am astonished and seek the cause of this. What is it all about? She becomes silent, replies in monosyllables, or when she speaks is evidently hinting at something. I begin to guess that the reason of it is that I have taken a walk in the garden with her cousin, with whom I never even thought of anything wrong, or there is some cause of that kind. I begin to guess at it but cannot mention it. Were I to do so I should confirm her suspicions. I begin to investigate and to interrogate her. She does not reply but guesses that I have understood what it is, and she feels still more strongly confirmed in her suspicions. "What is the matter with you?" I ask. "Nothing, I am the same as usual," she says; but like a lunatic she utters meaningless, inexplicable, and bitter words. Sometimes I endure it, but sometimes I burst out and become irritable myself, and then a flood of abuse pours forth and I am convicted of some imaginary offence. And all this is carried to an extreme with sobs and tears, and she rushes out of the house to most unusual places. I begin to search for her. I am uneasy as to what the servants and children will think but there is nothing for it. She is in such a state that I feel she may do anything. I run after her and look for her. I spend tormenting nights. And finally, with exhausted nerves, after most cruel words and accusations, we both become tranquillized again.'

[50] *The lithographed version varies here considerably from the printed version, though in some passages the one repeats the other. The lithography runs as follows:*

That is why they do not wish to suckle them: "If I suckle him," they say, "I shall love him too much—and what shall I do then if he dies?" It seems that they would prefer it if their children were gutta-percha, so that they could not be ill or die but could always be mended. Think what a muddle goes on in the heads and hearts of these unfortunate women. That is why they do nasty things to prevent births: so as not to love! Love—the most joyful condition of the soul—seems to them a danger. And why is this so? Because when a man or woman does not live as a human being should, he or she is much worse than a beast. You see, our women are unable to regard a child otherwise than as a pleasure. It is true that the birth is painful, but its little hands. . . . Ah, its little feet! Ah, it smiles! Ah, what a darling little body it has! Ah, and it smacks its lips and hiccups! In a word, the animal maternal instinct is sensual. There is in it no thought at all of the mysterious meaning of the arrival of a new human being who will replace us. There is nothing of what is said and done in baptism. You know, nobody believes in baptism, and yet that was really a reminder of the human importance of the baby. People have given that up, they do not believe in it, but they have not replaced it in any way, and only the ribbons and lace and little hands and feet have remained. The animal part has remained. But the thing is that an animal does not possess imagination or foresight or reflections or doctors—yes—again those doctors! Take a hen or a cow: when a chicken gets the pip or a calf dies she cackles a bit or lows a little, and goes on living as before. When among us a child falls ill— what happens? How is it to be treated? Where is it to be nursed? What doctor must we call in? Where is one to drive to? And if it should die—where will the little hands and little feet be then? Why has it all happened so? Why do we have this suffering? A cow does not ask this, and this is why our children are a torment. A cow has no imagination, and therefore cannot think of how she might have saved her offspring by doing so-and-so and so-and-so; and therefore her grief, mingling with her physical condition and continuing for a certain limited time, is not a condition of grief which is augmented by physical idleness and satiation till it becomes despair. She has not a reason which asks, "Why has this happened? Why were all these sufferings endured, why did I love the babies—if they had to die?" The cow has no reason which could say that in future it will be better not to bear offspring or if that happens accidentally then not to suckle it and in general not to love it, or things will be worse for her. But that is how our women reason. And it shows that when a human being does not live humanly, it is worse for him or her than for a beast.'

'Then what, in your opinion, is the human way in which one should treat children?' I asked.

'How? Love them humanly.'

'Well, don't mothers love their children?'

'Not like human beings, they hardly ever do that, and therefore they do not even love them in dog-fashion. Just notice: a hen, a goose, a she-wolf, are always unattainable models of animal love for our women. Few women would at the risk of their lives rush at an elephant to take their baby from him, but no hen, and no she-crow even, would fail to fly at a dog; and each of them would sacrifice itself for its children, while few women would do so. Notice that a human mother can refrain from physical love of her children while an animal cannot do so. Well, is that because a woman is inferior to an animal? No, but because she is superior (though "superior" is incorrect; she is not "superior," but is a different creature). She has other obligations—human ones; she can refrain from animal love and can transfer her love to the child's soul. That is becoming to a human mother, and that is what never is done in our society. We read of the heroism of mothers who sacrifice their children for the sake of something higher, and it seems to us that these cases are merely stories of ancient times, which have no relation to us. But yet I think that if a mother has nothing for the sake of which she can sacrifice her animal feelings for her child, and if she transfers the spiritual force, which has been left unapplied, to attempting the impossible—the physical preservation of her child—in which attempt the doctors will assist her, it will be much worse for her, and she will suffer, as she actually does suffer! So it was with my wife. Whether there was one child or five—it was always the same. It was even a little better when we had five of them. Our whole life was continually poisoned by fear on the children's account—fear of their real or imaginary illnesses —and even by their very presence. I at any rate, during my whole married life, always felt that my life and all my interests continually hung by a hair, and depended on the children's health and condition and lessons. Children are of course an important matter, but then we all have to live! In our times the grown-ups are not allowed to live. They have no proper life: the life of the whole family hangs every second by a hair; and family life, life for the married couple, is lacking. No matter what important affair you may have, if you suddenly hear that Vásya has vomited, or Lisa's motion shows signs of blood, everything has instantly to be left, forgotten, thrown away. Everything else is insignificant. . . . The only important things are the doctors, the enemas, the temperatures: not to mention the fact that you can never begin a conversation without it happening at the most interesting part that Pétya runs in with a troubled face to ask whether he is to eat an apple or which jacket he is to put on, or without the nurse bringing in a shrieking baby. There is no regular firm family life. How you are to live, where to live, and therefore what your occupation is to be, all depends on the children's health; while their health does not depend on anyone, but, thanks to the doctors who say that they can preserve their health, your whole life may be disturbed at any moment. There is no life; it is a constant peril.'

[51] Add: But besides this, the children were for her also a means of forgetting herself—an intoxication. I often noticed that when she was upset about anything she felt better if one of the children fell ill and she could revert to that state of intoxication. But it was an involuntary intoxication; there was nothing evil about it.

[52] Add: Of course the doctors confirmed all this with an air of importance and encouraged her in the belief. She would have been glad not to be afraid, but the doctor dropped a word or two about "blood-poisoning," "scarlatina," or (God forbid) "dysentery"—and it was all up! Nor could it be otherwise. You see, if among us women had, as in olden times, a belief that "The Lord gave, and the Lord hath taken away," that a young child's angel-

soul goes to God and it is better for him—the dead child
—to die in innocence than to die later on in sin, and so
forth, which is what people did believe, you know—if they
had any faith of that sort, they could bear the children's illnesses more quietly; but now there is nothing
of that sort left—not a trace of it. There is no belief of
that kind. But one must have faith in something, and they
have faith—a senseless faith—in medicine—and not even
in medicine but in doctors. One woman in I. I., and another in P. P.; and like religious believers they do not see
the absurdity of their faith but believe *quia absurdum*.
You know, if they did not believe irrationally, they would
see the absurdity of what those brigands prescribe—the
whole of it. Scarlatina is an infectious disease; on account
of it, in a large town, half the family has to move into a
hotel (they twice made us move in that way). But, you
see, everyone in a town is a centre of innumerable
diameters which carry the threads of all kinds of infection,
and there is no possibility of avoiding them: the baker,
the tailor, the laundress, and the cabman. So that for
everyone who moves out of his own house to another place
to escape an infection he knows of, I will undertake to
find, in that other place, another infection—if not the
very same infection—as near at hand. But that is not
enough. We all know of rich people who after diphtheria
have had everything in their house destroyed, and in that
house when freshly done up, have themselves fallen ill;
and we all know of dozens of people who have remained
with the sick ones and have not been infected. And so it
is with everything; one only need keep one's ears open.
One woman tells another that her doctor is a good one.
The other replies: "What are you saying? Why, he killed
so-and-so." And vice versa. Well, bring a country doctor
to a lady and she won't trust him; but bring another doctor in a carriage, who knows precisely as much and who
treats his patients on the basis of the same books and the
same experiments, and tell her that he must be paid $50
for each visit, and she will believe in him. The root of the
matter is that our women are savages. They have no faith
in God, and so some of them believe in an evil eye cast
by wicked people and others in Doctor I. P. because he
charges high fees. If they had faith they would know
that scarlatina and so forth is not at all so terrible, for it
cannot injure what one can and should love—namely, the

soul, and that sickness and death which none of us can avoid may occur. But as there is no faith in God they only love physically and all their energy is directed towards preserving life, which cannot be done, and which only the doctors assure fools, and especially she-fools, that they can save. And so they have to be called in. Therefore having children, far from improving our relations to one another, did not unite us but on the contrary divided us.

[53] *In the lithographed version the chapter continues*: At first we lived in the country, and later on in town. What I chiefly felt was that I was a man, and that a man, as I understood it, ought to be master, but that I had fallen under my wife's slipper, as the saying is, and could not manage to escape from under it. What chiefly kept me under her slipper was the children. I wished to get up and assert my authority, but it never came off. She had the children and, supporting herself on them, she ruled. I did not then understand that she was sure to rule, chiefly because when she married she was morally immeasureably superior to me as all maidens always are to man, because they are immeasureably purer than he. Notice this surprising fact, that a woman, an average woman of our circle, is usually a very poor creature, lacking moral bases, an egotist, a chatterbox, and wrong-headed, but a maiden, an ordinary maiden, a girl up to twenty years of age, is for the most part a charming creature ready for everything noble and good. Why is that so? Clearly it is because the husbands pervert their wives and bring them morally down to their own lower level. In fact if boys and girls are born equal the advantage on the girls' side is still enormous. In the first place a girl is not exposed to those vicious conditions to which we are exposed; she has not the smoking, the wine, the cards, the schools, the comrades, or the state-service we have, and secondly and chiefly she is physically virgin. And so a maiden when she marries is always superior to her husband. She is superior to him while she is a maiden, and when she becomes a married woman, in our circle where the men are under no direct compulsion to earn their own maintenance, she usually becomes superior to him also by the greater importance of her occupation when she begins to bear children and to feed them. A woman when bearing and nursing, clearly sees that her occupation is more important than the man's—who sits on the

County Council,* in Courts of Justice, or in the Senate. She knows that in all such affairs the one important thing is to get money. But money can be got in various other ways, and therefore the getting of it is not so indubitably necessary as the feeding of a child. So that the woman is certainly superior to the man and ought to rule him. But a man of our circle not only does not acknowledge this, but on the contrary always looks down on woman from the height of his grandeur, and despises her activity. So my wife despised me and my County activities, on the ground that she bore and nursed children. While I, supported by the established masculine view, considered that a woman's fussing: "swaddlings, teats, and teething," as I jokingly called it, is a most contemptible activity which one may and should jest about. "The women know how to attend to that." So besides all other causes we were also separated by mutual contempt.

54 *Instead of the next lines, read:* To people who were quite strangers to us she and I spoke of various subjects, but not with one another. Sometimes hearing how she spoke to other people in my presence, I said to myself: "What lies she is telling!" And I was surprised that the person she was speaking to did not see that she was pretending.

55 *Add:* The periods of what we called love occurred as often as before, but were barer, coarser, and lacked any cover. But they did not last long and were immediately followed by periods of quite causeless anger springing up on most unintelligible grounds.

56 *Add:* All these were occupations that were not directly necessary, but she always behaved as if her life and that of the children depended on the pies with the soup not being burnt, on the curtain being hung up, the dress finished, the lesson learnt, and some medicine or other taken. It was clear to me that all this was for her mainly a means of forgetting herself, an intoxication, such as was for me the intoxication of my service, shooting, or cards. It is true that besides these I also had intoxication in its direct meaning—drunkenness: with tobacco, of which I smoked an enormous quantity, and alcohol with which I did not actually get drunk, but of which I took some vodka before meals and a couple tumblers of wine during meals,

* The *Zémskoe Sobránie,* work in the administration of which was paid for.

so that a continual fog screened from us the discord of our life.

[57] *Add:* All this mental illness of ours occurred simply because we lived immorally. We suffered from our immoral life, and to smother our suffering we committed various abnormal acts—just what those doctors call "indications of mental disease"—hysterics. The cure for these illnesses does not lie with Charcot, nor with them. It cannot be cured by any suggestions or bromides, but it is necessary to recognize what the pain comes from. It is like sitting down on a nail: if you notice the nail, or see what is wrong in your life and cease to do it, the pain will cease and there will be nothing to smother. The wrongness of our life caused the pain, caused my torments of jealousy and my need of going out shooting, of cards, and above all of wine and tobacco to keep myself in a constant state of intoxication. From that wrongness of life arose her passionate relation to all her occupations, her instability of mood—now gloomy, now terribly gay—and her volubility—it all came from the constant need of diverting her attention from herself and her life. It was a constant intoxication with this or that work, which always had to be done in a hurry.

[58] *Add:* Unhappy people can get on better in town.

[59] *Instead of the following line, read:* Divorce, well then divorce!" My sister-in-law would not admit that idea.

[60] *Read:* but I have bound myself by my own words.

[61] *Read:* disliked him and understood that he was a dirty adulterer, and I began to be jealous of him even before he saw my wife.

[62] *Read:* why, in the important events of our life, in those which decide a man's fate—as mine was decided then—why, there is no distinction between past and future.

[63] *Instead of the following three lines, read:* I had a consciousness of some terrible calamity connected with that man. But for all that I could not help being affable with him.

[64] *Read:* He played excellently, with a strong and tender tone; difficulties did not exist for him. As soon as he began to play his face altered, became serious and far more sympathetic; he was of course a much better player than my wife and helped her simply and naturally.

[65] *Read:* . . . simple and pleasant. During the whole evening I seemed not only to the others, but to myself, to

be solely interested in the music, while in reality I was unceasingly tormented by jealousy. From the first moment that his eyes met my wife's I saw that he looked at her as a woman who was not unpleasant and with whom on occasion it would not be unpleasant to have a liaison. Had I been pure I should not have thought about what he might think of her, but like most men I also thought about women, and therefore understood him and was tormented by it.

[66] *Read*: his restrained voice and her refusal. She seemed to say "but no," and something more. It was as if someone was intentionally smothering the words. My God, what then arose in me! What I imagined!

[67] *Add*: She will disgrace me! I will go away—but I can't.

[68] *Add*: and advised me to see it out.

[69] *Add*: A husband ought not to think so, and still less should he shove his nose in and hinder things.

[70] *Read*: graceful, indolent, subtle figure,

[71] *Add*: or something of that kind about my character.

[72] *Instead of the next six lines, read*: and I turned her round and gave her a violent push. "What is the matter with you? Recollect yourself!" said she.

[73] *Add*: rolling my eyes.

[74] *Read*: I restrained myself and

[75] *Add*: We sent for the doctor, and I attended her all night.

[76] *Add*: . . . not so much on account of my wife's assurances, as on account of the tormenting suffering I had experienced from my jealousy.

[77] *Add*: He went to fetch his violin. My wife went to the piano and began selecting the music.

[78] *Add*: and long remained silent.

[79] *Add*: In this new condition jealousy had no place.

[80] *Add*: That music drew me into some world in which jealousy no longer had place. Jealousy and the feeling that evoked it seemed trifles not worth considering.

[81] *Instead of the next eleven lines, read*: I hardly felt jealous all the evening. I had to go to the Meetings in two days' time, and he, when leaving, collected all his music and inquired when I should be back, as he wished to say good-bye before his own departure. . . . It appeared that I should hardly be back before he left Moscow, so we bade one another a definite good-bye.

[82] *Add*: We spoke in very general terms of the impres-

sions produced by the music, but we were nearer and more friendly to one another that evening, in a way we had seldom been of late.

[83] *Read*: while it was still dark,

[84] *Add*: and as if I should drive on like that to the end of my life and of the world.

[85] *Add*: which was quite a new one,

[86] *Add*: one more cynical than another,

[87] *Add*: forgetting that there was no ground for this.

[88] *Instead of the next line, read*: I cried out, and began to groan.

[89] *Add*: and the same thing began again within me. I suffered as I never had suffered before. I did not know what to do with myself, and the thought occurred to me—and it pleased me very much—of getting out onto the line, lying down under the train, and finishing everything. The one thing that hindered my doing this was my self-pity, which immediately evoked hatred of her and of him. Of him not so much. Regarding him I had a strange feeling of my own humiliation and of his victory, but of her I felt terrible hatred. It will not do to finish myself off and to leave her, it is necessary that she should suffer.

[90] *Instead of the following words, read*: and read the shop signboards,

[91] *Instead of the next sentence, read*: I cannot at all explain to myself now why I was in such a hurry.

[92] *Read*: there arose in me an animal craving for physical, agile cunning, and decisive action.

[93] *Read*: and of the tormenting pleasure of punishing, and executing.

[94] *In the lithograph the chapter ends with the words*: I do not know how I went, with what steps, whether I ran or only walked, through which rooms I went on my way to the drawing-room, how I opened the door or how I entered the room—I remember nothing of all that.

[95] *In the lithograph this first sentence is omitted.*

[96] *Add*: as from a spring.

[97] *Add*:—a sister.

[98] *Read*: ' "Yes, if you had not killed me!" she suddenly exclaimed, and her eyes glittered feverishly.

[99] *The sentence ends*: the children, not even Lisa who rushed up to her.

[100] *In the lithograph the conclusion is different, the last*

paragraph being as follows: Yes, that is what I have done, and what I have gone through. Yes, a man should understand that the real meaning of the words in the Gospel—Matthew v. 28—where it says that everyone that looketh on a woman to lust after her commits adultery, relates to woman, his fellow human being—not merely to casual women or strangers, but above all to his own wife.

Master and Man

[1895]

I

It happened in the 'seventies in winter, on the day after St. Nicholas's Day. There was a fête in the parish and the innkeeper, Vasíli Andréevich Brekhunóv, a Second Guild merchant, being a church elder had to go to church, and had also to entertain his relatives and friends at home.

But when the last of them had gone he at once began to prepare to drive over to see a neighbouring proprietor about a grove which he had been bargaining over for a long time. He was now in a hurry to start, lest buyers from the town might forestall him in making a profitable purchase.

The youthful landowner was asking ten thousand rubles for the grove simply because Vasíli Andréevich was offering seven thousand. Seven thousand was, however, only a third of its real value. Vasíli Andréevich might perhaps have got it down to his own price, for the woods were in his district and he had a long-standing agreement with the other village dealers that no one should run up the price in another's district, but he had now learnt that some timber-dealers from town meant to bid for the Goryáchkin grove, and he resolved to go at once and get the matter settled. So as soon as the feast was over, he took seven hundred rubles from his strong box, added to them two thousand three hundred rubles of church money he had in his keeping, so as to make up the sum to three thousand; carefully counted the notes, and having put them into his pocket-book made haste to start.

Nikíta, the only one of Vasíli Andréevich's labourers who was not drunk that day, ran to harness the horse. Nikíta, though an habitual drunkard, was not drunk that day because since the last day before the fast, when he had drunk his coat and leather boots, he had sworn off drink and had kept his vow for two months, and was still keeping

453

it despite the temptation of the vodka that had been drunk everywhere during the first two days of the feast.

Nikíta was a peasant of about fifty from a neighbouring village, 'not a manager' as the peasants said of him, meaning that he was not the thrifty head of a household but lived most of his time away from home as a labourer. He was valued everywhere for his industry, dexterity, and strength at work, and still more for his kindly and pleasant temper. But he never settled down anywhere for long because about twice a year, or even oftener, he had a drinking bout, and then besides spending all his clothes on drink he became turbulent and quarrelsome. Vasíli Andréevich himself had turned him away several times, but had afterwards taken him back again—valuing his honesty, his kindness to animals, and especially his cheapness. Vasíli Andréevich did not pay Nikíta the eighty rubles a year such a man was worth, but only about forty, which he gave him haphazard, in small sums, and even that mostly not in cash but in goods from his own shop and at high prices.

Nikíta's wife Martha, who had once been a handsome vigorous woman, managed the homestead with the help of her son and two daughters, and did not urge Nikíta to live at home: first because she had been living for some twenty years already with a cooper, a peasant from another village who lodged in their house; and secondly because though she managed her husband as she pleased when he was sober, she feared him like fire when he was drunk. Once when he had got drunk at home, Nikíta, probably to make up for his submissiveness when sober, broke open her box, took out her best clothes, snatched up an axe, and chopped all her undergarments and dresses to bits. All the wages Nikíta earned went to his wife, and he raised no objection to that. So now, two days before the holiday, Martha had been twice to see Vasíli Andréevich and had got from him wheat flour, tea, sugar, and a quart of vodka, the lot costing three rubles, and also five rubles in cash, for which she thanked him as for a special favour, though he owed Nikíta at least twenty rubles.

'What agreement did we ever draw up with you?' said Vasíli Andréevich to Nikíta. 'If you need anything, take it; you will work it off. I'm not like others to keep you waiting, and making up accounts and reckoning fines. We deal straight-forwardly. You serve me and I don't neglect you.'

And when saying this Vasíli Andréevich was honestly convinced that he was Nikíta's benefactor, and he knew how to put it so plausibly that all those who depended on him for their money, beginning with Nikíta, confirmed him in the conviction that he was their benefactor and did not overreach them.

'Yes, I understand, Vasíli Andréevich. You know that I serve you and take as much pains as I would for my own father. I understand very well!' Nikíta would reply. He was quite aware that Vasíli Andréevich was cheating him, but at the same time he felt that it was useless to try to clear up his accounts with him or explain his side of the matter, and that as long as he had nowhere to go he must accept what he could get.

Now, having heard his master's order to harness, he went as usual cheerfully and willingly to the shed, stepping briskly and easily on his rather turned-in feet; took down from a nail the heavy tasselled leather bridle, and jingling the rings of the bit went to the closed stable where the horse he was to harness was standing by himself.

'What, feeling lonely, feeling lonely, little silly?' said Nikíta in answer to the low whinny with which he was greeted by the good-tempered, medium-sized bay stallion, with a rather slanting crupper, who stood alone in the shed. 'Now then, now then, there's time enough. Let me water you first,' he went on, speaking to the horse just as to someone who understood the words he was using, and having whisked the dusty, grooved back of the well-fed young stallion with the skirt of his coat, he put a bridle on his handsome head, straightened his ears and forelock, and having taken off his halter led him out to water.

Picking his way out of the dung-strewn stable, Mukhórty frisked, and making play with his hind leg pretended that he meant to kick Nikíta, who was running at a trot beside him to the pump.

'Now then, now then, you rascal!' Nikíta called out, well knowing how carefully Mukhórty threw out his hind leg just to touch his greasy sheepskin coat but not to strike him—a trick Nikíta much appreciated.

After a drink of the cold water the horse sighed, moving his strong wet lips, from the hairs of which transparent drops fell into the trough; then standing still as if in thought, he suddenly gave a loud snort.

'If you don't want any more, you needn't. But don't go

asking for any later,' said Nikíta quite seriously and fully explaining his conduct to Mukhórty. Then he ran back to the shed pulling the playful young horse, who wanted to gambol all over the yard, by the rein.

There was no one else in the yard except a stranger, the cook's husband, who had come for the holiday.

'Go and ask which sledge is to be harnessed—the wide one or the small one—there's a good fellow!'

The cook's husband went into the house, which stood on an iron foundation and was iron-roofed, and soon returned saying that the little one was to be harnessed. By that time Nikíta had put the collar and brass-studded belly-band on Mukhórty and, carrying a light, painted shaft-bow in one hand, was leading the horse with the other up to two sledges that stood in the shed.

'All right, let it be the little one!' he said, backing the intelligent horse, which all the time kept pretending to bite him, into the shafts, and with the aid of the cook's husband he proceeded to harness. When everything was nearly ready and only the reins had to be adjusted, Nikíta sent the other man to the shed for some straw and to the barn for a drugget.

'There, that's all right! Now, now, don't bristle up!' said Nikíta, pressing down into the sledge the freshly threshed oat straw the cook's husband had brought. 'And now let's spread the sacking like this, and the drugget over it. There, like that it will be comfortable sitting,' he went on, suiting the action to the words and tucking the drugget all round over the straw to make a seat.

'Thank you, dear man. Things always go quicker with two working at it!' he added. And gathering up the leather reins fastened together by a brass ring, Nikíta took the driver's seat and started the impatient horse over the frozen manure which lay in the yard, towards the gate.

'Uncle Nikíta! I say, Uncle, Uncle!' a high-pitched voice shouted, and a seven-year-old boy in a black sheepskin coat, new white felt boots, and a warm cap, ran hurriedly out of the house into the yard. 'Take me with you!' he cried, fastening up his coat as he ran.

'All right, come along, darling!' said Nikíta, and stopping the sledge he picked up the master's pale thin little son, radiant with joy, and drove out into the road.

It was past two o'clock and the day was windy, dull, and cold, with more than twenty degrees Fahrenheit of frost. Half the sky was hidden by a lowering dark cloud. In the yard it was quiet, but in the street the wind was felt more keenly. The snow swept down from a neighbouring shed and whirled about in the corner near the bath-house.

Hardly had Nikíta driven out of the yard and turned the horse's head to the house, before Vasíli Andréevich emerged from the high porch in front of the house with a cigarette in his mouth and wearing a cloth-covered sheepskin coat tightly girdled low at his waist, and stepped onto the hard-trodden snow which squeaked under the leather soles of his felt boots, and stopped. Taking a last whiff of his cigarette he threw it down, stepped on it, and letting the smoke escape through his moustache and looking askance at the horse that was coming up, began to tuck in his sheepskin collar on both sides of his ruddy face, clean-shaven except for the moustache, so that his breath should not moisten the collar.

'See now! The young scamp is there already!' he exclaimed when he saw his little son in the sledge. Vasíli Andréevich was excited by the vodka he had drunk with his visitors, and so he was even more pleased than usual with everything that was his and all that he did. The sight of his son, whom he always thought of as his heir, now gave him great satisfaction. He looked at him, screwing up his eyes and showing his long teeth.

His wife—pregnant, thin and pale, with her head and shoulders wrapped in a shawl so that nothing of her face could be seen but her eyes—stood behind him in the vestibule to see him off.

'Now really, you ought to take Nikíta with you,' she said timidly, stepping out from the doorway.

Vasíli Andréevich did not answer. Her words evidently annoyed him and he frowned angrily and spat.

'You have money on you,' she continued in the same plaintive voice. 'What if the weather gets worse! Do take him, for goodness' sake!'

'Why? Don't I know the road that I must needs take a guide?' exclaimed Vasíli Andréevich, uttering every word very distinctly and compressing his lips unnaturally, as he usually did when speaking to buyers and sellers.

'Really you ought to take him. I beg you in God's name!' his wife repeated, wrapping her shawl more closely round her head.

'There, she sticks to it like a leech! . . . Where am I to take him?'

'I'm quite ready to go with you, Vasíli Andréevich,' said Nikíta cheerfully. 'But they must feed the horses while I am away,' he added, turning to his master's wife.

'I'll look after them, Nikíta dear. I'll tell Simon,' replied the mistress.

'Well, Vasíli Andréevich, am I to come with you?' said Nikíta, awaiting a decision.

'It seems I must humour my old woman. But if you're coming you'd better put on a warmer cloak,' said Vasíli Andréevich, smiling again as he winked at Nikíta's short sheepskin coat, which was torn under the arms and at the back, was greasy and out of shape, frayed to a fringe round the skirt, and had endured many things in its lifetime.

'Hey, dear man, come and hold the horse!' shouted Nikíta to the cook's husband, who was still in the yard.

'No, I will myself, I will myself!' shrieked the little boy, pulling his hands, red with cold, out of his pockets, and seizing the cold leather reins.

'Only don't be too long dressing yourself up. Look alive!' shouted Vasíli Andréevich, grinning at Nikíta.

'Only a moment, Father, Vasíli Andréevich!' replied Nikíta, and running quickly with his inturned toes in his felt boots with their soles patched with felt, he hurried across the yard and into the workmen's hut.

'Arínushka! Get my coat down from the stove. I'm going with the master,' he said, as he ran into the hut and took down his girdle from the nail on which it hung.

The workmen's cook, who had had a sleep after dinner and was now getting the samovar ready for her husband, turned cheerfully to Nikíta, and infected by his hurry began to move as quickly as he did, got down his miserable worn-out cloth coat from the stove where it was drying, and began hurriedly shaking it out and smoothing it down.

'There now, you'll have a chance of a holiday with your good man,' said Nikíta, who from kindhearted politeness always said something to anyone he was alone with.

Then, drawing his worn narrow girdle round him, he drew in his breath, pulling in his lean stomach still more, and girdled himself as tightly as he could over his sheepskin.

'There now,' he said addressing himself no longer to the cook but the girdle, as he tucked the ends in at the waist, 'now you won't come undone!' And working his shoulders up and down to free his arms, he put the coat over his sheepskin, arched his back more strongly to ease his arms, poked himself under the armpits, and took down his leather-covered mittens from the shelf. 'Now we're all right!'

'You ought to wrap your feet up, Nikíta. Your boots are very bad.'

Nikíta stopped as if he had suddenly realized this.

'Yes, I ought to. . . . But they'll do like this. It isn't far!' and he ran out into the yard.

'Won't you be cold, Nikíta?' said the mistress as he came up to the sledge.

'Cold? No, I'm quite warm,' answered Nikíta as he pushed some straw up to the forepart of the sledge so that it should cover his feet, and stowed away the whip, which the good horse would not need, at the bottom of the sledge.

Vasíli Andréevich, who was wearing two fur-lined coats one over the other, was already in the sledge, his broad back filling nearly its whole rounded width, and taking the reins he immediately touched the horse. Nikíta jumped in just as the sledge started, and seated himself in front on the left side, with one leg hanging over the edge.

II

The good stallion took the sledge along at a brisk pace over the smooth-frozen road through the village, the runners squeaking slightly as they went.

'Look at him hanging on there! Hand me the whip, Nikíta!' shouted Vasíli Andréevich, evidently enjoying the sight of his 'heir,' who standing on the runners was hanging on at the back of the sledge. 'I'll give it you! Be off to mamma, you dog!'

The boy jumped down. The horse increased his amble and, suddenly changing foot, broke into a fast trot.

The Crosses, the village where Vasíli Andréevich lived, consisted of six houses. As soon as they had passed the blacksmith's hut, the last in the village, they realized that the wind was much stronger than they had thought. The road could hardly be seen. The tracks left by the sledge-runners were immediately covered by snow and the road was only distinguished by the fact that it was higher than the rest of the ground. There was a whirl of snow over the fields and the line where sky and earth met could not be seen. The Telyátin forest, usually clearly visible, now only loomed up occasionally and dimly through the driving snowy dust. The wind came from the left, insistently blowing over to one side the mane on Mukhórty's sleek neck and carrying aside even his fluffy tail, which was tied in a simple knot. Nikíta's wide coat-collar, as he sat on the windy side, pressed close to his cheek and nose.

'This road doesn't give him a chance—it's too snowy,' said Vasíli Andréevich, who prided himself on his good horse. 'I once drove to Pashútino with him in half an hour.'

'What?' asked Nikíta, who could not hear on account of his collar.

'I say I once went to Pashútino in half an hour,' shouted Vasíli Andréevich.

'It goes without saying that he's a good horse,' replied Nikíta.

They were silent for a while. But Vasíli Andréevich wished to talk.

'Well, did you tell your wife not to give the cooper any vodka?' he began in the same loud tone, quite convinced that Nikíta must feel flattered to be talking with so clever and important a person as himself, and he was so pleased with his jest that it did not enter his head that the remark might be unpleasant to Nikíta.

The wind again prevented Nikíta's hearing his master's words.

Vasíli Andréevich repeated the jest about the cooper in his loud, clear voice.

'That's their business, Vasíli Andréevich. I don't pry into their affairs. As long as she doesn't ill-treat our boy—God be with them.'

'That's so,' said Vasíli Andréevich. 'Well, and will you be buying a horse in spring?' he went on, changing the subject.

'Yes, I can't avoid it,' answered Nikíta, turning down his collar and leaning back towards his master.

The conversation now became interesting to him and he did not wish to lose a word.

'The lad's growing up. He must begin to plough for himself, but till now we've always had to hire someone,' he said.

'Well, why not have the lean-cruppered one. I won't charge much for it,' shouted Vasíli Andréevich, feeling animated, and consequently starting on his favourite occupation—that of horse-dealing—which absorbed all his mental powers.

'Or you might let me have fifteen rubles and I'll buy one at the horse-market,' said Nikíta, who knew that the horse Vasíli Andréevich wanted to sell him would be dear at seven rubles, but that if he took it from him it would be charged at twenty-five, and then he would be unable to draw any money for half a year.

'It's a good horse. I think of your interest as of my own —according to conscience. Brekhunóv isn't a man to wrong anyone. Let the loss be mine. I'm not like others. Honestly!' he shouted in the voice in which he hypnotized his customers and dealers. 'It's a real good horse.'

'Quite so!' said Nikíta with a sigh, and convinced that there was nothing more to listen to, he again released his collar, which immediately covered his ear and face.

They drove on in silence for about half an hour. The wind blew sharply onto Nikíta's side and arm where his sheepskin was torn.

He huddled up and breathed into the collar which covered his mouth, and was not wholly cold.

'What do you think—shall we go through Karamýshevo or by the straight road?' asked Vasíli Andréevich.

The road through Karamýshevo was more frequented and was well marked with a double row of high stakes. The straight road was nearer but little used and had no stakes, or only poor ones covered with snow.

Nikíta thought awhile.

'Though Karamýshevo is farther, it is better going,' he said.

'But by the straight road, when once we get through the hollow by the forest, it's good going—sheltered,' said Vasíli Andréevich, who wished to go the nearest way.

'Just as you please,' said Nikíta, and again let go of his collar.

Vasíli Andréevich did as he had said, and having gone about half a verst came to a tall oak stake which had a few dry leaves still dangling on it, and there he turned to the left.

On turning they faced directly against the wind, and snow was beginning to fall. Vasíli Andréevich, who was driving, inflated his cheeks, blowing the breath out through his moustache. Nikíta dosed.

So they went on in silence for about ten minutes. Suddenly Vasíli Andréevich began saying something.

'Eh, what?' asked Nikíta, opening his eyes.

Vasíli Andréevich did not answer, but bent over, looking behind them and then ahead of the horse. The sweat had curled Mukhórty's coat between his legs and on his neck. He went at a walk.

'What is it?' Nikíta asked again.

'What is it? What is it?' Vasíli Andréevich mimicked him angrily. 'There are no stakes to be seen! We must have got off the road!'

'Well, pull up then, and I'll look for it,' said Nikíta, and jumping down lightly from the sledge and taking the whip from under the straw, he went off to the left from his own side of the sledge.

The snow was not deep that year, so that it was possible to walk anywhere, but still in places it was knee-deep and got into Nikíta's boots. He went about feeling the ground with his feet and the whip, but could not find the road anywhere.

'Well, how is it?' asked Vasíli Andréevich when Nikíta came back to the sledge.

'There is no road this side. I must go to the other side and try there,' said Nikíta.

'There's something there in front. Go and have a look.'

Nikíta went to what had appeared dark, but found that it was earth which the wind had blown from the bare fields of winter oats and had strewn over the snow, colouring it. Having searched to the right also, he returned to the sledge, brushed the snow from his coat, shook it out of his boots, and seated himself once more.

'We must go to the right,' he said decidedly. 'The wind was blowing on our left before, but now it is straight in my face. Drive to the right,' he repeated with decision.

Vasíli Andréevich took his advice and turned to the right, but still there was no road. They went on in that direction for some time. The wind was as fierce as ever and it was snowing lightly.

'It seems, Vasíli Andréevich, that we have gone quite astray,' Nikíta suddenly remarked, as if it were a pleasant thing. 'What is that?' he added, pointing to some potato vines that showed up from under the snow.

Vasíli Andréevich stopped the perspiring horse, whose deep sides were heaving heavily.

'What is it?'

'Why, we are on the Zakhárov lands. See where we've got to!'

'Nonsense!' retorted Vasíli Andréevich.

'It's not nonsense, Vasíli Andréevich. It's the truth,' replied Nikíta. 'You can feel that the sledge is going over a potato-field, and there are the heaps of vines which have been carted here. It's the Zakhárov factory land.'

'Dear me, how we have gone astray!' said Vasíli Andréevich. 'What are we to do now?'

'We must go straight on, that's all. We shall come out somewhere—if not at Zakhárova, then at the proprietor's farm,' said Nikíta.

Vasíli Andréevich agreed, and drove as Nikíta had indicated. So they went on for a considerable time. At times they came onto bare fields and the sledge-runners rattled over frozen lumps of earth. Sometimes they got onto a winter-rye field, or a fallow field on which they could see stalks of wormwood, and straws sticking up through the snow and swaying in the wind; sometimes they came onto deep and even white snow, above which nothing was to be seen.

The snow was falling from above and sometimes rose from below. The horse was evidently exhausted, his hair had all curled up from sweat and was covered with hoarfrost, and he went at a walk. Suddenly he stumbled and sat down in a ditch or water-course. Vasíli Andréevich wanted to stop, but Nikíta cried to him:

'Why stop? We've got in and must get out. Hey, pet! Hey, darling! Gee up, old fellow!' he shouted in a cheerful tone to the horse, jumping out of the sledge and himself getting stuck in the ditch.

The horse gave a start and quickly climbed out onto the frozen bank. It was evidently a ditch that had been dug there.

'Where are we now?' asked Vasíli Andréevich.

'We'll soon find out!' Nikíta replied. 'Go on, we'll get somewhere.'

'Why, this must be the Goryáchkin forest!' said Vasíli Andréevich, pointing to something dark that appeared amid the snow in front of them.

'We'll see what forest it is when we get there,' said Nikíta. He saw that beside the black thing they had noticed, dry, oblong willow-leaves were fluttering, and so he knew it was not a forest but a settlement, but he did not wish to say so. And in fact they had not gone twenty-five yards beyond the ditch before something in front of them, evidently trees, showed up black, and they heard a new and melancholy sound. Nikíta had guessed right: it was not a wood, but a row of tall willows with a few leaves still fluttering on them here and there. They had evidently been planted along the ditch round a threshing-floor. Coming up to the willows, which moaned sadly in the wind, the horse suddenly planted his forelegs above the height of the sledge, drew up his hind legs also, pulling the sledge onto higher ground, and turned to the left, no longer sinking up to his knees in snow. They were back on a road.

'Well, here we are, but heaven only knows where!' said Nikíta.

The horse kept straight along the road through the drifted snow, and before they had gone another hundred yards the straight line of the dark wattle wall of a barn showed up black before them, its roof heavily covered with snow which poured down from it. After passing the barn the road turned to the wind and they drove into a snow-drift. But ahead of them was a lane with houses on either side, so evidently the snow had been blown across the road and they had to drive through the drift. And so in fact it was. Having driven through the snow they came out into a street. At the end house of the village some frozen clothes hanging on a line—shirts, one red and one white, trousers, leg-bands, and a petticoat—fluttered wildly in the wind. The white shirt in particular struggled desperately, waving its sleeves about.

'There now, either a lazy woman or a dead one has not taken her clothes down before the holiday,' remarked Nikíta, looking at the fluttering shirts.

III

At the entrance to the street the wind still raged and the road was thickly covered with snow, but well within the village it was calm, warm, and cheerful. At one house a dog was barking, at another a woman, covering her head with her coat, came running from somewhere and entered the door of a hut, stopping on the threshold to have a look at the passing sledge. In the middle of the village girls could be heard singing.

Here in the village there seemed to be less wind and snow, and the frost was less keen.

'Why, this is Gríshkino,' said Vasíli Andréevich.

'So it is,' responded Nikíta.

It really was Gríshkino, which meant that they had gone too far to the left and had travelled some six miles, not quite in the direction they aimed at, but towards their destination for all that.

From Gríshkino to Goryáchkin was about another four miles.

In the middle of the village they almost ran into a tall man walking down the middle of the street.

'Who are you?' shouted the man, stopping the horse, and recognizing Vasíli Andréevich he immediately took hold of the shaft, went along it hand over hand till he reached the sledge, and placed himself on the driver's seat.

He was Isáy, a peasant of Vasíli Andréevich's acquaintance, and well known as the principal horse-thief in the district.

'Ah, Vasíli Andréevich! Where are you off to?' said Isáy, enveloping Nikíta in the odour of the vodka he had drunk.

'We were going to Goryáchkin.'

'And look where you've got to! You should have gone through Molchánovka.'

'Should have, but didn't manage it,' said Vasíli Andréevich, holding in the horse.

'That's a good horse,' said Isáy, with a shrewd glance at Mukhórty, and with a practised hand he tightened the loosened knot high in the horse's bushy tail.

'Are you going to stay the night?'

'No, friend. I must get on.'

'Your business must be pressing. And who is this? Ah, Nikíta Stepánych!'

'Who else?' replied Nikíta. 'But I say, good friend, how are we to avoid going astray again?'

'Where can you go astray here? Turn back straight down the street and then when you come out keep straight on. Don't take to the left. You will come out onto the high road, and then turn to the right.'

'And where do we turn off the high road? As in summer, or the winter way?' asked Nikíta.

'The winter way. As soon as you turn off you'll see some

bushes, and opposite them there is a way-mark—a large
oak, one with branches—and that's the way.'

Vasíli Andréevich turned the horse back and drove
through the outskirts of the village.

'Why not stay the night?' Isáy shouted after them.

But Vasíli Andréevich did not answer and touched up
the horse. Four miles of good road, two of which lay
through the forest, seemed easy to manage, especially as
the wind was apparently quieter and the snow had stopped.

Having driven along the trodden village street, darkened
here and there by fresh manure, past the yard where the
clothes hung out and where the white shirt had broken
loose and was now attached only by one frozen sleeve,
they again came within sound of the weird moan of the
willows, and again emerged on the open fields. The storm,
far from ceasing, seemed to have grown yet stronger. The
road was completely covered with drifting snow, and only
the stakes showed that they had not lost their way. But
even the stakes ahead of them were not easy to see, since
the wind blew in their faces.

Vasíli Andréevich screwed up his eyes, bent down his
head, and looked out for the way-marks, but trusted mainly
to the horse's sagacity, letting it take its own way. And
the horse really did not lose the road but followed its
windings, turning now to the right and now to the left
and sensing it under his feet, so that though the snow fell
thicker and the wind strengthened they still continued to
see way-marks now to the left and now to the right of them.

So they travelled on for about ten minutes, when suddenly, through the slanting screen of wind-driven snow,
something black showed up which moved in front of the
horse.

This was another sledge with fellow-travellers. Mukhórty
overtook them, and struck his hoofs against the back of
the sledge in front of him.

'Pass on . . . hey there . . . get in front!' cried voices
from the sledge.

Vasíli Andréevich swerved aside to pass the other sledge.
In it sat three men and a woman, evidently visitors returning from a feast. One peasant was whacking the snow-
covered croup of their little horse with a long switch, and
the other two sitting in front waved their arms and shouted
something. The woman, completely wrapped up and

covered with snow, sat drowsing and bumping at the back.

'Who are you?' shouted Vasíli Andréevich.

'From A-a-a . . .' was all that could be heard.

'I say, where are you from?'

'From A-a-a-a!' one of the peasants shouted with all his might, but still it was impossible to make out who they were.

'Get along! Keep up!' shouted another, ceaselessly beating his horse with the switch.

'So you're from a feast, it seems?'

'Go on, go on! Faster, Simon! Get in front! Faster!'

The wings of the sledges bumped against one another, almost got jammed but managed to separate, and the peasants' sledge began to fall behind.

Their shaggy, big-bellied horse, all covered with snow, breathed heavily under the low shaft-bow and, evidently using the last of its strength, vainly endeavoured to escape from the switch, hobbling with its short legs through the deep snow which it threw up under itself.

Its muzzle, young-looking, with the nether lip drawn up like that of a fish, nostrils distended and ears pressed back from fear, kept up for a few seconds near Nikíta's shoulder and then began to fall behind.

'Just see what liquor does!' said Nikíta. 'They've tired that little horse to death. What pagans!'

For a few minutes they heard the panting of the tired little horse and the drunken shouting of the peasants. Then the panting and the shouts died away, and around them nothing could be heard but the whistling of the wind in their ears and now and then the squeak of their sledge-runners over a windswept part of the road.

This encounter cheered and enlivened Vasíli Andréevich, and he drove on more boldly without examining the way-marks, urging on the horse and trusting to him.

Nikíta had nothing to do, and as usual in such circumstances he drowsed, making up for much sleepless time. Suddenly the horse stopped and Nikíta nearly fell forward onto his nose.

'You know we're off the track again!' said Vasíli Andréevich.

'How's that?'

'Why, there are no way-marks to be seen. We must have got off the road again.'

'Well, if we've lost the road we must find it,' said Nikíta curtly, and getting out and stepping lightly on his pigeon-toed feet he started once more going about on the snow.

He walked about for a long time, now disappearing and now reappearing, and finally he came back.

'There is no road here. There may be farther on,' he said, getting into the sledge.

It was already growing dark. The snow-storm had not increased but had also not subsided.

'If we could only hear those peasants!' said Vasíli Andréevich.

'Well they haven't caught us up. We must have gone far astray. Or maybe they have lost their way too.'

'Where are we to go then?' asked Vasíli Andréevich.

'Why, we must let the horse take its own way,' said Nikíta. 'He will take us right. Let me have the reins.'

Vasíli Andréevich gave him the reins, the more willingly because his hands were beginning to feel frozen in his thick gloves.

Nikíta took the reins, but only held them, trying not to shake them and rejoicing at his favourite's sagacity. And indeed the clever horse, turning first one ear and then the other now to one side and then to the other, began to wheel round.

'The one thing he can't do is to talk,' Nikíta kept saying. 'See what he is doing! Go on, go on! You know best. That's it, that's it!'

The wind was now blowing from behind and it felt warmer.

'Yes, he's clever,' Nikíta continued, admiring the horse. 'A Kirgiz horse is strong but stupid. But this one—just see what he's doing with his ears! He doesn't need any telegraph. He can scent a mile off.'

Before another half-hour had passed they saw something dark ahead of them—a wood or a village—and stakes again appeared to the right. They had evidently come out onto the road.

'Why, that's Gríshkino again!' Nikíta suddenly exclaimed.

And indeed, there on their left was that same barn with the snow flying from it, and farther on the same line with the frozen washing, shirts and trousers, which still fluttered desperately in the wind.

Again they drove into the street and again it grew quiet,

warm, and cheerful, and again they could see the manure-stained street and hear voices and songs and the barking of a dog. It was already so dark that there were lights in some of the windows.

Half-way through the village Vasíli Andréevich turned the horse towards a large double-fronted brick house and stopped at the porch.

Nikíta went to the lighted snow-covered window, in the rays of which flying snow-flakes glittered, and knocked at it with his whip.

'Who is there?' a voice replied to his knock.

'From Krestý, the Brekhunóvs, dear fellow,' answered Nikíta. 'Just come out for a minute.'

Someone moved from the window, and a minute or two later there was the sound of the passage door as it came unstuck, then the latch of the outside door clicked and a tall white-bearded peasant, with a sheepskin coat thrown over his white holiday shirt, pushed his way out holding the door firmly against the wind, followed by a lad in a red shirt and high leather boots.

'Is that you, Andréevich?' asked the old man.

'Yes, friend, we've gone astray,' said Vasíli Andréevich. 'We wanted to get to Goryáchkin but found ourselves here. We went a second time but lost our way again.'

'Just see how you have gone astray!' said the old man. 'Petrúshka, go and open the gate!' he added, turning to the lad in the red shirt.

'All right,' said the lad in a cheerful voice, and ran back into the passage.

'But we're not staying the night,' said Vasíli Andréevich.

'Where will you go in the night? You'd better stay!'

'I'd be glad to, but I must go on. It's business, and it can't be helped.'

'Well, warm yourself at least. The samovar is just ready.'

'Warm myself? Yes, I'll do that,' said Vasíli Andréevich. 'It won't get darker. The moon will rise and it will be lighter. Let's go in and warm ourselves, Nikíta.'

'Well, why not? Let us warm ourselves,' replied Nikíta, who was stiff with cold and anxious to warm his frozen limbs.

Vasíli Andréevich went into the room with the old man, and Nikíta drove through the gate opened for him by Petrúshka, by whose advice he backed the horse under the penthouse. The ground was covered with manure and the tall bow over the horse's head caught against the beam. The hens and the cock had already settled to roost there, and clucked peevishly, clinging to the beam with their claws. The disturbed sheep shied and rushed aside trampling the frozen manure with their hooves. The dog yelped desperately with fright and anger and then burst out barking like a puppy at the stranger.

Nikíta talked to them all, excused himself to the fowls and assured them that he would not disturb them again, rebuked the sheep for being frightened without knowing why, and kept soothing the dog, while he tied up the horse.

'Now that will be all right,' he said, knocking the snow off his clothes. 'Just hear how he barks!' he added, turning to the dog. 'Be quiet, stupid! Be quiet. You are only troubling yourself for nothing. We're not thieves, we're friends. . . .'

'And these are, it's said, the three domestic counsellors,' remarked the lad, and with his strong arms he pushed under the pent-roof the sledge that had remained outside.

'Why counsellors?' asked Nikíta.

'That's what is printed in Paulson. A thief creeps to a house—the dog barks, that means, "Be on your guard!" The cock crows, that means, "Get up!" The cat licks herself—that means, "A welcome guest is coming. Get ready to receive him!"' said the lad with a smile.

Petrúshka could read and write and knew Paulson's primer, his only book, almost by heart, and he was fond of quoting sayings from it that he thought suited the occasion, especially when he had had something to drink, as to-day.

'That's so,' said Nikíta.

'You must be chilled through and through,' said Petrúshka.

'Yes, I am rather,' said Nikíta, and they went across the yard and the passage into the house.

IV

The household to which Vasíli Andréevich had come was one of the richest in the village. The family had five allotments, besides renting other land. They had six horses, three cows, two calves, and some twenty sheep. There were twenty-two members belonging to the homestead:

four married sons, six grandchildren (one of whom, Petrúshka, was married), two great-grandchildren, three orphans, and four daughters-in-law with their babies. It was one of the few homesteads that remained still undivided, but even here the dull internal work of disintegration which would inevitably lead to separation had already begun, starting as usual among the women. Two sons were living in Moscow as water-carriers, and one was in the army. At home now were the old man and his wife, their second son who managed the homestead, the eldest who had come from Moscow for the holiday, and all the women and children. Besides these members of the family there was a visitor, a neighbour who was godfather to one of the children.

Over the table in the room hung a lamp with a shade, which brightly lit up the tea-things, a bottle of vodka, and some refreshments, besides illuminating the brick walls, which in the far corner were hung with icons on both sides of which were pictures. At the head of the table sat Vasíli Andréevich in a black sheepskin coat, sucking his frozen moustache and observing the room and the people around him with his prominent hawk-like eyes. With him sat the old, bald, white-bearded master of the house in a white homespun shirt, and next him the son home from Moscow for the holiday—a man with a sturdy back and powerful shoulders and clad in a thin print shirt—then the second son, also broad-shouldered, who acted as head of the house, and then a lean red-haired peasant—the neighbour.

Having had a drink of vodka and something to eat, they were about to take tea, and the samovar standing on the floor beside the brick oven was already humming. The children could be seen in the top bunks and on the top of the oven. A woman sat on a lower bunk with a cradle beside her. The old housewife, her face covered with wrinkles which wrinkled even her lips, was waiting on Vasíli Andréevich.

As Nikíta entered the house she was offering her guest a small tumbler of thick glass which she had just filled with vodka.

'Don't refuse, Vasíli Andréevich, you mustn't! Wish us a merry feast. Drink it, dear!' she said.

The sight and smell of vodka, especially now when he was chilled through and tired out, much disturbed Nikíta's mind. He frowned, and having shaken the snow off his cap and coat, stopped in front of the icons as if not seeing anyone, crossed himself three times, and bowed to the icons. Then, turning to the old master of the house and bowing first to him, then to all those at table, then to the women who stood by the oven, and muttering: 'A merry holiday!' he began taking off his outer things without looking at the table.

'Why, you're all covered with hoar-frost, old fellow!' said the eldest brother, looking at Nikíta's snow-covered face, eyes, and beard.

Nikíta took off his coat, shook it again, hung it up beside the oven, and came up to the table. He too was offered vodka. He went through a moment of painful hesitation and nearly took up the glass and emptied the clear fragrant liquid down his throat, but he glanced at Vasíli Andréevich, remembered his oath and the boots that he had sold for drink, recalled the cooper, remembered his son for whom he had promised to buy a horse by spring, sighed, and declined it.

'I don't drink, thank you kindly,' he said frowning, and sat down on a bench near the second window.

'How's that?' asked the eldest brother.

'I just don't drink,' replied Nikíta without lifting his eyes but looking askance at his scanty beard and moustache and getting the icicles out of them.

'It's not good for him,' said Vasíli Andréevich, munching a cracknel after emptying his glass.

'Well, then, have some tea,' said the kindly old hostess. 'You must be chilled through, good soul. Why are you women dawdling so with the samovar?'

'It is ready,' said one of the young women, and after flicking with her apron the top of the samovar which was now boiling over, she carried it with an effort to the table, raised it, and set it down with a thud.

Meanwhile Vasíli Andréevich was telling how he had lost his way, how they had come back twice to this same village, and how they had gone astray and had met some drunken peasants. Their hosts were surprised, explained where and why they had missed their way, said who the tipsy people they had met were, and told them how they ought to go.

'A little child could find the way to Molchánovka from here. All you have to do is to take the right turning from

the high road. There's a bush you can see just there. But
you didn't even get that far!' said the neighbour.

'You'd better stay the night. The women will make up
beds for you,' said the old woman persuasively.

'You could go on in the morning and it would be
pleasanter,' said the old man, confirming what his wife had
said.

'I can't, friend. Business!' said Vasíli Andréevich. 'Lose
an hour and you can't catch it up in a year,' he added, remembering the grove and the dealers who might snatch
that deal from him. 'We shall get there, shan't we?' he
said, turning to Nikíta.

Nikíta did not answer for some time, apparently still
intent on thawing out his beard and moustache.

'If only we don't go astray again,' he replied gloomily.

He was gloomy because he passionately longed for some
vodka, and the only thing that could assuage that longing
was tea and he had not yet been offered any.

'But we have only to reach the turning and then we
shan't go wrong. The road will be through the forest the
whole way,' said Vasíli Andréevich.

'It's just as you please, Vasíli Andréevich. If we're to go,
let us go,' said Nikíta, taking the glass of tea he was offered.

'We'll drink our tea and be off.'

Nikíta said nothing but only shook his head, and carefully pouring some tea into his saucer began warming
his hands, the fingers of which were always swollen with
hard work, over the steam. Then, biting off a tiny bit of
sugar, he bowed to his hosts, said, 'Your health!' and drew
in the steaming liquid.

'If somebody would see us as far as the turning,' said
Vasíli Andréevich.

'Well, we can do that,' said the eldest son. 'Petrúshka
will harness and go that far with you.'

'Well, then, put in the horse, lad, and I shall be thankful to you for it.'

'Oh, what for, dear man?' said the kindly old woman.
'We are heartily glad to do it.'

'Petrúshka, go and put in the mare,' said the eldest
brother.

'All right,' replied Petrúshka with a smile, and promptly
snatching his cap down from a nail he ran away to harness.

While the horse was being harnessed the talk returned
to the point at which it had stopped when Vasíli Andréevich

drove up to the window. The old man had been complaining to his neighbour, the village elder, about his third son who had not sent him anything for the holiday though he had sent a French shawl to his wife.

'The young people are getting out of hand,' said the old man.

'And how they do!' said the neighbour. 'There's no managing them! They know too much. There's Demóchkin now, who broke his father's arm. It's all from being too clever, it seems.'

Nikíta listened, watched their faces, and evidently would have liked to share in the conversation, but he was too busy drinking his tea and only nodded his head approvingly. He emptied one tumbler after another and grew warmer and warmer and more and more comfortable. The talk continued on the same subject for a long time—the harmfulness of a household dividing up—and it was clearly not an abstract discussion—but concerned the question of a separation in that house; a separation demanded by the second son who sat there morosely silent.

It was evidently a sore subject and absorbed them all, but out of propriety they did not discuss their private affairs before strangers. At last, however, the old man could not restrain himself, and with tears in his eyes declared that he would not consent to a break-up of the family during his lifetime, that his house was prospering, thank God, but that if they separated they would all have to go begging.

'Just like the Matvéevs,' said the neighbour. 'They used to have a proper house, but now they've split up none of them has anything.'

'And that is what you want to happen to us,' said the old man, turning to his son.

The son made no reply and there was an awkward pause. The silence was broken by Petrúshka, who having harnessed the horse had returned to the hut a few minutes before this and had been listening all the time with a smile.

'There's a fable about that in Paulson,' he said. 'A father gave his sons a broom to break. At first they could not break it, but when they took it twig by twig they broke it easily. And it's the same here,' and he gave a broad smile. 'I'm ready!' he added.

'If you're ready, let's go,' said Vasíli Andréevich. 'And as to separating, don't you allow it, Grandfather. You got everything together and you're the master. Go to the Justice of the Peace. He'll say how things should be done.'

'He carries on so, carries on so,' the old man continued in a whining tone. 'There's no doing anything with him. It's as if the devil possessed him.'

Nikíta having meanwhile finished his fifth tumbler of tea laid it on its side instead of turning it upside down, hoping to be offered a sixth glass. But there was no more water in the samovar, so the hostess did not fill it up for him. Besides, Vasíli Andréevich was putting his things on, so there was nothing for it but for Nikíta to get up too, put back into the sugar-basin the lump of sugar he had nibbled all round, wipe his perspiring face with the skirt of his sheepskin, and go to put on his overcoat.

Having put it on he sighed deeply, thanked his hosts, said good-bye, and went out of the warm bright room into the cold dark passage, through which the wind was howling and where snow was blowing through the cracks of the shaking door, and from there into the yard.

Petrúshka stood in his sheepskin in the middle of the yard by his horse, repeating some lines from Paulson's primer. He said with a smile:

> 'Storms with mist the sky conceal,
> Snowy circles wheeling wild.
> Now like savage beast 'twill howl,
> And now 'tis wailing like a child.'

Nikíta nodded approvingly as he arranged the reins.

The old man, seeing Vasíli Andréevich off, brought a lantern into the passage to show him a light, but it was blown out at once. And even in the yard it was evident that the snowstorm had become more violent.

'Well, this is weather!' thought Vasíli Andréevich. 'Perhaps we may not get there after all. But there is nothing to be done. Business! Besides, we have got ready, our host's horse has been harnessed, and we'll get there with God's help!'

Their aged host also thought they ought not to go, but he had already tried to persuade them to stay and had not been listened to.

'It's no use asking them again. Maybe my age makes me timid. They'll get there all right, and at least we shall get to bed in good time and without any fuss,' he thought.

Petrúshka did not think of danger. He knew the road and the whole district so well, and the lines about 'snowy circles wheeling wild' described what was happening outside so aptly that it cheered him up. Nikíta did not wish to go at all, but he had been accustomed not to have his own way and to serve others for so long that there was no one to hinder the departing travellers.

V

Vasíli Andréevich went over to his sledge, found it with difficulty in the darkness, climbed in and took the reins.

'Go on in front!' he cried.

Petrúshka kneeling in his low sledge started his horse. Mukhórty, who had been neighing for some time past, now scenting a mare ahead of him started after her, and they drove out into the street. They drove again through the outskirts of the village and along the same road, past the yard where the frozen linen had hung (which, however, was no longer to be seen), past the same barn, which was now snowed up almost to the roof and from which the snow was still endlessly pouring, past the same dismally moaning, whistling, and swaying willows, and again entered into the sea of blustering snow raging from above and below. The wind was so strong that when it blew from the side and the travellers steered against it, it tilted the sledges and turned the horses to one side. Petrúshka drove his good mare in front at a brisk trot and kept shouting lustily. Mukhórty pressed after her.

After travelling so for about ten minutes, Petrúshka turned round and shouted something. Neither Vasíli Andréevich nor Nikíta could hear anything because of the wind, but they guessed that they had arrived at the turning. In fact Petrúshka had turned to the right, and now the wind that had blown from the side blew straight in their faces, and through the snow they saw something dark on their right. It was the bush at the turning.

'Well now, God speed you!'

'Thank you, Petrúshka!'

'Storms with mist the sky conceal!' shouted Petrúshka as he disappeared.

'There's a poet for you!' muttered Vasíli Andréevich, pulling at the reins.

'Yes, a fine lad—a true peasant,' said Nikíta.

They drove on.

Nikíta, wrapping his coat closely about him and pressing his head down so close to his shoulders that his short beard covered his throat, sat silently, trying not to lose the warmth he had obtained while drinking tea in the house. Before him he saw the straight lines of the shafts which constantly deceived him into thinking they were on a well-travelled road, and the horse's swaying crupper with his knotted tail blown to one side, and farther ahead the high shaft-bow and the swaying head and neck of the horse with its waving mane. Now and then he caught sight of a way-sign, so that he knew they were still on a road and that there was nothing for him to be concerned about.

Vasíli Andréevich drove on, leaving it to the horse to keep to the road. But Mukhórty, though he had had a breathing-space in the village, ran reluctantly, and seemed now and then to get off the road, so that Vasíli Andréevich had repeatedly to correct him.

'Here's a stake to the right, and another, and here's a third,' Vasíli Andréevich counted, 'and here in front is the forest,' thought he, as he looked at something dark in front of him. But what had seemed to him a forest was only a bush. They passed the bush and drove on for another hundred yards but there was no fourth way-mark nor any forest.

'We must reach the forest soon,' thought Vasíli Andréevich, and animated by the vodka and the tea he did not stop but shook the reins, and the good obedient horse responded, now ambling, now slowly trotting in the direction in which he was sent, though he knew that he was not going the right way. Ten minutes went by, but there was still no forest.

'There now, we must be astray again,' said Vasíli Andréevich, pulling up.

Nikíta silently got out of the sledge and holding his coat, which the wind now wrapped closely about him and now almost tore off, started to feel about in the snow, going first to one side and then to the other. Three or four times he was completely lost to sight. At last he returned and took the reins from Vasíli Andréevich's hand.

'We must go to the right,' he said sternly and peremptorily, as he turned the horse.

'Well, if it's to the right, go to the right,' said Vasíli
Andréevich, yielding up the reins to Nikíta and thrusting
his freezing hands into his sleeves.

Nikíta did not reply.

'Now then, friend, stir yourself!' he shouted to the horse,
but in spite of the shake of the reins Mukhórty moved only
at a walk.

The snow in places was up to his knees, and the sledge
moved by fits and starts with his every movement.

Nikíta took the whip that hung over the front of the
sledge and struck him once. The good horse, unused to
the whip, sprang forward and moved at a trot, but immediately fell back into an amble and then to a walk. So
they went on for five minutes. It was dark and the snow
whirled from above and rose from below, so that sometimes the shaft-bow could not be seen. At times the sledge
seemed to stand still and the field to run backwards. Suddenly the horse stopped abruptly, evidently aware of something close in front of him. Nikíta again sprang lightly
out, throwing down the reins, and went ahead to see what
had brought him to a standstill, but hardly had he made a
step in front of the horse before his feet slipped and he
went rolling down an incline.

'Whoa, whoa, whoa!' he said to himself as he fell, and
he tried to stop his fall but could not, and only stopped
when his feet plunged into a thick layer of snow that had
drifted to the bottom of the hollow.

The fringe of a drift of snow that hung on the edge of
the hollow, disturbed by Nikíta's fall, showered down on
him and got inside his collar.

'What a thing to do!' said Nikíta reproachfully, addressing the drift and the hollow and shaking the snow
from under his collar.

'Nikíta! Hey, Nikíta!' shouted Vasíli Andréevich from
above.

But Nikíta did not reply. He was too occupied in shaking out the snow and searching for the whip he had
dropped when rolling down the incline. Having found the
whip he tried to climb straight up the bank where he had
rolled down, but it was impossible to do so: he kept rolling
down again, and so he had to go along at the foot of the
hollow to find a way up. About seven yards farther on he
managed with difficulty to crawl up the incline on all
fours, then he followed the edge of the hollow back to

the place where the horse should have been. He could not see either horse or sledge, but as he walked against the wind he heard Vasíli Andréevich's shouts and Mukhórty's neighing, calling him.

'I'm coming! I'm coming! What are you cackling for?' he muttered.

Only when he had come up to the sledge could he make out the horse, and Vasíli Andréevich standing beside it and looking gigantic.

'Where the devil did you vanish to? We must go back, if only to Gríshkino,' he began reproaching Nikíta.

'I'd be glad to get back, Vasíli Andréevich, but which way are we to go? There is such a ravine here that if we once get in it we shan't get out again. I got stuck so fast there myself that I could hardly get out.'

'What shall we do, then? We can't stay here! We must go somewhere!' said Vasíli Andréevich.

Nikíta said nothing. He seated himself in the sledge with his back to the wind, took off his boots, shook out the snow that had got into them, and taking some straw from the bottom of the sledge, carefully plugged with it a hole in his left boot.

Vasíli Andréevich remained silent, as though now leaving everything to Nikíta. Having put his boots on again, Nikíta drew his feet into the sledge, put on his mittens and took up the reins, and directed the horse along the side of the ravine. But they had not gone a hundred yards before the horse again stopped short. The ravine was in front of him again.

Nikíta again climbed out and again trudged about in the snow. He did this for a considerable time and at last appeared from the opposite side to that from which he had started.

'Vasíli Andréevich, are you alive?' he called out.

'Here!' replied Vasíli Andréevich. 'Well, what now?'

'I can't make anything out. It's too dark. There's nothing but ravines. We must drive against the wind again.'

They set off once more. Again Nikíta went stumbling through the snow, again he fell in, again climbed out and trudged about, and at last quite out of breath he sat down beside the sledge.

'Well, how now?' asked Vasíli Andréevich.

'Why, I am quite worn out and the horse won't go.'

'Then what's to be done?'

'Why, wait a minute.'

Nikíta went away again but soon returned.

'Follow me!' he said, going in front of the horse.

Vasíli Andréevich no longer gave orders but implicitly did what Nikíta told him.

'Here, follow me!' Nikíta shouted, stepping quickly to the right, and seizing the rein he led Mukhórty down towards a snow-drift.

At first the horse held back, then he jerked forward, hoping to leap the drift, but he had not the strength and sank into it up to his collar.

'Get out!' Nikíta called to Vasíli Andréevich who still sat in the sledge, and taking hold of one shaft he moved the sledge closer to the horse. 'It's hard, brother!' he said to Mukhórty, 'but it can't be helped. Make an effort! Now, now, just a little one!' he shouted.

The horse gave a tug, then another, but failed to clear himself and settled down again as if considering something.

'Now, brother, this won't do!' Nikíta admonished him. 'Now once more!'

Again Nikíta tugged at the shaft on his side, and Vasíli Andréevich did the same on the other.

Mukhórty lifted his head and then gave a sudden jerk.

'That's it! That's it!' cried Nikíta. 'Don't be afraid—you won't sink!'

One plunge, another, and a third, and at last Mukhórty was out of the snow-drift, and stood still, breathing heavily and shaking the snow off himself. Nikíta wished to lead him farther, but Vasíli Andréevich, in his two fur coats, was so out of breath that he could not walk farther and dropped into the sledge.

'Let me get my breath!' he said, unfastening the kerchief with which he had tied the collar of his fur coat at the village.

'It's all right here. You lie there,' said Nikíta. 'I will lead him along.' And with Vasíli Andréevich in the sledge he led the horse by the bridle about ten paces down and then up a slight rise, and stopped.

The place where Nikíta had stopped was not completely in the hollow where the snow sweeping down from the hillocks might have buried them altogether, but still it was partly sheltered from the wind by the side of the ravine. There were moments when the wind seemed to abate a

little, but that did not last long and as if to make up for
that respite the storm swept down with tenfold vigour and
tore and whirled the more fiercely. Such a gust struck
them at the moment when Vasíli Andréevich, having recovered his breath, got out of the sledge and went up to
Nikíta to consult him as to what they should do. They
both bent down involuntarily and waited till the violence
of the squall should have passed. Mukhórty too laid back
his ears and shook his head discontentedly. As soon as
the violence of the blast had abated a little, Nikíta took
off his mittens, stuck them into his belt, breathed onto his
hands, and began to undo the straps of the shaft-bow.

'What's that you are doing there?' asked Vasíli Andréevich.

'Unharnessing. What else is there to do? I have no
strength left,' said Nikíta as though excusing himself.

'Can't we drive somewhere?'

'No, we can't. We shall only kill the horse. Why, the
poor beast is not himself now,' said Nikíta, pointing to
the horse, which was standing submissively waiting for
what might come, with his steep wet sides heaving heavily.
'We shall have to stay the night here,' he said, as if preparing to spend the night at an inn, and he proceeded to
unfasten the collar-straps. The buckles came undone.

'But shan't we be frozen?' remarked Vasíli Andréevich.

'Well, if we are we can't help it,' said Nikíta.

VI

Although Vasíli Andréevich felt quite warm in his two
fur coats, especially after struggling in the snow-drift, a
cold shiver ran down his back on realizing that he must
really spend the night where they were. To calm himself
he sat down in the sledge and got out his cigarettes and
matches.

Nikíta meanwhile unharnessed Mukhórty. He unstrapped
the belly-band and the back-band, took away the reins,
loosened the collar-strap, and removed the shaft-bow,
talking to him all the time to encourage him.

'Now come out! come out!' he said, leading him clear of
the shafts. 'Now we'll tie you up here and I'll put down
some straw and take off your bridle. When you've had a
bite you'll feel more cheerful.'

But Mukhórty was restless and evidently not comforted

by Nikíta's remarks. He stepped now on one foot and now on another, and pressed close against the sledge, turning his back to the wind and rubbing his head on Nikíta's sleeve. Then, as if not to pain Nikíta by refusing his offer of the straw he put before him, he hurriedly snatched a wisp out of the sledge, but immediately decided that it was now no time to think of straw and threw it down, and the wind instantly scattered it, carried it away, and covered it with snow.

'Now we will set up a signal,' said Nikíta, and turning the front of the sledge to the wind he tied the shafts together with a strap and set them up on end in front of the sledge. 'There now, when the snow covers us up, good folk will see the shafts and dig us out,' he said, slapping his mittens together and putting them on. 'That's what the old folk taught us!'

Vasíli Andréevich meanwhile had unfastened his coat, and holding its skirts up for shelter, struck one sulphur match after another on the steel box. But his hands trembled, and one match after another either did not kindle or was blown out by the wind just as he was lifting it to the cigarette. At last a match did burn up, and its flame lit up for a moment the fur of his coat, his hand with the gold ring on the bent forefinger, and the snow-sprinkled oat-straw that stuck out from under the drugget. The cigarette lighted, he eagerly took a whiff or two, inhaled the smoke, let it out through his moustache, and would have inhaled again, but the wind tore off the burning tobacco and whirled it away as it had done the straw.

But even these few puffs had cheered him.

'If we must spend the night here, we must!' he said with decision. 'Wait a bit, I'll arrange a flag as well,' he added, picking up the kerchief which he had thrown down in the sledge after taking it from round his collar, and drawing off his gloves and standing up on the front of the sledge and stretching himself to reach the strap, he tied the handkerchief to it with a tight knot.

The kerchief immediately began to flutter wildly, now clinging round the shaft, now suddenly streaming out, stretching and flapping.

'Just see what a fine flag!' said Vasíli Andréevich, admiring his handiwork and letting himself down into the sledge. 'We should be warmer together, but there's not room enough for two,' he added.

'I'll find a place,' said Nikíta. 'But I must cover up the horse first—he sweated so, poor thing. Let go!' he added, drawing the drugget from under Vasíli Andréevich.

Having got the drugget he folded it in two, and after taking off the breechband and pad, covered Mukhórty with it.

'Anyhow it will be warmer, silly!' he said, putting back the breechband and the pad on the horse over the drugget. Then having finished that business he returned to the sledge, and addressing Vasíli Andréevich, said: 'You won't need the sackcloth, will you? And let me have some straw.'

And having taken these things from under Vasíli Andréevich, Nikíta went behind the sledge, dug out a hole for himself in the snow, put straw into it, wrapped his coat well round him, covered himself with the sackcloth, and pulling his cap well down seated himself on the straw he had spread, and leant against the wooden back of the sledge to shelter himself from the wind and the snow.

Vasíli Andréevich shook his head disapprovingly at what Nikíta was doing, as in general he disapproved of the peasant's stupidity and lack of education, and he began to settle himself down for the night.

He smoothed the remaining straw over the bottom of the sledge, putting more of it under his side. Then he thrust his hands into his sleeves and settled down, sheltering his head in the corner of the sledge from the wind in front.

He did not wish to sleep. He lay and thought: thought ever of the one thing that constituted the sole aim, meaning, pleasure, and pride of his life—of how much money he had made and might still make, of how much other people he knew had made and possessed, and of how those others had made and were making it, and how he, like them, might still make much more. The purchase of the Goryáchkin grove was a matter of immense importance to him. By that one deal he hoped to make perhaps ten thousand rubles. He began mentally to reckon the value of the wood he had inspected in autumn, and on five acres of which he had counted all the trees.

'The oaks will go for sledge-runners. The undergrowth will take care of itself, and there'll still be some thirty sázheens of fire-wood left on each desyatín,' said he to himself. 'That means there will be at least two hundred and twenty-five rubles' worth left on each desyatín. Fifty-six desyatíns means fifty-six hundreds, and fifty-six hundreds, and fifty-six tens, and another fifty-six tens, and then fifty-six fives. . . .' He saw that it came out to more than twelve thousand rubles, but could not reckon it up exactly without a counting-frame. 'But I won't give ten thousand, anyhow. I'll give about eight thousand with a deduction on account of the glades. I'll grease the surveyor's palm—give him a hundred rubles, or a hundred and fifty, and he'll reckon that there are some five desyatíns of glade to be deducted. And he'll let it go for eight thousand. Three thousand cash down. That'll move him, no fear!' he thought, and he pressed his pocket-book with his forearm.

'God only knows how we missed the turning. The forest ought to be there, and a watchman's hut, and dogs barking. But the damned things don't bark when they're wanted.' He turned his collar down from his ear and listened, but as before only the whistling of the wind could be heard, the flapping and fluttering of the kerchief tied to the shafts, and the pelting of the snow against the woodwork of the sledge. He again covered up his ear.

'If I had known I would have stayed the night. Well, no matter, we'll get there to-morrow. It's only one day lost. And the others won't travel in such weather.' Then he remembered that on the 9th he had to receive payment from the butcher for his oxen. 'He meant to come himself, but he won't find me, and my wife won't know how to receive the money. She doesn't know the right way of doing things,' he thought, recalling how at their party the day before she had not known how to treat the police-officer who was their guest. 'Of course she's only a woman! Where could she have seen anything? In my father's time what was our house like? Just a rich peasant's house: just an oatmill and an inn—that was the whole property. But what have I done in these fifteen years? A shop, two taverns, a flour-mill, a grain-store, two farms leased out, and a house with an iron-roofed barn,' he thought proudly. 'Not as it was in Father's time! Who is talked of in the whole district now? Brekhunóv! And why? Because I stick to business. I take trouble, not like others who lie abed or waste their time on foolishness while I don't sleep of nights. Blizzard or no blizzard I start out. So business gets done. They think money-making is a joke. No, take pains and rack your brains! You get overtaken out of doors at night, like this, or keep awake night after night till the thoughts whirling in your head make the pillow turn,' he meditated with pride. 'They think people get on through luck. After all, the Mirónovs are now millionaires. And why? Take pains and God gives. If only He grants me health!'

The thought that he might himself be a millionaire like Mirónov, who began with nothing, so excited Vasíli Andréevich that he felt the need of talking to somebody. But there was no one to talk to. . . . If only he could have reached Goryáchkin he would have talked to the landlord and shown him a thing or two.

'Just see how it blows! It will snow us up so deep that we shan't be able to get out in the morning!' he thought, listening to a gust of wind that blew against the front of the sledge, bending it and lashing the snow against it. He raised himself and looked round. All he could see through the whirling darkness was Mukhórty's dark head, his back covered by the fluttering drugget, and his thick knotted tail; while all round, in front and behind, was the same fluctuating whity darkness, sometimes seeming to get a little lighter and sometimes growing denser still.

'A pity I listened to Nikíta,' he thought. 'We ought to have driven on. We should have come out somewhere, if only back to Gríshkino and stayed the night at Tarás's. As it is we must sit here all night. But what was I thinking about? Yes, that God gives to those who take trouble, but not to loafers, lie-abeds, or fools. I must have a smoke!'

He sat down again, got out his cigarette-case, and stretched himself flat on his stomach, screening the matches with the skirt of his coat. But the wind found its way in and put out match after match. At last he got one to burn and lit a cigarette. He was very glad that he had managed to do what he wanted, and though the wind smoked more of the cigarette than he did, he still got two or three puffs and felt more cheerful. He again leant back, wrapped himself up, started reflecting and remembering, and suddenly and quite unexpectedly lost consciousness and fell asleep.

Suddenly something seemed to give him a push and awoke him. Whether it was Mukhórty who had pulled some straw from under him, or whether something within him had startled him, at all events it woke him, and his heart began to beat faster and faster so that the sledge seemed to tremble under him. He opened his eyes. Everything around him was just as before. 'It looks lighter,' he thought. 'I expect it won't be long before dawn.' But he at once remembered that it was lighter because the moon had risen. He sat up and looked first at the horse. Mukhórty still stood with his back to the wind, shivering all over. One side of the drugget, which was completely covered with snow, had been blown back, the breeching had slipped down and the snow-covered head with its waving forelock and mane were now more visible. Vasíli Andréevich leant over the back of the sledge and looked behind. Nikíta still sat in the same position in which he had settled himself. The sacking with which he was covered, and his legs, were thickly covered with snow.

'If only that peasant doesn't freeze to death! His clothes are so wretched. I may be held responsible for him. What shiftless people they are—such a want of education,' thought Vasíli Andréevich, and he felt like taking the drugget off the horse and putting it over Nikíta, but it would be very cold to get out and move about and, more-over, the horse might freeze to death. 'Why did I bring him with me? It was all her stupidity!' he thought, recalling his unloved wife, and he rolled over into his old place at the front part of the sledge. 'My uncle once spent a whole night like this,' he reflected, 'and was all right.' But an-other case came at once to his mind. 'But when they dug Sebastian out he was dead—stiff like a frozen carcass. If I'd only stopped the night in Gríshkino all this would not have happened!'

And wrapping his coat carefully round him so that none of the warmth of the fur should be wasted but should warm him all over, neck, knees, and feet, he shut his eyes and tried to sleep again. But try as he would he could not get drowsy, on the contrary he felt wide awake and ani-mated. Again he began counting his gains and the debts due to him, again he began bragging to himself and feeling pleased with himself and his position, but all this was con-tinually disturbed by a stealthily approaching fear and by the unpleasant regret that he had not remained in Grísh-kino.

'How different it would be to be lying warm on a bench!' He turned over several times in his attempts to get into a more comfortable position more sheltered from the wind, he wrapped up his legs closer, shut his eyes, and lay still. But either his legs in their strong felt boots began to ache from being bent in one position, or the wind blew in some-where, and after lying still for a short time he again began to recall the disturbing fact that he might now have been lying quietly in the warm hut at Gríshkino. He again sat up, turned about, muffled himself up, and settled down once more.

Once he fancied that he heard a distant cock-crow. He felt glad, turned down his coat-collar and listened with strained attention, but in spite of all his efforts nothing could be heard but the wind whistling between the shafts, the flapping of the kerchief, and the snow pelting against the frame of the sledge.

Nikíta sat just as he had done all the time, not moving and not even answering Vasíli Andréevich who had addressed him a couple of times. 'He doesn't care a bit—he's probably asleep!' thought Vasíli Andréevich with vexation, looking behind the sledge at Nikíta who was covered with a thick layer of snow.

Vasíli Andréevich got up and lay down again some twenty times. It seemed to him that the night would never end. 'It must be getting near morning,' he thought, getting up and looking around. 'Let's have a look at my watch. It will be cold to unbutton, but if I only know that it's getting near morning I shall at any rate feel more cheerful. We could begin harnessing.'

In the depth of his heart Vasíli Andréevich knew that it could not yet be near morning, but he was growing more and more afraid, and wished both to get to know and yet to deceive himself. He carefully undid the fastening of his sheepskin, pushed in his hand, and felt about for a long time before he got to his waistcoat. With great difficulty he managed to draw out his silver watch with its enamelled flower design, and tried to make out the time. He could not see anything without a light. Again he went down on his knees and elbows as he had done when he lighted a cigarette, got out his matches, and proceeded to strike one. This time he went to work more carefully, and feeling with his fingers for a match with the largest head and the greatest amount of phosphorus, lit it at the first try. Bringing the face of the watch under the light he could hardly believe his eyes. . . . It was only ten minutes past twelve. Almost the whole night was still before him.

'Oh, how long the night is!' he thought, feeling a cold shudder run down his back, and having fastened his fur coats again and wrapped himself up, he snuggled into a corner of the sledge intending to wait patiently. Suddenly, above the monotonous roar of the wind, he clearly distinguished another new and living sound. It steadily strengthened, and having become quite clear diminished just as gradually. Beyond all doubt it was a wolf, and he was so near that the movement of his jaws as he changed his cry was brought down the wind. Vasíli Andréevich turned back the collar of his coat and listened attentively. Mukhórty too strained to listen, moving his ears, and when the wolf had ceased its howling he shifted from foot to foot and gave a warning snort. After this Vasíli Andréevich could not fall asleep again or even calm himself. The more he tried to think of his accounts, his business, his reputation, his worth and his wealth, the more and more was he mastered by fear, and regrets that he had not stayed the night at Gríshkino dominated and mingled in all his thoughts.

'Devil take the forest! Things were all right without it, thank God. Ah, if we had only put up for the night!' he said to himself. 'They say it's drunkards that freeze,' he thought, 'and I have had some drink.' And observing his sensations he noticed that he was beginning to shiver, without knowing whether it was from cold or from fear. He tried to wrap himself up and lie down as before, but could no longer do so. He could not stay in one position. He wanted to get up, to do something to master the gathering fear that was rising in him and against which he felt himself powerless. He again got out his cigarettes and matches, but only three matches were left and they were bad ones. The phosphorus rubbed off them all without lighting.

'The devil take you! Damned thing! Curse you!' he muttered, not knowing whom or what he was cursing, and he flung away the crushed cigarette. He was about to throw away the matchbox too, but checked the movement of his hand and put the box in his pocket instead. He was seized with such unrest that he could no longer remain in one spot. He climbed out of the sledge and standing with his back to the wind began to shift his belt again, fastening it lower down in the waist and tightening it.

'What's the use of lying and waiting for death? Better mount the horse and get away!' The thought suddenly occurred to him. 'The horse will move when he has someone on his back. As for him,' he thought of Nikíta—'it's all the same to him whether he lives or dies. What is his life worth? He won't grudge his life, but I have something to live for, thank God.'

He untied the horse, threw the reins over his neck and tried to mount, but his coats and boots were so heavy that he failed. Then he clambered up in the sledge and tried to mount from there, but the sledge tilted under his weight, and he failed again. At last he drew Mukhórty nearer to the sledge, cautiously balanced on one side of it, and managed to lie on his stomach across the horse's back. After lying like that for a while he shifted forward once and again, threw a leg over, and finally seated himself, supporting his feet on the loose breeching-straps. The shaking of the sledge awoke Nikíta. He raised himself, and it seemed to Vasíli Andréevich that he said something.

'Listen to such fools as you! Am I to die like this for nothing?' exclaimed Vasíli Andréevich. And tucking the loose skirts of his fur coat in under his knees, he turned the horse and rode away from the sledge in the direction in which he thought the forest and the forester's hut must be.

VII

From the time he had covered himself with the sackcloth and seated himself behind the sledge, Nikíta had not stirred. Like all those who live in touch with nature and have known want, he was patient and could wait for hours, even days, without growing restless or irritable. He heard his master call him, but did not answer because he did not want to move or talk. Though he still felt some warmth from the tea he had drunk and from his energetic struggle when clambering about in the snowdrift, he knew that this warmth would not last long and that he had no strength left to warm himself again by moving about, for he felt as tired as a horse when it stops and refuses to go further in spite of the whip, and its master sees that it must be fed before it can work again. The foot in the boot with a hole in it had already grown numb, and he could no longer feel his big toe. Besides that, his whole body began to feel colder and colder.

The thought that he might, and very probably would, die that night occurred to him, but did not seem particularly unpleasant or dreadful. It did not seem particularly un-

pleasant, because his whole life had been not a continual
holiday, but on the contrary an unceasing round of toil of
which he was beginning to feel weary. And it did not seem
particularly dreadful, because besides the masters he had
served here, like Vasíli Andréevich, he always felt himself
dependent on the Chief Master, who had sent him into this
life, and he knew that when dying he would still be in that
Master's power and would not be ill-used by Him. 'It
seems a pity to give up what one is used to and accustomed to. But there's nothing to be done, I shall get used to
the new things.'

'Sins?' he thought, and remembered his drunkenness, the
money that had gone on drink, how he had offended his
wife, his cursing, his neglect of church and of the fasts,
and all the things the priest blamed him for at confession.
'Of course they are sins. But then, did I take them on of
myself? That's evidently how God made me. Well, and the
sins? Where am I to escape to?'

So at first he thought of what might happen to him that
night, and then did not return to such thoughts but gave
himself up to whatever recollections came into his head of
themselves. Now he thought of Martha's arrival, of the
drunkenness among the workers and his own renunciation
of drink, then of their present journey and of Tarás's
house and the talk about the breaking-up of the family,
then of his own lad, and of Mukhórty now sheltered under
the drugget, and then of his master who made the sledge
creak as he tossed about in it. 'I expect you're sorry yourself that you started out, dear man,' he thought. 'It would
seem hard to leave a life such as his! It's not like the likes
of us.'

Then all these recollections began to grow confused and
got mixed in his head, and he fell asleep.

But when Vasíli Andréevich, getting on the horse, jerked
the sledge, against the back of which Nikíta was leaning,
and it shifted away and hit him in the back with one of
its runners, he awoke and had to change his position
whether he liked it or not. Straightening his legs with
difficulty and shaking the snow off them he got up, and an
agonizing cold immediately penetrated his whole body. On
making out what was happening he called to Vasíli Andréevich to leave him the drugget which the horse no longer
needed, so that he might wrap himself in it.

But Vasíli Andréevich did not stop, but disappeared amid the powdery snow.

Left alone, Nikíta considered for a moment what he should do. He felt that he had not the strength to go off in search of a house. It was no longer possible to sit down in his old place—it was by now all filled with snow. He felt that he could not get warmer in the sledge either, for there was nothing to cover himself with, and his coat and sheepskin no longer warmed him at all. He felt as cold as though he had nothing on but a shirt. He became frightened. 'Lord, heavenly Father!' he muttered, and was comforted by the consciousness that he was not alone but that there was One who heard him and would not abandon him. He gave a deep sigh, and keeping the sackcloth over his head he got inside the sledge and lay down in the place where his master had been.

But he could not get warm in the sledge either. At first he shivered all over, then the shivering ceased and little by little he began to lose consciousness. He did not know whether he was dying or falling asleep, but felt equally prepared for the one as for the other.

VIII

Meanwhile Vasíli Andréevich, with his feet and the ends of the reins, urged the horse on in the direction in which for some reason he expected the forest and forester's hut to be. The snow covered his eyes and the wind seemed intent on stopping him, but bending forward and constantly lapping his coat over and pushing it between himself and the cold harness pad which prevented him from sitting properly, he kept urging the horse on. Mukhórty ambled on obediently though with difficulty, in the direction in which he was driven.

Vasíli Andréevich rode for about five minutes straight ahead, as he thought, seeing nothing but the horse's head and the white waste, and hearing only the whistle of the wind about the horse's ears and his coat collar.

Suddenly a dark patch showed up in front of him. His heart beat with joy, and he rode towards the object, already seeing in imagination the walls of village houses. But the dark patch was not stationary, it kept moving; and it was not a village but some tall stalks of wormwood sticking up through the snow on the boundary between two fields, and desperately tossing about under the pressure of the wind which beat it all to one side and whistled through it. The sight of that wormwood tormented by the pitiless wind made Vasíli Andréevich shudder, he knew not why, and he hurriedly began urging the horse on, not noticing that when riding up to the wormwood he had quite changed his direction and was now heading the opposite way, though still imagining that he was riding towards where the hut should be. But the horse kept making towards the right, and Vasíli Andréevich kept guiding it to the left.

Again something dark appeared in front of him. Again he rejoiced, convinced that now it was certainly a village. But once more it was the same boundary line overgrown with wormwood, once more the same wormwood desperately tossed by the wind and carrying unreasoning terror to his heart. But its being the same wormwood was not all, for beside is there was a horse's track partly snowed over. Vasíli Andréevich stopped, stooped down and looked carefully. It was a horse-track only partially covered with snow, and could be none but his own horse's hoofprints. He had evidently gone round in a small circle. 'I shall perish like that!' he thought, and not to give way to his terror he urged on the horse still more, peering into the snowy darkness in which he saw only flitting and fitful points of light. Once he thought he heard the barking of dogs or the howling of wolves, but the sounds were so faint and indistinct that he did not know whether he heard them or merely imagined them, and he stopped and began to listen intently.

Suddenly some terrible, deafening cry resounded near his ears, and everything shivered and shook under him. He seized Mukhórty's neck, but that too was shaking all over and the terrible cry grew still more frightful. For some seconds Vasíli Andréevich could not collect himself or understand what was happening. It was only that Mukhórty, whether to encourage himself or to call for help, had neighed loudly and resonantly. 'Ugh, you wretch! How you frightened me, damn you!' thought Vasíli Andréevich. But even when he understood the cause of his terror he could not shake it off.

'I must calm myself and think things over,' he said to himself, but yet he could not stop, and continued to urge the horse on, without noticing that he was now going with the wind instead of against it. His body, especially between his legs where it touched the pad of the harness and was not covered by his overcoats, was getting painfully cold, especially when the horse walked slowly. His legs and arms trembled and his breathing came fast. He saw himself perishing amid this dreadful snowy waste, and could see no means of escape.

Suddenly the horse under him tumbled into something and, sinking into a snow-drift, began to plunge and fell on his side. Vasíli Andréevich jumped off, and in so doing dragged to one side the breechband on which his foot was resting, and twisted round the pad to which he held as he dismounted. As soon as he had jumped off, the horse struggled to his feet, plunged forward, gave one leap and another, neighed again, and dragging the drugget and the breechband after him, disappeared, leaving Vasíli Andréevich alone on the snow-drift.

The latter pressed on after the horse, but the snow lay so deep and his coats were so heavy that, sinking above his knees at each step, he stopped breathless after taking not more than twenty steps. 'The copse, the oxen, the lease-hold, the shop, the tavern, the house with the iron-roofed barn, and my heir,' thought he. 'How can I leave all that? What does this mean? It cannot be!' These thoughts flashed through his mind. Then he thought of the wormwood tossed by the wind, which he had twice ridden past, and he was seized with such terror that he did not believe in the reality of what was happening to him. 'Can this be a dream?' he thought, and tried to wake up but could not. It was real snow that lashed his face and covered him and chilled his right hand from which he had lost the glove, and this was a real desert in which he was now left alone like that wormwood, awaiting an inevitable, speedy, and meaningless death.

'Queen of Heaven! Holy Father Nicholas, teacher of temperance!' he thought, recalling the service of the day before and the holy icon with its black face and gilt frame, and the tapers which he sold to be set before that icon and which were almost immediately brought back to him scarcely burnt at all, and which he put away in the store-chest. He began to pray to that same Nicholas the Wonder-Worker to save him, promising him a thanksgiving service and some candles. But he clearly and indubitably realized that the icon, its frame, the candles, the priest, and the thanksgiving service, though very important and necessary in church, could do nothing for him here, and that there was and could be no connexion between those candles and services and his present disastrous plight. 'I must not despair,' he thought. 'I must follow the horse's track before it is snowed under. He will lead me out, or I may even catch him. Only I must not hurry, or I shall stick fast and be more lost than ever.'

But in spite of his resolution to go quietly, he rushed forward and even ran, continually falling, getting up and falling again. The horse's track was already hardly visible in places where the snow did not lie deep. 'I am lost!' thought Vasíli Andréevich. 'I shall lose the track and not catch the horse.' But at that moment he saw something black. It was Mukhórty, and not only Mukhórty, but the sledge with the shafts and the kerchief. Mukhórty, with the sacking and the breechband twisted round to one side, was standing not in his former place but nearer to the shafts, shaking his head which the reins he was stepping on drew downwards. It turned out that Vasíli Andréevich had sunk in the same ravine Nikíta had previously fallen into, and that Mukhórty had been bringing him back to the sledge and he had got off his back no more than fifty paces from where the sledge was.

IX

Having stumbled back to the sledge Vasíli Andréevich caught hold of it and for a long time stood motionless, trying to calm himself and recover his breath. Nikíta was not in his former place, but something, already covered with snow, was lying in the sledge and Vasíli Andréevich concluded that this was Nikíta. His terror had now quite left him, and if he felt any fear it was lest the dreadful terror should return that he had experienced when on the horse and especially when he was left alone in the snowdrift. At any cost he had to avoid that terror, and to keep it away he must do something—occupy himself with something. And the first thing he did was to turn his back to the wind and open his fur coat. Then, as soon as he recovered his breath a little, he shook the snow out of his boots and out of his left-hand glove (the right-hand glove was hopelessly lost and by this time probably lying somewhere under a dozen inches of snow); then as was his custom when going out of his shop to buy grain from the peasants, he pulled his girdle low down and tightened it and prepared for action. The first thing that occurred to him was to free Mukhórty's leg from the rein. Having done that, and tethered him to the iron cramp at the front of the sledge where he had been before, he was going round the horse's quarters to put the breechband and pad straight and cover him with the cloth, but at that moment he noticed that something was moving in the sledge and Nikíta's head rose up out of the snow that covered it. Nikíta, who was half frozen, rose with great difficulty and sat up, moving his hand before his nose in a strange manner just as if he were driving away flies. He waved his hand and said something, and seemed to Vasíli Andréevich to be calling him. Vasíli Andréevich left the cloth unadjusted and went up to the sledge.

'What is it?' he asked. 'What are you saying?'

'I'm dy . . . ing, that's what,' said Nikíta brokenly and with difficulty. 'Give what is owing to me to my lad, or to my wife, no matter.'

'Why, are you really frozen?' asked Vasíli Andréevich.

'I feel it's my death. Forgive me for Christ's sake . . .' said Nikíta in a tearful voice, continuing to wave his hand before his face as if driving away flies.

Vasíli Andréevich stood silent and motionless for half a minute. Then suddenly, with the same resolution with which he used to strike hands when making a good purchase, he took a step back and turning up his sleeves began raking the snow off Nikíta and out of the sledge. Having done this he hurriedly undid his girdle, opened out his fur coat, and having pushed Nikíta down, lay down on top of him, covering him not only with his fur coat but with the whole of his body, which glowed with warmth. After pushing the skirts of his coat between Nikíta and the sides of the sledge, and holding down its hem with his knees, Vasíli Andréevich lay like that face down, with his head pressed against the front of the sledge. Here he no longer heard the horse's movements or the whistling of the wind, but only Nikíta's breathing. At first and for a long time Nikíta lay motionless, then he sighed deeply and moved.

'There, and you say you are dying! Lie still and get warm, that's our way . . .' began Vasíli Andréevich.

But to his great surprise he could say no more, for tears

came to his eyes and his lower jaw began to quiver rapidly. He stopped speaking and only gulped down the risings in his throat. 'Seems I was badly frightened and have gone quite weak,' he thought. But this weakness was not only not unpleasant, but gave him a peculiar joy such as he had never felt before.

'That's our way!' he said to himself, experiencing a strange and solemn tenderness. He lay like that for a long time, wiping his eyes on the fur of his coat and tucking under his knee the right skirt, which the wind kept turning up.

But he longed so passionately to tell somebody of his joyful condition that he said: 'Nikíta!'

'It's comfortable, warm!' came a voice from beneath.

'There, you see, friend, I was going to perish. And you would have been frozen, and I should have . . .'

But again his jaws began to quiver and his eyes to fill with tears, and he could say no more.

'Well, never mind,' he thought. 'I know about myself what I know.'

He remained silent and lay like that for a long time.

Nikíta kept him warm from below and his fur coats from above. Only his hands, with which he kept his coat-skirts down round Nikíta's sides, and his legs which the wind kept uncovering, began to freeze, especially his right hand which had no glove. But he did not think of his legs or of his hands but only of how to warm the peasant who was lying under him. He looked out several times at Mukhórty and could see that his back was uncovered and the drugget and breeching lying on the snow, and that he ought to get up and cover him, but he could not bring himself to leave Nikíta and disturb even for a moment the joyous condition he was in. He no longer felt any kind of terror.

'No fear, we shan't lose him this time!' he said to himself, referring to his getting the peasant warm with the same boastfulness with which he spoke of his buying and selling.

Vasíli Andréevich lay in that way for one hour, another, and a third, but he was unconscious of the passage of time. At first impressions of the snow-storm, the sledge-shafts, and the horse with the shaft-bow shaking before his eyes, kept passing through his mind, then he remembered Nikíta lying under him, then recollections of the festival, his wife, the police-officer, and the box of candles, began to mingle with these; then again Nikíta, this time lying under that box, then the peasants, customers and traders, and the white walls of his house with its iron roof with Nikíta lying underneath, presented themselves to his imagination. Afterwards all these impressions blended into one nothingness. As the colours of the rainbow unite into one white light, so all these different impressions mingled into one, and he fell asleep.

For a long time he slept without dreaming, but just before dawn the visions recommenced. It seemed to him that he was standing by the box of tapers and that Tíkhon's wife was asking for a five-kopek taper for the Church fête. He wished to take one out and give it to her, but his hands would not lift, being held tight in his pockets. He wanted to walk round the box but his feet would not move and his new clean goloshes had grown to the stone floor, and he could neither lift them nor get his feet out of the goloshes. Then the taper-box was no longer a box but a bed, and suddenly Vasíli Andréevich saw himself lying in his bed at home. He was lying in his bed and could not get up. Yet it was necessary for him to get up because Iván Matvéich, the police-officer, would soon call for him and he had to go with him—either to bargain for the forest or to put Mukhórty's breeching straight.

He asked his wife: 'Nikoláevna, hasn't he come yet?' 'No, he hasn't,' she replied. He heard someone drive up to the front steps. 'It must be him.' 'No, he's gone past.' 'Nikoláevna! I say, Nikoláevna, isn't he here yet?' 'No.' He was still lying on his bed and could not get up, but was always waiting. And this waiting was uncanny and yet joyful. Then suddenly his joy was completed. He whom he was expecting came; not Iván Matvéich the police-officer, but someone else—yet it was he whom he had been waiting for. He came and called him; and it was he who had called him and told him to lie down on Nikíta. And Vasíli Andréevich was glad that that one had come for him.

'I'm coming!' he cried joyfully, and that cry awoke him, but woke him up not at all the same person he had been when he fell asleep. He tried to get up but could not, tried to move his arm and could not, to move his leg and also could not, to turn his head and could not. He was surprised but not at all disturbed by this. He understood that this was death, and was not at all disturbed by that either.

He remembered that Nikíta was lying under him and that he had got warm and was alive, and it seemed to him that he was Nikíta and Nikíta was he, and that his life was not in himself but in Nikíta. He strained his ears and heard Nikíta breathing and even slightly snoring. 'Nikíta is alive, so I too am alive!' he said to himself triumphantly.

And he remembered his money, his shop, his house, the buying and selling, and Mirónov's millions, and it was hard for him to understand why that man, called Vasíli Brekhunóv, had troubled himself with all those things with which he had been troubled.

'Well, it was because he did not know what the real thing was,' he thought, concerning that Vasíli Brekhunóv. 'He did not know, but now I know and know for sure. Now I know!' And again he heard the voice of the one who had called him before. 'I'm coming! Coming!' he responded gladly, and his whole being was filled with joyful emotion. He felt himself free and that nothing could hold him back any longer.

After that Vasíli Andréevich neither saw, heard, nor felt anything more in this world.

All around the snow still eddied. The same whirlwinds of snow circled about, covering the dead Vasíli Andréevich's fur coat, the shivering Mukhórty, the sledge, now scarcely to be seen, and Nikíta lying at the bottom of it, kept warm beneath his dead master.

X

Nikíta awoke before daybreak. He was aroused by the cold that had begun to creep down his back. He had dreamt that he was coming from the mill with a load of his master's flour and when crossing the stream had missed the bridge and let the cart get stuck. And he saw that he had crawled under the cart and was trying to lift it by arching his back. But strange to say the cart did not move, it stuck to his back and he could neither lift it nor get out from under it. It was crushing the whole of his loins. And how cold it felt! Evidently he must crawl out. 'Have done!' he exclaimed to whoever was pressing the cart down on him. 'Take out the sacks!' But the cart pressed down colder and colder, and then he heard a strange knocking, awoke completely, and remembered everything. The cold cart was his dead and frozen master lying upon him. And the knock was produced by Mukhórty, who had twice struck the sledge with his hoof.

'Andréevich! Eh, Andréevich!' Nikíta called cautiously, beginning to realize the truth, and straightening his back. But Vasíli Andréevich did not answer and his stomach and legs were stiff and cold and heavy like iron weights.

'He must have died! May the Kingdom of Heaven be his!' thought Nikíta.

He turned his head, dug with his hand through the snow about him and opened his eyes. It was daylight; the wind was whistling as before between the shafts, and the snow was falling in the same way, except that it was no longer driving against the frame of the sledge but silently covered both sledge and horse deeper and deeper, and neither the horse's movements nor his breathing were any longer to be heard.

'He must have frozen too,' thought Nikíta of Mukhórty, and indeed those hoof knocks against the sledge, which had awakened Nikíta, were the last efforts the already numbed Mukhórty had made to keep on his feet before dying.

'O Lord God, it seems Thou art calling me too!' said Nikíta. 'Thy Holy Will be done. But it's uncanny. . . . Still, a man can't die twice and must die once. If only it would come soon!'

And he again drew in his head, closed his eyes, and became unconscious, fully convinced that now he was certainly and finally dying.

It was not till noon that day that peasants dug Vasíli Andréevich and Nikíta out of the snow with their shovels, not more than seventy yards from the road and less than half a mile from the village.

The snow had hidden the sledge, but the shafts and the kerchief tied to them were still visible. Mukhórty, buried up to his belly in snow, with the breeching and drugget hanging down, stood all white, his dead head pressed against his frozen throat: icicles hung from his nostrils, his eyes were covered with hoar-frost as though filled with tears, and he had grown so thin in that one night that he was nothing but skin and bone.

Vasíli Andréevich was stiff as a frozen carcass, and when they rolled him off Nikíta his legs remained apart and his arms stretched out as they had been. His bulging hawk eyes were frozen, and his open mouth under his clipped moustache was full of snow. But Nikíta though chilled through was still alive. When he had been brought to, he felt sure that he was already dead and that what was taking place with him was no longer happening in this world but in the next. When he heard the peasants shouting as they dug him out and rolled the frozen body of Vasíli Andréevich from off him, he was at first surprised that in the other world peasants should be shouting in the same old way and had the same kind of body, and then when he realized that he was still in this world he was sorry rather than glad, especially when he found that the toes on both his feet were frozen.

Nikíta lay in hospital for two months. They cut off three of his toes, but the others recovered so that he was still able to work and went on living for another twenty years, first as a farm-labourer, then in his old age as a watchman. He died at home as he had wished, only this year, under the icons with a lighted taper in his hands. Before he died he asked his wife's forgiveness and forgave her for the cooper. He also took leave of his son and grandchildren, and died sincerely glad that he was relieving his son and daughter-in-law of the burden of having to feed him, and that he was now really passing from this life of which he was weary into that other life which every year and every hour grew clearer and more desirable to him. Whether he is better or worse off there where he awoke after his death, whether he was disappointed or found there what he expected, we shall all soon learn.

Father Sergius

[1898]

I

In Petersburg in the eighteen-forties a surprising event occurred. An officer of the Cuirassier Life Guards, a handsome prince who everyone predicted would become aidede-camp to the Emperor Nicholas I and have a brilliant career, left the service, broke off his engagement to a beautiful maid of honour, a favourite of the Empress's, gave his small estate to his sister, and retired to a monastery to become a monk.

This event appeared extraordinary and inexplicable to those who did not know his inner motives, but for Prince Stepán Kasátsky himself it all occurred so naturally that he could not imagine how he could have acted otherwise.

His father, a retired colonel of the Guards, had died when Stepán was twelve, and sorry as his mother was to part from her son, she entered him at the Military College as her deceased husband had intended.

The widow herself, with her daughter Varvára, moved to Petersburg to be near her son and have him with her for the holidays.

The boy was distinguished both by his brilliant ability and by his immense self-esteem. He was first both in his studies—especially in mathematics, of which he was particularly fond—and also in drill and in riding. Though of more than average height, he was handsome and agile, and he would have been an altogether exemplary cadet had it not been for his quick temper. He was remarkably truthful, and was neither dissipated nor addicted to drink. The only faults that marred his conduct were fits of fury to which he was subject and during which he lost control of himself and became like a wild animal. He once nearly threw out of the window another cadet who had begun to tease him about his collection of minerals. On another occasion he came almost completely to grief by flinging a whole dish of cutlets at an officer who was acting as

steward, attacking him and, it was said, striking him for
having broken his word and told a barefaced lie. He would
certainly have been reduced to the ranks had not the
Director of the College hushed up the whole matter and
dismissed the steward.

By the time he was eighteen he had finished his College
course and received a commission as lieutenant in an
aristocratic regiment of the Guards.

The Emperor Nicholas Pávlovich (Nicholas I) had
noticed him while he was still at the College, and continued to take notice of him in the regiment, and it was
on this account that people predicted for him an appointment as aide-de-camp to the Emperor. Kasátsky himself
strongly desired it, not from ambition only but chiefly
because since his cadet days he had been passionately
devoted to Nicholas Pávlovich. The Emperor had often
visited the Military College and every time Kasátsky saw
that tall erect figure, with breast expanded in its military
overcoat, entering with brisk step, saw the cropped side-
whiskers, the moustache, the aquiline nose, and heard the
sonorous voice exchanging greetings with the cadets, he
was seized by the same rapture that he experienced later
on when he met the woman he loved. Indeed, his passionate
adoration of the Emperor was even stronger: he wished
to sacrifice something—everything, even himself—to prove
his complete devotion. And the Emperor Nicholas was
conscious of evoking this rapture and deliberately aroused
it. He played with the cadets, surrounded himself with
them, treating them sometimes with childish simplicity,
sometimes as a friend, and then again with majestic
solemnity. After that affair with the officer, Nicholas
Pávlovich said nothing to Kasátsky, but when the latter
approached he waved him away theatrically, frowned,
shook his finger at him, and afterwards when leaving, said:
'Remember that I know everything. There are some things
I would rather not know, but they remain here,' and he
pointed to his heart.

When on leaving College the cadets were received by
the Emperor, he did not again refer to Kasátsky's offence,
but told them all, as was his custom, that they should serve
him and the fatherland loyally, that he would always be
their best friend, and that when necessary they might approach him direct. All the cadets were as usual greatly
moved, and Kasátsky even shed tears, remembering the

past, and vowed that he would serve his beloved Tsar with all his soul.

When Kasátsky took up his commission his mother moved with her daughter first to Moscow and then to their country estate. Kasátsky gave half his property to his sister and kept only enough to maintain himself in the expensive regiment he had joined.

To all appearance he was just an ordinary, brilliant young officer of the Guards making a career for himself; but intense and complex strivings went on within him. From early childhood his efforts had seemed to be very varied, but essentially they were all one and the same. He tried in everything he took up to attain such success and perfection as would evoke praise and surprise. Whether it was his studies or his military exercises, he took them up and worked at them till he was praised and held up as an example to others. Mastering one subject he took up another, and obtained first place in his studies. For example, while still at College he noticed in himself an awkwardness in French conversation, and contrived to master French till he spoke it as well as Russian, and then he took up chess and became an excellent player.

Apart from his main vocation, which was the service of his Tsar and the fatherland, he always set himself some particular aim, and however unimportant it was, devoted himself completely to it and lived for it until it was accomplished. And as soon as it was attained another aim would immediately present itself, replacing its predecessor. This passion for distinguishing himself, or for accomplishing something in order to distinguish himself, filled his life. On taking up his commission he set himself to acquire the utmost perfection in knowledge of the service, and very soon became a model officer, though still with the same fault of ungovernable irascibility, which here in the service again led him to commit actions inimical to his success. Then he took to reading, having once in conversation in society felt himself deficient in general education—and again achieved his purpose. Then, wishing to secure a brilliant position in high society, he learnt to dance excellently and very soon was invited to all the balls in the best circles, and to some of their evening gatherings. But this did not satisfy him: he was accustomed to being first, and in this society was far from being so.

The highest society then consisted, and I think always

and everywhere does consist, of four sorts of people: rich
people who are received at Court, people not wealthy
but born and brought up in Court circles, rich people who
ingratiate themselves into the Court set, and people neither
rich nor belonging to the Court but who ingratiate themselves into the first and second sets.

Kasátsky did not belong to the first two sets, but was
readily welcomed in the others. On entering society he
determined to have relations with some society lady, and
to his own surprise quickly accomplished this purpose.
He soon realized, however, that the circles in which he
moved were not the highest, and that though he was
received in the highest spheres he did not belong to them.
They were polite to him, but showed by their whole manner
that they had their own set and that he was not of it. And
Kasátsky wished to belong to that inner circle. To attain
that end it would be necessary to be an aide-de-camp to
the Emperor—which he expected to become—or to marry
into that exclusive set, which he resolved to do. And his
choice fell on a beauty belonging to the Court, who not
merely belonged to the circle into which he wished to be
accepted, but whose friendship was coveted by the very
highest people and those most firmly established in that
highest circle. This was Countess Korotkóva. Kasátsky
began to pay court to her, and not merely for the sake of
his career. She was extremely attractive and he soon fell
in love with her. At first she was noticeably cool towards
him, but then suddenly changed and became gracious, and
her mother gave him pressing invitations to visit them.
Kasátsky proposed and was accepted. He was surprised
at the facility with which he attained such happiness. But
though he noticed something strange and unusual in the
behaviour towards him of both mother and daughter,
he was blinded by being so deeply in love, and did not
realize what almost the whole town knew—namely, that
his fiancée had been the Emperor Nicholas's mistress the
previous year.

Two weeks before the day arranged for the wedding,
Kasátsky was at Tsárskoe Seló at his fiancée's country
place. It was a hot day in May. He and his betrothed had
walked about the garden and were sitting on a bench in a
shady linden alley. Mary's white muslin dress suited her
particularly well, and she seemed the personification of
innocence and love as she sat, now bending her head,

now gazing up at the very tall and handsome man who was speaking to her with particular tenderness and self-restraint, as if he feared by word or gesture to offend or sully her angelic purity.

Kasátsky belonged to those men of the eighteen-forties (they are now no longer to be found) who while deliberately and without any conscientious scruples condoning impurity in themselves, required ideal and angelic purity in their women, regarded all unmarried women of their circle as possessed of such purity, and treated them accordingly. There was much that was false and harmful in this outlook, as concerning the laxity the men permitted themselves, but in regard to the women that old-fashioned view (sharply differing from that held by young people to-day who see in every girl merely a female seeking a mate) was, I think, of value. The girls, perceiving such adoration, endeavoured with more or less success to be goddesses.

Such was the view Kasátsky held of women, and that was how he regarded his fiancée. He was particularly in love that day, but did not experience any sensual desire for her. On the contrary he regarded her with tender adoration as something unattainable.

He rose to his full height, standing before her with both hands on his sabre.

'I have only now realized what happiness a man can experience! And it is you, my darling, who have given me this happiness,' he said with a timid smile.

Endearments had not yet become usual between them, and feeling himself morally inferior he felt terrified at this stage to use them to such an angel.

'It is thanks to you that I have come to know myself. I have learnt that I am better than I thought.'

'I have known that for a long time. That was why I began to love you.'

Nightingales trilled near by and the fresh leafage rustled, moved by a passing breeze.

He took her hand and kissed it, and tears came into his eyes.

She understood that he was thanking her for having said she loved him. He silently took a few steps up and down, and then approached her again and sat down.

'You know . . . I have to tell you . . . I was not disinterested when I began to make love to you. I wanted

to get into society; but later . . . how unimportant that
became in comparison with you—when I got to know you.
You are not angry with me for that?'

She did not reply but merely touched his hand. He
understood that this meant: 'No, I am not angry.'

'You said . . .' He hesitated. It seemed too bold to
say. 'You said that you began to love me. I believe it—
but there is something that troubles you and checks your
feeling. What is it?'

'Yes—now or never!' thought she. 'He is bound to know
of it anyway. But now he will not forsake me. Ah, if he
should, it would be terrible!' And she threw a loving
glance at his tall, noble, powerful figure. She loved him
now more than she had loved the Tsar, and apart from the
Imperial dignity would not have preferred the Emperor
to him.

'Listen! I cannot deceive you. I have to tell you. You
ask what it is? It is that I have loved before.'

She again laid her hand on his with an imploring
gesture. He was silent.

'You want to know who it was? It was—the Emperor.'

'We all love him. I can imagine you, a schoolgirl at the
Institute . . .'

'No, it was later. I was infatuated, but it passed . . . I
must tell you . . .'

'Well, what of it?'

'No, it was not simply—' She covered her face with
her hands.

'What? You gave yourself to him?'

She was silent.

'His mistress?'

She did not answer.

He sprang up and stood before her with trembling jaws,
pale as death. He now remembered how the Emperor,
meeting him on the Névsky, had amiably congratulated
him.

'O God, what have I done! Stíva!'

'Don't touch me! Don't touch me! Oh, how it pains!'

He turned away and went to the house. There he met
her mother.

'What is the matter, Prince? I . . .' She became silent
on seeing his face. The blood had suddenly rushed to his
head.

'You knew it, and used me to shield them! If you

weren't a woman . . . !' he cried, lifting his enormous fist, and turning aside he ran away.

Had his fiancée's lover been a private person he would have killed him, but it was his beloved Tsar.

Next day he applied both for furlough and his discharge, and professing to be ill, so as to see no one, he went away to the country.

He spent the summer at his village arranging his affairs. When summer was over he did not return to Petersburg, but entered a monastery and there became a monk.

His mother wrote to try to dissuade him from this decisive step, but he replied that he felt God's call which transcended all other considerations. Only his sister, who was as proud and ambitious as he, understood him.

She understood that he had become a monk in order to be above those who considered themselves his superiors. And she understood him correctly. By becoming a monk he showed contempt for all that seemed most important to others and had seemed so to him while he was in the service, and he now ascended a height from which he could look down on those he had formerly envied. . . . But it was not this alone, as his sister Varvára supposed, that influenced him. There was also in him something else —a sincere religious feeling which Varvára did not know, which intertwined itself with the feeling of pride and the desire for pre-eminence, and guided him. His disillusionment with Mary, whom he had thought of angelic purity, and his sense of injury, were so strong that they brought him to despair, and the despair led him—to what? To God, to his childhood's faith which had never been destroyed in him.

II

Kasátsky entered the monastery on the feast of the Intercession of the Blessed Virgin. The Abbot of that monastery was a gentleman by birth, a learned writer and a *stárets,* that is, he belonged to that succession of monks originating in Walachia who each choose a director and teacher whom they implicitly obey. This Superior had been a disciple of the *stárets* Ambrose, who was a disciple of Makarius, who was a disciple of the *stárets* Leonid, who was a disciple of Païssy Velichkóvsky.

To this Abbot Kasátsky submitted himself as to his

chosen director. Here in the monastery, besides the feeling of ascendency over others that such a life gave him, he felt much as he had done in the world: he found satisfaction in attaining the greatest possible perfection outwardly as well as inwardly. As in the regiment he had been not merely an irreproachable officer but had even exceeded his duties and widened the borders of perfection, so also as a monk he tried to be perfect, and was always industrious, abstemious, submissive, and meek, as well as pure both in deed and in thought, and obedient. This last quality in particular made life far easier for him. If many of the demands of life in the monastery, which was near the capital and much frequented, did not please him and were temptations to him, they were all nullified by obedience: 'It is not for me to reason; my business is to do the task set me, whether it be standing beside the relics, singing in the choir, or making up accounts in the monastery guest-house.' All possibility of doubt about anything was silenced by obedience to the *stárets*. Had it not been for this, he would have been oppressed by the length and monotony of the church services, the bustle of the many visitors, and the bad qualities of the other monks. As it was, he not only bore it all joyfully but found in it solace and support. 'I don't know why it is necessary to hear the same prayers several times a day, but I know that it is necessary; and knowing this I find joy in them.' His director told him that as material food is necessary for the maintenance of the life of the body, so spiritual food—the church prayers—is necessary for the maintenance of the spiritual life. He believed this, and though the church services, for which he had to get up early in the morning, were a difficulty, they certainly calmed him and gave him joy. This was the result of his consciousness of humility, and the certainty that whatever he had to do, being fixed by the *stárets*, was right.

The interest of his life consisted not only in an ever greater and greater subjugation of his will, but in the attainment of all the Christian virtues, which at first seemed to him easily attainable. He had given his whole estate to his sister and did not regret it, he had no personal claims, humility towards his inferiors was not merely easy for him but afforded him pleasure. Even victory over the sins of the flesh, greed and lust, was easily attained. His director had specially warned him against the latter sin, but Kasátsky felt free from it and was glad.

One thing only tormented him—the remembrance of his fiancée; and not merely the remembrance but the vivid image of what might have been. Involuntarily he recalled a lady he knew who had been a favourite of the Emperor's, but had afterwards married and become an admirable wife and mother. The husband had a' high position, influence and honour, and a good and penitent wife.

In his better hours Kasátsky was not disturbed by such thoughts, and when he recalled them at such times he was merely glad to feel that the temptation was past. But there were moments when all that made up his present life suddenly grew dim before him, moments when, if he did not cease to believe in the aims he had set himself, he ceased to see them and could evoke no confidence in them but was seized by a remembrance of, and—terrible to say—a regret for, the change of life he had made.

The only thing that saved him in that state of mind was obedience and work, and the fact that the whole day was occupied by prayer. He went through the usual forms of prayer, he bowed in prayer, he even prayed more than usual, but it was lip-service only and his soul was not in it. This condition would continue for a day, or sometimes for two days, and would then pass of itself. But those days were dreadful. Kasátsky felt that he was neither in his own hands nor in God's, but was subject to something else. All he could do then was to obey the *stárets*, to restrain himself, to undertake nothing, and simply to wait. In general all this time he lived not by his own will but by that of the *stárets,* and in this obedience he found a special tranquillity.

So he lived in his first monastery for seven years. At the end of the third year he received the tonsure and was ordained to the priesthood by the name of Sergius. The profession was an important event in his inner life. He had previously experienced a great consolation and spiritual exaltation when receiving communion, and now when he himself officiated, the performance of the preparation filled him with ecstatic and deep emotion. But subsequently that feeling became more and more deadened, and once when he was officiating in a depressed state of mind he felt that the influence produced on him by the service would not endure. And it did in fact weaken till only the habit remained.

In general in the seventh year of his life in the monastery Sergius grew weary. He had learnt all there was to learn and had attained all there was to attain, there was nothing more to do and his spiritual drowsiness increased. During this time he heard of his mother's death and his sister Varvára's marriage, but both events were matters of indifference to him. His whole attention and his whole interest were concentrated on his inner life.

In the fourth year of his priesthood, during which the Bishop had been particularly kind to him, the *stárets* told him that he ought not to decline it if he were offered an appointment to higher duties. Then monastic ambition, the very thing he had found so repulsive in other monks, arose within him. He was assigned to a monastery near the metropolis. He wished to refuse but the *stárets* ordered him to accept the appointment. He did so, and took leave of the *stárets* and moved to the other monastery.

The exchange into the metropolitan monastery was an important event in Sergius's life. There he encountered many temptations, and his whole will-power was concentrated on meeting them.

In the first monastery, women had not been a temptation to him, but here that temptation arose with terrible strength and even took definite shape. There was a lady known for her frivolous behaviour who began to seek his favour. She talked to him and asked him to visit her. Sergius sternly declined, but was horrified by the definiteness of his desire. He was so alarmed that he wrote about it to the *stárets*. And in addition, to keep himself in hand, he spoke to a young novice and, conquering his sense of shame, confessed his weakness to him, asking him to keep watch on him and not let him go anywhere except to service and to fulfil his duties.

Besides this, a great pitfall for Sergius lay in the fact of his extreme antipathy to his new Abbot, a cunning worldly man who was making a career for himself in the Church. Struggle with himself as he might, he could not master that feeling. He was submissive to the Abbot, but in the depths of his soul he never ceased to condemn him. And in the second year of his residence at the new monastery that ill-feeling broke out.

The Vigil service was being performed in the large

church on the eve of the feast of the Intercession of the Blessed Virgin, and there were many visitors. The Abbot himself was conducting the service. Father Sergius was standing in his usual place and praying: that is, he was in that condition of struggle which always occupied him during the service, especially in the large church when he was not himself conducting the service. This conflict was occasioned by his irritation at the presence of fine folk, especially ladies. He tried not to see them or to notice all that went on: how a soldier conducted them, pushing the common people aside, how the ladies pointed out the monks to one another—especially himself and a monk noted for his good looks. He tried as it were to keep his mind in blinkers, to see nothing but the light of the candles on the altar-screen, the icons, and those conducting the service. He tried to hear nothing but the prayers that were being chanted or read, to feel nothing but self-oblivion in consciousness of the fulfilment of duty—a feeling he always experienced when hearing or reciting in advance the prayers he had so often heard.

So he stood, crossing and prostrating himself when necessary, and struggled with himself, now giving way to cold condemnation and now to a consciously evoked obliteration of thought and feeling. Then the sacristan, Father Nicodemus—also a great stumbling-block to Sergius who involuntarily reproached him for flattering and fawning on the Abbot—approached him and, bowing low, requested his presence behind the holy gates. Father Sergius straightened his mantle, put on his biretta, and went circumspectly through the crowd.

'*Lise, regarde à droite, c'est lui!*' he heard a woman's voice say.

'*Où, où? Il n'est pas tellement beau.*'

He knew that they were speaking of him. He heard them and, as always at moments of temptation, he repeated the words, 'Lead us not into temptation', and bowing his head and lowering his eyes went past the ambo and in by the north door, avoiding the canons in their cassocks who were just then passing the altar-screen. On entering the sanctuary he bowed, crossing himself as usual and bending double before the icons. Then, raising his head but without turning, he glanced out of the corner of his eye at the Abbot, whom he saw standing beside another glittering figure.

The Abbot was standing by the wall in his vestments. Having freed his short plump hands from beneath his chasuble he had folded them over his fat body and protruding stomach, and fingering the cords of his vestments was smilingly saying something to a military man in the uniform of a general of the Imperial suite, with its insignia and shoulder-knots which Father Sergius's experienced eye at once recognized. This general had been the commander of the regiment in which Sergius had served. He now evidently occupied an important position, and Father Sergius at once noticed that the Abbot was aware of this and that his red face and bald head beamed with satisfaction and pleasure. This vexed and disgusted Father Sergius, the more so when he heard that the Abbot had only sent for him to satisfy the general's curiosity to see a man who had formerly served with him, as he expressed it.

'Very pleased to see you in your angelic guise,' said the general, holding out his hand. 'I hope you have not forgotten an old comrade.'

The whole thing—the Abbot's red, smiling face amid its fringe of grey, the general's words, his well-cared-for face with its self-satisfied smile and the smell of wine from his breath and of cigars from his whiskers—revolted Father Sergius. He bowed again to the Abbot and said:

'Your reverence deigned to send for me?'—and stopped, the whole expression of his face and eyes asking why.

'Yes, to meet the General,' replied the Abbot.

'Your reverence, I left the world to save myself from temptation,' said Father Sergius, turning pale and with quivering lips. 'Why do you expose me to it during prayers and in God's house?'

'You may go! Go!' said the Abbot, flaring up and frowning.

Next day Father Sergius asked pardon of the Abbot and of the brethren for his pride, but at the same time, after a night spent in prayer, he decided that he must leave this monastery, and he wrote to the *stárets* begging permission to return to him. He wrote that he felt his weakness and incapacity to struggle against temptation without his help, and penitently confessed his sin of pride. By return of post came a letter from the *stárets*, who wrote that Sergius's pride was the cause of all that had happened. The old man pointed out that his fits of anger were due to the fact that in refusing all clerical honours he humiliated himself not for the sake of God but for the sake of his pride. 'There now, am I not a splendid man not to want anything?' That was why he could not tolerate the Abbot's action. 'I have renounced everything for the glory of God, and here I am exhibited like a wild beast!' 'Had you renounced vanity for God's sake you would have borne it. Worldly pride is not yet dead in you. I have thought about you, Sergius my son, and prayed also, and this is what God has suggested to me. At the Tambóv hermitage the anchorite Hilary, a man of saintly life, has died. He had lived there eighteen years. The Tambóv Abbot is asking whether there is not a brother who would take his place. And here comes your letter. Go to Father Païssy of the Tambóv Monastery. I will write to him about you, and you must ask for Hilary's cell. Not that you can replace Hilary, but you need solitude to quell your pride. May God bless you!'

Sergius obeyed the *stárets*, showed his letter to the Abbot, and having obtained his permission, gave up his cell, handed all his possessions over to the monastery, and set out for the Tambóv hermitage.

There the Abbot, an excellent manager of merchant origin, received Sergius simply and quietly and placed him in Hilary's cell, at first assigning to him a lay brother but afterwards leaving him alone, at Sergius's own request. The cell was a dual cave, dug into the hillside, and in it Hilary had been buried. In the back part was Hilary's grave, while in the front was a niche for sleeping, with a straw mattress, a small table, and a shelf with icons and books. Outside the outer door, which fastened with a hook, was another shelf on which, once a day, a monk placed food from the monastery.

And so Sergius became a hermit.

III

At Carnival time, in the sixth year of Sergius's life at the hermitage, a merry company of rich people, men and women from a neighbouring town, made up a troyka-party, after a meal of carnival-pancakes and wine. The company consisted of two lawyers, a wealthy landowner, an officer, and four ladies. One lady was the officer's wife, another the wife of the landowner, the third his sister—

a young girl—and the fourth a divorcée, beautiful, rich, and eccentric, who amazed and shocked the town by her escapades.

The weather was excellent and the snow-covered road smooth as a floor. They drove some seven miles out of town, and then stopped and consulted as to whether they should turn back or drive farther.

'But where does this road lead to?' asked Makóvkina, the beautiful divorcée.

'To Tambóv, eight miles from here,' replied one of the lawyers, who was having a flirtation with her.

'And then where?'

'Then on to L——, past the Monastery.'

'Where that Father Sergius lives?'

'Yes.'

'Kasátsky, the handsome hermit?'

'Yes.'

'*Mesdames and messieurs,* let us drive on and see Kasátsky! We can stop at Tambóv and have something to eat.'

'But we shouldn't get home to-night!'

'Never mind, we will stay at Kasátsky's.'

'Well, there is a very good hostelry at the Monastery. I stayed there when I was defending Mákhin.'

'No, I shall spend the night at Kasátsky's!'

'Impossible! Even your omnipotence could not accomplish that!'

'Impossible? Will you bet?'

'All right! If you spend the night with him, the stake shall be whatever you like.'

'*A discrétion!*'

'But on your side too!'

'Yes, of course. Let us drive on.'

Vodka was handed to the drivers, and the party got out a box of pies, wine, and sweets for themselves. The ladies wrapped up in their white dogskins. The drivers disputed as to whose troyka should go ahead, and the youngest, seating himself sideways with a dashing air, swung his long knout and shouted to the horses. The troyka-bells tinkled and the sledge-runners squeaked over the snow.

The sledges swayed hardly at all. The shaft-horse, with his tightly bound tail under his decorated breechband, galloped smoothly and briskly; the smooth road seemed to

run rapidly backwards, while the driver dashingly shook
the reins. One of the lawyers and the officer sitting opposite talked nonsense to Makóvkina's neighbour, but
Makóvkina herself sat motionless and in thought, tightly
wrapped in her fur. 'Always the same and always nasty!
The same red shiny faces smelling of wine and cigars!
The same talk, the same thoughts, and always about the
same things! And they are all satisfied and confident
that it should be so, and will go on living like that till they
die. But I can't. It bores me. I want something that would
upset it all and turn it upside down. Suppose it happened
to us as to those people—at Sarátov was it?—who kept on
driving and froze to death. . . . What would our people
do? How would they behave? Basely, for certain. Each
for himself. And I too should act badly. But I at any rate
have beauty. They all know it. And how about that monk?
Is it possible that he has become indifferent to it? No!
That is the one thing they all care for—like that cadet
last autumn. What a fool he was!'

'Iván Nikoláevich!' she said aloud.

'What are your commands?'

'How old is he?'

'Who?'

'Kasátsky.'

'Over forty, I should think.'

'And does he receive all visitors?'

'Yes, everybody, but not always.'

'Cover up my feet. Not like that—how clumsy you are!
No! More, more—like that! But you need not squeeze
them!'

So they came to the forest where the cell was.

Makóvkina got out of the sledge, and told them to drive
on. They tried to dissuade her, but she grew irritable and
ordered them to go on.

When the sledges had gone she went up the path in
her white dogskin coat. The lawyer got out and stopped
to watch her.

It was Father Sergius's sixth year as a recluse, and he
was now forty-nine. His life in solitude was hard—not on
account of the fasts and the prayers (they were no hardship to him) but on account of an inner conflict he had not
at all anticipated. The sources of that conflict were two:
doubts, and the lust of the flesh. And these two enemies

always appeared together. It seemed to him that they were
two foes, but in reality they were one and the same. As
soon as doubt was gone so was the lustful desire. But
thinking them to be two different fiends he fought them
separately.

'O my God, my God!' thought he. 'Why dost thou
not grant me faith? There is lust, of course: even the
saints had to fight that—Saint Anthony and others. But
they had faith, while I have moments, hours, and days,
when it is absent. Why does the whole world, with all its
delights, exist if it is sinful and must be renounced? Why
hast Thou created this temptation? Temptation? Is it not
rather a temptation that I wish to abandon all the joys of
earth and prepare something for myself there where perhaps there is nothing?' And he became horrified and filled
with disgust at himself. 'Vile creature! And it is you who
wish to become a saint!' he upbraided himself, and he began
to pray. But as soon as he started to pray he saw himself
vividly as he had been at the Monastery, in a majestic
post in biretta and mantle, and he shook his head. 'No,
that is not right. It is deception. I may deceive others, but
not myself or God. I am not a majestic man, but a
pitiable and ridiculous one!' And he threw back the folds
of his cassock and smiled as he looked at his thin legs
in their underclothing.

Then he dropped the folds of the cassock again and
began reading the prayers, making the sign of the cross
and prostrating himself. 'Can it be that this couch will be
my bier?' he read. And it seemed as if a devil whispered
to him: 'A solitary couch is itself a bier. Falsehood!' And
in imagination he saw the shoulders of a widow with
whom he had lived. He shook himself, and went on reading.
Having read the precepts he took up the Gospels, opened
the book, and happened on a passage he often repeated
and knew by heart: 'Lord, I believe. Help thou my un-
belief!'—and he put away all the doubts that had arisen.
As one replaces an object of insecure equilibrium, so he
carefully replaced his belief on its shaky pedestal and
carefully stepped back from it so as not to shake or upset
it. The blinkers were adjusted again and he felt tranquillized, and repeating his childhood's prayer: 'Lord, receive
me, receive me!' he felt not merely at ease, but thrilled
and joyful. He crossed himself and lay down on the
bedding on his narrow bench, tucking his summer cassock

under his head. He fell asleep at once, and in his light
slumber he seemed to hear the tinkling of sledge bells. He
did not know whether he was dreaming or awake, but a
knock at the door aroused him. He sat up, distrusting his
senses, but the knock was repeated. Yes, it was a knock
close at hand, at his door, and with it the sound of a
woman's voice.

'My God! Can it be true, as I have read in the *Lives
of the Saints,* that the devil takes on the form of a woman?
Yes—it is a woman's voice. And a tender, timid, pleasant
voice. Phui!' And he spat to exorcise the devil. 'No, it was
only my imagination,' he assured himself, and he went to
the corner where his lectern stood, falling on his knees
in the regular and habitual manner which of itself gave
him consolation and satisfaction. He sank down, his hair
hanging over his face, and pressed his head, already going
bald in front, to the cold damp strip of drugget on the
draughty floor. He read the psalm old Father Pímon had
told him warded off temptation. He easily raised his light
and emaciated body on his strong sinewy legs and tried
to continue saying his prayers, but instead of doing so
he involuntarily strained his hearing. He wished to hear
more. All was quiet. From the corner of the roof regular
drops continued to fall into the tub below. Outside was a
mist and fog eating into the snow that lay on the ground.
It was still, very still. And suddenly there was a rustling
at the window and a voice—that same tender, timid voice,
which could only belong to an attractive woman—said:

'Let me in, for Christ's sake!'

It seemed as though his blood had all rushed to his
heart and settled there. He could hardly breathe. 'Let God
arise and let his enemies be scattered . . .'

'But I am not a devil!' It was obvious that the lips that
uttered this were smiling. 'I am not a devil, but only a
sinful woman who has lost her way, not figuratively but
literally!' She laughed. 'I am frozen and beg for shelter.'

He pressed his face to the window, but the little icon-
lamp was reflected by it and shone on the whole pane. He
put his hands to both sides of his face and peered between
them. Fog, mist, a tree, and—just opposite him—she herself. Yes, there, a few inches from him, was the sweet,
kindly frightened face of a woman in a cap and a coat
of long white fur, leaning towards him. Their eyes met
with instant recognition: not that they had ever known one

another, they had never met before, but by the look they exchanged they—and he particularly—felt that they knew and understood one another. After that glance to imagine her to be a devil and not a simple, kindly, sweet, timid woman, was impossible.

'Who are you? Why have you come?' he asked.

'Do please open the door!' she replied, with capricious authority. 'I am frozen. I tell you I have lost my way.'

'But I am a monk—a hermit.'

'Oh, do please open the door—or do you wish me to freeze under your window while you say your prayers?'

'But how have you . . .'

'I shan't eat you. For God's sake let me in! I am quite frozen.'

She really did feel afraid, and said this in an almost tearful voice.

He stepped back from the window and looked at an icon of the Saviour in His crown of thorns. 'Lord, help me! Lord, help me!' he exclaimed, crossing himself and bowing low. Then he went to the door, and opening it into the tiny porch, felt for the hook that fastened the outer door and began to lift it. He heard steps outside. She was coming from the window to the door. 'Ah!' she suddenly exclaimed, and he understood that she had stepped into the puddle that the dripping from the roof had formed at the threshold. His hands trembled, and he could not raise the hook of the tightly closed door.

'Oh, what are you doing? Let me in! I am all wet. I am frozen! You are thinking about saving your soul and are letting me freeze to death . . .'

He jerked the door towards him, raised the hook, and without considering what he was doing, pushed it open with such force that it struck her.

'Oh—*pardon!*' he suddenly exclaimed, reverting completely to his old manner with ladies.

She smiled on hearing that *pardon*. 'He is not quite so terrible, after all,' she thought. 'It's all right. It is you who must pardon me,' she said, stepping past him. 'I should never have ventured, but such an extraordinary circumstance . . .'

'If you please!' he uttered, and stood aside to let her pass him. A strong smell of fine scent, which he had long not encountered, struck him. She went through the little porch into the cell where he lived. He closed the outer door without fastening the hook, and stepped in after her.

'Lord Jesus Christ, Son of God, have mercy on me a sinner! Lord, have mercy on me a sinner!' he prayed unceasingly, not merely to himself but involuntarily moving his lips. 'If you please!' he said to her again. She stood in the middle of the room, moisture dripping from her to the floor as she looked him over. Her eyes were laughing.

'Forgive me for having disturbed your solitude. But you see what a position I am in. It all came about from our starting from town for a sledge-drive, and my making a bet that I would walk back by myself from the Vorobëvka to the town. But then I lost my way, and if I had not happened to come upon your cell . . .' She began lying, but his face confused her so that she could not continue, but became silent. She had not expected him to be at all such as he was. He was not as handsome as she had imagined, but was nevertheless beautiful in her eyes: his greyish hair and beard, slightly curling, his fine, regular nose, and his eyes like glowing coal when he looked at her, made a strong impression on her.

He saw that she was lying.

'Yes . . . so,' said he, looking at her and again lowering his eyes. 'I will go in there, and this place is at your disposal.'

And taking down the little lamp, he lit a candle, and bowing low to her went into the small cell beyond the partition, and she heard him begin to move something about there. 'Probably he is barricading himself in from me!' she thought with a smile, and throwing off her white dogskin cloak she tried to take off her cap, which had become entangled in her hair and in the woven kerchief she was wearing under it. She had not got at all wet when standing under the window, and had said so only as a pretext to get him to let her in. But she really had stepped into the puddle at the door, and her left foot was wet up to the ankle and her overshoe full of water. She sat down on his bed—a bench only covered by a bit of carpet—and began to take off her boots. The little cell seemed to her charming. The narrow little room, some seven feet by nine, was as clean as glass. There was nothing in it but the bench on which she was sitting, the book-shelf above it, and a lectern in the corner. A sheepskin coat and a cassock hung on nails by the door. Above the lectern was the little lamp and an icon of Christ in His crown of thorns. The room smelt strangely of perspiration and of earth. It all pleased her—even that smell. Her wet feet, especially one of them, were uncomfortable, and she quickly began to take off her boots and stockings without ceasing to smile, pleased not so much at having achieved her object as because she perceived that she had abashed that charming, strange, striking, and attractive man. 'He did not respond, but what of that?' she said to herself.

'Father Sergius! Father Sergius! Or how does one call you?'

'What do you want?' replied a quiet voice.

'Please forgive me for disturbing your solitude, but really I could not help it. I should simply have fallen ill. And I don't know that I shan't now. I am all wet and my feet are like ice.'

'Pardon me,' replied the quiet voice. 'I cannot be of any assistance to you.'

'I would not have disturbed you if I could have helped it. I am only here till daybreak.'

He did not reply and she heard him muttering something, probably his prayers.

'You will not be coming in here?' she asked, smiling. 'For I must undress to dry myself.'

He did not reply, but continued to read his prayers.

'Yes, that is a man!' thought she, getting her dripping boot off with difficulty. She tugged at it, but could not get it off. The absurdity of it struck her and she began to laugh almost inaudibly. But knowing that he would hear her laughter and would be moved by it just as she wished him to be, she laughed louder, and her laughter—gay, natural, and kindly—really acted on him just in the way she wished.

'Yes, I could love a man like that—such eyes and such a simple noble face, and passionate too despite all the prayers he mutters!' thought she. 'You can't deceive a woman in these things. As soon as he put his face to the window and saw me, he understood and knew. The glimmer of it was in his eyes and remained there. He began to love me and desired me. Yes—desired!' said she, getting her overshoe and her boot off at last and starting to take off her stockings. To remove those long stockings fastened with elastic it was necessary to raise her skirts. She felt embarrassed and said:

'Don't come in!'

But there was no reply from the other side of the wall. The steady muttering continued and also a sound of moving.

'He is prostrating himself to the ground, no doubt,' thought she. 'But he won't bow himself out of it. He is thinking of me just as I am thinking of him. He is thinking of these feet of mine with the same feeling that I have!' And she pulled off her wet stockings and put her feet up on the bench, pressing them under her. She sat a while like that with her arms round her knees and looking pensively before her. 'But it is a desert, here in this silence. No one would ever know. . . .'

She rose, took her stockings over to the stove, and hung them on the damper. It was a queer damper, and she turned it about, and then, stepping lightly on her bare feet, returned to the bench and sat down there again with her feet up.

There was complete silence on the other side of the partition. She looked at the tiny watch that hung round her neck. It was two o'clock. 'Our party should return about three!' She had not more than an hour before her. 'Well, am I to sit like this all alone? What nonsense! I don't want to. I will call him at once.'

'Father Sergius, Father Sergius! Sergéy Dmítrich! Prince Kasátsky!'

Beyond the partition all was silent.

'Listen! This is cruel. I would not call you if it were not necessary. I am ill. I don't know what is the matter with me!' she exclaimed in a tone of suffering. 'Oh! Oh!' she groaned, falling back on the bench. And strange to say she really felt that her strength was failing, that she was becoming faint, that everything in her ached, and that she was shivering with fever.

'Listen! Help me! I don't know what is the matter with me. Oh! Oh!' She unfastened her dress, exposing her breast, and lifted her arms, bare to the elbow. 'Oh! Oh!'

All this time he stood on the other side of the partition and prayed. Having finished all the evening prayers, he now stood motionless, his eyes looking at the end of his nose, and mentally repeated with all his soul: 'Lord Jesus Christ, Son of God, have mercy upon me!'

But he had heard everything. He had heard how the silk rustled when she took off her dress, how she stepped with bare feet on the floor, and had heard how she rubbed her feet with her hand. He felt his own weakness, and that he might be lost at any moment. That was why he prayed unceasingly. He felt rather as the hero in the fairy-tale must have felt when he had to go on and on without looking round. So Sergius heard and felt that danger and destruction were there, hovering above and around him, and that he could only save himself by not looking in that direction for an instant. But suddenly the desire to look seized him. At the same instant she said:

'This is inhuman. I may die. . . .'

'Yes, I will go to her, but like the Saint who laid one hand on the adulteress and thrust his other into the brazier. But there is no brazier here.' He looked round. The lamp! He put his finger over the flame and frowned, preparing himself to suffer. And for a rather long time, as it seemed to him, there was no sensation, but suddenly—he had not yet decided whether it was painful enough—he writhed all over, jerked his hand away, and waved it in the air. 'No, I can't stand that!'

'For God's sake come to me! I am dying! Oh!'

'Well—shall I perish? No, not so!'

'I will come to you directly,' he said, and having opened his door, he went without looking at her through the cell into the porch where he used to chop wood. There he felt for the block and for an axe which leant against the wall.

'Immediately!' he said, and taking up the axe with his right hand he laid the forefinger of his left hand on the block, swung the axe, and struck with it below the second joint. The finger flew off more lightly than a stick of similar thickness, and bounding up, turned over on the edge of the block and then fell to the floor.

He heard it fall before he felt any pain, but before he had time to be surprised he felt a burning pain and the warmth of flowing blood. He hastily wrapped the stump in the skirt of his cassock, and pressing it to his hip went back into the room, and standing in front of the woman, lowered his eyes and asked in a low voice: 'What do you want?'

She looked at his pale face and his quivering left cheek, and suddenly felt ashamed. She jumped up, seized her fur cloak, and throwing it round her shoulders, wrapped herself up in it.

'I was in pain . . . I have caught cold . . . I . . . Father Sergius . . . I . . .'

He let his eyes, shining with a quiet light of joy, rest upon her, and said:

'Dear sister, why did you wish to ruin your immortal soul? Temptations must come into the world, but woe to him by whom temptation comes. Pray that God may forgive us!'

She listened and looked at him. Suddenly she heard the sound of something dripping. She looked down and saw that blood was flowing from his hand and down his cassock.

'What have you done to your hand?' She remembered the sound she had heard, and seizing the little lamp ran out into the porch. There on the floor she saw the bloody finger. She returned with her face paler than his and was about to speak to him, but he silently passed into the back cell and fastened the door.

'Forgive me!' she said. 'How can I atone for my sin?'

'Go away.'

'Let me tie up your hand.'

'Go away from here.'

She dressed hurriedly and silently, and when ready sat waiting in her furs. The sledge-bells were heard outside.

'Father Sergius, forgive me!'

'Go away. God will forgive.'

'Father Sergius! I will change my life. Do not forsake me!'

'Go away.'

'Forgive me—and give me your blessing!'

'In the name of the Father and of the Son and of the Holy Ghost!'—she heard his voice from behind the partition. 'Go!'

She burst into sobs and left the cell. The lawyer came forward to meet her.

'Well, I see I have lost the bet. It can't be helped. Where will you sit?'

'It is all the same to me.'

She took a seat in the sledge, and did not utter a word all the way home.

A year later she entered a convent as a novice, and lived a strict life under the direction of the hermit Arsény, who wrote letters to her at long intervals.

IV

Father Sergius lived as a recluse for another seven years.

At first he accepted much of what people brought him —tea, sugar, white bread, milk, clothing, and fire-wood. But as time went on he led a more and more austere life, refusing everything superfluous, and finally he accepted nothing but rye-bread once a week. Everything else that was brought him he gave to the poor who came to him. He spent his entire time in his cell, in prayer or in conversation with callers, who became more and more numerous as time went on. Only three times a year did he go out to church, and when necessary he went out to fetch water and wood.

The episode with Makóvkina had occurred after five years of his hermit life. That occurrence soon became generally known—her nocturnal visit, the change she underwent, and her entry into a convent. From that time Father Sergius's fame increased. More and more visitors came to see him, other monks settled down near his cell, and a church was erected there and also a hostelry. His fame, as usual exaggerating his feats, spread ever more and more widely. People began to come to him from a distance, and began bringing invalids to him whom they declared he cured.

His first cure occurred in the eighth year of his life as a hermit. It was the healing of a fourteen-year-old boy, whose mother brought him to Father Sergius insisting that he should lay his hand on the child's head. It had never occurred to Father Sergius that he could cure the sick. He would have regarded such a thought as a great sin of pride; but the mother who brought the boy implored him insistently, falling at his feet and saying: 'Why do you, who heal others, refuse to help my son?' She besought him in Christ's name. When Father Sergius assured her that only God could heal the sick, she replied that she only wanted him to lay his hands on the boy and pray for him. Father Sergius refused and returned to his cell. But next day (it was in autumn and the nights were already cold) on going out for water he saw the same mother with her son, a pale boy of fourteen, and was met by the same petition.

He remembered the parable of the unjust judge, and though he had previously felt sure that he ought to refuse, he now began to hesitate and, having hesitated, took to prayer and prayed until a decision formed itself in his soul. This decision was, that he ought to accede to the woman's request and that her faith might save her son. As for himself, he would in this case be but an insignificant instrument chosen by God.

And going out to the mother he did what she asked—laid his hand on the boy's head and prayed.

The mother left with her son, and a month later the boy recovered, and the fame of the holy healing power of the *stárets* Sergius (as they now called him) spread throughout the whole district. After that, not a week passed without sick people coming, riding or on foot, to Father Sergius; and having acceded to one petition he could not refuse others, and he laid his hands on many and prayed. Many recovered, and his fame spread more and more.

So seven years passed in the Monastery and thirteen in his hermit's cell. He now had the appearance of an old man: his beard was long and grey, but his hair, though thin, was still black and curly.

V

For some weeks Father Sergius had been living with one persistent thought: whether he was right in accepting the position in which he had not so much placed himself as been placed by the Archimandrite and the Abbot. That position had begun after the recovery of the fourteen-year-old boy. From that time, with each month, week, and day that passed, Sergius felt his own inner life wasting away and being replaced by external life. It was as if he had been turned inside out.

Sergius saw that he was a means of attracting visitors and contributions to the monastery, and that therefore the authorities arranged matters in such a way as to make as much use of him as possible. For instance, they rendered it impossible for him to do any manual work. He was supplied with everything he could want, and they only demanded of him that he should not refuse his blessing to those who came to seek it. For his convenience they appointed days when he would receive. They arranged a reception-room for men, and a place was railed in so that he should not be pushed over by the crowds of women visitors, and so that he could conveniently bless those who came.

They told him that people needed him, and that fulfilling Christ's law of love he could not refuse their demand to see him, and that to avoid them would be cruel. He could not but agree with this, but the more he gave himself up to such a life the more he felt that what was internal became external, and that the fount of living water within him dried up, and that what he did now was done more and more for men and less and less for God.

Whether he admonished people, or simply blessed them, or prayed for the sick, or advised people about their lives, or listened to expressions of gratitude from those he had helped by precepts, or alms, or healing (as they assured him)—he could not help being pleased at it, and could not be indifferent to the results of his activity and to the influence he exerted. He thought himself a shining light, and the more he felt this the more was he conscious of a weakening, a dying down of the divine light of truth that shone within him.

'In how far is what I do for God and in how far is it for men?' That was the question that insistently tormented him and to which he was not so much unable to give himself an answer as unable to face the answer.

In the depth of his soul he felt that the devil had substituted an activity for men in place of his former activity for God. He felt this because, just as it had formerly been hard for him to be torn from his solitude so now that solitude itself was hard for him. He was oppressed and wearied by visitors, but at the bottom of his heart he was glad of their presence and glad of the praise they heaped upon him.

There was a time when he decided to go away and hide. He even planned all that was necessary for that purpose. He prepared for himself a peasant's shirt, trousers, coat, and cap. He explained that he wanted these to give to those who asked. And he kept these clothes in his cell, planning how he would put them on, cut his hair short, and go away. First he would go some three hundred versts by train, then he would leave the train and walk from village to village. He asked an old man who had been a soldier how he tramped: what people gave him, and what shelter they allowed him. The soldier told him where people were most charitable, and where they would take a wanderer in for the night, and Father Sergius intended to avail himself of this information. He even put on those clothes one night in his desire to go, but he could not decide what was best—to remain or to escape. At first he was in doubt, but afterwards this indecision passed. He submitted to custom and yielded to the devil, and only the peasant garb reminded him of the thought and feeling he had had.

Every day more and more people flocked to him and less and less time was left him for prayer and for renewing his spiritual strength. Sometimes in lucid moments he thought he was like a place where there had once been a spring. 'There used to be a feeble spring of living water which flowed quietly from me and through me. That was true life, the time when she tempted me!' (He always thought with ecstasy of that night and of her who was now Mother Agnes.) She had tasted of that pure water, but since then there had not been time for it to collect before thirsty people came crowding in and pushing one another aside. And they had trampled everything down and nothing was left but mud.

So he thought in rare moments of lucidity, but his usual state of mind was one of weariness and a tender pity for himself because of that weariness.

It was in spring, on the eve of the mid-Pentecostal feast. Father Sergius was officiating at the Vigil Service in his hermitage church, where the congregation was as large as the little church could hold—about twenty people. They were all well-to-do proprietors or merchants. Father Sergius admitted anyone, but a selection was made by the monk in attendance and by an assistant who was sent to the hermitage every day from the monastery. A crowd of some eighty people—pilgrims and peasants, and especially peasant-women—stood outside waiting for Father Sergius to come out and bless them. Meanwhile he conducted the service, but at the point at which he went out to the tomb of his predecessor, he staggered and would have fallen had he not been caught by a merchant standing behind him and by the monk acting as deacon.

'What is the matter, Father Sergius? Dear man! O Lord!' exclaimed the women. 'He is as white as a sheet!'

But Father Sergius recovered immediately, and though

very pale, he waved the merchant and the deacon aside and continued to chant the service.

Father Seraphim, the deacon, the acolytes, and Sófya Ivánovna, a lady who always lived near the hermitage and tended Father Sergius, begged him to bring the service to an end.

'No, there's nothing the matter,' said Father Sergius, slightly smiling from beneath his moustache and continuing the service. 'Yes, that is the way the Saints behaved!' thought he.

'A holy man—an angel of God!' he heard just then the voice of Sófya Ivánovna behind him, and also of the merchant who had supported him. He did not heed their entreaties, but went on with the service. Again crowding together they all made their way by the narrow passages back into the little church, and there, though abbreviating it slightly, Father Sergius completed vespers.

Immediately after the service Father Sergius, having pronounced the benediction on those present, went over to the bench under the elm tree at the entrance to the cave. He wished to rest and breathe the fresh air—he felt in need of it. But as soon as he left the church the crowd of people rushed to him soliciting his blessing, his advice, and his help. There were pilgrims who constantly tramped from one holy place to another and from one *stárets* to another, and were always entranced by every shrine and every *stárets*. Father Sergius knew this common, cold, conventional, and most irreligious type. There were pilgrims, for the most part discharged soldiers, unaccustomed to a settled life, poverty-stricken, and many of them drunken old men, who tramped from monastery to monastery merely to be fed. And there were rough peasants and peasant-women who had come with their selfish requirements, seeking cures or to have doubts about quite practical affairs solved for them: about marrying off a daughter, or hiring a shop, or buying a bit of land, or how to atone for having overlaid a child or having an illegitimate one.

All this was an old story and not in the least interesting to him. He knew he would hear nothing new from these folk, that they would arouse no religious emotion in him; but he liked to see the crowd to which his blessing and advice was necessary and precious, so while that crowd oppressed him it also pleased him. Father Seraphim began to drive them away, saying that Father Sergius was tired.

But Father Sergius, remembering the words of the Gospel: 'Forbid them' (children) 'not to come unto me', and feeling tenderly towards himself at this recollection, said they should be allowed to approach.

He rose, went to the railing beyond which the crowd had gathered, and began blessing them and answering their questions, but in a voice so weak that he was touched with pity for himself. Yet despite his wish to receive them all he could not do it. Things again grew dark before his eyes, and he staggered and grasped the railings. He felt a rush of blood to his head and first went pale and then suddenly flushed.

'I must leave the rest till to-morrow. I cannot do more to-day,' and, pronouncing a general benediction, he returned to the bench. The merchant again supported him, and leading him by the arm helped him to be seated.

'Father!' came voices from the crowd. 'Dear Father! Do not forsake us. Without you we are lost!'

The merchant, having seated Father Sergius on the bench under the elm, took on himself police duties and drove the people off very resolutely. It is true that he spoke in a low voice so that Father Sergius might not hear him, but his words were incisive and angry.

'Be off, be off! He has blessed you, and what more do you want? Get along with you, or I'll wring your necks! Move on there! Get along, you old woman with your dirty leg-bands! Go, go! Where are you shoving to? You've been told that it is finished. To-morrow will be as God wills, but for to-day he has finished!'

'Father! Only let my eyes have a glimpse of his dear face!' said an old woman.

'I'll glimpse you! Where are you shoving to?'

Father Sergius noticed that the merchant seemed to be acting roughly, and in a feeble voice told the attendant that the people should not be driven away. He knew that they would be driven away all the same, and he much desired to be left alone and to rest, but he sent the attendant with that message to produce an impression.

'All right, all right! I am not driving them away. I am only remonstrating with them,' replied the merchant. 'You know they wouldn't hesitate to drive a man to death. They have no pity, they only consider themselves. . . . You've been told you cannot see him. Go away! To-morrow!' And he got rid of them all.

He took all these pains because he liked order and liked to domineer and drive the people away, but chiefly because he wanted to have Father Sergius to himself. He was a widower with an only daughter who was an invalid and unmarried, and whom he had brought fourteen hundred versts to Father Sergius to be healed. For two years past he had been taking her to different places to be cured: first to the university clinic in the chief town of the province, but that did no good; then to a peasant in the province of Samára, where she got a little better; then to a doctor in Moscow to whom he paid much money, but this did no good at all. Now he had been told that Father Sergius wrought cures, and had brought her to him. So when all the people had been driven away he approached Father Sergius, and suddenly falling on his knees loudly exclaimed:

'Holy Father! Bless my afflicted offspring that she may be healed of her malady. I venture to prostrate myself at your holy feet.'

And he placed one hand on the other, cup-wise. He said and did all this as if he were doing something clearly and firmly appointed by law and usage—as if one must and should ask for a daughter to be cured in just this way and no other. He did it with such conviction that it seemed even to Father Sergius that it should be said and done in just that way, but nevertheless he bade him rise and tell him what the trouble was. The merchant said that his daughter, a girl of twenty-two, had fallen ill two years ago, after her mother's sudden death. She had moaned (as he expressed it) and since then had not been herself. And now he had brought her fourteen hundred versts and she was waiting in the hostelry till Father Sergius should give orders to bring her. She did not go out during the day, being afraid of the light, and could only come after sunset.

'Is she very weak?' asked Father Sergius.

'No, she has no particular weakness. She is quite plump, and is only "nerastenic" the doctors say. If you will only let me bring her this evening, Father Sergius, I'll fly like a spirit to fetch her. Holy Father! Revive a parent's heart, restore his line, save his afflicted daughter by your prayers!' And the merchant again threw himself on his knees and bending sideways, with his head resting on his clenched fists, remained stock still. Father Sergius again

told him to get up, and thinking how heavy his activities
were and how he went through with them patiently notwithstanding, he sighed heavily and after a few seconds
of silence, said:

'Well, bring her this evening. I will pray for her, but
now I am tired . . .' and he closed his eyes. 'I will send
for you.'

The merchant went away, stepping on tiptoe, which
only made his boots creak the louder, and Father Sergius
remained alone.

His whole life was filled by Church services and by
people who came to see him, but to-day had been a particularly difficult one. In the morning an important official
had arrived and had had a long conversation with him;
after that a lady had come with her son. This son was a
sceptical young professor whom the mother, an ardent
believer and devoted to Father Sergius, had brought that
he might talk to him. The conversation had been very
trying. The young man, evidently not wishing to have a
controversy with a monk, had agreed with him in everything as with someone who was mentally inferior. Father
Sergius saw that the young man did not believe but yet
was satisfied, tranquil, and at ease, and the memory of
that conversation now disquieted him.

'Have something to eat, Father,' said the attendant.

'All right, bring me something.'

The attendant went to a hut that had been arranged
some ten paces from the cave, and Father Sergius remained alone.

The time was long past when he had lived alone doing
everything for himself and eating only rye-bread, or rolls
prepared for the Church. He had been advised long since
that he had no right to neglect his health, and he was
given wholesome, though Lenten, food. He ate sparingly,
though much more than he had done, and often he ate
with much pleasure, and not as formerly with aversion
and a sense of guilt. So it was now. He had some gruel,
drank a cup of tea, and ate half a white roll.

The attendant went away, and Father Sergius remained
alone under the elm tree.

It was a wonderful May evening, when the birches,
aspens, elms, wild cherries, and oaks, had just burst into
foliage.

The bush of wild cherries behind the elm tree was in

full bloom and had not yet begun to shed its blossoms, and the nightingales—one quite near at hand and two or three others in the bushes down by the river—burst into full song after some preliminary twitters. From the river came the far-off songs of peasants returning, no doubt, from their work. The sun was setting behind the forest, its last rays glowing through the leaves. All that side was brilliant green, the other side with the elm tree was dark. The cockchafers flew clumsily about, falling to the ground when they collided with anything.

After supper Father Sergius began to repeat a silent prayer: 'O Lord Jesus Christ, Son of God, have mercy upon us!' and then he read a psalm, and suddenly in the middle of the psalm a sparrow flew out from the bush, alighted on the ground, and hopped towards him chirping as it came, but then it took fright at something and flew away. He said a prayer which referred to his abandonment of the world, and hastened to finish it in order to send for the merchant with the sick daughter. She interested him in that she presented a distraction, and because both she and her father considered him a saint whose prayers were efficacious. Outwardly he disavowed that idea, but in the depths of his soul he considered it to be true.

He was often amazed that this had happened, that he, Stepán Kasátsky, had come to be such an extraordinary saint and even a worker of miracles, but of the fact that he was such there could not be the least doubt. He could not fail to believe in the miracles he himself witnessed, beginning with the sick boy and ending with the old woman who had recovered her sight when he had prayed for her.

Strange as it might be, it was so. Accordingly the merchant's daughter interested him as a new individual who had faith in him, and also as a fresh opportunity to confirm his healing powers and enhance his fame. 'They bring people a thousand versts and write about it in the papers. The Emperor knows of it, and they know of it in Europe, in unbelieving Europe'—thought he. And suddenly he felt ashamed of his vanity and again began to pray. 'Lord, King of Heaven, Comforter, Soul of Truth! Come and enter into me and cleanse me from all sin and save and bless my soul. Cleanse me from the sin of worldly vanity that troubles me!' he repeated, and he remembered how often he had prayed about this and how vain till now his prayers had been in that respect. His prayers worked miracles for others, but in his own case God had not granted him liberation from this petty passion.

He remembered his prayers at the commencement of his life at the hermitage, when he prayed for purity, humility, and love, and how it seemed to him then that God heard his prayers. He had retained his purity and had chopped off his finger. And he lifted the shrivelled stump of that finger to his lips and kissed it. It seemed to him now that he had been humble then when he had always seemed loathsome to himself on account of his sinfulness; and when he remembered the tender feelings with which he had then met an old man who was bringing a drunken soldier to him to ask alms; and how he had received *her*, it seemed to him that he had then possessed love also. But now? And he asked himself whether he loved anyone, whether he loved Sófya Ivánovna, or Father Seraphim, whether he had any feeling of love for all who had come to him that day—for that learned young man with whom he had had that instructive discussion in which he was concerned only to show off his own intelligence and that he had not lagged behind the times in knowledge. He wanted and needed their love, but felt none towards them. He now had neither love nor humility nor purity.

He was pleased to know that the merchant's daughter was twenty-two, and he wondered whether she was good-looking. When he inquired whether she was weak, he really wanted to know if she had feminine charm.

'Can I have fallen so low?' he thought. 'Lord, help me! Restore me, my Lord and God!' And he clasped his hands and began to pray.

The nightingales burst into song, a cockchafer knocked against him and crept up the back of his neck. He brushed it off. 'But does He exist? What if I am knocking at a door fastened from outside? The bar is on the door for all to see. Nature—the nightingales and the cockchafers —is that bar. Perhaps the young man was right.' And he began to pray aloud. He prayed for a long time till these thoughts vanished and he again felt calm and confident. He rang the bell and told the attendant to say that the merchant might bring his daughter to him now.

The merchant came, leading his daughter by the arm. He led her into the cell and immediately left her.

She was a very fair girl, plump and very short, with

a pale, frightened, childish face and a much developed feminine figure. Father Sergius remained seated on the bench at the entrance and when she was passing and stopped beside him for his blessing he was aghast at himself for the way he looked at her figure. As she passed by him he was acutely conscious of her femininity, though he saw by her face that she was sensual and feeble-minded. He rose and went into the cell. She was sitting on a stool waiting for him, and when he entered she rose.

'I want to go back to Papa,' she said.

'Don't be afraid,' he replied. 'What are you suffering from?'

'I am in pain all over,' she said, and suddenly her face lit up with a smile.

'You will be well,' said he. 'Pray!'

'What is the use of praying? I have prayed and it does no good'—and she continued to smile. 'I want you to pray for me and lay your hands on me. I saw you in a dream.'

'How did you see me?'

'I saw you put your hands on my breast like that.' She took his hand and pressed it to her breast. 'Just here.'

He yielded his right hand to her.

'What is your name?' he asked, trembling all over and feeling that he was overcome and that his desire had already passed beyond control.

'Marie. Why?'

She took his hand and kissed it, and then put her arm round his waist and pressed him to herself.

'What are you doing?' he said. 'Marie, you are a devil!'

'Oh, perhaps. What does it matter?'

And embracing him she sat down with him on the bed.

At dawn he went out into the porch.

'Can this all have happened? Her father will come and she will tell him everything. She is a devil! What am I to do? Here is the axe with which I chopped off my finger.' He snatched up the axe and moved back towards the cell.

The attendant came up.

'Do you want some wood chopped? Let me have the axe.'

Sergius yielded up the axe and entered the cell. She was lying there asleep. He looked at her with horror, and passed on beyond the partition, where he took down the peasant clothes and put them on. Then he seized a pair of scissors, cut off his long hair, and went out along the path down the hill to the river, where he had not been for more than three years.

A road ran beside the river and he went along it and walked till noon. Then he went into a field of rye and lay down there. Towards evening he approached a village, but without entering it went towards the cliff that over-hung the river. There he again lay down to rest.

It was early morning, half an hour before sunrise. All was damp and gloomy and a cold early wind was blowing from the west. 'Yes, I must end it all. There is no God. But how am I to end it? Throw myself into the river? I can swim and should not drown. Hang myself? Yes, just throw this sash over a branch.' This seemed so feasible and so easy that he felt horrified. As usual at moments of despair he felt the need of prayer. But there was no one to pray to. There was no God. He lay down resting on his arm, and suddenly such a longing for sleep overcame him that he could no longer support his head on his hand, but stretched out his arm, laid his head upon it, and fell asleep. But that sleep lasted only for a moment. He woke up im-mediately and began not to dream but to remember.

He saw himself as a child in his mother's home in the country. A carriage drives up, and out of it steps Uncle Nicholas Sergéevich, with his long, spade-shaped, black beard, and with him Páshenka, a thin little girl with large mild eyes and a timid pathetic face. And into their com-pany of boys Páshenka is brought and they have to play with her, but it is dull. She is silly, and it ends by their making fun of her and forcing her to show how she can swim. She lies down on the floor and shows them, and they all laugh and make a fool of her. She sees this and blushes red in patches and becomes more pitiable than before, so pitiable that he feels ashamed and can never forget that crooked, kindly, submissive smile. And Sergius remembered having seen her since then. Long after, just before he became a monk, she had married a landowner who squandered all her fortune and was in the habit of beating her. She had had two children, a son and a daughter, but the son had died while still young. And Sergius remembered having seen her very wretched. Then again he had seen her in the monastery when she was a widow. She had been still the same, not exactly stupid, but insipid, insignificant, and pitiable. She had come with her daughter and her daughter's fiancé. They were already poor at that time and later on he had heard that she was living in a small provincial town and was very poor.

'Why am I thinking about her?' he asked himself, but he could not cease doing so. 'Where is she? How is she getting on? Is she still as unhappy as she was then when she had to show us how to swim on the floor? But why should I think about her? What am I doing? I must put an end to myself.'

And again he felt afraid, and again, to escape from that thought, he went on thinking about Páshenka.

So he lay for a long time, thinking now of his unavoidable end and now of Páshenka. She presented herself to him as a means of salvation. At last he fell asleep, and in his sleep he saw an angel who came to him and said: 'Go to Páshenka and learn from her what you have to do, what your sin is, and wherein lies your salvation.'

He awoke, and having decided that this was a vision sent by God, he felt glad, and resolved to do what had been told him in the vision. He knew the town where she lived. It was some three hundred versts (two hundred miles) away, and he set out to walk there.

VI

Páshenka had already long ceased to be Páshenka and had become old, withered, wrinkled Praskóvya Mikháylovna, mother-in-law of that failure, the drunken official Mavríkyev. She was living in the country town where he had had his last appointment, and there she was supporting the family: her daughter, her ailing neurasthenic son-in-law, and her five grandchildren. She did this by giving music lessons to tradesmen's daughters, giving four and sometimes five lessons a day of an hour each, and earning in this way some sixty rubles (£6) a month. So they lived for the present, in expectation of another appointment. She had sent letters to all her relations and acquaintances asking them to obtain a post for her son-in-law, and among the rest she had written to Sergius, but that letter had not reached him.

It was a Saturday, and Praskóvya Mikháylovna was herself mixing dough for currant bread such as the serf-cook on her father's estate used to make so well. She wished to give her grandchildren a treat on the Sunday.

Másha, her daughter, was nursing her youngest child, the eldest boy and girl were at school, and her son-in-law was asleep, not having slept during the night. Praskóvya Mikháylovna had remained awake too for a great part of the night, trying to soften her daughter's anger against her husband.

She saw that it was impossible for her son-in-law, a weak creature, to be other than he was, and realized that his wife's reproaches could do no good—so she used all her efforts to soften those reproaches and to avoid recrimination and anger. Unkindly relations between people caused her actual physical suffering. It was so clear to her that bitter feelings do not make anything better, but only make everything worse. She did not in fact think about this: she simply suffered at the sight of anger as she would from a bad smell, a harsh noise, or from blows on her body.

She had—with a feeling of self-satisfaction—just taught Lukérya how to mix the dough, when her six-year-old grandson Mísha, wearing an apron and with darned stockings on his crooked little legs, ran into the kitchen with a frightened face.

'Grandma, a dreadful old man wants to see you.'

Lukérya looked out at the door.

'There is a pilgrim of some kind, a man . . .'

Praskóvya Mikháylovna rubbed her thin elbows against one another, wiped her hands on her apron and went upstairs to get a five-kopek piece [about a penny] out of her purse for him, but remembering that she had nothing less than a ten-kopek piece she decided to give him some bread instead. She returned to the cupboard, but suddenly blushed at the thought of having grudged the ten-kopek piece, and telling Lukérya to cut a slice of bread, went upstairs again to fetch it. 'It serves you right,' she said to herself. 'You must now give twice over.'

She gave both the bread and the money to the pilgrim, and when doing so—far from being proud of her generosity—she excused herself for giving so little. The man had such an imposing appearance.

Though he had tramped two hundred versts as a beggar, though he was tattered and had grown thin and weather-beaten, though he had cropped his long hair and was wearing a peasant's cap and boots, and though he bowed very humbly, Sergius still had the impressive appearance that made him so attractive. But Praskóvya Mikháylovna did not recognize him. She could hardly do so, not having seen him for almost twenty years.

'Don't think ill of me, Father. Perhaps you want something to eat?'

He took the bread and the money, and Praskóvya Mikháylovna was surprised that he did not go, but stood looking at her.

'Páshenka, I have come to you! Take me in . . .'

His beautiful black eyes, shining with the tears that started in them, were fixed on her with imploring insistence. And under his greyish moustache his lips quivered piteously.

Praskóvya Mikháylovna pressed her hands to her withered breast, opened her mouth, and stood petrified, staring at the pilgrim with dilated eyes.

'It can't be! Stëpa! Sergéy! Father Sergius!'

'Yes, it is I,' said Sergius in a low voice. 'Only not Sergius, or Father Sergius, but a great sinner, Stepán Kasátsky—a great and lost sinner. Take me in and help me!'

'It's impossible! How have you so humbled yourself? But come in.'

She reached out her hand, but he did not take it and only followed her in.

But where was she to take him? The lodging was a small one. Formerly she had had a tiny room, almost a closet, for herself, but later she had given it up to her daughter, and Másha was now sitting there rocking the baby.

'Sit here for the present,' she said to Sergius, pointing to a bench in the kitchen.

He sat down at once, and with an evidently accustomed movement slipped the straps of his wallet first off one shoulder and then off the other.

'My God, my God! How you have humbled yourself, Father! Such great fame, and now like this . . .'

Sergius did not reply, but only smiled meekly, placing his wallet under the bench on which he sat.

'Másha, do you know who this is?'—And in a whisper Praskóvya Mikháylovna told her daughter who he was, and together they then carried the bed and the cradle out of the tiny room and cleared it for Sergius.

Praskóvya Mikháylovna led him into it.

'Here you can rest. Don't take offence . . . but I must go out.'

'Where to?'

'I have to go to a lesson. I am ashamed to tell you, but I teach music!'

'Music? But that is good. Only just one thing, Praskóvya Mikháylovna, I have come to you with a definite object. When can I have a talk with you?'

'I shall be very glad. Will this evening do?'

'Yes. But one thing more. Don't speak about me, or say who I am. I have revealed myself only to you. No one knows where I have gone to. It must be so.'

'Oh, but I have told my daughter.'

'Well, ask her not to mention it.'

And Sergius took off his boots, lay down, and at once fell asleep after a sleepless night and a walk of nearly thirty miles.

When Praskóvya Mikháylovna returned, Sergius was sitting in the little room waiting for her. He did not come out for dinner, but had some soup and gruel which Lukérya brought him.

'How is it that you have come back earlier than you said?' asked Sergius. 'Can I speak to you now?'

'How is it that I have the happiness to receive such a guest? I have missed one of my lessons. That can wait . . . I had always been planning to go to see you. I wrote to you, and now this good fortune has come.'

'Páshenka, please listen to what I am going to tell you as to a confession made to God at my last hour. Páshenka, I am not a holy man, I am not even as good as a simple ordinary man; I am a loathsome, vile, and proud sinner who has gone astray, and who, if not worse than everyone else, is at least worse than most very bad people.'

Páshenka looked at him at first with staring eyes. But she believed what he said, and when she had quite grasped it she touched his hand, smiled pityingly, and said:

'Perhaps you exaggerate, Stíva?'

'No, Páshenka. I am an adulterer, a murderer, a blasphemer, and a deceiver.'

'My God! How is that?' exclaimed Praskóvya Mikháylovna.

'But I must go on living. And I, who thought I knew

everything, who taught others how to live—I know nothing and ask you to teach me.'

'What are you saying, Stíva? You are laughing at me. Why do you always make fun of me?'

'Well, if you think I am jesting you must have it as you please. But tell me all the same how you live, and how you have lived your life.'

'I? I have lived a very nasty, horrible life, and now God is punishing me as I deserve. I live so wretchedly, so wretchedly . . .'

'How was it with your marriage? How did you live with your husband?'

'It was all bad. I married because I fell in love in the nastiest way. Papa did not approve. But I would not listen to anything and just got married. Then instead of helping my husband I tormented him by my jealousy, which I could not restrain.'

'I heard that he drank . . .'

'Yes, but I did not give him any peace. I always reproached him, though you know it is a disease! He could not refrain from it. I now remember how I tried to prevent his having it, and the frightful scenes we had!'

And she looked at Kasátsky with beautiful eyes, suffering from the remembrance.

Kasátsky remembered how he had been told that Páshenka's husband used to beat her, and now, looking at her thin withered neck with prominent veins behind her ears, and her scanty coil of hair, half grey half auburn, he seemed to see just how it had occurred.

'Then I was left with two children and no means at all.'

'But you had an estate!'

'Oh, we sold that while Vásya was still alive, and the money was all spent. We had to live, and like all our young ladies I did not know how to earn anything. I was particularly useless and helpless. So we spent all we had. I taught the children and improved my own education a little. And then Mítya fell ill when he was already in the fourth form, and God took him. Másha fell in love with Ványa, my son-in-law. And—well, he is well-meaning but unfortunate. He is ill.'

'Mamma!'—her daughter's voice interrupted her—'Take Mítya! I can't be in two places at once.'

Praskóvya Mikháylovna shuddered, but rose and went

out of the room, stepping quickly in her patched shoes. She soon came back with a boy of two in her arms, who threw himself backwards and grabbed at her shawl with his little hands.

'Where was I? Oh yes, he had a good appointment here, and his chief was a kind man too. But Ványa could not go on, and had to give up his position.'

'What is the matter with him?'

'Neurasthenia—it is a dreadful complaint. We consulted a doctor, who told us he ought to go away, but we had no means. . . . I always hope it will pass of itself. He has no particular pain, but . . .'

'Lukérya!' cried an angry and feeble voice. 'She is always sent away when I want her. Mamma . . .'

'I'm coming!' Praskóvya Mikháylovna again interrupted herself. 'He has not had his dinner yet. He can't eat with us.'

She went out and arranged something, and came back wiping her thin dark hands.

'So that is how I live. I always complain and am always dissatisfied, but thank God the grandchildren are all nice and healthy, and we can still live. But why talk about me?'

'But what do you live on?'

'Well, I earn a little. How I used to dislike music, but how useful it is to me now!' Her small hand lay on the chest of drawers beside which she was sitting, and she drummed an exercise with her thin fingers.

'How much do you get for a lesson?'

'Sometimes a ruble, sometimes fifty kopeks, or sometimes thirty. They are all so kind to me.'

'And do your pupils get on well?' asked Kasátsky with a slight smile.

Praskóvya Mikháylovna did not at first believe that he was asking seriously, and looked inquiringly into his eyes.

'Some of them do. One of them is a splendid girl—the butcher's daughter—such a good kind girl! If I were a clever woman I ought, of course, with the connexions Papa had, to be able to get an appointment for my son-in-law. But as it is I have not been able to do anything, and have brought them all to this—as you see.'

'Yes, yes,' said Kasátsky, lowering his head. 'And how is it, Páshenka—do you take part in Church life?'

'Oh, don't speak of it. I am so bad that way, and have

neglected it so! I keep the fasts with the children and sometimes go to church, and then again sometimes I don't go for months. I only send the children.'

'But why don't you go yourself?'

'To tell the truth' (she blushed) 'I am ashamed, for my daughter's sake and the children's, to go there in tattered clothes, and I haven't anything else. Besides, I am just lazy.'

'And do you pray at home?'

'I do. But what sort of prayer is it? Only mechanical. I know it should not be like that, but I lack real religious feeling. The only thing is that I know how bad I am . . .'

'Yes, yes, that's right!' said Kasátsky, as if approvingly.

'I'm coming! I'm coming!' she replied to a call from her son-in-law, and tidying her scanty plait she left the room.

But this time it was long before she returned. When she came back, Kasátsky was sitting in the same position, his elbows resting on his knees and his head bowed. But his wallet was strapped on his back.

When she came in, carrying a small tin lamp without a shade, he raised his fine weary eyes and sighed very deeply.

'I did not tell them who you are,' she began timidly. 'I only said that you are a pilgrim, a nobleman, and that I used to know you. Come into the dining-room for tea.'

'No . . .'

'Well then, I'll bring some to you here.'

'No, I don't want anything. God bless you, Páshenka! I am going now. If you pity me, don't tell anyone that you have seen me. For the love of God don't tell anyone. Thank you. I would bow to your feet but I know it would make you feel awkward. Thank you, and forgive me for Christ's sake!'

'Give me your blessing.'

'God bless you! Forgive me for Christ's sake!'

He rose, but she would not let him go until she had given him bread and butter and rusks. He took it all and went away.

It was dark, and before he had passed the second house he was lost to sight. She only knew he was there because the dog at the priest's house was barking.

'So that is what my dream meant! Páshenka is what I ought to have been but failed to be. I lived for men on the pretext of living for God, while she lives for God imagining that she lives for men. Yès, one good deed—a cup of water given without thought of reward—is worth more than any benefit I imagined I was bestowing on people. But after all was there not some share of sincere desire to serve God?' he asked himself, and the answer was: 'Yes, there was, but it was all soiled and overgrown by desire for human praise. Yes, there is no God for the man who lives, as I did, for human praise. I will now seek Him!'

And he walked from village to village as he had done on his way to Páshenka, meeting and parting from other pilgrims, men and women, and asking for bread and a night's rest in Christ's name. Occasionally some angry housewife scolded him, or a drunken peasant reviled him, but for the most part he was given food and drink and even something to take with him. His noble bearing disposed some people in his favour, while others on the contrary seemed pleased at the sight of a gentleman who had come to beggary.

But his gentleness prevailed with everyone.

Often, finding a copy of the Gospels in a hut he would read it aloud, and when they heard him the people were always touched and surprised, as at something new yet familiar.

When he succeeded in helping people, either by advice, or by his knowledge of reading and writing, or by settling some quarrel, he did not wait to see their gratitude but went away directly afterwards. And little by little God began to reveal Himself within him.

Once he was walking along with two old women and a soldier. They were stopped by a party consisting of a lady and gentleman in a gig and another lady and gentleman on horseback. The husband was on horseback with his daughter, while in the gig his wife was driving with a Frenchman, evidently a traveller.

The party stopped to let the Frenchman see the pilgrims who, in accord with a popular Russian superstition, tramped about from place to place instead of working.

They spoke French, thinking that the others would not understand them.

'*Demandez-leur,*' said the Frenchman, '*s'ils sont bien sûr de ce que leur pèlerinage est agréable à Dieu.*'

The question was asked, and one old woman replied:

'As God takes it. Our feet have reached the holy places, but our hearts may not have done so.'

They asked the soldier. He said that he was alone in the world and had nowhere else to go.

They asked Kasátsky who he was.

'A servant of God.'

'*Qu'est-ce qu'il dit? Il ne répond pas.*'

'*Il dit qu'il est un serviteur de Dieu. Cela doit être un fils de prêtre. Il a de la race. Avez-vous de la petite monnaie?*'

The Frenchman found some small change and gave twenty kopeks to each of the pilgrims.

'*Mais dites-leur que ce n'est pas pour les cierges que je leur donne, mais pour qu'ils se régalent de thé. Chay, chay pour vous, mon vieux!*' he said with a smile. And he patted Kasátsky on the shoulder with his gloved hand.

'May Christ bless you,' replied Kasátsky without replacing his cap and bowing his bald head.

He rejoiced particularly at this meeting, because he had disregarded the opinion of men and had done the simplest, easiest thing—humbly accepted twenty kopeks and given them to his comrade, a blind beggar. The less importance he attached to the opinion of men the more did he feel the presence of God within him.

For eight months Kasátsky tramped on in this manner, and in the ninth month he was arrested for not having a passport. This happened at a night-refuge in a provincial town where he had passed the night with some pilgrims. He was taken to the police-station, and when asked who he was and where was his passport, he replied that he had no passport and that he was a servant of God. He was classed as a tramp, sentenced, and sent to live in Siberia.

In Siberia he has settled down as the hired man of a well-to-do peasant, in which capacity he works in the kitchen-garden, teaches children, and attends to the sick.

Hadji Murád

[1904]

[A list of Tartar words used in *Hadji Murád* is given alphabetically in an appendix at the end of the story.]

I

I was returning home by the fields. It was midsummer, the hay harvest was over and they were just beginning to reap the rye. At that season of the year there is a delightful variety of flowers—red, white, and pink scented tufty clover; milk-white ox-eye daisies with their bright yellow centres and pleasant spicy smell; yellow honey-scented rape blossoms; tall campanulas with white and lilac bells, tulip-shaped; creeping vetch; yellow, red, and pink scabious; faintly scented, neatly arranged purple plantains with blossoms slightly tinged with pink; cornflowers, the newly opened blossoms bright blue in the sunshine but growing paler and redder towards evening or when growing old; and delicate almond-scented dodder flowers that withered quickly. I gathered myself a large nosegay and was going home when I noticed in a ditch, in full bloom, a beautiful thistle plant of the crimson variety, which in our neighbourhood they call 'Tartar' and carefully avoid when mowing—or, if they do happen to cut it down, throw out from among the grass for fear of pricking their hands. Thinking to pick this thistle and put it in the centre of my nosegay, I climbed down into the ditch, and after driving away a velvety humble-bee that had penetrated deep into one of the flowers and had there fallen sweetly asleep, I set to work to pluck the flower. But this proved a very difficult task. Not only did the stalk prick on every side—even through the handkerchief I wrapped round my hand—but it was so tough that I had to struggle with it for nearly five minutes, breaking the fibres one by one; and when I had at last plucked it, the stalk was all frayed and the flower itself no longer seemed so fresh and beautiful. Moreover, owing to its coarseness and stiffness, it did not seem in place among the delicate blossoms of my nosegay. I threw it away feeling sorry to have vainly destroyed a flower that looked beautiful in its proper place.

'But what energy and tenacity! With what determination it defended itself, and how dearly it sold its life!' thought I, remembering the effort it had cost me to pluck the flower. The way home led across black-earth fields that had just been ploughed up. I ascended the dusty path. The ploughed field belonged to a landed proprietor and was so large that on both sides and before me to the top of the hill nothing was visible but evenly furrowed and moist earth. The land was well tilled and nowhere was there a blade of grass or any kind of plant to be seen, it was all black. 'Ah, what a destructive creature is man. . . . How many different plant-lives he destroys to support his own existence!' thought I, involuntarily looking around for some living thing in this lifeless black field. In front of me to the right of the road I saw some kind of little clump, and drawing nearer I found it was the same kind of thistle as that which I had vainly plucked and thrown away. This 'Tartar' plant had three branches. One was broken and stuck out like the stump of a mutilated arm. Each of the other two bore a flower, once red but now blackened. One stalk was broken, and half of it hung down with a soiled flower at its tip. The other, though also soiled with black mud, still stood erect. Evidently a cartwheel had passed over the plant but it had risen again, and that was why, though erect, it stood twisted to one side, as if a piece of its body had been torn from it, its bowels drawn out, an arm torn off, and one of its eyes plucked out. Yet it stood firm and did not surrender to man who had destroyed all its brothers around it. . . .

'What vitality!' I thought. 'Man has conquered everything and destroyed millions of plants, yet this one won't submit.' And I remembered a Caucasian episode of years ago, which I had partly seen myself, partly heard of from eye-witnesses, and in part imagined.

The episode, as it has taken shape in my memory and imagination, was as follows.

*   *   *

It happened towards the end of 1851.

On a cold November evening Hadji Murád rode into Makhmet, a hostile Chechen *aoul* that lay some fifteen miles from Russian territory and was filled with the scented smoke of burning *kizyák*. The strained chant of the muezzin had just ceased, and through the clear mountain air, impregnated with *kizyák* smoke, above the lowing of the cattle and the bleating of the sheep that were dispersing among the *sáklyas* (which were crowded together like the cells of honeycomb), could be clearly heard the guttural voices of disputing men, and sounds of women's and children's voices rising from near the fountain below.

This Hadji Murád was Shamil's *naïb*, famous for his exploits, who used never to ride out without his banner and some dozens of *murids*, who caracoled and showed off before him. Now wrapped in hood and *búrka*, from under which protruded a rifle, he rode, a fugitive, with one *murid* only, trying to attract as little attention as possible and peering with his quick black eyes into the faces of those he met on his way.

When he entered the *aoul*, instead of riding up the road leading to the open square, he turned to the left into a narrow side street, and on reaching the second *sáklya*, which was cut into the hill-side, he stopped and looked round. There was no one under the penthouse in front, but on the roof of the *sáklya* itself, behind the freshly plastered clay chimney, lay a man covered with a sheepskin. Hadji Murád touched him with the handle of his leather-plaited whip and clicked his tongue, and an old man, wearing a greasy old *beshmét* and a nightcap, rose from under the sheepskin. His moist red eyelids had no lashes, and he blinked to get them unstuck. Hadji Murád, repeating the customary '*Selaam aleikum!*' uncovered his face. '*Aleikum, selaam!*' said the old man, recognizing him, and smiling with his toothless mouth. And raising himself on his thin legs he began thrusting his feet into the wooden-heeled slippers that stood by the chimney. Then he leisurely slipped his arms into the sleeves of his crumpled sheepskin, and going to the ladder that leant against the roof he descended backwards, while he dressed and as he climbed down he kept shaking his head on its thin, shrivelled sunburnt neck and mumbling something with his toothless mouth. As soon as he reached the ground he hospitably seized Hadji Murád's bridle and right stirrup; but the strong active *murid* had quickly dismounted and, motioning the old man aside, took his place. Hadji Murád also dismounted, and walking with a slight limp, entered under the penthouse. A boy of fifteen, coming quickly out of the door, met him and wonderingly fixed his sparkling eyes, black as ripe sloes, on the new arrivals.

'Run to the mosque and call your father,' ordered the old man as he hurried forward to open the thin, creaking door into the *sáklya*.

As Hadji Murád entered the outer door, a slight, spare, middle-aged woman in a yellow smock, red *beshmét,* and wide blue trousers came through an inner door carrying cushions.

'May thy coming bring happiness!' said she, and bending nearly double began arranging the cushions along the front wall for the guest to sit on.

'May thy sons live!' answered Hadji Murád, taking off his *búrka,* his rifle, and his sword, and handing them to the old man who carefully hung the rifle and sword on a nail beside the weapons of the master of the house, which were suspended between two large basins that glittered against the clean clay-plastered and carefully whitewashed wall.

Hadji Murád adjusted the pistol at his back, came up to the cushions, and wrapping his Circassian coat closer round him, sat down. The old man squatted on his bare heels beside him, closed his eyes, and lifted his hands palms upwards. Hadji Murád did the same; then after repeating a prayer they both stroked their faces, passing their hands downwards till the palms joined at the end of their beards.

'*Ne habar?*' ('Is there anything new?') asked Hadji Murád, addressing the old man.

'*Habar yok*' ('Nothing new'), replied the old man, looking with his lifeless red eyes not at Hadji Murád's face but at his breast. 'I live at the apiary and have only to-day come to see my son. . . . He knows.'

Hadji Murád, understanding that the old man did not wish to say what he knew and what Hadji Murád wanted to know, slightly nodded his head and asked no more questions.

'There is no good news,' said the old man. 'The only news is that the hares keep discussing how to drive away the eagles, and the eagles tear first one and then another of them. The other day the Russian dogs burnt the hay in the Mitchit *aoul*. . . . May their faces be torn!' he added hoarsely and angrily.

Hadji Murád's *murid* entered the room, his strong legs

striding softy over the earthen floor. Retaining only his dagger and pistol, he took off his *búrka,* rifle, and sword as Hadji Murád had done, and hung them up on the same nails as his leader's weapons.

'Who is he?' asked the old man, pointing to the newcomer.

'My *murid.* Eldár is his name,' said Hadji Murád.

'That is well,' said the old man, and motioned Eldár to a place on a piece of felt beside Hadji Murád. Eldár sat down, crossing his legs and fixing his fine ram-like eyes on the old man who, having now started talking, was telling how their brave fellows had caught two Russian soldiers the week before and had killed one and sent the other to Shamil in Vedén.

Hadji Murád heard him absently, looking at the door and listening to the sounds outside. Under the penthouse steps were heard, the door creaked, and Sado, the master of the house, came in. He was a man of about forty, with a small beard, long nose, and eyes as black, though not as glittering, as those of his fifteen-year-old son who had run to call him home and who now entered with his father and sat down by the door. The master of the house took off his wooden slippers at the door, and pushing his old and much-worn cap to the back of his head (which had remained unshaved so long that it was beginning to be overgrown with black hair), at once squatted down in front of Hadji Murád.

He too lifted his palms upwards, as the old man had done, repeated a prayer, and then stroked his face downwards. Only after that did he begin to speak. He told how an order had come from Shamil to seize Hadji Murád alive or dead, that Shamil's envoys had left only the day before, that the people were afraid to disobey Shamil's orders, and that therefore it was necessary to be careful.

'In my house,' said Sado, 'no one shall injure my *kunák* while I live, but how will it be in the open fields? . . . We must think it over.'

Hadji Murád listened with attention and nodded approvingly. When Sado had finished he said:

'Very well. Now we must send a man with a letter to the Russians. My *murid* will go but he will need a guide.'

'I will send brother Bata,' said Sado. 'Go and call Bata,' he added, turning to his son.

The boy instantly bounded to his nimble feet as if he

were on springs, and swinging his arms, rapidly left the *sáklya*. Some ten minutes later he returned with a sinewy, short-legged Chechen, burnt almost black by the sun, wearing a worn and tattered yellow Circassian coat with frayed sleeves, and crumpled black leggings.

Hadji Murád greeted the newcomer, and again without wasting a single word, immediately asked:

'Canst thou conduct my *murid* to the Russians?'

'I can,' gaily replied Bata. 'I can certainly do it. There is not another Chechen who would pass as I can. Another might agree to go and might promise anything, but would do nothing; but I can do it!'

'All right,' said Hadji Murád. 'Thou shalt receive three for thy trouble,' and he held up three fingers.

Bata nodded to show that he understood, and added that it was not money he prized, but that he was ready to serve Hadji Murád for the honour alone. Every one in the mountains knew Hadji Murád, and how he slew the Russian swine.

'Very well. . . . A rope should be long but a speech short,' said Hadji Murád.

'Well then I'll hold my tongue,' said Bata.

'Where the river Argun bends by the cliff,' said Hadji Murád, 'there are two stacks in a glade in the forest—thou knowest?'

'I know.'

'There my four horsemen are waiting for me,' said Hadji Murád.

'Aye,' answered Bata, nodding.

'Ask for Khan Mahomá. He knows what to do and what to say. Canst thou lead him to the Russian Commander, Prince Vorontsóv?'

'Yes, I'll take him.'

'Canst thou take him and bring him back again?'

'I can.'

'Then take him there and return to the wood. I shall be there too.'

'I will do it all,' said Bata, rising, and putting his hands on his heart he went out.

Hadji Murád turned to his host.

'A man must also be sent to Chekhi,' he began, and took hold of one of the cartridge pouches of his Circassian coat, but let his hand drop immediately and became silent on seeing two women enter the *sáklya*.

One was Sado's wife—the thin middle-aged woman who had arranged the cushions. The other was quite a young girl, wearing red trousers and a green *beshmét*. A necklace of silver coins covered the whole front of her dress, and at the end of the short but thick plait of hard black hair that hung between her thin shoulder-blades a silver ruble was suspended. Her eyes, as sloe-black as those of her father and brother, sparkled brightly in her young face which tried to be stern. She did not look at the visitors, but evidently felt their presence.

Sado's wife brought in a low round table on which stood tea, pancakes in butter, cheese, *churek* (that is, thinly rolled out bread), and honey. The girl carried a basin, a ewer, and a towel.

Sado and Hadji Murád kept silent as long as the women, with their coin ornaments tinkling, moved softly about in their red soft-soled slippers, setting out before the visitors the things they had brought. Eldár sat motionless as a statue, his ram-like eyes fixed on his crossed legs, all the time the women were in the *sáklya*. Only after they had gone and their soft footsteps could no longer be heard behind the door, did he give a sigh of relief.

Hadji Murád having pulled out a bullet from one of the cartridge-pouches of his Circassian coat, and having taken out a rolled-up note that lay beneath it, held it out, saying:

'To be handed to my son.'

'Where must the answer be sent?'

'To thee; and thou must forward it to me.'

'It shall be done,' said Sado, and placed the note in a cartridge-pocket of his own coat. Then he took up the metal ewer and moved the basin towards Hadji Murád.

Hadji Murád turned up the sleeves of his *beshmét* on his white muscular arms, held out his hands under the clear cold water which Sado poured from the ewer, and having wiped them on a clean unbleached towel, turned to the table. Eldár did the same. While the visitors ate, Sado sat opposite and thanked them several times for their visit. The boy sat by the door never taking his sparkling eyes off Hadji Murád's face, and smiled as if in confirmation of his father's words.

Though he had eaten nothing for more than twenty-four hours Hadji Murád ate only a little bread and cheese; then, drawing out a small knife from under his dagger, he spread some honey on a piece of bread.

'Our honey is good,' said the old mán, evidently pleased
to see Hadji Murád eating his honey. 'This year, above all
other years, it is plentiful and good.'

'I thank thee,' said Hadji Murád and turned from the
table. Eldár would have liked to go on eating but he followed his leader's example, and having moved away from
the table, handed him the ewer and basin.

Sado knew that he was risking his life by receiving such
a guest in his house, for after his quarrel with Shamil the
latter had issued a proclamation to all the inhabitants of
Chechnya forbidding them to receive Hadji Murád on pain
of death. He knew that the inhabitants of the *aoul* might at
any moment become aware of Hadji Murád's presence in
his house and might demand his surrender. But this not
only did not frighten Sado, it even gave him pleasure: he
considered it his duty to protect his guest though it should
cost him his life, and he was proud and pleased with himself because he was doing his duty.

'Whilst thou art in my house and my head is on my
shoulders no one shall harm thee,' he repeated to Hadji
Murád.

Hadji Murád looked into his glittering eyes and understanding that this was true, said with some solemnity—

'Mayest thou receive joy and life!'

Sado silently laid his hand on his heart in token of
thanks for these kind words.

Having closed the shutters of the *sáklya* and laid some
sticks in the fireplace, Sado, in an exceptionally bright and
animated mood, left the room and went into that part of
his *sáklya* where his family all lived. The women had not
yet gone to sleep, and were talking about the dangerous
visitors who were spending the night in their guest-chamber.

II

At Vozvízhensk, the advanced fort situated some ten
miles from the *aoul* in which Hadji Murád was spending
the night, three soldiers and a non-commissioned officer
left the fort and went beyond the Shahgirínsk Gate. The
soldiers, dressed as Caucasian soldiers used to be in those
days, wore sheepskin coats and caps, and boots that reached
above their knees, and they carried their cloaks tightly
rolled up and fastened across their shoulders. Shouldering

arms, they first went some five hundred paces along the road and then turned off it and went some twenty paces to the right—the dead leaves rustling under their boots—till they reached the blackened trunk of a broken plane tree just visible through the darkness. There they stopped. It was at this plane tree that an ambush party was usually placed.

The bright stars, that had seemed to be running along the tree-tops while the soldiers were walking through the forest, now stood still, shining brightly between the bare branches of the trees.

'A good job it's dry,' said the non-commissioned officer Panóv, bringing down his long gun and bayonet with a clang from his shoulder and placing it against the plane tree.

The three soldiers did the same.

'Sure enough I've lost it!' muttered Panóv crossly. 'Must have left it behind or I've dropped it on the way.'

'What are you looking for?' asked one of the soldiers in a bright, cheerful voice.

'The bowl of my pipe. Where the devil has it got to?'

'Have you got the stem?' asked the cheerful voice.

'Here it is.'

'Then why not stick it straight into the ground?'

'Not worth bothering!'

'We'll manage that in a minute.'

Smoking in ambush was forbidden, but this ambush hardly deserved the name. It was rather an outpost to prevent the mountaineers from bringing up a cannon unobserved and firing at the fort as they used to. Panóv did not consider it necessary to forego the pleasure of smoking, and therefore accepted the cheerful soldier's offer. The latter took a knife from his pocket and made a small round hole in the ground. Having smoothed it, he adjusted the pipe-stem to it, then filled the hole with tobacco and pressed it down, and the pipe was ready. A sulphur match flared and for a moment lit up the broad-cheeked face of the soldier who lay on his stomach, the air whistled in the stem, and Panóv smelt the pleasant odour of burning tobacco.

'Fixed it up?' said he, rising to his feet.

'Why, of course!'

'What a smart chap you are, Avdéev! . . . As wise as a judge! Now then, lad.'

Avdéev rolled over on his side to make room for Panóv, letting smoke escape from his mouth.

Panóv lay down prone, and after wiping the mouthpiece with his sleeve, began to inhale.

When they had had their smoke the soldiers began to talk.

'They say the commander has had his fingers in the cashbox again,' remarked one of them in a lazy voice. 'He lost at cards, you see.'

'He'll pay it back again,' said Panóv.

'Of course he will! He's a good officer,' assented Avdéev.

'Good! good!' gloomily repeated the man who had started the conversation. 'In my opinion the company ought to speak to him. "If you've taken the money, tell us how much and when you'll repay it." '

'That will be as the company decides,' said Panóv, tearing himself away from the pipe.

'Of course. "The community is a strong man," ' assented Avdéev, quoting a proverb.

'There will be oats to buy and boots to get towards spring. The money will be wanted, and what shall we do if he's pocketed it?' insisted the dissatisfied one.

'I tell you it will be as the company wishes,' repeated Panóv. 'It's not the first time; he takes it and gives it back.'

In the Caucasus in those days each company chose men to manage its own commissariat. They received 6 rubles 50 kopeks a month per man from the treasury, and catered for the company. They planted cabbages, made hay, had their own carts, and prided themselves on their well-fed horses. The company's money was kept in a chest of which the commander had the key, and it often happened that he borrowed from the chest. This had just happened again, and the soldiers were talking about it. The morose soldier, Nikítin, wished to demand an account from the commander, while Panóv and Avdéev considered that unnecessary.

After Panóv, Nikítin had a smoke, and then spreading his cloak on the ground sat down on it leaning against the trunk of the plane tree. The soldiers were silent. Far above their heads the crowns of the trees rustled in the wind and suddenly, above this incessant low rustling, rose the howling, whining, weeping, and chuckling of jackals.

'Just listen to those accursed creatures—how they cater-waul!'

'They're laughing at you because your mouth's all on one side,' remarked the high voice of the third soldier, an Ukrainian.

All was silent again, except for the wind that swayed the branches, now revealing and now hiding the stars.

'I say, Panóv,' suddenly asked the cheerful Avdéev, 'do you ever feel dull?'

'Dull, why?' replied Panóv reluctantly.

'Well, I do. . . . I feel so dull sometimes that I don't know what I might not be ready to do to myself.'

'There now!' was all Panóv replied.

'That time when I drank all the money it was from dull-ness. It took hold of me . . . took hold of me till I thought to myself, "I'll just get blind drunk!" '

'But sometimes drinking makes it still worse.'

'Yes, that's happened to me too. But what is a man to do with himself?'

'But what makes you feel so dull?'

'What, me? . . . Why, it's the longing for home.'

'Is yours a wealthy home then?'

'No; we weren't wealthy, but things went properly—we lived well.' And Avdéev began to relate what he had already told Panóv many times.

'You see, I went as a soldier of my own free will, instead of my brother,' he said. 'He has children. They were five in family and I had only just married. Mother began beg-ging me to go. So I thought, "Well, maybe they will remember what I've done." So I went to our proprietor . . . he was a good master and he said, "You're a fine fel-low, go!" So I went instead of my brother.'

'Well, that was right,' said Panóv.

'And yet, will you believe me, Panóv, it's chiefly because of that that I feel so dull now? "Why did you go instead of your brother?" I say to myself. "He's living like a king now over there, while you have to suffer here;" and the more I think of it the worse I feel. . . . It seems just a piece of ill-luck!'

Avdéev was silent.

'Perhaps we'd better have another smoke,' said he after a pause.

'Well then, fix it up!'

But the soldiers were not to have their smoke. Hardly had Avdéev risen to fix the pipe-stem in its place when above the rustling of the trees they heard footsteps along the road. Panóv took his gun and pushed Nikítin with his foot.

Nikítin rose and picked up his cloak.

The third soldier, Bondarénko, rose also, and said:

'And I have dreamt such a dream, mates. . . .'

'Sh!' said Avdéev, and the soldiers held their breath, listening. The footsteps of men in soft-soled boots were heard approaching. The fallen leaves and dry twigs could be heard rustling clearer and clearer through the darkness. Then came the peculiar guttural tones of Chechen voices. The soldiers could now not only hear men approaching, but could see two shadows passing through a clear space between the trees; one shadow taller than the other. When these shadows had come in line with the soldiers, Panóv, gun in hand, stepped out on to the road, followed by his comrades.

'Who goes there?' cried he.

'Me, friendly Chechen,' said the shorter one. This was Bata. 'Gun, *yok!* . . . sword, *yok!*' said he, pointing to himself. 'Prince, want!'

The taller one stood silent beside his comrade. He too was unarmed.

'He means he's a scout, and wants the Colonel,' explained Panóv to his comrades.

'Prince Vorontsóv . . . much want! Big business!' said Bata.

'All right, all right! We'll take you to him,' said Panóv. 'I say, you'd better take them,' said he to Avdéev, 'you and Bondarénko; and when you've given them up to the officer on duty come back again. Mind,' he added, 'be careful to make them keep in front of you!'

'And what of this?' said Avdéev, moving his gun and bayonet as though stabbing someone. 'I'd just give a dig, and let the steam out of him!'

'What'll he be worth when you've stuck him?' remarked Bondarénko.

'Now, march!'

When the steps of the two soldiers conducting the scouts could no longer be heard, Panóv and Nikítin returned to their post.

'What the devil brings them here at night?' said Nikítin.

'Seems it's necessary,' said Panóv. 'But it's getting chilly,' he added, and unrolling his cloak he put it on and sat down by the tree.

About two hours later Avdéev and Bondarénko returned.

'Well, have you handed them over?'

'Yes. They weren't yet asleep at the Colonel's—they were taken straight in to him. And do you know, mates, those shaven-headed lads are fine!' continued Avdéev. 'Yes, really. What a talk I had with them!'

'Of course you'd talk,' remarked Nikítin disapprovingly.

'Really they're just like Russians. One of them is married. "Molly," says I, *"bar?"* *"Bar,"* he says. Bondarénko, didn't I say *"bar?"* *"Many bar?"* "A couple," says he. A couple! Such a good talk we had! Such nice fellows!'

'Nice, indeed!' said Nikítin. 'If you met him alone he'd soon let the guts out of you.'

'It will be getting light before long,' said Panóv.

'Yes, the stars are beginning to go out,' said Avdéev, sitting down and making himself comfortable.

And the soldiers were silent again.

III

The windows of the barracks and the soldiers' houses had long been dark in the fort; but there were still lights in the windows of the best house.

In it lived Prince Simon Mikhaílovich Vorontsóv, Commander of the Kurín Regiment, an Imperial Aide-de-Camp and son of the Commander-in-Chief. Vorontsóv's wife, Márya Vasílevna, a famous Petersburg beauty, was with him and they lived in this little Caucasian fort more luxuriously than any one had ever lived there before. To Vorontsóv, and even more to his wife, it seemed that they were not only living a very modest life, but one full of privations, while to the inhabitants of the place their luxury was surprising and extraordinary.

Just now, at midnight, the host and hostess sat playing cards with their visitors, at a card-table lit by four candles, in the spacious drawing-room with its carpeted floor and rich curtains drawn across the windows. Vorontsóv, who had a long face and wore the insignia and gold cords of an aide-de-camp, was partnered by a shaggy young man of gloomy appearance, a graduate of Petersburg University whom Princess Vorontsóv had lately had sent to the Caucasus to be tutor to her little son (born of her first marriage). Against them played two officers: one a broad, red-faced man, Poltorátsky, a company commander who had exchanged out of the Guards; and the other the regimental adjutant, who sat very straight on his chair with a cold expression on his handsome face.

Princess Márya Vasílevna, a large-built, large-eyed, black-browed beauty, sat beside Poltorátsky—her crinoline touching his legs—and looked over his cards. In her words, her looks, her smile, her perfume, and in every movement of her body, there was something that reduced Poltorátsky to obliviousness of everything except the consciousness of her nearness, and he made blunder after blunder, trying his partner's temper more and more.

'No . . . that's too bad! You've wasted an ace again,' said the regimental adjutant, flushing all over as Poltorátsky threw out an ace.

Poltorátsky turned his kindly, wide-set black eyes towards the dissatisfied adjutant uncomprehendingly, as though just aroused from sleep.

'Do forgive him!' said Márya Vasílevna, smiling. 'There, you see! Didn't I tell you so?' she went on, turning to Poltorátsky.

'But that's not at all what you said,' replied Poltorátsky, smiling.

'Wasn't it?' she queried, with an answering smile, which excited and delighted Poltorátsky to such a degree that he blushed crimson and seeing the cards began to shuffle.

'It isn't your turn to deal,' said the adjutant sternly, and with his white ringed hand he began to deal himself, as though he wished to get rid of the cards as quickly as possible.

The prince's valet entered the drawing-room and announced that the officer on duty wanted to speak to him.

'Excuse me, gentlemen,' said the prince, speaking Russian with an English accent. 'Will you take my place, Márya?'

'Do you all agree?' asked the princess, rising quickly and lightly to her full height, rustling her silks, and smiling the radiant smile of a happy woman.

'I always agree to everything,' replied the adjutant, very pleased that the princess—who could not play at all—was now going to play against him.

Poltorátsky only spread out his hands and smiled.

The rubber was nearly finished when the prince returned to the drawing-room, animated and obviously very pleased.

'Do you know what I propose?'

'What?'

'That we have some champagne.'

'I am always ready for that,' said Poltorátsky.

'Why not? We shall be delighted!' said the adjutant.

'Bring some, Vasíli!' said the prince.

'What did they want you for?' asked Márya Vasílevna.

'It was the officer on duty and another man.'

'Who? What about?' asked Márya Vasílevna quickly.

'I mustn't say,' said Vorontsóv, shrugging his shoulders.

'You mustn't say!' repeated Márya Vasílevna. 'We'll see about that.'

When the champagne was brought each of the visitors drank a glass, and having finished the game and settled the scores they began to take their leave.

'Is it your company that's ordered to the forest to-morrow?' the prince asked Poltorátsky as they said good-bye.

'Yes, mine . . . why?'

'Then we shall meet to-morrow,' said the prince, smiling slightly.

'Very pleased,' replied Poltorátsky, not quite under-standing what Vorontsóv was saying to him and preoc-cupied only by the thought that he would in a minute be pressing Márya Vasílevna's hand.

Márya Vasílevna, according to her wont, not only pressed his hand firmly but shook it vigorously, and again reminding him of his mistake in playing diamonds, she gave him what he took to be a delightful, affectionate, and meaning smile.

Poltorátsky went home in an ecstatic condition only to be understood by people like himself who, having grown up and been educated in society, meet a woman belonging to their own circle after months of isolated military life, and moreover a woman like Princess Vorontsóv.

When he reached the little house in which he and his comrade lived he pushed the door, but it was locked. He knocked, with no result. He felt vexed, and began kicking the door and banging it with his sword. Then he heard a sound of footsteps and Vovílo—a domestic serf of his—undid the cabin-hook which fastened the door.

'What do you mean by locking yourself in, blockhead?'

'But how is it possible, sir . . . ?'

'You're tipsy again! I'll show you "how it is possible!" ' and Poltorátsky was about to strike Vovílo but changed his mind. 'Oh, go to the devil! . . . Light a candle.'

'In a minute.'

Vovílo was really tipsy. He had been drinking at the name-day party of the ordnance-sergeant, Iván Petróvich. On returning home he began comparing his life with that of the latter. Iván Petróvich had a salary, was married, and hoped in a year's time to get his discharge.

Vovílo had been taken 'up' when a boy—that is, he had been taken into his owner's household service—and now although he was already over forty he was not married, but lived a campaigning life with his harum-scarum young master. He was a good master, who seldom struck him, but what kind of a life was it? 'He promised to free me when we return from the Caucasus, but where am I to go with my freedom? . . . It's a dog's life!' thought Vovílo, and he felt so sleepy that, afraid lest someone should come in and steal something, he fastened the hook of the door and fell asleep.

* * *

Poltorátsky entered the bedroom which he shared with his comrade Tíkhonov.

'Well, have you lost?' asked Tíkhonov, waking up.

'No, as it happens, I haven't. I've won seventeen rubles, and we drank a bottle of Cliquot!'

'And you've looked at Márya Vasílevna?'

'Yes, and I've looked at Márya Vasílevna,' repeated Poltorátsky.

'It will soon be time to get up,' said Tíkhonov. 'We are to start at six.'

'Vovílo!' shouted Poltorátsky, 'see that you wake me up properly to-morrow at five!'

'How can I wake you if you fight?'

'I tell you you're to wake me! Do you hear?'

'All right.' Vovílo went out, taking Poltorátsky's boots and clothes with him. Poltorátsky got into bed and smoked a cigarette and put out his candle, smiling the while. In the dark he saw before him the smiling face of Márya Vasílevna.

* * *

The Vorontsóvs did not go to bed at once. When the visitors had left, Márya Vasílevna went up to her husband and standing in front of him, said severely—

'Eh bien! Vous allez me dire ce que c'est.'

'Mais, ma chère . . .'

'Pas de "ma chère"! C'était un émissaire, n'est-ce pas?'

'Quand même, je ne puis pas vous le dire.'

'Vous ne pouvez pas? Alors, c'est moi qui vais vous le dire!'

'Vous?'

'It was Hadji Murád, wasn't it?' said Márya Vasílevna, who had for some days past heard of the negotiations and thought that Hadji Murád himself had been to see her husband. Vorontsóv could not altogether deny this, but disappointed her by saying that it was not Hadji Murád himself but only an emissary to announce that Hadji Murád would come to meet him next day at the spot where a wood-cutting expedition had been arranged.

In the monotonous life of the fortress the young Vorontsóvs—both husband and wife—were glad of this occurrence, and it was already past two o'clock when, after speaking of the pleasure the news would give his father, they went to bed.

IV

After the three sleepness nights he had passed flying from the *murids* Shamil had sent to capture him, Hadji Murád fell asleep as soon as Sado, having bid him goodnight, had gone out of the *sáklya*. He slept fully dressed with his head on his hand, his elbow sinking deep into the red down-cushions his host had arranged for him.

At a little distance, by the wall, slept Eldár. He lay on his back, his strong young limbs stretched out so that his high chest, with the black cartridge-pouches sewn into the front of his white Circassian coat, was higher than his freshly shaven, blue-gleaming head, which had rolled off the pillow and was thrown back. His upper lip, on which a little soft down was just appearing, pouted like a child's, now contracting and now expanding, as though he were sipping something. Like Hadji Murád he slept with pistol and dagger in his belt. The sticks in the grate burnt low, and a night-light in a niche in the wall gleamed faintly.

In the middle of the night the floor of the guest-chamber

creaked, and Hadji Murád immediately rose, putting his hand to his pistol. Sado entered, treading softly on the earthen floor.

'What is it?' asked Hadji Murád, as if he had not been asleep at all.

'We must think,' replied Sado, squatting down in front of him. 'A woman from her roof saw you arrive and told her husband, and now the whole *aoul* knows. A neighbour has just been to tell my wife that the Elders have assembled in the mosque and want to detain you.'

'I must be off!' said Hadji Murád.

'The horses are saddled,' said Sado, quickly leaving the *sáklya*.

'Eldár!' whispered Hadji Murád. And Eldár, hearing his name, and above all his master's voice, leapt to his feet, setting his cap straight as he did so.

Hadji Murád put on his weapons and then his *búrka*. Eldár did the same, and they both went silently out of the *sáklya* into the penthouse. The black-eyed boy brought their horses. Hearing the clatter of hoofs on the hard-beaten road, someone stuck his head out of the door of a neighbouring *sáklya*, and a man ran up the hill towards the mosque, clattering with his wooden shoes. There was no moon, but the stars shone brightly in the black sky so that the outlines of the *sáklya* roofs could be seen in the darkness, the mosque with its minarets in the upper part of the village rising above the other buildings. From the mosque came a hum of voices.

Quickly seizing his gun, Hadji Murád placed his foot in the narrow stirrup, and silently and easily throwing his body across, swung himself onto the high cushion of the saddle.

'May God reward you!' he said, addressing his host while his right foot felt instinctively for the stirrup, and with his whip he lightly touched the lad who held his horse, as a sign that he should let go. The boy stepped aside, and the horse, as if it knew what it had to do, started at a brisk pace down the lane towards the principal street. Eldár rode behind him. Sado in his sheepskin followed, almost running, swinging his arms and crossing now to one side and now to the other of the narrow sidestreet. At the place where the streets met, first one moving shadow and then another appeared in the road.

'Stop . . . who's that? Stop!' shouted a voice, and several men blocked the path.

Instead of stopping, Hadji Murád drew his pistol from his belt and increasing his speed rode straight at those who blocked the way. They separated, and without looking round he started down the road at a swift canter. Eldár followed him at a sharp trot. Two shots cracked behind them and two bullets whistled past without hitting either Hadji Murád or Eldár. Hadji Murád continued riding at the same pace, but having gone some three hundred yards he stopped his slightly panting horse and listened.

In front of him, lower down, gurgled rapidly running water. Behind him in the *aoul* cocks crowed, answering one another. Above these sounds he heard behind him the approaching tramp of horses and the voices of several men. Hadji Murád touched his horse and rode on at an even pace. Those behind him galloped and soon overtook him. They were some twenty mounted men, inhabitants of the *aoul*, who had decided to detain Hadji Murád or at least to make a show of detaining him in order to justify themselves in Shamil's eyes. When they came near enough to be seen in the darkness, Hadji Murád stopped, let go his bridle, and with an accustomed movement of his left hand unbuttoned the cover of his rifle, which he drew forth with his right. Eldár did the same.

'What do you want?' cried Hadji Murád. 'Do you wish to take me? . . . Take me, then!' and he raised his rifle. The men from the *aoul* stopped, and Hadji Murád, rifle in hand, rode down into the ravine. The mounted men followed him but did not draw any nearer. When Hadji Murád had crossed to the other side of the ravine the men shouted to him that he should hear what they had to say. In reply he fired his rifle and put his horse to a gallop. When he reined it in his pursuers were no longer within hearing and the crowing of the cocks could also no longer be heard; only the murmur of the water in the forest sounded more distinctly and now and then came the cry of an owl. The black wall of the forest appeared quite close. It was in this forest that his *murids* awaited him.

On reaching it Hadji Murád paused, and drawing much air into his lungs he whistled and then listened silently. The next minute he was answered by a similar whistle from the forest. Hadji Murád turned from the road and entered it. When he had gone about a hundred paces he saw among the trunks of the trees a bonfire, the shadows of some men sitting round it, and, half lit-up by the firelight, a hobbled horse which was saddled. Four men were seated by the fire.

One of them rose quickly, and coming up to Hadji Murád took hold of his bridle and stirrup. This was Hadji Murád's sworn brother who managed his household affairs for him.

'Put out the fire,' said Hadji Murád, dismounting.

The men began scattering the pile and trampling on the burning branches.

'Has Bata been here?' asked Hadji Murád, moving towards a *búrka* that was spread on the ground.

'Yes, he went away long ago with Khan Mahomá.'

'Which way did they go?'

'That way,' answered Khanéfi pointing in the opposite direction to that from which Hadji Murád had come.

'All right,' said Hadji Murád, and unslinging his rifle he began to load it.

'We must take care—I have been pursued,' he said to a man who was putting out the fire.

This was Gamzálo, a Chechen. Gamzálo approached the *búrka*, took up a rifle that lay on it wrapped in its cover, and without a word went to that side of the glade from which Hadji Murád had come.

When Eldár had dismounted he took Hadji Murád's horse, and having reined up both horses' heads high, tied them to two trees. Then he shouldered his rifle as Gamzálo had done and went to the other side of the glade. The bonfire was extinguished, the forest no longer looked as black as before, but in the sky the stars still shone, though faintly.

Lifting his eyes to the stars and seeing that the Pleiades had already risen half-way up the sky, Hadji Murád calculated that it must be long past midnight and that his nightly prayer was long overdue. He asked Khanéfi for a ewer (they always carried one in their packs), and putting on his *búrka* went to the water.

Having taken off his shoes and performed his ablutions, Hadji Murád stepped onto the *búrka* with bare feet and then squatted down on his calves, and having first placed his fingers in his ears and closed his eyes, he turned to the south and recited the usual prayer.

When he had finished he returned to the place where the saddle-bags lay, and sitting down on the *búrka* he leant his elbows on his knees and bowed his head and fell into deep thought.

Hadji Murád always had great faith in his own fortune. When planning anything he always felt in advance firmly convinced of success, and fate smiled on him. It had been so, with a few rare exceptions, during the whole course of his stormy military life; and so he hoped it would be now. He pictured to himself how—with the army Vorontsóv would place at his disposal—he would march against Shamil and take him prisoner, and revenge himself on him; and how the Russian Tsar would reward him and how he would again rule not only over Avaria, but over the whole of Chechnya, which would submit to him. With these thoughts he unwittingly fell asleep.

He dreamt how he and his brave followers rushed at Shamil with songs and with the cry, 'Hadji Murád is coming!' and how they seized him and his wives and how he heard the wives crying and sobbing. He woke up. The song, *Lya-il-allysha*, and the cry, 'Hadji Murád is coming!' and the weeping of Shamil's wives, was the howling, weeping, and laughter of jackals that awoke him. Hadji Murád lifted his head, glanced at the sky which, seen between the trunks of the trees, was already growing light in the east, and inquired after Khan Mahomá of a *murid* who sat at some distance from him. On hearing that Khan Mahomá had not yet returned, Hadji Murád again bowed his head and at once fell asleep.

He was awakened by the merry voice of Khan Mahomá returning from his mission with Bata. Khan Mahomá at once sat down beside Hadji Murád and told him how the soldiers had met them and had led them to the prince himself, and how pleased the prince was and how he promised to meet them in the morning where the Russians would be felling trees beyond the Mitchík in the Shalín glade. Bata interrupted his fellow-envoy to add details of his own.

Hadji Murád asked particularly for the words with which Vorontsóv had answered his offer to go over to the Russians, and Khan Mahomá and Bata replied with one voice that the prince promised to receive Hadji Murád as a guest, and to act so that it should be well for him.

Then Hadji Murád questioned them about the road,

and when Khan Mahomá assured him that he knew the way well and would conduct him straight to the spot, Hadji Murád took out some money and gave Bata the promised three rubles. Then he ordered his men to take out of the saddle-bags his gold-ornamented weapons and his turban, and to clean themselves up so as to look well when they arrived among the Russians.

While they cleaned their weapons, harness, and horses, the stars faded away, it became quite light, and an early morning breeze sprang up.

V

Early in the morning, while it was still dark, two companies carrying axes and commanded by Poltorátsky marched six miles beyond the Shahgirínsk Gate, and having thrown out a line of sharpshooters set to work to fell trees as soon as the day broke. Towards eight o'clock the mist which had mingled with the perfumed smoke of the hissing and crackling damp green branches on the bonfires began to rise and the wood-fellers—who till then had not seen five paces off but had only heard one another—began to see both the bonfires and the road through the forest, blocked with fallen trees. The sun now appeared like a bright spot in the fog and now again was hidden.

In the glade, some way from the road, Poltorátsky, his subaltern Tíkhonov, two officers of the Third Company, and Baron Freze, an ex-officer of the Guards and a fellow-student of Poltorátsky's at the Cadet College, who had been reduced to the ranks for fighting a duel, were sitting on drums. Bits of paper that had contained food, cigarette stumps, and empty bottles, lay scattered around them. The officers had had some vódka and were now eating, and drinking porter. A drummer was uncorking their third bottle.

Poltorátsky, although he had not had enough sleep, was in that peculiar state of elation and kindly careless gaiety which he always felt when he found himself among his soldiers and with his comrades where there was a possibility of danger.

The officers were carrying on an animated conversation, the subject of which was the latest news: the death of General Sleptsóv. None of them saw in this death that most important moment of a life, its termination and return to the source whence it sprang—they saw in it only the valour of a gallant officer who rushed at the mountaineers sword in hand and hacked them desperately.

Though all of them—and especially those who had been in action—knew and could not help knowing that in those days in the Caucasus, and in fact anywhere and at any time, such hand-to-hand hacking as is always imagined and described never occurs (or if hacking with swords and bayonets ever does occur, it is only those who are running away that get hacked), that fiction of hand-to-hand fighting endowed them with the calm pride and cheerfulness with which they sat on the drums—some with a jaunty air, others on the contrary in a very modest pose, and drank and joked without troubling about death, which might overtake them at any moment as it had overtaken Sleptsóv. And in the midst of their talk, as if to confirm their expectations, they heard to the left of the road the pleasant stirring sound of a rifle-shot; and a bullet, merrily whistling somewhere in the misty air, flew past and crashed into a tree.

'Hullo!' exclaimed Poltorátsky in a merry voice; 'why that's at our line. . . . There now, Kóstya,' and he turned to Freze, 'now's your chance. Go back to the company. I will lead the whole company to support the cordon and we'll arrange a battle that will be simply delightful . . . and then we'll make a report.'

Freze jumped to his feet and went at a quick pace towards the smoke-enveloped spot where he had left his company.

Poltorátsky's little Kabardá dapple-bay was brought to him, and he mounted and drew up his company and led it in the direction whence the shots were fired. The outposts stood on the skirts of the forest in front of the bare descending slope of a ravine. The wind was blowing in the direction of the forest, and not only was it possible to see the slope of the ravine, but the opposite side of it was also distinctly visible. When Poltorátsky rode up to the line the sun came out from behind the mist, and on the other side of the ravine, by the outskirts of a young forest, a few horsemen could be seen at a distance of a quarter of a mile. These were the Chechens who had pursued Hadji Murád and wanted to see him meet the Russians. One of them fired at the line. Several soldiers fired back. The Chechens retreated and the firing ceased.

But when Poltorátsky and his company came up he nevertheless gave orders to fire, and scarcely had the word been passed than along the whole line of sharpshooters the incessant, merry, stirring rattle of our rifles began, accompanied by pretty dissolving cloudlets of smoke. The soldiers, pleased to have some distraction, hastened to load and fired shot after shot. The Chechens evidently caught the feeling of excitement, and leaping forward one after another fired a few shots at our men. One of these shots wounded a soldier. It was that same Avdéev who had lain in ambush the night before.

When his comrades approached him he was lying prone, holding his wounded stomach with both hands, and rocking himself with a rhythmic motion moaned softly. He belonged to Poltorátsky's company, and Poltorátsky, seeing a group of soldiers collected, rode up to them.

'What is it, lad? Been hit?' said Poltorátsky. 'Where?'

Avdéev did not answer.

'I was just going to load, your honour, when I heard a click,' said a soldier who had been with Avdéev; 'and I look and see he's dropped his gun.'

'Tut, tut, tut!' Poltorátsky clicked his tongue. 'Does it hurt much, Avdéev?'

'It doesn't hurt but it stops me walking. A drop of vódka now, your honour!'

Some vódka (or rather the spirit drunk by the soldiers in the Caucasus) was found, and Panóv, severely frowning, brought Avdéev a can-lid full. Avdéev tried to drink it but immediately handed back the lid.

'My soul turns against it,' he said. 'Drink it yourself.'

Panóv drank up the spirit.

Avdéev raised himself but sank back at once. They spread out a cloak and laid him on it.

'Your honour, the colonel is coming,' said the sergeant-major to Poltorátsky.

'All right. Then will you see to him?' said Poltorátsky, and flourishing his whip he rode at a fast trot to meet Vorontsóv.

Vorontsóv was riding his thoroughbred English chestnut gelding, and was accompanied by the adjutant, a Cossack, and a Chechen interpreter.

'What's happening here?' asked Vorontsóv.

'Why, a skirmishing party attacked our advanced line,' Poltorátsky answered.

'Come, come—you arranged the whole thing yourself!'

'Oh no, Prince, not I,' said Poltorátsky with a smile; 'they pushed forward of their own accord.'

'I hear a soldier has been wounded?'

'Yes, it's a great pity. He's a good soldier.'

'Seriously?'

'Seriously, I believe . . . in the stomach.'

'And do you know where I am going?' Vorontsóv asked.

'I don't.'

'Can't you guess?'

'No.'

'Hadji Murád has surrendered and we are now going to meet him.'

'You don't mean to say so?'

'His envoy came to me yesterday,' said Vorontsóv, with difficulty repressing a smile of pleasure. 'He will be waiting for me at the Shalín glade in a few minutes. Place sharpshooters as far as the glade, and then come and join me.'

'I understand,' said Poltorátsky, lifting his hand to his cap, and rode back to his company. He led the sharpshooters to the right himself, and ordered the sergeant-major to do the same on the left side.

The wounded Avdéev had meanwhile been taken back to the fort by some of the soldiers.

On his way back to rejoin Vorontsóv, Poltorátsky noticed behind him several horsemen who were overtaking him. In front on a white-maned horse rode a man of imposing appearance. He wore a turban and carried weapons with gold ornaments. This man was Hadji Murád. He approached Poltorátsky and said something to him in Tartar. Raising his eyebrows, Poltorátsky made a gesture with his arms to show that he did not understand, and smiled. Hadji Murád gave him smile for smile, and that smile struck Poltorátsky by its childlike kindliness. Poltorátsky had never expected to see the terrible mountain chief look like that. He had expected to see a morose, hard-featured man, and here was a vivacious person whose smile was so kindly that Poltorátsky felt as if he were an old acquaintance. He had only one peculiarity: his eyes, set wide apart, which gazed from under their black brows calmly, attentively, and penetratingly into the eyes of others.

Hadji Murád's suite consisted of five men, among them was Khan Mahomá, who had been to see Prince Vorontsóv that night. He was a rosy, round-faced fellow with black lashless eyes and a beaming expression, full of the joy of life. Then there was the Avar Khanéfi, a thick-set, hairy man, whose eyebrows met. He was in charge of all Hadji Murád's property and led a stud-bred horse which carried tightly packed saddle-bags. Two men of the suite were particularly striking. The first was a Lesghian: a youth, broad-shouldered but with a waist as slim as a woman's, beautiful ram-like eyes, and the beginnings of a brown beard. This was Eldár. The other, Gamzálo, was a Chechen with a short red beard and no eyebrows or eyelashes; he was blind in one eye and had a scar across his nose and face. Poltorátsky pointed out Vorontsóv, who had just appeared on the road. Hadji Murád rode to meet him, and putting his right hand on his heart said something in Tartar and stopped. The Chechen interpreter translated.

'He says, "I surrender myself to the will of the Russian Tsar. I wish to serve him," he says. "I wished to do so long ago but Shamil would not let me."'

Having heard what the interpreter said, Vorontsóv stretched out his hand in its wash-leather glove to Hadji Murád. Hadji Murád looked at it hesitatingly for a moment and then pressed it firmly, again saying something and looking first at the interpreter and then at Vorontsóv.

'He says he did not wish to surrender to any one but you, as you are the son of the Sirdar and he respects you much.'

Vorontsóv nodded to express his thanks. Hadji Murád again said something, pointing to his suite.

'He says that these men, his henchmen, will serve the Russians as well as he.'

Vorontsóv turned towards them and nodded to them too. The merry, black-eyed, lashless Chechen, Khan Mahomá, also nodded and said something which was probably amusing, for the hairy Avar drew his lips into a smile, showing his ivory-white teeth. But the red-haired Gamzálo's one red eye just glanced at Vorontsóv and then was again fixed on the ears of his horse.

When Vorontsóv and Hadji Murád with their retinues rode back to the fort. the soldiers released from the lines gathered in groups and made their own comments.

'What a lot of men that damned fellow has destroyed! And now see what a fuss they will make of him!'

'Naturally. He was Shamil's right hand, and now—no fear!'

'Still there's no denying it! he's a fine fellow—a regular *dzhigít!*'

'And the red one! He squints at you like a beast!'

'Ugh! He must be a hound!'

They had all specially noticed the red one. Where the wood-felling was going on the soldiers nearest to the road ran out to look. Their officer shouted to them, but Vorontsóv stopped him.

'Let them have a look at their old friend.'

'You know who that is?' he added, turning to the nearest soldier, and speaking the words slowly with his English accent.

'No, your Excellency.'

'Hadji Murád. . . . Heard of him?'

'How could we help it, your Excellency? We've beaten him many a time!'

'Yes, and we've had it hot from him too.'

'Yes, that's true, your Excellency,' answered the soldier, pleased to be talking with his chief.

Hadji Murád understood that they were speaking about him, and smiled brightly with his eyes.

Vorontsóv returned to the fort in a very cheerful mood.

VI

Young Vorontsóv was much pleased that it was he, and no one else, who had succeeded in winning over and receiving Hadji Murád—next to Shamil Russia's chief and most active enemy. There was only one unpleasant thing about it: General Meller-Zakomélsky was in command of the army at Vozdvízhensk, and the whole affair ought to have been carried out through him. As Vorontsóv had done everything himself without reporting it there might be some unpleasantness, and this thought rather interfered with his satisfaction. On reaching his house he entrusted Hadji Murád's henchmen to the regimental adjutant and himself showed Hadji Murád into the house.

Princess Márya Vasílevna, elegantly dressed and smiling, and her little son, a handsome curly-headed child of six, met Hadji Murád in the drawing-room. The latter placed his hands on his heart, and through the interpreter—who had entered with him—said with solemnity that he regarded himself as the prince's *kunák,* since the prince had brought him into his own house; and that a *kunák's* whole family was as sacred as the *kunák* himself.

Hadji Murád's appearance and manners pleased Márya Vasílevna, and the fact that he flushed when she held out her large white hand to him inclined her still more in his favour. She invited him to sit down, and having asked him whether he drank coffee, had some served. He, however, declined it when it came. He understood a little Russian but could not speak it. When something was said which he could not understand he smiled, and his smile pleased Márya Vasílevna just as it had pleased Poltorátsky. The curly-haired, keen-eyed little boy (whom his mother called Búlka) standing beside her did not take his eyes off Hadji Murád, whom he had always heard spoken of as a great warrior.

Leaving Hadji Murád with his wife, Vorontsóv went to his office to do what was necessary about reporting the fact of Hadji Murád's having come over to the Russians. When he had written a report to the general in command of the left flank—General Kozlóvsky—at Grózny, and a letter to his father, Vorontsóv hurried home, afraid that his wife might be vexed with him for forcing on her this terrible stranger, who had to be treated in such a way that he should not take offense, and yet not too kindly. But his fears were needless. Hadji Murád was sitting in an armchair with little Búlka, Vorontsóv's stepson, on his knee, and with bent head was listening attentively to the interpreter who was translating to him the words of the laughing Márya Vasílevna. Márya Vasílevna was telling him that if every time a *kunák* admired anything of his he made him a present of it, he would soon have to go about like Adam. . . .

When the prince entered, Hadji Murád rose at once and, surprising and offending Búlka by putting him off his knee, changed the playful expression of his face to a stern and serious one. He only sat down again when Vorontsóv had himself taken a seat.

Continuing the conversation he answered Márya Vasílevna by telling her that it was a law among his people that anything your *kunák* admired must be presented to him.

'Thy son, *kunák!*' he said in Russian, patting the curly head of the boy who had again climbed on his knee.

'He is delightful, your brigand!' said Márya Vasílevna to her husband in French. 'Búlka has been admiring his dagger, and he has given it to him.'

Búlka showed the dagger to his father. *'C'est un objet de prix!'* added she.

'Il faudra trouver l'occasion de lui faire cadeau,' said Vorontsóv.

Hadji Murád, his eyes turned down, sat stroking the boy's curly hair and saying: *'Dzhigít, dzhigít!'*

'A beautiful, beautiful dagger,' said Vorontsóv, half drawing out the sharpened blade which had a ridge down the centre. 'I thank thee!'

'Ask him what I can do for him,' he said to the interpreter.

The interpreter translated, and Hadji Murád at once replied that he wanted nothing but that he begged to be taken to a place where he could say his prayers.

Vorontsóv called his valet and told him to do what Hadji Murád desired.

As soon as Hadji Murád was alone in the room allotted to him his face altered. The pleased expression, now kindly and now stately, vanished, and a look of anxiety showed itself. Vorontsóv had received him far better than Hadji Murád had expected. But the better the reception the less did Hadji Murád trust Vorontsóv and his officers. He feared everything: that he might be seized, chained, and sent to Siberia, or simply killed; and therefore he was on his guard. He asked Eldár, when the latter entered his room, where his *murids* had been put and whether their arms had been taken from them, and where the horses were. Eldár reported that the horses were in the prince's stables; that the men had been placed in a barn; that they retained their arms, and that the interpreter was giving them food and tea.

Hadji Murád shook his head in doubt, and after undressing said his prayers and told Eldár to bring him his silver dagger. He then dressed, and having fastened his belt sat down on the divan with his legs tucked under him, to await what might befall him.

At four in the afternoon the interpreter came to call him to dine with the prince.

At dinner he hardly ate anything except some *pilau*,

to which he helped himself from the very part of the dish
from which Márya Vasílevna had helped herself.

'He is afraid we shall poison him,' Márya Vasílevna remarked to her husband. 'He has helped himself from the
place where I took my helping.' Then instantly turning to
Hadji Murád she asked him through the interpreter when
he would pray again. Hadji Murád lifted five fingers and
pointed to the sun. 'Then it will soon be time,' and
Vorontsóv drew out his watch and pressed a spring. The
watch struck four and one quarter. This evidently surprised
Hadji Murád, and he asked to hear it again and to be
allowed to look at the watch.

'*Voilà l'occasion! Donnez-lui la montre,*' said the princess
to her husband.

Vorontsóv at once offered the watch to Hadji Murád.

The latter placed his hand on his breast and took the
watch. He touched the spring several times, listened, and
nodded his head approvingly.

After dinner, Meller-Zakomélsky's aide-de-camp was
announced.

The aide-de-camp informed the prince that the general,
having heard of Hadji Murád's arrival, was highly displeased that this had not been reported to him, and required Hadji Murád to be brought to him without delay.
Vorontsóv replied that the general's command should be
obeyed, and through the interpreter informed Hadji Murád
of these orders and asked him to go to Meller with him.

When Márya Vasílevna heard what the aide-de-camp
had come about, she at once understood that unpleasantness might arise between her husband and the general, and
in spite of all her husband's attempts to dissuade her, decided to go with him and Hadji Murád.

'*Vous feriez bien mieux de rester—c'est mon affaire, non
pas la vôtre. . . .*'

'*Vous ne pouvez pas m'empêcher d'aller voir madame la
générale!*'

'You could go some other time.'

'But I wish to go now!'

There was no help for it, so Vorontsóv agreed, and they
all three went.

When they entered, Meller with sombre politeness conducted Márya Vasílevna to his wife and told his aide-de-
camp to show Hadji Murád into the waiting-room and not
let him out till further orders.

'Please . . .' he said to Vorontsóv, opening the door of his study and letting the prince enter before him.

Having entered the study he stopped in front of Vorontsóv and, without offering him a seat, said:

'I am in command here and therefore all negotiations with the enemy have to be carried on through me! Why did you not report to me that Hadji Murád had come over?'

'An emissary came to me and announced his wish to capitulate only to me,' replied Vorontsóv growing pale with excitement, expecting some rude expression from the angry general and at the same time becoming infected with his anger.

'I ask you why I was not informed?'

'I intended to inform you, Baron, but . . .'

'You are not to address me as "Baron," but as "Your Excellency"!' And here the baron's pent-up irritation suddenly broke out and he uttered all that had long been boiling in his soul.

'I have not served my sovereign twenty-seven years in order that men who began their service yesterday, relying on family connexions, should give orders under my very nose about matters that do not concern them!'

'Your Excellency, I request you not to say things that are incorrect!' interrupted Vorontsóv.

'I am saying what is correct, and I won't allow . . .' said the general, still more irritably.

But at that moment Márya Vasílevna entered, rustling with her skirts and followed by a modest-looking little lady, Meller-Zakomélsky's wife.

'Come, come, Baron! Simon did not wish to displease you,' began Márya Vasílevna.

'I am not speaking about that, Princess. . . .'

'Well, well, let's forget it all! . . . You know, "A bad peace is better than a good quarrel!" . . . Oh dear, what am I saying?' and she laughed.

The angry general capitulated to the enchanting laugh of the beauty. A smile hovered under his moustache.

'I confess I was wrong,' said Vorontsóv, 'but——'

'And I too got rather carried away,' said Meller, and held out his hand to the prince.

Peace was re-established, and it was decided to leave Hadji Murád with the general for the present, and then to send him to the commander of the left flank.

Hadji Murád sat in the next room and though he did

not understand what was said, he understood what it was
necessary for him to understand—namely, that they were
quarrelling about him, that his desertion of Shamil was a
matter of immense importance to the Russians, and that
therefore not only would they not exile or kill him, but
that he would be able to demand much from them. He
also understood that though Meller-Zakomélsky was the
commanding-officer, he had not as much influence as his
subordinate Vorontsóv, and that Vorontsóv was important
and Meller-Zakomélsky unimportant; and therefore when
Meller-Zakomélsky sent for him and began to question
him, Hadji Murád bore himself proudly and ceremoniously,
saying that he had come from the mountains to serve the
White Tsar and would give account only to his Sirdar,
meaning the commander-in-chief, Prince Vorontsóv senior,
in Tiflis.

VII

The wounded Avdéev was taken to the hospital—a
small wooden building roofed with boards at the entrance
of the fort—and was placed on one of the empty beds in
the common ward. There were four patients in the ward:
one ill with typhus and in high fever; another, pale, with
dark shadows under his eyes, who had ague, was just expecting another attack and yawned continually; and two
more who had been wounded in a raid three weeks before:
one in the hand—he was up—and the other in the
shoulder. The latter was sitting on a bed. All of them except the typhus patient surrounded and questioned the
newcomer and those who had brought him.

'Sometimes they fire as if they were spilling peas over
you, and nothing happens . . . and this time only about
five shots were fired,' related one of the bearers.

'Each man gets what fate sends!'

'Oh!' groaned Avdéev loudly, trying to master his pain
when they began to place him on the bed; but he stopped
groaning when he was on it, and only frowned and moved
his feet continually. He held his hands over his wound
and looked fixedly before him.

The doctor came, and gave orders to turn the wounded
man over to see whether the bullet had passed out behind.

'What's this?' the doctor asked, pointing to the large

white scars that crossed one another on the patient's back and loins.

'That was done long ago, your honour!' replied Avdéev with a groan.

They were scars left by the flogging Avdéev had received for the money he drank.

Avdéev was again turned over, and the doctor probed in his stomach for a long time and found the bullet, but failed to extract it. He put a dressing on the wound, and having stuck plaster over it went away. During the whole time the doctor was probing and bandaging the wound Avdéev lay with clenched teeth and closed eyes, but when the doctor had gone he opened them and looked around as though amazed. His eyes were turned on the other patients and on the surgeon's orderly, though he seemed to see not them but something else that surprised him.

His friends Panóv and Serógin came in, but Avdéev continued to lie in the same position looking before him with surprise. It was long before he recognized his comrades, though his eyes gazed straight at them.

'I say, Peter, have you no message to send home?' said Panóv.

Avdéev did not answer, though he was looking Panóv in the face.

'I say, haven't you any orders to send home?' again repeated Panóv, touching Avdéev's cold, large-boned hand.

Avdéev seemed to come to.

'Ah! . . . Panóv!'

'Yes, I'm here. . . . I've come! Have you nothing for home? Serógin would write a letter.'

'Serógin . . .' said Avdéev moving his eyes with difficulty towards Serógin, 'will you write? . . . Well then, write so: "Your son," say, "Peter, has given orders that you should live long. He envied his brother" . . . I told you about that today . . . "and now he is himself glad. Don't worry him. . . . Let him live. God grant it him. I am glad!" Write that.'

Having said this he was silent for some time with his eyes fixed on Panóv.

'And did you find your pipe?' he suddenly asked.

Panóv did not reply.

'Your pipe . . . your pipe! I mean, have you found it?' Avdéev repeated.

'It was in my bag.'

'That's right! . . . Well, and now give me a candle to hold . . . I am going to die,' said Avdéev.

Just then Poltorátsky came in to inquire ⸣after his soldier.

'How goes it, my lad! Badly?' said he.

Avdéev closed his eyes and shook his head negatively. His broad-cheeked face was pale and stern. He did not reply, but again said to Panóv:

'Bring a candle. . . . I am going to die.'

A wax taper was placed in his hand but his fingers would not bend, so it was placed between them and held up for him.

Poltorátsky went away, and five minutes later the orderly put his ear to Avdéev's heart and said that all was over.

Avdéev's death was described in the following manner in the report sent to Tiflis:

'*23rd Nov.*—Two companies of the Kurín regiment advanced from the fort on a wood-felling expedition. At midday a considerable number of mountaineers suddenly attacked the wood-fellers. The sharpshooters began to retreat, but the 2nd Company charged with the bayonet and overthrew the mountaineers. In this affair two privates were slightly wounded and one killed. The mountaineers lost about a hundred men killed and wounded.'

VIII

On the day Peter Avdéev died in the hospital at Vozdvízhensk, his old father with the wife of the brother in whose stead he had enlisted, and that brother's daughter —who was already approaching womanhood and almost of age to get married—were threshing oats on the hardfrozen threshing-floor.

There had been a heavy fall of snow the previous night, followed towards morning by a severe frost. The old man woke when the cocks were crowing for the third time, and seeing the bright moonlight through the frozen windowpanes got down from the stove, put on his boots, his sheepskin coat and cap, and went out to the threshing-floor. Having worked there for a couple of hours he returned to the hut and awoke his son and the women. When the woman and the girl came to the threshing-floor they found it ready swept, with a wooden shovel sticking in the dry white snow, beside which were birch brooms with the twigs upwards and two rows of oat-sheaves laid ears to ears in a long line the whole length of the clean threshing-floor. They chose their flails and started threshing, keeping time with their triple blows. The old man struck powerfully with his heavy flail, breaking the straw, the girl struck the ears from above with measured blows, and the daughter-in-law turned the oats over with her flail.

The moon had set, dawn was breaking, and they were finishing the line of sheaves when Akím, the eldest son, in his sheepskin and cap, joined the threshers.

'What are you lazing about for?' shouted his father to him, pausing in his work and leaning on his flail.

'The horses had to be seen to.'

' "Horses seen to!" ' the father repeated, mimicking him. 'The old woman will look after them. . . . Take your flail! You're getting too fat, you drunkard!'

'Have you been standing me treat?' muttered the son.

'What?' said the old man, frowning sternly and missing a stroke.

The son silently took a flail and they began threshing with four flails.

'Trak, tapatam . . . trak, tapatam . . . trak . . .' came down the old man's heavy flail after the three others.

'Why, you've got a nape like a goodly gentleman! . . . Look here, my trousers have hardly anything to hang on!' said the old man, omitting his stroke and only swinging his flail in the air so as not to get out of time.

They had finished the row, and the women began removing the straw with rakes.

'Peter was a fool to go in your stead. They'd have knocked the nonsense out of you in the army, and he was worth five of such as you at home!'

'That's enough, father,' said the daughter-in-law, as she threw aside the binders that had come off the sheaves.

'Yes, feed the six of you and get no work out of a single one! Peter used to work for two. He was not like . . .'

Along the trodden path from the house came the old man's wife, the frozen snow creaking under the new bark shoes she wore over her tightly wound woollen leg-bands. The men were shovelling the unwinnowed grain into heaps, the woman and the girl sweeping up what remained.

'The Elder has been and orders everybody to go and

work for the master, carting bricks,' said the old woman.
'I've got breakfast ready. . . . Come along, won't you?'

'All right. . . . Harness the roan and go,' said the old
man to Akím, 'and you'd better look out that you don't
get me into trouble as you did the other day! . . . I can't
help regretting Peter!'

'When he was at home you used to scold him,' retorted
Akím. 'Now he's away you keep nagging at me.'

'That shows you deserve it,' said his mother in the same
angry tones. 'You'll never be Peter's equal.'

'Oh, all right,' said the son.

' "All right," indeed! You've drunk the meal, and now
you say "all right!" '

'Let bygones be bygones!' said the daughter-in-law.

The disagreements between father and son had begun
long ago—almost from the time Peter went as a soldier.
Even then the old man felt that he had parted with an eagle
for a cuckoo. It is true that it was right—as the old man
understood it—for a childless man to go in place of a
family man. Akím had four children and Peter had none;
but Peter was a worker like his father, skilful, observant,
strong, enduring, and above all industrious. He was always at work. If he happened to pass by where people
were working he lent a helping hand as his father would
have done, and took a turn or two with the scythe, or
loaded a cart, or felled a tree, or chopped some wood.
The old man regretted his going away, but there was no
help for it. Conscription in those days was like death. A
soldier was a severed branch, and to think about him at
home was to tear one's heart uselessly. Only occasionally,
to prick his elder son, did the father mention him, as he
had done that day. But his mother often thought of her
younger son, and for a long time—more than a year now
—she had been asking her husband to send Peter a little
money, but the old man had made no response.

The Kúrenkovs were a well-to-do family and the old
man had some savings hidden away, but he would on no
account have consented to touch what he had laid by. Now
however the old woman having heard him mention their
younger son, made up her mind to ask him again to send
him at least a ruble after selling the oats. This she did.
As soon as the young people had gone to work for the
proprietor and the old folk were left alone together, she
persuaded him to send Peter a ruble out of the oats-money.

So when ninety-six bushels of the winnowed oats had been packed onto three sledges lined with sacking carefully pinned together at the top with wooden skewers, she gave her husband a letter the church clerk had written at her dictation, and the old man promised when he got to town to enclose a ruble and send it off to the right address.

The old man, dressed in a new sheepskin with a homespun cloak over it, his legs wrapped round with warm white woollen leg-bands, took the letter, placed it in his wallet, said a prayer, got into the front sledge, and drove to town. His grandson drove in the last sledge. When he reached town the old man asked the innkeeper to read the letter to him, and listened to it attentively and approvingly.

In her letter Peter's mother first sent him her blessing, then greetings from everybody and the news of his godfather's death, and at the end she added that Aksínya (Peter's wife) had not wished to stay with them but had gone into service, where they heard she was living honestly and well. Then came a reference to the present of a ruble, and finally a message which the old woman, yielding to her sorrows, had dictated with tears in her eyes and the church clerk had taken down exactly, word for word:

'One thing more, my darling child, my sweet dove, my own Peterkin! I have wept my eyes out lamenting for thee, thou light of my eyes. To whom hast thou left me? . . .' At this point the old woman had sobbed and wept, and said: 'That will do!' So the words stood in the letter; but it was not fated that Peter should receive the news of his wife's having left home, nor the present of the ruble, nor his mother's last words. The letter with the money in it came back with the announcement that Peter had been killed in the war, 'defending his Tsar, his Fatherland, and the Orthodox Faith.' That is how the army clerk expressed it.

The old woman, when this news reached her, wept for as long as she could spare time, and then set to work again. The very next Sunday she went to church and had a requiem chanted and Peter's name entered among those for whose souls prayers were to be said, and she distributed bits of holy bread to all the good people in memory of Peter, the servant of God.

Aksínya, his widow, also lamented loudly when she heard of the death of her beloved husband with whom she had lived but one short year. She regretted her husband

and her own ruined life, and in her lamentations mentioned Peter's brown locks and his love, and the sadness of her life with her little orphaned Vánka, and bitterly reproached Peter for having had pity on his brother but none on her—obliged to wander among strangers!

But in the depth of her soul Aksínya was glad of her husband's death. She was pregnant a second time by the shopman with whom she was living, and no one would now have a right to scold her, and the shopman could marry her as he had said he would when he was persuading her to yield.

IX

Michael Semënovich Vorontsóv, being the son of the Russian Ambassador, had been educated in England and possessed a European education quite exceptional among the higher Russian officials of his day. He was ambitious, gentle and kind in his manner with inferiors, and a finished courtier with superiors. He did not understand life without power and submission. He had obtained all the highest ranks and decorations and was looked upon as a clever commander, and even as the conqueror of Napoleon at Krásnoe.

In 1852 he was over seventy, but young for his age, he moved briskly, and above all was in full possession of a facile, refined, and agreeable intellect which· he used to maintain his power and strengthen and increase his popularity. He possessed large means—his own and his wife's (who had been a Countess Branítski)—and received an enormous salary as Viceroy, and he spent a great part of his means on building a palace and laying out a garden on the south coast of the Crimea.

On the evening of December the 4th, 1852, a courier's troyka drew up before his palace in Tiflis. An officer, tired and black with dust, sent by General Kozlóvski with the news of Hadji Murád's surrender to the Russians, entered the wide porch, stretching the stiffened muscles of his legs as he passed the sentinel. It was six o'clock, and Vorontsóv was just going in to dinner when he was informed of the courier's arrival. He received him at once, and was therefore a few minutes late for dinner.

When he entered the drawing-room the thirty persons invited to dine, who were sitting beside Princess Elizabeth

Ksavérevna Vorontsóva, or standing in groups by the windows, turned their faces towards him. Vorontsóv was dressed in his usual black military coat, with shoulder-straps but no epaulets, and wore the White Cross of the Order of St. George at his neck.

His clean-shaven, foxlike face wore a pleasant smile as, screwing up his eyes, he surveyed the assembly. Entering with quick soft steps he apologized to the ladies for being late, greeted the men, and approaching Princess Manana Orbelyáni—a tall, fine, handsome woman of Oriental type about forty-five years of age—he offered her his arm to take her in to dinner. Princess Elizabeth Ksavérevna Vorontsóva gave her arm to a red-haired general with bristly moustaches who was visiting Tiflis. A Georgian prince offered his arm to Princess Vorontsóva's friend, Countess. Choiseuil. Doctor Andréevsky, the aide-de-camp, and others, with ladies or without, followed these first couples. Footmen in livery and knee-breeches drew back and replaced the guests' chairs when they sat down, while the major-domo ceremoniously ladled out steaming soup from a silver tureen.

Vorontsóv took his place in the centre of one side of the long table, and his wife sat opposite, with the general on her right. On the prince's right sat his lady, the beautiful Orbelyáni; and on his left was a graceful, dark, red-cheeked Georgian woman, glittering with jewels and incessantly smiling.

'*Excellentes, chère amie!*' replied Vorontsóv to his wife's inquiry about what news the courier had brought him. '*Simon a eu de la chance!*' And he began to tell aloud, so that everyone could hear, the striking news (for him alone not quite unexpected, because negotiations had long been going on) that Hadji Murád, the bravest and most famous of Shamil's officers, had come over to the Russians and would in a day or two be brought to Tiflis.

Everybody—even the young aides-de-camp and officials who sat at the far ends of the table and who had been quietly laughing at something among themselves—became silent and listened.

'And you, General, have you ever met this Hadji Murád?' asked the princess of her neighbour, the carroty general with the bristly moustaches, when the prince had finished speaking.

'More than once, Princess.'

And the general went on to tell how Hadji Murád, after the mountaineers had captured Gergebel in 1843, had fallen upon General Pahlen's detachment and killed Colonel Zolotúkhin almost before their very eyes.

Vorontsóv listened to the general and smiled amiably, evidently pleased that the latter had joined in the conversation. But suddenly his face assumed an absent-minded and depressed expression.

The general, having started talking, had begun to tell of his second encounter with Hadji Murád.

'Why, it was he, if your Excellency will please remember,' said the general, 'who arranged the ambush that attacked the rescue party in the "Biscuit" expedition.'

'Where?' asked Vorontsóv, screwing up his eyes.

What the brave general spoke of as the 'rescue' was the affair in the unfortunate Dargo campaign in which a whole detachment, including Prince Vorontsóv who commanded it, would certainly have perished had it not been rescued by the arrival of fresh troops. Every one knew that the whole Dargo campaign under Vorontsóv's command —in which the Russians lost many killed and wounded and several cannon—had been a shameful affair, and therefore if any one mentioned it in Vorontsóv's presence they did so only in the aspect in which Vorontsóv had reported it to the Tsar—as a brilliant achievement of the Russian army. But the word 'rescue' plainly indicated that it was not a brilliant victory but a blunder costing many lives. Everybody understood this and some pretended not to notice the meaning of the general's words, others nervously waited to see what would follow, while a few exchanged glances, and smiled. Only the carroty general with the bristly moustaches noticed nothing, and carried away by his narrative quietly replied:

'At the rescue, your Excellency.'

Having started on his favourite theme, the general recounted circumstantially how Hadji Murád had so cleverly cut the detachment in two that if the rescue party had not arrived (he seemed to be particularly fond of repeating the word 'rescue') not a man in the division would have escaped, because . . . He did not finish his story, for Manana Orbelyáni, having understood what was happening, interrupted him by asking if he had found comfortable quarters in Tiflis. The general, surprised, glanced at everybody all round and saw his aides-de-camp from the end of the table looking fixedly and significantly at him, and he suddenly understood! Without replying to the princess's question, he frowned, became silent, and began hurriedly swallowing the delicacy that lay on his plate, the appearance and taste of which both completely mystified him.

Everybody felt uncomfortable, but the awkwardness of the situation was relieved by the Georgian prince—a very stupid man but an extraordinarily refined and artful flatterer and courtier—who sat on the other side of Princess Vorontsóva. Without seeming to have noticed anything he began to relate how Hadji Murád had carried off the widow of Akhmet Khan of Mekhtulí.

'He came into the village at night, seized what he wanted, and galloped off again with the whole party.'

'Why did he want that particular woman?' asked the princess.

'Oh, he was her husband's enemy, and pursued him but could never once succeed in meeting him right up to the time of his death, so he revenged himself on the widow.'

The princess translated this into French for her old friend Countess Choiseuil, who sat next to the Georgian prince.

'*Quelle horreur!*' said the countess, closing her eyes and shaking her head.

'Oh no!' said Vorontsóv, smiling. 'I have been told that he treated his captive with chivalrous respect and afterwards released her.'

'Yes, for a ransom!'

'Well, of course. But all the same he acted honourably.'

These words of Vorontsóv's set the tone for the further conversation. The courtiers understood that the more importance was attributed to Hadji Murád the better the prince would be pleased.

'The man's audacity is amazing. A remarkable man!'

'Why, in 1849 he dashed into Temir Khan Shurá and plundered the shops in broad daylight.'

An Armenian sitting at the end of the table, who had been in Temir Khan Shurá at the time, related the particulars of that exploit of Hadji Murád's.

In fact, Hadji Murád was the sole topic of conversation during the whole dinner.

Everybody in succession praised his courage, his ability, and his magnanimity. Someone mentioned his having or-

dered twenty-six prisoners to be killed, but that too was
met by the usual rejoinder, 'What's to be done? *À la guerre,
comme à la guerre!*'

'He is a great man.'

'Had he been born in Europe he might have been another Napoleon,' said the stupid Georgian prince with a
gift of flattery.

He knew that every mention of Napoleon was pleasant
to Vorontsóv, who wore the White Cross at his neck as a
reward for having defeated him.

'Well, not Napoleon perhaps, but a gallant cavalry
general if you like,' said Vorontsóv.

'If not Napoleon, then Murat.'

'And his name is Hadji *Murád!*'

'Hadji Murád has surrendered and now there'll be an
end to Shamil too,' someone remarked.

'They feel that now' (this 'now' meant under Vorontsóv)
'they can't hold out,' remarked another.

'*Tout cela est grâce à vous!*' said Manana Orbelyáni.

Prince Vorontsóv tried to moderate the waves of flattery
which began to flow over him. Still, it was pleasant, and in
the best of spirits he led his lady back into the drawing-
room.

After dinner, when coffee was being served in the
drawing-room, the prince was particularly amiable to
everybody, and going up to the general with the red
bristly moustaches he tried to appear not to have noticed
his blunder.

Having made a round of the visitors he sat down to the
card-table. He only played the old-fashioned game of
ombre. His partners were the Georgian prince, an Armenian general (who had learnt the game of ombre from
Prince Vorontsóv's valet), and Doctor Andréevsky, a man
remarkable for the great influence he exercised.

Placing beside him his gold snuff-box with a portrait of
Alexander I on the lid, the prince tore open a pack of
highly glazed cards and was going to spread them out,
when his Italian valet brought him a letter on a silver
tray.

'Another courier, your Excellency.'

Vorontsóv laid down the cards, excused himself, opened
the letter, and began to read.

The letter was from his son, who described Hadji

Murád's surrender and his own encounter with Meller-Zakomélsky.

The princess came up and inquired what their son had written.

'It's all about the same matter. . . . *Il a eu quelques désagréments avec le commandant de la place. Simon a eu tort.* . . . But "All's well that ends well," ' he added in English, handing the letter to his wife; and turning to his respectfully waiting partners he asked them to draw cards.

When the first round had been dealt Vorontsóv did what he was in the habit of doing when in a particularly pleasant mood: with his white, wrinkled old hand he took out a pinch of French snuff, carried it to his nose, and released it.

X

When Hadji Murád appeared at the prince's palace next day, the waiting-room was already full of people. Yesterday's general with the bristly moustaches was there in full uniform with all his decorations, having come to take leave. There was the commander of a regiment who was in danger of being court-martialled for misappropriating commissariat money, and there was a rich Armenian (patronized by Doctor Andréevsky) who wanted to obtain from the Government a renewal of his monopoly for the sale of vódka. There, dressed in black, was the widow of an officer who had been killed in action. She had come to ask for a pension, or for free education for her children. There was a ruined Georgian prince in a magnificent Georgian costume who was trying to obtain for himself some confiscated Church property. There was an official with a large roll of paper containing a new plan for subjugating the Caucasus. There was also a Khan who had come solely to be able to tell his people at home that he had called on the prince.

They all waited their turn and were one by one shown into the prince's cabinet and out again by the aide-de-camp, a handsome, fair-haired youth.

When Hadji Murád entered the waiting-room with his brisk though limping step all eyes were turned towards him and he heard his name whispered from various parts of the room.

He was dressed in a long white Circassian coat over a brown *beshmét* trimmed round the collar with fine silver lace. He wore black leggings and soft shoes of the same colour which were stretched over his instep as tight as gloves. On his head he wore a high cap draped turban-fashion—that same turban for which, on the denunciation of Akhmet Khan, he had been arrested by General Klüge-nau and which had been the cause of his going over to Shamil.

He stepped briskly across the parquet floor of the waiting-room, his whole slender figure swaying slightly in consequence of his lameness in one leg which was shorter than the other. His eyes, set far apart, looked calmly before him and seemed to see no one.

The handsome aide-de-camp, having greeted him, asked him to take a seat while he went to announce him to the prince, but Hadji Murád declined to sit down and, putting his hand on his dagger, stood with one foot advanced, looking round contemptuously at all those present.

The prince's interpreter, Prince Tarkhánov, approached Hadji Murád and spoke to him. Hadji Murád answered abruptly and unwillingly. A Kumýk prince, who was there to lodge a complaint against a police official, came out of the prince's room, and then the aide-de-camp called Hadji Murád, led him to the door of the cabinet, and showed him in.

The Commander-in-Chief received Hadji Murád stand-ing beside his table, and his old white face did not wear yesterday's smile but was rather stern and solemn.

On entering the large room with its enormous table and great windows with green venetian blinds, Hadji Murád placed his small sunburnt hands on his chest just where the front of his white coat overlapped, and lowering his eyes began, without hurrying, to speak distinctly and re-spectfully, using the Kumýk dialect which he spoke well.

'I place myself under the powerful protection of the great Tsar and of yourself,' said he, 'and promise to serve the White Tsar in faith and truth to the last drop of my blood, and I hope to be useful to you in the war with Shamil who is my enemy and yours.'

Having heard the interpreter out, Vorontsóv glanced at Hadji Murád and Hadji Murád glanced at Vorontsóv.

The eyes of the two men met, and expressed to each other much that could not have been put into words and that was not at all what the interpreter said. Without words they told each other the whole truth. Vorontsóv's eyes said that he did not believe a single word Hadji Murád was saying, and that he knew he was and always would be an enemy to everything Russian and had surrendered only because he was obliged to. Hadji Murád understood this and yet continued to give assurances of his fidelity. His eyes said, 'That old man ought to be thinking of his death and not of war, but though he is old he is cunning, and I must be careful.' Vorontsóv understood this also, but nevertheless spoke to Hadji Murád in the way he considered necessary for the success of the war.

'Tell him,' said Vorontsóv, 'that our sovereign is as merciful as he is mighty and will probably at my request pardon him and take him into his service. . . . Have you told him?' he asked, looking at Hadji Murád. . . . 'Until I receive my master's gracious decision, tell him I take it on myself to receive him and make his sojourn among us pleasant.'

Hadji Murád again pressed his hands to the centre of his chest and began to say something with animation.

'He says,' the interpreter translated, 'that formerly, when he governed Avaria in 1839, he served the Russians faithfully and would never have deserted them had not his enemy, Akhmet Khan, wishing to ruin him, calumniated him to General Klügenau.'

'I know, I know,' said Vorontsóv (though if he had ever known he had long forgotten it). 'I know,' he repeated, sitting down and motioning Hadji Murád to the divan that stood beside the wall. But Hadji Murád did not sit down. Shrugging his powerful shoulders as a sign that he could not bring himself to sit in the presence of so important a man, he went on, addressing the interpreter:

'Akhmet Khan and Shamil are both my enemies. Tell the prince that Akhmet Khan is dead and I cannot revenge myself on him, but Shamil lives and I will not die without taking vengeance on him,' said he, knitting his brows and tightly closing his mouth.

'Yes, yes; but how does he want to revenge himself on Shamil?' said Vorontsóv quietly to the interpreter. 'And tell him he may sit down.'

Hadji Murád again declined to sit down, and in answer to the question replied that his object in coming over to the Russians was to help them to destroy Shamil.

'Very well, very well,' said Vorontsóv; 'but what exactly does he wish to do? . . . Sit down, sit down!'

Hadji Murád sat down, and said that if only they would send him to the Lesghian line and would give him an army, he would guarantee to raise the whole of Daghestan and Shamil would then be unable to hold out.

'That would be excellent. . . . I'll think it over,' said Vorontsóv.

The interpreter translated Vorontsóv's words to Hadji Murád.

Hadji Murád pondered.

'Tell the Sirdar one thing more,' Hadji Murád began again, 'that my family are in the hands of my enemy, and that as long as they are in the mountains I am bound and cannot serve him. Shamil would kill my wife and my mother and my children if I went openly against him. Let the prince first exchange my family for the prisoners he has, and then I will destroy Shamil or die!'

'All right, all right,' said Vorontsóv. 'I will think it over. . . . Now let him go to the chief of the staff and explain to him in detail his position, intentions, and wishes.'

Thus ended the first interview between Hadji Murád and Vorontsóv.

That evening an Italian opera was performed at the new theatre, which was decorated in Oriental style. Vorontsóv was in his box when the striking figure of the limping Hadji Murád wearing a turban appeared in the stalls. He came in with Lóris-Mélikov, Vorontsóv's aide-de-camp, in whose charge he was placed, and took a seat in the front row. Having sat through the first act with Oriental Mohammedan dignity, expressing no pleasure but only obvious indifference, he rose and looking calmly round at the audience went out, drawing to himself everybody's attention.

The next day was Monday and there was the usual evening party at the Vorontsóvs'. In the large brightly lighted hall a band was playing, hidden among trees. Young women and women not very young wearing dresses that displayed their bare necks, arms, and breasts, turned round and round in the embrace of men in bright uniforms. At the buffet, footmen in red swallow-tail coats and wearing shoes and knee-breeches, poured out champagne and served sweetmeats to the ladies. The 'Sirdar's' wife also, in spite of her age, went about half-dressed among the visitors smiling affably, and through the interpreter said a few amiable words to Hadji Murád who glanced at the visitors with the same indifference he had shown yesterday in the theatre. After the hostess, other half-naked women came up to him and all of them stood shamelessly before him and smilingly asked him the same question: How he liked what he saw? Vorontsóv himself, wearing gold epaulets and gold shoulder-knots with his white cross and ribbon at his neck, came up and asked him the same question, evidently feeling sure, like all the others, that Hadji Murád could not help being pleased at what he saw. Hadji Murád replied to Vorontsóv as he had replied to them all, that among his people nothing of the kind was done, without expressing an opinion as to whether it was good or bad that it was so.

Here at the ball Hadji Murád tried to speak to Vorontsóv about buying out his family, but Vorontsóv, pretending that he had not heard him, walked away, and Lóris-Mélikov afterwards told Hadji Murád that this was not the place to talk about business.

When it struck eleven Hadji Murád, having made sure of the time by the watch the Vorontsóvs had given him, asked Lóris-Mélikov whether he might now leave. Lóris-Mélikov said he might, though it would be better to stay. In spite of this Hadji Murád did not stay, but drove in the phaeton placed at his disposal to the quarters that had been assigned to him.

XI

On the fifth day of Hadji Murád's stay in Tiflis Lóris-Mélikov, the Viceroy's aide-de-camp, came to see him at the latter's command.

'My head and my hands are glad to serve the Sirdar,' said Hadji Murád with his usual diplomatic expression, bowing his head and putting his hands to his chest. 'Command me!' said he, looking amiably into Lóris-Mélikov's face.

Lóris-Mélikov sat down in an arm-chair placed by the table and Hadji Murád sank onto a low divan opposite and, resting his hands on his knees, bowed his head and listened attentively to what the other said to him.

Lóris-Mélikov, who spoke Tartar fluently, told him that though the prince knew about his past life, he yet wanted to hear the whole story from himself.

'Tell it me, and I will write it down and translate it into Russian and the prince will send it to the Emperor.'

Hadji Murád remained silent for a while (he never interrupted anyone but always waited to see whether his interlocutor had not something more to say), then he raised his head, shook back his cap, and smiled the peculiar child-like smile that had captivated Márya Vasílevna.

'I can do that,' said he, evidently flattered by the thought that his story would be read by the Emperor.

'Thou must tell me' (in Tartar nobody is addressed as 'you') 'everything, deliberately from the beginning,' said Lóris-Mélikov drawing a notebook from his pocket.

'I can do that, only there is much—very much—to tell! Many events have happened!' said Hadji Murád.

'If thou canst not do it all in one day thou wilt finish it another time,' said Lóris-Mélikov.

'Shall I begin at the beginning?'

'Yes, at the very beginning . . . where thou wast born and where thou didst live.'

Hadji Murád's head sank and he sat in that position for a long time. Then he took a stick that lay beside the divan, drew a little knife with an ivory gold-inlaid handle, sharp as a razor, from under his dagger, and started whittling the stick with it and speaking at the same time.

'Write: Born in Tselméss, a small *aoul*, "the size of an ass's head," as we in the mountains say,' he began. 'Not far from it, about two cannon-shots, lies Khunzákh where the Khans lived. Our family was closely connected with them.

'My mother, when my eldest brother Osman was born, nursed the eldest Khan, Abu Nutsal Khan. Then she nursed the second son of the Khan, Umma Khan, and reared him; but Akhmet my second brother died, and when I was born and the Khansha bore Bulách Khan, my mother would not go as wet-nurse again. My father ordered her to, but she would not. She said: "I should again kill my own son, and I will not go." Then my father, who was passionate, struck her with a dagger and would have killed her had they not rescued her from him. So she did not give me up, and later on she composed a song . . . but I need not tell that.'

'Yes, you must tell everything. It is necessary,' said Lóris-Mélikov.

Hadji Murád grew thoughtful. He remembered how his mother had laid him to sleep beside her under a fur coat on the roof of the *sáklya,* and he had asked her to show him the place in her side where the scar of her wound was still visible.

He repeated the song, which he remembered:

'My white bosom was pierced by the blade of bright steel,
But I laid my bright sun, my dear boy, close upon it
Till his body was bathed in the stream of my blood.
And the wound healed without aid of herbs or of grass.
As I feared not death, so my boy will ne'er fear it.'

'My mother is now in Shamil's hands,' he added, 'and she must be rescued.'

He remembered the fountain below the hill, when holding on to his mother's *sharováry* (loose Turkish trousers) he had gone with her for water. He remembered how she had shaved his head for the first time, and how the reflection of his round bluish head in the shining brass vessel that hung on the wall had astonished him. He remembered a lean dog that had licked his face. He remembered the strange smell of the *lepéshki* (a kind of flat cake) his mother had given him—a smell of smoke and of sour milk. He remembered how his mother had carried him in a basket on her back to visit his grandfather at the farmstead. He remembered his wrinkled grandfather with his grey hairs, and how he had hammered silver with his sinewy hands.

'Well, so my mother did not go as nurse,' he said with a jerk of his head, 'and the Khansha took another nurse but still remained fond of my mother, and my mother used to take us children to the Khansha's palace, and we played with her children and she was fond of us.

'There were three young Khans: Abu Nutsal Khan my brother Osman's foster-brother; Umma Khan my own sworn brother; and Bulách Khan the youngest—whom Shamil threw over the precipice. But that happened later.

'I was about sixteen when *murids* began to visit the *aouls.* They beat the stones with wooden scimitars and cried, "Mussulmans, *Ghazavát!*" The Chechens all went over to Muridism and the Avars began to go over too. I was then living in the palace like a brother of the Khans.

I could do as I liked, and I became rich. I had horses and weapons and money. I lived for pleasure and had no care, and went on like that till the time when Kazi-Mulla, the Imám, was killed and Hamzád succeeded him. Hamzád sent envoys to the Khans to say that if they did not join the *Ghazavát* he would destroy Khunzákh.

'This needed consideration. The Khans feared the Russians, but were also afraid to join in the Holy War. The old Khansha sent me with her second son, Umma Khan, to Tiflis to ask the Russian Commander-in-Chief for help against Hamzád. The Commander-in-Chief at Tiflis was Baron Rosen. He did not receive either me or Umma Khan. He sent word that he would help us, but did nothing. Only his officers came riding to us and played cards with Umma Khan. They made him drunk with wine and took him to bad places, and he lost all he had to them at cards. His body was as strong as a bull's and he was as brave as a lion, but his soul was weak as water. He would have gambled away his last horses and weapons if I had not made him come away.

'After visiting Tiflis my ideas changed and I advised the old Khansha and the Khans to join the *Ghazavát.* . . .'

'What made you change your mind?' asked Lóris-Mélikov. 'Were you not pleased with the Russians?'

Hadji Murád paused.

'No, I was not pleased,' he answered decidedly, closing his eyes. 'And there was also another reason why I wished to join the *Ghazavát.*'

'What was that?'

'Why, near Tselméss the Khan and I encountered three *murids,* two of whom escaped but the third one I shot with my pistol.

'He was still alive when I approached to take his weapons. He looked up at me, and said, "Thou hast killed me . . . I am happy; but thou art a Mussulman, young and strong. Join the *Ghazavát!* God wills it!"'

'And did you join it?'

'I did not, but it made me think,' said Hadji Murád, and he went on with his tale.

'When Hamzád approached Khunzákh we sent our Elders to him to say that we would agree to join the *Ghazavát* if the Imám would send a learned man to explain it to us. Hamzád had our Elders' moustaches shaved off, their nostrils pierced, and cakes hung to their noses, and in that condition he sent them back to us.

'The Elders brought word that Hamzád was ready to send a sheik to teach us the *Ghazavát*, but only if the Khansha sent him her youngest son as a hostage. She took him at his word and sent her youngest son, Bulách Khan. Hamzád received him well and sent to invite the two elder brothers also. He sent word that he wished to serve the Khans as his father had served their father. . . . The Khansha was a weak, stupid, and conceited woman, as all women are when they are not under control. She was afraid to send away both sons and sent only Umma Khan. I went with him. We were met by *murids* about a mile before we arrived and they sang and shot and caracoled around us, and when we drew near, Hamzád came out of his tent and went up to Umma Khan's stirrup and received him as a Khan. He said, "I have not done any harm to thy family and do not wish to do any. Only do not kill me and do not prevent my bringing the people over to the *Ghazavát*, and I will serve you with my whole army as my father served your father! Let me live in your house and I will help you with my advice, and you shall do as you like!"

'Umma Khan was slow of speech. He did not know how to reply and remained silent. Then I said that if this was so, let Hamzád come to Khunzákh and the Khansha and the Khans would receive him with honour. . . . But I was not allowed to finish—and here I first encountered Shamil, who was beside the Imám. He said to me, "Thou hast not been asked. . . . It was the Khan!"

'I was silent, and Hamzád led Umma Khan into his tent. Afterwards Hamzád called me and ordered me to go to Khunzákh with his envoys. I went. The envoys began persuading the Khansha to send her eldest son also to Hamzád. I saw there was treachery and told her not to send him; but a woman has as much sense in her head as an egg has hair. She ordered her son to go. Abu Nutsal Khan did not wish to. Then she said, "I see thou art afraid!" Like a bee she knew where to sting him most painfully. Abu Nutsal Khan flushed and did not speak to her any more, but ordered his horse to be saddled. I went with him.

'Hamzád met us with even greater honour than he had

shown Umma Khan. He himself rode out two rifle-shot lengths down the hill to meet us. A large party of horsemen with their banners followed him, and they too sang, shot, and caracoled.

'When we reached the camp, Hamzád led the Khan into his tent and I remained with the horses. . . .

'I was some way down the hill when I heard shots fired in Hamzád's tent. I ran there and saw Umma Khan lying prone in a pool of blood, and Abu Nutsal was fighting the *murids*. One of his cheeks had been hacked off and hung down. He supported it with one hand and with the other stabbed with his dagger at all who came near him. I saw him strike down Hamzád's brother and aim a blow at another man, but then the *murids* fired at him and he fell.'

Hadji Murád stopped and his sunburnt face flushed a dark red and his eyes became bloodshot.

'I was seized with fear and ran away.'

'Really? . . . I thought thou never wast afraid,' said Lóris-Mélikov.

'Never after that. . . . Since then I have always remembered that shame, and when I recalled it I feared nothing!'

XII

'But enough! It is time for me to pray,' said Hadji Murád drawing from an inner breast-pocket of his Circassian coat Vorontsóv's repeater watch and carefully pressing the spring. The repeater struck twelve and a quarter. Hadji Murád listened with his head on one side, repressing a childlike smile.

'*Kunák* Vorontsóv's present,' he said, smiling.

'It is a good watch,' said Lóris-Mélikov. 'Well then, go thou and pray, and I will wait.'

'*Yakshí*. Very well,' said Hadji Murád and went to his bedroom.

Left by himself, Lóris-Mélikov wrote down in his notebook the chief things Hadji Murád had related, and then lighting a cigarette began to pace up and down the room. On reaching the door opposite the bedroom he heard animated voices speaking rapidly in Tartar. He guessed that the speakers were Hadji Murád's *murids*, and opening the door he went in to them.

The room was impregnated with that special leathery

acid smell peculiar to the mountaineers. On a *búrka* spread
out on the floor sat the one-eyed, red-haired Gamzálo, in
a tattered greasy *beshmét*, plaiting a bridle. He was saying
something excitedly, speaking in a hoarse voice, but when
Lóris-Mélikov entered he immediately became silent and
continued his work without paying any attention to him.

In front of Gamzálo stood the merry Khan Mahomá
showing his white teeth, his black lashless eyes glittering,
and saying something over and over again. The handsome
Eldár, his sleeves turned up on his strong arms, was polish-
ing the girths of a saddle suspended from a nail. Khanéfi,
the principal worker and manager of the household, was not
there, he was cooking their dinner in the kitchen.

'What were you disputing about?' asked Lóris-Mélikov
after greeting them.

'Why, he keeps on praising Shamil,' said Khan Mahomá
giving his hand to Lóris-Mélikov. 'He says Shamil is a
great man, learned, holy, and a *dzhigít*.'

'How is it that he has left him and still praises him?'

'He has left him and still praises him,' repeated Khan
Mahomá, his teeth showing and his eyes glittering.

'And does he really consider him a saint?' asked Lóris-
Mélikov.

'If he were not a saint the people would not listen to
him,' said Gamzálo rapidly.

'Shamil is no saint, but Mansúr was!' replied Khan
Mahomá. 'He was a real saint. When he was Imám the
people were quite different. He used to ride through the
aouls and the people used to come out and kiss the hem
of his coat and confess their sins and vow to do no evil.
Then all the people—so the old men say—lived like saints:
not drinking, nor smoking, nor neglecting their prayers,
and forgiving one another their sins even when blood had
been spilt. If anyone then found money or anything, he
tied it to a stake and set it up by the roadside. In those
days God gave the people success in everything—not as
now.'

'In the mountains they don't smoke or drink now,' said
Gamzálo.

'Your Shamil is a *lamorey*,' said Khan Mahomá, winking at Lóris-Mélikov. (*Lamorey* was a contemptuous term
for a mountaineer.)

'Yes, *lamorey* means mountaineer,' replied Gamzálo.
'It is in the mountains that the eagles dwell.'

'Smart fellow! Well hit!' said Khan Mahomá with a grin, pleased at his adversary's apt retort.

Seeing the silver cigarette-case in Lóris-Mélikov's hand, Khan Mahomá asked for a cigarette, and when Lóris-Mélikov remarked that they were forbidden to smoke, he winked with one eye and jerking his head in the direction of Hadji Murád's bedroom replied that they could do it as long as they were not seen. He at once began smoking —not inhaling—and pouting his red lips awkwardly as he blew out the smoke.

'That is wrong!' said Gamzálo severely, and left the room. Khan Mahomá winked in his direction, and while smoking asked Lóris-Mélikov where he could best buy a silk *beshmét* and a white cap.

'Why, hast thou so much money?'

'I have enough,' replied Khan Mahomá with a wink.

'Ask him where he got the money,' said Eldár, turning his handsome smiling face towards Lóris-Mélikov.

'Oh, I won it!' said Khan Mahomá quickly, and related how while walking in Tiflis the day before he had come upon a group of men—Russians and Armenians—playing at *orlyánka* (a kind of heads-and-tails). The stake was a large one: three gold pieces and much silver. Khan Mahomá at once saw what the game consisted in, and jingling the coppers he had in his pocket he went up to the players and said he would stake the whole amount.

'How couldst thou do it? Hadst thou so much?' asked Lóris-Mélikov.

'I had only twelve kopeks,' said Khan Mahomá, grinning.

'But if thou hadst lost?'

'Why, this!' said Khan Mahomá pointing to his pistol.

'Wouldst thou have given that?'

'Give it indeed! I should have run away, and if anyone had tried to stop me I should have killed him—that's all!'

'Well, and didst thou win?'

'Aye, I won it all and went away!'

Lóris-Mélikov quite understood what sort of men Khan Mahomá and Eldár were. Khan Mahomá was a merry fellow, careless and ready for any spree. He did not know what to do with his superfluous vitality. He was always gay and reckless, and played with his own and other people's lives. For the sake of that sport with life he had now come over to the Russians, and for the same sport he might go back to Shamil to-morrow.

Eldár was also quite easy to understand. He was a man entirely devoted to his *murshíd;* calm, strong, and firm.

The red-haired Gamzálo was the only one Lóris-Mélikov did not understand. He saw that that man was not only loyal to Shamil but felt an insuperable aversion, contempt, repugnance, and hatred for all Russians, and Lóris-Mélikov could therefore not understand why he had come over to them. It occurred to him that, as some of the higher officials suspected, Hadji Murád's surrender and his tales of hatred of Shamil might be false, and that perhaps he had surrendered only to spy out the Russians' weak spots that, after escaping back to the mountains, he might be able to direct his forces accordingly. Gamzálo's whole person strengthened this suspicion.

'The others, and Hadji Murád himself, know how to hide their intentions, but this one betrays them by his open hatred,' thought he.

Lóris-Mélikov tried to speak to him. He asked whether he did not feel dull. 'No, I don't!' he growled hoarsely without stopping his work, and glancing at his questioner out of the corner of his one eye. He replied to all Lóris-Mélikov's other questions in a similar manner.

While Lóris-Mélikov was in the room Hadji Murád's fourth *murid* came in, the Avar Khanéfi; a man with a hairy face and neck and an arched chest as rough as if it were overgrown with moss. He was strong and a hard worker, always engrossed in his duties, and like Eldár unquestioningly obedient to his master.

When he entered the room to fetch some rice, Lóris-Mélikov stopped him and asked where he came from and how long he had been with Hadji Murád.

'Five years,' replied Khanéfi. 'I come from the same *aoul* as he. My father killed his uncle and they wished to kill me,' he said calmly, looking from under his joined eyebrows straight into Lóris-Mélikov's face. 'Then I asked them to adopt me as a brother.'

'What do you mean by "adopt as a brother"?'

'I did not shave my head nor cut my nails for two months, and then I came to them. They let me in to Patimát, his mother, and she gave me the breast and I became his brother.'

Hadji Murád's voice could be heard from the next room and Eldár, immediately answering his call, promptly wiped his hands and went with large strides into the drawing-room.

'He asks thee to come,' said he, coming back.

Lóris-Mélikov gave another cigarette to the merry Khan Mahomá and went into the drawing-room.

XIII

When Lóris-Mélikov entered the drawing-room Hadji Murád received him with a bright face.

'Well, shall I continue?' he asked, sitting down comfortably on the divan.

'Yes, certainly,' said Lóris-Mélikov. 'I have been in to have a talk with thy henchmen. . . . One is a jolly fellow!' he added.

'Yes, Khan Mahomá is a frivolous fellow,' said Hadji Murád.

'I liked the young handsome one.'

'Ah, that's Eldár. He's young but firm—made of iron!'

They were silent for a while.

'So I am to go on?'

'Yes, yes!'

'I told thee how the Khans were killed. . . . Well, having killed them Hamzád rode into Khunzákh and took up his quarters in their palace. The Khansha was the only one of the family left alive. Hamzád sent for her. She reproached him, so he winked to his *murid* Aseldár, who struck her from behind and killed her.'

'Why did he kill her?' asked Lóris-Mélikov.

'What could he do? . . . Where the forelegs have gone the hind legs must follow! He killed off the whole family. Shamil killed the youngest son—threw him over a precipice. . . .

'Then the whole of Avaria surrendered to Hamzád. But my brother and I would not surrender. We wanted his blood for the blood of the Khans. We pretended to yield, but our only thought was how to get his blood. We consulted our grandfather and decided to await the time when he would come out of his palace, and then to kill him from an ambush. Someone overheard us and told Hamzád, who sent for grandfather and said, "Mind, if it be true that thy grandsons are planning evil against me, thou and they shall hang from one rafter. I do God's work and cannot be hindered. . . . Go, and remember what I have said!"

'Our grandfather came home and told us.

'Then we decided not to wait but to do the deed on the first day of the feast in the mosque. Our comrades would not take part in it but my brother and I remained firm.

'We took two pistols each, put on our *búrkas*, and went to the mosque. Hamzád entered the mosque with thirty *murids*. They all had drawn swords in their hands. Aseldár, his favourite *murid* (the one who had cut off Khansha's head), saw us, shouted to us to take off our *búrkas*, and came towards me. I had my dagger in my hand and I killed him with it and rushed at Hamzád; but my brother Osman had already shot him. He was still alive and rushed at my brother dagger in hand, but I gave him a finishing blow on the head. There were thirty *murids* and we were only two. They killed my brother Osman, but I kept them at bay, leapt through the window, and escaped.

'When it was known that Hamzád had been killed all the people rose. The *murids* fled and those of them who did not flee were killed.'

Hadji Murád paused, and breathed heavily.

'That was very good,' he continued, 'but afterwards everything was spoilt.

'Shamil succeeded Hamzád. He sent envoys to me to say that I should join him in attacking the Russians, and that if I refused he would destroy Khunzákh and kill me.

'I answered that I would not join him and would not let him come to me. . . .'

'Why didst thou not go with him?' asked Lóris-Mélikov.

Hadji Murád frowned and did not reply at once.

'I could not. The blood of my brother Osman and of Abu Nutsal Khan was on his hands. I did not go to him. General Rosen sent me an officer's commission and ordered me to govern Avaria. All this would have been well but that Rosen appointed as Khan of Kazi-Kumúkh, first Mahómet-Murza, and afterwards Akhmet Khan, who hated me. He had been trying to get the Khansha's daughter, Sultanetta, in marriage for his son, but she would not give her to him, and he believed me to be the cause of this. . . . Yes, Akhmet Khan hated me and sent his henchmen to kill me, but I escaped from them. Then he spoke ill of me to General Klügenau. He said that I told the Avars not to supply wood to the Russian soldiers, and he also said that I had donned a turban—this one' (Hadji Murád touched his turban) 'and that this meant that I had gone over to Shamil. The general did not believe him and gave orders that I should not be touched. But when the general went to Tiflis, Akhmet Khan did as he pleased. He sent a company of soldiers to seize me, put me in chains, and tied me to a cannon.

'So they kept me six days,' he continued. 'On the seventh day they untied me and started to take me to Temir-Khan-Shurá. Forty soldiers with loaded guns had me in charge. My hands were tied and I knew that they had orders to kill me if I tried to escape.

'As we approached Mansokha the path became narrow, and on the right was an abyss about a hundred and twenty yards deep. I went to the right—to the very edge. A soldier wanted to stop me, but I jumped down and pulled him with me. He was killed outright but I, as you see, remained alive.

'Ribs, head, arms, and leg—all were broken! I tried to crawl but grew giddy and fell asleep. I awoke wet with blood. A shepherd saw me and called some people who carried me to an *aoul*. My ribs and head healed, and my leg too, only it has remained short,' and Hadji Murád stretched out his crooked leg. 'It still serves me, however, and that is well,' said he.

'The people heard the news and began coming to me. I recovered and went to Tselméss. The Avars again called on me to rule over them,' he went on, with tranquil, confident pride, 'and I agreed.'

He rose quickly and taking a portfolio out of a saddlebag, drew out two discoloured letters and handed one of them to Lóris-Mélikov. They were from General Klügenau. Lóris-Mélikov read the first letter, which was as follows:

'Lieutenant Hadji Murád, thou hast served under me and I was satisfied with thee and considered thee a good man.

'Recently Akhmet Khan informed me that thou art a traitor, that thou hast donned a turban and hast intercourse with Shamil, and that thou hast taught the people to disobey the Russian Government. I ordered thee to be arrested and brought before me but thou fledst. I do not know whether this is for thy good or not, as I do not know whether thou art guilty or not.

'Now hear me. If thy conscience is pure, if thou art not guilty in anything towards the great Tsar, come to me, fear no one. I am thy defender. The Khan can do nothing to thee, he is himself under my command, so thou hast nothing to fear.'

Klügenau added that he always kept his word and was just, and he again exhorted Hadji Murád to appear before him.

When Lóris-Mélikov had read this letter Hadji Murád, before handing him the second one, told him what he had written in reply to the first.

'I wrote that I wore a turban not for Shamil's sake but for my soul's salvation; that I neither wished nor could go over to Shamil, because he had caused the death of my father, my brothers, and my relations; but that I could not join the Russians because I had been dishonoured by them. (In Khunzákh, a scoundrel had spat on me while I was bound, and I could not join your people until that man was killed.) But above all I feared that liar, Akhmet Khan.

'Then the general sent me this letter,' said Hadji Murád, handing Lóris-Mélikov the other discoloured paper.

'Thou hast answered my first letter and I thank thee,' read Lóris-Mélikov. 'Thou writest that thou art not afraid to return but that the insult done thee by a certain giaour prevents it, but I assure thee that the Russian law is just and that thou shalt see him who dared to offend thee punished before thine eyes. I have already given orders to investigate the matter.

'Hear me, Hadji Murád! I have a right to be displeased with thee for not trusting me and my honour, but I forgive thee, for I know how suspicious mountaineers are in general. If thy conscience is pure, if thou hast put on a turban only for thy soul's salvation, then thou art right and mayst look me and the Russian Government boldly in the eye. He who dishonoured thee shall, I assure thee, be punished and *thy property shall be restored to thee*, and thou shalt see and know what Russian law is. Moreover we Russians look at things differently, and thou hast not sunk in our eyes because some scoundrel has dishonoured thee.

'I myself have consented to the Chimrints wearing turbans, and I regard their actions in the right light, and therefore I repeat that thou hast nothing to fear. Come to me with the man by whom I am sending thee this letter.

He is faithful to me and is not the slave of thy enemies, but is the friend of a man who enjoys the special favour of the Government.'

Further on Klügenau again tried to persuade Hadji Murád to come over to him.

'I did not believe him,' said Hadji Murád when Lóris-Mélikov had finished reading, 'and did not go to Klügenau. The chief thing for me was to revenge myself on Akhmet Khan, and that I could not do through the Russians. Then Akhmet Khan surrounded Tselméss and wanted to take me or kill me. I had too few men and could not drive him off, and just then came an envoy with a letter from Shamil promising to help me to defeat and kill Akhmet Khan and making me ruler over the whole of Avaria. I considered the matter for a long time and then went over to Shamil, and from that time I have fought the Russians continually.'

Here Hadji Murád related all his military exploits, of which there were very many and some of which were already familiar to Lóris-Mélikov. All his campaigns and raids had been remarkable for the extraordinary rapidity of his movements and the boldness of his attacks, which were always crowned with success.

'There never was any friendship between me and Shamil,' said Hadji Murád at the end of his story, 'but he feared me and needed me. But it so happened that I was asked who should be Imám after Shamil, and I replied: "He will be Imám whose sword is sharpest!"

'This was told to Shamil and he wanted to get rid of me. He sent me into Tabasarán. I went, and captured a thousand sheep and three hundred horses, but he said I had not done the right thing and dismissed me from being *Naïb*, and ordered me to send him all the money. I sent him a thousand gold pieces. He sent his *murids* and they took from me all my property. He demanded that I should go to him, but I knew he wanted to kill me and I did not go. Then he sent to take me. I resisted and went over to Vorontsóv. Only I did not take my family. My mother, my wives, and my son are in his hands. Tell the Sirdar that as long as my family is in Shamil's power I can do nothing.'

'I will tell him,' said Lóris-Mélikov.

'Take pains, try hard! . . . What is mine is thine, only help me with the Prince! I am tied up and the end of the rope is in Shamil's hands,' said Hadji Murád concluding his story.

XIV

On the 20th of December Vorontsóv wrote to Chernyshóv, the Minister of War. The letter was in French:

'I did not write to you by the last post, dear Prince, as I wished first to decide what we should do with Hadji Murád, and for the last two or three days I have not been feeling quite well.

'In my last letter I informed you of Hadji Murád's arrival here. He reached Tiflis on the 8th, and next day I made his acquaintance, and during the following seven or eight days have spoken to him and considered what use we can make of him in the future, and especially what we are to do with him at present, for he is much concerned about the fate of his family, and with every appearance of perfect frankness says that while they are in Shamil's hands he is paralysed and cannot render us any service or show his gratitude for the friendly reception and forgiveness we have extended to him.

'His uncertainty about those dear to him makes him restless, and the persons I have appointed to live with him assure me that he does not sleep at night, eats hardly anything, prays continually, and asks only to be allowed to ride out accompanied by several Cossacks—the sole recreation and exercise possible for him and made necessary to him by life-long habit. Every day he comes to me to know whether I have any news of his family, and to ask me to have all the prisoners in our hands collected and offered to Shamil in exchange for them. He would also give a little money. There are people who would let him have some for the purpose. He keeps repeating to me: "Save my family and then give me a chance to serve thee" (preferably, in his opinion, on the Lesghian line), "and if within a month I do not render you great service, punish me as you think fit." I reply that to me all this appears very just, and that many among us would even not trust him so long as his family remain in the mountains and are not in our hands as hostages, and that I will do everything possible to collect the prisoners on our frontier, that I have no power under our laws to give him money for the ransom of his family in addition to the sum he may himself be able to raise, but that I may perhaps find some other means of helping him. After that I told him frankly that in my opinion Shamil would not in any case give up the family, and that Shamil might tell him so straight out and promise him a full pardon and his former posts, and might threaten if Hadji Murád did not return, to kill his mother, his wives, and his six children. I asked him whether he could say frankly what he would do if he received such an announcement from Shamil. He lifted his eyes and arms to heaven, and said that everything is in God's hands, but that he would never surrender to his foe, for he is certain Shamil would not forgive him and he would therefore not have long to live. As to the destruction of his family, he did not think Shamil would act so rashly: firstly, to avoid making him a yet more desperate and dangerous foe, and secondly, because there were many people, and even very influential people, in Daghestan, who would dissuade Shamil from such a course. Finally, he repeated several times that whatever God might decree for him in the future, he was at present interested in nothing but his family's ransom, and he implored me in God's name to help him and allow him to return to the neighbourhood of the Chechnya, where he could, with the help and consent of our commanders, have some intercourse with his family and regular news of their condition and of the best means to liberate them. He said that many people, and even some *Naïbs* in that part of the enemy's territory, were more or less attached to him, and that among the whole of the population already subjugated by Russia or neutral it would be easy with our help to establish relations very useful for the attainment of the aim which gives him no peace day or night, and the attainment of which would set him at ease and make it possible for him to act for our good and win our confidence.

'He asks to be sent back to Grózny with a convoy of twenty or thirty picked Cossacks who would serve him as a protection against foes and us as a guarantee of his good faith.

'You will understand, dear Prince, that I have been much perplexed by all this, for do what I will a great responsibility rests on me. It would be in the highest degree rash to trust him entirely, yet in order to deprive him of all means of escape we should have to lock him up, and in my opinion that would be both unjust and impolitic. A measure of that kind, the news of which would soon spread over the whole of Daghestan, would do us great harm by keeping back those who are now inclined more or less openly to oppose Shamil (and there are many such), and who are keenly watching to see how we treat the Imám's bravest and most adventurous officer now that he has found himself obliged to place himself in our hands. If we treat Hadji Murád as a prisoner all the good effect of the situation will be lost. Therefore I think that I could not act otherwise than as I have done, though at the same time I feel that I may be accused of having made a great mistake if Hadji Murád should take it into his head to escape again. In the service, and especially in a complicated situation such as this, it is difficult, not to say impossible, to follow any one straight path without risking mistakes and without accepting responsibility, but once a path seems to be the right one I must follow it, happen what may.

'I beg of you, dear Prince, to submit this to his Majesty the Emperor for his consideration; and I shall be happy if it pleases our most august monarch to approve my action.

'All that I have written above I have also written to Generals Zavodóvsky and Kozlóvsky, to guide the latter when communicating direct with Hadji Murád whom I have warned not to act or go anywhere without Kozlóvsky's consent. I also told him that it would be all the better for us if he rode out with our convoy, as otherwise Shamil might spread a rumour that we were keeping him prisoner, but at the same time I made him promise never to go to Vozdvízhensk, because my son, to whom he first surrendered and whom he looks upon as his *kunák* (friend), is not the commander of that place and some unpleasant misunderstanding might easily arise. In any case Vozdvízhensk lies too near a thickly populated hostile settlement, while for the intercourse with his friends which he desires, Grózny is in all respects suitable.

'Besides the twenty chosen Cossacks who at his own request are to keep close to him, I am also sending Captain Lóris-Mélikov—a worthy, excellent, and highly intelligent officer who speaks Tartar, and knows Hadji Murád well and apparently enjoys his full confidence. During the ten days that Hadji Murád has spent here, he has, however, lived in the same house with Lieutenant-Colonel Prince Tarkhánov, who is in command of the Shoushín District and is here on business connected with the service. He is a truly worthy man whom I trust entirely. He also has won Hadji Murád's confidence, and through him alone—as he speaks Tartar perfectly—we have discussed the most delicate and secret matters. I have consulted Tarkhánov about Hadji Murád, and he fully agrees with me that it was necessary either to act as I have done, or to put Hadji Murád in prison and guard him in the strictest manner (for if we once treat him badly he will not be easy to hold), or else to remove him from the country altogether. But these two last measures would not only destroy all the advantage accruing to us from Hadji Murád's quarrel with Shamil, but would inevitably check any growth of the present insubordination, and possible future revolt, of the people against Shamil's power. Prince Tarkhánov tells me he himself has no doubt of Hadji Murád's truthfulness, and that Hadji Murád is convinced that Shamil will never forgive him but would have him executed in spite of any promise of forgiveness. The only thing Tarkhánov has noticed in his intercourse with Hadji Murád that might cause any anxiety, is his attachment to his religion. Tarkhánov does not deny that Shamil might influence Hadji Murád from that side. But as I have already said, he will never persuade Hadji Murád that he will not take his life sooner or later should the latter return to him.

'This, dear Prince, is all I have to tell you about this episode in our affairs here.'

XV

The report was dispatched from Tiflis on the 24th of December 1851, and on New Year's Eve a courier, having overdriven a dozen horses and beaten a dozen drivers till they bled, delivered it to Prince Chernyshóv who at that time was Minister of War; and on the 1st of January 1852 Chernyshóv took Vorontsóv's report, among other papers, to the Emperor Nicholas.

Chernyshóv disliked Vorontsóv because of the general respect in which the latter was held and because of his immense wealth, and also because Vorontsóv was a real aristocrat while Chernyshóv, after all, was a *parvenu*, but especially because the Emperor was particularly well disposed towards Vorontsóv. Therefore at every opportunity Chernyshóv tried to injure Vorontsóv.

When he had last presented a report about Caucasian

affairs he had succeeded in arousing Nicholas's displeasure against Vorontsóv because—through the carelessness of those in command—almost the whole of a small Caucasian detachment had been destroyed by the mountaineers. He now intended to present the steps taken by Vorontsóv in relation to Hadji Murád in an unfavourable light. He wished to suggest to the Emperor that Vorontsóv always protected and even indulged the natives to the detriment of the Russians, and that he had acted unwisely in allowing Hadji Murád to remain in the Caucasus for there was every reason to suspect that he had only come over to spy on our means of defence, and that it would therefore be better to transport him to Central Russia and make use of him only after his family had been rescued from the mountaineers and it had become possible to convince ourselves of his loyalty.

Chernyshóv's plan did not succeed merely because on that New Year's Day Nicholas was in particularly bad spirits, and out of perversity would not have accepted any suggestion whatever from anyone, least of all from Chernyshóv whom he only tolerated—regarding him as indispensable for the time being but looking upon him as a blackguard, for Nicholas knew of his endeavours at the trial of the Decembrists to secure the conviction of Zacháry Chernyshóv, and of his attempt to obtain Zacháry's property for himself. So thanks to Nicholas's ill temper Hadji Murád remained in the Caucasus, and his circumstances were not changed as they might have been had Chernyshóv presented his report at another time.

* * *

It was half-past nine o'clock when through the mist of the cold morning (the thermometer showed 13 degrees below zero Fahrenheit) Chernyshóv's fat, bearded coachman, sitting on the box of a small sledge (like the one Nicholas drove about in) with a sharp-angled, cushion-shaped azure velvet cap on his head, drew up at the entrance of the Winter Palace and gave a friendly nod to his chum, Prince Dolgorúky's coachman—who having brought his master to the palace had himself long been waiting outside, in his big coat with the thickly wadded skirts, sitting on the reins and rubbing his numbed hands together. Chernyshóv had on a long cloak with a large cape and a fluffy collar of silver beaver, and a regulation three-cornered hat with cocks' feathers. He threw back the bearskin apron of the sledge and carefully disengaged his chilled feet, on which he had no over-shoes (he prided himself on never wearing any). Clanking his spurs with an air of bravado he ascended the carpeted steps and passed through the hall door which was respectfully opened for him by the porter, and entered the hall. Having thrown off his cloak which an old Court lackey hurried forward to take, he went to a mirror and carefully removed the hat from his curled wig. Looking at himself in the mirror, he arranged the hair on his temples and the tuft above his forehead with an accustomed movement of his old hands, and adjusted his cross, the shoulder-knots of his uniform, and his large-initialled epaulets, and then went up the gently ascending carpeted stairs, his not very reliable old legs feebly mounting the shallow steps. Passing the Court lackeys in gala livery who stood obsequiously bowing, Chernyshóv entered the waiting-room. He was respectfully met by a newly appointed aide-de-camp of the Emperor's in a shining new uniform with epaulets and shoulder-knots, whose face was still fresh and rosy and who had a small black moustache, and the hair on his temples brushed towards his eyes in the same way as the Emperor.

Prince Vasíli Dolgorúky, Assistant-Minister of War, with an expression of *ennui* on his dull face—which was ornamented with similar whiskers, moustaches, and temple tufts brushed forward like Nicholas's—greeted him.

'*L'empereur?*' said Chernyshóv, addressing the aide-de-camp and looking inquiringly towards the door leading to the cabinet.

'*Sa majesté vient de rentrer,*' replied the aide-de-camp, evidently enjoying the sound of his own voice, and stepping so softly and steadily that had a tumbler of water been placed on his head none of it would have been spilt, he approached the door and disappeared, his whole body evincing reverence for the spot he was about to visit.

Dolgorúky meanwhile opened his portfolio to see that it contained the necessary papers, while Chernyshóv, frowning, paced up and down to restore the circulation in his numbed feet, and thought over what he was about to report to the Emperor. He was near the door of the cabinet when it opened again and the aide-de-camp, even more radiant and respectful than before, came out and with a gesture invited the minister and his assistant to enter.

The Winter Palace had been rebuilt after a fire some considerable time before this, but Nicholas was still occupying rooms in the upper story. The cabinet in which he received the reports of his ministers and other high officials was a very lofty apartment with four large windows. A big portrait of the Emperor Alexander I hung on the front side of the room. Two bureaux stood between the windows, and several chairs were ranged along the walls. In the middle of the room was an enormous writing-table, with an arm-chair before it for Nicholas, and other chairs for those to whom he gave audience.

Nicholas sat at the table in a black coat with shoulder-straps but no epaulets, his enormous body—with his over-grown stomach tightly laced in—was thrown back, and he gazed at the newcomers with fixed, lifeless eyes. His long pale face, with its enormous receding forehead between the tufts of hair which were brushed forward and skilfully joined to the wig that covered his bald patch, was specially cold and stony that day. His eyes, always dim, looked duller than usual, the compressed lips under his upturned moustaches, the high collar which supported his chin, and his fat freshly shaven cheeks on which symmetrical sausage-shaped bits of whiskers had been left, gave his face a dissatisfied and even irate expression. His bad mood was caused by fatigue, due to the fact that he had been to a masquerade the night before, and while walking about as was his wont in his Horse Guards' uniform with a bird on the helmet, among the public which crowded round and timidly made way for his enormous, self-assured figure, he had again met the mask who at the previous masquerade had aroused his senile sensuality by her white-ness, her beautiful figure, and her tender voice. At that former masquerade she had disappeared after promising to meet him at the next one.

At yesterday's masquerade she had come up to him, and this time he had not let her go, but had led her to the box specially kept ready for that purpose, where he could be alone with her. Having arrived in silence at the door of the box Nicholas looked round to find the attendant, but he was not there. He frowned and pushed the door open himself, letting the lady enter first.

'*Il y a quelqu'un!*' said the mask, stopping short.

And the box actually was occupied. On the small velvet-covered sofa, close together, sat an Uhlan officer and a pretty, fair curly-haired young woman in a domino, who had removed her mask. On catching sight of the angry figure of Nicholas drawn up to its full height, she quickly replaced her mask, but the Uhlan officer, rigid with fear, gazed at Nicholas with fixed eyes without rising from the sofa.

Used as he was to the terror he inspired in others, that terror always pleased Nicholas, and by way of contrast he sometimes liked to astound those plunged in terror by addressing kindly words to them. He did so on this occasion.

'Well, friend!' said he to the officer, 'You are younger than I and might give up your place to me.'

The officer jumped to his feet, and growing first pale and then red and bending almost double, he followed his partner silently out of the box, leaving Nicholas alone with his lady.

She proved to be a pretty, twenty-year-old virgin, the daughter of a Swedish governess. She told Nicholas how when quite a child she had fallen in love with him from his portraits; how she adored him and had made up her mind to attract his attention at any cost. Now she had succeeded and wanted nothing more—so she said.

The girl was taken to the place where Nicholas usually had rendezvous with women, and there he spent more than an hour with her.

When he returned to his room that night and lay on the hard narrow bed about which he prided himself, and covered himself with the cloak which he considered to be (and spoke of as being) as famous as Napoleon's hat, it was a long time before he could fall asleep. He thought now of the frightened and elated expression on that girl's fair face, and now of the full, powerful shoulders of his established mistress, Nelídova, and he compared the two. That profligacy in a married man was a bad thing did not once enter his head, and he would have been greatly surprised had anyone censured him for it. Yet though convinced that he had acted rightly, some kind of unpleasant after-taste remained, and to stifle that feeling he dwelt on a thought that always tranquilized him—the thought of his own greatness.

Though he had fallen asleep so late, he rose before eight, and after attending to his toilet in the usual way—rubbing his big well-fed body all over with ice—and saying his prayers (repeating those he had been used to from childhood—the prayer to the Virgin, the Apostles' Creed, and the Lord's Prayer, without attaching any kind of meaning to the words he uttered), he went out through the smaller portico of the palace onto the embankment in his military cloak and cap.

On the embankment he met a student in the uniform of the School of Jurisprudence, who was as enormous as himself. On recognizing the uniform of that school, which he disliked for its freedom of thought, Nicholas frowned, but the stature of the student and the painstaking manner in which he drew himself up and saluted, ostentatiously sticking out his elbow, mollified his displeasure.

'Your name?' said he.

'Polosátov, your Imperial Majesty.'

'. . . fine fellow!'

The student continued to stand with his hand lifted to his hat.

Nicholas stopped.

'Do you wish to enter the army?'

'Not at all, your Imperial Majesty.'

'Blockhead!' And Nicholas turned away and continued his walk, and began uttering aloud the first words that came into his head.

'Kopervine . . . Kopervine——' he repeated several times (it was the name of yesterday's girl). 'Horrid . . . horrid——' He did not think of what he was saying, but stifled his feelings by listening to the words.

'Yes, what would Russia be without me?' said he, feeling his former dissatisfaction returning. 'What would—not Russia alone but Europe be, without me?' and calling to mind the weakness and stupidity of his brother-in-law the King of Prussia, he shook his head.

As he was returning to the small portico, he saw the carriage of Helena Pávlovna, with a red-liveried footman, approaching the Saltykóv entrance of the palace.

Helena Pávlovna was to him the personification of that futile class of people who discussed not merely science and poetry, but even the ways of governing men: imagining that they could govern themselves better than he, Nicholas, governed them! He knew that however much he crushed such people they reappeared again and again, and he recalled his brother, Michael Pávlovich, who had died not long before. A feeling of sadness and vexation came over him and with a dark frown he again began whispering the first words that came into his head, which he only ceased doing when he re-entered the palace.

On reaching his apartments he smoothed his whiskers and the hair on his temples and the wig on his bald patch, and twisted his moustaches upwards in front of the mirror, and then went straight to the cabinet in which he received reports.

He first received Chernyshóv, who at once saw by his face, and especially by his eyes, that Nicholas was in a particularly bad humour that day, and knowing about the adventure of the night before he understood the cause. Having coldly greeted him and invited him to sit down, Nicholas fixed on him a lifeless gaze. The first matter Chernyshóv reported upon was a case of embezzlement by commissariat officials which had just been discovered; the next was the movement of troops on the Prussian frontier; then came a list of rewards to be given at the New Year to some people omitted from a former list; then Vorontsóv's report about Hadji Murád; and lastly some unpleasant business concerning an attempt by a student of the Academy of Medicine on the life of a professor.

Nicholas heard the report of the embezzlement silently with compressed lips, his large white hand—with one ring on the fourth finger—stroking some sheets of paper, and his eyes steadily fixed on Chernyshóv's forehead and on the tuft of hair above it.

Nicholas was convinced that everybody stole. He knew he would have to punish the commissariat officials now, and decided to send them all to serve in the ranks, but he also knew that this would not prevent those who succeeded them from acting in the same way. It was a characteristic of officials to steal, but it was his duty to punish them for doing so, and tired as he was of that duty he conscientiously performed it.

'It seems there is only one honest man in Russia!' said he.

Chernyshóv at once understood that this one honest man was Nicholas himself, and smiled approvingly.

'It looks like it, your Imperial Majesty,' said he.

'Leave it—I will give a decision,' said Nicholas, taking the document and putting it on the left side of the table.

Then Chernyshóv reported the rewards to be given and about moving the army on the Prussian frontier.

Nicholas looked over the list and struck out some names, and then briefly and firmly gave orders to move two divisions to the Prussian frontier. He could not forgive the King of Prussia for granting a Constitution to his people after the events of 1848, and therefore while expressing most friendly feelings to his brother-in-law in letters and conversation, he considered it necessary to keep an army near the frontier in case of need. He might want to use these troops to defend his brother-in-law's throne if the people of Prussia rebelled (Nicholas saw a readiness for rebellion everywhere) as he had used troops to suppress the rising in Hungary a few years previously. They were also of use to give more weight and influence to such advice as he gave to the King of Prussia.

'Yes—what would Russia be like now if it were not for me?' he again thought.

'Well, what else is there?' said he.

'A courier from the Caucasus,' said Chernyshóv, and he reported what Vorontsóv had written about Hadji Murád's surrender.

'Well, well!' said Nicholas. 'It's a good beginning!'

'Evidently the plan devised by your Majesty begins to bear fruit,' said Chernyshóv.

This approval of his strategic talents was particularly pleasant to Nicholas because, though he prided himself upon them, at the bottom of his heart he knew that they did not really exist, and he now desired to hear more detailed praise of himself.

'How do you mean?' he asked.

'I mean that if your Majesty's plans had been adopted before, and we had moved forward slowly and steadily, cutting down forests and destroying the supplies of food, the Caucasus would have been subjugated long ago. I attribute Hadji Murád's surrender entirely to his having come to the conclusion that they can hold out no longer.'

'True,' said Nicholas.

Although the plan of a gradual advance into the enemy's territory by means of felling forests and destroying the food supplies was Ermólov's and Velyamínov's plan, and was quite contrary to Nicholas's own plan of seizing

Shamil's place of residence and destroying that nest of robbers—which was the plan on which the Dargo expedition in 1845 (that cost so many lives) had been undertaken—Nicholas nevertheless attributed to himself also the plan of a slow advance and a systematic felling of forests and devastation of the country. It would seem that to believe the plan of a slow movement by felling forests and destroying food supplies to have been his own would have necessitated hiding the fact that he had insisted on quite contrary operations in 1845. But he did not hide it and was proud of the plan of the 1845 expedition as well as of the plan of a slow advance—though the two were obviously contrary to one another. Continual brazen flattery from everybody round him in the teeth of obvious facts had brought him to such a state that he no longer saw his own inconsistencies or measured his actions and words by reality, logic, or even simple common sense; but was quite convinced that all his orders, however senseless, unjust, and mutually contradictory they might be, became reasonable, just, and mutually accordant simply because he gave them. His decision in the case next reported to him—that of the student of the Academy of Medicine—was of that senseless kind.

The case was as follows: A young man who had twice failed in his examinations was being examined a third time, and when the examiner again would not pass him, the young man whose nerves were deranged, considering this to be an injustice, seized a pen-knife from the table in a paroxysm of fury, and rushing at the professor inflicted on him several trifling wounds.

'What's his name?' asked Nicholas.

'Bzhezóvski.'

'A Pole?'

'Of Polish descent and a Roman Catholic,' answered Chernyshóv.

Nicholas frowned. He had done much evil to the Poles. To justify that evil he had to feel certain that all Poles were rascals, and he considered them to be such and hated them in proportion to the evil he had done them.

'Wait a little,' he said, closing his eyes and bowing his head.

Chernyshóv, having more than once heard Nicholas say so, knew that when the Emperor had to take a decision it

was only necessary for him to concentrate his attention
for a few moments and the spirit moved him, and the best
possible decision presented itself as though an inner voice
had told him what to do. He was now thinking how most
fully to satisfy the feeling of hatred against the Poles which
this incident had stirred up within him, and the inner
voice suggested the following decision. He took the report
and in his large handwriting wrote on its margin with
three orthographical mistakes:

'*Diserves deth; but, thank God, we have no capitle
punishment, and it is not for me to introduce it. Make him
run the gauntlet of a thousand men twelve times.—
Nicholas.*'

He signed, adding his unnaturally huge flourish.

Nicholas knew that twelve thousand strokes with the
regulation rods were not only certain death with torture,
but were a superfluous cruelty, for five thousand strokes
were sufficient to kill the strongest man. But it pleased him
to be ruthlessly cruel and it also pleased him to think that
we have abolished capital punishment in Russia.

Having written his decision about the student, he pushed
it across to Chernyshóv.

'There,' he said, 'read it.'

Chernyshóv read it, and bowed his head as a sign of respectful amazement at the wisdom of the decision.

'Yes, and let all the students be present on the drill-
ground at the punishment,' added Nicholas.

'It will do them good! I will abolish this revolutionary
spirit and will tear it up by the roots!' he thought.

'It shall be done,' replied Chernyshóv; and after a short
pause he straightened the tuft on his forehead and returned
to the Caucasian report.

'What do you command me to write in reply to Prince
Vorontsóv's dispatch?'

'To keep firmly to my system of destroying the dwellings
and food supplies in Chechnya and to harass them by
raids,' answered Nicholas.

'And what are your Majesty's commands with reference
to Hadji Murád?' asked Chernyshóv.

'Why, Vorontsóv writes that he wants to make use of
him in the Caucasus.'

'Is it not dangerous?' said Chernyshóv, avoiding Nicholas's gaze. 'Prince Vorontsóv is too confiding, I am afraid.'

'And you—what do you think?' asked Nicholas sharply, detecting Chernyshóv's intention of presenting Vorontsóv's decision in an unfavourable light.

'Well, I should have thought it would be safer to deport him to Central Russia.'

'You would have thought!' said Nicholas ironically. 'But I don't think so, and agree with Vorontsóv. Write to him accordingly.'

'It shall be done,' said Chernyshóv, rising and bowing himself out.

Dolgorúky also bowed himself out, having during the whole audience only uttered a few words (in reply to a question from Nicholas) about the movement of the army.

After Chernyshóv, Nicholas received Bíbikov, General-Governor of the Western Provinces. Having expressed his approval of the measures taken by Bíbikov against the mutinous peasants who did not wish to accept the Orthodox Faith, he ordered him to have all those who did not submit tried by court-martial. That was equivalent to sentencing them to run the gauntlet. He also ordered the editor of a newspaper to be sent to serve in the ranks of the army for publishing information about the transfer of several thousand State peasants to the Imperial estates.

'I do this because I consider it necessary,' said Nicholas, 'and I will not allow it to be discussed.'

Bíbikov saw the cruelty of the order concerning the Uniate peasants and the injustice of transferring State peasants (the only free peasants in Russia in those days) to the Crown, which meant making them serfs of the Imperial family. But it was impossible to express dissent. Not to agree with Nicholas's decisions would have meant the loss of that brilliant position which it had cost Bíbikov forty years to attain and which he now enjoyed; and he therefore submissively bowed his dark head (already touched with grey) to indicate his submission and his readiness to fulfil the cruel, insensate, and dishonest supreme will.

Having dismissed Bíbikov, Nicholas stretched himself, with a sense of duty well fulfilled, glanced at the clock, and went to get ready to go out. Having put on a uniform with epaulets, orders, and a ribbon, he went out into the reception hall where more than a hundred persons—men in uniforms and women in elegant low-necked dresses, all standing in the places assigned to them—awaited his arrival with agitation.

He came out to them with a lifeless look in his eyes, his chest expanded, his stomach bulging out above and below its bandages, and feeling everybody's gaze tremulously and obsequiously fixed upon him he assumed an even more triumphant air. When his eyes met those of people he knew, remembering who was who, he stopped and addressed a few words to them sometimes in Russian and sometimes in French, and transfixing them with his cold glassy eye listened to what they said.

Having received all the New Year congratulations he passed on to church, where God, through His servants the priests, greeted and praised Nicholas just as worldly people did; and weary as he was of these greetings and praises Nicholas duly accepted them. All this was as it should be, because the welfare and happiness of the whole world depended on him, and wearied though he was he would still not refuse the universe his assistance.

When at the end of the service the magnificently arrayed deacon, his long hair crimped and carefully combed, began the chant *Many Years*, which was heartily caught up by the splendid choir, Nicholas looked round and noticed Nelídova, with her fine shoulders, standing by a window, and he decided the comparison with yesterday's girl in her favour.

After Mass he went to the Empress and spent a few minutes in the bosom of his family, joking with the children and his wife. Then passing through the Hermitage, he visited the Minister of the Court, Volkónski, and among other things ordered him to pay out of a special fund a yearly pension to the mother of yesterday's girl. From there he went for his customary drive.

Dinner that day was served in the Pompeian Hall. Besides the younger sons of Nicholas and Michael there were also invited Baron Lieven, Count Rzhévski, Dolgorúky, the Prussian Ambassador, and the King of Prussia's aide-de-camp.

While waiting for the appearance of the Emperor and Empress an interesting conversation took place between Baron Lieven and the Prussian Ambassador concerning the disquieting news from Poland.

'*La Pologne et le Caucase, ce sont les deux cautères de la Russie,*' said Lieven. '*Il nous faut cent mille hommes à peu près, dans chacun de ces deux pays.*'

The Ambassador expressed a fictitious surprise that it should be so.

'*Vous dites, la Pologne—*' began the Ambassador.

'*Oh, oui, c'était un coup de maître de Metternich de nous en avoir laissé l'embarras. . . .*'

At this point the Empress, with her trembling head and fixed smile, entered followed by Nicholas.

At dinner Nicholas spoke of Hadji Murád's surrender and said that the war in the Caucasus must now soon come to an end in consequence of the measures he was taking to limit the scope of the mountaineers by felling their forests and by his system of erecting a series of small forts.

The Ambassador, having exchanged a rapid glance with the aide-de-camp—to whom he had only that morning spoken about Nicholas's unfortunate weakness for considering himself a great strategist—warmly praised this plan which once more demonstrated Nicholas's great strategic ability.

After dinner Nicholas drove to the ballet where hundreds of women marched round in tights and scanty clothing. One of them specially attracted him, and he had the German ballet-master sent for and gave orders that a diamond ring should be presented to her.

The next day when Chernyshóv came with his report, Nicholas again confirmed his order to Vorontsóv—that now that Hadji Murád had surrendered, the Chechens should be more actively harassed than ever and the cordon round them tightened.

Chernyshóv wrote in that sense to Vorontsóv; and another courier, overdriving more horses and bruising the faces of more drivers, galloped to Tiflis.

XVI

In obedience to this command of Nicholas a raid was immediately made in Chechnya that same month, January 1852.

The detachment ordered for the raid consisted of four infantry battalions, two companies of Cossacks, and eight guns. The column marched along the road; and on both sides of it in a continuous line, now mounting, now descending, marched *Fägers* in high boots, sheepskin coats, and tall caps, with rifles on their shoulders and cartridges in their belts.

As usual when marching through a hostile country, silence was observed as far as possible. Only occasionally the guns jingled jolting across a ditch, or an artillery horse snorted or neighed, not understanding that silence was ordered, or an angry commander shouted in a hoarse subdued voice to his subordinates that the line was spreading out too much or marching too near or too far from the column. Only once was the silence broken, when from a bramble patch between the line and the column a gazelle with a white breast and grey back jumped out followed by a buck of the same colour with small backward-curving horns. Doubling up their forelegs at each big bound they took, the beautiful timid creatures came so close to the column that some of the soldiers rushed after them laughing and shouting, intending to bayonet them, but the gazelles turned back, slipped through the line of *Fägers,* and pursued by a few horsemen and the company's dogs, fled like birds to the mountains.

It was still winter, but towards noon, when the column (which had started early in the morning) had gone three miles, the sun had risen high enough and was powerful enough to make the men quite hot, and its rays were so bright that it was painful to look at the shining steel of the bayonets or at the reflections—like little suns—on the brass of the cannons.

The clear and rapid stream the detachment had just crossed lay behind, and in front were tilled fields and meadows in shallow valleys. Farther in front were the dark mysterious forest-clad hills with crags rising beyond them, and farther still on the lofty horizon were the ever-beautiful ever-changing snowy peaks that played with the light like diamonds.

At the head of the 5th Company, Butler, a tall handsome officer who had recently exchanged from the Guards, marched along in a black coat and tall cap, shouldering his sword. He was filled with a buoyant sense of the joy of living, the danger of death, a wish for action, and the consciousness of being part of an immense whole directed by a single will. This was his second time of going into action and he thought how in a moment they would be fired at, and he would not only not stoop when the shells flew overhead, or heed the whistle of the bullets, but would carry his head even more erect than before and would look round at his comrades and the soldiers with smiling eyes, and begin to talk in a perfectly calm voice about quite other matters.

The detachment turned off the good road onto a little-used one that crossed a stubbly maize field, and they were drawing near the forest when, with an ominous whistle, a shell flew past amid the baggage wagons—they could not see whence—and tore up the ground in the field by the roadside.

'It's beginning,' said Butler with a bright smile to a comrade who was walking beside him.

And so it was. After the shell a thick crowd of mounted Chechens appeared with their banners from under the shelter of the forest. In the midst of the crowd could be seen a large green banner, and an old and very far-sighted sergeant-major informed the short-sighted Butler that Shamil himself must be there. The horsemen came down the hill and appeared to the right, at the highest part of the valley nearest the detachment, and began to descend. A little general in a thick black coat and tall cap rode up to Butler's company on his ambler, and ordered him to the right to encounter the descending horsemen. Butler quickly led his company in the direction indicated, but before he reached the valley he heard two cannon shots behind him. He looked round: two clouds of grey smoke had risen above two cannon and were spreading along the valley. The mountaineers' horsemen—who had evidently not expected to meet artillery—retired. Butler's company began firing at them and the whole ravine was filled with the smoke of powder. Only higher up above the ravine could the mountaineers be seen hurriedly retreating, though still firing back at the Cossacks who pursued them. The company followed the mountaineers farther, and on the slope of a second ravine came in view of an *aoul*.

Following the Cossacks, Butler and his company entered the *aoul* at a run, to find it deserted. The soldiers were ordered to burn the corn and the hay as well as the *sáklyas*, and the whole *aoul* was soon filled with pungent smoke amid which the soldiers rushed about dragging out of the *sáklyas* what they could find, and above all catching and shooting the fowls the mountaineers had not been able to take away with them.

The officers sat down at some distance beyond the smoke, and lunched and drank. The sergeant-major brought them some honeycombs on a board. There was no sign of any Chechens and early in the afternoon the order was given to retreat. The companies formed into a column behind the *aoul* and Butler happened to be in the rear-guard. As soon as they started Chechens appeared, following and firing at the detachment, but they ceased this pursuit as soon as they came out into an open space.

Not one of Butler's company had been wounded, and he returned in a most happy and energetic mood. When after fording the same stream it had crossed in the morning, the detachment spread over the maize fields and the meadows, the singers of each company came forward and songs filled the air.

'Very diff'rent, very diff'rent, *Fägers* are, *Fägers* are!' sang Butler's singers, and his horse stepped merrily to the music. Trezórka, the shaggy grey dog belonging to the company, ran in front, with his tail curled up with an air of responsibility like a commander. Butler felt buoyant, calm, and joyful. War presented itself to him as consisting only in his exposing himself to danger and to possible death, thereby gaining rewards and the respect of his comrades here, as well as of his friends in Russia. Strange to say, his imagination never pictured the other aspect of war: the death and wounds of the soldiers, officers, and mountaineers. To retain his poetic conception he even unconsciously avoided looking at the dead and wounded. So that day when we had three dead and twelve wounded, he passed by a corpse lying on its back and did not stop to look, seeing only with one eye the strange position of the waxen hand and a dark red spot on the head. The hillsmen appeared to him only a mounted *dzhigits* from whom he had to defend himself.

'You see, my dear sir,' said his major in an interval between two songs, 'it's not as it is with you in Petersburg—"Eyes right! Eyes left!" Here we have done our job, and now we go home and Másha will set a pie and some nice cabbage soup before us. That's life—don't you think so? —Now then! *As the Dawn Was Breaking!*' He called for his favourite song.

There was no wind, the air was fresh and clear and so
transparent that the snow hills nearly a hundred miles
away seemed quite near, and in the intervals between the
songs the regular sound of the footsteps and the jingle
of the guns was heard as a background on which each song
began and ended. The song that was being sung in Butler's
company was composed by a cadet in honour of the
regiment, and went to a dance tune. The chorus was:
'Very diff'rent, very diff'rent, *Fägers* are, *Fägers* are!'

Butler rode beside the officer next in rank above him,
Major Petróv, with whom he lived, and he felt he could
not be thankful enough to have exchanged from the Guards
and come to the Caucasus. His chief reason for exchanging was that he had lost all he had at cards and was afraid
that if he remained there he would be unable to resist
playing though he had nothing more to lose. Now all that
was over, his life was quite changed and was such a
pleasant and brave one! He forgot that he was ruined,
and forgot his unpaid debts. The Caucasus, the war, the
soldiers, the officers—those tipsy, brave, good-natured fellows—and Major Petróv himself, all seemed so delightful
that sometimes it appeared too good to be true that he
was not in Petersburg—in a room filled with tobacco-
smoke, turning down the corners of cards and gambling,
hating the holder of the bank and feeling a dull pain in
his head—but was really here in this glorious region
among these brave Caucasians.

The major and the daughter of a surgeon's orderly,
formerly known as Másha, but now generally called by
the more respectful name of Márya Dmítrievna, lived together as man and wife. Márya Dmítrievna was a handsome, fair-haired, very freckled, childless woman of thirty.
Whatever her past may have been she was now the major's
faithful companion and looked after him like a nurse—a
very necessary matter, since he often drank himself into
oblivion.

When they reached the fort everything happened as the
major had foreseen. Márya Dmítrievna gave him and
Butler, and two other officers of the detachment who had
been invited, a nourishing and tasty dinner, and the major
ate and drank till he was unable to speak, and then went
off to his room to sleep.

Butler, having drunk rather more chikhír wine than was
good for him, went to his bedroom, tired but contented,

and hardly had time to undress before he fell into a sound, dreamless, and unbroken sleep with his hand under his handsome curly head.

XVII

The *aoul* which had been destroyed was that in which Hadji Murád had spent the night before he went over to the Russians. Sado and his family had left the *aoul* on the approach of the Russian detachment, and when he returned he found his *sáklya* in ruins—the roof fallen in, the door and the posts supporting the penthouse burned, and the interior filthy. His son, the handsome bright-eyed boy who had gazed with such ecstasy at Hadji Murád, was brought dead to the mosque on a horse covered with a *búrka:* he had been stabbed in the back with a bayonet. The dignified woman who had served Hadji Murád when he was at the house now stood over her son's body, her smock torn in front, her withered old breasts exposed, her hair down, and she dug her nails into her face till it bled, and wailed incessantly. Sado, taking a pick-axe and spade, had gone with his relatives to dig a grave for his son. The old grandfather sat by the wall of the ruined *sáklya* cutting a stick and gazing stolidly in front of him. He had only just returned from the apiary. The two stacks of hay there had been burnt, the apricot and cherry trees he had planted and reared were broken and scorched, and worse still all the beehives and bees had been burnt. The wailing of the women and the little children, who cried with their mothers, mingled with the lowing of the hungry cattle for whom there was no food. The bigger children, instead of playing, followed their elders with frightened eyes. The fountain was polluted, evidently on purpose, so that the water could not be used. The mosque was polluted in the same way, and the Mullah and his assistants were cleaning it out. No one spoke of hatred of the Russians. The feeling experienced by all the Chechens, from the youngest to the oldest, was stronger than hate. It was not hatred, for they did not regard those Russian dogs as human beings, but it was such repulsion, disgust, and perplexity at the senseless cruelty of these creatures, that the desire to exterminate them—like the desire to exterminate rats, poisonous spiders, or wolves—was as natural an instinct as that of self-preservation.

The inhabitants of the *aoul* were confronted by the choice of remaining there and restoring with frightful effort what had been produced with such labour and had been so lightly and senselessly destroyed, facing every moment the possibility of a repetition of what had happened; or to submit to the Russians—contrary to their religion and despite the repulsion and contempt they felt for them. The old men prayed, and unanimously decided to send envoys to Shamil asking him for help. Then they immediately set to work to restore what had been destroyed.

XVIII

On the morning after the raid, not very early, Butler left the house by the back porch meaning to take a stroll and a breath of fresh air before breakfast, which he usually had with Petróv. The sun had already risen above the hills and it was painful to look at the brightly lit-up white walls of the houses on the right side of the street. But then as always it was cheerful and soothing to look to the left, at the dark receding and ascending forest-clad hills and at the dim line of snow peaks, which as usual pretended to be clouds. Butler looked at these mountains, inhaling deep breaths and rejoicing that he was alive, that it was just he that was alive, and that he lived in this beautiful place.

He was also rather pleased that he had behaved so well in yesterday's affair both during the advance and especially during the retreat when things were pretty hot; he was also pleased to remember how Másha (or Márya Dmítrievna), Petróv's mistress, had treated them at dinner on their return after the raid, and how she had been particularly nice and simple with everybody, but specially kind—as he thought—to him.

Márya Dmítrievna with her thick plait of hair, her broad shoulders, her high bosom, and the radiant smile on her kindly freckled face, involuntarily attracted Butler, who was a healthy young bachelor. It sometimes even seemed to him that she wanted him, but he considered that that would be doing his good-natured simple-hearted comrade a wrong, and he maintained a simple, respectful attitude towards her and was pleased with himself for doing so.

He was thinking of this when his meditations were disturbed by the tramp of many horses' hoofs along the dusty road in front of him, as if several men were riding that way. He looked up and saw at the end of the street a group of horsemen coming towards him at a walk. In front of a score of Cossacks rode two men: one in a white Circassian coat with a tall turban on his head, the other an officer in the Russian service, dark, with an aquiline nose, and much silver on his uniform and weapons. The man with the turban rode a fine chestnut horse with mane and tail of a lighter shade, a small head, and beautiful eyes. The officer's was a large, handsome Karabákh horse. Butler, a lover of horses, immediately recognized the great strength of the first horse and stopped to learn who these people were.

The officer addressed him. 'This the house of commanding officer?' he asked, his foreign accent and his words betraying his foreign origin.

Butler replied that it was. 'And who is that?' he added, coming nearer to the officer and indicating the man with the turban.

'That Hadji Murád. He come here to stay with the commander,' said the officer.

Butler knew about Hadji Murád and about his having come over to the Russians, but he had not at all expected to see him here in this little fort. Hadji Murád gave him a friendly look.

'Good day, *kotkildy*,' said Butler, repeating the Tartar greeting he had learnt.

'*Saubul!*' ('Be well!') replied Hadji Murád, nodding. He rode up to Butler and held out his hand, from two fingers of which hung his whip.

'Are you the chief?' he asked.

'No, the chief is in here. I will go and call him,' said Butler addressing the officer, and he went up the steps and pushed the door. But the door of the visitors' entrance, as Márya Dmítrievna called it, was locked, and as it still remained closed after he had knocked, Butler went round to the back door. He called his orderly but received no reply, and finding neither of the two orderlies he went into the kitchen, where Márya Dmítrievna—flushed, with a kerchief tied round her head and her sleeves rolled up on her plump white arms—was rolling pastry, white as her hands, and cutting it into small pieces to make pies of.

'Where have the orderlies gone to?' asked Butler.

'Gone to drink,' replied Márya Dmítrievna. 'What do you want?'

'To have the front door opened. You have a whole horde of mountaineers in front of your house. Hadji Murád has come!'

'Invent something else!' said Márya Dmítrievna, smiling.

'I am not joking, he is really waiting by the porch!'

'Is it really true?' said she.

'Why should I wish to deceive you? Go and see, he's just at the porch!'

'Dear me, here's a go!' said Márya Dmítrievna pulling down her sleeves and putting up her hand to feel whether the hairpins in her thick plait were all in order. 'Then I will go and wake Iván Matvéich.'

'No, I'll go myself. And you Bondarénko, go and open the door,' said he to Petróv's orderly who had just appeared.

'Well, so much the better!' said Márya Dmítrievna and returned to her work.

When he heard that Hadji Murád had come to his house, Iván Matvéich Petróv, the major, who had already heard that Hadji Murád was in Grózny, was not at all surprised. Sitting up in bed he rolled a cigarette, lit it, and began to dress, loudly clearing his throat and grumbling at the authorities who had sent 'that devil' to him.

When he was ready he told his orderly to bring him some medicine. The orderly knew that 'medicine' meant vódka, and brought some.

'There is nothing so bad as mixing,' muttered the major when he had drunk the vódka and taken a bite of rye bread. 'Yesterday I drank a little chikhír and now I have a headache. . . . Well, I'm ready,' he added, and went to the parlour, into which Butler had already shown Hadji Múrad and the officer who accompanied him.

The officer handed the major orders from the commander of the left flank to the effect that he should receive Hadji Murád and should allow him to have intercourse with the mountaineers through spies, but was on no account to allow him to leave the fort without a convoy of Cossacks.

Having read the order the major looked intently at Hadji Murád and again scrutinized the paper. After passing his eyes several times from one to the other in this manner, he at last fixed them on Hadji Murád and said:

'*Yakshí, Bek; yakshí!* ('Very well, sir, very well!') Let him stay here, and tell him I have orders not to let him out—and what is commanded is sacred! Well, Butler, where do you think we'd better lodge him? Shall we put him in the office?'

Butler had not time to answer before Márya Dmítrievna —who had come from the kitchen and was standing in the doorway—said to the major:

'Why? Keep him here! We will give him the guest-chamber and the storeroom. Then at any rate he will be within sight,' said she, glancing at Hadji Murád; but meeting his eyes she turned quickly away.

'Do you know, I think Márya Dmítrievna is right,' said Butler.

'Now then, now then, get away! Women have no business here,' said the major frowning.

During the whole of this discussion Hadji Murád sat with his hand on the hilt of his dagger and a faint smile of contempt on his lips. He said it was all the same to him where he lodged, and that he wanted nothing but what the Sirdar had permitted—namely, to have communication with the mountaineers, and that he therefore wished they should be allowed to come to him.

The major said this should be done, and asked Butler to entertain the visitors till something could be got for them to eat and their rooms prepared. Meanwhile he himself would go across to the office to write what was necessary and to give some orders.

Hadji Murád's relations with his new acquaintances were at once very clearly defined. From the first he was repelled by and contemptuous of the major, to whom he always behaved very haughtily. Márya Dmítrievna, who prepared and served up his food, pleased him particularly. He liked her simplicity and especially the—to him—foreign type of her beauty, and he was influenced by the attraction she felt towards him and unconsciously conveyed. He tried not to look at her or speak to her, but his eyes involuntarily turned towards her and followed her movements. With Butler, from their first acquaintance, he immediately made friends and talked much and willingly with him, questioning him about his life, telling him of his own, communicating to him the news the spies brought him of his family's condition, and even consulting him as to how he ought to act.

The news he received through the spies was not good. During the first four days of his stay in the fort they came to see him twice and both times brought bad news.

XIX

Hadji Murád's family had been removed to Vedenó soon after his desertion to the Russians, and were there kept under guard awaiting Shamil's decision. The women —his old mother Patimát and his two wives with their five little children—were kept under guard in the *sáklya* of the officer Ibrahim Raschid, while Hadji Murád's son Yusúf, a youth of eighteen, was put in prison—that is, into a pit more than seven feet deep, together with seven criminals, who like himself were awaiting a decision as to their fate.

The decision was delayed because Shamil was away on a campaign against the Russians.

On January 6, 1852, he returned to Vedenó after a battle, in which according to the Russians he had been vanquished and had fled to Vedenó; but in which according to him and all the *murids* he had been victorious and had repulsed the Russians. In this battle he himself fired his rifle—a thing he seldom did—and drawing his sword would have charged straight at the Russians had not the *murids* who accompanied him held him back. Two of them were killed on the spot at his side.

It was noon when Shamil, surrounded by a party of *murids* who caracoled around him firing their rifles and pistols and continually singing *Lya illyah il Allah!* rode up to his place of residence.

All the inhabitants of the large *aoul* were in the street or on their roofs to meet their ruler, and as a sign of triumph they also fired off rifles and pistols. Shamil rode a white Arab steed which pulled at its bit as it approached the house. The horse had no gold or silver ornaments, its equipment was of the simplest—a delicately worked red leather bridle with a stripe down the middle, metal cup-shaped stirrups, and a red saddlecloth showing a little from under the saddle. The Imám wore a brown cloth cloak lined with black fur showing at the neck and sleeves, and was tightly girded round his long thin waist with a black strap which held a dagger. On his head he wore a tall cap with flat crown and black tassel, and round it was wound a white turban, one end of which hung down on his neck. He wore green slippers, and black leggings trimmed with plain braid.

He wore nothing bright—no gold or silver—and his tall, erect, powerful figure, clothed in garments without any ornaments, surrounded by *murids* with gold and silver on their clothes and weapons, produced on the people just the impression and influence he desired and knew how to produce. His pale face framed by a closely trimmed reddish beard, with his small eyes always screwed up, was as immovable as though hewn out of stone. As he rode through the *aoul* he felt the gaze of a thousand eyes turned eagerly on him, but he himself looked at no one.

Hadji Murád's wives had come out into the penthouse with the rest of the inmates of the *sáklya* to see the Imám's entry. Only Patimát, Hadji Murád's old mother, did not go out but remained sitting on the floor of the *sáklya* with her grey hair down, her long arms encircling her thin knees, blinking with her fiery black eyes as she watched the dying embers in the fireplace. Like her son she had always hated Shamil, and now she hated him more than ever and had no wish to see him. Neither did Hadji Murád's son see Shamil's triumphal entry. Sitting in the dark and fetid pit he heard the firing and singing, and endured tortures such as can only be felt by the young who are full of vitality and deprived of freedom. He only saw his unfortunate, dirty, and exhausted fellow-prisoners—embittered and for the most part filled with hatred of one another. He now passionately envied those who, enjoying fresh air and light and freedom, caracoled on fiery steeds around their chief, shooting and heartily singing: *Lya illyah il Allah!*

When he had crossed the *aoul* Shamil rode into the large courtyard adjoining the inner court where his seraglio was. Two armed Lesghians met him at the open gates of this outer court, which was crowded with people. Some had come from distant parts about their own affairs, some had come with petitions, and some had been summoned by Shamil to be tried and sentenced. As the Imám rode in, they all respectfully saluted him with their hands on their breasts, some of them kneeling down and remaining on their knees while he rode across the court from the outer to the inner gates. Though he recognized among the people who waited in the court many whom he disliked, and many tedious petitioners who wanted his attention, Shamil passed them all with the same immovable, stony expression on his face, and having entered the inner court dismounted at the penthouse in front of his apartment, to the left of the gate. He was worn out, mentally rather than physically, by the strain of the campaign, for in spite of the public declaration that he had been victorious he knew very well that his campaign had been unsuccessful, that many Chechen *aouls* had been burnt down and ruined, and that the unstable and fickle Chechens were wavering and those nearest the border line were ready to go over to the Russians.

All this had to be dealt with, and it oppressed him, for at that moment he did not wish to think at all. He only desired one thing: rest and the delights of family life, and the caresses of his favourite wife, the black-eyed quick-footed eighteen-year-old Aminal, who at that very moment was close at hand behind the fence that divided the inner court and separated the men's from the women's quarters (Shamil felt sure she was there with his other wives, looking through a chink in the fence while he dismounted). But not only was it impossible for him to go to her, he could not even lie down on his feather cushions and rest from his fatigue; he had first of all to perform the midday rites for which he had just then not the least inclination, but which as the religious leader of the people he could not omit, and which moreover were as necessary to him himself as his daily food. So he performed his ablutions and said his prayers and summoned those who were waiting for him.

The first to enter was Jemal Eddin, his father-in-law and teacher, a tall grey-haired good-looking old man with a beard white as snow and a rosy red face. He said a prayer and began questioning Shamil about the incidents of the campaign and telling him what had happened in the mountains during his absence.

Among events of many kinds—murders connected with blood-feuds, cattle-stealing, people accused of disobeying

the Tarikát (smoking and drinking wine)—Jemal Eddin
related how Hadji Murád had sent men to bring his family
over to the Russians, but that this had been detected and
the family had been brought to Vedenó where they were
kept under guard and awaited the Imám's decision. In
the next room, the guest-chamber, the Elders were assembled to discuss all these affairs, and Jemal Eddin advised Shamil to finish with them and let them go that same
day, as they had already been waiting three days for him.

After eating his dinner—served to him in his room by
Zeidát, a dark, sharp-nosed, disagreeable-looking woman
whom he did not love but who was his eldest wife—
Shamil passed into the guest-chamber.

The six old men who made up his council—white, grey,
or red-bearded, with tall caps on their heads, some with
turbans and some without, wearing new *beshméts* and Circassian coats girdled with straps on which their daggers
were suspended—rose to greet him on his entrance. Shamil
towered a head above them all. On entering the room he,
as well as all the others, lifted his hands, palms upwards,
closed his eyes and recited a prayer, and then stroked his
face downwards with both hands, uniting them at the end
of his beard. Having done this they all sat down, Shamil
on a larger cushion than the others, and discussed the
various cases before them.

In the case of the criminals the decisions were given
according to the Shariát: two were sentenced to have a
hand cut off for stealing, one man to be beheaded for
murder, and three were pardoned. Then they came to
the principal business: how to stop the Chechens from going over to the Russians. To counteract that tendency
Jemal Eddin drew up the following proclamation:

'I wish you eternal peace with God the Almighty!

'I hear that the Russians flatter you and invite you to
surrender to them. Do not believe what they say, and do
not surrender but endure. If ye be not rewarded for it in
this life ye shall receive your reward in the life to come.
Remember what happened before when they took your
arms from you! If God had not brought you to reason
then, in 1840, ye would now be soldiers, and your wives
would be dishonoured and would no longer wear trousers.

'Judge of the future by the past. It is better to die in
enmity with the Russians than to live with the Unbelievers.

Endure for a little while and I will come with the Koran
and the sword and will lead you against the enemy. But
now I strictly command you not only to entertain no intention, but not even a thought, of submitting to the Russians!'

Shamil approved this proclamation, signed it, and had
it sent out.

After this business they considered Hadji Murád's case.
This was of the utmost importance to Shamil. Although he
did not wish to admit it, he knew that if Hadji Murád with
his agility, boldness, and courage, had been with him,
what had now happened in Chechnya would not have occurred. It would therefore be well to make it up with
Hadji Murád and have the benefit of his services again.
But as this was not possible it would never do to allow
him to help the Russians, and therefore he must be en-
ticed back and killed. They might accomplish this either
by sending a man to Tiflis who would kill him there, or
by inducing him to come back and then killing him. The
only means of doing the latter was by making use of his
family and especially his son, whom Shamil knew he
loved passionately. Therefore they must act through the
son.

When the councillors had talked all this over, Shamil
closed his eyes and sat silent.

The councillors knew that this meant that he was listening to the voice of the Prophet, who spoke to him and
told him what to do.

After five minutes of solemn silence Shamil opened his
eyes, and narrowing them more than usual, said:

'Bring Hadji Murád's son to me.'

'He is here,' replied Jemal Eddin, and in fact Yusúf,
Hadji Murád's son, thin, pale, tattered, and evil-smelling,
but still handsome in face and figure, with black eyes that
burnt like his grandmother Patimát's, was already standing
by the gate of the outside court waiting to be called in.

Yusúf did not share his father's feelings towards Shamil.
He did not know all that had happened in the past, or if
he knew it, not having lived through it he still did not understand why his father was so obstinately hostile to
Shamil. To him who wanted only one thing—to continue
living the easy, loose life that, as the naïb's son, he had
led in Khunzákh—it seemed quite unnecessary to be at

enmity with Shamil. Out of defiance and a spirit of contradiction to his father he particularly admired Shamil, and shared the ecstatic adoration with which he was regarded in the mountains. With a peculiar feeling of tremulous veneration for the Imám he now entered the guest-chamber. As he stopped by the door he met the steady gaze of Shamil's half-closed eyes. He paused for a moment, and then approached Shamil and kissed his large, long-fingered hand.

'Thou art Hadji Murád's son?'

'I am, Imám.'

'Thou knowest what he has done?'

'I know, Imám, and deplore it.'

'Canst thou write?'

'I was preparing myself to be a Mullah——'

'Then write to thy father that if he will return to me now, before the Feast of Bairam, I will forgive him and everything shall be as it was before; but if not, and if he remains with the Russians'—and Shamil frowned sternly—'I will give thy grandmother, thy mother, and the rest to the different *aouls*, and thee I will behead!'

Not a muscle of Yusúf's face stirred, and he bowed his head to show that he understood Shamil's words.

'Write that and give it to my messenger.'

Shamil ceased speaking, and looked at Yusúf for a long time in silence.

'Write that I have had pity on thee and will not kill thee, but will put out thine eyes as I do to all traitors! . . . Go!'

While in Shamil's presence Yusúf appeared calm, but when he had been led out of the guest-chamber he rushed at his attendant, snatched the man's dagger from its sheath and tried to stab himself, but he was seized by the arms, bound, and led back to the pit.

That evening at dusk after he had finished his evening prayers, Shamil put on a white fur-lined cloak and passed out to the other side of the fence where his wives lived, and went straight to Aminal's room, but he did not find her there. She was with the older wives. Then Shamil, trying to remain unseen, hid behind the door and stood waiting for her. But Aminal was angry with him because he had given some silk stuff to Zeidát and not to her. She saw him come out and go into her room looking for her, and she purposely kept away. She stood a long time at the door of Zeidát's room, laughing softly at Shamil's white figure that kept going in and out of her room.

Having waited for her in vain, Shamil returned to his own apartments when it was already time for the midnight prayers.

XX

Hadji Murád had been a week in the major's house at the fort. Although Márya Dmítrievna quarrelled with the shaggy Khanéfi (Hadji Murád had only brought two of his *murids*, Khanéfi and Eldár, with him) and had turned him out of her kitchen—for which he nearly killed her—she evidently felt a particular respect and sympathy for Hadji Murád. She now no longer served him his dinner, having handed that duty over to Eldár, but she seized every opportunity of seeing him and rendering him service. She always took the liveliest interest in the negotiations about his family, knew how many wives and children he had, and their ages, and each time a spy came to see him she inquired as best she could into the results of the negotiations.

Butler during that week had become quite friendly with Hadji Murád. Sometimes the latter came to Butler's room, sometimes Butler went to Hadji Murád's: sometimes they conversed by the help of the interpreter, and sometimes they got on as best they could with signs and especially with smiles.

Hadji Murád had evidently taken a fancy to Butler, as could be gathered from Eldár's relations with the latter. When Butler entered Hadji Murád's room Eldár met him with a pleased smile showing his glittering teeth, and hurried to put down a cushion for him to sit on and to relieve him of his sword if he was wearing one.

Butler also got to know, and became friendly with, the shaggy Khanéfi, Hadji Murád's sworn brother. Khanéfi knew many mountain songs and sang them well, and to please Butler, Hadji Murád often made Khanéfi sing, choosing the songs he considered best. Khanéfi had a high tenor voice and sang with extraordinary clearness and expression. One of the songs Hadji Murád specially liked impressed Butler by its solemnly mournful tone and he asked the interpreter to translate it.

The subject of the song was the very blood-feud that had existed between Khanéfi and Hadji Murád. It ran as follows:

'The earth will dry on my grave,
    Mother, my Mother!
And thou wilt forget me!
And over me rank grass will wave,
    Father, my Father!
Nor wilt thou regret me
When tears cease thy dark eyes to lave,
    Sister, dear Sister!
No more will grief fret thee!

'But thou, my Brother the elder, wilt never forget,
    With vengeance denied me!
And thou, my Brother the younger, wilt ever regret,
    Till thou liest beside me!

'Hotly thou camest, O death-bearing ball that I spurned,
    For thou wast my slave!
And thou, black earth, that battle-steed trampled and
    churned,
    Wilt cover my grave!

'Cold art Thou, O Death, yet I was thy Lord and thy
    Master!
My body sinks fast to the earth, my soul to Heaven flies
    faster.'

Hadji Murád always listened to this song with closed eyes and when it ended on a long gradually dying note he always remarked in Russian—

'Good song! Wise song!'

After Hadji Murád's arrival and his intimacy with him and his *murids*, the poetry of the stirring mountain life took a still stronger hold on Butler. He procured for himself a *beshmét* and a Circassian coat and leggings, and imagined himself a mountaineer living the life those people lived.

On the day of Hadji Murád's departure the major invited several officers to see him off. They were sitting, some at the table where Márya Dmítrievna was pouring out tea, some at another table on which stood vódka, chikhír, and light refreshments, when Hadji Murád dressed for the journey came limping into the room with soft, rapid footsteps.

They all rose and shook hands with him. The major offered him a seat on the divan, but Hadji Murád thanked him and sat down on a chair by the window.

The silence that followed his entrance did not at all abash him. He looked attentively at all the faces and fixed an indifferent gaze on the tea-table with the samovar and refreshments. Petróvsky, a lively officer who now met Hadji Murád for the first time, asked him through the interpreter whether he liked Tiflis.

'*Alya!*' he replied.

'He says "Yes",' translated the interpreter.

'What did he like there?'

Hadji Murád said something in reply.

'He liked the theatre best of all.'

'And how did he like the ball at the house of the commander-in-chief?'

Hadji Murád frowned. 'Every nation has its own customs! Our women do not dress in such a way,' said he, glancing at Márya Dmítrievna.

'Well, didn't he like it?'

'We have a proverb,' said Hadji Murád to the interpreter, ' "The dog gave meat to the ass and the ass gave hay to the dog, and both went hungry," ' and he smiled. 'Its own customs seem good to each nation.'

The conversation went no farther. Some of the officers took tea, some other refreshments. Hadji Murád accepted the tumbler of tea offered him and put it down before him.

'Won't you have cream and a bun?' asked Márya Dmítrievna, offering them to him.

Hadji Murád bowed his head.

'Well, I suppose it is good-bye!' said Butler, touching his knee. 'When shall we meet again?'

'Good-bye, good-bye!' said Hadji Murád, in Russian, with a smile. '*Kunák bulug*. Strong *kunák* to thee! Time— ayda—go!' and he jerked his head in the direction in which he had to go.

Eldár appeared in the doorway carrying something large and white across his shoulder and a sword in his hand. Hadji Murád beckoned to him and he crossed the room with big strides and handed him a white *búrka* and the sword. Hadji Murád rose, took the *búrka*, threw it over his arm, and saying something to the interpreter handed it to Márya Dmítrievna.

'He says thou hast praised the *búrka,* so accept it,' said the interpreter.

'Oh, why?' said Márya Dmítrievna blushing.

'It is necessary. Like Adam,' said Hadji Murád.

'Well, thank you,' said Márya Dmítrievna, taking the *búrka.* 'God grant that you rescue your son,' she added. '*Ulan yakshi.* Tell him that I wish him success in releasing his son.'

Hadji Murád glanced at Márya Dmítrievna and nodded his head approvingly. Then he took the sword from Eldár and handed it to the major. The major took it and said to the interpreter, 'Tell him to take my chestnut gelding. I have nothing else to give him.'

Hadji Murád waved his hand in front of his face to show that he did not want anything and would not accept it. Then, pointing first to the mountains and then to his heart, he went out.

All the household followed him as far as the door, while the officers who remained inside the room drew the sword from its scabbard, examined its blade, and decided that it was a real Gurda.

Butler accompanied Hadji Murád to the porch, and then came a very unexpected incident which might have ended fatally for Hadji Murád had it not been for his quick observation, determination, and agility.

The inhabitants of the Kumúkh *aoul,* Tash-Kichu, which was friendly to the Russians, respected Hadji Murád greatly and had often come to the fort merely to look at the famous *naïb.* They had sent messengers to him three days previously to ask him to visit their mosque on the Friday. But the Kumúkh princes who lived in Tash-Kichu hated Hadji Murád because there was a blood-feud between them, and on hearing of this invitation they announced to the people that they would not allow him to enter the mosque. The people became excited and a fight occurred between them and the princes' supporters. The Russian authorities pacified the mountaineers and sent word to Hadji Murád not to go to the mosque.

Hadji Murád did not go and everyone supposed that the matter was settled.

But at the very moment of his departure, when he came out into the porch before which the horses stood waiting, Arslán Khan, one of the Kumúkh princes and an acquaintance of Butler and the major, rode up to the house.

When he saw Hadji Murád he snatched a pistol from his belt and took aim, but before he could fire, Hadji Murád in spite of his lameness rushed down from the porch like a cat towards Arslán Khan who missed him.

Seizing Arslán Khan's horse by the bridle with one hand, Hadji Murád drew his dagger with the other and shouted something to him in Tartar.

Butler and Eldár both ran at once towards the enemies and caught them by the arms. The major, who had heard the shot, also came out.

'What do you mean by it, Arslán—starting such a nasty business on my premises?' said he, when he heard what had happened. 'It's not right, friend! "To the foe in the field you need not yield!"—but to start this kind of slaughter in front of my house——'

Arslán Khan, a little man with black moustaches, got off his horse pale and trembling, looked angrily at Hadji Murád, and went into the house with the major. Hadji Murád, breathing heavily and smiling, returned to the horses.

'Why did he want to kill him?' Butler asked the interpreter.

'He says it is a law of theirs,' the interpreter translated Hadji Murád's reply. 'Arslán must avenge a relation's blood and so he tried to kill him.'

'And supposing he overtakes him on the road?' asked Butler.

Hadji Murád smiled.

'Well, if he kills me it will prove that such is Allah's will. . . . Good-bye,' he said again in Russian, taking his horse by the withers. Glancing round at everybody who had come out to see him off, his eyes rested kindly on Márya Dmítrievna.

'Good-bye, my lass,' said he to her. 'I thank you.'

'God help you—God help you to rescue your family!' repeated Márya Dmítrievna.

He did not understand her words, but felt her sympathy for him and nodded to her.

'Mind, don't forget your *kunák*,' said Butler.

'Tell him I am his true friend and will never forget him,' answered Hadji Murád to the interpreter, and in spite of his short leg he swung himself lightly and quickly into the high saddle, barely touching the stirrup, and automatically feeling for his dagger and adjusting his sword. Then, with

that peculiarly proud look with which only a Caucasian
hill-man sits his horse—as though he were one with it—
he rode away from the major's house. Khanéfi and Eldár
also mounted and having taken a friendly leave of their
hosts and of the officers, rode off at a trot, following their
murshíd.

As usual after a departure, those who remained behind
began to discuss those who had left.

'Plucky fellow! He rushed at Arslán Khan like a wolf!
His face quite changed!'

'But he'll be up to tricks—he's a terrible rogue, I should
say,' remarked Petróvsky.

'It's a pity there aren't more Russian rogues of such a
kind!' suddenly put in Márya Dmítrievna with vexation.
'He has lived a week with us and we have seen nothing but
good from him. He is courteous, wise, and just,' she added.

'How did you find that out?'

'No matter, I did find it out!'

'She's quite smitten, and that's a fact!' said the major,
who had just entered the room.

'Well, and if I am smitten? What's that to you? Why
run him down if he's a good man? Though he's a Tartar
he's still a good man!'

'Quite true, Márya Dmítrievna,' said Butler, 'and you're
quite right to take his part!'

XXI

Life in our advanced forts in the Chechen lines went
on as usual. Since the events last narrated there had been
two alarms when the companies were called out and militiamen galloped about; but both times the mountaineers who
had caused the excitement got away, and once at Vozdvízhensk they killed a Cossack and succeeded in carrying off eight Cossack horses that were being watered.
There had been no further raids since the one in which the
aoul was destroyed, but an expedition on a large scale was
expected in consequence of the appointment of a new commander of the left flank, Prince Baryátinsky. He was an
old friend of the Viceroy's and had been in command of
the Kabardá Regiment. On his arrival at Grózny as commander of the whole left flank he at once mustered a detachment to continue to carry out the Tsar's commands
as communicated by Chernyshóv to Vorontsóv. The de-

tachment mustered at Vozdvízhensk left the fort and took up a position towards Kurín, where the troops were encamped and were felling the forest. Young Vorontsóv lived in a splendid cloth tent, and his wife, Márya Vasílevna, often came to the camp and stayed the night. Baryátinsky's relations with Márya Vasílevna were no secret to anyone, and the officers who were not in the aristocratic set and the soldiers abused her in coarse terms —for her presence in camp caused them to be told off to lie in ambush at night. The mountaineers were in the habit of bringing guns within range and firing shells at the camp. The shells generally missed their aim and therefore at ordinary times no special measures were taken to prevent such firing, but now men were placed in ambush to hinder the mountaineers from injuring or frightening Márya Vasílevna with their cannon. To have to be always lying in ambush at night to save a lady from being frightened, offended and annoyed them, and therefore the soldiers, as well as the officers not admitted to the higher society, called Márya Vasílevna bad names.

Having obtained leave of absence from his fort, Butler came to the camp to visit some old mess-mates from the cadet corps and fellow officers of the Kurín regiment who were serving as adjutants and orderly officers. When he first arrived he had a very good time. He put up in Poltorátsky's tent and there met many acquaintances who gave him a hearty welcome. He also called on Vorontsóv, whom he knew slightly, having once served in the same regiment with him. Vorontsóv received him very kindly, introduced him to Prince Baryátinsky, and invited him to the farewell dinner he was giving in honour of General Kozlóvsky, who until Baryátinsky's arrival had been in command of the left flank.

The dinner was magnificent. Special tents were erected in a line, and along the whole length of them a table was spread as for a dinner-party, with dinner-services and bottles. Everything recalled life in the Guards in Petersburg. Dinner was served at two o'clock. Kozlóvsky sat in the middle on one side. Baryátinsky on the other. At Kozlóvsky's right and left hand sat the Vorontsóvs, husband and wife. All along the table on both sides sat the officers of the Kabardá and Kurín regiments. Butler sat next to Poltorátsky and they both chatted merrily and drank with the officers around them. When the roast was served and the orderlies had gone round and filled the champagne glasses, Poltorátsky said to Butler, with real anxiety:

'Our Kozlóvsky will disgrace himself!'

'Why?'

'Why, he'll have to make a speech, and what good is he at that? . . . It's not as easy as capturing entrenchments under fire! And with a lady beside him too, and these aristocrats!'

'Really it's painful to look at him,' said the officers to one another. And now the solemn moment had arrived. Baryátinsky rose and lifting his glass, addressed a short speech to Kozlóvsky. When he had finished, Kozlóvsky— who always had a trick of using the word 'how' superfluously—rose and stammeringly began:

'In compliance with the august will of his Majesty I am leaving you—parting from you, gentlemen,' said he. 'But consider me as always remaining among you. The truth of the proverb, how "One man in the field is no warrior", is well known to you, gentlemen. . . . Therefore, how every reward I have received . . . how all the benefits showered on me by the great generosity of our sovereign the Emperor . . . how all my position—how my good name . . . how everything decidedly . . . how . . .' (here his voice trembled) '. . . how I am indebted to you for it, to you alone, my friends!' The wrinkled face puckered up still more, he gave a sob and tears came into his eyes. 'How from my heart I offer you my sincerest, heartfelt gratitude!'

Kozlóvsky could not go on but turned round and began to embrace the officers. The princess hid her face in her handkerchief. The prince blinked, with his mouth drawn awry. Many of the officers' eyes grew moist and Butler, who had hardly known Kozlóvsky, could also not restrain his tears. He liked all this very much.

Then followed other toasts. Healths were drunk to Baryátinsky, Vorontsóv, the officers, and the soldiers, and the visitors left the table intoxicated with wine and with the military elation to which they were always so prone. The weather was wonderful, sunny and calm, and the air fresh and bracing. Bonfires crackled and songs resounded on all sides. It might have been thought that everybody was celebrating some joyful event. Butler went to Poltorátsky's in the happiest, most emotional mood. Several officers had gathered there and a card-table was set. An adjutant started a bank with a hundred rubles. Two or three times Butler left the tent with his hand gripping the purse in his trousers-pocket, but at last he could resist the temptation no longer, and despite the promise he had given to his brother and to himself not to play, he began to do so. Before an hour was past, very red, perspiring, and soiled with chalk, he was sitting with both elbows on the table and writing on it—under cards bent for 'corners' and 'transports'—the figures of his stakes. He had already lost so much that he was afraid to count up what was scored against him. But he knew without counting that all the pay he could draw in advance, added to the value of his horse, would not suffice to pay what the adjutant, a stranger to him, had written down against him. He would still have gone on playing, but the adjutant sternly laid down the cards he held in his large clean hands and added up the chalked figures of the score of Butler's losses. Butler, in confusion, began to make excuses for being unable to pay the whole of his debt at once, and said he would send it from home. When he said this he noticed that everybody pitied him and that they all—even Poltorátsky—avoided meeting his eye. That was his last evening there. He reflected that he need only have refrained from playing and gone to the Vorontsóvs who had invited him, and all would have been well, but now it was not only not well—it was terrible.

Having taken leave of his comrades and acquaintances he rode home and went to bed, and slept for eighteen hours as people usually sleep after losing heavily. From the fact that he asked her to lend him fifty kopeks to tip the Cossack who had escorted him, and from his sorrowful looks and short answers, Márya Dmítrievna guessed that he had lost at cards and she reproached the major for having given him leave of absence.

When he woke up at noon next day and remembered the situation he was in he longed again to plunge into the oblivion from which he had just emerged, but it was impossible. Steps had to be taken to repay the four hundred and seventy rubles he owed to the stranger. The first step he took was to write to his brother, confessing his sin and imploring him, for the last time, to lend him five hundred rubles on the security of the mill they still owned in common. Then he wrote to a stingy relative asking her to lend him five hundred rubles at whatever rate of interest she liked. Finally he went to the major, knowing that he—or rather Márya Dmítrievna—had some money, and asked him to lend him five hundred rubles.

'I'd let you have them at once,' said the major, 'but Másha won't! These women are so close-fisted—who the devil can understand them? . . . And yet you must get out of it somehow, devil take him! . . . Hasn't that brute the canteen-keeper got something?'

But it was no use trying to borrow from the canteen-keeper, so Butler's salvation could only come from his brother or his stingy relative.

XXII

Not having attained his aim in Chechnya, Hadji Murád returned to Tiflis and went every day to Vorontsóv's, and whenever he could obtain audience he implored the Viceroy to gather together the mountaineer prisoners and exchange them for his family. He said that unless that were done his hands were tied and he could not serve the Russians and destroy Shamil as he desired to do. Vorontsóv vaguely promised to do what he could, but put it off, saying that he would decide when General Argutínski reached Tiflis and he could talk the matter over with him.

Then Hadji Murád asked Vorontsóv to allow him to go to live for a while in Nukhá, a small town in Transcaucasia where he thought he could better carry on negotiations about his family with Shamil and with the people who were attached to himself. Moreover Nukhá, being a Mohammedan town, had a mosque where he could more conveniently perform the rites of prayer demanded by the Mohammedan law. Vorontsóv wrote to Petersburg about it but meanwhile gave Hadji Murád permission to go to Nukhá.

For Vorontsóv and the authorities in Petersburg, as well as for most Russians acquainted with Hadji Murád's history, the whole episode presented itself as a lucky turn in the Caucasian war, or simply as an interesting event. For Hadji Murád it was a terrible crisis in his life—especially laterally. He had escaped from the mountains partly to save himself and partly out of hatred of Shamil, and difficult as this flight had been he had attained his object, and for a time was glad of his success and really devised a plan to attack Shamil, but the rescue of his family—which he had thought would be easy to arrange—had proved more difficult than he expected.

Shamil had seized the family and kept them prisoners, threatening to hand the women over to the different *aouls* and to blind or kill the son. Now Hadji Murád had gone to Nukhá intending to try by the aid of his adherents in Daghestan to rescue his family from Shamil by force or by cunning. The last spy who had come to see him in Nukhá informed him that the Avars, who were devoted to him, were preparing to capture his family and themselves bring them over to the Russians, but that there were not enough of them and they could not risk making the attempt in Vedenó, where the family was at present imprisoned, but could do so only if the family were moved from Vedenó to some other place—in which case they promised to rescue them on the way.

Hadji Murád sent word to his friends that he would give three thousand rubles for the liberation of his family.

At Nukhá a small house of five rooms was assigned to Hadji Murád near the mosque and the Khan's palace. The officers in charge of him, his interpreter, and his henchmen, stayed in the same house. Hadji Murád's life was spent in the expectation and reception of messengers from the mountains and in rides he was allowed to take in the neighborhood.

On 24th April, returning from one of these rides, Hadji Murád learnt that during his absence an official sent by Vorontsóv had arrived from Tiflis. In spite of his longing to know what message the official had brought him he went to his bedroom and repeated his noonday prayer before going into the room where the officer in charge and the official were waiting. This room served him both as drawing- and reception-room. The official who had come from Tiflis, Councillor Kiríllov, informed Hadji Murád of Vorontsóv's wish that he should come to Tiflis on the 12th to meet General Argutínski.

'*Yakshi!*' said Hadji Murád angrily. The councillor did not please him. 'Have you brought money?'

'I have,' answered Kiríllov.

'For two weeks now,' said Hadji Murád, holding up first both hands and then four fingers. 'Give here!'

'We'll give it you at once,' said the official, getting his purse out of his travelling-bag. 'What does he want with the money?' he went on in Russian, thinking that Hadji

Murád would not understand. But Hadji Murád had understood, and glanced angrily at him. While getting out the money the councillor, wishing to begin a conversation with Hadji Murád in order to have something to tell Prince Vorontsóv on his return, asked through the interpreter whether he was not feeling dull there. Hadji Murád glanced contemptuously out of the corner of his eye at the fat, unarmed little man dressed as a civilian, and did not reply. The interpreter repeated the question.

'Tell him that I cannot talk with him! Let him give me the money!' and having said this, Hadji Murád sat down at the table ready to count it.

Hadji Murád had an allowance of five gold pieces a day, and when Kiríllov had got out the money and arranged it in seven piles of ten gold pieces each and pushed them towards Hadji Murád, the latter poured the gold into the sleeve of his Circassian coat, rose, quite unexpectedly smacked Councillor Kiríllov on his bald pate, and turned to go.

The councillor jumped up and ordered the interpreter to tell Hadji Murád that he must not dare to behave like that to him who held a rank equal to that of colonel! The officer in charge confirmed this, but Hadji Murád only nodded to signify that he knew, and left the room.

'What is one to do with him?' said the officer in charge. 'He'll stick his dagger into you, that's all! One cannot talk with those devils! I see that he is getting exasperated.'

As soon as it began to grow dusk two spies with hoods covering their faces up to their eyes, came to him from the hills. The officer in charge led them to Hadji Murád's room. One of them was a fleshy, swarthy Tavlinian, the other a thin old man. The news they brought was not cheering. Hadji Murád's friends who had undertaken to rescue his family now definitely refused to do so, being afraid of Shamil, who threatened to punish with most terrible tortures anyone who helped Hadji Murád. Having heard the messengers he sat with his elbows on his crossed legs, and bowing his turbaned head remained silent a long time.

He was thinking and thinking resolutely. He knew that he was now considering the matter for the last time and that it was necessary to come to a decision. At last he raised his head, gave each of the messengers a gold piece, and said: 'Go!'

'What answer will there be?'

'The answer will be as God pleases. . . . Go!'

The messengers rose and went away, and Hadji Murád continued to sit on the carpet leaning his elbows on his knees. He sat thus a long time and pondered.

'What am I to do? To take Shamil at his word and return to him?' he thought. 'He is a fox and will deceive me. Even if he did not deceive me it would still be impossible to submit to that red liar. It is impossible . . . because now that I have been with the Russians he will not trust me,' thought Hadji Murád; and he remembered a Tavlinian fable about a falcon who had been caught and lived among men and afterwards returned to his own kind in the hills. He returned, wearing jesses with bells, and the other falcons would not receive him. 'Fly back to where they hung those silver bells on thee!' said they. 'We have no bells and no jesses.' The falcon did not want to leave his home and remained, but the other falcons did not wish to let him stay there and pecked him to death.

'And they would peck me to death in the same way,' thought Hadji Murád. 'Shall I remain here and conquer Caucasia for the Russian Tsar and earn renown, titles, riches?'

'That could be done,' thought he, recalling his interviews with Vorontsóv and the flattering things the prince had said; 'but I must decide at once, or Shamil will destroy my family.'

That night he remained awake, thinking.

XXIII

By midnight his decision had been formed. He had decided that he must fly to the mountains, and break into Vedenó with the Avars still devoted to him, and either die or rescue his family. Whether after rescuing them he would return to the Russians or escape to Khunzákh and fight Shamil, he had not made up his mind. All he knew was that first of all he must escape from the Russians into the mountains, and he at once began to carry out his plan.

He drew his black wadded *beshmét* from under his pillow and went into his henchmen's room. They lived on the other side of the hall. As soon as he entered the hall, the outer door of which stood open, he was at once enveloped

by the dewy freshness of the moonlit night and his ears
were filled by the whistling and trilling of several nightingales in the garden by the house.

Having crossed the hall he opened the door of his
henchmen's room. There was no light there, but the moon
in its first quarter shone in at the window. A table and two
chairs were standing on one side of the room, and four of
his henchmen were lying on carpets or on *búrkas* on the
floor. Khanéfi slept outside with the horses. Gamzálo
heard the door creak, rose, turned round, and saw him. On
recognizing him he lay down again, but Eldár, who lay
beside him, jumped up and began putting on his *beshmét*,
expecting his master's orders. Khan Mahomá and Bata
slept on. Hadji Murád put down the *beshmét* he had
brought on the table, which it hit with a dull sound,
caused by the gold sewn up in it.

'Sew these in too,' said Hadji Murád, handing Eldár
the gold pieces he had received that day. Eldár took them
and at once went ino the moonlight, drew a small knife
from under his dagger and started unstitching the lining
of the *beshmét*. Gamzálo raised himself and sat up with
his legs crossed.

'And you, Gamzálo, tell the men to examine the rifles
and pistols and get the ammunition ready. To-morrow we
shall go far,' said Hadji Murád.

'We have bullets and powder, everything shall be ready,'
replied Gamzálo, and roared out something incomprehensible. He understood why Hadji Murád had ordered
the rifles to be loaded. From the first he had desired only
one thing—to slay and stab as many Russians as possible
and to escape to the hills—and this desire had increased
day by day. Now at last he saw that Hadji Murád also
wanted this and he was satisfied.

When Hadji Murád went away Gamzálo roused his
comrades, and all four spent the rest of the night examining their rifles, pistols, flints, and accoutrements; replacing
what was damaged, sprinkling fresh powder onto the pans,
and stoppering with bullets wrapped in oiled rags, packets
filled with the right amount of powder for each charge,
sharpening their swords and daggers and greasing the
blades with tallow.

Before daybreak Hadji Murád again came out into the
hall to get water for his ablutions. The songs of the night-

ingales that had burst into ecstasy at dawn were now even louder and more incessant, while from his henchmen's room, where the daggers were being sharpened, came the regular screech and rasp of iron against stone.

Hadji Murád got himself some water from a tub, and was already at his own door when above the sound of the grinding he heard from his *murids'* room the high tones of Khanéfi's voice singing a familiar song. He stopped to listen. The song told of how a *dzhigít*, Hamzád, with his brave followers captured a herd of white horses from the Russians, and how a Russian prince followed him beyond the Térek and surrounded him with an army as large as a forest; and then the song went on to tell how Hamzád killed the horses, entrenched his men behind this gory bulwark, and fought the Russians as long as they had bullets in their rifles, daggers in their belts, and blood in their veins. But before he died Hamzád saw some birds flying in the sky and cried to them:

'Fly on, ye winged ones, fly to our homes!
Tell ye our mothers, tell ye our sisters,
Tell the white maidens, that fighting we died
For Ghazavát! Tell them our bodies
Never will lie and rest in a tomb!
Wolves will devour and tear them to pieces,
Ravens and vultures will pluck out our eyes.'

With that the song ended, and at the last words, sung to a mournful air, the merry Bata's vigorous voice joined in with a loud shout of *'Lya-il-lyakha-il Allakh!'* finishing with a shrill shriek. Then all was quiet again, except for the *tchuk, tchuk, tchuk, tchuk* and whistling of the nightingales from the garden and from behind the door the even grinding, and now and then the whiz, of iron sliding quickly along the whetstone.

Hadji Murád was so full of thought that he did not notice how he tilted his jug till the water began to pour out. He shook his head at himself and re-entered his room. After performing his morning ablutions he examined his weapons and sat down on his bed. There was nothing more for him to do. To be allowed to ride out he would have to get permission from the officer in charge, but it was not yet daylight and the officer was still asleep.

Khanéfi's song reminded him of the song his mother had composed just after he was born—the song addressed to his father that Hadji Murád had repeated to Lóris-Mélikov.

And he seemed to see his mother before him—not wrinkled and grey-haired, with gaps between her teeth, as he had lately left her, but young and handsome, and strong enough to carry him in a basket on her back across the mountains to her father's when he was a heavy five-year-old boy.

And the recollection of himself as a little child reminded him of his beloved son, Yusúf, whose head he himself had shaved for the first time; and now this Yusúf was a handsome young *dzhigít*. He pictured him as he was when last he saw him on the day he left Tselmess. Yusúf had brought him his horse and asked to be allowed to accompany him. He was ready dressed and armed, and led his own horse by the bridle, and his rosy handsome young face and the whole of his tall slender figure (he was taller than his father) breathed of daring, youth, and the joy of life. The breadth of his shoulders, though he was so young, the very wide youthful hips, the long slender waist, the strength of his long arms, and the power, flexibility, and agility of all his movements had always rejoiced Hadji Murád, who admired his son.

'Thou hadst better stay. Thou wilt be alone at home now. Take care of thy mother and thy grandmother,' said Hadji Murád. And he remembered the spirited and proud look and the flush of pleasure with which Yusúf had replied that as long as he lived no one should injure his mother or grandmother. All the same, Yusúf had mounted and accompanied his father as far as the stream. There he turned back, and since then Hadji Murád had not seen his wife, his mother, or his son. And it was this son whose eyes Shamil threatened to put out! Of what would be done to his wife Hadji Murád did not wish to think.

These thoughts so excited him that he could not sit still any longer. He jumped up and went limping quickly to the door, opened it, and called Eldár. The sun had not yet risen, but it was already quite light. The nightingales were still singing.

'Go and tell the officer that I want to go out riding, and saddle the horses,' said he.

XXIV

Butler's only consolation all this time was the poetry of warfare, to which he gave himself up not only during his hours of service but also in private life. Dressed in his Circassian costume, he rode and swaggered about, and twice went into ambush with Bogdanóvich, though neither time did they discover or kill anyone. This closeness to and friendship with Bogdanóvich, famed for his courage, seemed pleasant and warlike to Butler. He had paid his debt, having borrowed the money of a Jew at an enormous rate of interest—that is to say, he had postponed his difficulties but had not solved them. He tried not to think of his position, and to find oblivion not only in the poetry of warfare but also in wine. He drank more and more every day, and day by day grew morally weaker. He was now no longer the chaste Joseph he had been towards Márya Dmítrievna, but on the contrary began courting her grossly, meeting to his surprise with a strong and decided repulse which put him to shame.

At the end of April there arrived at the fort a detachment with which Baryátinsky intended to effect an advance right through Chechnya, which had till then been considered impassable. In that detachment were two companies of the Kabardá regiment, and according to Caucasian custom these were treated as guests by the Kurín companies. The soldiers were lodged in the barracks, and were treated not only to supper, consisting of buckwheat-porridge and beef, but also to vódka. The officers shared the quarters of the Kurín officers, and as usual those in residence gave the new-comers a dinner at which the regimental singers performed and which ended up with a drinking-bout. Major Petróv, very drunk and no longer red but ashy pale, sat astride a chair and, drawing his sword, hacked at imaginery foes, alternately swearing and laughing, now embracing someone and now dancing to the tune of his favourite song.

'Shamil, he began to riot
In the days gone by;
Try, ry, rataty,
In the years gone by!'

Butler was there too. He tried to see the poetry of warfare in this also, but in the depth of his soul he was sorry for the major. To stop him, however, was quite impossible; and Butler, feeling that the fumes were mounting to his own head, quietly left the room and went home.

The moon lit up the white houses and the stones on the road. It was so light that every pebble, every straw, every little heap of dust was visible. As he approached the house he met Márya Dmítrievna with a shawl over her head and neck. After the rebuff she had given him Butler had avoided her, feeling rather ashamed, but now in the moonlight and after the wine he had drunk he was pleased to meet her and wished to make up to her again.

'Where are you off to?' he asked.

'Why, to see after my old man,' she answered pleasantly. Her rejection of Butler's advances was quite sincere and decided, but she did not like his avoiding her as he had done lately.

'Why bother about him? He'll soon come back.'

'But will he?'

'If he doesn't they'll bring him.'

'Just so. . . . That's not right, you know! . . . But you think I'd better not go?'

'Yes, I do. We'd better go home.'

Márya Dmítrievna turned back and walked beside him. The moon shone so brightly that a halo seemed to move along the road round the shadows of their heads. Butler was looking at this halo and making up his mind to tell her that he liked her as much as ever, but he did not know how to begin. She waited for him to speak, and they walked on in silence almost to the house, when some horsemen appeared from round the corner. These were an officer with an escort.

'Who's that coming now?' said Márya Dmítrievna, stepping aside. The moon was behind the rider so that she did not recognize him until he had almost come up to them. It was Peter Nikoláevich Kámenev, an officer who had formerly served with the major and whom Márya Dmítrievna therefore knew.

'Is that you, Peter Nikoláevich?' said she, addressing him.

'It's me,' said Kámenev. 'Ah, Butler, how d'you do? . . . Not asleep yet? Having a walk with Márya

Dmítrievna! You'd better look out or the major will give it you. . . . Where is he?'

'Why, there. . . . Listen!' replied Márya Dmítrievna pointing in the direction whence came the sounds of a *tulumbas* and songs. 'They're on the spree.'

'Why? Are your people having a spree on their own?'

'No; some officers have come from Hasav-Yurt, and they are being entertained.'

'Ah, that's good! I shall be in time. . . . I just want the major for a moment.'

'On business?' asked Butler.

'Yes, just a little business matter.'

'Good or bad?'

'It all depends. . . . Good for us but bad for some people,' and Kámenev laughed.

By this time they had reached the major's house.

'Chikhirév,' shouted Kámenev to one of his Cossacks, 'come here!'

A Don Cossack rode up from among the others. He was dressed in the ordinary Don Cossack uniform with high boots and a mantle, and carried saddle-bags behind.

'Well, take the thing out,' said Kámenev, dismounting.

The Cossack also dismounted, and took a sack out of his saddle-bag. Kámenev took the sack from him and inserted his hand.

'Well, shall I show you a novelty? You won't be frightened, Márya Dmítrievna?'

'Why should I be frightened?' she replied.

'Here it is!' said Kámenev taking out a man's head and holding it up in the light of the moon. 'Do you recognize it?'

It was a shaven head with salient brows, black short-cut beard and moustaches, one eye open and the other half-closed. The shaven skull was cleft, but not right through, and there was congealed blood in the nose. The neck was wrapped in a blood-stained towel. Notwithstanding the many wounds on the head, the blue lips still bore a kindly childlike expression.

Márya Dmítrievna looked at it, and without a word turned away and went quickly into the house.

Butler could not tear his eyes from the terrible head. It was the head of that very Hadji Murád with whom he had so recently spent his evenings in such friendly intercourse.

'What does this mean? Who has killed him?' he asked.

'He wanted to give us the slip, but was caught,' said Kámenev, and he gave the head back to the Cossack and went into the house with Butler.

'He died like a hero,' he added.

'But however did it all happen?'

'Just wait a bit. When the major comes I'll tell you all about it. That's what I am sent for. I take it round to all the forts and *aouls* and show it.'

The major was sent for, and came back accompanied by two other officers as drunk as himself, and began embracing Kámenev.

'And I have brought you Hadji Murád's head,' said Kámenev.

'No? . . . Killed?'

'Yes; wanted to escape.'

'I always said he would bamboozle them! . . . And where is it? The head, I mean. . . . Let's see it.'

The Cossack was called, and brought in the bag with the head. It was taken out and the major looked long at it with drunken eyes.

'All the same, he was a fine fellow,' said he. 'Let me kiss him!'

'Yes, it's true. It was a valiant head,' said one of the officers.

When they had all looked at it, it was returned to the Cossack who put it in his bag, trying to let it bump against the floor as gently as possible.

'I say, Kámenev, what speech do you make when you show the head?' asked an officer.

'No! . . . Let me kiss him. He gave me a sword!' shouted the major.

Butler went out into the porch.

Márya Dmítrievna was sitting on the second step. She looked round at Butler and at once turned angrily away again.

'What's the matter, Márya Dmítrievna?' asked he.

'You're all cut-throats! . . . I hate it! You're cut-throats, really,' and she got up.

'It might happen to anyone,' remarked Butler, not knowing what to say. 'That's war.'

'War? War, indeed! . . . Cut-throats and nothing else. A dead body should be given back to the earth, and they're

grinning at it there! . . . Cut-throats, really,' she repeated,
as she descended the steps and entered the house by the
back door.

Butler returned to the room and asked Kámenev to tell
them in detail how the thing had happened.

And Kámenev told them.

This is what had happened.

XXV

Hadji Murád was allowed to go out riding in the neighbourhood of the town, but never without a convoy of
Cossacks. There was only half a troop of them altogether
in Nukhá, ten of whom were employed by the officers, so
that if ten were sent out with Hadji Murád (according to
the orders received) the same men would have had to go
every other day. Therefore after ten had been sent out the
first day, it was decided to send only five in future and
Hadji Murád was asked not to take all his henchmen with
him. But on April the 25th he rode out with all five. When
he mounted, the commander, noticing that all five henchmen were going with him, told him that he was forbidden to
take them all, but Hadji Murád pretended not to hear,
touched his horse, and the commander did not insist.

With the Cossacks rode a non-commissioned officer,
Nazárov, who had received the Cross of St. George for
bravery. He was a young, healthy, brown-haired lad, as
fresh as a rose. He was the eldest of a poor family belonging to the sect of Old Believers, had grown up without a
father, and had maintained his old mother, three sisters,
and two brothers.

'Mind, Nazárov, keep close to him!' shouted the commander.

'All right, your honour!' answered Nazárov, and rising
in his stirrups and adjusting the rifle that hung at his back
he started his fine large roan gelding at a trot. Four Cossacks followed him: Ferapóntov, tall and thin, a regular
thief and plunderer (it was he who had sold gunpowder
to Gamzálo); Ignátov, a sturdy peasant who boasted of
his strength, though he was no longer young and had
nearly completed his service; Míshkin, a weakly lad at
whom everybody laughed; and the young fair-haired Petrakóv, his mother's only son, always amiable and jolly.

The morning had been misty, but it cleared up later on and the opening foliage, the young virgin grass, the sprouting corn, and the ripples of the rapid river just visible to the left of the road, all glittered in the sunshine.

Hadji Murád rode slowly along followed by the Cossacks and by his henchmen. They rode out along the road beyond the fort at a walk. They met women carrying baskets on their heads, soldiers driving carts, and creaking wagons drawn by buffaloes. When he had gone about a mile and a half Hadji Murád touched up his white Kabardá horse, which started at an amble that obliged the henchmen and Cossacks to ride at a quick trot to keep up with him.

'Ah, he's got a fine horse under him,' said Ferapóntov. 'If only he were still an enemy I'd soon bring him down.'

'Yes, mate. Three hundred rubles were offered for that horse in Tiflis.'

'But I can get ahead of him on mine,' said Nazárov.

'You get ahead? A likely thing!'

Hadji Murád kept increasing his pace.

'Hey, *kunák*, you mustn't do that. Steady!' cried Nazárov, starting to overtake Hadji Murád.

Hadji Murád looked round, said nothing, and continued to ride at the same pace.

'Mind, they're up to something, the devils!' said Ignátov. 'See how they are tearing along.'

So they rode for the best part of a mile in the direction of the mountains.

'I tell you it won't do!' shouted Nazárov.

Hadji Murád did not answer or look round, but only increased his pace to a gallop.

'Humbug! You won't get away!' shouted Nazárov, stung to the quick. He gave his big roan gelding a cut with his whip and, rising in his stirrups and bending forward, flew full speed in pursuit of Hadji Murád.

The sky was so bright, the air so clear, and life played so joyously in Nazárov's soul as, becoming one with his fine strong horse, he flew along the smooth road behind Hadji Murád, that the possibility of anything sad or dreadful happening never occurred to him. He rejoiced that with every step he was gaining on Hadji Murád.

Hadji Murád judged by the approaching tramp of the big horse behind him that he would soon be overtaken, and seizing his pistol with his right hand, with his left he began slightly to rein in his Kabardá horse which was excited by hearing the tramp of hoofs behind it.

'You mustn't, I tell you!' shouted Nazárov, almost level with Hadji Murád and stretching out his hand to seize the latter's bridle. But before he reached it a shot was fired. 'What are you doing?' he screamed, clutching at his breast. 'At them, lads!' and he reeled and fell forward on his saddle-bow.

But the mountaineers were beforehand in taking to their weapons, and fired their pistols at the Cossacks and hewed at them with their swords.

Nazárov hung on the neck of his horse, which careered round his comrades. The horse under Ignátov fell, crushing his leg, and two of the mountaineers, without dismouting, drew their swords and hacked at his head and arms. Petrakóv was about to rush to his comrade's rescue when two shots—one in his back and the other in his side— stung him, and he fell from his horse like a sack.

Míshkin turned round and galloped off towards the fortress. Khanéfi and Bata rushed after him, but he was already too far away and they could not catch him. When they saw that they could not overtake him they returned to the others.

Petrakóv lay on his back, his stomach ripped open, his young face turned to the sky, and while dying he gasped for breath like a fish.

Gamzálo having finished off Ignátov with his sword, gave a cut to Nazárov too and threw him from his horse. Bata took their cartridge-pouches from the slain. Khanéfi wished to take Nazárov's horse, but Hadji Murád called out to him to leave it, and dashed forward along the road. His *murids* galloped after him, driving away Nazárov's horse that tried to follow them. They were already among rice-fields more than six miles from Nukhá when a shot was fired from the tower of that place to give the alarm.

* * *

'O good Lord! O God! my God! What have they done?' cried the commander of the fort seizing his head with his hands when he heard of Hadji Murád's escape. 'They've done for me! They've let him escape, the villains!' cried he, listening to Míshkin's account.

An alarm was raised everywhere and not only the Cossacks of the place were sent after the fugitives but also all the militia that could be mustered from the pro-Russian *aouls*. A thousand rubles reward was offered for the capture of Hadji Murád alive or dead, and two hours after he and his followers had escaped from the Cossacks more than two hundred mounted men were following the officer in charge at a gallop to find and capture the runaways.

After riding some miles along the high road Hadji Murád checked his panting horse, which, wet with sweat, had turned from white to grey.

To the right of the road could be seen the *sáklyas* and minarets of the *aoul* Benerdzhík, on the left lay some fields, and beyond them the river. Although the way to the mountains lay to the right, Hadji Murád turned to the left, in the opposite direction, assuming that his pursuers would be sure to go to the right, while he, abandoning the road, would cross the Alazán and come out onto the high road on the other side where no one would expect him— ride along it to the forest, and then after recrossing the river make his way to the mountains.

Having come to this conclusion he turned to the left; but it proved impossible to reach the river. The rice-field which had to be crossed had just been flooded, as is always done in spring, and had become a bog in which the horses' legs sank above their pasterns. Hadji Murád and his henchmen turned now to the left, now to the right, hoping to find drier ground; but the field they were in had been equally flooded all over and was now saturated with water. The horses drew their feet out of the sticky mud into which they sank, with a pop like that of a cork drawn from a bottle, and stopped, panting, after every few steps. They struggled in this way so long that it began to grow dusk and they had still not reached the river. To their left lay a patch of higher ground overgrown with shrubs and Hadji Murád decided to ride in among these clumps and remain there till night to rest their exhausted horses and let them graze. The men themselves ate some bread and cheese they had brought with them. At last night came on and the moon that had been shining at first, hid behind the hill and it became dark. There were a great many nightingales in that neighbourhood and there were two of them in these shrubs. As long as Hadji Murád and his men were making a noise among the bushes the nightingales had been silent, but when they became still the birds again began to call to one another and to sing.

Hadji Murád, awake to all the sounds of night, listened to them involuntarily, and their trills reminded him of the song about Hamzád which he had heard the night before when he went to get water. He might now at any moment find himself in the position in which Hamzád had been. He fancied that it would be so, and suddenly his soul became serious. He spread out his *búrka* and performed his ablutions, and scarcely had he finished before a sound was heard approaching their shelter. It was the sound of many horses' feet plashing through the bog.

The keen-sighted Bata ran out to one edge of the clump, and peering through the darkness saw black shadows, which were men on foot and on horseback. Khanéfi discerned a similar crowd on the other side. It was Kargánov, the military commander of the district, with his militia.

'Well, then, we shall fight like Hamzád,' thought Hadji Murád.

When the alarm was given, Kargánov with a troop of militiamen and Cossacks had rushed off in pursuit of Hadji Murád, but had been unable to find any trace of him. He had already lost hope and was returning home when, towards evening, he met an old man and asked him if he had seen any horsemen about. The old man replied that he had. He had seen six horsemen floundering in the rice-field, and then had seen them enter the clump where he himself was getting wood. Kargánov turned back, taking the old man with him, and seeing the hobbled horses he made sure that Hadji Murád was there. In the night he surrounded the clump and waited till morning to take Hadji Murád alive or dead.

Having understood that he was surrounded, and having discovered an old ditch among the shrubs, Hadji Murád decided to entrench himself in it and to resist as long as strength and ammunition lasted. He told his comrades this, and ordered them to throw up a bank in front of the ditch, and his henchmen at once set to work to cut down branches, dig up the earth with their daggers, and make an entrenchment. Hadji Murád himself worked with them.

As soon as it began to grow light the commander of the militia troop rode up to the clump and shouted:

'Hey! Hadji Murád, surrender! We are many and you are few!'

In reply came the report of a rifle, a cloudlet of smoke rose from the ditch and a bullet hit the militiaman's horse, which staggered under him and began to fall. The rifles of the militiamen who stood at the outskirts of the clump of shrubs began cracking in their turn, and their bullets whistled and hummed, cutting off leaves and twigs and striking the embankment, but not the men entrenched behind it. Only Gamzálo's horse, that had strayed from the others, was hit in the head by a bullet. It did not fall, but breaking its hobbles and rushing among the bushes it ran to the other horses, pressing close to them and watering the young grass with its blood. Hadji Murád and his men fired only when any of the militiamen came forward, and rarely missed their aim. Three militiamen were wounded, and the others, far from making up their minds to rush the entrenchment, retreated farther and farther back, only firing from a distance and at random.

So it continued for more than an hour. The sun had risen to about half the height of the trees, and Hadji Murád was already thinking of leaping on his horse and trying to make his way to the river, when the shouts were heard of many men who had just arrived. These were Hadji Aga of Mekhtulí with his followers. There were about two hundred of them. Hadji Aga had once been Hadji Murád's *kunák* and had lived with him in the mountains, but he had afterwards gone over to the Russians. With him was Akhmet Khan, the son of Hadji Murád's old enemy.

Like Kargánov, Hadji Aga began by calling to Hadji Murád to surrender, and Hadji Murád answered as before with a shot.

'Swords out, my men!' cried Hadji Aga, drawing his own; and a hundred voices were raised by men who rushed shrieking in among the shrubs.

The militiamen ran in among the shrubs, but from behind the entrenchment came the crack of one shot after another. Some three men fell, and the attackers stopped at the outskirts of the clump and also began firing. As they fired they gradually approached the entrenchment, running across from behind one shrub to another. Some succeeded in getting across, others fell under the bullets of Hadji

Murád or of his men. Hadji Murád fired without missing; Gamzálo too rarely wasted a shot, and shrieked with joy every time he saw that his bullet had hit its aim. Khan Mahomá sat at the edge of the ditch singing *'Il lyakha il Allakh!'* and fired leisurely, but often missed. Eldár's whole body trembled with impatience to rush dagger in hand at the enemy, and he fired often and at random, constantly looking round at Hadji Murád and stretching out beyond the entrenchment. The shaggy Khanéfi, with his sleeves rolled up, did the duty of a servant even here. He loaded the guns which Hadji Murád and Khan Mahomá passed to him, carefully driving home with a ramrod the bullets wrapped in greasy rags, and pouring dry powder out of the powder-flask onto the pans. Bata did not remain in the ditch as the others did, but kept running to the horses, driving them away to a safer place and, shrieking incessantly, fired without using a prop for his gun. He was the first to be wounded. A bullet entered his neck and he sat down spitting blood and swearing. Then Hadji Murád was wounded, the bullet piercing his shoulder. He tore some cotton wool from the lining of his *beshmét*, plugged the wound with it, and went on firing.

'Let us fly at them with our swords!' said Eldár for the third time, and he looked out from behind the bank of earth ready to rush at the enemy; but at that instant a bullet struck him and he reeled and fell backwards onto Hadji Murád's leg. Hadji Murád glanced at him. His eyes, beautiful like those of a ram, gazed intently and seriously at Hadji Murád. His mouth, the upper lip pouting like a child's, twitched without opening. Hadji Murád drew his leg away from under him and continued firing.

Khanéfi bent over the dead Eldár and began taking the unused ammunition out of the cartridge-cases of his coat.

Khan Mahomá meanwhile continued to sing, loading leisurely and firing. The enemy ran from shrub to shrub, hallooing and shrieking and drawing ever nearer and nearer.

Another bullet hit Hadji Murád in the left side. He lay down in the ditch and again pulled some cotton wool out of his *beshmét* and plugged the wound. This wound in the side was fatal and he felt that he was dying. Memories and pictures succeeded one another with extraordinary rapidity in his imagination. Now he saw the powerful Abu Nutsal Khan, dagger in hand and holding up his severed cheek he rushed at his foe; then he saw the weak, bloodless old Vorontsóv with his cunning white face, and heard his soft voice; then he saw his son Yusúf, his wife Sofiát, and then the pale, red-bearded face of his enemy Shamil with its half-closed eyes. All these images passed through his mind without evoking any feeling within him—neither pity nor anger nor any kind of desire: everything seemed so insignificant in comparison with what was beginning, or had already begun, within him.

Yet his strong body continued the thing that he had commenced. Gathering together his last strength he rose from behind the bank, fired his pistol at a man who was just running towards him, and hit him. The man fell. Then Hadji Murád got quite out of the ditch, and limping heavily went dagger in hand straight at the foe.

Some shots cracked and he reeled and fell. Several militiamen with triumphant shrieks rushed towards the fallen body. But the body that seeemd to be dead suddenly moved. First the uncovered, bleeding, shaven head rose; then the body with hands holding to the trunk of a tree. He seemed so terrible, that those who were running towards him stopped short. But suddenly a shudder passed through him, he staggered away from the tree and fell on his face, stretched out at full length like a thistle that had been mown down, and he moved no more.

He did not move, but still he felt.

When Hadji Aga, who was the first to reach him, struck him on the head with a large dagger, it seemed to Hadji Murád that someone was striking him with a hammer and he could not understand who was doing it or why. That was his last consciousness of any connexion with his body. He felt nothing more and his enemies kicked and hacked at what had no longer anything in common with him.

Hadji Aga placed his foot on the back of the corpse and with two blows cut off the head, and carefully—not to soil his shoes with blood—rolled it away with his foot. Crimson blood spurted from the arteries of the neck, and black blood flowed from the head, soaking the grass.

Kargánov and Hadji Aga and Akhmet Khan and all the militiamen gathered together—like sportsmen round a slaughtered animal—near the bodies of Hadji Murád and his men (Khanéfi, Khan Mahomá, and Gamzálo they bound), and amid the powder-smoke which hung over the bushes they triumphed in their victory.

The nightingales, that had hushed their songs while the firing lasted, now started their trills once more: first one quite close, then others in the distance.

* * *

It was of this death that I was reminded by the crushed thistle in the midst of the ploughed field.

A List of Tartar Words Used in *Hadji Murád*

Aoul	A Tartar village.
Bar	Have.
Beshmét	A Tartar undergarment with sleeves.
Búrka	A long round felt cape.
Dzhigít	The same as a *brave* among the Red Indians, but the word is inseparably connected with the idea of skilful horsemanship.
Gazavát	A holy war against the infidels.
Imám	The leader in the holy war, uniting in himself supreme spiritual and temporal power.
Khansha	The wife of a khan.
Kizyák	A fuel made of straw and manure.
Kunák	A sworn friend, an adopted brother.
Murid	A disciple or follower: 'One who desires' to find the way in Muridism.
Muridism	Almost identical with Sufism.
Murshéd	'One who shows' the way in Muridism.
Naïb	A Tartar lieutenant or governor.
Pilau	An Oriental dish prepared with rice and mutton or chicken.
Sáklya	A Caucasian house, clay-plastered and often built of earth.
Shariát	The written Mohammedan law.
Tarikát	'The Path' leading to the higher life.
Yok	No, not.

Alyosha the Pot

[1905]

The following translation of "Aljoša Goršok" was made especially for this anthology by S. A. Carmack from the Russian text in Povesti i rasskazy: 1903–1910, *the fourteenth volume of the collected works of Tolstoy published in Moscow in 1964 by Izdatel'stvo Xudožestvennaja Literatura.*

Alyosha was a younger brother. He was nicknamed "the Pot", because once, when his mother sent him with a pot of milk for the deacon's wife, he stumbled and broke it. His mother thrashed him soundly, and the children in the village began to tease him, calling him "the Pot". Alyosha the Pot: and this is how he got his nickname.

Alyosha was a skinny little fellow, lop-eared—his ears stuck out like wings—and with a large nose. The children always teased him about this, too, saying "Alyosha has a nose like a gourd on a pole!"

There was a school in the village where Alyosha lived, but reading and writing and such did not come easy for him, and besides there was no time to learn. His older brother lived with a merchant in town, and Alyosha had begun helping his father when still a child. When he was only six years old, he was already watching over his family's cow and sheep with his younger sister in the common pasture. And long before he was grown, he had started taking care of their horses day and night. From his twelfth year he plowed and carted. He hardly had the strength for all these chores, but he did have a certain manner—he was always cheerful. When the children laughed at him, he fell silent or laughed himself. If his father cursed him, he stood quietly and listened. And when they finished and ignored him again, he smiled and went back to whatever task was before him.

When Alyosha was nineteen years old, his brother was taken into the army; and his father arranged for Alyosha to take his brother's place as a servant in the merchant's household. He was given his brother's old boots and his father's cap and coat and was taken into town. Alyosha was very pleased with his new clothes, but the merchant was quite dissatisfied with his appearance.

"I thought you would bring me a young man just like

Semyon" said the merchant, looking Alyosha over carefully. "But you've brought me such a sniveller. What's he good for?"

"Ah, he can do anything—harness and drive anywhere you like. And he's a glutton for work. Only looks like a stick. He's really very wiry."

"That much is plain. Well, we shall see."

"And above all he's a meek one. Loves to work."

"Well, what can I do? Leave him."

And so Alyosha began to live with the merchant.

The merchant's family was not large. There were his wife, his old mother and three children. His older married son, who had only completed grammar school, was in business with his father. His other son, a studious sort, had been graduated from the high school and was for a time at the university, though he had been expelled and now lived at home. And there was a daughter, too, a young girl in the high school.

At first they did not like Alyosha. He was too much the peasant and was poorly dressed. He had no manners and addressed everyone familiarly as in the country. But soon they grew used to him. He was a better servant than his brother and was always very responsive. Whatever they set him to do he did willingly and quickly, moving from one task to another without stopping. And at the merchant's, just as at home, all the work was given to Alyosha. The more he did, the more everyone heaped upon him. The mistress of the household and her old mother-in-law, and the daughter, and the younger son, even the merchant's clerk and the cook—all sent him here and sent him there and ordered him to do everything that they could think of. The only thing that Alyosha ever heard was "Run do this, fellow", or "Alyosha, fix this up now", or "Did you forget, Alyosha? Look here, fellow, don't you forget!" And Alyosha ran, and fixed, and looked, and did not forget, and managed to do everything and smiled all the while.

Alyosha soon wore out his brother's boots, and the merchant scolded him sharply for walking about in tatters with his bare feet sticking out and ordered him to buy new boots in the market. These boots were truly new, and Alyosha was very happy with them; but his feet remained old all the same, and by evening they ached so from running that he got mad at them. Alyosha was afraid that when his father came to collect his wages, he would be very annoyed that the master had deducted the cost of the new boots from his pay.

In winter Alyosha got up before dawn, chopped firewood, swept out the courtyard, fed grain to the cow and the horses and watered them. Afterwards, he lit the stoves, cleaned the boots and coats of all the household, got out the samovars and polished them. Then, either the clerk called him into the shop to take out the wares or the cook ordered him to knead the dough and to wash the pans. And later he would be sent into town with a message, or to the school for the daughter, or to fetch lamp oil or something else for the master's old mother. "Where have you been loafing, you worthless thing?" one would say to him, and then another. Or among themselves they would say "Why go yourself? Alyosha will run for you. Alyosha, Alyosha!" And Alyosha would run.

Alyosha always ate breakfast on the run and was seldom in time for dinner. The cook was always chiding him, because he never took meals with the others, but for all that she did feel sorry for him and always left him something hot for dinner and for supper.

Before and during holidays there was a lot more work for Alyosha, though he was happier during holidays, because then everyone gave him tips, not much, only about sixty kopeks usually; but it was his own money, which he could spend as he chose. He never laid eyes on his wages, for his father always came into town and took from the merchant Alyosha's pay, giving him only the rough edge of his tongue for wearing out his brother's boots too quickly. When he had saved two rubles altogether from tips, Alyosha bought on the cook's advice a red knitted sweater. When he put it on for the first time and looked down at himself, he was so surprised and delighted that he just stood in the kitchen gaping and gulping.

Alyosha said very little, and when he did speak, it was always to say something necessary abruptly and briefly. And when he was told to do something or other or was asked if he could do it, he always answered without the slightest hesitation "I can do it". And he would immediately throw himself into the job and do it.

Alyosha did not know how to pray at all. His mother

had once taught him the words, but he had forgot even as she spoke. Nonetheless, he did pray, morning and evening, but simply, just with his hands, crossing himself.

Thus Alyosha lived for a year and a half, and then, during the second half of the second year, the most unusual experience of his life occurred. This experience was his sudden discovery, to his complete amazement, that besides those relationships between people that arise from the need that one may have for another, there also exist other relationships that are completely different: not a relationship that a person has with another because that other is needed to clean boots, to run errands or to harness horses; but a relationship that a person has with another who is in no way necessary to him, simply because that other one wants to serve him and to be loving to him. And he discovered, too, that he, Alyosha, was just such a person. He realized all this through the cook Ustinja. Ustinja was an orphan, a young girl yet, and as hard a worker as Alyosha. She began to feel sorry for Alyosha, and Alyosha for the first time in his life felt that he himself, not his services, but he himself was needed by another person. When his mother had been kind to him or had felt sorry for him, he took no notice of it, because it seemed to him so natural a thing, just the same as if he felt sorry for himself. But suddenly he realized that Ustinja, though completely a stranger, felt sorry for him, too. She always left him a pot of kasha with butter, and when he ate, she sat with him, watching him with her chin propped upon her fist. And when he looked up at her and she smiled, he, too, smiled.

It was all so new and so strange that at first Alyosha was frightened. He felt that it disturbed his work, his serving, but he was nonetheless very happy. And when he happened to look down and notice his trousers, which Ustinja had mended for him, he would shake his head and smile. Often while he was working or running an errand, he would think of Ustinja and mutter warmly "Ah, that Ustinja!" Ustinja helped him as best she could, and he helped her. She told him all about her life, how she had been orphaned when very young, how an old aunt had taken her in, how this aunt later sent her into town to

work, how the merchant's son had tried stupidly to seduce
her, and how she put him in his place. She loved to talk,
and he found listening to her very pleasant. Among other
things he heard that in town it often happened that peasant boys who came to serve in households would marry
the cooks. And once she asked him if his parents would
marry him off soon. He replied that he didn't know and
that there was no one in his village whom he wanted.

"What, then, have you picked out someone else?" she
asked.

"Yes. I'd take you. Will you?"

"O Pot, my Pot, how cunningly you put it to me!" she
said, cuffing him playfully on the back with her ladle.

At Shrovetide Alyosha's old father came into town again
to collect his son's wages. The merchant's wife had found
out that Alyosha planned to marry Ustinja, and she was
not at all pleased. "She will just get pregnant, and then
what good will she be!" she complained to her husband.

The merchant counted out Alyosha's money to his
father. "Well, is my boy doing all right by you?" asked
the old man. "I told you he was a meek one, would do
anything you say."

"Meek or no, he's done something stupid. He has got
it into his head to marry the cook. And I will not keep
married servants. It doesn't suit us."

"Eh, that little fool! What a fool! How can he think to
do such a stupid thing! But don't worry over it. I'll make
him forget all that nonsense."

The old man walked straight into the kitchen and sat
down at the table to wait for his son. Alyosha was, as
always, running an errand, but he soon came in all out
of breath.

"Well, I thought you were a sensible fellow, but what
nonsense you've thought up!" Aloysha's father greeted
him.

"I've done nothing."

"What d'you mean nothing! You've decided to marry.
I'll marry you when the time comes, and I'll marry you
to whoever I want, not to some town slut."

The old man said a great deal more of the same sort.
Alyosha stood quietly and sighed. When his father finished,
he smiled.

"So I'll forget about it" he said.

"See that you do right now" the old man said curtly as he left.

When his father had gone and Alyosha remained alone with Ustinja, who had been standing behind the kitchen door listening while his father was talking, he said to her: "Our plan won't work out. Did you hear? He was furious, won't let us."

Ustinja began to cry quietly into her apron. Alyosha clucked his tongue and said "How could I not obey him? Look, we must forget all about it."

In the evening, when the merchant's wife called him to close the shutters, she said to him "Are you going to obey your father and forget all this nonsense about marrying?"

"Yes. Of course. I've forgot it" Alyosha said quickly, then smiled and immediately began weeping.

From that time Alyosha did not speak again to Ustinja about marriage and lived as he had before.

One morning during Lent the clerk sent Alyosha to clear the snow off the roof. He crawled up onto the roof, shovelled it clean and began to break up the frozen snow near the gutters when his feet slipped out from under him and he fell headlong with his shovel. As ill luck would have it, he fell not into the snow, but onto an entry-way with an iron railing. Ustinja ran up to him, followed by the merchant's daughter.

"Are you hurt, Alyosha?"

"Yes. But it's nothing. Nothing."

He wanted to get up, but he could not and just smiled. Others came and carried him down into the yard-keeper's lodge. An orderly from the hospital arrived, examined him and asked where he hurt. "It hurts all over" he replied. "But it's nothing. Nothing. Only the master will be annoyed. Must send word to Papa."

Alyosha lay abed for two full days, and then, on the third day, they sent for a priest.

"You're not going to die, are you?" asked Ustinja.

"Well, we don't all live forever. It must be some time" he answered quickly, as always. "Thank you, dear Ustinja, for feeling sorry for me. See, it's better they didn't let us marry, for nothing would have come of it. And now all is fine."

He prayed with the priest, but only with his hands and with his heart. And in his heart he felt that if he was good here, if he obeyed and did not offend, then there all would be well.

He said little. He only asked for something to drink and smiled wonderingly. Then he seemed surprised at something, and stretched out and died.

A Chronology

1828	Born into what Prince Mirsky described as "the best Russian nobility", the son of Count Nikolaj Tolstoy and his wife, the former Princess Volkonsky, on the 28th August in the old style, at the Yasnaya Polyana, Tolstoy estate in the province of Tula, located some one hundred and twenty miles south of Moscow.
1830	Countess Tolstoy dies.
1837	Count Tolstoy dies, leaving young Leo to be brought up largely by his aunt.
1844–1847	Matriculates at the University of Kazan, where he studies first oriental languages and afterwards the law, but leaves without taking a degree.
1849	Settles at Yasnaya Polyana to improve the living and working conditions of his serfs and begins to keep a diary.
1851	In frustration of his plans of improvement travels with his brother Nikolaj to the Caucasus, where he volunteers for service in the army. Winters in Tiflis, where he writes *Childhood*, which was published in the following year by Nekrasov in *Sovremennik* with immediate and great acclaim.
1852–1853	Serves in the Caucasian campaign, completes *Adolescence*, begins *The Cossacks* and plans a novel on his experiences as a landowner.
1855	Serving in the area of Sevastopol and writes *Sevastopol Sketches* and *The Woodfelling* and starts *Youth*.
1856	Writes *Two Hussars*.
1857	Visits Europe.

1858–1859	Continues *The Cossacks* and writes *Family Happiness.*
1859	Organizes a school at Yasnaya Polyana.
1862	Marries Sofya Andreyevna Behrs, daughter of a court physician, and completes *The Cossacks.*
1863–1869	In residence at Yasnaya, with visits to Moscow. Writing *War and Peace.*
1870	Studies Greek and suffers bad health. Takes a cure in Samara.
1873–1877	Writing *Anna Karenina.*
1878	Undergoes a great moral crisis and "conversion".
1879–1883	Makes intensive theological study.
1883	Writing *What I Believe.*
1884	*What I Believe* banned. Writes *Memoirs of a Madman.*
1885	Visits Crimea.
1886	Finishes *What Then Must We Do?* and writes *The Death of Ivan Ilych* and other short stories.
1889	Finishes *The Kreutzer Sonata* and *The Devil.*
1890	Writes the postscript to *The Kreutzer Sonata.* Writes *Father Sergius* (finished 1898).
1891	Renounces copyrights and divides property among family.
1895	Death of son Ivan. Writes *Master and Man.*
1898	Finishes *What is Art?*
1899	Finishes *Resurrection.*
1901	Visit to Yalta. Writing *Hadji Murád* (finished 1904).
1902	Finishes *What is Religion?* Returns to Yasnaya.
1903	Protests against pogroms.
1904	Outbreak of Russo-Japanese War. Tolstoy's protest, *Bethink Yourselves!*
1904–1905	First Revolution.
1905	Writes "Alyosha the Pot".
1906	Death of daughter Masha.
1908	Finishes *I Cannot be Silent!*—a protest against hangings in suppression of the First Revolution. Jubilee celebration of Tolstoy's birthday.

Writes articles on violence and capital punishment.

1908–1909   Quarrels of Tolstoy with his wife. Tolstoy keeps Secret Diary.

1909   Writes educational articles. Makes wills.

1910   July. Signs last will. October. Leaves home. 9th November, old style. Dies at Astapovo in the province of Ryazan. Buried at Yasnaya Polyana.

A Bibliography in English

Works, translated by Louise and Aylmer Maude for The Centenary Edition, in 21 volumes (Oxford, 1928–1937). An excellent translation of many of the most important fictional and non-fictional works, with Aylmer Maude's *Life.* The Maude translations of a number of the works are reprinted in The World's Classics. *Works,* translated by Leo Wiener, in 24 volumes (Boston and London, 1904–1905). An accurate translation which includes some of the works not translated by the Maudes, but does not contain others. *Stories and Dramas, hitherto unpublished,* translated by L. Turin (London and New York, 1926). Some of the fiction is also available in other translations, e.g. in the Everyman Library and in Penguin Translations, the Signet Library etc. His diaries for the years 1853–1857 have been translated by Louise and Aylmer Maude (London, 1927); 1895–1899 by Rose Strunsky (New York, 1917).

LETTERS

Some eight thousand of Tolstoy's letters are extant, though many, especially early ones, are known to have been lost. Especially interesting are his correspondences with the following: his wife Countess S. A. Tolstoy, his cousin Countess A. A. Tolstoy, his friends A. A. Fet, N. N. Strakhov, A. I. Herzen, L. D. Urusov, V. V. Stasov, V. G. Chertkov, M. K. Gandhi. Very little of this material exists in English, but there are *The Letters of Tolstoy and his cousin Countess Alexandra Tolstoy (1857–1903),* translated by L. Islavin (London, 1929), a fairly large but incomplete selection, and *Tolstoy's Love Letters* (to Valerya Arseneva), 1856–1857, translated by S. S. Koteliansky and V. Woolf (London, 1923).

REMINISCENCES

The Diary of Tolstoy's Wife, 1860–1891, translated by A. Werth (London, 1928).

Countess Tolstoy's Later Diary, 1891–1897, translated by A. Werth (London, 1929).

The Autobiography of Countess Sophie Tolstoy, translated by S. S. Koteliansky and L. Woolf, with preface and notes by V. Spiridonov (London, 1922).

Recollections of Count Tolstoy, by S. A. Behrs, Tolstoy's brother-in-law, translated by C. E. Turner (London, 1893).

Reminiscences of Tolstoy, by Count I. L. Tolstoy, Tolstoy's son, translated by G. Calderan (London, 1914).

The Truth About My Father, by Count L. L. Tolstoy, Tolstoy's son (London, 1924).

Family Views of Tolstoy, translated by Louise and Aylmer Maude (London, 1926).

How Count Tolstoy Lives and Works, by A. P. Sergeyenko, translated by I. Hapgood (London, 1899).

Talks with Tolstoi, by A. B. Goldenweizer, translated by S. S. Koteliansky and V. Woolf (London, 1923).

The Last Days of Tolstoy, by V. G. Chertkov, translated by N. Duddington (London, 1922).

Reminiscences of Tolstoy, Chekhov, and Andreyev, by M. Gorki, translated by K. Mansfield, S. S. Koteliansky, and L. Woolf (London, 1934).

BIOGRAPHY

The best biographies in English are Aylmer Maude, *The Life of Tolstoy*, 2 volumes (included in the Oxford Centenary Edition, also reprinted in World's Classics [Oxford, 1930]); E. J. Simmons, *Leo Tolstoy* (London, 1949); D. Leon, *Tolstoy, His Life and Work* (London, 1944). More specialised are R. Rolland, *Tolstoy*, translated by B. Miall (London, 1911); G. R. Noyes, *Tolstoy* (London, 1919); H. I'A. Fausset, *Tolstoy: The inner drama* (London, 1927). (An interesting psychological study); Thomas Mann, 'Goethe and Tolstoy' in *Three Essays*, translated by H. T. Lowe-Porter (New York, 1929, London, 1932), and reprinted in Mann's *Essays of Three Decades*, translated by H. T. Lowe-Porter (London, 1947). (a brilliant long essay); A. I. Nazarov, *Tolstoy, the Inconstant Genius* (London, 1930); G. Abraham, *Tolstoy* (London, 1935). (A well-written brief life). S. Zweig, *Adepts in Self-Por-*

traiture (Casanova, Stendhal, Tolstoy), translated by E. and C. Paul (London, 1952). Countess A. Tolstoy, Tolstoy's daughter, *Tolstoy: A Life of My Father* (London. 1953).

CRITICISM

M. Arnold, 'Count Leo Tolstoi', first published in 1887, reproduced in *Essays in Criticism, Second Series*. W. D. Howells, in *My Literary Passions* (New York, 1895). D. S. Merezhkowsky, *Tolstoy as Man and Artist: with an essay on Dostoievsky* (Westminster, 1902). P. Kropotkin, in *Ideals and Realities in Russian Literature* (London, 1905). M. de Vogüé, in *The Russian Novel*, translated by H. A. Sawyer (London, 1913). T. G. Masaryk, in *The Spirit of Russia* (New York, 1919). G. Wilson Knight, *Shakespeare and Tolstoy* (London, 1934). J. Lavrin, *Tolstoy: an Approach* (London, 1944). D. S. Mirsky, in *A History of Russian Literature* (London, 1949). G. Lukacs, in *Studies in European Realism*, translated by E. Bone (London, 1950). G. H. Phelps, in *The Russian Novel in English Fiction* (London, 1956). Isaiah Berlin, *The Hedgehog and the Fox* (New York: Simon and Schuster, Inc., 1953). The New American Library of World Literature, Inc. (Mentor Books, 1957). George Steiner, *Tolstoy or Dostoevsky* (New York: Alfred A. Knopf, Inc., 1959). Theodore Redpath, *Tolstoy* (London: Bowes and Bowes, 1960). John Bayley, *Tolstoy and the Novel* (London: Chatto and Windus, 1966; New York: Viking Press, 1967).

About the Author

LEO TOLSTOY was born in 1828. He died in 1910, having written some of the most timeless works in all of literature, including *War and Peace* and *Anna Karenina*.

PERENNIAL ✚ CLASSICS

The Classic Writings of First-Class Writers:

GREAT SHORT WORKS OF LEO TOLSTOY
ISBN 0-06-058697-4 (paperback) • INTRODUCTION BY JOHN BAYLEY
Of all Russian writers, Leo Tolstoy is probably the best known to the Western world, largely because of *War and Peace* and *Anna Karenina*. Here, reprinted in one volume, are his eight finest short novels, including "Family Happiness."

GREAT SHORT WORKS OF HERMAN MELVILLE
ISBN 0-06-058654-0 (paperback) • INTRODUCTION BY WARNER BERTHOFF
"Billy Budd, Sailor" and "Bartleby, the Scrivener" are two of the most revered shorter works of ever written. Here they are along with 19 other stories, in a collection that represents the best short work of an American master.

Coming Soon:

GREAT SHORT WORKS OF STEPHEN CRANE
ISBN 0-06-072648-2 (paperback) • INTRODUCTION BY JAMES COLVERT
Stephen Crane died at the age of 28 in Germany. In his short life, he produced stories that are among the most enduring in the history of American fiction, including "The Red Badge of Courage" and "Maggie: A Girl of the Streets."

GREAT SHORT WORKS OF FYODOR DOSTOEVSKY
ISBN 0-06-072646-6 (paperback) • INTRODUCTION BY RONALD HINGLEY
The short works of Dostoevsky exist in the very large shadow of his astonishing longer novels, but they, too, are among the best works in the history of literature, including the classics "The Gambler" and "Notes from the Underground."

GREAT SHORT WORKS OF MARK TWAIN
ISBN 0-06-072786-1 (paperback)
This masterpiece collection—featuring classics such as "Old Times on the Mississippi," "The Mysterious Stranger," "The Jumping Frog," and more—belongs on every bookshelf.

GREAT SHORT WORKS OF EDGAR ALLAN POE
ISBN 0-06-072785-3 (paperback)
A solid sampling of the literary achievements of one of the undisputed giants of American literature—from the best of his comic and satiric works to the best of his Gothic works.

Don't miss the next book by your favorite author.
Sign up for AuthorTracker by visiting *www.AuthorTracker.com*.

Available wherever books are sold, or call 1-800-331-3761 to order.